P9-DLZ-539

Playing
for
the Ashes

Also by Elizabeth George

A Great Deliverance
Payment in Blood
Well-Schooled in Murder
A Suitable Vengeance
For the Sake of Elena
Missing Joseph

Playing
for
the Ashes

ELIZABETH GEORGE

BANTAM BOOKS
New York · Toronto · London · Sydney · Auckland

PLAYING FOR THE ASHES
A Bantam Book / August 1994

All rights reserved.
Copyright © 1994 by Susan Elizabeth George

Book design by Maria Carella

No part of this book may be reproduced or transmitted in any form or by any means, electronic or
mechanical, including photocopying, recording, or by any information storage and retrieval system,
without permission in writing from the publisher.
For information address: Bantam Books.

Library of Congress Cataloging-in-Publication Data
George, Elizabeth.
Playing for the ashes / Elizabeth George.
p.   cm.
ISBN 0-553-09262-6
1. Lynley, Thomas (Fictitious character)—Fiction.   2. Havers,
Barbara (Fictitious character)—Fiction.   3. Police—England—
Yorkshire—Fiction.   4. Yorkshire (England)—Fiction.   I. Title.
PS3557.E478P58   1994
813'.54—dc20   93-50153
                                                       CIP

Published simultaneously in the United States and Canada

Bantam Books are published by Bantam Books, a division of Bantam Doubleday Dell Publishing Group, Inc.
Its trademark, consisting of the words "Bantam Books" and the portrayal of a rooster, is Registered in U.S.
Patent and Trademark Office and in other countries. Marca Registrada. Bantam Books, 1540 Broadway, New
York, New York 10036.

PRINTED IN THE UNITED STATES OF AMERICA

BVG   0 9 8 7 6 5 4 3 2 1

FOR FREDDIE LACHAPELLE
with love

The earth and the sand are burning. Put your face on the burning sand and on the earth of the road, since all those who are wounded by love must have the imprint on their face, and the scar must be seen.

THE CONFERENCE OF THE BIRDS
by Farīd al-Dīn ʿAṭṭār

AUTHOR'S NOTE

In England the term "the Ashes" signifies victory in test cricket (cricket played at the national level) against Australia.

This expression arises from the following bit of cricket history:

When the Australian national team defeated the English national team in a test series in August of 1882, it was the first time England had been defeated on her own soil. In reaction to the loss, the *Sporting Times* ran a mock obituary in which the paper declared that English cricket had "died at the Oval on 29th August 1882." The obituary was followed by a note informing readers that "the body will be cremated and the ashes taken to Australia."

After that fatal match, the English team left for Australia for another series of matches. Captained by Ivo Bligh, the team was said to be on a pilgrimage to *recover the Ashes*. After the second defeat of the Australian team, some women from Melbourne took one of the bails (the pieces of wood that lie across three vertical stumps and with them comprise the wicket that the batsman is defending against the bowler), burned the bail, and presented the ashes to Bligh. These ashes now reside at Lord's Cricket Ground in London, the Mecca of English cricket.

While no trophy exchanges hands at the end of a series between England and Australia, whenever they meet for the five matches that constitute what is called a test series, they play for the Ashes.

Playing
for
the Ashes

OLIVIA

Chris has taken the dogs for a run along the canal. I can still see them because they haven't yet come to the Warwick Avenue bridge. Beans is loping along on the right, flirting with falling into the water. Toast is on the left. About every ten strides, Toast forgets he only has three legs and he starts to go down onto his shoulder.

Chris said he wouldn't be gone for long, because he knows how I'm feeling about writing this. But he likes the exercise and once he gets going, the sun and the breeze will make him forget. He'll end up running all the way to the zoo. I'll try not to be cheesed off about this. I need Chris more than ever right now, so I'll tell myself that he always means well and I'll try to believe it.

When I worked at the zoo, sometimes the three of them would come to fetch me in mid-afternoon, and we'd have a coffee in the refreshment pavilion, outside if the weather was fine, sitting on a bench where we could see the facade of Cumberland Terrace. We'd study the curve of those statues lined up on the pediment, and we'd make up stories about who they were. Sir Boffing Bigtoff, Chris would call one for a start, him that got his arse blown off at the battle of Waterloo. Dame Tartsie Twit, I'd call another, her that posed as a witless wonder but was actually a female Pimpernel. Or Makus Sictus for someone in a toga, him that lost his courage and his breakfast with the Ides of March. And then we'd snicker at our idiocy, and we'd watch the dogs play at stalking the birds and the tourists.

I'll wager you can't see me doing that, can you, weaving dim tales with my chin on my knees and a cup of coffee, along with Chris Faraday, on the bench beside me. And not even wearing black like I do these days, but instead khaki trousers and an olive shirt, the uniform we always had on at the zoo.

I thought I knew who I was back then. I had myself sorted out. Appearances go for nothing, I'd decided a good ten years past, and if people can't deal with my chopped-up hair, if people have problems with my ink-pot roots, if a nose ring gives them the willies and ear-studs lined up like medieval weapons make their stomachs do flip-flops, then to hell with them. They can't look beyond the surface, can they? They don't want to see me as I really am.

So who am I, really? What am I? I could have told you eight days ago because I knew then. I had a philosophy conveniently bastardized from Chris's beliefs. I'd mixed it with what I'd picked up from my mates during the two years I spent at university, and I'd blended it well with what I learned from five years of crawling out of sticky-sheeted beds with my head exploding and my mouth like sawdust and no memory at all of the night that had passed or the name of the bloke who was snoring next to me. I knew the woman who'd walked through all that. She was angry. She was hard. She was unforgiving.

I'm still those things, and with good cause. But I'm something more. I can't identify it. But I feel it every time I pick up a newspaper, read the stories, and know the trial is looming ahead.

At first I told myself I was sick to death of being accosted by head-lines. I was tired of reading about the sodding murder. I was weary with seeing all the relevant faces peering out at me from the *Daily Mail* and the *Evening Standard.* I thought I could escape the whole rotten mess by reading only *The Times* instead, because the one thing I knew I could rely upon was *The Times'* dedication to the facts and its general refusal to wallow in gossip. But even *The Times* has picked up on the story, and I find I can't avoid it any longer. *Who gives a shit* doesn't cut it right now as a means of distraction. Because I do give a shit, and I know it. Chris knows it as well, which is the real reason he's taken the dogs and given me this time alone. He said, "You know, I think we'll have a longer run this morning, Livie," and he changed to his tracksuit. He hugged me in that asexual way of his—a side hug offering practically no body contact—and off he went. I'm on the deck of the barge with a yellow lined pad on my knees, a packet of Marlboros in my pocket, and a tin filled with pencils beside my foot. The pencils each have been sharpened to a pinpoint. Chris saw to that before he left.

I look across the pool to Browning's Island where the willows dip branches towards the tiny pier. The trees are finally in full leaf which means it's nearly summer. Summer was always a time of forgetting, when the sun baked problems away. So I tell myself that if I hold on for just a few more weeks and wait for summer, all this will be past. I won't have to think about it. I won't have to take action. I tell myself it's not my problem. But that's not quite the truth, and I know it.

When I can't shirk looking at the newspapers any longer, I start with the pictures. I look the most at his. I see the way he holds his head, and I know that he thinks he's taken himself to a place where no one can hurt him.

I understand. I thought I'd finally arrived at that place myself at one time. But the truth is that once you start to believe in someone, once you allow yourself to be touched by another's essential goodness—and it does exist, you know, this basic goodness that some people are blessed with—then it's all over. Not only have the walls been breached, but the armour's been pierced. And you bleed like a piece of ripe fruit, skin slit by a knife and flesh exposed for consumption. He doesn't know this yet. He will, eventually.

So I'm writing, I suppose, because of him. And because at the core of this dreary shamble of lives and loves, I know I'm the one who's responsible for everything.

The story begins with my father, actually, and the fact that I'm the one who caused his death. This wasn't my first crime, as you will see, but it's the one my mother couldn't forgive. And because she couldn't forgive me for killing him, our lives got sticky. And people got hurt.

This is tricky business, writing about Mother. It's probably going to seem like mud-slinging, a perfect opportunity to get mine back. But here's one characteristic about Mother that you need to know up front if you're going to read this: She likes to keep secrets. So while, given the chance, she would doubtlessly explain with some delicacy that she and I fell out round ten years ago over my "unfortunate involvement" with a middle-aged musician called Richie Brewster, she'd never mention everything. She wouldn't want you to know that I was a married bloke's "other woman" for a time, that he put me up the duff and then did a runner, that I took him back and let him give me herpes, that I ended up on the job in Earl's Court, doing it in cars for fifteen quid a go when I needed to score some coke real bad and couldn't be bothered wasting time taking blokes to a room. Mother wouldn't ever tell you that. She'd hold back the facts and convince herself she was protecting me. But all the time the real story is that Mother's always hidden facts to protect herself.

From what? you ask.

From the truth, I reply. About her life, about her dissatisfaction, and most of all about her marriage. Which is what—my own unsavoury behaviour aside—I believe set Mother on the path that finally led her to believe that she was possessed of some sort of divine right to meddle in the affairs of others.

Naturally, most people engaged in dissecting my mother's life wouldn't see her as a meddler. Rather, they would see her as a woman of admirable social conscience. She certainly has the credentials: former teacher of English literature in a nasty-smelling comprehensive on the Isle of Dogs, one-time volunteer reader to the blind at weekends, assistant director of recreation for the retarded on school holidays and at half-terms, a gold medal fund-raiser for whatever disease was media darling of the moment. From a superficial observation of her, Mother looks like a woman with one hand in the vitamin bottle and the other on the first rung of the sainthood ladder.

"There are concerns beyond our own," she always said to me when she wasn't saying sadly, "Are you going to be difficult again today, Olivia?"

But there's more to Mother than the woman who rushed round London like a twentieth-century Dr. Barnardo for thirty years. There's the reason why. And that's where protecting herself comes in.

Living in the same house with her, I had plenty of time to try to understand Mother's passion for doing good works. I came to realise that she served others in order to serve herself simultaneously. As long as she kept bustling through the wretched world of London's unfortunates, she never had to think much about her own world. Particularly, she didn't have to think about my father.

I realise that it's quite the fashion to examine the marital condition of one's parents during one's childhood. What better way to excuse the excesses, the paucities, and the downright infirmities of one's own character? But bear with me, please, in this minor expedition through my family's history. It explains why Mother is who Mother is. And Mother is the person you must understand.

While she'd never admit it, I think my mother accepted my father not because she loved him but because he was suitable. He hadn't served in the war, which was slightly problematical as far as his level of social desirability went. But despite a heart murmur, a cracked kneecap, and congenital deafness in his right ear, Dad at least had the grace to feel guilty for having escaped military service. He assuaged his guilt in 1952 by joining one of the societies dedicated to rebuilding London. There he met my mother. She assumed his presence indicated a social conscience on a par with her own and not a desire to forget the fortune he and his father had made from printing propaganda for the government from their business in Stepney from 1939 until the war's end.

They married in 1958. Even now with Dad all these years dead, I still sometimes wonder what the early days of marriage must have been like for my parents. I wonder how long it took Mother to realise that Dad's repertoire of passion didn't run much further than a short gamut from silence to a whimsical, sweet smile. I used to think their times together in bed must have been something along the order of clutch, grope, sweat, poke, groan, with a "very nice, my dear" thrown in at the end, which was how I explained to myself that I was their only child. I came along in 1962, a little package of bonhomie engendered by what I'm sure was a bimonthly encounter in the missionary position.

To her credit, Mother played the role of dutiful wife for three years. She'd got herself a husband, achieving one of the goals set forth for postwar womankind, and she tried to do her best by him. But the more she came to know this Gordon Whitelaw, the more she realised that he'd sold himself to her on false pretences. He wasn't the man of passion she had hoped to wed. He wasn't a rebel. He had no cause. He was at heart just a printer from Stepney, a good man, but one whose world was circumscribed by paper mills and print runs, by keeping the machinery up and running and keeping the unions from bleeding him dry. He ran his business, came home, read the newspaper, ate his dinner, watched the telly, and went to bed. He had few interests. He had little to say. He was solid, faithful, dependable, and predictable. In short, he was boring.

So Mother cast about for something to colour her world. She could have chosen either adultery or alcohol, but she chose good works instead.

She'd never admit to any of this. Admitting that she always wanted to have more in her life than what Dad provided would have meant admitting that her marriage wasn't all she'd hoped it would be. Even now if you went to Kensington and asked her, she'd no doubt paint a picture of life with Gordon Whitelaw that was bliss from the first. Since it wasn't that, she worked on her social responsibilities. For Mother, doing good took the place of feeling good. Nobility of effort took the place of physical passion and love.

In return, Mother had a place to turn when she was feeling low. She had a sense of accomplishment, and a feeling of worth. She received the honest and heartfelt gratitude of those to whose needs she daily ministered. She got herself praised from the classroom to the boardroom to the sickroom. She got her hands shaken. She got her cheeks kissed. She got to hear a thousand different voices say, "Bless you, Mrs. Whitelaw. God love you, Mrs. Whitelaw." She got to distract herself till the day Dad died. She got everything she herself needed, in fact, from keeping the needs of society foremost in her mind. And in the end, when my father was dead, she got herself Kenneth Fleming as well.

Yes, indeed. All those years ago. *The* Kenneth Fleming.

CHAPTER
1

Less than quarter of an hour before Martin Snell discovered the crime scene, he was delivering milk. He'd already completed his rounds in two of the three Springburns, Greater and Middle, and he was on his way to Lesser Springburn, cruising along Water Street in his blue and white milk-float, enjoying his favourite part of the route.

Water Street was the narrow country lane that kept the villages of Middle and Lesser Springburn detached from Greater Springburn, the market town. The lane wound between tawny ragstone walls, bypassing apple orchards and fields of rape. It dipped and climbed with the undulations of the land it bisected, overhung by ash trees, limes, and alders whose leaves were finally beginning to unfold in a springtime arc of green.

The day was glorious, no rain and no clouds. Just a breeze from the east, a milky blue sky, and the sun winking in reflection against the oval picture frame that swung on a silver chain from the milk-float's rearview mirror.

"Quite a day, Majesty," Martin said to the photograph. "Beautiful morning, don't you think? Hear that there? It's the cuckoo again. And there . . . one of them larks is going off now as well. Lovely sound, i'n't it? Sound o' spring, it is."

Martin's habit had long been to chat companionably with his photograph of the Queen. He saw nothing odd in this. She was the country's monarch, and as far as he was concerned, no one was likely to appreciate England's beauty more than the woman who sat on its throne.

Their daily discussions encompassed more than an evaluation of flora and fauna, however. The Queen was Martin's companion of the heart, the recipient of his deepest thoughts. What he liked about her was that, despite her noble birth, she was a decidedly friendly woman. Unlike his wife, who had been born again with a pious vengeance at the hands of a Bible-wielding cement maker some five years back, the Queen never fell to her knees in prayer in the midst of one of his bumbling attempts at communication. Unlike his son, who was given to the secretive silences of the seventeen-year-old with copulation and complexion weighing equally on his mind, she never rebuffed one of Martin's approaches. She always leaned forward slightly and smiled with encouragement, one hand raised to wave from the coach as she was driven eternally to her coronation.

Of course, Martin didn't tell the Queen everything. She knew about Lee's devotion to the Church of the Reborn and Saved. He'd described at great length and more than once the spanner that religion had put into the works of his once jovial dinner hours. And she knew about Danny's job at Tesco's where he kept the shelves stocked with everything from peas to dried beans and about the girl from the tea shop that the boy was so wild about. With his skin going hot, Martin had even disclosed to the Queen only last week his belated attempt at explaining the facts of life to his son. How she had chuckled—how Martin had been forced to chuckle as well —at the thought of him pawing through the second-hand books in Greater Springburn, looking for something to do with biology and coming up with a diagram of frogs instead. He'd presented this to his son along with a packet of condoms he'd had in his chest of drawers since approximately 1972. These'll do for conversation starters, he'd thought. "What're the frogs for, Dad" would lead inescapably to a revelation of what his own father had mysteriously called "the marital embrace."

Not that he and the Queen discussed marital embraces as such. Martin had far too much respect for Her Majesty to do anything more than hint at the topic and then move on.

But for the last four weeks, their milk-route conversations had pe-tered off at the high point of Water Street, where the countryside stretched to the east in hop fields and fell to the west in a grass-covered slope that dropped to a spring where watercress grew. Here, Martin had taken to pulling the milk-float onto the narrow strip of pigweed that served as verge in order to spend a few minutes in quiet contemplation.

This morning he did no differently. He let the engine idle. He gazed at the hop field.

The poles had been up for more than a month, row upon row of slim chestnuts some twenty feet tall from which strings crisscrossed to the ground below. The strings made a diamond-paned lattice up which the hops would eventually grow. The twiddlers had seen to the hops at long last, Martin realised as he surveyed the land. Sometime since yesterday morning they had worked the field, twirling the juvenile plants eighteen inches up the string. The hops would do the rest in the coming months, creating a maze of heavy green drapery as they stretched towards the sun.

Martin sighed with pleasure. The sight would grow lovelier day by day. The field would be cool between the rows of plants as they grew to maturity. He and his love would walk there, just the two of them, hand in hand. Earlier in the year—yesterday, in fact—he would have shown her how to wind the tender tendrils of the plant onto the string. She would have been kneeling in the dirt, her gauzy blue skirt spread out like spilled water, her firm young bottom resting against her bare heels. New to the job and desperate for money to . . . to send to her poor mother who was the widow of a fisherman in Whitstable and left with eight young children to feed, she would struggle with the vine and be afraid to ask for help lest she somehow betray her ignorance and lose the only source of income that her starving brothers and sisters have except for the money her mother brings in making lace to dress up ladies' collars and hats, money that her father ruthlessly swills away in the pub, falling down drunk and staying away all night when he isn't drowning in the sea in a storm while trying to catch enough cod to pay for the operation that would save his youngest child's life. She's wearing a white blouse, with short puffy sleeves and a low neck scooped out so that when he, the burly overseer of the job, bends to help her, he sees the beads of perspiration no bigger than pinheads glistening on her breasts and her breasts rising and falling so quickly because of his nearness and his maleness. He takes her hands and shows her how to twirl the hop plants on the string so the shoots don't break. And her breath comes quicker with the touch of him and her breasts rise higher and he can feel her hair so soft and blonde against his cheek. He says, This is how you do it, Miss. Her fingers tremble. She can't meet his eyes. She's never been touched by a man before. She doesn't want him to leave. She doesn't want him to stop. His hands on hers make her feel quite faint. So she swoons. Yes, she swoons and he carries her to the edge of the field, her long skirt sweeping against his legs as he strides manfully between the rows and her head lolling back with her neck so white so pure so exposed. He lays her on the ground. He holds water to her lips, water in a little tin cup that is handed to him by the toothless crone who follows the field workers in her dogcart and sells them water for tuppence a cup. Her eyelids flutter open. She sees him. She smiles. He raises her hand to his lips. He kisses—

A horn honked behind him. Martin started. The driver of a large red Mercedes was apparently unwilling to risk the wings of her car by easing between the hedgerow on one side and the milk-float on the other. Martin waved and put the float into gear. He looked sheepishly at the Queen to see if she knew about the pictures he'd been painting in his head. But she gave no sign of disapproval. She merely smiled, her hand raised and her tiara shimmering as she rode to the abbey.

He pointed the float down the hill towards Celandine Cottage, a fifteenth-century weaver's workplace and home that stood behind a rag-stone wall on a slight rise of land where Water Street veered off to the northeast and a footpath led west to Lesser Springburn. He glanced at the Queen once more, and despite her sweet face telling him that she didn't judge him ill, he felt the need to make an excuse.

"She doesn't *know*, Majesty," he said to his monarch. "I've never said anything. I've never done . . . Well, I wouldn't do, would I? You know that."

Her Majesty smiled. Martin could tell she didn't quite believe him.

At the bottom of the drive, he parked the float, pulling off the lane so that the Mercedes that had interrupted his daydream could glide quietly past. The woman driving it gave him a scowl and two fingers. Londoner, he thought with resignation. Kent had started going to the devil the very day they had opened the M20 and made it easier for Londoners to live in the country and commute to work.

He hoped Her Majesty hadn't seen the woman's rude gesture. Or the one that he'd made in return once the Mercedes had swung round the bend and sailed off towards Maidstone.

Martin adjusted the rear-view mirror so that he could study his reflection. He checked to make sure there was no stubble on his cheeks. He gave a feather-light pat to his hair. This he carefully combed and sprayed every morning after spending ten minutes massaging a tablespoon of GroMore SuperStrength into his scalp. He'd been actively involved in improving his personal appearance for just over a month now, ever since the first morning when Gabriella Patten had drifted out to the gate of Celandine Cottage to fetch the milk from him in person.

Gabriella Patten. The very thought of her made him sigh. Gabriella. In an ebony silk dressing gown that whispered when she walked. With the sleep still clouding her cornflower eyes and her tousled hair shining like wheat in the sun.

When the order had come to start delivering milk to Celandine Cottage once again, Martin had filed the information in the part of his brain that took him through his delivery route on automatic pilot. He hadn't bothered to wonder why the regular request for two pints had been changed to one. He merely parked at the base of the drive one morning, rustled in the float for the cool glass bottle, wiped the moisture off it with the rag he kept on the floor, and pushed through the white wooden gate that fenced the cottage drive from Water Street.

He was putting the milk into the shaded box at the top of the drive where it nestled at the base of a silver fir when he heard footsteps coming along the path that curved from the drive to the kitchen door. He looked up, ready to say, "Morning to you," but the words caught somewhere between his throat and his tongue when he saw Gabriella Patten for the very first time.

She was yawning, stumbling slightly on the uneven bricks, with her unbelted dressing gown fluttering as she walked. She was naked beneath it.

He knew he ought to turn away, but he found himself mesmerised by the contrast of the dressing gown against her pale skin. And such skin, like the underside petals of granny's nightcap, white as shelduck's down and edged in pink. The pink of her burned him in the eyes, throat, and groin. He stared and said, "Jesus." It was as much thanksgiving as it was surprise.

She gave a gasp and drew the dressing gown round her. "Good Lord, I'd no idea . . ." She raised three fingers to her upper lip and smiled behind them. "I'm awfully sorry, but I didn't expect anyone. And certainly not you. I always thought the milk came at dawn."

He'd begun backing away at once, saying, "Nope. No. Just about this time. Just about ten A.M. is the usual hereabouts." He reached for his peaked cap to give it a pull and cover more of his face, which felt like embers were burning down it. Only he hadn't worn a cap that morning. He never wore a cap from April Fools' on, no matter the weather. So he ended up tugging at his hair like some simpleton on one of those fancy-dress television programmes.

"Well, I've a lot to learn about the country then, haven't I, Mister . . . ?"

"Martin," he said. "That is, Snell. Martin."

"Ah. Mr. Martin Snell Martin." She came out of the latticework gate that separated the drive from the lawn. She bent—he averted his eyes—and flipped up the top of the milk box. She said, "This is quite lovely. Thank you," and when he turned back, she'd taken the pint of milk and was holding it between her breasts, in the V made by the closure of her dressing gown. "It's cold," she said.

"Forecast is for sun today," he replied stoutly. "We should see it by noon or thereabouts."

She smiled again. She had the softest eyes when she smiled. "I meant the milk. How do you keep it so cold?"

"Oh. The float. I got some holders're insulated special."

"Do you promise I'll always be able to fetch it like this?" She gave the bottle a turn so it seemed to rest more deeply between her breasts. "Cold, that is."

"Oh, yes. Sure. Cold," he said.

"Thank you," she said. "Mr. Martin Snell Martin."

He saw her several times a week after that, but never again in her dressing gown. Not that he needed reminding what the sight of her had been like.

Gabriella. Gabriella. He loved the sound of it inside his head, trembling like it was set to violins.

Martin readjusted the rearview mirror, satisfied that he looked his best. Even if his hair wasn't much thicker than it had been before he started his treatments, it was far less wispy since he'd begun with the spray. He rustled in the back of the float to find the pint of milk he always kept coldest. He wiped off its moisture and polished its foil top on the front of his shirt.

He pushed through the drive's gate. He noticed that it was off the latch and he said, "Gate, gate, gate," just above a whisper to remind himself to mention it to her. The gate didn't have a lock, of course, but there was no need to make it easier for anyone who might want to intrude on her privacy.

The cuckoo he'd pointed out to Her Majesty was calling again, from somewhere beyond the paddock that lay to the north of the cottage. The lark's song had been joined by the twittering of redpolls perched in the conifers that edged the drive. A horse whinnied softly and a rooster crowed. It was, Martin thought, a glory of a day.

He lifted the top of the milk box. He started to place his delivery inside. He stopped. He frowned. Something wasn't right.

Yesterday's milk hadn't been fetched. The bottle was warm. Whatever condensation had gathered on the glass and dripped to the bottle's base had long since evaporated.

Well, he thought at first, she's a flighty one, is Miss Gabriella. She's gone off somewhere without leaving a note about her milk. He picked up yesterday's bottle and tucked it under his arm. He'd stop delivering till he heard from her again.

He started back towards the gate, but then he remembered. The gate, the gate. Off the latch, he thought, and he felt a flutter of trepidation.

Slowly, he retraced his steps to the milk box. He stood in front of the garden gate. Her newspapers hadn't been fetched either, he saw. Yesterday's and today's—one copy each of the *Daily Mail* and *The Times*—were in their respective holders. And when he squinted at the front door with its iron slot for the post, he saw a small triangle of white resting against the weathered oak and he thought, She's not fetched the post either; she must be gone. But the curtains were opened at the windows, which didn't seem practical or wise if she'd taken off. Not that Miss Gabriella appeared to be either practical or wise by nature, but she'd know enough not to leave the cottage so obviously unoccupied. Wouldn't she?

He wasn't certain. He looked over his shoulder at the garage, a brick and clapboard structure at the top of the drive. Best to check, he decided. He wouldn't need to go in or even to open the door all the way. He'd just need a peek to make sure she'd gone. Then he'd take away the milk, he'd carry the newspapers off to the rubbish, and he'd be on his way. After a peek.

The garage was big enough for two cars, and the doors to it opened in the centre. They usually had a padlock, but Martin could see without a close inspection that the lock wasn't currently being used. One of the doors stood open a good three inches. Martin went to the door and with an indrawn breath and a glance in the direction of the cottage, he eased it open one inch more and pressed his face to the crack.

He saw a glimmer of chrome as the light struck the bumper of the silver Aston Martin that he'd seen her spinning along the lanes in, a dozen times or more. Martin felt a peculiar buzzing in his head at the sight of it. He looked back at the cottage.

If the car was here and she was here, then why had she not taken in her milk?

Perhaps she'd been gone all day yesterday from early morning, he answered himself. Perhaps she'd got home late and forgotten about the milk altogether.

But what about the newspapers? Unlike the milk, they were in plain sight in their holders. She'd have had to walk right past them to go into the cottage. Why wouldn't she have taken them with her?

Because she'd been shopping in London and her arms were filled with packages and she'd simply forgotten to fetch the newspapers later, once she'd set the packages down.

And the post? It would be lying right inside the front door. Why would she have left it there?

Because it was late, she was tired, she wanted to go to bed, and she hadn't gone in the front door anyway. She'd gone in through the kitchen so she hadn't seen the post. She had walked right by it and gone up to bed where even now she was still asleep.

Asleep, asleep. Sweet Gabriella. In a black silk gown with her hair curled against it and her lashes like buttercup filaments against her skin.

It wouldn't hurt to check, Martin thought. Most definitely, it wouldn't hurt to check. She wouldn't be miffed. That wasn't her way. She'd be touched that he thought of her, a woman alone out here in the country without a man to see to her welfare. She'd likely ask him in.

He settled his shoulders, took the newspapers, and pushed open the gate. He made his way along the path. The sun hadn't struck this part of the garden yet, so the dew still lay like a beaded shawl on the bricks and the lawn. Against both sides of the old front door, lavender and wallflowers were planted. Buds on the first sent up a sharp fragrance. Flowers on the second nodded with the weight of the morning's moisture.

Martin reached for the bell-pull and heard its jangle just inside the door. He waited for the sound of her footsteps or her voice calling out or the whirl and clank of the key in the lock. But none of that happened.

Perhaps, he thought, she was having her bath, or perhaps she was in the kitchen where, perhaps again, she couldn't hear the bell. It would be wise to check.

He did so, going round to thump on the back door and wondering how people managed to use it without knocking themselves senseless on the lintel, which hung only five feet from the ground. Which then made him think . . . Could she have been in a rush to get in or get out? Could she have rendered her sweet self unconscious? There was neither answer nor movement behind the white panels. Could she be lying this very moment on the cold kitchen floor, waiting for someone to find her?

To the right of the door, beneath an arbour, a casement window looked into the kitchen. And Martin looked into the window. But he couldn't see anything beyond a small linen-covered table, the work top, the Aga, the sink, and the closed door to the dining room. He'd have to find another window. And one preferably on this side of the house because he was feeling decidedly uneasy about peering through the windows like a Peeping Tom. It wouldn't do to be seen from the road. God alone knew what it would do to business if someone drove by and saw Martin Snell, milkman and monarchist, having a peek where he oughtn't.

He had to climb through a flower-bed to get to the dining room window on this same side of the house. He did his best not to trample the violets. He squeezed behind a lilac bush and gained the glass.

Odd, he thought. He couldn't see through it. He could see the shape of curtains against it, open like the others, but nothing more. It seemed to be dirty, filthy in fact, which was even stranger because the kitchen window had been clean as brook water and the cottage itself was as white as a lamb. He rubbed his fingers against the glass. Strangest of all. The glass wasn't dirty. At least, not on the outside.

Something jangled in his mind, some sort of warning that he couldn't identify. It sounded like a flock of snow buntings in flight, soft then loud then louder again. The noise in his head made his arms feel weak.

He climbed out of the flower bed. He retraced his steps. He tried the back door. Locked. He hurried to the front door. Locked as well. He strode round the south side of the house where wisteria grew against the exposed black timbers. He turned the corner and made his way along the flagstone path that bordered the structure's west wall. At the far end, he found the other dining room window.

This one wasn't dirty, either outside or in. He grasped onto its sill. He took a breath. He looked.

Everything seemed normal upon a first glance. The burl-topped dining table, the chairs surrounding it, the open fireplace with its iron fire-back and its copper bedwarmers hanging upon the bricks. Everything looked fine. The pine dresser held dishes, an antique washstand displayed the makings of drinks. To one side of the fireplace stood a heavy armchair and across the room from it, at the foot of the stairs the matching armchair—

Martin tightened his fingers against the window-sill. He felt a splinter dig into his palm. He said, "Oh Majesty Majesty Gabriella Miss Miss," and plunged one hand frantically into his pocket, looking in vain for something that he could use to jemmy the casement open. All the time his eyes were fixed on that chair.

It stood at an angle at the foot of the stairs, facing into the dining room. One corner of it abutted the wall underneath the window that had been too dirty to look through. Only now Martin saw from his position on the other side of the house that the window wasn't dirty at all in the conventional sense. Instead, it was stained black from smoke: smoke that had risen in an ugly dense cloud from the wingback chair, smoke that had risen in the shape of a tornado that blackened the window, blackened the curtains, blackened the wall, smoke that left its mark on the stairway as it was sucked upwards towards the bedroom where even now Miss Gabriella, Miss Sweet Gabriella . . .

Martin shoved himself away from the window. He ran across the lawn. He clambered over the wall. He dashed down the footpath in the direction of the spring.

It was shortly after noon when Detective Inspector Isabelle Ardery first saw Celandine Cottage. The sun was high in the sky, casting small pools of shadow at the base of the fir trees that lined the drive. This had been sealed off with yellow police tape. One panda car, a red Sierra, and a blue and white milk-float were lined up on the lane.

She parked behind the milk-float and surveyed the area, feeling grim despite her initial pleasure at being called out on another case so soon. For information gathering, the location didn't look promising. There were several houses farther along the lane, timber-framed with peg-tiled roofs like the cottage in which the fire had occurred, but they were each surrounded with enough land to give them quiet and privacy. So if the fire in question turned out to be arson—as was suggested by the words *question-able ignition* scrawled at the bottom of the note Ardery had received from her chief constable not an hour ago—it might prove unlikely that any of the neighbours had heard or seen someone or something suspicious.

With her collection kit in hand, she ducked under the tape and swung open the gate at the end of the drive. Across a paddock to the east where a bay mare was grazing, half a dozen onlookers leaned against a split chestnut fence. She could hear their murmured speculation as she walked up the drive. Yes, indeed, she told them mentally as she passed through a smaller gate into the garden, a woman investigator, even for a fire. Welcome to the waning years of our century.

"Inspector Ardery?" It was a female voice. Isabelle turned to see another woman waiting on the brick path that led in two directions: to the front door and round towards the back of the house. She'd apparently come from this latter direction. "DS Coffman," she said cheerfully. "Greater Springburn CID."

Isabelle joined her. She offered her hand.

Coffman said, "The guv's not here at the moment. He rode with the body to Pembury Hospital."

Isabelle frowned at this oddity. Greater Springburn's chief superintendent had been the one to request her presence in the first place. It was a breach of police etiquette for him to leave the site before her arrival. "The hospital?" she asked. "Have you no medical examiner to accompany the body?"

Coffman gave her eyes a quick rise heavenward. "Oh, he was here as well, graciously assuring us that the corpse was dead. But there's to be a news conference when they i.d. the victim, and the guv loves that stuff. Give him a microphone, five minutes of your time, and he does a fairly decent John Thaw."

"Who's still here, then?"

"Couple of probationary DCs getting their first chance to suss things out. And the bloke who discovered the mess. Snell, he's called."

"What about the fire brigade?"

"They've been and gone. Snell phoned emergency from next door, house across from the spring. Emergency sent the fire team."

"And?"

Coffman smiled. "Luck for your side. Once they got in, they could see the fire'd been out for hours. They didn't touch a thing. They just phoned CID and waited till we got here."

That fact, at least, was a blessing. One of the biggest difficulties in arson investigation was the necessary existence of the fire brigade. They were trained to two tasks: saving lives and extinguishing fires. Intent upon that, more often than not they axed down doors, flooded rooms, collapsed ceilings, and in the process obliterated evidence.

Isabelle ran her gaze over the building. She said, "All right. I'll take a moment out here, first."

"Shall I—"

"Alone, please."

Coffman said, "Quite. I'll leave you to it," and strode off towards the back of the house. She paused at the northeast corner of the building, turning back and pushing a curl of oak-coloured hair from her face. "The hot spot's this way when you're ready," she said. She began to raise an index finger in comradely salute, apparently thought better of it, and disappeared round the side of the house.

Isabelle stepped off the brick path and crossed the lawn, walking to the far corner of the property. There she turned back and gazed first at the cottage and then at the grounds that surrounded it.

If arson had been committed here, finding evidence outside the building wasn't going to be easy. It would take hours to conduct a search on the grounds because Celandine Cottage was an amateur gardener's dream: hung on the south end by wisteria just coming into bloom, surrounded by flower beds from which grew everything from forget-me-nots to heather, from white violets to lavender, from pansies to tulips. Where there weren't flower-beds, there was lawn, thick and lush. Where there wasn't lawn, there were shrubs in bloom. Where there weren't shrubs, there were trees. These last provided a partial screen from the lane and another from the nearest neighbour. If there were footprints, tyre prints, discarded tools, fuel containers, or matchbooks, it was going to take some effort to find them.

Isabelle circled the house carefully, moving east to northwest. She examined windows. She scanned the ground. She gave her attention to roof and to doors. In the end, she made her way to the back where the kitchen door stood open and where, under an arbour across which a grapevine was beginning to unfurl its leaves, a middle-aged man sat at a wicker table, with his head sunk into his chest and his hands pressed together between his knees. A glass of water stood, untouched, before him.

"Mr. Snell?"

The man lifted his head. "Took the body, they did," he said. "She was covered up all from head to toe. She was wrapped up and tied down. It looked like they'd put her in some sort of bag. It's not proper, that, is it? It's not quite decent. It's not even respectful."

Isabelle joined him, pulling out a chair and setting her collection kit on the concrete. She felt an instant's duty to comfort him, but making an effort at compassion seemed pointless. Dead was dead no matter what anyone said or did. Nothing changed that fact for the living. "Mr. Snell, were the doors locked or unlocked when you arrived?"

"I tried to get in when she didn't answer. But I couldn't. So I looked in the window." He squeezed his hands together and took a tremulous breath. "She wouldn't have suffered, would she? I heard one of them say the body wasn't even burnt and that's why they could tell who it was straightaway. Did she die from the smoke, then?"

"We won't know anything for certain until a postmortem is done," DS Coffman said. She'd come to the doorway. Her answer sounded professionally cautious.

The man seemed to accept it. He said, "What about them kittens?"

"Kittens?" Isabelle asked.

"Miss Gabriella's kittens. Where're they? No one's brought them out."

Coffman said, "They must be outside somewhere. We've not run across them in the house."

"But she got herself two little 'uns last week. Two kittens. From over by the spring. Someone'd dumped them in a cardboard box next to the footpath. She brought them home. She was caring for them. They slept in the kitchen in their own little basket and—" Snell wiped the back of his wrist against his eyes. "I got to see to the milk delivery. Before it goes bad."

"Have you got his statement?" Isabelle asked Coffman as she ducked beneath the low lintel of the doorway to join the DS in the kitchen.

"For what it's worth. Thought you might want to have a chat with him yourself. Shall I send him off?"

"If we've got his address."

"Right. I'll see to it. We're in through there." Coffman gestured towards an inner door. Beyond it, Isabelle could see the curve of a dining table and the end of a wall-sized fireplace.

"Who's been inside?"

"Three blokes from the fire brigade. The CID lot."

"Crime team?"

"Just the photographer and the pathologist. I thought it best to keep the rest out till you had a look."

She led Isabelle into the dining room. Two probationary detective constables stood on either side of what was left of a wingback chair positioned at an angle at the base of the stairway. They were frowning down at it, each of them a picture of contemplation. One looked earnest. The other looked offended by the acrid smell of incinerated upholstery. Neither could have been more than twenty-three years old.

"Inspector Ardery," Coffman said by way of introducing Isabelle. "Maidstone Constabulary's hot shot of hot spots. You two move back and give her some space. And try taking a few notes while you're at it."

Isabelle nodded at the young men and gave her attention to what was obviously the point of ignition. She set her collection kit on the table, put the tape measure into her jacket pocket along with tweezers and pliers, took out her notebook, and made a preliminary sketch of the room, saying, "Nothing's been moved?"

"Not a stitch or a hair," Coffman replied. "Which is why I phoned for the guv when I had a look. It's that chair by the stairs. Look. It doesn't seem right."

Isabelle didn't agree with the sergeant readily. She knew the other woman was heading towards a logical question: What was the chair doing sitting at such an angle at the foot of the stairs? One would have to skirt it to climb to the first floor. Its position suggested its having been moved there.

But, on the other hand, the room was also crowded with other furniture, none of it burned but all of it either discoloured by smoke or covered with soot. In addition to the dining table and its four chairs, an old-fashioned nursing chair and a second wingback stood on either side of the fireplace. Against one wall leaned a dresser holding china, against another a table covered with decanters, against a third a chest of drawers displaying porcelain. And on every wall also hung paintings and prints. The walls themselves had apparently been white. One was now scorched black; the others were varying degrees of grey. As were the lace curtains, which hung limply on their rods, crusted with grime.

"Have you examined the carpet?" Isabelle asked the sergeant. "If that chair's been moved, we'll find its prints somewhere else. Perhaps in another room.''

"That's just it," Coffman said. "Have a look here."

Isabelle said, "A moment," and completed the drawing, shading in the pattern of scorching on the wall. She created a quick floor-plan next and labelled its components—furniture, fireplace, windows, doorways, and stairs. And only then did she approach the source of ignition. Here she made a third drawing of the chair itself, noting the distinct burn pattern in the upholstery. It was standard stuff.

A localised fire such as this spread in a V, with the origin of the burn at the V's tip. This fire had behaved in a normal fashion. Along the chair's right side, which ran at a forty-five-degree angle from the stairway, the charring was heaviest. The fire had first smouldered—probably for several hours—then flamed through both upholstery and stuffing, eating its way upwards to the chair's frame on the right side before dying out. On this same right side, the burn pattern rose in two angles from the flame source, one oblique and one acute, roughly forming a V. Upon Isabelle's preliminary inspection, nothing about the chair suggested arson.

"It looks like a cigarette smoulder if you ask me," one of the two young detective constables said. He sounded restless. It was after noon. He was hungry. Isabelle saw Sergeant Coffman shoot the man a narrow-eyed look that clearly declared, "But no one's asking you, are they, laddie?" He quickly adjusted his attitude by saying, "What I don't get is why the whole place didn't burn to the ground."

"Were all the windows closed?" Isabelle asked the sergeant.

"They were."

Isabelle said over her shoulder in explanation to the constable, "The fire in the chair consumed what oxygen there was in the cottage. Afterwards, it died."

Sergeant Coffman squatted next to the charred armchair. Isabelle joined her. The fitted carpet had been a solid colour—beige. Beneath the chair it wore a heavy snowfall of black grit. Coffman pointed to three shallow depressions, each one by measurement two and a half inches from a corresponding leg of the chair. She said, "This is what I was talking about."

Isabelle fetched a brush from her collection kit, saying, "It's a possibility," and she gently flicked the soot from the nearest cavity and then from another. When she'd done them all, she saw that they were perfectly lined up with each other, the impressions the chair had made in its original position.

"You see. It's been moved. Pivoted on one leg."

Isabelle rested back on her heels and studied the chair's position in relation to the rest of the room. "Someone could have run into it."

"But don't you think—"

"We need more."

She moved closer to the chair. She examined the point of the fire's origin, an uneven carbon wound from which bled wiry lengths of kindled stuffing. As was the case in so many smouldering fires, the chair had burnt slowly, sending up a steady, noxious stream of smoke as a glowing means of primary ignition—like an ember—had eaten through upholstery to the stuffing beneath it. But true to the smouldering fire as well, the chair had only been partially demolished, because once complete ignition occurred, available oxygen had already been eaten and the fire died.

Thus, Isabelle was able to probe the carbon wound, delicately moving aside charred fabric in order to follow the descent of the ember as it sank through the right side of the chair. It was painstaking work, a wordless scrutiny of every centimetre by light of a torch, which Coffman held steady over her shoulder. More than quarter of an hour passed before Isabelle found what she was looking for.

She used the tweezers to pull the prize out. She gave it a satisfied scrutiny before she held it up.

"Cigarette after all." Coffman sounded disappointed.

"No." In contrast to the sergeant, Isabelle felt decidedly pleased. "It's an incendiary device." She looked at the detective constables whose expressions awakened with interest at her words. "We'll need to start outside with a perimeter search," she told them. "Use a spiral pattern. Look for footprints, tyre prints, a matchbox, tools, containers of any kind, anything unusual. Chart it first. Then photograph and collect it. Understand?"

"Ma'am," one said as "Right," said the other. They headed for the kitchen and from there outside.

Coffman was frowning at the stub of cigarette that Isabelle still held. "I don't get it," she said.

Isabelle pointed out the scalloped condition of the cigarette's casing.

"So?" Coffman said. "Still looks like a cigarette to me."

"That's what it's meant to look like. Bring the light closer. Keep as clear from the chair as you can. Fine. Right there."

"You mean it isn't a cigarette?" Coffman asked as Isabelle continued to probe. "It's not a real cigarette?"

"It is and it isn't."

"I don't get it."

"Which is, of course, the arsonist's hope."

"But—"

"If I'm not mistaken—and we'll know in a few minutes because this chair's going to tell us—what we've got is a primitive timing device. It gives the fire raiser four to seven minutes to be gone before the actual flames begin."

Coffman jiggled the torch as she started to speak, caught herself, said, "Sorry," and redirected the light as before. She went on with, "If that's the case, when the flames *did* begin, why didn't the entire chair go up? Wouldn't the arsonist have wanted it that way? I know the windows were closed, but surely the fire had enough time to go from the chair to the curtains and up the wall before the oxygen ran out. So why didn't it do that? Why didn't the windows break from the heat and let in more air? Why didn't the whole blooming cottage go up?"

Isabelle continued the process of delicate probing. It was an operation not unlike taking the chair apart a single strand at a time. "You're talking about the speed of the fire," she said. "Speed depends upon the chair's upholstery and stuffing, along with the amount of draft in the room. It.depends upon the weave of the fabric. And the age of the stuffing and how and if it's been chemically treated." She fingered an edge of the singed material. "We'll have to run tests to get the answers. But there's one thing I'd lay money on."

"Arson?" Coffman said. "Meant to look like something else?"

"That's what I'd say."

Coffman glanced at the stairway beyond the chair. "That makes things real dicey, then." Her words were uneasy.

"I dare say. Arson usually does." Isabelle brought forth from the bowels of the chair the first sliver of wood that she'd been seeking. She dropped it into a collection jar with a gratified smile. "Excellent," she murmured. "As lovely a sight as you can hope to see." There would be, she was certain, at least five more wooden slivers buried within the charred remains of the chair. She went back to her probing, separating, and sifting. "Who was she, by the way?"

"Who was who?"

"The victim. The woman with the kittens."

"That's the problem," Coffman replied. "That's why the guv's gone to Pembury with the body. That's why there'll be a news conference later. That's why it's all so dicey now."

"Why?"

"A woman lives here, you see."

"A film star or something? Someone important?"

"She isn't that. She isn't even a she."

Isabelle raised her head. "What's going on?"

"Snell doesn't know. No one knows but us."

"No one knows what?"

"The body upstairs was a man's."

CHAPTER
2

When the police showed up at Billingsgate Market, it was mid-afternoon, and by all rights Jeannie shouldn't even have been there because at that hour the London fish market was as dead and as empty as an underground station at three in the morning. But she *was* there, waiting for a repairman who was on his way to Crissys Café to fix the cooker. It had broken down at the worst possible time, in the middle of the rush that usually came around half past nine after the fishmongers had dealt with the buyers from the city's posh restaurants and the rubbish crew had finished ridding the vast car park of Styrofoam crates and mollusc nets.

The girls—for they were always called *the girls* at Crissys, no matter that the oldest was fifty-eight and the youngest was Jeannie herself, thirty-two—had managed to coax the cooker into working at half heat for the rest of the morning, which allowed them to continue competently setting out fried bacon and bread, eggs, blood pudding, welsh rabbit, and toasted sausage sandwiches as if nothing were the matter. But if they were to avoid a mutiny among their customers—worse, if they were to avoid losing their customers to Catons upstairs—the small caff's cooker would have to be fixed at once.

The girls drew lots for the responsibility in the same way they'd been drawing lots for the fifteen years Jeannie had worked with them. They lit wooden matches simultaneously and watched them burn down. The first person to drop hers lost.

Jeannie was as good as any of them at holding on till the flame licked her fingers, but today she wanted to lose the burn. Winning meant she'd have to go home. Staying and waiting God knew how long for the repairman to show up meant she could avoid trying to think what to do about Jimmy a while longer. Everyone from her nearest neighbours to the school authorities was using the word *juvenile* in a way Jeannie didn't like when they talked about her son. They said it the way they'd say *yob* or *bloody little sod* or *thug*, none of which applied. But they wouldn't know that, would they, because they only saw the surface of the boy and they didn't stop to think what might be underneath.

Underneath, Jimmy hurt. He had four years of hurting that matched her own.

Jeannie was sitting at one of the tables by a window, having a cuppa and munching from a bag of carrot sticks that she always brought from home, when she finally heard the car door slam. She assumed it was the repairman at last. She glanced at the wall clock. It was after three. She closed her copy of *Woman's Own* upon "How Do You Know If You're Good in Bed?", rolled the magazine into a tube that she tucked into the pocket of her smock, and pushed back her chair. It was then that she saw it was a panda car, occupied by a man and a woman. And because one of them *was* a woman, who looked grave and searched the length of the sprawling brick building with sombre eyes as she set her shoulders and adjusted the triangular tips of the collar of her blouse, Jeannie felt a quiver of warning run across her skin.

Automatically, she looked at the clock a second time and thought of Jimmy. She offered a prayer that, despite his disappointment at the ruin of his sixteenth birthday holiday, her oldest child had gone to school. If he hadn't, if he'd done yet another bunk, if he'd been picked up somewhere he oughtn't be, if this woman and this man—and why were there two of them?—had come to inform his mother of another piece of mischief . . . It didn't bear thinking what might have happened since Jeannie had left the house at ten till four that morning.

She went to the counter and fumbled a packet of cigarettes from where one of the other girls kept her secret stash. She lit it, felt the smoke burn against her throat and fill her lungs, felt the immediate sense of light in her head.

She met the man and woman at the door to Crissys. The woman was exactly Jeannie's height, and like Jeannie, she had smooth skin that crinkled round the eyes, and light hair that couldn't rightly be called either blonde or brown. She introduced herself and presented an identification that Jeannie didn't look at, once she heard her name and title. Coffman, she said. Detective Sergeant. Agnes, she added, as if having a Christian name somehow might soften the effect of her presence. She said she was from Greater Springburn CID and she introduced the young man with her, giving his name as Detective Constable Dick Payne or Nick Dane or some variation thereof. Jeannie didn't catch it because she heard nothing else clearly once the woman said Greater Springburn.

"You're Jean Fleming?" Sergeant Coffman said.

"Was," Jeannie said. "Eleven years of Jean Fleming. It's Cooper now. Jean Cooper. Why? Who wants to know?"

The sergeant touched a knuckle to the spot between her eyebrows as if this helped her to think. She said, "I've been made to understand . . . You *are* the wife of Kenneth Fleming?"

"I got no decree yet, if that's what you're thinking. So I s'pose we're still married," Jeannie replied. "But being married's not exactly the same as being someone's wife, is it?"

"No. I suppose not." But there was something about the way the sergeant said those four words and something even more in the way the sergeant looked at Jeannie as she said them that made her suck in hard on her cigarette. "Mrs. Fleming . . . Miss Cooper . . . Ms. Cooper . . ." Sergeant Agnes Coffman went on. The young constable with her dropped his head.

And then Jeannie knew. The real message was contained in the piling up of names. Jeannie didn't even need her to say the words. Kenny was dead. He was smashed on the motorway or knifed on the platform of Kensington High Street Station or thrown two hundred feet from a zebra crossing or hit by a bus or . . . What did it matter? However it had happened, it was over at last. He couldn't come back yet another time and sit across the kitchen table from her and talk and smile. He couldn't make her want to reach out and touch the red-gold hairs on the back of his hand.

She'd thought more than once in the last four years that she would be glad at this moment. She'd thought, If something could just wipe him off the face of the earth and free me of loving the bastard even now when he's left and everyone knows I wasn't good enough, we weren't good enough, we weren't family enough . . . I wanted him to die and die and die a thousand times, I wanted him to be gone, I wanted him to be smashed into bits, I wanted him to suffer.

She thought how odd it was that she wasn't even shaking. She said, "Is Kenny dead then, Sergeant?"

"We need an official identification. We need you to view the body. I'm terribly sorry."

She wanted to say, "Why not ask her to do it? She was hot enough to view the body when he was alive."

Instead, she said, "If you'll excuse me, I'll need to use the phone, first," and the sergeant said of course she could and then retreated with the detective constable to the other side of the caff where they looked out of the windows, across the harbour to the pyramid-topped glass towers of Canary Wharf, another failing promise of hope, jobs, and redevelopment that those toffs from the City periodically flung at the lower East End.

Jeannie phoned her parents, hoping to get her mother but getting Derrick instead. She tried to manage her voice and give nothing away. Upon hearing a simple request, her mother would have gone to Jeannie's and waited with the children and not asked questions. But with Derrick, Jeannie had to be careful. Her brother always wanted to be in too close.

So she lied, telling Derrick that the repairman she was waiting for at the caff was going to be hours and would he go to her place and see to the kids? Get them their tea? Try to keep Jimmy from doing a bunk this evening? Make sure Stan brushed his teeth proper? Help Sharon with her school work?

The request appealed to Derrick's need to replace the two families he'd already lost to divorce. Going to Jeannie's meant he'd have to miss his nightly session with his weights—continuing the process of sculpting every muscle on his body to a monstrous kind of perfection—but in its place would be a chance to play Dad without the attendant lifelong responsibilities.

Jeannie turned to the police and said, "I'm ready, then," and followed them out to their car.

It took ages to get there because for some reason that Jeannie didn't understand they didn't use the siren or the twirly lights. Rush hour had begun. They crossed the river and crawled through the suburbs, passing endless postwar buildings of sooty brick. When they finally made it to the motorway, the going was little better.

They changed motorways once and then left the second one altogether when the signposts started announcing Tonbridge. They wound through two villages, zipped between hedges in the open country, and slowed as they finally came into a town. They eventually stopped at the rear entrance to a hospital where behind a makeshift barrier of rubbish bins half a dozen photographers began clicking and popping with their cameras the moment the Payne-Dane constable opened Jeannie's door.

Jeannie hesitated, clutching her handbag. She said, "Can't you make them . . . ?"

To which Sergeant Coffman said over the back of her seat, "I'm sorry. We've been holding them off since noon."

"But how d'they *know*? Have you said? Have you told?"

"No."

"Then how . . . ?"

Coffman got out and came to Jeannie's door. "Someone works the police beat. Someone else listens in to radio transmissions with a scanner. Someone else—at the station, sorry to say—usually has a loose tongue. The press put things together. But they don't know anything for sure yet, and you don't have to tell them. All right?"

Jeannie nodded.

"Good. Here. Quick now. Let me take your arm."

Jeannie ran her hand against her smock and felt its coarse material against her palm. She stepped out of the car. Voices began to shout, "Mrs. Fleming! Can you tell us . . ." as cameras whirred. Between the young detective constable and the sergeant, she hurried inside the glass doors that swung open at their approach.

They went in through the casualty ward where the air stung their eyes with the smell of disinfectant and someone was crying, "It's my chest, goddamn you!" At first, Jeannie was aware of little but the prevalence of white. The moving bodies in laboratory coats and in uniforms, the sheets on trolleys, the papers on charts, the shelves that seemed covered with gauze and cotton wool. And then, she started to hear the sounds. Feet on the linoleum floor, the *shoosh* of a door swinging shut, the creaking wheels of a cart. And the voices, in an auditory rainbow:

"It's his heart. I know it."

"Won't one of you look . . ."

". . . off his feed for two days . . ."

"We'll need an ECG."

". . . Solu Cortef. Stat!"

And someone clattering past, shouting, "Give way," pushing a trolley on which sat a machine with cords, dials, and knobs.

Through it all, Jeannie could feel Sergeant Coffman's hand on her arm, curved just above her elbow, warm and firm. The constable didn't touch her, but he kept close by her side. They walked down a first corridor, then another. They finally came to more white and a new sensation—cold—in an area of quiet with a metal door. Jeannie knew they were there.

Sergeant Coffman said, "Would you like something first? Tea? Coffee? A Coke? Some water?"

Jeannie shook her head. "I'm all right," she said.

"Are you feeling faint? You've gone rather pale. Here. Sit down."

"I'm all right. I'll stand."

Sergeant Coffman peered at her face for a moment as if doubting her words. Then she nodded at the constable who gave a knock on the door and disappeared through it. Sergeant Coffman said, "It won't be long." Jeannie thought it had been quite long enough, years in the making. But she said, "Fine."

The constable was gone less than a minute. When he popped his head round the door and said, "They're ready for you," Sergeant Coffman took Jeannie's arm again and they walked inside.

She'd been expecting to confront his body immediately, laid out and washed like they did in old films, with chairs all round it, suitable for viewing. But instead they walked into an office where a secretary was watching paper spew out of a printer. On either side of her desk, two doors stood closed. A man in green surgical garb was positioned next to one of them, his hand on its knob.

He said, "In here," in a quiet voice. He swung his door open and as Jeannie approached it, she heard Sergeant Coffman say softly, "Got the salts?" and she felt the green man take her other arm as he said, "Yes."

Inside, it was cold. It was bright. It was spotless. There seemed to be stainless steel everywhere. There were lockers, long work tops, cupboards on the walls, and a single trolley angling out beneath them. A green sheet covered this, the same split-pea colour as the green man's medical garb. They approached as if on their way to an altar. And just like at church, when they stopped, they were silent as if experiencing awe. Jeannie realised the others were waiting for her to give them a sign that she was prepared. So she said, "Let's see him, then," and the green man bent forward and rolled the sheet back to expose the face.

She said, "Why's he so pink?"

The green man said, "Is this your husband?"

Sergeant Coffman said, "Carbon monoxide flushes the skin when it gets into the bloodstream."

The green man said, "Is this your husband, Mrs. Fleming?"

So easy to say yes, have done with it, and be out of there. So easy to turn, walk back down those corridors, face the cameras and the questions without giving answers because there were none really—there never had been. So easy just to slip into the car, to be driven off and to ask for sirens to make the going quick. But she couldn't form the right word. *Yes.* It seemed so simple. But she couldn't say it.

Instead she said, "Pull down the sheet."

The green man hesitated. Sergeant Coffman said, "Mrs. . . . Ms. . . ." and sounded in pain.

"Pull down the sheet."

They wouldn't understand, but that didn't matter because in another few hours they'd be out of her life. Kenny, on the other hand, would be there forever: in the faces of her children, in the unexpected slide of footsteps on the stairs, in the eternal whip-crack of a leather ball as somewhere in the world on a clipped green field the willow wood hit it soaring over the boundary for another six.

She could tell that the sergeant and the green man were looking at each other, wondering exactly what they ought to do. But it was her decision, wasn't it, to see the rest. It had nothing at all to do with them.

The green man folded the sheet with both hands, starting at the body's shoulders. He did it neatly, each fold a precise three inches across, and slowly enough so that he could stop the moment she told him she'd seen enough.

Except she'd never see enough. Jeannie knew this fact at the very same moment as she knew she'd never forget the sight of Kenny Fleming dead.

Ask them questions, she told herself. Ask them the questions anyone would ask. You got to. You must.

Who found him? Where was he? Was he naked like this? Why's he look so peaceful? How'd he die? When? Was she with him? Is her body nearby?

But instead she took a step nearer the trolley and thought about how she'd loved the clean angles of his collar bone and the muscles of his shoulders and arms. She remembered how his stomach was hard, how the hair grew thick and coarse round his penis, how his thighs were roped with the sinews of a runner, how his legs were lean. She thought about the twelve-year-old boy he'd been, fumbling with her knickers the very first time behind the packing crates on Invicta Wharf. She thought about the man he'd become and the woman she was and how even on the afternoon he'd driven that fancy car of his into Cubitt Town and sat in the kitchen and shared a cuppa and said the word *divorce* that she'd been expecting him to say for four years now, their fingers still finally managed to find each other and to grasp like blind things with a will of their own.

She thought of the years together—KennyandJean—that would trail her like hungry insistent dogs for the rest of her life. She thought of the years without him that unspooled before her in a ribbon of grief. She wanted to grab his body and throw it to the floor and drive her heel into his face. She wanted to claw at his chest and pound her fists into his throat. Hate beat in her skull and made a vice of her chest and told her how much she still loved him. Which made her hate him all the more. Which made her wish he could only die again and again right into eternity.

She said, "Yes," and stepped back from the trolley.

"It's Kenneth Fleming?" Sergeant Coffman said.

"It's him." Jeannie turned away. She disengaged the sergeant's hand from her arm. She adjusted her handbag so that its handle fit snugly into the bend of her elbow. She said, "I'd like to buy some fags. I don't suppose you got a tobacconist hereabouts?"

Sergeant Coffman said she'd see about the cigarettes as soon as she could. There were papers to be signed. If Mrs. Fleming—

"Cooper," Jeannie said.

If Ms. Cooper would come this way. . . .

The green man stayed behind with the corpse. Jeannie heard him give a low whistle-breath between his teeth as he rolled the trolley towards a hanging dome of light in the centre of the room. Jeannie thought she heard him mutter the word *Jesus*, but by that time the door had shut behind them and she was being seated at a desk beneath a poster of a long-haired dachshund puppy wearing a tiny straw hat.

Sergeant Coffman said something in a quiet voice to her constable, and Jeannie caught the word *cigarette*, so she said, "Make them Embassys, won't you?'' and began signing her name on the forms where the secretary had placed neat red *x*'s. She didn't know what the forms were or why she had to sign or what, indeed, she might be signing away or giving her permission to be done. She just kept signing and when she was through, the Embassys were sitting on the edge of the desk along with a box of matches. She lit up. The secretary and the constable coughed discreetly. Jeannie inhaled with deep satisfaction.

"That's finished things for now," Sergeant Coffman said. "If you'd like to come this way, we can take you out quickly and get you home."

"Right," Jeannie said. She got to her feet. She tucked the cigarettes and matches into her handbag. She followed the sergeant back into the corridor.

The questions hammered at them and the cameras' lights popped the moment they stepped into the evening air.

"It's Fleming, then?''

"Suicide?''

"Accident?''

"Can you tell us what happened? Anything, Mrs. Fleming.''

It's Cooper, Jeannie thought. Jean Stella Cooper.

Detective Inspector Thomas Lynley climbed the front steps of the Onslow Square building that housed the flat of Lady Helen Clyde. He hummed the same ten random notes of music that had been plaguing his brain like hungry mosquitoes ever since he'd left his office. He'd tried to drive them off with several quick recitations of the opening soliloquy from *Richard III*, but every time he directed his thoughts to dive down to his soul to herald the entrance of George, that wiliest Duke of Clarence, the blasted notes returned.

It wasn't until he had actually let himself into Helen's building and was bounding up the stairs to her flat that the source of his musical torment dawned upon him. And then he had to smile at the unconscious mind's ability to communicate through a medium he hadn't considered part of his world in years. He liked to think of himself as a classical music man, preferably a Russian classical music man. Rod Stewart singing "Tonight's the Night" was hardly the choice he himself would have made to underscore the evening's significance. Although, it was appropriate enough. As was Richard's soliloquy, come to think of it, since like Richard, plots he had laid and although his inductions were not at all dangerous, they were intended to lead in one direction. The concert, a late dinner, a postprandial stroll to that decidedly quiet and underlit restaurant just off the King's Road where, in the bar, one could depend upon soft music supplied by a harpist whose instrument rendered her incapable of wandering among the tables and interrupting conversations crucial to one's future. . . . Yes, Rod Stewart was perhaps more appropriate than *Richard III*, for all his scheming. Because tonight was indeed the night.

"Helen?" he called as he shut the door. "Are you ready, darling?"

Silence was the response. He frowned at this. He'd spoken to her at nine this morning. He'd told her he'd be by at a quarter past seven. While that gave them forty-five minutes to make a ten-minute drive, he knew Helen well enough to realise that he had to allow a lengthy margin for error and indecision when it came to her preparations for an evening out. Still, she usually made a reply, calling out, "In here, Tommy," from the bedroom where he would invariably find her attempting to resolve herself over six or eight different pairs of earrings.

He went in search of her and found her in the drawing room, stretched out on the sofa and surrounded by a mound of green and gold shopping bags whose logo he only too well recognised. Suffering the agonies of a woman who consistently disregards common sense in the selection of her footwear, she was an eloquent testament to the rigours involved in the simultaneous pursuit of bargain and fashion. She had one arm crooked over her head. When he said her name a second time, she groaned.

"It was like a war zone," she murmured from beneath her arm. "I've never actually seen such a crowd in Harrods. And rapacious. Tommy, the word doesn't even do justice to the women I had to fight through simply to get to the lingerie. Lingerie, for heaven's sake. One would think they were battling over limited half pints from the fountain of youth."

"Didn't you tell me you were working with Simon today?" Lynley went to the sofa, uncrooked her arm, kissed her, and replaced the arm in position. "Wasn't he supposed to be up to his ears preparing to testify for . . . What was it, Helen?"

"Oh, I did and he was. It's something to do with distinguishing sensitisers in water-gel explosives. Amines, amino acids, silica gel, cellulose plates. I was positively dizzy with all the lingo by half past two. And the beastly man was in such a rush that he even insisted we go without lunch. *Lunch*, Tommy.''

"Dire straits indeed," Lynley said. He lifted her legs, sat down, and rested her feet in his lap.

"I was willing to cooperate till half past three, working at the word processor till I was nearly blind, but at that point—faint with hunger, mind you—I bid him farewell."

"And went to Harrods. Faint with hunger though you were."

She lifted her arm, gave him a scowl, lowered the arm again. "I had you in mind all along."

"Had you? How?"

She gestured weakly towards the shopping bags that surrounded them. "There. That."

"There what?"

"The shopping."

Blankly, he looked at the bags, saying, "You've been shopping for me?" and wondering how to interpret such unique behaviour. It wasn't that Helen never surprised him with something amusing that she managed to ferret out in Portobello Road or the Berwick Street Market, but such largesse. . . . He examined her surreptitiously and wondered if, anticipating his designs, plans and inductions she had laid herself.

She sighed and swung her legs to the floor. She began rustling round in the bags. She discarded one that seemed filled with tissue and silk, then another containing cosmetics. She burrowed into a third and then a fourth and finally said, "Ah. Here it is." She handed him the bag and continued her search, saying, "I've one as well."

"One what?"

"Look and see."

He pulled out a mound of tissue, wondering how much Harrods was contributing to the inevitable defoliation of the planet. He began to unseal and then to unwrap. He sat staring down at the navy tracksuit and pondered the message behind it.

"Lovely, isn't it?" Helen said.

"Perfectly," he said. "Thank you, darling. It's exactly what I . . .''

"You *do* need it, don't you?" She rose from her prowl through the shopping bags and emerged triumphant with a tracksuit of her own, navy like his, although relieved with white piping. "I've been seeing them everywhere."

"Tracksuits?"

"Joggers. Getting themselves fit. In Hyde Park. In Kensington Gardens. Along the Embankment. It's time we joined them. Won't that be fun?"

"Jogging?"

"Of course. Jogging. It's just the very thing. Exposure to fresh air after a day indoors."

"You're proposing we do this after work? At night?"

"Or before a day indoors."

"You're proposing we do this at dawn?"

"Or at lunch or at tea. Instead of lunch. Instead of tea. We aren't getting any younger and it's time we did something to fend off middle age."

"You're thirty-three, Helen."

"And destined to be reduced to flab if I don't do something positive now." She returned to the shopping bags. "There are shoes as well. Somewhere. I wasn't entirely sure of your size, but you can always return them. Now where could they be . . . Ah. Here." She brought them forth, triumphant. "It's early yet, isn't it, and we could easily change and have a quick jog round the square a few times. Just the very thing to work ourselves up to . . ." She lifted her head, face suddenly pensive. She seemed to regard his clothing for the very first time. The dinner jacket, the bow tie, the pristinely shined shoes. "Lord. Tonight. We were going . . . Tonight . . ." Her cheeks took on colour and she continued hastily. "Tommy. Darling. We've an engagement, haven't we?"

"You've forgotten."

"Not at all. Truly. It's the fact I haven't eaten. I haven't eaten a thing."

"Nothing? You didn't seek sustenance somewhere between Simon's lab, Harrods, and Onslow Square? Why is it I have difficulty believing that?"

"I had only a cup of tea." When he raised a sceptical eyebrow, Helen added, "Oh, all right. Perhaps one or two pastries at Harrods. But they were the smallest of eclairs, and you know what they're like. Completely hollow."

"I seem to recall their being filled with . . . What is it? custard? whipped cream?"

"A dollop," she asserted. "A pathetic little teaspoonful. That's hardly enough to be counted as anything and it's certainly not a meal.

Frankly, I'm lucky to be among the living at the moment, with so little to sustain me from dawn to dusk.''

"We shall have to do something about that."

Her face brightened. "It *is* dinner, then. Lovely. I thought so. And somewhere quite wonderful because you've put yourself into that ghastly bow tie which I know you loathe." She rose from her shopping bags with renewed energy. "It's a good thing I've not eaten then, isn't it? Nothing shall spoil my dinner."

"True. Afterwards."

"After—?"

He reached for his pocket watch and flicked it open. "It's twenty-five past seven and we've only got till eight. We need to be off."

"Where?"

"The Albert Hall."

Helen blinked.

"The philharmonic, Helen. The tickets I nearly sold my soul to get. Strauss. More Strauss. And when you're tired of him, Strauss. Is this sounding familiar?"

Her face became radiant. "Tommy! Strauss? You're actually taking me to hear Strauss? This isn't a trick? We don't have Stravinsky after the interval? *The Rite of Spring* or something equally loathsome?"

"Strauss," Lynley said. "Before and after the interval. Followed by dinner."

"Thai food?" she asked eagerly.

"Thai," he replied.

"My God, this is an evening from heaven," she declared. She picked up her shoes and an armful of shopping bags. "I won't be ten minutes."

He smiled and scooped up the remaining shopping bags. Things were moving according to plan.

He followed her out of the drawing room and along the corridor past the kitchen where a glance inside told him that Helen was adhering to her usual mode of indifferent housekeeping. The breakfast dishes were scattered on the work top. The coffee maker's light still shone. The coffee itself had long since evaporated, leaving a deposit of sludge at the bottom of the glass carafe and the scent of overworked grounds permeating the air. He said, "Helen, for God's sake. Don't you notice that smell? You've left the coffee on all day."

She hesitated in the bedroom doorway. "Have I? What a nuisance. Those machines ought to shut themselves off automatically."

"And the plates ought to dance themselves into the dishwasher as well?"

"It would certainly show good breeding if they did." She disappeared into her bedroom where he heard her dropping her packages to the floor. He placed his own on the table, took off his jacket, switched off the coffee maker, and went to the work top. Water, detergent, and ten minutes set the kitchen in order, although the coffee carafe would need a good soak to put it right. He left it in the sink.

He found Helen standing alongside her bed in a teal-coloured dressing gown, pursing her lips thoughtfully as she studied three ensembles she'd put together. "Which says '*Blue Danube* followed by seraphic Thai food' to you?"

"The black."

"Hmm." She took a step back. "I don't know, darling. It seems to me—"

"The black's fine, Helen. Put it on. Comb your hair. Let's go. All right?"

She tapped her cheek. "I don't know, Tommy. One always wants to be elegant at a concert but at the same time not overdressed for dinner. Don't you think this might be too understated for the one and too overstated for the other?"

He picked up the dress, unzipped it, handed it to her. He went to her dressing table. There, unlike the kitchen, every item was arranged with an attention to order that one might give to assembling surgical instruments in an operating theatre. He opened her jewellery box and drew out a necklace, earrings, two bracelets. He went to the wardrobe and rustled up shoes. He returned to the bed, tossed down jewellery and shoes, turned her to face him, and untied the belt of her dressing gown.

"You're being excessively naughty this evening," he said.

She smiled. "But look where it's got me. You're taking off my clothes."

He pushed the gown from her shoulders. It fell to the floor. "You don't have to be naughty to get me to do that. But I expect you know that already, don't you?" He kissed her, sliding his hands into her hair. It felt like cool water between his fingers. He kissed her again. For all the frustrations of having his heart enmeshed in her life, he still loved the touch of her, the powdery scent of her, the taste of her mouth.

He felt her fingers working at his shirt. She loosened his tie. Her hands slid to his chest. He said against her mouth, "Helen, I thought you wanted dinner this evening."

She said, "Tommy, I thought you wanted me dressed."

"Yes. Right. But first things first." He brushed the clothing to the floor and drew her to the bed. He slid his hand up her thigh.

The telephone rang.

He said, "Damn."

"Ignore it. I'm not expecting anyone. The machine will pick it up."

"I'm on rota this weekend."

"You're not."

"Sorry."

They both watched the phone. It continued to ring.

"Well," Helen said. The ringing continued. "Does the Yard know you're here?"

"Denton knows where I am. He would have told them."

"We might have already left for all they know."

"They have the car phone and the seat numbers at the concert."

"Well, perhaps it's nothing. Perhaps it's my mother."

"Perhaps we ought to see."

"Perhaps." She touched her fingers to his face, sketching a pattern across his cheek to his lips. Her own lips parted.

He drew in a breath. His lungs felt oddly hot. Her fingers moved from his face to his hair. The phone stopped ringing and in a moment from the other room a disembodied voice spoke into Helen's answering machine. It was an only too recognisable disembodied voice, belonging to Dorothea Harriman, secretary to Lynley's divisional superintendent. When she went to the effort of tracking him down, it always meant the worst. Lynley sighed. Helen's hands dropped to her lap. "I'm sorry, darling," he said to her and reached for the telephone on the bedside table, interrupting the message that Harriman was leaving by saying, "Yes. Hello, Dee. I'm here."

"Detective Inspector Lynley?"

"None other. What is it?"

As he spoke, he reached out for Helen once more. But she was already moving away from him, slipping from the bed and bending to retrieve her dressing gown from where it lay in a heap on the floor.

CHAPTER
3

Three weeks into her new domestic arrangements, Detective Sergeant Barbara Havers decided that what she liked best about her solitary life in Chalk Farm was the choices it gave her in the area of transportational anxiety. If she wished to avoid dwelling upon the implications behind twenty-one days of not yet having spoken to a soul in her neighbourhood aside from a Sri Lankan girl called Bhimani who worked the till in the local grocery, all she had to concentrate on was the hair-pulling happiness of her daily commute to and from New Scotland Yard.

Even before she'd acquired it, her tiny cottage had long been a symbol to Barbara. It meant liberation from a life that had held her chained for years to duty and ailing parents. But while making the move had given her the freedom from responsibility that she had dreamed of having, that same freedom brought a solitude that closed in on her at moments when she was least prepared to encounter it. So Barbara had taken a distinct if sardonic pleasure in the discovery that there were two means of getting to

work each morning, both of them teeming with teeth-grating, ulcer-caus-
ing, and—best of all—loneliness-displacing distractions.

She could fight the traffic in her ageing Mini, battling her way down
Camden High Street to Mornington Crescent where she could choose at
least three different routes, all of which wound through the sort of life-in-
a-medieval-city congestion that every day seemed to become more hopeless of remedy. Or she could take the underground, which meant sinking
into the bowels of Chalk Farm Station and waiting for a train with ever-
decreasing hope among the faithful but understandably irascible riders of
the capricious Northern Line. And even then, not just any train would do,
but one that passed through Embankment Station where she could catch
yet another train to St. James's Park.

It was a situation based firmly in the realm of cliché: On a daily basis,
Barbara could choose between the devil and the deep blue sea. This day,
in deference to her car's increasingly ominous rattles, she'd chosen the
sea, wading past her fellow-commuters on escalators, in tunnels, and on
platforms, clinging to a stainless steel pole as the train hurtled through the
darkness and jostled its riders onto one another's feet.

She endured the irritants with resignation. Another bloody commute. Another chance to conclude conveniently that her loneliness was
really of no account because there was neither time nor energy at the end
of the day for social interaction anyway.

It was half past seven when she began her trudge up Chalk Farm
Road. She stopped in Jaffri's Fine Groceries, a shop crammed with so
many "delicacies to delight the discriminating palate" that the resulting
space was the approximate width of a Victorian railway carriage and just
about as well lit. She scrunched past a teetering display of soup tins—Mr.
Jaffri was deeply committed to "savoury soups from the seven seas"—and
struggled with the glass door to the freezer where a sign declared that row
upon row of Häagen-Dazs ice cream represented "absolutely every flavour under the sun." It wasn't the Häagen-Dazs she wanted, although salt
and vinegar crisps with a chaser of vanilla almond fudge didn't sound half-
bad for dinner. Instead she wanted the one item that sheer mercantile
inspiration had prompted Mr. Jaffri to stock, so certain was he that the
slow gentrification of the neighbourhood and the inevitable drinks parties
that would follow would place it in high demand. She wanted ice. Mr.
Jaffri sold it by the bagful, and ever since moving into her new digs,
Barbara had been using it in a bucket beneath her kitchen sink as a primitive means of preserving her perishables.

She dug one bag out of the freezer and lugged it to the counter where Bhimani was perched, awaiting another opportunity to pound upon the keys of the new till that not only chimed like Big Ben when the total was presented but also informed her in bright blue numbers the exact amount of change she was supposed to hand over to the customer. As always, the purchase was made in silence, with Bhimani ringing up the price, smiling close-lipped, and nodding eagerly at the total when it appeared on the digital screen.

She never spoke. Barbara had thought at first that she was mute. But one evening she had caught the girl in the middle of a yawn and got a glimpse of the gold that capped most of her teeth. She'd wondered since then if Bhimani didn't smile because she wished to conceal the value of her dental work or because, in coming to England and observing the common man, she'd realised how unusual it was and didn't care to display it.

Barbara said, "Thanks. See you," and scooped up her ice once Bhimani had presented her with seventy-five pence in change. She hauled her shoulder bag up her arm, locked the ice onto her hip, and went back to the street.

She continued up the road. She passed the local pub on the opposite pavement, and she gave brief thought to squeezing in among the boozers, ice and all. They appeared to be at least a depressing decade her junior, but she hadn't had her weekly pint of Bass yet and its seductive call made her theorise about how much energy it would take to inch inside to the bar, order the pint, light up a fag, and act friendly. The ice could act as a conversation piece, couldn't it? And how much of it would realistically melt if she took quarter of an hour to mingle with the Friday-after-work crowd? Who knew what could come of it? She might strike up an acquaintance with someone. She might make a friend. Even if she didn't, she was feeling parched as the desert. She needed some liquid. She could do with a spirit-lifter as well. She was feeling tired from the day and thirsty from the walk and hot from the tube. A relatively cool drink would be perfect. Wouldn't it?

She paused and gazed across the street. Three men were surrounding a long-legged girl, all four of them laughing, all four of them drinking. The girl, standing with her hips against a window-sill of the pub, lifted and drained her glass. Two of the men reached for it simultaneously. The girl laughed and tossed her head. Her thick hair rippled like a horse's mane, and the men moved in closer.

Perhaps another night, Barbara decided.

She plodded on, keeping her head down, making her eyes concentrate on the pavement. *Step on a crack, break your mother's back. Step on a line, break your mother's* . . . No. It wasn't the topic she wished to dwell on at the moment. She cleared her head of the doggerel by whistling. She chose the first tune that came into her mind: "Get Me to the Church on Time." It wasn't exactly appropriate to her situation, but it served its purpose. And as she whistled she realised that she must have thought of it because of Inspector Lynley's big plan for Popping the Question tonight. She chortled inwardly at the thought of his expression of surprise—and dismay, of course, since he didn't exactly want his plans to be public information—when she'd stopped by his office and said, "Good luck. I hope she says yes this time," before she left the Yard. At first, he'd attempted to act nonplussed by her comment, but she'd heard him phoning round for concert tickets all week and she'd witnessed his grilling of fellow officers in an attempt to discover the perfect Thai restaurant, and since she knew that Strauss and Thai food meant an evening designed to please Lady Helen Clyde, she deduced the rest. "Elementary," she'd said into his startled silence. "I know you hate Strauss." She waggled her fingers at him in farewell. "My, my, Inspector. What we do for love."

She made the turn into Steele's Road and passed beneath the newly leafing lime trees. In them, birds were settling for the evening as were the families in the grit-stained brick houses that lined the street. When she reached Eton Villas, she turned yet again. She hiked the ice bag higher on her hip and cheered herself with the thought that, her abysmal social circumstances aside, at least this was the final time she would have to haul ice from Jaffri's Fine Groceries.

For three weeks she had lived in her digs without aid of modern refrigeration, stowing her milk, her butter, her eggs, and her cheese in a metal bucket. She had spent those three weeks—evenings and weekends and the odd lunch hour—in search of a refrigerator that she could afford. She'd finally located it last Sunday afternoon, the perfect appliance that fit the size of her cottage and the size of her purse. It wasn't exactly what she'd been looking for: barely a metre tall and decorated with hideous, yellowing floral transfers. But when she handed over the cash and established ownership over the appliance, which—in addition to its unappealing decoration of roses, daisies, fuchsias, and flax—also gave a portentous *crankle-clank* whenever its door was slammed, Barbara had thought philosophically about beggars and choosers. The move from Acton to Chalk

Farm had cost her more than she had anticipated, she needed to econo-
mise, the refrigerator would do. And since the owner's son had a son who
drove an open-back lorry for a gardening service, and since that son's son
was willing to drop by his dear old gran's at the weekend and pick up the
refrigerator and transport it all the way up to Chalk Farm from Fulham for
a mere ten quid, Barbara had been willing to overlook the fact that not
only did the appliance probably have a limited life span, but also that she
would have to spend a good six hours scraping off dear old gran's transfers. Anything for a bargain.

She used her knee to open the gate of the semi-detached Edwardian
house in Eton Villas behind which her small cottage stood. The house was
yellow, with a cinnamon door recessed into a white front porch. This was
overhung with wisteria that climbed from a small square of earth next to
the french doors of the ground floor flat. Through the doors this evening,
Barbara could see a small, dark girl laying plates on a table. She wore a
school uniform and her waist-length hair had been plaited neatly and tied
up with tiny ribbons at the end. She was chatting to someone over her
shoulder and as Barbara watched, she skipped happily out of sight. Family
dinner, Barbara thought. Then she deleted the modifier, set her shoulders,
and headed down the concrete path that ran next to the house and led to
the garden.

Her cottage abutted the wall at the bottom of the garden, with a false
acacia tree looming above it and four casement windows looking out on
the grass. It was small, built of brick, with woodwork painted the same
yellow that had been used on the main house, and a new slate roof that
sloped up to a terra-cotta chimney. The building was a square that had
been elongated to a rectangle through the addition of a tiny kitchen and
an even tinier bathroom.

Barbara unlocked the door and flipped on the ceiling light. It was
dim. She kept forgetting to buy a stronger bulb.

She set her shoulder bag on the table and her ice on the work top.
She gave a grunt as she lifted the bucket from beneath the sink, and she
waddled with it towards the door and cursed when some of the cool water
sloshed onto her shoe. She emptied it, carried it back to the kitchen, and
began repacking it and thinking about dinner.

She assembled her meal quickly—ham salad, a two-day-old roll, and
the rest of a tin of beetroot—then went to the bookshelves that stood on
either side of the minuscule fireplace. She'd left her book there before

turning off her light last night and as she recalled the hero Flint Southern was just about to sweep the sassy heroine Star Flaxen into his arms where she was going to feel not only his muscular thighs encased in tight blue jeans but also his throbbing member, which, of course, was throbbing and had always throbbed only for her. They would consummate this desperate throbbing within the next few pages, accompanied by hardening nipples and birds taking flight, after which they would lie in each other's arms and wonder why it had taken them one hundred and eighty pages to reach this miraculous moment. There was nothing like great literature to accompany a fine meal.

Barbara grabbed the novel and was about to head back to the table when she saw that her answering machine was blinking. One blink, one call. She watched it for a moment.

She was on rota this weekend, but it was hard to believe that she was being called back to work less than two hours after having left it. That being the case and her number being ex-directory, the only other caller would be Florence Magentry, Mrs. Flo, her mother's keeper.

Barbara meditated on the possibilities presented by pushing the button and listening to the message. If it was the Yard, she was back at work with barely time to cool her heels or eat her meal. If it was Mrs. Flo, she would be embarking on another trip on the Great Guilt Railway. Barbara hadn't gone to Greenford last weekend to see her mother as scheduled. She hadn't gone to Greenford the weekend before. She knew that she had to go this weekend if she was to continue to live with herself, but she didn't want to, she didn't want to think why she didn't want to, and talking to Florence Magentry—even listening to her voice on the machine —would lead her to consider the nature of her avoidance and ask her to begin assigning it the appropriate labels: selfishness, thoughtlessness, and all the rest.

Her mother had been in Hawthorne Lodge for nearly six months now. Barbara had managed a visit at least every two weeks. The move to Chalk Farm had finally provided her with an excuse not to go and she'd grabbed on to it happily, substituting her presence with telephone calls in which she catalogued for Mrs. Flo all the reasons why there would have to be yet another unfortunate delay in her regularly scheduled appearances in Greenford. And they *were* good reasons, as Mrs. Flo herself assured Barbara during one or another of their usual Monday/Thursday chats. Barbie wasn't to pick at herself if she wasn't able to get out to Mum right away. Barbie had a life as well, dear, and no one expected her to try not to live it. "You get yourself settled into that new house of yours," Mrs. Flo said. "Mum'll do just fine in the meanwhile, Barbie. See if she won't."

Barbara hit the play button on her answering machine and returned to the table where her ham salad waited.

"Hello, Barbie." The greeting was spoken by the soporific read-me-a-bedtime-story voice of Mrs. Flo. "I wanted to let you know that Mum's a touch under the weather, dear. I thought it best to phone and tell you at once."

Barbara hurried back to the telephone, ready to punch in Mrs. Flo's number. As if anticipating this, Mrs. Flo continued.

"Now, I don't think a doctor's visit is called for in the least, Barbie, but Mum's temperature is up two degrees and she's had herself a bit of a cough these last few days . . ." There was a pause during which Barbara could hear one of Mrs. Flo's other houseguests singing along with Deborah Kerr, who was in the process of inviting Yul Brynner to dance. It had to be Mrs. Salkild. *The King and I* was her favourite video, and she insisted upon seeing it at least once a week. "Actually, dear," Mrs. Flo went on carefully, "Mum's been asking for you as well. It's just been since lunchtime, so I don't want you to put yourself into a dither over this, but since she so rarely mentions anyone by name, I thought it might cheer Mum up to hear your voice. You know how it is when one's not quite feeling one hundred percent, don't you, dear? Do ring if you can. Cheerie bye, Barbie."

Barbara reached for the phone.

"How lovely that you called, dear," Mrs. Flo said when she heard Barbara's voice, as if she hadn't telephoned first to prompt the call.

"How is she?" Barbara asked.

"I've just now come from having a peep in her room, and she's sleeping like a lamb."

Barbara held her wrist up to the dim cottage light. It was not yet eight o'clock. "Sleeping? But why's she in bed? She doesn't usually go to bed this early. Are you sure—"

"She was off her food at dinner, dear, so we both decided that a bit of a lie down with the music box playing would be just the thing to settle her tummy. So she had herself a nice listen and drifted off as sweet as could be. You know how she loves that music box."

"Look," Barbara said, "I could be out there by half past eight. Or quarter to nine. Traffic didn't look so bad this evening. I'll drive it."

"After a long day at work? Don't be foolish, Barbie. Mum's fine as can be and since she's asleep, she won't even know that you're here, will she? But I'll tell her you've phoned."

"She won't know who you mean," Barbara protested. Unless she was given the visual stimulus of a photograph or the auditory stimulus of a voice on the phone, the name Barbara meant virtually nothing to Mrs. Havers at this point. Even with visual or auditory back-up, whether she recognised her only daughter was still a coin toss.

"Barbie," Mrs. Flo said with gentle firmness, "I shall make certain she knows who I mean. She mentioned you several times this afternoon, so she'll know who Barbara is when I tell her you rang."

But knowing who Barbara was on Friday afternoon didn't mean Mrs. Havers would have any idea who Barbara was on Saturday morning over poached eggs and toast. "I'll be out tomorrow," Barbara said. "In the morning. I've collected some brochures on New Zealand. Will you tell her that? Tell her we'll plan another holiday for her album."

"Of course, my dear."

"And ring if she asks for me again. I don't care what time it is. Will you ring me, Mrs. Flo?"

Of course she would ring, Mrs. Flo said. Barbie was to eat a nice meal, to put her feet on the hassock, to have a quiet evening so that she would be right as rain to make the trip out to Greenford tomorrow.

"Mum will look forward to that," Mrs. Flo said. "I dare say that'll take care of her tummy."

They rang off. Barbara went back to her meal. The slice of ham looked even less appealing than it had done when she first slapped it onto the plate. The beetroot, spooned from the tin and arranged like a hand of five-card stud, appeared in the light to bear a greenish tinge. And the leaves of lettuce, which lay like open palms cradling both the ham and the beetroot, were limp from exposure to water and black at the edges from too close contact with the ice in the pail. So much for dinner, Barbara thought. She shoved the plate away and thought about walking to the falafel house back on Chalk Farm Road. Or treating herself to a Chinese dinner, sitting at a table in the restaurant like a real person. Or going back to that pub for bangers or shepherd's pie. . . .

She brought herself up sharply. What the hell was she thinking of? Her mother wasn't well. No matter Mrs. Flo's words, her mother needed to see her. Now. So she would climb in the Mini and drive to Greenford. And if her mother was still asleep, she'd sit by the bed until she awoke.

Even if it took until morning. Because that's what daughters did for their mothers, especially if more than three weeks had passed since they'd last laid eyes on them.

As Barbara reached for her shoulder bag and her keys, the phone rang again. She froze for an instant. She thought inanely, No, my God, she couldn't have, not that quickly. And she walked with dread to answer it.

"We're on," Lynley said at the other end of the line when he heard her voice.

"Hell."

"I agree. I hope I've not interrupted anything particularly interesting in your life."

"No. I was heading out to see Mum. And hoping for dinner."

"The first, I can't help you with, rota being what it is. The second can be remedied with a quick sashay through the officers' canteen."

"Now there's a real stimulant to the appetite."

"I've always seen it that way. How much time do you need?"

"A good thirty minutes if the traffic's bad near Tottenham Court Road."

"And when isn't it?" he asked pleasantly. "I'll keep your beans on toast warm at this end."

"Great. I love spending time with a real gent."

He laughed and rang off.

Barbara did likewise. Tomorrow, she thought. First thing in the morning. Tomorrow she would make the trip out to Greenford.

She left her Mini in the underground car park of New Scotland Yard after flashing her identification at the uniformed constable who looked up from his magazine long enough to yawn and make sure he wasn't entertaining a visit from the IRA. She pulled next to Lynley's silver Bentley. She managed to squeeze in as close as possible, snickering at how he would shudder at the idea of her car door possibly nicking the precious paint job on his.

She punched the button for the lift and rustled up a cigarette. She smoked it as furiously as possible, to bulk up on the nicotine before she was forced to enter Lynley's piously smoke-free domain. She'd been trying to woo him back to the siren weed for more than a year, believing that it would make their partnership so much easier if they shared at least one loathsome habit. But she'd got no further than one or two moans of addicted anguish when she blew smoke in his face during the first six months of his abstinence. It had been sixteen months now since he'd given up tobacco, and he was beginning to act like the newly converted.

She found him in his office, elegantly dressed for his aborted romantic evening with Helen Clyde. He was sitting behind his desk, drinking black coffee. He wasn't alone, however, and at the sight of his companion, Barbara frowned and paused in the doorway.

Two chairs were drawn up to the front of his desk, and a woman sat in one of them. She was youthful looking, with long legs that she kept uncrossed. She wore fawn trousers and a herringbone jacket, she wore an ivory blouse and well-polished pumps with sensible heels. She sipped something from a plastic cup and watched gravely as Lynley read through a sheaf of papers. As Barbara took stock of her and wondered who the hell she was and what the hell she was doing in New Scotland Yard on a Friday night, the woman paused in her drinking to shake from her cheek a wing-shaped lock of amber hair that had fallen out of place. It was a sensual gesture that raised Barbara's hackles. Automatically, she looked to the row of filing cabinets against the far wall, assuring herself that Lynley had not surreptitiously removed the photograph of Helen prior to waltzing Miss Deluxe Fashionplate into his office. The photo was in place. So exactly what the hell was going on?

"Evening," Barbara said.

Lynley looked up. The woman turned in her chair. Her face betrayed nothing, and Barbara noticed that Miss Deluxe Fashionplate didn't bother to evaluate her appearance the way another woman might. Even Barbara's red high-top trainers went completely disregarded.

"Ah. Good," Lynley said. He set down his paperwork and took off his spectacles. "Havers. At last."

She saw that a sandwich wrapped in cellophane, a packet of crisps, and a cup with a lid sat waiting for her on the desk in front of the empty chair. She sauntered over to it and picked up the sandwich, which she unwrapped and sniffed suspiciously. She lifted the bread. The mixture inside looked like liver paste blended with spinach. It smelled like fish. She shuddered.

"It was the best I could do," Lynley said.

"Ptomaine on whole wheat?"

"With an antidote of Bovril to wash it down."

"You're spoiling me with your thoughtfulness, sir." To the woman,

Barbara gave a nod designed to acknowledge her presence at the same time as it communicated disapproval. That social nicety taken care of, she plopped into the chair. At least the crisps were salt and vinegar. She ripped open the bag and began to munch.

"So what's up?" she asked. Her voice was casual but her meaningful look in the direction of the other woman said the rest: Who the hell is the beauty queen and what the hell is she doing here and where the dickens is Helen if you need a companion on the very Friday night when you meant to ask her to marry you and did she refuse again and is this how quickly you've managed to rebound from the disappointment you blighter you dog?

Lynley received the message, pushed back his chair, and regarded Havers evenly. After a moment he said, "Sergeant, this is Detective Inspector Isabelle Ardery, Maidstone CID. She's been good enough to bring us some information. Can you tear yourself away from speculations entirely unrelated to the case and listen to the facts?" Beneath the question she read his unspoken response to her unspoken allegations: Give me a modicum of credit, please.

Barbara winced and said, "Sorry, sir." She wiped her hand on her trousers and extended it to Inspector Ardery.

Ardery shook. She glanced between them but didn't pretend to understand their exchange. In fact, she didn't seem interested in it. Her lips curved fractionally in Barbara's direction, but what went for a smile was merely a cool, professional obligation. Perhaps she wasn't Lynley's type after all, Barbara decided.

"What have we got?" She unlidded her Bovril and took a sip.

"Arson," Lynley said. "A body as well. Inspector, if you'd put my sergeant in the picture. . . ."

In a formal, steady tone Inspector Ardery listed the details: a fifteenth-century restored cottage not far from a market town called Greater Springburn in Kent, a woman in residence, the milkman making his morning delivery, the newspaper and post gone uncollected, a peek through the windows, a burned chair, a trail of deadly smoke against window and wall, a stairway that acted—as all stairways do when a fire breaks out—like a chimney, a body upstairs, and finally the source of ignition.

She opened her shoulder bag which lay on the floor next to her foot. From it, she brought forth a packet of cigarettes, a box of wooden matches, and an elastic band. For a moment Barbara thought, with a rush of delight, that the inspector was actually going to light up, giving Barbara herself an excuse to do likewise. But instead, she spilled six matches from the box onto the desk and shook a cigarette on top of them.

"The fire raiser used an incendiary device," Ardery said. "It was primitive but nonetheless quite effective." Approximately an inch from the tobacco end of the filtered cigarette, she created a sheafing of matches, their heads up. She fastened them in place with the elastic band and held the contrivance in the palm of her hand. "It acts like a timer. Anyone can make one."

Barbara took the cigarette from Ardery's palm and examined it. The inspector continued to speak. "The fire raiser lights the tobacco and places the cigarette where he wants the blaze, in this case tucked between the cushion and the arm of a wingback chair. He leaves. In four to seven minutes, the cigarette burns down and the matches flame. The fire starts."

"Why the exact time span?" Barbara asked.

"Each brand of cigarette burns at a different rate."

"Do we know the brand?" Lynley had replaced his spectacles on his nose. He was glancing through the report again.

"Not at the moment. My lab has the works—the cigarette, the matches, and the band that held them together. We'll—"

"You're testing for saliva and latent prints?"

She offered another half-smile. "As you'd expect, Inspector, we've a fine lab in Kent and we do know how to use it. But as far as prints go, we're unlikely to come up with anything more than partials, so I'm afraid you can't expect too much help there."

Lynley, Barbara noted, ignored the unspoken reproach. "As to the brand?" he asked.

"We'll know the brand for a certainty. The cigarette end will tell us."

Lynley handed Barbara a set of photographs as Ardery said, "It was meant to look like an accident. What the raiser didn't know is that the cigarette, the matches, and the elastic band wouldn't burn completely. That's not, of course, an unreasonable mistake for the raiser to have made. And the benefit is ours as it tells he was a nonprofessional."

"Why didn't they burn?" Barbara asked. She began to flip through the pictures. They matched Inspector Ardery's description of the scene: the gutted chair, the patterns on the wall, the deadly trail of smoke. She set them aside and looked up for an answer before going on to the pictures of the body. "Why didn't they burn?" she repeated.

"Because cigarettes and matches generally remain on the top of ashes and debris."

Barbara nodded thoughtfully. She dug out the last of her crisps, ate them, and balled up the bag, which she lobbed into the rubbish. "So why're we in on it?" she asked Lynley. "This could be a suicide, couldn't it? Made to look like an accident for insurance purposes?"

"That possibility can't be overlooked," Ardery said. "The chair put out as much carbon monoxide as an engine's exhaust."

"So couldn't the victim have set the chair ready to go up in flames, lit the cigarette, popped six or eight pills, had a few drinks, and Bob's your grim-reaping uncle?"

"No one's discounting that," Lynley said, "although all things considered, it seems unlikely."

"All things? What things?"

"The postmortem's not done. They took the body directly to autopsy. According to Inspector Ardery, the medical examiner has leap-frogged over three other corpses to get his hands on this one. We'll have the preliminary facts on the amount of carbon monoxide in the blood straightaway. But the drug screen's going to take some time."

Barbara looked from Lynley to Ardery. "Right," she said slowly. "Okay. I've got it. But the drug screen'll take weeks. So why'd we get the call now?"

"Because of the corpse."

"The corpse?" She picked up the rest of the pictures. They had been taken in a low-ceilinged bedroom. The body of a man lay diagonally across a brass bed. He was on his stomach, partially clothed in grey trousers, black socks, and a pale blue shirt with the sleeves rolled above the elbows. His left arm cushioned his head on the pillow. His right arm was extended towards the bedside table on which sat an empty glass and a bottle of Bushmills. He'd been photographed from every possible angle, near and far. Barbara flipped to the close-ups.

His eyes were seven-eighths shut, with a crescent of white showing. His skin was flushed unevenly, nearly red in the lips and on the cheeks, closer to pink on the one exposed temple, the forehead, and the chin. A thin line of froth bubbled at one corner of his mouth. It too was stained pink. Barbara studied his face. It looked vaguely familiar, but she couldn't place it. Politician? she wondered. Television actor?

"Who is he?" she asked.

"Kenneth Fleming."

She looked up from the pictures to Lynley, then to Ardery. "Not . . . ?"

"Yes."

She held the photographs sideways and examined the face. "Do the media know?"

Inspector Ardery answered. "The local CID's chief superintendent was waiting for formal identification of the body, which—" she turned her wrist and examined the face of a fine-looking gold watch, "will have occurred long before now. But that's merely a formality as Mr. Fleming's identification was there in the bedroom, in his jacket pocket."

"Still," Barbara said, "that could be misdirection if this bloke looks enough like him and someone wanted people to think—"

Lynley stopped her by raising his hand. "Unlikely, Havers. The local police recognised him themselves."

"Ah." She had to admit that recognising Kenneth Fleming would have been easy enough for anyone who fancied cricket. Fleming was currently the country's foremost batsman, and he'd been something of a legend for the last two years. He'd been chosen to play for England for the first time at the unusual age of thirty. He'd not come up in the typical way: either through secondary school and university cricket grounds or through experience with the colts and the county seconds. Rather he had played in an East End league for a factory team, of all things, where a retired coach from the Kent county side had seen him one day and had offered to take him on. A long spate of private coaching, it was. Which was one mark against him, something people called a variation of the silver spoon syndrome.

His initial appearance at the wicket for England had ended in a humiliating golden duck, effected at Lord's in front of a near capacity crowd when one of the New Zealand fielders managed to catch his first and only shot. Which was a second mark against him.

Fleming left the field to the jeers of his countrymen, suffered the ignominy of trudging past the unforgiving and unforgetful members of the Marylebone Cricket Club who as always were holding court in the amber-bricked Pavilion, and he responded to a muted catcall in the Long Room by making a decidedly unsportsmanlike gesture. Which was a third mark against him.

All the marks were the stuff of journalism and the even greater stuff of the daily tabloids. Within a week the country's cricket-lovers were divided evenly between give-the-poor-bloke-a-chance and cut-off-his-cobblers. Never a group to cave in to public opinion when a test match was at stake, the national selectors decided upon the former. Kenneth Fleming defended the wicket for a second time in a match at Old Trafford. He took guard in a combination of silence and grave reservations. By the time he was through, he'd scored a century. When the bowler finally managed to dismiss him, he'd put 125 runs on the scoreboard for England. He'd never looked back.

Lynley was saying, "Greater Springburn called in their divisional people at Maidstone. Maidstone"—with a nod to Inspector Ardery—"made the decision to hand us the case."

Ardery demurred. She didn't sound happy about it. "Not I, Inspector. It was my CC's call."

"Just because it's Fleming?" Barbara asked. "I'd think you lot would be anxious to keep the case to yourselves."

"I'd prefer it that way," Ardery said. "Unfortunately, the principals involved in this particular death appear to be spread all over London."

"Ah. Politics."

"Indeed."

All three of them knew how it worked. London was divided into individual policing districts. Protocol would require the Kent police to clear with the resident district commanding officer every invasion into his patch to conduct an interrogation or an interview. The paperwork, phone calls, and political manoeuvring could take as much time as the investigation itself. Far easier to hand it over to the higher-ups at New Scotland Yard.

"Inspector Ardery will handle the case in Kent," Lynley said.

"It's already long in motion, Inspector," Ardery clarified. "Our crime scene team has been at the cottage since one this afternoon."

"While we do our part in London," Lynley finished.

Barbara frowned at the irregularity of what they were setting up. But she phrased her objection carefully, aware of Inspector Ardery's understandable inclination to protect her turf. "Won't that get everyone's wires crossed, sir? The left hand not knowing. The blind leading the deaf. You know what I mean."

"It shouldn't be a problem. Inspector Ardery and I shall coordinate the investigation."

Inspector Ardery and I. He made the statement in an easy, generous fashion, but Barbara heard the implications beneath it as well as if he'd shared them aloud. Ardery herself had wanted the case. Her higher-ups had snatched it from her. Lynley and Havers would do very well to keep Ardery's feathers oiled if they expected the cooperation they were going to need from her crime scene team.

"Oh," Barbara said. "Right. Right. What's first, then?"

Ardery got to her feet in a single lithe movement. She was, Barbara saw, exceedingly tall. When Lynley stood as well, his height of six feet and two inches gave him only the two inches over her.

Ardery said, "You've things to discuss at this point, Inspector. I dare say you won't be needing me further. I've put my number at the top of the report."

"You have." Lynley fished in the drawer of his desk, brought out a card, and handed it to her.

She put it in her shoulder bag without glancing at it. "I'll phone you in the morning. I should have some information from the lab by then."

"Fine." He picked up the report she'd brought with her. He tapped the photographs into place underneath the documents. He placed the report in the centre of the blotter that was itself in the centre of his desk. Clearly, he was waiting for her to take her leave and she was waiting for him to make some sort of comment prior to that. *Looking forward to working with you* might have done it, but it also would have danced a quick tango with the truth.

"Good evening, then," Inspector Ardery finally said. She added with a deliberate, amused smile at Lynley's manner of dress, "And I do apologise for however I may have disrupted your weekend plans." She nodded at Barbara, said the single-word farewell of "Sergeant," and left them.

Her footsteps echoed sharply as she made her way from Lynley's office to the lift. Barbara said, "You think they keep her on ice in Maidstone and only defrost her for special occasions?"

"I think she's got a rough job in a rougher profession." He returned to his seat and began flipping through some papers. Barbara looked at him shrewdly.

"Blimey. Did you *like* her? She's pretty enough and I admit when I first saw her sitting here I thought that you . . . Well, you guessed that, didn't you? But did you actually like her?"

"I'm not required to like her," Lynley said. "I'm merely required to work with her. With you as well. So shall we begin?"

He was pulling rank, something he rarely did. Barbara felt like grousing about it, but she knew that the equality of rank between him and

Ardery meant that they would stick together when the going got tricky. There was no point to arguing. So she said, "Right."

He referred to the report. "We have several interesting facts. According to the preliminary report, Fleming died Wednesday night or early Thursday morning. Right now they're estimating somewhere between midnight and three." He read for a moment and ticked off something in the report with a pencil. "He was found this morning . . . at quarter to eleven, by the time the Greater Springburn police arrived and managed to get into the cottage."

"Why's that interesting?"

"Because—fact of interest number one—from Wednesday night until Friday morning, no one reported Kenneth Fleming missing."

"Perhaps he'd gone off for a few days to spend time by himself."

"That leads us to fact of interest number two. In taking himself to this particular cottage in the Springburns, he wasn't choosing solitude. There was a woman staying there. Gabriella Patten."

"Is she important?"

"She's the wife of Hugh Patten."

"Who is . . . ?"

"The director of a company called Powersource. They're sponsoring this summer's test matches against Australia. And she—Gabriella, his wife—has gone missing. But her car's still at the cottage in the garage. What does that suggest to you?"

"We've got a suspect?"

"Quite possibly, I'd say."

"Or a kidnapping?"

He teetered his hand back and forth in an I-truly-doubt-it gesture. He went on. "Fact of interest number three. Although Fleming was found in the bedroom, his body—as you saw—was fully clothed save for his jacket. And there was no overnight case in the bedroom or in the cottage."

"He hadn't intended to stay? He may have been knocked unconscious and dragged up there to make it look like he'd decided to have a kip?"

"And fact of interest number four. His wife and family live on the Isle of Dogs. But Fleming himself lives in Kensington and has done for the last two years."

"So they're separated, right? So why's that fact of interest number four?"

"Because he lives—in Kensington—with the woman who owns the cottage in Kent."

"This Gabriella Patten?"

"No. A third woman altogether. Someone called—" Lynley ran his finger down the page, "Miriam Whitelaw."

Barbara put her ankle on her knee and played with the lace of her red high-top trainer. "Busy bloke, this Fleming, when he wasn't playing cricket. A wife on the Isle of Dogs, a what . . . a lover in Kensington?"

"It seems that way."

"Then what was she in Kent?"

"That's the question," Lynley said. He got to his feet. "Let's start looking for the answer."

CHAPTER
4

The houses in Staffordshire Terrace ran across the southern slope of Campden Hill and reflected the apogee of Victorian architecture in the northern part of Kensington. They were classical Italianate in style, complete with balustrades, bay windows, dog-toothed cornices, and other white stucco ornamentation that served to decorate what would otherwise be plain, solid structures of pepper-coloured bricks. Behind black wrought-iron fences, they lined the narrow street with repetitive dignity, their exteriors differing from one another only through the choice of flowers growing in window boxes and planters.

At Number 18, the flower was jasmine, and it grew in dense, undisciplined profusion from a bay window's three boxes. Unlike most of the other houses in the street, Number 18 had not been converted into flats. There was no panel of doorbells, just a single bell, which Lynley and

Havers rang some twenty-five minutes after Inspector Ardery had left them.

"Pish posh." Havers jerked her head in the direction of the street. "I counted three BMW's, two Range Rovers, a Jaguar, and a Coupe de Ville."

"Coupe de Ville?" Lynley said, looking back at the street upon which the Victorian lampposts were shedding a yellow glow. "Is Chuck Berry in the neighbourhood?"

Havers grinned. "And I thought you never listened to rock 'n' roll."

"Some things one knows through osmosis, Sergeant, through exposure to a common cultural experience that slyly becomes part of one's stockpile of knowledge. I call it subliminal assimilation." He looked to the fan window above the door. Light shone through it. "You did phone her, didn't you?"

"Just before we left."

"Saying?"

"That we wanted to talk to her about the cottage and the fire."

"Then where—"

Behind the door a firm voice said, "Who is it, please?"

Lynley identified himself and his sergeant. They heard the sound of a deadlock being turned. The door swung open, bringing them face-to-face with a grey-haired woman stylishly dressed in a navy sheath with a matching jacket that hung nearly to the hem of the dress. She wore fashionable, large-framed spectacles that winked in the light as she looked from Lynley to Havers.

"We're here to see Miriam Whitelaw," Lynley said, offering the woman his warrant card.

"Yes," she said. "I know. I'm she. Please come in."

Lynley felt rather than saw Sergeant Havers shoot a look in his direction. He knew she was doing exactly what he was: deciding whether they ought to make a rapid reassessment of their previous conclusions about the nature of the relationship between Kenneth Fleming and the woman with whom he lived. Miriam Whitelaw, although beautifully dressed and groomed, appeared to be somewhere in her late sixties, more than thirty years older than the dead man in Kent. In the modern age, the term *living with* carried an unmistakable connotation. Both Lynley and Havers had bought into it without thinking. Which, Lynley realised with some self-disgust, wasn't the most propitious of signs indicating how they were going to fare as the case progressed.

Miriam Whitelaw stepped back from the door and beckoned them into the entry. She said, "Shall we go up to the drawing room?" and led them down a corridor towards the stairway. "I've a fire burning there."

A fire would be needed, Lynley thought. Despite the month, the interior of the house seemed only several degrees warmer than a walk-in refrigerator.

Miriam Whitelaw apparently read his thoughts, because she said over her shoulder, "My late husband and I put in central heating after my father had a stroke in the late sixties. I don't use it much. I suppose I'm rather more like my father than I would have expected. Except for the electricity, which he finally accepted just after the Second World War, he wanted the house to remain as his parents had fashioned it in the 1870s. Sentimental, I know. But there you have it."

Lynley couldn't see that her father's wishes had been in any way ignored. Stepping into the entry of Number 18 Staffordshire Terrace was like walking into a time capsule filled with William Morris paper, countless prints on the walls, Persian rugs on the floor, blue-globed former gaslights serving as sconces, and a velvet-topped fireplace in the centre of which dangled a bronze gong. It was decidedly odd.

The anachronic sensation only increased as they climbed the stairs, initially passing walls given over to a display of faded sporting prints and then after the mezzanine, an entire wall of framed caricatures from *Punch*. These were arranged according to year. They began with 1858.

Lynley heard Havers breathe, "Jesus," as she looked about. He saw her shiver, and he knew it had nothing to do with the cold.

The room to which Miriam Whitelaw led them could have served as either an admirable set for a television costume drama or a museum's reproduction of a Victorian drawing room. It had two tiled fireplaces, both with marble surrounds and overmantels of gilt Venetian mirrors in front of which sat ormolu clocks, Etruscan vases, and small bronze sculptures favouring Mercury, Diana, and sinewy men wrestling each other in the nude. A fire burned in the farther of the two fireplaces, and Miriam Whitelaw walked towards this. As she passed a baby grand piano, the fringe on a silk shawl covering the top of it caught on a ring she was wearing. She paused to untangle it, to straighten the shawl, and to right one of the dozen or more photographs that stood in silver frames on the piano top. It wasn't so much a room as it was an obstacle course consisting

of tassels, velvet, arrangements of dried flowers, nursing chairs, and minuscule footstools that threatened the unwary with a headlong fall.
Lynley idly wondered if a Miss Havisham were in residence.

Again as if reading his thoughts, Mrs. Whitelaw said, "It's the sort of
thing one actually gets used to, Inspector. This was a magical place to visit
when I was a child. All these intriguing knick-knacks to stare at, think
about, and weave stories from. When the house came to me, I couldn't
bring myself to alter it. Please. Sit down."

She herself chose a nursing chair covered in green velvet. She motioned them towards the armchairs nearer the hard coal fire that was
putting off a blaze of heat. The armchairs were deep and plushly upholstered. In them, one didn't so much sit as sink.

Next to the nursing chair stood a tripod table on which sat a decanter
and small, stemmed glasses. One of these was half-full. Miriam Whitelaw
drank from it, saying, "I've always had sherry after dinner. A social sole-
cism, I know. Brandy or cognac would be more appropriate. But I've
never liked either. Would you like a sherry?"

Lynley said no. Havers looked as if she would have jumped at the
chance to have a Glenlivet had it been offered. But she shook her head
and plunged her hand into her shoulder bag, bringing forth her notebook.

Lynley explained to Mrs. Whitelaw how the case would be handled,
coordinated from the two locations of Kent and London. He gave her
Inspector Ardery's name. He handed her one of his cards. She took it,
read it, and turned it over. She laid it next to her glass.

"Forgive me," she said. "I don't quite understand. What do you
mean, 'coordinated'?"

"Have you not spoken to the Kent police?" Lynley asked. "Or the
fire brigade?"

"I spoke to the fire brigade. Sometime after lunch. I can't recall the
gentleman's name. He phoned me at work."

"Where's this?" Lynley saw Havers beginning to write.

"A printing factory. In Stepney."

At this, Havers raised her head. Miriam Whitelaw didn't exactly look
the part of either Stepney or a factory worker.

"Whitelaw Printworks," she clarified. "I run it." She reached in her
pocket and brought out a handkerchief, which she held in her palm,
curling her fingers round it. "Can you tell me exactly what's going on,
please?"

"What have you been told so far?" Lynley asked.

"The gentleman from the fire brigade told me there'd been a fire in the cottage. He said they'd had to break through the door. He said they'd found that the fire was out and there wasn't much damage aside from smoke and soot. I wanted to go out and have a look for myself, but he told me that they'd sealed off the cottage and I wouldn't be able to get in until the investigation was completed. I asked him what investigation. I asked him why we needed an investigation if the fire was out. He asked me who was staying in the cottage. I told him. He said thank you and rang off." She curled the handkerchief further against her palm. "I phoned down there twice during the afternoon. No one would tell me anything. They took my name and my number each time and said thank you very much and they'd be in touch directly they had some news. That was the extent of it. Now you're here and . . . Please. What's happened?"

"You told them a woman called Gabriella Patten was staying in the cottage," Lynley said.

"She is. The gentleman who phoned asked how to spell her name. He asked if anyone was staying with her. I told him no, as far as I knew. Gabriella had gone out there for seclusion, and I couldn't imagine she'd be up to entertaining. I asked the gentleman if Gabriella was all right. He said he'd be in touch as soon as he knew." She raised the handkerchief hand to the necklace she was wearing. This was gold, constructed of heavy links. Her earrings matched it. "As soon as he *knew*," she said pensively. "How could he not know . . . ? Was she hurt, Inspector? Is that why you've come? Is Gabriella in hospital?"

"The fire started in the dining room," Lynley said.

"That much I know. Was it the carpet? Gabriella likes fires, and if an ember shot out from the fireplace while she was in another room—"

"Actually, it was a cigarette in an armchair. Several nights ago."

"Cigarette?" Miriam Whitelaw's eyes lowered. Her expression altered. She didn't look as understanding as she had done at the thought of an unfortunate fireplace ember being the cause of the blaze.

Lynley leaned forward. "Mrs. Whitelaw, we've come to talk to you about Kenneth Fleming."

"Ken? Why?"

"Because, unfortunately, there's been a death at your cottage. And we need to gather some information in order to sort out what happened."

She didn't stir at first. Then it was only her fingers on the handkerchief, another tight roll along its hem. "A death? But the fire brigade didn't say. They asked me how to spell her name. They said they'd let me know the moment they discovered anything . . . And now you're saying that all along they *knew*—'' She drew a breath. ''Why didn't they tell me? They had me on the phone and they didn't even bother to say that someone was dead. *Dead*. In my cottage. And Gabriella. . . . Oh my God, I must notify Ken.''

In her words, Lynley heard the fleeting echo of the thane's distraught wife in Inverness: *What, in our house?* He said, ''There's been a death, but it wasn't Gabriella Patten's, Mrs. Whitelaw.''

''Wasn't . . . ?'' She looked from Lynley to Havers. She stiffened in her chair, as if she suddenly realised that a horror was about to befall her. ''Then that's why the gentleman wanted to know if someone else was staying there with her.'' She swallowed. ''Who? Tell me. Please.''

''I'm sorry to say it's Kenneth Fleming.''

Her face altered to a perfect blank. Then it became perplexed. She said, ''Ken? That's not possible.''

''I'm afraid it is. We've had a formal identification of the body.''

''By whom?''

''His—''

''No,'' she said. The colour was rapidly draining from her face. ''There's been a mistake. Ken's not even in England.''

''His wife identified his body late this afternoon.''

''It can't be. It can not be. Why wasn't *I* asked . . . ?'' She reached out to Lynley. She said, ''Ken's not here. He's gone with Jimmy. They're sailing. . . . They've gone sailing. They've taken a brief holiday and . . . They're sailing and I can't remember. Where did he . . . ? Where?''

She struggled to her feet as if standing upright would allow her to think. She looked right and left. Her eyes rolled back dangerously in her head. She crashed to the floor, knocking over the tripod table and its drink.

Havers said, ''Holy hell!''

The crystal decanter and glasses scattered. The liquor sloshed onto the Persian rug. The scent of sherry was honey-sweet.

Lynley had risen to his feet as Mrs. Whitelaw got to hers, but he wasn't quick enough to catch her. Now he moved swiftly to her crumpled body. He checked her pulse, removed her spectacles, and lifted her eyelids. He took her hand between his. Her skin felt clammy and cold.

"Find a blanket somewhere," Lynley said. "There'll be bedrooms above."

He heard Havers dash from the room. She pounded up the stairs. He removed Mrs. Whitelaw's shoes, pulled one of the tiny footstools over, and elevated her feet. He checked her pulse again. It was strong. Her breathing was normal. He took off his dinner jacket and covered her with it. He rubbed her hands. As Sergeant Havers bounded back into the room, a pale green counterpane in her arms, Mrs. Whitelaw's eyelids fluttered. Her forehead creased, deepening the incision-like line between her eyebrows.

"You're all right," Lynley said. "You've fainted. Lie still."

He replaced his jacket with the counterpane, which Havers had apparently ripped from an upstairs bed. He righted the tripod table as his sergeant collected the glasses and decanter and used a packet of tissues to sop up at least part of the sherry that had pooled out in the shape of Gibraltar, soaking into the rug.

Beneath the counterpane, Mrs. Whitelaw trembled. The fingers of one hand crept out from beneath the cover. She clutched at its edge.

"Shall I get her something?" Havers asked. "Water? A whisky?"

Mrs. Whitelaw's lips twitched with the effort at talking. She fastened her eyes on Lynley. He covered her fingers with his hand and said to his sergeant, "She's all right, I think." And to Mrs. Whitelaw, "Just be still."

Her eyes squeezed shut. Her breathing grew ragged, but it appeared to be a battle for emotional control rather than an indication of a physical crisis.

Havers added another several coals to the fire. Mrs. Whitelaw raised her hand to her temple. "Head," she whispered. "God. The hammering."

"Shall we phone for your doctor? You may have hit it badly."

She shook her head weakly. "Comes and goes. Migraines." Her eyes filled with tears and she widened them, it seemed, in an effort to keep the tears from spilling over. "Ken . . . he knew."

"He knew?"

"What to do." Her lips looked dry. Her skin seemed cracked, like old glaze on porcelain. "My head. He knew. He could always make the pain go."

But not this pain, Lynley thought. He said, "Are you alone here in the house, Mrs. Whitelaw?" She nodded. "Shall we phone for someone?" Her lips formed the word *no*. "My sergeant can stay with you the night."

Her hand shook the counterpane in a gesture of refusal. "I . . . I shall be . . ." She blinked hard. "I shall be . . . all right presently," she said, although her voice was faint. "Forgive me, please. So sorry. The shock."

"Don't apologise. It's quite all right."

They waited in a silence broken only by the hissing of the coal as it burned and the ticking of several clocks in the room. Lynley felt oppression closing in on all sides. He wanted to throw open the stained and painted windows. Instead, he remained where he was, one hand on Mrs. Whitelaw's shoulder.

She began to raise herself. Sergeant Havers came to her side. She and Lynley eased the older woman to a sitting position and from there to her feet. She wobbled. They kept their hands on her elbows and guided her to one of the overstuffed chairs. Sergeant Havers handed her her spectacles. Lynley found her handkerchief under the nursing chair and returned it to her. He wrapped the counterpane round her shoulders.

She cleared her throat and said, "Thank you," with some dignity. She put on her spectacles and straightened her clothes. She said tentatively, "If you don't mind . . . If I might have my shoes as well," and waited until she had them on before she spoke again. When she did, it was with the trembling fingers of her right hand pressed into her temple in an attempt to master whatever pounding she felt in her skull. She said in a quiet voice, "Are you certain?"

"That it was Fleming?"

"If there was a fire, surely it's possible that the body was . . ." She pressed her lips together so hard that the impressions of her teeth showed against her skin. "There could be a mistake, couldn't there?"

"You've forgotten. It wasn't that kind of fire," Lynley said. "He wasn't burned. The body was only discoloured." When she flinched, he said quickly to reassure her, "From carbon monoxide. Smoke inhalation. His skin would have been deeply flushed. But it wouldn't have prevented his wife from recognising him."

"No one told me," she said dully. "No one even phoned."

"The police generally notify the family first. The family takes it from there."

"The family," she repeated. "Yes. Well."

Lynley took her place in the nursing chair as Sergeant Havers returned to her original position and picked up her notebook. Mrs. Whitelaw's colour was still bad, and Lynley wondered how much questioning they could expect her to endure.

She stared at the pattern in the Persian rug. Her voice was slow, as if she recalled each fact moments before stating it.

"Ken said he was going . . . It was Greece. A few days' boating in Greece, he said. With his son."

"You mentioned Jimmy."

"Yes. His son. Jimmy. For his birthday. That's the reason Ken was cutting some training to go. He had . . . they had a flight from Gatwick."

"When was this?"

"Wednesday night. He'd had it planned for months. It was Jimmy's birthday present. Just the two of them were going."

"You're certain about the trip? You're certain he meant to leave Wednesday night?"

"I helped him carry his luggage to the car."

"A taxi?"

"No. His car. I'd said I'd drive him to the airport, but he'd only had the car for a few weeks. He loved the excuse to take it out on the road. He was going to fetch Jimmy and then they'd be off. Just the two of them. On a boat. Round the islands. For just a few days because we're so close now to the first test match." Her eyes filled with tears. She pressed her handkerchief beneath them and cleared her throat. "Forgive me."

"Please. It's all right." Lynley waited a moment as she tried to regain her composure. He said, "What sort of car did he have?"

"A Lotus."

"The model?"

"I don't know. It was old. Restored. Low to the ground. Headlamps like pods."

"A Lotus-7?"

"It was green."

"There was no Lotus at the cottage. Just an Aston Martin in the garage."

"That would have been Gabriella's," she said. She moved her handkerchief to press it against her upper lip. She spoke from behind her hand. More tears pooled in her eyes. "I can't think that he's dead. He was here on Wednesday. We had an early dinner together. We talked about the printworks. We talked about the test matches this summer. The Australian spin bowler. The challenge he would be for a batsman. Ken was worrying over whether he'd be selected for the England team again. He always has doubts every time the selectors begin to choose. I tell him his fears are ridiculous. He's such a fine player. His form's never off. Why should he ever worry about not being selected? He's . . . Present tense. Oh God, I'm using present tense. It's because he's been . . . he was . . . Forgive me, please. If you will. Please. If I can only piece myself together. I mustn't fall apart. I mustn't. Later. I can fall apart later. There are things to be seen to. I know that. I do.''

Lynley managed to get several tablespoons of sherry from what was left in the decanter. He offered the glass to her and held her hand steady. She gulped the liquor like medicine.

"Jimmy," she said. "He wasn't at the cottage as well?"

"Only Fleming."

"Only Ken." She moved her gaze to the fire. Lynley saw her swallow, saw her fingers begin to tighten, then relax.

"What is it?" he said.

"Nothing. It isn't important in the least."

"Let me be the one to decide that, Mrs. Whitelaw."

Her tongue passed over her lips. "Jimmy would have been expecting his father to fetch him for the flight on Wednesday. If Ken didn't show up, he'd have phoned here to know why."

"And he didn't?"

"No."

"You were here at home once Fleming left Wednesday evening? You didn't go out yourself? Even for a few minutes? Could you have missed a call from him?"

"I was here. No one phoned." Her eyes widened marginally as she said the last word. "No. No, that's not quite true."

"Someone phoned?"

"Earlier. Just before dinner. For Ken, not for me."

"Do you know who it was?"

"Guy Mollison."

Longtime captain of the England team, Lynley thought. It wasn't strange that he'd be phoning Fleming. But the timing was interesting. "Did you hear Fleming's end of the conversation?"

"I answered the phone in the kitchen. Ken took the call in the morning room."

"Did you listen in?"

She looked away from the fire to him. She appeared too exhausted to be offended by the question. But, still, her voice was reserved when she replied, "Of course not."

"Not even before you replaced the receiver? Not for a moment to make sure Fleming was on the line? It would be natural to do that."

"I heard Ken's voice. Then Guy's. That's all."

"Saying?"

"I'm not certain. Something . . . Ken said hullo. And Guy said something about a row."

"An argument between them?"

"He said something about wanting the Ashes back. Something like, 'We want the bloody Ashes back, don't we? Can we forget the row and get on with things?' It was test-match talk. Nothing more."

"And the row?"

"I don't know. Ken didn't say. I assumed it had something to do with cricket, with Guy's influence over the selectors, perhaps."

"How long was their conversation?"

"He came down to the kitchen five minutes, perhaps ten minutes later."

"He said nothing about it then? Or over dinner?"

"Nothing."

"Did he seem changed after he talked to Mollison? More subdued, perhaps? More agitated, more pensive?"

"Not at all."

"And in the past few days? The past week? Had he seemed changed at all to you?"

"Changed? No. He was the same as ever." She cocked her head. "Why? What are you asking, Inspector?"

Lynley considered how best to answer the question. The police had the advantage at the moment, in the form of knowledge only the arsonist would possess. He said carefully, "There are some irregularities about the fire at the cottage."

"You said a cigarette? In one of the armchairs?"

"Had he been despondent in the last several weeks?"

"Despondent? Of course he wasn't despondent. Worried, yes, about being chosen to play for England. Perhaps a bit concerned about going off with his son for a few days in the midst of his training. But that was the extent of it. What on earth had he to be despondent about?"

"Had he personal troubles? Family troubles? We know his wife and children live apart from him. Were there difficulties with them?"

"No more than usual. Jimmy—the eldest—was a source of worry to Ken, but what sixteen-year-old isn't a worry to his parents?"

"Would Fleming have left you a note?"

"A note? Why? What sort of note?"

Lynley leaned forward in his chair. "Mrs. Whitelaw, we must rule out suicide before we can proceed in any other direction."

She stared at him. He could see her trying to work her way through the emotional mire created first by the shock of Fleming's death and now by the allegation of suicide.

"May we check his bedroom?"

She swallowed but did not reply.

"Consider it a necessary formality, Mrs. Whitelaw."

Tentatively, she rose, one hand grasping the arm of her chair. She said quietly, "This way, then," and led them out of the room and up another flight of stairs.

Kenneth Fleming's room was on the second floor overlooking the back garden. Most of the space was dominated by a large brass bed across from which an enormous oriental fan spread across the fireplace. As Mrs. Whitelaw took a seat in the room's only chair—a wingback tucked into the corner—Lynley went to a chest of drawers that stood beneath the window while Havers opened a mirrored wardrobe.

"These are his children?" Lynley asked. From the top of the chest of drawers, he picked up one photograph after another. There were nine of them, haphazardly framed snapshots of babies, toddlers, and children.

"He has three children," Mrs. Whitelaw said. "They've grown since those were taken."

"No recent pictures?"

"Ken wanted to take them, but Jimmy wouldn't cooperate whenever Ken got the camera out. As Jimmy goes, so go his brother and sister."

"There was friction between Fleming and the older boy?"

"Jimmy's sixteen," she told them once again. "It's a difficult age."

Lynley couldn't disagree. His own sixteenth year had been the start of a downhill slide in parental relationships that had only ended when he was thirty-two.

There was nothing else on the top of the chest of drawers, nothing but soap and a folded towel on the washstand, nothing propped up on the pillows of the bed awaiting notice, and only a worn copy of Graham Swift's *Waterland* on the bedside table. Lynley flipped through this. Nothing fell out.

He began to go through the chest of drawers. He saw that Fleming was compulsively neat. Every jersey and sweatshirt was identically folded.

Even his socks were arranged in their drawer by colour. Across the room, Sergeant Havers was apparently drawing this same conclusion from the row of shirts on their hangers, followed by trousers, followed by jackets, with shoes lined up in a row beneath them.

"Blimey," she said. "Not a stitch out of place. They do that sometimes, don't they, sir?"

"Do what?" Miriam Whitelaw asked.

Havers looked as if she was sorry she had spoken. "Suicides," Lynley said. "They generally put everything in order first."

"They generally leave a note as well, don't they?" Mrs. Whitelaw said.

"Not always. Especially if they want the suicide to look like an accident."

"But it *was* an accident," Mrs. Whitelaw said. "It had to be an accident. Ken didn't smoke. So if he were going to kill himself and make it look like an accident, why would he have used a cigarette?"

To cast suspicion on someone else, Lynley thought. To make it look like a murder. He answered her question with one of his own. "What can you tell us about Gabriella Patten?"

Mrs. Whitelaw didn't answer at first. She seemed to be evaluating the implications behind Lynley's having asked the question on the heels of her own. She said, "What do you want to know?"

"Is she a smoker, for example?"

Mrs. Whitelaw looked towards the window in which they all were reflected against the nighttime panes. She appeared to be trying to picture Gabriella Patten both with and without a cigarette. She finally said, "She never smoked here, in this house. Because I don't. Ken doesn't . . . didn't. Otherwise, I don't know. She may be a smoker."

"What was her relationship to Fleming?"

"They were lovers." And to Lynley's raised eyebrows, she added, "It wasn't general knowledge. But I knew. We talked about it most nights—Ken and I—and had done since the situation first developed between them."

"The situation?"

"He was in love with her. He wanted to marry her."

"And she?"

"She said at times that she wanted to marry him."

"At times only?"

"That was her way. She liked to keep him off guard. They'd been seeing each other since . . ." Her hand rose to touch her necklace as she thought. "It was sometime last autumn when they began the affair. He knew straightaway that he wanted to marry her. She was less certain."

"She's married, I understand."

"Separated."

"When they began seeing each other?"

"No. Not then."

"And now?"

"Formally?" she asked.

"And legally."

"She had her solicitors ready, as far as I know. Her husband had his. According to Ken, they'd met five or six times, but they hadn't reached an agreement on anything."

"But a divorce was pending?"

"On her part? Probably, but I couldn't say."

"What did Fleming say?"

"Ken sometimes felt she was dragging her feet, but he was like that . . . impatient to have things settled in his life as soon as possible. He was always that way when he made up his mind about something."

"And in his own life? Had he settled things?"

"He'd finally talked to Jean about divorcing, if that's what you mean."

"When was this?"

"About the same time Gabriella left her husband. Early last month."

"Did his wife agree to the divorce?"

"They've lived apart for four years, Inspector. Her agreement wasn't really an issue, was it?"

"Nonetheless, did she agree?"

Mrs. Whitelaw hesitated. She shifted in the chair. A spring creaked beneath her. "Jean loved Ken. She wanted him back. That never changed all the years he was gone, so I can't imagine it changed just because he finally mentioned divorce."

"And Mr. Patten? What do you know of him? Where did he stand in all this? Did he know about his wife's relationship with Fleming?"

"I doubt it. They tried to be discreet."

"But if she was staying in your cottage," Sergeant Havers put in, turning from the wardrobe where she was systematically going through Fleming's clothes, "that pretty much makes an announcement of the situation, wouldn't you say?"

"As far as I know, Gabriella didn't tell anyone where she was staying. She needed a place to live once she left Hugh. Ken asked me if she could use the cottage. I agreed."

"Your way of giving tacit approval to their relationship?" Lynley asked.

"Ken didn't ask for my approval."

"If he had?"

"He's been like my son for years. I wanted to see him happy. If he believed that marriage to Gabriella was the source of his happiness, that was fine with me."

It was an interesting answer, Lynley thought. There was a world of meaning beneath the word *believed*. He said, "Mrs. Patten's gone missing. Have you any idea where she might be?"

"None at all, unless she's gone back to Hugh. She threatened to do that whenever she and Ken had a row. She might have made good on her words."

"Had they had a row?"

"I doubt it. Ken and I usually talked it over when they had."

"They quarrelled frequently?"

"Gabriella likes to have things her way. Ken does as well. Occasionally they found it difficult to compromise. That's all." She seemed to see where the questions were heading, because she added, "Really, you can't think Gabriella . . . That's unlikely, Inspector."

"Who knew she was at the cottage, aside from you and Fleming?"

"The neighbours would have known, of course. The postman. The milkman. People from Lesser Springburn if she went into the village."

"I mean here, in London."

"No one," she said.

"Besides yourself."

Her face was grave but unoffended. "That's right," she said. "No one besides myself. And Ken."

She met Lynley's eyes as if she were waiting for the accusation and expecting him to make it. Lynley said nothing. She claimed Kenneth Fleming was like a son to her. He wondered about that.

"Ah. Here's something," Sergeant Havers said. She was opening a narrow folder that she had taken from a pocket of one of the jackets. "Plane tickets," she said and looked up. "Greece."

"Is there a flight date on them?"

Havers held them towards the light. Her forehead wrinkled as she scanned the writing. "Here. Yes. They're for—" She did a mental calculation with the date. "Last Wednesday."

"He must have forgotten them," Mrs. Whitelaw said.

"Or never intended to take them in the first place."

"But his luggage, Inspector," Mrs. Whitelaw said. "He had his luggage. I watched him pack. I helped him carry his things to the car. Wednesday. Wednesday night."

Havers tapped the tickets pensively against her open hand. "He may have changed his mind. Postponed the trip. Delayed his departure. That would explain why his son never phoned when Fleming failed to show up to fetch him for the flight."

"But it doesn't explain why he packed as if he intended to go on in the first place," Mrs. Whitelaw insisted. "Or why he said, 'I'll send you a card from Mykonos,' before he drove off."

"That's easy enough," Havers said. "For some reason he wanted you to think that he was still going to Greece. Right then."

"Or perhaps he didn't want you to think he was going to Kent first," Lynley added.

He waited as Mrs. Whitelaw made an effort to assimilate the information. The fact that it was an effort for her was made evident by the distress that caused her gaze to falter. She tried, and failed, to fix on her face an expression that would communicate to them that she was unsurprised by the knowledge that Kenneth Fleming had lied to her.

Just like a son, Lynley thought. He wondered if Fleming's lie made him more or less son-like to Mrs. Whitelaw.

OLIVIA

When the tour barges pass, I can feel our barge do a little bob-and-sway on the water. Chris says I imagine it because those are singles and leave practically no wake while ours is a double and impossible to move. Still, I swear I can feel the rise and fall of the water. If I'm having a lie down and I've made my room dark, it's like being in the womb, I expect.

Farther down, in the direction of Regent's Park, all the barges are singles. They're painted brightly and lined up something like railway carriages along both sides of the canal. The tourists going to Regent's Park or Camden Lock take photographs of them. They probably try to imagine what it's like, living on a barge in the middle of a city. They probably assume that one can forget one's in the middle of a city altogether.

Our barge isn't photographed often. Chris built it to be practical, not to be coy, so it's not much to look at, but it does for a home. I spend most of my time here in the cabin. I watch Chris do the sketches for his mouldings. I take care of the dogs.

Chris hasn't returned from his run yet. I knew he'd be an age. If he got as far as the park and took the dogs inside, he won't be back for hours. But, if that's the case, he'll also bring a take-away meal back with him. Unfortunately, it'll be tandoori something. He'll forget I don't like it. I won't blame him for that. He's got a lot on his mind.

So do I.

I can't get away from seeing his face. This is something that would have made me rave at one time—the idea of a person I don't even know having the cheek to make an ethical demand upon me, asking me to have principles, for God's sake. But curiously this unspoken request has given me the oddest sense of peace. Chris would say it's because I've finally reached a decision and am acting on it. Perhaps he's right. Mind you, I don't relish the thought of sharing any of my dirty laundry with you, but I've seen his face again and again—I *keep* seeing his face—and his face is what's made me come to terms with the fact that if I declare myself responsible, then I must explain how and why.

You see, I was something of a disappointment in my parents' lives although who I was and what I did affected my mother far more than Dad. That's to say that Mother was more forthcoming with her reactions to my behaviour. She labelled me in capitals: Such A Disappointment. She talked in terms of washing her hands of me. And she dealt with the trouble I caused in her usual manner: by distracting herself.

You read my bitterness, don't you? You probably won't believe me when I say I feel little enough of it now. But I did then. I felt bitter in spades. I'd spent a childhood watching her run from this meeting to that fund-raising event, listening to her tales of the poor-but-gifted in her fifth form English class, and trying to increase her level of interest in me through various means, all categorised under the heading Olivia Being Difficult Again. Which indeed I was. By the time I was twenty years old, I was as angry as a cornered warthog and about as attractive. Richie Brewster was my ploy to communicate my feelings of disgruntlement to Mother. However, I didn't see that at the time. What I saw was love.

I met Richie on a Friday night in Soho. He was playing saxophone in a club called Julip's. It's closed down now, but you probably remember it, about three hundred square feet of cigarette smoke and sweating bodies in a cellar on Greek Street. In those days, it sported blue lights on the ceiling, which were very in vogue despite the fact that they made everyone look like heroin addicts on the prowl for a score. It boasted the presence of the occasional minor royal with *paparazzi* in attendance. Actors, painters, and writers hung out there. It was the place to go if you wanted to see or be seen.

I didn't want either. I was with friends. We'd come down from university for a concert in Earl's Court, four twenty-year-old females looking for a break before exams.

We ended up in Julip's by chance. There was a crowd on the pavement waiting to get in, so we joined them to see what was what. It didn't take long to discover that about half a dozen joints were being passed round. We indulged ourselves.

These days, cannabis is like Lethe for me. When the future looks the worst, I smoke and drift. But then, it was a key to good times. I loved getting high. I could take a few hits and be someone new, Liv Whitelaw the Outlaw, unafraid and outrageous. So I was the one who tracked down the source of the weed: three blokes from Wales, medical students out for an evening of music, drinks, dope, and twat. It was clear they had access to the first three already. When they met us, they had access to the rest. But the numbers were off, as we all could see. And unless one of the blokes was willing to do a double poke, one of the women was going to end up in the cold. I'd never been much good at pulling men. I assumed from the first that the loser would be me.

None of the blokes appealed to me anyway. Two of them were too short. The third had breath that smelled like a sewer. My friends could have them.

Once we were inside the nightclub, they involved themselves in some serious groping on the dance floor. That was part of the scene in Julip's, so no one paid much attention. I mostly watched the band.

Two of my mates had already left the place, saying, "See you back in college, Liv," which was their way of telling me not to wait round while they got themselves stuffed, when the band took a break. I leaned back in my chair and started to light a cigarette. Richie Brewster lit it for me.

How lame it seems now, that moment when the lighter spurted its flame six inches from my face and illuminated his. But Richie had seen every old black and white film in creation, and he thought of himself as something between Humphrey Bogart and David Niven. He said, "Mind if I join you?" Liv Whitelaw the Outlaw said, "Do what you want," and arranged her face in a perfect display of b-o-r-e-d. From what I could see, Richie was old, way over forty, maybe closer to fifty. His skin was sagging round his jaw, his eyes were baggy. I wasn't interested.

So why did I go with him that night when the band played its last set and Julip's locked up? I could tell you that the last train to Cambridge had left and I had no other place to stay, but the truth is that I could have gone home to Kensington. Instead, when Richie packed up his sax, lit two cigarettes, handed one to me, and invited me out for a drink, I saw the possibility of excitement and experience. I said, "Sure, why not?" and thus changed the direction of the rest of my life.

We went to Bayswater in a taxi. Richie said to the driver, "The Commodore, on Queensway," and he put his hand high up on my thigh and squeezed.

All the manoeuvring seemed so illicit and adult. An exchange of cash at the hotel desk, two bottles procured, a climb to the room, unlocking the door. Through it all, Richie kept glancing in my direction and I kept smiling conspiratorily at him. I was Liv Whitelaw the Outlaw, sexual animal, a woman with a man completely in her power, eyelids drooped and breasts thrust out suggestively. God, what a fool.

Richie unwrapped the plastic from the drinking glasses that stood on a wobbly chest of drawers. He had three short vodkas fast. He poured a longer fourth and drank that down before he poured me a gin. He snatched up the bottles between his fingers and carried them, along with his drink, to the circular table between the room's two chairs. These were done up in pea-soup vinyl, and the pink Chinese lantern covering the ceiling light turned them the colour of dying leaves on a rose bush. Richie sat, lit a cigarette, and began to talk.

I can still recall his choice of subjects: music, art, theatre, travel, books, and films. I listened, awestruck by his erudition. I made few replies. I later discovered that silence and the appearance of attention were all that were required of me, but at the moment I thought it was pretty bloody something to be round a man who really Knew How To Open Up To A Woman.

What I didn't understand was that talking was foreplay for Richie Brewster. He had no interest in fondling female bodies. He got heated up by caressing the airwaves instead. When he'd worked himself up to performance level that night, he rose from his chair, pulled me from mine, put his tongue in my mouth, unzipped his trousers, and pulled out his dick. He wrapped my hand round it while he lowered my blue jeans and probed with two fingers to see if I was ready. He backed me to the bed. He smiled at me, saying, "Oh yes" with great meaning, and took off his trousers. He had no underpants on. He told me later that he never wore them, they got in the way. He peeled my jeans and my pants off one leg.

He said, "That's nice, baby," apropos of nothing. He took my butt in his hands. He raised my hips. He dived in.

He pumped with a lot of energy. He twined my legs round his back. He caught my hair in his fingers. He breathed, groaned, and sighed in my ear. He said *God* and *Jesus* a hundred times. And when he came, he shouted, "Liv Liv Liv."

Afterwards, he went into the bathroom. The water ran, then shut off. He swaggered back with a towel, which he threw to me with a smile, saying, "You always that wet?" I took it for a compliment. He went to the chest of drawers and poured us both another drink. He said, "Hell, I feel good," and sauntered back to the bed where he nuzzled my neck, murmuring, "You're something. Some*thing*. I haven't come like that in years."

How mighty I felt. How insignificant seemed the sex I'd had before. Until this night at the Commodore, my encounters had been nothing more than sweaty clutching with boys, children who didn't know the first sodding thing about Making Love.

Richie touched my hair. It was dun then, not blonde like now, and long and straight as a railway track. He fingered a length of it, saying, "Hmm. Soft." He held my gin glass to my lips. He yawned. He rubbed his head. He said, "Shit, it feels like I've known you for years," and that was the moment I decided I loved him.

I stayed in London. I realised I'd never fitted in at Cambridge, surrounded by toffs, by poofs, and by clots. Who the hell wanted a career in social science—that was Mother's idea in the first place, and hadn't she pulled every string in the book to get Girton to take me?—when I could have a hotel room in Bayswater and a real man who paid for it and came round every day for some grunt-and-groan on a lumpy mattress?

Girton sent out the alarm after a week when my mates decided that covering any longer for my absence in college wasn't going to go far in enhancing their status. The senior tutor phoned my parents. My parents phoned the police. The only lead they had to give the cops was Julip's in Soho, but as I was of age, and since no female corpses bearing my description had been tossed into the Thames of late, and since the IRA had been developing a recent taste for planting bombs in cars, department stores, and tube stations, the police didn't get on to the case like hounds. So three weeks passed before Mother showed up with Dad at her elbow.

I was thoroughly pissed when they got there. It was just after eight in the evening, and I'd been drinking since four. When I heard the knock, I thought it was the desk clerk coming up for the rent. He'd been up twice already. I'd told him the money was Richie's business. I'd told him he'd have to wait. But he was one of those persistent West Indian types—half smarm and half bluster—and he wouldn't give it up.

I thought, goddamn it you little nig-nog leave me alone. I threw open the door ready for battle, and there they were. I can see them to this day: Mother dressed in one of those sheaths of hers that she's been wearing in one variation or another since Jackie Kennedy first made them popular, Dad outfitted in a suit and tie as if he was going on a social call.

I'm sure Mother can see me to this day as well: in one of Richie's shrunken T-shirts and nothing else. I don't know what she expected to find in the Commodore when she dropped by that evening. But it was clear from her expression that she hadn't expected Liv Whitelaw the Outlaw to open the door.

She said, "Olivia. My God." Dad looked at me once, dropped his eyes, looked again. He seemed to shrivel inside his clothes.

I stood at the door with one hand on the knob and the other on the jamb. I said, "What's the problem?" and sounded like a victim of terminal ennui. I could see what was coming—guilt, tears, and a round of manipulation, not to mention an attempt to get me out of the Commodore—and I knew it was going to be dreary as hell.

She said, "What's happened to you?"

"I met a bloke. We're together. That's the story."

She said, "The college phoned. Your supervisors are frantic. Your friends are making themselves sick with worry."

"Cambridge isn't part of the picture any longer."

"Your education, your future, your life," she said. She was speaking carefully. "What on earth are you thinking?"

I pulled on my lip. "Thinking? Hmmm . . . Of fucking Richie Brewster as soon as he gets back."

Mother seemed to grow taller. Dad lowered his eyes to the floor. His lips moved on a reply that I didn't catch.

I said, "Wha's that, Pops?" and arched my back against the door-jamb. I was still keeping my other hand on the knob, however. I wasn't a fool. Give my mother access to that room and life with Richie was over.

But she appeared to be heading for a different course, featuring reason and the hope of Bringing Olivia Back To Her Senses. She said, "We've spoken to the master and the senior tutor. They'll take you back on probation. You'll need to pack your things."

"No."

"Olivia—"

"You don't get it, do you? I love him. He loves me. We've got a life here."

"This isn't a life." She looked left and right, as if evaluating the corridor for its potential to contribute to my education and future. She sounded reasonable when she went on. "You're inexperienced. You've been seduced. It's understandable that you think you're in love with this man, that you think he loves you. But this . . . What you've got here, Olivia . . ." I could see she was trying not to lose control. She was trying to seem like Mother of the Year. But she was coming on the stage too late with her maternal act. Faced with it, I could feel my hackles rising.

"Yes?" I said. "What I've got here?"

"This is nothing more than cheap gin in exchange for sex. You must see that."

"What I see," I said, squinting at them both because the light from the corridor was beginning to burn my eyes, "is that I've got a hell of a lot more than you can imagine. But we can't expect miracles of understanding, can we? You've hardly got experience in the passion department."

My father said, "Livie," and raised his head.

My mother said, "You've had too much to drink. It's distorted your thinking." She pressed her fingers to her temple. She closed her eyes briefly. I knew the symptoms. She was fighting off a migraine. A few more minutes and the battle was mine. "We'll phone the college and tell them tomorrow or the next day. Right now, we need to get you home."

"No. We only need to say good night. I'm through with Cambridge. Who can walk on the grass. Who wears what gown. Who's going to pick apart your essays this term. That isn't living. It never was. This is."

"With a married man?"

My father took her arm. Clearly, this was the trump card they'd been holding.

"Waiting for when he has time off from his wife?" And then, because she knew how to use the moment, Mother reached for me, saying, "Olivia. Oh my dearest Olivia," but I shook her off.

I hadn't known, you see, and Mother damn well knew it. Foolish little twenty-year-old, full of herself, sexual animal, Liv Whitelaw the Outlaw with a middle-aged man eating out of her hand, I hadn't known. I should have put it all together, but I hadn't because everything between us was all so different, so new, so down-and-dirty exciting. But when the facts flashed before me in the way facts do when one's had a shock, I knew my mother was telling me the truth. He didn't always spend the night. He claimed it was a gig in another city and in a way it was: in Brighton, with his wife and his kids, at home.

Mother said, "You didn't know, did you, darling?" and the pity in her voice gave me the bollocks for an answer.

"Who gives a shit, anyway," I said and followed up with, "Of course I knew. I'm not exactly a cretin."

But I was. Because I didn't walk out on Richie Brewster then and there.

You're wondering why, aren't you? It was simple enough. I saw no choices. Where could I have gone? Back to Cambridge to play at being a model student while every eye watched me for one false move? Home to Kensington where Mother would act noble as she ministered to my emotional ills? Out on the street? No. None of that was on. I wasn't going anywhere. I was in control of my life and I was about to demonstrate that fact indisputably. I said, "He's leaving his wife, if you need to know," and I shut the door. I made sure it was locked.

They knocked for a while. At least Mother did. I could hear Dad saying, "Miriam, that's enough," in a low voice that sounded far away. I rooted through the chest of drawers for a new packet of cigarettes. I lit up, poured myself another drink, and waited for them to give up and shove off. And all the time I thought of what I would say and what I would do when Richie showed up and I brought him to his knees.

I had a hundred scenarios, all of them ending with Richie begging for mercy. But he didn't return to the Commodore for two weeks. He'd got the word somehow. And when he finally showed his face, I'd already known for three days that I was pregnant.

OLIVIA

It's a clear sky today—you can't see any clouds—but its colour's not blue and I don't know why. It rises like the back of an unpolished shield behind that dreary monolith of wet-sand flats they've built where Robert Browning once lived, and I sit here looking at it and letting my mind play with reasons why it's lost its colour. I can't remember the last time I saw a truly blue sky and that worries me. Perhaps the sun's eating the blue away, scorching the sky along the edges first the way flames burn paper, then sneaking inward with gathering speed until all that ultimately will be left above us is a spinning white fireball hurtling towards what's already become an ember.

No one else seems to notice this difference in the sky. When I point it out to Chris, he shields his eyes with his hands and he gives it a look. He says, "Yes. Indeed. By my calculations, we've got another two hours of breathable air in our current environment. Shall we live it up or make a run for the Alps?" Then he ruffles my hair and goes down into the cabin where I can hear him start whistling and unshelving all his architecture books.

He's at work on matching a piece of cornice from a house in Queen's Park. It's a fairly easy job because the cornice is wood, which he generally prefers to work with over plaster. He says plaster makes him nervous. He says, "Jesus, Livie, who am I to mess about with an Adam ceiling?" I once thought this was false modesty on his part, considering how many people ask him to work on their houses once the word goes out that another neighbourhood's being gentrified, but that was before I knew him well. I assumed he was a bloke who'd managed to clean the cobwebs of doubt from every corner of his life. I learned over time that that was a persona he adopted when leadership was called for. The real Chris is just like the rest of us, in possession of a score of uncertainties. He has a nighttime mask that he can pull on when the situation calls for it. In the daytime, however, when power doesn't count as far as he's concerned, he is who he is.

I've wished from the first that I could be more like Chris. Even when I was the most cheesed off at him—in the beginning when I dragged other blokes back here to the barge with that nasty, knowing little smile of mine and shagged them till they howled and I was sure Chris knew what I was doing and to whom—I still wanted to be like him. I yearned to exchange bodies and souls with him. I wanted to feel free to lay myself out and say, "Here, this is who I am underneath all the cock," just like Chris and because I couldn't do that, because I couldn't *be* him, I tried to hurt him instead. I sought to push him to the edge and over. I wanted to destroy him, because if I could destroy him, then it meant his entire way of living was a lie. And I needed that to be the case.

I'm ashamed of the person I was. Chris says there's no point to shame. He says, "You were what you had to be, Livie. Let it go," but I'm never able to do that. Every time I think I'm close to opening my hand, spreading my fingers, and letting memory spill out into the water like sand, something jars me and stops me. Sometimes it's a piece of music I hear or a woman's laughter when it's high-pitched and false. Sometimes it's the sour smell of laundry left unwashed too long. Sometimes it's the sight of a face gone hard with sudden anger or a glance exchanged with a stranger whose eyes look opaque with despair. And then I'm an unwilling traveller, swept back through time and deposited on the doorstep of who I was. "I can't forget," I tell Chris, especially if I've woken him when the cramps take my legs and he's come to my room with Beans and Toast at his heels and a glass of warm milk, which he insists I drink. "You don't have to forget," he says as the dogs settle on the floor at his feet. "Forgetting means you're afraid to learn from the past. But you've got to forgive." And I drink the milk even though I don't want it, with both hands lifting the glass to my mouth, trying to keep from groaning with the pain. Chris notices. He sets to with massaging. The muscles loosen again.

When this happens, I say, "I'm sorry." He says, "What've you got to be sorry for, Livie?"

There's the question, all right. When I hear him ask it, it's like the music, the laughter, the laundry, the sight of a face, the casual exchange of a glance. I'm the traveller again, swept back and swept back to face who I was.

Twenty years old and pregnant. I called it the thing. I didn't see it as a baby growing inside of me as much as I saw it as an inconvenience. Richie saw it as an excuse to clear out. He was gracious enough to settle the account with the desk clerk before he disappeared, but he was ungracious enough to let the desk clerk know that I was officially "on my own" from that time on. I'd burned enough bridges with the Commodore's staff. They were only too happy to evict me.

Once I was on the street, I had a cup of coffee and a sausage roll in a caff across from Bayswater Station. I considered my options. I stared at the familiar red, white, and blue of the underground sign until its logic and the cure for my ills became apparent. There it was, the entrance to both the Circle and District lines, barely thirty yards from where I was sitting. And just two stops to the south was High Street Kensington. What the hell, I thought. I decided then and there that the least I could do in this lifetime was give Mother a chance to drop her Elizabeth Fry act in exchange for a good bout of Florence Nightingale. I went home.

You're wondering why they took me back. I expect you're one of the sort who never cause their parents a moment's grief, aren't you, so you probably can't fathom why someone such as myself would have been welcomed back anywhere. You've forgotten the basic definition of home: a place where you go, you knock on the door, you look repentant, and they let you in. Once you're inside with your bags unpacked, you break whatever bad news has brought you there in the first place.

I waited two days to tell Mother about the pregnancy, coming upon her while she was marking papers from one of her English classes. She was in the dining room at the front of the house, with three stacks of essays piled on the table in front of her and a pot of Darjeeling tea steaming at her elbow. I picked a paper from the top of a stack and idly read the first sentence. I can still remember it: "In exploring the character of Maggie Tulliver, the reader is left to ponder the distinction between fate and doom." How prophetic.

I tossed the paper down. Mother looked up, raising her eyes above the level of her reading glasses without lifting her head.

"I'm pregnant," I told her.

She set her pencil down. She took off her glasses. She poured herself another cup of tea. No milk, no sugar, but she stirred it anyway. "Does he know?"

"Obviously."

"Why obviously?"

"He's done a runner, hasn't he?"

She sipped. "I see." She picked up her pencil and tapped it against her little finger. She smiled for a moment. She shook her head. She was wearing gold earrings in the shape of coiled ropes and a necklace to match. I remember how they all glittered in the light.

"What?" I said.

"Nothing," she said. Another sip of tea. "I thought you'd come to your senses and broken away from him. I thought that's why you'd returned."

"What difference does it make? It's over. I'm back. Isn't that good enough?"

"What do you intend to do now?"

"About the kid?"

"About your life, Olivia."

I hated the schoolmarm in her tone. I said, "It's my business, isn't it? Maybe I'll have the kid. Maybe I won't."

I knew what I intended to do, but I wanted her to be the one to suggest it. She'd been posing as a woman of Great Social Conscience for so many years, and I felt the need to unmask her.

She said, "I'll need to think about this," and went back to her papers.

I said, "Whatever," and began to leave the room.

As I passed her chair, she put out her hand to stop me, resting it for a minute—and I suppose unintentionally—on my stomach where her grandchild grew. "We won't be telling your father," she said. So I knew what she meant to do.

I shrugged. "I doubt he'd understand. Is Dad clear on where babies come from in the first place?"

"Don't make a mockery of your father, Olivia. He's more of a man than what walked out on you."

I used my index finger and thumb to remove her hand from my body. I left the room.

I heard her get up and go to the sideboard; she opened a drawer and rustled round for a moment. Then she went to the morning room, punched some numbers into the phone, and began to talk.

She made the arrangements for three weeks later. Clever of her. She wanted me to stew. In the meantime, we play-acted at something between normal family life and a guarded truce. Mother tried several times to engage me in conversation about the past—largely dominated by Richie Brewster—and the future—a return to Girton College. But never did she mention the baby.

It was nearly a month after Richie left me at the Commodore when I had the abortion. Mother drove me, with her hands high on the steering wheel and her foot pumping the accelerator in fits and starts. She'd chosen a clinic as far north in Middlesex as one could go, and as she drove us there through a dreary morning of rain and diesel fumes, I wondered if she'd picked this particular clinic to make certain we didn't come across any of her acquaintances. That would be exactly like her, I thought, that would be utterly in hypocritical character. I hunched in my seat. I shoved my hands into the opposite arms of my jacket. I felt my mouth tighten.

I said, "I need a fag."

She said, "Not in the car."

"I want a fag."

"That's not possible."

"I want it!"

She pulled over to the pavement. She said, "Olivia, you simply cannot—"

"Cannot what? Can't smoke or it'll hurt the baby? What shit."

I wasn't looking at her. I was staring out of the window, watching two men unload dry cleaning from a yellow van and rustle it into the doorway of a Sketchley's. I could feel Mother's anger and her attempt to master it. I enjoyed the fact that not only was I still able to provoke her, but that she had to battle to keep her persona in place whenever she and I were together.

She said with great care, "I was going to say that you cannot go on like this, Olivia."

Brilliant. Another lecture. I settled my body and rolled my eyes.

"Let's just get on with our business," I replied. I gestured towards the road with a wiggle of my fingers. "Let's move it along, Miriam, all right?"

I'd never called her by her first name before, and as I made the shift from *Mother* to *Miriam*, I felt the balance of power swing my way.

"You take pleasure out of petty cruelty, don't you?"

"Oh please. Let's not start."

"I don't understand that sort of nature in a person," she said in her I'm-the-voice-of-reason tone. "I try but I can't understand it. Tell me. Where does your nastiness come from? How am I supposed to deal with it?"

"Look, just drive. Take me to the clinic so that we can get on with business."

"Not until we talk."

"Oh Jesus. What in hell do you want from me? If you expect me to kiss your hand like all those sods whose lives you're messing about with, it's not going to happen."

She said reflectively, "All those sods . . ." and then, "Olivia. My dear." She moved in her seat and I could tell she was facing me. I could imagine well enough what her expression was because I could hear it in her tone and I could read it from her choice of words. *My dear* meant I'd given her an opening to display a rush of comprehension and its attendant compassion. *My dear* set my teeth on edge and skilfully wrenched the power back. She said, "Olivia, have you done all this because of me?"

"Don't flatter yourself."

"Because of my projects, my career, my . . ." She touched my shoulder. "Have you been thinking I don't love you? Darling, have you been trying to—"

"Christ! Will you shut up and drive! Can you do that much? Can you bloody well drive and keep your eyes on the road and your sticky hands off me?"

After a moment to let my words bounce round the car for maximum effect, she said, "Yes. Of course," and I realised I'd played the game her way once again. I'd allowed her to feel the injured party.

That was the way things were with my mother. Whenever I thought I had the upper hand, she was quick to show me what was really what.

Once we arrived at the clinic and filled out the paperwork, the procedure itself didn't take long. A little scrape, a little suction, and the inconvenience in our lives was gone. Afterwards I lay in a narrow white room in a narrow white bed and thought about what Mother expected of me.

Weeping and gnashing of teeth, no doubt. Regret. Guilt. Evidence of any kind that I had Learned My Lesson. A plan for the future. Whatever it was, I wasn't about to accommodate the bitch.

I spent two days in the clinic to take care of some bleeding and an infection that the doctors didn't like. They wanted to keep me for a week, but that wasn't on as far as I was concerned. I checked myself out and went home by taxi. Mother met me at the door. She had a fountain pen in one hand, a buff-coloured envelope in the other, and her reading glasses on the end of her nose. She said, "Olivia, what on earth . . . The doctor told me that—"

I said, "I need cash for the taxi," and I left her to deal with it while I went to the dining room and poured myself a drink. I stood by the sideboard and gave serious thought to what I was going to do next. Not with my life, with the evening.

I tossed back one gin. I poured another. I heard the front door close. Mother's footsteps came down the corridor and stopped in the dining room doorway. She spoke to my back.

"The doctor told me there was some haemorrhaging. An infection."

"It's under control." I swirled the gin in my glass.

"Olivia, I'd like you to know that I didn't come to see you because you made it quite clear you wouldn't have me there."

"That's right, Miriam." I tapped my fingernail against my glass, noting how the sound got deeper when I moved from bottom to top, in direct reversal of what one would expect.

"When I couldn't bring you home the same night, I had to tell your father something so—"

"He can't deal with the truth?"

"So I told him that you've been in Cambridge, seeing about what you'll need to do to be readmitted."

I laughed through my nose.

"And that's what I want you to do," she said.

"I see." I drained my glass. I thought about having a third drink, but the first two were acting on me more quickly than I had expected. "And if I don't?"

"I imagine you can guess the consequences."

"What's that supposed to mean?"

"That your father and I have decided we're willing to support you at the University but nowhere else. That neither one of us is going to stand by and watch you throw your life away."

"Ah. Thanks. Got it." I set my glass on the sideboard, crossed the room, and pushed through the doorway.

"You can think about it until tomorrow," she said. "I'll want your decision in the morning."

"All right," I said and I thought, Stupid cow.

I went upstairs. My room was on the top floor of the house, and by the end of the climb my legs were shaking and the back of my neck was damp. I stood for a moment with my forehead resting against the door, thinking, Fuck her, fuck this, fuck them all. I needed to get out for the night. That was the cure and the ticket all at once. I headed for the bathroom where the light was better for fixing up my face. That was when Richie Brewster phoned.

"I miss you, baby," he said. "It's over. I left her. I want to make you feel good again."

He was phoning from Julip's, he said. The band had just signed on for a six-month gig. They'd been playing a circuit in The Netherlands. They'd scored some decent hashish in Amsterdam, they'd smuggled it out, Richie's share had *Sweet Liv* imprinted all over it, it was just sitting back stage waiting for me to smoke it.

He said, "Remember how good things were at the Commodore? It'll be better this time between us. I was a fool to walk out on you, Liv. You're the best thing that's happened in my life in years. I need you, baby. You make me make the music like no one else."

I said, "I got rid of the kid. Three days ago. I'm not in the mood. Okay?"

Richie was nothing if not a musician. He didn't miss a beat. He said, "Oh, baby. Baby. Oh hell." I could hear him breathing. His voice got tight. "What can I say? I got scared, Liv. I ran. You came in too close. You made me feel things that I didn't expect. Look, what I felt was too much for me. It was like nothing I've ever felt before. So I got scared. But my head's on right this time. Let me make it up to you. Let me do things over. I love you, baby."

"I don't have the time for this sort of bullshit."

"It won't end like before. It won't end at all."

"Right."

"Give me a chance, Liv. If I balls it up, I lose you. But give me a chance." And then he just waited and breathed.

I let him do both. I liked the possibility of having Richie Brewster right where I wanted him.

He said, "Come on, Liv. Remember how it was? It'll be better."

I weighed the alternatives. There seemed to be three: a return to Cambridge and the noose-round-the-neck life that Cambridge implied, a stint on the streets trying to make it on my own, and another try with Richie. Richie who had a job, who had money, who had dope, and who was telling me he also had a place to live now, a ground-floor flat in Shepherd's Bush. And there was more, he said. But he didn't have to tell me what it was. I knew because I knew him: parties, people, music, and action. How could I choose either Cambridge or the streets when, if I merely took myself to Soho this moment, I'd be in the middle of a real life?

I finished working on my face. I grabbed my bag and a coat. I told Mother I was going out. She was in the morning room at Grandmother's davenport, addressing a stack of envelopes. She took her glasses off and pushed back her chair. She asked me where I was going.

I repeated myself. "Out."

She knew, the way mothers always do. "You've heard from him, haven't you? That was he on the phone."

That was he. English teachers. Even in a crisis, they keep their guard up against the grammar police. I didn't reply.

She said, "Olivia, don't do this. You can make something of your life. You've had a bad time, darling, but it doesn't have to mean the end of your dreams. I'll help you. Your father will help you. But you must meet us halfway."

I could tell that she was building up a good head of preaching steam. Her eyes were taking on that fiery look.

I said, "Save it, Miriam. I'm out of here. I'll be back later."

The last was a lie, but I wanted her off my back. She quickly changed directions. "Olivia, you're not well. You've had a bout of serious bleeding, not to mention an infection. You've had"—was it my imagination or did her lips have a hard time forming the word?—"surgery only three days ago."

"I had an abortion," I said and was pleased to see the shudder of aversion pass over her.

"I think it's best that we forget and go on."

"Right. Yes. You forget your way back to your envelopes while I go on."

"Your father . . . Olivia. Don't do this."

"Dad'll get over it. So will you." I turned.

Her voice changed from reason to calculation. She said, "Olivia, if you leave this house tonight—after everything you've been through, after all our attempts to help you . . ." She faltered. I turned back. She was clutching her fountain pen like a dagger although her face looked perfectly calm.

"Yes?"

"I'll wash my hands of you."

"Get out the soap."

I left her working on the appropriate bereft-mother expression. I went out into the night.

At Julip's, I stood by the bar, watched the crowd, and listened to Richie play. At the end of the first set, he shouldered his way through the bodies, ignoring everyone who spoke to him, his eyes fixed on me like lead to a magnet. He took my hand and we went to the back, behind the stage. He said, "Liv. Oh, baby," and he held me like crystal and played with my hair.

For the rest of the evening, I stayed back stage. We smoked hash between sets. He held me on his lap. He kissed my neck and my palms. He told the other blokes in the band to shove off when they came near us. He said that he was nothing without me.

We went out to a caff for coffee when Julip's closed for the night. The lights were bright there, and I noticed right off that Richie didn't look good. His eyes were more like a basset hound's than they'd ever been. His skin was loose. I asked him had he been ill. He said that breaking off with his wife had been tougher on him than he thought it would be. He said, "Loretta still loves me, baby. I need you to know that because there's not going to be any lies between us any longer. She didn't want me to leave. She wants me back even now. But I can't face things that way. Not without you." He said the first week without me had shown him the truth. He said he'd spent the rest of the time trying to get up his courage to act on the truth. He said, "I'm weak, baby. But you give me strength like no one else." He kissed the tips of my fingers. He said, "Let's go home, Liv. Let me do it right."

Things were different this time, just like he'd said. We weren't dossing in some smelly dump three floors up with carpet squares on the floor and mice in the walls. We had a first-floor conversion with its own bay window and posh Corinthian pillars on either side of the porch. We had a fireplace decked out in ironwork and tiles. We had a bedroom and a kitchen and a bathtub with claws. We went to Julip's each night where

Richie's band made the music. When the place closed down, we went on the town. We partied, we drank. We did coke whenever we got the chance. We even hit on some LSD. We danced, we shagged in the back of taxis, and we never once got home before three. We ate Chinese take-away in bed. We bought watercolours and painted on each other's bodies. One night we got drunk, and he pierced my nose. In the late afternoons Richie jammed with the band, and when he got tired, he always turned to me.

This was it this time. I wasn't a ninny. I knew the real thing when it slapped me in the face. But just to make sure, I waited two weeks for Richie to cock things up. When he didn't, I went home to Kensington and collected my things.

Mother wasn't there when I arrived. It was a Tuesday afternoon and the wind was blowing in gusts that came and went in that waving kind of pattern that always feels like someone in the sky is shaking out a big sheet. I rang the bell first. I waited, shoulders raised against the wind, and rang again. Then I remembered that Tuesday afternoons had always been Mother's late day down on the Isle of Dogs, when she tutored the great minds from her fifth form classes, willing them to be unlocked so she could fill them with Truth. I had my house keys with me, so I let myself in.

I skipped up the stairs, feeling with every step like I was shedding yet another aspect of constipated, constrictive, bourgeois family life. What need had I for the smothering tedium prescribed by generations of English womanhood—not to mention my mother—doing the done thing? I had Richie Brewster and a real life to take the place of everything implied by this looming mausoleum in Kensington.

Out of here, I thought, out of here, out . . . of . . . here.

Mother had anticipated me. She'd gone to Cambridge and collected my gear. She'd packed it, along with every other possession of mine, in cardboard boxes which sat on my bedroom floor, neatly sealed with Sello-tape.

Thanks, Mir, I thought. Old cow, old girl, old mackerel tart. Thanks ever so much for seeing to things in your competent fashion.

I went through the boxes, decided what I wanted, and dumped the rest on the bed or the floor. Afterwards, I spent a half-hour wandering round the house. Richie had said that money was getting tight, so I took what I could to help him out: a piece of silver here, a pewter jug there, one or two porcelains, three or four rings, a few miniatures laid out on a table in the drawing room. It was all part of my eventual inheritance. I was merely getting a head start on things.

Money stayed tight for months on end. The flat and our expenses were tallying up to more than Richie made. To help out, I took a job stuffing jacket potatoes in a caff in Charing Cross Road, but for Richie and me holding on to money was as easy as chasing feathers in a gale. So Richie decided the only answer was for him to pick up a few extra gigs out of town. "I don't want you working more than you already are," he said. "Let me take this gig in Bristol"—or Exeter or York or Chichester—"to set us right, Liv."

Looking back, I realise that I should have seen what it all meant: the tightness of finances in combination with all those extra gigs. But I didn't, at first. Not because I didn't want to, but because I couldn't allow myself to. I had far more than money invested in Richie, but I wasn't about to consider that. So I lied and donned blinkers. I told myself we were hard pressed for cash and it was reasonable that he might have to travel to make it. But when the cash got tighter and his travelling didn't make a difference in what we were bringing in, I was forced to put the facts together. He wasn't bringing it in because he was laying it out.

I accused. He admitted. He was drowning in expenses. He had his wife in Brighton, he had me in London, he had a tart called Sandy in Southend-on-Sea.

Not that he mentioned Sandy at first. He wasn't a fool. He kept me focussed on his wife, the martyred Loretta, who still loved him, couldn't make herself part with him, was the mother of his children, and all the etceteras. He'd taken to dropping down to Brighton for a visit now and again, as any dutiful father might. He'd extended his visits with three or four—or was it five, Richie?—safaris into Loretta's knickers. She was pregnant.

He cried when he told me. He said what could he do, they'd been married for years, she was the mother of his children, he couldn't turn away from her love when she offered it to him, when she couldn't get over him, when she'd never get over him . . . It didn't *mean* anything, she didn't mean anything, together the two of them didn't mean anything because "You're the one, Liv. You make me make the music. Everything else is crap."

Except Sandy, as things turned out. I found out about Sandy on a Wednesday morning, directly the doctor explained how what I thought was an inconvenient and uncomfortable infection was really herpes. I was through with Richie by Thursday night. I had just enough strength to throw his belongings down the front steps and make arrangements to change the lock on the door. By Friday night, I thought I was dying. On Saturday, the doctor called it "a most interesting and prodigious infection," which was his way of saying he'd never seen anything like it.

And what was it like? Like fever and burning, like screaming into a towel when I went to the toilet, like rats taking large bites out of my twat. I had six weeks to think about Sandy, Richie, and Southend-on-Sea while I travelled from the doctor to the loo to my bed and felt that gangrene couldn't be any worse than what was tearing through me.

I got down quickly to no food in the flat, filthy laundry piled in doorways, and crockery broken against walls and doors. I got down quickly to having no money. National Health took care of the doctor, but no one took care of anything else.

I remember sitting by the telephone and thinking, Hellfire and hot ice, I finally qualify. I remember laughing. I'd been drinking the last of the gin all morning, and it took a mixture of gin and desperation to place the call. It was Sunday, noon.

Dad answered. I said, "I need help."

He said, "Livie? Where in God's name are you? What's happened, my dear?"

When had I spoken to him last? I couldn't recall. Had he always sounded so gentle? Had his voice been at once so kind and so low?

He said, "You're not well, are you? Has there been an accident? Are you hurt? Are you in hospital?"

I felt the oddest sensation. His words acted like anaesthetic and scalpel. I opened to him painlessly.

I told him everything. When I was done, I said, "Daddy, help me. Please help me get out of this."

He said, "Let me work on things here. Let me do what I can. Your mother's—"

"I can't hold on here," I told him. I began to cry. I hated myself for it because he'd tell her I was weeping and she'd talk to him about children who engage in manipulation and parents who stand firm and keep true to their word and their law and their miserable belief that theirs is the only right way to live. "Daddy!" I must have wailed because I could hear the word in the flat long after I said it into the phone.

He said gently, "Give me your phone number, Livie. Give me your address. I'll speak to your mother. I'll be in touch."

"But I—"

"You must trust me."

"Promise."

"I'll do what I can. This isn't going to be easy."

I suppose he presented his case as best he could, but Mother had always been the expert when it came to Family Troubles. She held true to her position. Two days later she sent me fifty pounds inside an envelope. A sheet of white paper was folded round the notes. She'd written on it, "A home has to be a place where the children learn to live by their parents' rules. When you're capable of guaranteeing you'll adhere to our rules, please let us know. Tears and pleas for help are simply not enough at this point. We love you, darling. We always will." And that was that.

Miriam, I thought. Good old Miriam. I could read between the lines of her perfect handwriting. This was all about washing one's hands of one's children. As far as Mother was concerned, I'd got what I deserved.

Well, to hell with her, I thought. I wished upon her every curse I could think of. Every disease, every ill fortune, every unhappiness. Since she was taking pleasure in my condition, I would take heady pleasure in hers.

It's odd to think how things work out.

OLIVIA

The sun feels warm against my cheeks. I smile, lean back, and close my eyes. I count a minute off the way I was taught: one thousand and one, one thousand and two, and so forth. I ought to go to three hundred, but sixty is just about my limit right now. And even then, once I hit one thousand and forty, I tend to rush things to get to the end. I call the minute "taking a rest," which is what I'm supposed to do several times a day. I don't know why. I think "take a rest" is what they tell you when they don't have anything more productive to say. They want you to close your eyes and slowly drift off. I fight that idea. It's rather like asking someone to get used to the inevitable before she's ready, isn't it?

Except the inevitable is something black, cold, and infinite while here on the barge in my canvas chair, I see the red streaks of sunlight against my eyelids and I feel the warmth press like fingers against my face. My jersey soaks up heat. My leggings distribute it along my shins. And everything—the world especially—seems so terribly forg

.   .   .

Sorry. I drifted off completely. My trouble is that I fight sleep all night, so there are times in the day when it takes me unaware. It's better that way, actually, because it's a peaceful thing, like slowly being drawn from shore with the tide. And the dreams which come with a daytime sleep that seduces one from consciousness . . . those are the sweetest.

I was with Chris in my dream. I knew it was him because I felt so sure that he wouldn't drop me. I clung to his back and we soared high above a green-and-black rocky coastline like the Cliffs of Moher where the ocean sends spray a thousand feet in the air. And his hair was long for some reason, not like Chris's hair at all, long and pure black and straight as the shaft of a spear. It covered me as we flew. And I could feel his shoulders, the strength of his legs, and the wind on my face. When we landed, it was in a barren place like the Burren, and he said, This is where it will happen, Livie. I said, What? He said, Children spring from the stones. And when he smiled, I saw he had changed to my father.

I killed my father. I live with that knowledge, along with everything else. Chris tells me I don't bear nearly the amount of responsibility for Dad's death that I seem to want to bear. But Chris didn't know me then. He hadn't tumbled me out of the rubbish heap and challenged me, in that perfectly reasonable way of his, to act as big as I talked, to talk as big as he believed I could be. I've asked him since that time why he took me on; he shrugs and says, "Instinct, Livie. I could see who you were. It was in your eyes." I say, "It's because I reminded you of them." He says, "Them? Who?" but he knows who I mean, and we both know it's the truth. "Rescue," I say. "That's your real forte, isn't it?" He says, "You needed something to believe in. Like we all do." But the fact of the matter is that Chris has always seen more of me than was really there. He sees my heart as good. I see it as absent.

Which is what it was the last time I came face to face with my father.

I saw Mother and Dad right outside Covent Garden Station on a Friday night. They'd been to the opera. Even in my state, I could tell that much because Mother was head-to-toe in black, wearing a quadruple strand of pearls. It was a choker, something I'd always told her shortened her neck and made her look like Winston Churchill in drag. Dad was in a dinner jacket that smelled of lavender. He'd had his hair cut recently, and it was much too short. His ears looked like conch shells pressed against his head. They gave him an air of surprise and innocence. Somewhere he'd unearthed a pair of patent leather shoes, which he'd polished to mirror quality.

I hadn't seen or spoken to either of them since I'd talked to Dad that day on the phone when I called for help. Nearly two years had passed. I'd had six different jobs, gone through five flatmates, and lived my life as I saw fit, answerable to no one and liking it that way.

I was with two blokes that I'd met on King Street in a pub called something like the Ram or the Ox. We were heading for a party rumoured to be blowing off the rooftops in Brixton. At least, I was heading there. The blokes were following. We'd snorted some coke in the gentlemen's toilet and afterwards—when things seemed funnier than they would otherwise—we'd had ourselves a good laugh about doing a three-some with me taking it in both ends at once. They were sweating to do it to me, swearing how much I was going to like it because they were war-riors, they were kings, they were absolute studs. They were grabbing, poking, and working themselves up, while I was sweating for the coke. I could see it was a case of who was going to get what from who when, and I was clever enough to know that the minute I put out the way that they wanted, I'd be shut out and finished.

You shudder as you read this, don't you? You lay these pages aside. You look out the window until some exterior beauty there fortifies you enough to come back to me.

Because your life hasn't been like mine, has it? I imagine you've never done drugs, so you don't know what sort of human slime you can end up slithering through when you want to get high. You can't see your-self, can you, kneeling on the cracked tiles in the gentlemen's toilet while some bloke who plays banker in the City all day fumbles with the zip on his I'm-incognito leather trousers and laughs while he grabs your head and says, "Come on. Do it." You can't imagine that, can you? You can't even imagine *considering* it in the first place because you can't think what it's like in the aftermath, when those few obliging if somewhat nasty minutes in the gentlemen's toilet on your knees with your head in someone's crotch buy you power, wit, energy, brilliance, and the knowledge that you are the most superior creature God ever put on earth.

Because that's what it's like when the stuff shoots up your nose and sets your eyeballs on fire. But I wasn't so far gone in the need for coke that I'd forgotten how to play for what I wanted. So I laughed along with them, kneeling on those tiles with the broken edge of one knifing through my jeans, and I gave each of those blokes just enough mouth to act as a preview of future delight. When they were hot, I leaned back on my heels. I yawned, eyelids drooping. I said, "I need another hit," because as far as I was concerned, neither one of them was getting anything more off me till I'd gone through my fair share of their dope.

They were simple blokes, for all their public school received pronunciation and their posh jobs in the City. They thought they had me where they wanted me, so they decided it was time to be mean with the drug. I suppose they thought that a good spot of stinginess would keep me interested.

They were wrong. I said, "Buzz off then, nancies," and that was enough to make them decide a show of good faith was in order if their grubby little dreams were going to come true. We paused long enough to do a couple of lines on the boot of a car, then we arm-in-armed it up to the station. I don't know about them, but I felt eighty feet tall.

Clark was singing "Satisfaction" with a new set of lyrics designed for what he expected his future sexual circumstances to be. Barry was alternating between sticking his middle finger in my mouth and rubbing himself up to keep in shape for the fun. Like a hot knife through whipping cream, we parted the herd of pedestrians that are always mucking round Covent Garden. One glance in our direction and people simply stepped off the pavement. Until we ran into my parents.

I still don't understand what they were doing at the station that night. When she isn't able to drive her own car, Mother has always been strictly a taxi person, one of those women who act as if they'd allow their toenails to be pulled out one by one before they'd wander through the entrails of London transport. Dad never minded the tube. To him a ride on the underground was a ride on the underground, efficient, inexpensive, and relatively trouble-free. He went from home to work and back again on the District Line every Monday to Saturday, and I doubt he ever gave a passing thought to who was sitting next to him or to what might be implied by arriving at the printing factory in anything less than a Ferrari.

Perhaps that night, he had won her over to his means of transport. Perhaps there had been not enough taxis available when they left the opera. Or perhaps Dad had suggested they save a few quid towards the yearly summer's holiday on Jersey by taking a rumble along the Piccadilly Line. At any rate, there they were where I least expected to see them.

Mother didn't speak. Dad didn't recognise me at first, which is understandable. I'd cut my hair short and coloured it cherry red and tarted it up with purple on the ends. I wasn't wearing clothes he'd seen before—other than the blue jeans—and my earrings were different. There were more of them as well.

I was just strung out enough to make a scene. I threw out my arms in the fashion of a singer about to hit high C. I said, "Jesus in a jumpsuit. Lads, here's the loins I'm the fruit of."

"Whose loins?" Barry asked. He hung his chin on my shoulder, reached down, and cupped me between my legs. "Does a bird have loins? D'you know, Clark?"

Clark didn't know much of anything at that point. He was weaving on my left. I began giggling and rotating against the hand that held me. I leaned against him and said, "Better stop that, Barry. You're going to make Mummy dead jealous."

"Why? She want some too?" He pushed me to one side and staggered towards her. "Don't you get it regular?" Barry asked, landing a hand on her shoulder. "Don't he give it to you like a good boy should?"

"He's a good boy," I said. "He knows what's what." I reached out and patted Dad on the lapel. He flinched.

Mother disengaged Barry's hand from her shoulder. She looked at me. "Just how far is it that you'd like to sink?" she said.

And that's when Dad seemed to realise that he wasn't being confronted by three hooligans intent upon roughing him up and humiliating his wife. He was face to face with his daughter.

He said, "Good God. Is it Livie?"

Mother took his arm. She said, "Gordon."

He said, "No. It's enough. You're coming home, Livie."

I winked at him broadly. "Can't," I said. "Got to suck dick tonight." Clark came up behind me and rubbed me up good. "Ohhh. Nasty stuff, that," I said. "But not as good as the real thing. Do you like to fuck, Daddy?"

Mother's mouth barely moved as she said, "Gordon. Let's go."

I brushed Clark's hand off me. I went to my father. I patted his chest and leaned my forehead against him. He felt like wood. I turned my head and gazed at my mother. "Well, does he?" I asked her.

"Gordon," she repeated.

"He hasn't answered. Why won't he answer?" I put my arms round his waist and tipped my head back to look at him. "D'you like to fuck, Daddy?"

"Gordon, we have nothing to discuss with her when she's in this condition."

"Me?" I asked. "Condition?" I asked. I moved closer and rotated my hips against my father. "Okay. Let's change the question, then. D'you want to fuck me? Barry and Clark do. They'd do it here in the street if they could. Would you? If I said yes? Cause I might, you know."

"All *right*." Clark moved behind me again so that the three of us made an undulating sexual sandwich on the pavement.

Barry began laughing. He said, "Do it," and I made a sing-song of "Daddy wants to do it, to do it, to do it."

The crowd on the pavement gave us a wide berth.

I felt like one of those coloured scraps at the end of a kaleidoscope. I was part of a swirling mass that shifted when I tossed my head. I was alone. Then I was in the centre of the action. I was dominatrix. Then I was slave.

From another planet, Mother's voice said, "Gordon, for the love of God . . ."

Someone said, "Do it."

Someone shouted, "Whooooahhhh."

Someone called out, "Ride her."

And then hot irons went round my wrists.

I hadn't realised Dad was so strong. When he took my arms, unlocked them from round him, and thrust me away, I felt the pain of it right through my shoulders.

I said, "Hey!"

He stepped back. He took out a handkerchief and pressed it to his mouth. Someone said, "Do you need help here, sir?" and I saw a flash of silver in the corner of my eye. A bobby's helmet.

I snickered. "Saved by the local constab. Lucky you, Dad."

Mother said to the constable, "Thank you. These three . . ."

Dad said, "It's nothing."

"Gordon." Mother's voice was all admonition. Here was their chance to teach their little hell-spawn a proper lesson.

"A misunderstanding," Dad said. "Thank you, Officer. We'll be on our way." He placed his hand beneath my mother's elbow. He said, "Miriam," and his meaning was clear.

Mother was trembling. I could tell by the way her pearls shuddered in the light. She said to me, "You're a monster."

I said, "What about him?" And as they walked off, I shouted, "Because we know, Dad, don't we? But don't you worry. It'll be our secret. I'll never tell.''

I'd aroused him, you see. He'd gone hard as a fire iron. And I loved the joke of it, the beautiful power of it. The thought of him walking through the lights of that station with all the world to see the bulge in his trousers—with Miriam to see the bulge in his trousers—made me weak with amusement. To have got a reaction from taciturn, passionless Gordon Whitelaw. If I could do that, here in public, in front of God only knows how many witnesses, I could do anything. I was omnipotence personified.

The copper said to us, "Move off, you lot," and "Nothing more to see here," to what remained of the spectators.

Barry, Clark, and I never found the party in Brixton. We never actually tried. Instead, we made our own party in the flat in Shepherd's Bush. We did two threesomes, one twosome, and ended up with three onesomes with each of us egging the other on. We had enough dope to last the night, at the end of which Clark and Barry decided they liked the action well enough to move in as my flatmates, which was fine with me. I shared their dope. They shared me. It was an arrangement that promised to benefit all of us.

At the end of our first week together, we prepared to celebrate our seventh-day anniversary. We were happily spread out on the floor, with three grams of coke and a half litre of eucalyptus body oil, when the telegram arrived. Somehow she'd managed to have it delivered, rather than phoned. She no doubt wanted the effect to be an unforgettable one.

I didn't read it at first. I was watching Barry whip a razor blade through the coke, and all my attention was fixed on two words: *how soon*.

Clark answered the door. He brought the telegram into the sitting room. He said, "For you, Liv," and dropped it into my lap. He put on music and he uncapped the body oil. I pulled off my jersey, then my jeans. He said, "Aren't you going to read it?"

I said, "Later." He poured the oil and started. I closed my eyes and felt the ripples of pleasure take my shoulders and arms first, then my breasts and my thighs. I smiled and listened to the *chick chick chick* of Barry's razor blade making the magic powder. When it was ready, he giggled and said, "Let the games begin."

I forgot about the telegram until the next morning when I woke in a fog with the taste of melted aspirin in my throat. Always the quickest of us to recover, Clark was shaving, getting ready to head into the City for another day of financial wizardry. Barry was still out cold where we'd left him, sprawled half on and half off the sofa. He was lying on his stomach with his little arse looking like two pink muffins and his fingers jerking spasmodically as if he was trying to grab something in his dream.

I plodded into the sitting room and slapped his bum. He didn't wake up. Clark said, "He's not going to make it today. Can you wake him enough so he can phone in?"

I prodded Barry with my foot. He groaned. I prodded again. He turned his head into the sofa. "No," I told Clark.

"Can you be his sister? On the phone, I mean."

"Why? Does he say he lives with his sister?"

"He has been until now. And it would be easier if you—"

"Shit. All right." I made the call. Flu, I told them. Barry spent the night with his head in the toilet. He's just gone off to sleep. "Done," I said when I rang off.

Clark nodded. He adjusted his tie. He seemed to hesitate and he watched me too carefully. "Liv," he said, "about last night." He'd slicked his hair back in a way I didn't like. I reached up to mess it about. He tilted his head away. He said again, "About last night."

"What about it? Didn't get enough? Want more? Now?"

"I'd prefer you didn't let Barry know. All right?"

I frowned. "What?"

"Don't say anything to him. We'll talk later." He glanced at his watch. It was a Rolex, a present from his proud mummy when he left the London School of Economics. "I must go. I've a meeting at half past nine."

I blocked his way. I didn't like the persona that was Clark when he was straight—all pish-posh language rolling delicately off the tongue—and I liked it even less this morning. "Not till you tell me what you mean. Don't tell Barry what? And why?"

He sighed. "That it was just the two of us. Last night. Liv, you know what I'm talking about."

"Who cares? He was out of it. He couldn't have if he'd even wanted to."

"I'm aware of that fact, but it's not quite the point." He shifted from one foot to the other. "Just don't say anything to him. We had a bargain, he and I. I don't want to mess it up."

"What kind of bargain?"

"It's not important. I can't explain it now anyway."

I was still in his path. "You'd better explain it. If you want to make your meeting, that is."

He sighed and said *hell* under his breath.

"What deal, Clark? About last night."

"Very well. Before we moved in with you we agreed we'd never—" he cleared his throat, "we agreed that without the other one we'd never . . ." He ran his hand through his hair and messed it up himself. "We'd both always be there, all right? With you. That was the bargain."

"I see. You'd shag me together, you mean. The threesome would only do a twosome if we had a onesome for an audience."

"If you feel it's necessary to put it that way."

"Is there another way to put it?"

"I suppose not."

"Fine. Just as long as we know what we're talking about."

He licked his lips. "Good," he said. "See you tonight."

"Right." I stepped to one side and watched him walk to the door. "Oh Clark?" He turned. "In case you can't feel it, you've got snot dripping out of your nose. I'd hate you to look bad for your meeting."

I wiggled my fingers at him in farewell and when the door closed on him, I went to Barry. We would see what we would see about who had Liv and when.

I smacked his bum. He groaned. I tickled his bollocks. He smiled. I said, "Come on, you hunk of meat. We've got business to attend to," and I squatted down to turn him over. That's when I saw the telegram again, lying on the floor with Barry's sleeping fingers mincing across it.

I kicked it to one side at first and sank onto the floor to work on Barry. But when I saw that nothing was going to bring him out of the stupor, let alone make it possible for him to perform, I said, "Hell," and reached for the telegram.

I was clumsy, so when I ripped the envelope open, I ripped the message in half. I read *crematorium* and *Tuesday*, and I thought initially that I was holding a grisly advert for how to prepare for the afterlife. But then I saw *father* at the top. And near it the word *underground*. I put the two halves together and squinted at the message.

She'd told me as little as possible. He had died on the underground between Knightsbridge and South Kensington stations, going home from the opera on the night of our encounter. He'd been cremated three days later. On the fourth day, the memorial service had been held.

Later—much later when things were different between us—I learned the rest from her. That he'd been standing with her in the God-awful pack that always smash into the square of space right near the carriage doors, that he'd not even fallen at first but instead leaned with a tremendous sigh into a young woman who thought he was coming on to her and shoved him away, that he'd sunk to his knees and then toppled to his side when the carriage doors opened and the bodies shifted at South Kensington Station.

To do his fellow passengers credit, they did help Mother get him out onto the platform, and someone ran for help. But it was more than twenty minutes before he arrived at the nearest hospital, and if anything had been able to save him, that time had long since passed.

The doctors said that his death had been swift. Heart failure, they said. Quite possibly he was dead before he hit the floor.

But, as I've said, I learned all that later. At the moment I only had the meagre but explicit information contained in the telegram and the abundant but implicit information contained between the telegram's lines.

I remember thinking, Why, you sodding little bitch! You miserable cow! I felt tight and hot. I felt a burning band sinking into my head. I had to act. I had to act now. I balled up the telegram and crammed it hard between Barry's cheeks. I filled my hand with his hair and yanked his head back.

I laughed and shouted, "Wake up, you twit. Wake up. Wake up. Goddamn you. Wake up." He moaned. I shoved his head into the sofa. I strode to the kitchen. I filled a pot with water. It sloshed onto my feet as I carried it back to the sofa, all the time shouting, "Up, up, up!" I jerked Barry's arm and his body came after it, right where I wanted, onto the floor. I flipped him over and doused him with water. His eyes fluttered open. He said, "Hey. Wha'?" and that was enough.

I fell upon him. I hit him. I scratched and punched. His arms flailed like windmills. He said, "Wha' the hell!" and tried to pin me but he was still too far gone to have much strength.

I laughed then screamed, "You bloody bastards!"

He said, "Hey! Liv!" and writhed away on his stomach.

I went after him. I rode him, smacking him, biting his shoulder, shrieking, "The two of you! Bastards! You want it! You want it?"

"What is this?" he said. "What the fu—"

I grabbed the bottle of what remained of the eucalyptus oil that lay on the floor along with the plates from our dinner. I smashed him on the head with it. It didn't break. I hit him on the neck, then the shoulders. All the time I screamed. And laughed and laughed. He managed to rise to his knees. I got one more good blow in before he threw me backwards. I landed near the fireplace. I grabbed the poker. I began to swing it. "Hate you! No! The two of you! Scum! Worms!" And with every word I swung the poker again.

Barry shouted, "Holy shit!" and headed for the bedroom. He slammed the door. I beat against it with the poker. I felt the splinters flying out from the wood. When my shoulders were sore and my arms couldn't lift the poker again, I threw it the length of the passage and slid down the wall to the floor.

Which is where I finally began to weep, saying, "You're gonna, Barry. To me. Right. Now."

The door cracked open after a minute or two. My head was on my knees and I didn't look up. I heard Barry mutter, "Crazy bitch," as he eased past me. Then he was speaking to voices raised in the corridor outside our flat. I heard *disagreement* and *temper* and *female thing* and *misunderstanding* in that BBC voice of his. I leaned my head back against the wall and slammed my skull against it.

"You will," I sobbed. "To me. Right now. You will."

I dragged myself to my knees. I fixed my mind on the two of them—Barry and Clark—and I began to rage through the flat. What was breakable, I broke. I smashed plates against work tops and glasses against walls and lamps against the floor. What was made of or covered by cloth, I hacked with a knife. What little furniture we had, I toppled and trampled as best I could. In the end, I fell onto the tattered, stained mattress of our bed, and I curled into a foetal ball.

But doing that forced me to think about him. And Covent Garden Station. . . . I couldn't afford to think. I had to get out. I had to be above it all. I had to fly. I needed power. I needed something, someone, it didn't matter what or who just as long as the end result was getting me out of here away from these walls that were shifting towards me and the mess the smell and what cock to think Shepherd's Bush had anything to offer when there was a world out there just waiting for me to conquer it so who needed this shit anyway who even wanted it who asked for it to be part of life.

I left the flat and never went back. The flat meant thinking of Clark and Barry. Clark and Barry meant thinking of Dad. Better to score drugs. Better to pop pills. Better to find some greasy-haired bloke who'd put out the money for gin in the hope of having it off with me in the back seat of his car. Better to anything. Better to be safe.

I started out in Shepherd's Bush. I worked my way over to Notting Hill where I crawled round Ladbroke Road for a while. I had only twenty pounds with me—hardly enough money to do the sort of damage I wanted—so I wasn't as drunk as I would have liked to be by the time I finally made it to Kensington. But I was drunk enough.

I'd not given any thought to what I would do. I just wanted to see her face once more so that I could spit in it.

I stumbled down that street of proper white houses with their Doric columns and white-lace bay windows. I weaved between the parked cars. I muttered, "See *you*, Miriam-cow. In your ugly fat face," and I staggered to a halt directly across the street from that shiny black front door. I leaned against an antique Deux Chevaux and peered at the steps. I counted them. Seven. They seemed to be moving. Or perhaps it was me. Except that the entire street seemed to tilt in the oddest way. And a mist fell between me and my destination, then cleared away, then fell again. I began to perspire and to shiver simultaneously. My stomach roiled once. And then it heaved.

I was sick on the bonnet of that Deux Chevaux. Then again on the pavement and in the gutter.

"It's you," I said to the woman inside that house across the street. "This is you."

Not *for* you. Not *because of* you. But *you*. What was I thinking? I wonder that even now. Perhaps I thought that an indissoluble connection could be got rid of through such a simple means as vomiting it up in the street.

Now I know that's not the case. There are more profound and lasting ways to break a tie between mother and child.

When I could stand, I lurched along the pavement the way I had come. I scrubbed my mouth against my jersey. I thought, Bitch, witch, shrew. She blamed me for his death and I knew it. She had punished me using the best method she could find. Well, I could blame and punish as well. We would see, I thought, who was expert.

So I set about the project and worked like a master at blame and punishment for the next five years.

OLIVIA

Chris is back. He's brought take-away with him, as I thought he might, but it isn't tandoori. It's Thai, from a place called Bangkok Hideaway. He held the bag beneath my nose, saying, "Mmmm, smell, Livie. We've not tried this yet, have we? They cook peanuts and bean sprouts with the noodles," and he took it below, through his workroom and into the galley where I can hear him banging crockery about. He's singing as well. He loves American country western music, and right now he's doing "Crazy" only slightly less well than Patsy Cline. He likes the part about tryin' and cryin'. He belts those lines out, and he always makes *crazy* into three syllables: *cuh-RAY-zee*. I'm so used to the way Chris sings it that when he plays Patsy Cline on his stereo, I can't adjust to hearing her instead of him.

From my spot on the barge deck, I could see Chris coming along Blomfield Road with the dogs. They weren't running any longer, and from the way Chris was walking, I could tell he was juggling the dogs' leads, a bag, and something else, which was tucked into the bend of his arm. The dogs seemed interested in this something else. Beans kept trying to jump up to give a look. Toast kept hobbling and nudging Chris's arm, perhaps in the hope that whatever was there would fall. It didn't, and when they all came on board—the dogs first, dragging their leads behind them—I saw the rabbit. He was shaking so hard that he looked like a grey and brown blur with floppy ears and eyes that resembled chocolate under glass. I looked from him to Chris.

"The park," he said. "Beans routed him from beneath a hydrangea. People make me want to be sick sometimes."

I knew what he meant. Someone had got tired of the trouble of a pet and decided he'd be ever so much happier if he was free. Never mind that he wasn't born wild. He'd get used to it and love it, so long as some dog or cat didn't get to him first.

"He's lovely," I said. "What shall we call him?"

"Felix."

"Isn't that a cat's name?"

"It's also Latin for *happy*. Which I expect he is, now he's out of the park." And he went below.

Chris has just come on deck with the dogs now. He's got their bowls, and he means to feed them. He usually feeds them below, but I know he wants me to have the company. He puts the bowls near my canvas chair and watches the dogs tuck into their kibble. He stretches, then arcs his arms upward. The late afternoon sunlight makes his head look covered with rust-coloured down. He gazes across the pool to Browning's Island. He smiles.

I say, "What?" in reference to that smile.

He says, "There's something about willow trees in leaf. Look how the breeze makes the branches sway. They look like dancers. They remind me of Yeats."

"And that makes you smile? Yeats makes you smile?"

"How can we know the dancer from the dance?" he says.

"What?"

"That's Yeats. 'How can we know the dancer from the dance.' Appropriate, isn't it?" He squats by my chair. He notices how many pages I've filled. He picks up my tin of those jumbo child's pencils and sees how many I've worn down so far. "Shall I sharpen these up?" is his way of asking how it's going and if I feel up to continuing.

My way of saying all right to both is, "Where've you put Felix?"

"On the table in the galley for the moment. He's having his tea. Perhaps I should check on him. Want to come below?"

"Not just yet."

He nods. He straightens up and when he does my pencil tin rises with him. He says to the dogs, "You lot stay on board. Beans. Toast. D'you hear me? No prowling. You keep an eye on Livie."

Their tails wag. Chris goes below. I hear the whirring of the pencil sharpener. I lean back and smile. *Keep an eye on Livie*. As if I'm going somewhere.

We've developed this peculiar shorthand way of talking, Chris and I. It's comforting to be able to speak one's mind without having to touch on the subject. The only problem I find with it is that sometimes I don't have all the words I want, and the message gets confused. For example, I haven't yet come up with the way to tell Chris I love him. Not that it would make any difference to our situation if I did tell him. Chris doesn't love me—not the way one ordinarily thinks of love—and he never has. Nor does he want me. Nor did he ever. I used to accuse him of being queer. *Bum-boy*, I called him, *pansy*, *ginger beer*. And he'd lean forward in his chair with his elbows on his knees and his hands clasped beneath his chin, and he'd say earnestly, "Listen to your language of choice. Notice what it says. Don't you see how that tunnel vision of yours is indicative of a greater ill, Livie? And what's fascinating is that you're really not to blame for it. Society's to blame. For where else do we develop our attitudes if not from the society in which we move?" And my mouth would hang open. I would want to rail. But one can't fight with a man who doesn't carry weapons.

Chris comes back with my pencil tin. He's brought a cup of tea as well. He says, "Felix has started eating the telephone book."

I say, "Good thing I haven't got anyone to ring."

He touches my cheek. "You're getting chilled. I'll fetch a blanket."

"You needn't. I'll want to come below in a while."

"But until then . . ." And he's gone. He'll bring the blanket. He'll tuck it round me. He'll squeeze my shoulder or perhaps he'll kiss the top of my head. He'll direct the dogs to lie on either side of my chair. Then he'll set out dinner. And when it's ready, he'll come for me. He'll say, "If I may escort Mademoiselle to her table . . . ?" Because *escort* is part of our shorthand as well.

The light's growing dim as we lose the day's sun, and along the canal I can see reflections in the water from the lamps burning in the other barges. They're shimmering oblongs the colour of sultanas, and against them the occasional shadow moves.

It's quiet. I've always found that odd because one would think you'd hear noise from Warwick Avenue, Harrow Road, or either of the bridges, but there's something about being beneath the roadways that sends sound off in another direction. Chris would be able to explain it to me. I must remember to ask him. If he finds the question odd, he won't say. He'll merely look pensive, run a finger through the scrap of hair that curls behind his right ear, and say, "It has to do with the sound waves and the surrounding buildings and the effect of the trees," and if I look interested, he'll get out paper and pencil—or take mine from me—and say, "Let me show you what I mean," and begin to sketch. I used to think that he made up these explanations he seems to have for everything. Who is he, after all? Some skinny bloke with pock-marked cheeks who dropped out of university to "make real change, Livie. There's only one way to do that, you know. And it has nothing to do with being part of either the structure or the infrastructure keeping the beast alive." I used to think that anyone who mixed his metaphors like that with so little conscience could hardly be educated enough to know anything, let alone to be part of some great social change in the future. I used to say with great boredom, "I think you mean 'keeping the building's foundations sound,' " in an effort to embarrass him. But that was, aside from an obvious need to belittle, the daughter of my mother speaking. My mother who was the English teacher, the illuminator of minds.

That's the role Miriam Whitelaw played in Kenneth Fleming's life at first. But you probably know that already since it's part of the Fleming legend.

Kenneth and I are of an age, although I look years older. But our birthdays are actually a week apart, a fact among many that I learned about Kenneth at home over dinner, somewhere between the soup and the pudding. I first heard about him when we were both fifteen. He was a pupil in Mother's English class on the Isle of Dogs. He lived in Cubitt Town with his parents in those days and what athletic prowess he possessed was demonstrated mostly on the river-damp playing fields of Millwall Park. I don't know if the comprehensive had a cricket team. It probably had, and Kenneth may well have played on the first eleven. But if he did, that was part of the Fleming legend that I never heard. And I heard most of it, night after night, with roast beef, chicken, plaice, or pork.

I've never been a teacher, so I don't know what it is to have a star pupil. And since I was never disciplined enough or interested enough to attend to my studies, I certainly don't know what it is to be a star pupil and to find a mentor among the instructors who drone endlessly on at the front of the classroom. But that was what Kenneth Fleming and my mother were to each other from the very beginning.

I think he was what she'd always believed she could find, cultivate, and encourage to grow from the sodden river soil and the dreary council housing that constituted life on the Isle of Dogs. He was the point she had been trying to make with her life. He was possibility personified.

One week into Autumn term, she began to talk about "this clever young man I've got in class," which is how she introduced him to Dad and me as a regular dinnertime topic. He was articulate, she told us. He was amusing. He was self-deprecating in the most charming of ways. He was completely at ease with his peers and with adults. In the classroom, he had astonishing insight into theme, motivation, and character when they were discussing Dickens, Austen, Shakespeare, Brontë. He read Sartre and Beckett in his free time. At lunch, he argued the merits of Pinter. And he wrote—"Gordon, Olivia, this is what's so lovely about the boy" —he wrote like a real scholar. He had a questioning mind and a ready wit. He engaged in discussion, he didn't merely proffer ideas that he knew the instructor wanted to hear. In short, he was a dream come true. And through Autumn, Spring, and Summer terms, he didn't miss a single day of school.

I loathed him. Who wouldn't have done? He was everything I wasn't and he'd managed it all without having a single Social or Economic Advantage.

"His father's a docker," Mother informed us. She seemed all agog at the fact that the son of a docker could possibly be what she'd always claimed the son of a docker could be: successful. "His mother's a housewife. He's the eldest of five children. He gets up at half past four to do his prep for school because he helps with the children at night. He gave the most stunning presentation to the class today. The one I was telling you I'd assigned them on the self. He's been studying—What is it? Judo? Karate?—and he paced back and forth at the front of the room in that pyjama-thing they wear. He talked about the art and the discipline of mind and then . . . Gordon, Olivia, he broke a brick with his hand!"

My father nodded, smiled, and said, "Good Lord. A brick. Fancy that." I yawned. What a bore it was, she was, he was. The next thing I would learn, no doubt, was that darling Kenneth walked across the Thames without aid of a bridge.

There was no doubt that he would fly through his O-levels. Or that he'd put his name in lights. He'd make himself the pride of his parents, my mother, and the entire comprehensive. And he'd doubtlessly do it all with one hand tied behind his back, standing on his head in a bucket of vinegar. After which he'd go on to the lower and upper sixth, distinguishing himself in every area possible to a single pupil. After which he'd go to Oxford for a first in an arcane subject. After which he'd bow to civic duty and become prime minister. And through it all, no doubt, the name on his lips most frequently spoken when it came time for acknowledging the secret of his success would be Miriam Whitelaw, beloved teacher. Because she was beloved to Kenneth, my mother. He made her the keeper of the flame of his dreams. He shared with her the intimate parts of his soul.

That's why she knew about Jean Cooper long before anyone else did. And we learned about Jean—Dad and I—at the same time as we learned about Kenneth.

Jean was his girl. She'd been his girl from the time they were twelve-year-olds when having a girl doesn't mean much more than knowing who's going to lean against the schoolyard wall with whom. She was Scandinavian pretty, with light hair and blue eyes. She was slender like a willow branch and quick like a colt. She looked on the world from an adolescent's face, but with adult eyes. She went to school only when the mood was upon her. When it wasn't, she did a bunk with her mates and went through the footway tunnel to Greenwich. When she wasn't doing that, she'd pinch her sisters' copies of *Just 17* and spend the day reading about music and fashions. She'd paint her face, shorten her skirts, and style her hair.

I listened to my mother's tales of Jean Cooper with considerable interest. I knew that if anyone was going to put a cog in the works of Kenneth Fleming's unstoppable rise to glory, it was going to be Jean.

From what I gathered over the dinner table, Jean knew what she wanted, and it didn't have anything to do with O-levels, going on to the lower and upper sixth, A-levels, and university. It did, however, have to do with Kenneth Fleming. At least that's the way my mother told it.

Kenneth and Jean both took their O-levels. Kenneth passed his brilliantly. Jean fluffed hers. That outcome was a surprise to no one. But it gratified my mother because I'm sure she believed that the intellectual imbalance in the relationship between Kenneth and his girlfriend would finally become apparent to the boy. Once it was apparent to him, Kenneth would act to remove Jean from his life in order to get on with his education. It's rather an amusing idea, that, isn't it? I'm not sure how Mother ever reached the conclusion that relationships between teenagers are about intellectual balance in the first place.

Jean went from the comprehensive to a job at the old Billingsgate Market. Kenneth went on a governors' scholarship to a small public school in West Sussex. There he *did* play on the cricket first eleven, shining so brightly that on more than one occasion scouts from one county side or another stopped by a school match to watch him hit fours and sixes, without apparent effort.

He came home at weekends. Dad and I heard about this as well because Kenneth always stopped by the comprehensive to give Mother an update on his progress in school. It seems that he played every sport, belonged to every society, distinguished himself in every one of his subjects, endeared himself to the headmaster, the members of the staff, his fellow pupils, his housemaster, the matron, and every blade of grass upon which he trod. When he wasn't bent upon either achieving greatness or having it thrust upon him, he was home at the weekend, helping out with his brothers and sisters. And when he wasn't helping out with his brothers and sisters, he was at the comprehensive chatting up Mother and posing as an example, for all the fifth formers, of what a pupil could achieve once he set his sights on a goal. Kenneth's goal was Oxford, a blue in cricket, a good fifteen years playing for England if he could manage it, and all the benefits that can accompany playing for the England team: the travel, the notoriety, the product endorsements, the money.

With all this on his plate, Mother concluded happily that he couldn't possibly have time any longer for "that Cooper creature," as she called Jean with a curling of her lip. She couldn't have been more wrong.

Kenneth continued seeing Jean in much the same way as he'd been seeing her for the past several years. They merely moved their meetings to the weekend, every Saturday night. They did what they had been doing since they were fourteen years old with two years of getting acquainted behind them: they went to a film or they found a party or they listened to music with some of their mates or they took a long walk or they had dinner with one of their families or they made their way by bus to Trafalgar Square and wandered in the crowds and watched the water stream from the fountains. The prelude never made much difference to what followed, because what followed was always the same. They had sex.

When Kenneth came to Mother's classroom that Friday in May of his lower sixth year, her mistake was not giving herself enough time to think the situation through after he told her that Jean was pregnant. She saw hopelessness mix with the shame on his face, and she said the first thing that came into her mind: "No!" And then she followed it up with, "She can't be. Not now. It's not possible."

He told her it was. It was far more than possible, in fact. Then he apologised.

She knew what the apology was going to precede and she sought to head him off, saying, "Ken, you're upset but you must listen to me. Do you know for certain that she's pregnant?"

He said that Jean had told him as much.

"But have you spoken to her doctor? Has she even seen a doctor? Has she been to a clinic? Has she had a test?"

He didn't reply. He looked so miserable that Mother was sure he'd run from the room before she had the chance to clarify the situation. She went hurriedly on. "She may be mistaken. She may have miscounted the days."

He said no, there was no mistake. She hadn't miscounted. She'd told him it was a possibility two weeks ago. The possibility had turned to reality this week.

Mother rallied carefully with "Is it at all possible that she's trying to trap you because you've been gone and she's missed you, Ken? The tale of a pregnancy now to get you out of school. A false miscarriage in a month or two should you marry."

He said no, that wasn't it. That wasn't Jean.

"How do you know?" Mother asked. "If you haven't seen her doctor, if you haven't yet read the results of her test for yourself, how on earth do you know she's telling you the truth?"

He said she'd been to the doctor. He'd seen the test results. He was so sorry. He'd let everyone down. He'd let his parents down. He'd let Mrs. Whitelaw and the comprehensive down. He'd let the board of governors down. He'd let—

"Oh God, you mean to marry her, don't you?" Mother said. "You mean to leave school, throw everything away, and marry her. But you mustn't do that."

There wasn't another way, he said. He was equally responsible for what had happened.

"How can you say that?"

Because Jean'd run out of pills. She'd told him as much. She hadn't wanted . . . And *he* was the one—not Jean—who said she'd not get pregnant the very first time they did it once she'd stopped taking the pills. It'll be okay, he'd told her. But it wasn't. And now . . . He lifted his hands and dropped them, those skilful hands that held the bat that hit the ball, those very same hands that held the pen that wrote the wonderful essays, those hands whose one blow cracked through a brick as he calmly talked about a definition of self.

"Ken." Mother tried to stay calm, which wasn't easy considering all that appeared to be riding on this one conversation. "Listen to me, dear. You've got a future ahead of you. You've got your education. A career."

Not any longer, he said.

"Yes! It's still there. And you mustn't even think about throwing it away for a cheap bit of stuff who wouldn't recognise your potential if she had it explained to her point by point."

Jean was more than that, he said. She was all right, he said. They'd known each other for next to forever. He'd see to it they muddled through somehow. He was so sorry. He'd let everyone down. Especially Mrs. Whitelaw, who'd been so good to him.

It was clear he meant the conversation to be over. Mother played her trump card carefully. "Well, you must do as you see fit, but . . . I don't wish to hurt you. Still, it must be said. Please think about whether you can be sure it's your baby in the first place, Ken." He looked stricken enough for Mother to continue. She said, "You don't know everything, my dear. You can't know everything. And you especially can't know what goes on here when you're in West Sussex, can you?" She gathered up her belongings and placed them gently into her brief case. "Sometimes, dear Ken, a young girl who sleeps with one boy is only too willing . . . You know what I mean."

What she wanted to say was, "That nasty little tart's been sleeping around for years. God only knows who put her in the club. It could have been anyone. It could have been everyone."

He said in a low voice that of course it was his baby. Jeannie didn't sleep around and she didn't lie.

"Perhaps you've just never caught her," Mother said. "Doing either." She went on in the kindest possible voice, "You've gone off to school. You've risen beyond her. It's understandable that she'd want to bring you back somehow. One can't malign her for doing that." And she ended with, "Just think things through, Ken. Don't do anything hasty. Promise me that. Promise me you'll wait at least another week before doing anything or telling anyone about the situation."

Along with a blow-by-blow description of her encounter with Kenneth, we heard Mother's thoughts on this new Fall of Man over dinner the very night he came to see her. Dad's response was, "Oh dear. How dreadful for everyone." My response was a smirk. "End of the reign of another tin god," I remarked to the ceiling. Mother shot me a look and said we would see who was tin and who was not.

She went to see Jean the very next Monday, taking a day off from school in order to do it. She didn't want to see her at home, and she wanted the advantage of surprise. So she went to the old Billingsgate Market where Jean was working in some sort of caff.

Mother was fully confident of how her meeting with Jean Cooper would play itself out. She had had many such meetings with unwed mothers-to-be before, and her track record of orchestrating those encounters to a successful conclusion was a stellar one. Most of the girls who had fallen within Mother's purview had seen reason in the end. Mother was expert in the art of gentle persuasion, her focus always fixed on the baby's future, the mother's future, and a delicate division between the two. There was no reason to think she would have any difficulty with Jean Cooper, who was her mental, emotional, and social inferior.

She found Jean not in the caff but in the Ladies' where she was having a break, smoking a cigarette and flicking its ash into the basin. She wore a white smock brindled with grease spots. She'd haphazardly bunched her hair beneath a cap. A ladder in her stockings shot up her right leg from inside her shoe. If comparative appearances were anything to go by, Mother had the upper hand from the first.

Jean hadn't been one of her pupils. Streaming was very much the vogue at that time, and Jean had spent her years at the comprehensive swimming among the lesser fish. But Mother knew who she was. One couldn't know Kenneth Fleming without knowing who Jean Cooper was. And Jean knew who Mother was as well. No doubt she'd heard enough from Kenneth about his teacher to have had her fill of Mrs. Whitelaw long before their encounter at Billingsgate Market.

"Kenny looked dead grey in the face when I saw him Friday evening," was the first thing Jean said. "He wouldn't talk. He went back to school on Saturday instead of Sunday night. I expect you had a hand in that, didn't you?"

Mother began with her standard line. "I'd like to have a chat about the future."

"Whose future? Mine? The baby's? Or Kenny's?"

"All three of your futures."

Jean nodded. "I bet you've got yourself in a real dither about my future, haven't you, Mrs. Whitelaw? I bet you're losing sleep about my future. I bet you've got my future all mapped out for me and all's I have to do is listen while you tell me how things'll be." She dropped her cigarette to the cracked linoleum floor, crushed it out with her toe, and immediately lit another.

"Jean, that's not good for the baby," Mother said.

"I'll decide what's good for the baby, thank you very much. Me and Kenny'll decide. On our own."

"Is either of you in a position to decide? On your own, that is."

"We know what we know."

"Ken's a student, Jean. He has no work experience. If he leaves school now, you'll be caught up in a life with neither future nor promise. You must see that."

"I see lots. I see that I love him and he loves me and we want a life together and we mean to have it."

"*You* mean to have it," Mother said. "You. Jean. Ken isn't a part of the wanting. No boy has that sort of wanting in him when he's sixteen years old. And Ken's just *turned* seventeen. He's little more than a child. And you yourself are . . . Jean, do you want to take such a step as this—marriage and a baby, one right after the other—when you're so young? When you've so few resources? When you'll have to rely upon your families for assistance and your families are merely scraping by as it is? Is that what you think is best for the three of you? For Ken, for the child, for yourself?"

"I see lots," Jeannie said. "I see that we been together for years and what we have is good and it's always been good and him going to some posh school isn't going to change that not one bit. No matter what you want."

"I want nothing but what's best for both of you."

Jean snorted and attended to her cigarette, all the time watching Mother through the smoke. "I see lots," she repeated. "I see you talked to Kenny and twisted him round and got him upset."

"He was already upset. Heavens, you must know that he wouldn't exactly greet this news"—with a gesture at Jean's stomach—"with joy. It's made a muddle of his life."

"I see you made him look at me with his eyes gone doubtful. I see the questions you had him ask. I see him thinking, What if Jeannie's dishing it out for three or four other blokes as well as for me, and I see where he got the idea in the first place because she's standing right in front of me bigger'n life."

Jean tossed her cigarette to the floor and ground it out beside the other. "I got to get back to work. If you excuse me," and she ducked her head and wiped at her cheeks as she passed my mother.

Mother said, "You're upset. That's understandable. But Ken's questions are legitimate. If you're going to ask him to throw away his future, then you've got to accept the fact that he might want first to be assured that—"

She swung back so quickly that Mother faltered. "I'm asking for nothing. The baby's his and I told him as much because I thought he had a right to know. If he decides he wants to leave school and be with us, fine. If he doesn't, we'll get on without him."

"But there are other options," Mother said. "You needn't have the baby in the first place. Even if you do, you needn't keep it. There are thousands of men and women eager to adopt, longing for a child. There's no reason to bring an unwanted child into the world."

Jeannie grasped Mother's arm so hard that later—at dinner that night when she showed them to us—bruises rose in the spots where her fingers dug in. "Don't you call it unwanted, you nasty-minded slag. Don't you bloody *dare.*"

That's when she saw the real Jean Cooper, Mother reported to us in a wavering voice. A girl who'd do anything to get what she wanted. A girl capable of any act, even violence. And she meant to be violent, there was no doubt of that. She meant to strike Mother and she would have done if one of the market secretaries hadn't come in at that moment, teetering on high heels and catching herself on a rip in the lino. She said, "Damn! Oh, sorry. Am I interrupting?" Jean said, "No," flung Mother's arm to one side, and left.

Mother followed. "It won't work. The two of you. Jean, don't do this to him. Or at the very least wait until—"

"—you've had an even chance to get him for yourself?" Jean finished.

Mother stopped a few feet away, safely choosing a distance from which Jean couldn't reach her. "Don't be ridiculous. Don't be absurd."

But she was neither, was Jean Cooper. She was sixteen years old and a seer of the future, although she couldn't have known it at the time. At the time, she must have thought only, I've won, because Kenneth did leave school at the end of the term. They didn't marry at once. Rather, they surprised everyone by waiting, working, squirrelling away their money, and finally marrying six months after their first son Jimmy was born.

After that, we ate our meals in peace in Kensington. We heard nothing more of Kenneth Fleming. I don't know how Dad felt about the sudden absence of dining conversation, but I myself spent many a happy hour celebrating the fact that the god-boy of the Isle of Dogs had turned out to be yet another mortal with feet of clay. As for her part, Mother didn't abandon Kenneth entirely. That wasn't her style. Instead, she persuaded Dad to make a place for him in the printworks so he'd have a steady job and be able to take care of his family. But Kenneth Fleming was no longer the sterling example of youth's promise fulfilled as she'd obviously once hoped he might be. And thus there was no reason for her to nightly trot out him and his triumphant escapades for our admiration.

Mother washed her hands of Kenneth Fleming in much the same way as she washed her hands of me some three years later. The only difference was that when the opportunity arose not long after my father's death, she picked up a towel and dried them.

Kenneth was twenty-six at the time. Mother was sixty.

CHAPTER
5

"Kenneth Fleming," the ITN news correspondent finished, speaking into his microphone with a solemnity that he seemed to feel appropriate for the occasion, "dead at thirty-two. The world of cricket has much to mourn this night." The camera panned over his shoulder to the swag-topped walls and ornate wrought iron of the Grace Gate at Lord's Cricket Ground, which served as backdrop to his report. "We'll have reactions in a moment from his fellow team members, and from Guy Mollison, England's captain."

Jeannie Cooper left her position at the sitting room window. She stabbed her finger into the television's *off* button. She watched the screen dissolve from image to black, going fuzzy on the edges first. It seemed to leave a residue behind.

She thought, Got to get a new telly, wonder how much new televisions cost.

It was a convenient area to send her thoughts scurrying: what kind of telly she would buy; how big a screen it would have; did she want stereo speakers and a VCR to go with it; did she want one in a cabinet like she had now, a hulking monster as big as a fridge and as old as Jimmy.

As her son's name fluttered unbidden in her mind, Jeannie bit down hard on the inside of her lip. She tried to draw blood. A cut lip, she decided, was a pain she could manage. Wondering where Jimmy had taken himself off to all this long day was decidedly not.

"Jimmy never came home?" she'd asked her brother when the police returned her from the horror of Kent.

"Didn't go to school neither, from what Shar told me. He's done a proper bunk this time." Derrick snagged two of his weight-training devices from the coffee table. These looked like pincers, and he squeezed them alternately in each hand, muttering, "Adductor, flexor, pronator, yeah."

"You didn't look for him, Der? You didn't go to the park?"

Derrick watched his massive arm muscles contract and relax. "Tell you one thing about that little sod, Pook. Wherever he is ain't likely to be the park."

She and her brother had had that conversation at half past six, just before his departure. It was after ten now. Her two younger children had been in bed for more than an hour. And ever since closing each of their doors and descending the stairs, Jeannie had stood at the window, listening to the drone of the television voices, and watching the night for a sign of Jimmy.

She went to the coffee table for her cigarettes and dug in her pocket for the box of matches. She was still dressed for work in the smock and crêpe-soled shoes she'd put on at half past three that morning. They were beginning to feel as if they'd melded on to her, like a second skin. The only article of clothing she'd removed all day was her cap, and this she'd left near the till in Crissys before leaving for Kent. That had been in another life, it seemed, the part she would henceforth label Before the Police Came to Billingsgate.

Jeannie drew in on her cigarette. She went from the coffee table back to the front window and tipped the curtain away from the glass.

She saw movement on the pavement three doors down. She hoped against reason and experience that the figure heading in her direction was her oldest child. The figure *was* tall and spare, she decided, he walked with the same energy, he was lean like his dad . . . She allowed herself a moment to feel the spring-release of tension that comes with relief. Then she saw it wasn't Jimmy at all, but Mr. Newton taking his corgi for her nightly stroll to Crossharbour Station and back.

Jeannie thought about setting out on a search for Jimmy. She rejected the idea. There were things she had to discover from her son, and the only way to ferret them out was to stay where she was, in this room, so that she could be the first member of the family that Jimmy saw when he finally walked in. Until that happened, she told herself, she had to be calm. She had to wait. She had to pray.

Except that she knew she couldn't pray to change what had already happened.

From the ten o'clock news she had gathered the details she'd not asked for earlier: when Kenny had died, the unofficial cause of his death pending formal autopsy, where his body had been found, the fact that he was alone. "The police have verified at this time that the cottage fire was started by a cigarette smouldering in an armchair," the news reader had said. He'd looked at the camera and his regretful shake of the head had said the rest: "Ladies and gentlemen, mind my words. Cigarettes do kill in more ways than one."

Jeannie left the window to stub hers out in a metal ashtray shaped like a clam shell and stamped with the gold words *Weston-Super-Mare*. She lit another, picked up the ashtray, returned to her post.

She would have liked to argue that the bike was the problem, that all her troubles with Jimmy had started the very day he brought the bloody motorbike home. But the truth was more complicated than a series of arguments between mother and son over ownership of a means of transportation. The truth lay in everything they had avoided for years as a subject of conversation.

She let the curtain fall back into place over the window. She straightened it neatly along the ledge. She wondered how much of her life she had spent standing at windows like this, hoping to see an arrival that would never occur.

She moved across the sitting room to the old grey couch, part of the dismal three-piece suite she and Kenny had inherited from her parents upon their marriage. She picked up a tattered copy of *Woman's Own* and perched on the edge of one of the cushions. It was so worn that its stuffing had long ago been packed into tight little pellets. They afforded all the comfort of having a sit on a patch of wet sand. Kenny had wanted to replace the old furniture with something grand when he first started to play for England. But he'd been already two years gone from their lives when he made the offer, and Jeannie'd refused him.

She opened *Woman's Own* on her knees. She bent over the pages. She tried to read. She began "The Diary of a Wedding Dress," but after four tries at the same paragraph recounting the remarkable adventures of a wedding dress for hire, she tossed the magazine back on the coffee table, brought her fists to her forehead, squeezed her eyes shut, and tried to pray.

"God," she whispered. "God, if you'll please . . ." What, she asked herself. What should God do? Alter reality? Change the facts?

Against her will she saw him again: stretched out motionless in that cool room of closed cupboards and stainless steel, flushed to the colour of salmon's roe, still as marble where once he'd been filled with restless energy and breath and flight. . . .

Quickly, she pushed herself off the couch and began to pace the width of the room. She beat the knuckles of her right hand hard into the palm of her left. Where is he, where is he, where *is* he, she thought.

The sound of the motorbike stopped her. It sputtered down the walk that separated the houses on Cardale Street from those behind them. It idled long at the back garden's gate, as if its rider were trying to decide what to do. Then the gate creaked as it opened and shut, the rumble of an engine came closer, and the motorbike belched once and died just on the other side of the kitchen door.

Jeannie went back to the couch and sat. She heard the kitchen door swing open then shut. Footsteps crossed the lino and there he was, metal-tipped Doc Martens loosely laced, beltless blue jeans hanging round hips, grimy T-shirt spotted with holes at the neck. He used his hand to shove his long hair behind one ear, and he shifted his weight to one foot so that a skinny hip jutted out.

Aside from his clothing and the fact that he was as filthy as a beggar, he looked so much like his father at sixteen years old that a fog seemed to come between Jeannie and him. She felt like a spear was pressing just beneath her left breast, and she held her breath to make the pain dissolve.

"Where you been, Jim?"

"Out." He held his head like he always did, cocked to one side as if he wanted to disguise his height.

"You take your specs with you?"

"No."

"I don't like you driving that bike without your specs. It's dangerous."

He used the heel of his hand to shove his hair off his forehead. His shoulders moved in an indifferent shrug.

"Go to school today?"

He flicked his glance to the stairway. He fingered the belt loop of his jeans.

"You know about Dad?"

His adolescent Adam's apple bobbled in his neck. His eyes skittered to her and then back to the stairs. "He got the chop."

"How'd you find out?"

He shifted his weight. The other hip jutted. He was so thin that it made Jeannie's palms ache whenever she looked at him.

He shoved his fist into one of his pockets and brought out a crumpled packet of JPS. He dug a grimy index finger inside and crooked it round a cigarette. He put it in his mouth. He looked to the coffee table, from there to the top of the television set.

Jeannie's fingers closed round the box of matches in her pocket. She felt the corner of it dig into her thumb.

"How'd you find out, Jim?" she asked again.

"Heard it on the telly."

"Where?"

"BBC."

"Where? Whose telly?"

"Some bloke's in Deptford."

"What's his name?"

Jimmy twisted the cigarette in his lips, like he was tightening a screw. "You don't know him. I never brought him round."

"What's he called?"

"Brian." He looked steadily at her, always a certain sign that he was fibbing. "Brian. Jones."

"That where you were today? With this Brian Jones in Deptford?"

His hands returned to his pockets, front then back. He patted himself down. He frowned.

Jeannie put the box of matches on the coffee table and nodded at them. Jimmy hesitated as if expecting a trick. Then he shambled forward. He snatched the matches quickly and lit one on the edge of his thumbnail. When he held it to the cigarette, he watched his mother.

"Dad died in a fire," Jeannie said. "At the cottage."

Jimmy took a long drag and raised his head to the ceiling as if that would help get the smoke into his lungs and keep it there longer. His hair hung stiffly back from his skull in greasy segments that looked like rats' tails. It was strawberry blond like his dad's, but so long unwashed that its colour resembled straw sodden with piss in a horse's stall.

"You hear me, Jim?" Jeannie tried to keep her voice steady, like the reader on the news. "Dad died in a fire. At the cottage. Wednesday night."

He took another drag. He wouldn't look at her. But his Adam's apple kept bobbing like a spool on a string.

"Jim."

"What?"

"It was a cigarette caused the fire. A cigarette in a chair. Dad was upstairs. He was asleep. He breathed in the smoke. Carbon monox—"

"Who *gives* a shit?"

"You, I expect. Stan, Sharon, me."

"Oh, too right. Like *he* would of cared if one of us died? What a fucking joke. He wouldn't of come to the funeral."

"Don't talk like that."

"Like what?"

"You know. Don't play that you don't."

"Like fuck and shit? Or like telling the truth?"

She didn't reply. He shoved his fingers through his hair, paced to the window and back, and stopped himself from pacing. She tried to read him and wondered exactly when she had lost the knack of knowing in an instant what was going on in his head.

"Don't talk nasty in this house," she said quietly. "You're to set the example. You've a brother and sister who look to you as a guide."

"And aren't they a proper mess?" He snorted. "Stan's a baby needs a dummy to suck. And Shar's—"

"Don't you dirty-talk them."

"Shar's thick as a brick with mash for brains. You sure we're all related to each other? You sure someone 'sides Dad didn't put you in the club?"

Jeannie got to her feet. She began to take a step towards her son but his words held her back.

"You could of done it with other blokes, right? How 'bout at the market? Sliding round in the fish guts on the floor after hours?" He flicked ash from his cigarette onto the leg of his jeans. He rubbed his finger through it. He snickered, then grinned, then slapped himself on the forehead, hard. "Oy, that's it! Why di'n't I get it before?"

"Get it? What?"

"How we got different dads. Mine's the famous batsman, which gives me the advantage in looks and brains—"

"You hold your tongue, Jimmy."

"Shar's's the postman, which is why she looks like her face's been cancelled."

"I said that's enough."

"And Stan's's one of the blokes't bring eels from the fens. How'd you ever do it with an eelman, Mum? Course I s'pose one poke's good as another if you keep your eyes closed and don't mind the smell."

Jeannie came round the coffee table. "Where'd you get this crap, Jim?"

"I c'n see what it's like. All those blokes. All that fish. The smell must remind them of what they're missing." His face brightened and his voice began to rise. "So if they find a tart who's not too fussy about who she lets poke her and where and when—"

"I'll wash your mouth, boy."

"—then they just go ahead and take it out of their trousers."

"You stop this. Now!"

"She sees it's hard and she says with a giggle Cor what a pretty sight I see and she lowers her knickers and he backs her into one of those fridges where she don't mind the cold because he's panting over her like some gorilla and—"

"Jimmy!"

"—he fucks her till she's dizzy and what d'you know then she's banged up good and it don't matter at all who she fucks after that until the kid pops out ugly as a potato with legs." He sucked in heavily on his cigarette. His hands were shaking.

Jeannie felt a burning behind her eyes. She blinked it away. She understood. "Oh Jimmy," she murmured. "Daddy never meant you to hurt. You got to know that."

Rigidly, he put his hands over his ears. His voice grew louder. "So, the next day she takes on another bloke, see. Everyone watches and she likes it that way. There's a circle round them, cheering them on."

"Dad's dead, Jim. He's gone."

His face pinched closed. "First one finishes her. Then another takes her on. She snorts. She squeals. She says Come on and get me the lot of you I can cope I can I like it this way."

Jeannie went to him, put her hands on his. She tried to bring them down from his ears, but all she managed to do was knock the cigarette away. It fell to the carpet. She picked it up, stubbed it out in an ashtray.

"So they climb on her, see, the whole flaming lot. They hump her to bits and she never gets enough." His voice wavered. His hands moved from his ears to his eyes. His fingers scrabbled at his flesh.

Jeannie touched his arm. He gave a cry, pulled away.

She said, "Your dad loved you. He loved you. *Always.*"

He countered behind his hands with, "So they do that to her. They do it. They do. And when they're through with her and she's lying in the fish guts with a smarmy smile plastered on her stupid face she thinks she's got what she wanted what she . . . what she wanted because she's got all these blokes, see, even if she couldn't keep him and she thinks she thinks she can't even think that this is what it's s'posed to be like." He began to weep.

Jeannie put her arm round his shoulders. He tore himself away from her and ran for the stairs.

"Why di'n't you divorce him?" he sobbed. "Why di'n't you? Why di'n't you? Jesus, Mum. You could of divorced him."

Jeannie watched him climb. She wanted to follow. She lacked the strength.

She went into the kitchen where the pots and dishes from an uneaten dinner of chops, chips, and sprouts were scattered on the table and the work top. She gathered and scraped them. She stacked them in the sink. She squeezed Fairy Liquid over them, turned on the hot water, and watched the bubbles begin to froth, just like lace on a bridal gown.

It was nearly eleven when Lynley telephoned the husband of Gabriella Patten from the Bentley, as he and Havers headed up Campden Hill in the direction of Hampstead. Hugh Patten didn't seem surprised to be receiving a telephone call from the police. He didn't question why an interview was necessary nor did he try to put Lynley off with a request that their meeting be postponed until the morning. He merely gave the necessary directions and told them to ring the bell three times when they got there.

"I've been rather more bothered by journalists than I like," was his explanation.

"Who is this bloke when he's somebody?" Havers asked as they made the turn onto Holland Park Avenue.

"You know as much as I, at the moment," Lynley said.

"Cuckolded husband."

"So it seems."

"Potential killer."

"There's that to be discovered."

"And the sponsor of the test match series with Australia."

The drive to Hampstead was lengthy. They finished it in silence. They wound up the High Street, where several coffee bars accommodated a late evening crowd, and then farther up Holly Hill to a point where houses gave way to mansions. They found Patten's home behind a stone wall overgrown with clematis, pale pink flowers feather-striped with red.

"Nice digs," Havers said with a nod at the house as she hopped from the car. "He's not too pushed for lolly, is he?"

Two other cars stood on the drive, a late model Range Rover and a small Renault with its left rear light smashed. As Havers strolled along the edge of the semi-circular drive, Lynley walked to a second drive that veered off from this main one. Perhaps thirty yards along, a large garage stood. It was newish looking but built in the same Georgian manner as the house itself, and like the house, it was lit with ground lights that fanned illumination in intervals along its brick exterior. The garage was large enough to house three cars. He slid one of the doors open to see the gleam of a white Jaguar inside. It appeared to be freshly washed. It bore neither scratches nor dents. When Lynley squatted to scrutinise them, even the tyres looked clean to their treads.

"Anything?" Havers asked when he returned to her.

"Jaguar. Recently washed."

"There's mud on the Rover. And the Renault's rear light—"

"Yes. I saw it. Make a note."

"Done."

They went to the front door, which stood between two terra-cotta urns of goldheart ivy. Lynley pushed the bell, waited, then pushed twice more.

A man's voice spoke quietly behind the door, not to Lynley but to someone else whose response was muted. The man spoke again and then after a short delay, the door opened.

He looked them over. His glance took in Lynley's dinner jacket. His eyes moved to Sergeant Havers and travelled the length of her, from her overgrown haircut to her red high-top trainers. His mouth twitched. "Police, I assume? Since it's not Halloween."

"Mr. Patten?" Lynley said.

"This way," he replied.

He led them across a polished parquet floor beneath a brass candelabrum burning lightbulb flames. He was a good-size man with a decent physique encased in blue jeans and a faded plaid shirt, which he'd rolled up to the elbows. A blue sweater—cashmere by the look of it—was knotted casually round his neck. He had nothing on his feet and, like the rest of him, they were just tanned enough to suggest Mediterranean holidays and not labour in the sun.

Like most Georgian houses, Patten's was constructed on a simple plan. The large entry gave way to a long salon, which itself gave way to several closed doors leading to the right and to the left and a bank of french doors opening onto a terrace. It was through these doors that Hugh Patten strode, leading them to a chaise longue, two chairs, and a table that formed a seating area on the flagstones, half in shadow and half in light from the house. Perhaps ten yards from this, the garden sloped down to a lily pond beyond which the lights of London spread out in a vast, glittering ocean without apparent horizon.

On the table stood four glasses, a tray, and three bottles of The MacAllan, each one stamped with a distillery date: 1965, 1967, 1973. The '65 was half-empty. The '73 hadn't yet been opened.

Patten poured a quarter glassful of the '67 and used the glass to gesture to the bottles. "Will you try some? Or is that not allowed? You're on duty, I take it?"

"A swallow won't hurt," Lynley said. "I'll try the '65."

Havers chose the '67. When they had their drinks, Patten made for the chaise longue, and he sat with his right arm curled behind his head and his eyes on the view. "Hell, I love this damn place. Sit down. Take a moment to enjoy yourselves."

Light from the far end of the salon filtered through the french doors, lying in neat parallelograms on the flagstones. But as they took their seats,

Lynley noticed that Patten had positioned the furniture so that only the top of his head was illuminated. This would allow them to gather one initial and potentially useless fact about the man from his appearance: His dark hair bore that peculiar metallic tinge that sometimes accompanies surreptitious colouring done outside of a hairdressing salon.

"I've heard about Fleming." Patten lifted his drink, his eyes still on the view. "The word went out around three this afternoon. Guy Mollison phoned. He was letting this summer's sponsor know. Only the sponsor, he said, so for God's sake keep it under your hat until the announcement's official." Patten shook his head derisively and swirled the whisky in his glass. "Always has England's interests in mind."

"Mollison?"

"He'll be chosen captain again, after all."

"Are you sure about the time?"

"I'd just come in from lunch."

"Odd that he knew it was Fleming, then. He was phoning before the body was identified," Lynley said.

"Before the wife identified it. The police already knew who he was." Patten turned from the view. "Or didn't they tell you that much?"

"You appear to have a great deal of information."

"My money's involved."

"More than money, as I understand it."

Patten swung himself off the chaise longue. He walked to the edge of the terrace where the flagstones gave way to the gentle slope of lawn. He stood, ostensibly admiring the view.

"Millions of them." He gestured with his glass. "Dragging through their lives every day without the slightest thought as to what it's all about. And by the time they conclude that life might actually be about something besides grubbing for money, eating, eliminating, and coupling in the dark, it's too late for most of them to do anything about it."

"That's certainly the case for Fleming."

Patten kept his eyes on the shimmering lights of London. "He was a rare one, our Ken. He knew there was more than what he had in hand. He meant to have it."

"Your wife, for example."

Patten made no reply. He tossed back the rest of his whisky and returned to the table. He reached for the unopened 1973 bottle. He broke the seal and removed the cap.

"How much did you know about your wife and Kenneth Fleming?" Lynley asked.

Patten returned to the chaise longue and sat on its edge. He looked amused when Sergeant Havers crinkled through her notebook's pages to find a clean sheet. "Am I being given the caution for some reason?"

"That's rather premature," Lynley said. "Although if you'd like your solicitor present—"

Patten laughed. "Francis has heard enough from me this past month to keep him in his favourite port wine for a year. I think I can soldier on without him."

"You've legal problems, then?"

"I've divorce problems, then."

"You knew about your wife's affair?"

"I hadn't a clue until she said she was leaving me. And even then, I didn't know an affair was at the bottom of things at first. I just thought I hadn't been giving her enough attention. Ego, if you will." His mouth curved with a wry smile. "We had one hell of a row when she said she was leaving. I bullied her a bit. 'Who d'you suppose is going to want to pick up a thick-headed piece of fluff like you, Gabriella? Where in Christ's name do you think you'll find another bloke willing to take on a tart without a brain in her head? Do you actually think you can walk out on me and not become what you were when I found you in the first place? A six-quid-an-hour office temp with nothing to recommend her but a somewhat erratic ability to alphabetise?' It was one of those nasty marital scenes, over dinner at the Capital Hotel. In Knightsbridge."

"Odd that she chose a public place for the conversation."

"Not odd when you consider Gabriella. It would have appealed to her sense of drama, although I dare say she imagined me sobbing into my consommé rather than losing my temper."

"When was this?"

"The conversation? I don't know. Sometime early last month."

"And she told you she was leaving you for Fleming?"

"Not on your life. She had a good-size divorce settlement on her mind, and she was clever enough to realise she'd have a bloody rough time getting what she wanted from me financially if I knew she had someone she'd been screwing on the side. She merely defended herself at first. You can imagine how it ran: 'Fat lot you know, Hugh, I can find another bloke, I can walk out of here as easy as pie, I'm not a piece of mindless fluff to everyone, son.' " Patten set his glass on the flagstones and swung his legs onto the chaise longue. He resumed his earlier position, right arm cushioning his head.

"But she said nothing about Fleming?"

"Gabriella's no simpleton despite the fact that she occasionally acts like one. And she's no fool when it comes to positioning herself financially. The last thing she'd have been likely to do is to burn her bridges with me before she was certain there was going to be a new way to get across the river." He ran his hand back through his hair, fingers spread, in a gesture that seemed designed to emphasise its thickness. "I knew she'd been flirting with Fleming. Hell, I'd *seen* her flirt with him. But I thought nothing of it because pulling men was nothing out of the ordinary for Gabriella. She's on automatic pilot when it comes to blokes. Always has been."

"Doesn't that bother you?" Sergeant Havers asked the question. She'd finished her whisky and pushed the glass to join the other that Patten had earlier moved to one side of the table.

Patten's answer consisted of the word, "Listen," and he held up his fingers to still their conversation. From the far right side of the garden where a bank of poplars formed a boundary, a bird had begun to call. Its song was liquid and warbling, rising to a crescendo. Patten smiled. "Nightingale. Magnificent, isn't it? It almost—but not quite—makes one believe in God." And then to Sergeant Havers, he said, "I liked knowing other men found my wife desirable. It was part of the turn-on, at first."

"And now?"

"Everything loses its amusement value, Sergeant. After a time."

"How long have you been married?"

"Two months short of five years."

"And before?"

"What?"

"Is she your first wife?"

"What's that got to do with the price of petrol?"

"I don't know. Is she?"

Abruptly, Patten looked back at the view. His eyes narrowed against it, as if the lights were too bright. "My second," he said.

"And your first?"

"What about her?"

"What happened to her?"

"We were divorced."

"When?"

"Two months short of five years ago."

"Ah." Sergeant Havers wrote rapidly.

"Am I to know what *ah* means, Sergeant?" Patten said.

"You divorced your first wife to marry Gabriella?"

"That's what Gabriella wanted if I wanted Gabriella. And I wanted Gabriella. I've never wanted anyone quite as much, in fact."

"And now?" Lynley asked.

"I wouldn't take her back, if that's what you're asking. I've no particular interest in her any longer, and even if I had, things went too far."

"In what way?"

"People knew."

"That she'd left you for Fleming?"

"One draws the line somewhere. With me, it's infidelity."

"Your own?" Havers asked. "Or just your wife's?"

Patten's head, still leaning back against the chaise longue, turned in her direction. He slowly smiled. "The male-female double standard. It's not very attractive. But I am what I am, a hypocrite when it comes to the women I love."

"How did you find out it was Fleming?" Lynley asked.

"I had her followed."

"To Kent?"

"She tried to lie at first. She said she was just staying at Miriam Whitelaw's cottage while she sorted out her thoughts about what to do with her life. Fleming was just a friend, she said, helping her out. There was nothing between them. If she was having an affair with him, if she'd left me for him, wouldn't she be living with him openly? But she wasn't, was she, and that proved there was no adultery involved, that proved she'd been a good and faithful wife to me and I'd better instruct my solicitor to keep that in mind when he met with hers to talk about the settlement." Patten rubbed his thumb along his jawline where a dark stubble of whiskers was shadowing his face. "So I showed her the photographs. They, at least, cowed her."

They were photographs of her and Fleming, he went on without embarrassment, taken at the cottage in Kent. Fond greetings at the doorway in the evening, passionate goodbyes in the drive at dawn, energetic grapplings in an apple orchard not far from the cottage, one enthusiastic mating on the garden lawn.

When she saw the photos, she also saw her future financial status dwindle rapidly, he told them. She flew at him like a spitting cat, she threw the photos in the dining room fire, but she knew she'd lost the larger part of the game.

"So you've been to the cottage?" Lynley said.

Oh yes, he'd been there. Once, when he'd delivered the photographs to her. A second time when Gabriella phoned with a request to talk things out and see if they couldn't arrive at a reasonable and civilised manner of ending their marriage. "That was a euphemism, the talking," he added. "Using her mouth for speech has never been Gabriella's forte."

"Your wife's gone missing," Havers said. Lynley glanced in her direction when he heard the unmistakably even and deathly polite tone of the remark.

"Has she?" Patten enquired. "I wondered why there was no mention of her on the news. I thought at first she'd managed to get to all the journalists and make it worth their while to keep her out of the story. Although that would have been a monumental project, even for someone with Gabriella's power of suction."

"Where were you on Wednesday night, Mr. Patten?" Havers jabbed her pencil against the paper as she wrote. Lynley wondered if she was going to be able to read her notes later. "Thursday morning as well."

"Why?" He looked interested.

"Just answer the question."

"I shall, once I know what it's got to do with anything."

Havers was bristling. Lynley intervened. "Kenneth Fleming may well have been murdered," he said.

Patten set his glass down on the table. He kept his fingers on the rim. He seemed to be trying to read Lynley's face for its degree of levity. "Murdered."

"So you can understand our interest in your whereabouts," Lynley said.

The nightingale's song rose from the trees again. Nearby, a single cricket gave answer. "Wednesday night, Thursday morning," Patten murmured, more to himself than to them. "I was at the Cherbourg Club."

"Berkeley Square?" Lynley asked. "How long were you there?"

"It must have been two or three before I left. I've an itch for baccarat and I was winning for once."

"Was anyone with you?"

"One doesn't play baccarat alone, Inspector."

"A companion," Havers said testily.

"For part of the evening."

"Which part?"

"The beginning. I sent her off in a taxi around . . . I don't know. Half past one? Two?"

"And afterwards?"

"I continued to play. I came home, went to bed." Patten moved his glance from Lynley to Havers. He seemed to be waiting for more questions. He finally went on. "You know, I'd hardly be likely to kill Fleming, if that's where we're heading, as it appears we are."

"Who followed your wife?"

"Who what?"

"Who took the pictures. We'll need the name."

"All right. You'll get it. Look, Fleming may have been screwing my wife, but he was a damn fine cricket player—the best batsman we've had in half a century. If I wanted to put an end to his affair with Gabriella, I would have killed her, not him. At least that way the bloody test matches wouldn't have been affected. Besides I didn't even know he was in Kent on Wednesday. How could I have known?"

"You could have had him followed."

"What would be the point?"

"Revenge."

"If I wanted him dead. But I didn't."

"And Gabriella?"

"What about Gabriella?"

"Did you want her dead?"

"Certainly. It would be far more cost-effective than having to divorce her. But I like to think I'm rather more civilised than the average husband whose wife betrays him."

"You haven't heard from her?" Lynley asked.

"From Gabriella? Not a word."

"She isn't here in the house?"

Patten looked genuinely surprised, eyebrows lifted. "Here? No." Then he seemed to realise why the question had been asked. "Oh. That wasn't Gabriella."

"If you wouldn't mind substantiating the fact."

"If it's necessary."

"Thank you."

Patten sauntered into the house. Havers slouched in her chair, watching him through narrowed eyes. "What a pig," she muttered.

"You've got the Cherbourg information?"

"I'm still breathing, Inspector."

"Sorry." Lynley gave her the number plates of the Jaguar in the garage. "We'll want Kent to check if there's been a sighting of either the Jag or the Range Rover near the Springburns. The Renault as well. The one on the drive."

She snorted. "You think he'd stoop to rattling round in that?"

"If he'd stoop to murder."

One of the farthest french doors opened. Patten returned. He was accompanied by a girl, no more than twenty years old. She was wearing an oversize sweater and leggings. Her body moved sinuously as she crossed the flagstones on slim bare feet. Patten put his hand on the back of her neck, just beneath her hair, which was blacker than seemed natural and cut in a short geometric style that made her eyes look large. He pulled her closer to him and, for a moment, he appeared to breathe in whatever scent was coming from her scalp.

"Jessica," he said by way of introduction.

"Your daughter?" Havers asked blandly.

"Sergeant," Lynley said.

The girl seemed to understand the intention behind the exchange. She slid her index finger through a belt loop of Patten's jeans and said, "You coming up now, Hugh? It's getting late."

He ran his hand down her back, in very much the same way a man strokes a prize race horse. "A few minutes," he said. And to Lynley, "Inspector?"

Lynley lifted his hand in wordless indication of the fact that he had no questions to put to the girl. He waited until she had returned to the house before saying, "Where might your wife be, Mr. Patten? She's disappeared. As has Fleming's car. Have you any idea where she may have headed?"

Patten began to recap the whisky bottles. He set them on a tray along with the glasses. "None whatsoever. Although wherever she is, I doubt she's alone."

"Like yourself," Havers said, flipping her notebook closed.

Patten regarded her. His face was untroubled. "Yes. In that respect Gabriella and I have always been remarkably similar."

CHAPTER
6

Lynley reached for the folder of information from Kent. He began to flip through the crime scene photographs, his eyebrows drawn together above his spectacles. Barbara watched him, wondering how he was managing to look so wide awake.

She herself was knackered. It was nearly one in the morning. She'd had three cups of coffee since their return to New Scotland Yard, and despite the caffeine—or perhaps because of it—her brain was doing flip-flops but her body had decided to cash in its chips. She wanted to put her head on Lynley's desk and snore, but instead she got to her feet, stretched, and walked to the window. No one was on the street below them. Above them, the sky was soot grey, rendered incapable of ever achieving true darkness because of the teeming megalopolis beneath it.

She pulled thoughtfully on her lower lip as she studied the view. "Let's suppose Patten did it," she said. Lynley made no reply. He set the photographs aside. He read part of Inspector Ardery's report and raised his head. His expression became thoughtful. "He's got motive enough," Barbara continued. "If he rubs out Fleming, he's got his revenge on the bloke that was rolling in Gabriella's knickers."

Lynley bracketed off a paragraph. Then a second one. One in the morning, Barbara thought with disgust, and he was still going strong.

"Well?" she asked him.

"May I see your notes?"

She returned to her chair, dug her notebook from her shoulder bag, handed it over. As she walked back to the window, Lynley ran his finger along the first and second pages of their interview with Mrs. Whitelaw. He read something on the third, something else on the fourth. He turned another page and twirled his pencil against it.

"He told us he draws the line at infidelity," Barbara said. "Maybe his line is murder."

Lynley looked in her direction. "Don't let antipathy become your bedmate, Sergeant. We don't have enough facts."

"Still and all, Inspector—"

He gestured with the pencil to stop her, saying, "When we do, I expect they'll support his presence at the Cherbourg Club on Wednesday night."

"Being at the Cherbourg Club doesn't exactly eliminate him as a suspect. He could have hired someone to set the fire. He's already admitted hiring someone to have Gabriella followed. And he didn't exactly go skulking round the bushes himself to take those pictures of her and Fleming that he was talking about. So there's another hiring for you."

"Neither of which is illegal. Questionable, perhaps. Tasteless, to be sure. But not illegal."

Barbara guffawed and returned to her chair. She flopped into it. "Pardon me, Inspector, but did our little Hugh manage to give you the impression he wouldn't stoop to something as *tasteless* as murder? When did this occur? Before he talked about his wife's amazing talents at fellatio or after he trotted out whatsername and gave her bum a nice squeeze just in case us rozzers were too thick to figure out what was what between them?"

"I'm not ruling him out," Lynley said.

"Well, praised be Jesus."

"But accepting Patten as the premeditated killer of Fleming presupposes he knew where Fleming was on Wednesday night. He's denied knowing. I'm not convinced we can prove otherwise." Lynley replaced photographs and reports in the folder. He removed his spectacles and rubbed his fingers on either side of the bridge of his nose.

"If Fleming phoned Gabriella and told her to expect him," Barbara pointed out, "she could have phoned Patten and dropped him the word. Not deliberately, mind you. Not with the intention of Patten's running out there to make Fleming cold meat. Just a bit of the old in-your-face-Hugh. That follows what he's told us about her. There were other blokes who wanted her, and here was the proof."

Lynley appeared to consider his sergeant's words. "The telephone," he said reflectively.

"What about it?"

"The conversation Fleming had with Mollison. He may have mentioned his Kent plans to him."

"If you're thinking a phone call's the key, then his family must have known where Fleming was going as well. He had to cancel the trip to Greece, didn't he? Or at least postpone it. He would have told them something. He *had* to have told them something since the son . . . what was his name?"

Lynley looked through her notes, flipping forward two more pages. "Jimmy."

"Right. Since Jimmy didn't phone Mrs. Whitelaw on Wednesday when his dad failed to show. And if Jimmy knew why the trip was cancelled, he may have told his mum. That would have been natural. She was expecting the boy to be gone. He wasn't. She would have asked what happened. He would have explained. So where does that take us?"

Lynley pulled a lined pad from the top side drawer of his desk. "Mollison," he said as he wrote. "Fleming's wife. His son."

"Patten," Barbara added.

"Gabriella," Lynley finished. He underlined the name once, then a second time. He considered it thoughtfully. He underlined it again.

Barbara watched him for a moment, then said, "As to Gabriella, I don't know, Inspector. It doesn't really make sense. What'd she do? Pick off her lover and then blithely drive away in his car? It's too easy. It's too obvious. What's she got for brains, if she did something like that? Wet cotton wool?"

"According to Patten."

"We're back to him. See? It's the natural direction."

"He has motive enough. As to the rest—" Lynley indicated the file and the photographs, "we'll have to see how the evidence stacks up.

Maidstone's crime scene team will have finished with the cottage by mid-morning. If there's something to be found, they'll be bound to find it."

"At least we know it wasn't a suicide," Barbara said.

"It wasn't that. But it may not be a murder."

"You can't say it was an accident. Not with the cigarette and the matches that Ardery found in the chair."

"I'm not saying it was an accident." Lynley yawned, dropped his chin into his palm, and grimaced as the stubble on his face seemed to give him an idea of what hour it was. "We'll need the number plates on Fleming's car," he said. "We'll need to circulate a description. Green, Mrs. White-law said. A Lotus. Possibly a Lotus-7. There must be paperwork on it somewhere. At the Kensington house, I should guess."

"Right." Barbara reached for her notebook and scrawled a reminder in it. "Did you notice the extra door in his bedroom by any chance? At the Whitelaw house?"

"Fleming's?"

"Next to the wardrobe. Did you see it? A bathrobe was hanging from a hook in it."

Lynley stared at his office door as if attempting recollection. "Brown velour," he said, "with green stripes running through it. Yes. What about it?"

"The door, not the bathrobe. It leads to her room. That's where I got the bedspread earlier."

"Mrs. Whitelaw's bedroom?"

"Interesting, don't you think? Adjoining bedrooms. What does that suggest to you?"

Lynley got to his feet. "Sleeping," he said. "Which is what we both ought to be doing at the moment." He reached for the set of reports and photographs, tucking them neatly under his arm. "Come along, Sergeant. We'll need to make an early start in the morning."

When Jeannie couldn't put it off any longer, she climbed the stairs. She'd done the washing up from the dinner that no one had eaten. She'd folded the tea towel neatly on the rod that was suctioned to the side of the fridge, just below a display of Stan's school papers and a perky sketch of one of Sharon's birds. She'd cleaned the cooker and moved on to wipe down the old red oilcloth that served to cover the kitchen table. Then she'd stood back and, without wanting to, remembered him picking at a worn spot in the oilcloth as he said, "It isn't you, girl. It's me. It's her. It's wanting something with her and not knowing what it is and not feeling right about you and the kids sitting here waiting for me to decide what's to happen to the lot of you. Jeannie, I'm in a bad patch. Don't you see that? I don't know what I want. Oh damn it, Jean, don't cry. Here. Please. I hate you to cry." She remembered, without wanting to, his fingers wiping at her cheeks, his hand closing over her wrist, his arm circling her shoulders, his mouth against her hair, saying, "Please, please. Make it easy for us, Jean." Which she could not do.

She blasted the image from her head by sweeping the floor. She went on to scour the sink. She scraped away at the insides of the oven. She even took down the daisy curtains from the window in order to give them a thorough wash. But they couldn't be washed now, so late at night, so she balled them up, left them on a chair, and knew it was time to see to her children.

She climbed the stairs slowly, shaking off the weariness that made her legs quake. She stopped in the bathroom and splashed her face with cold water. She removed her smock, slipped into her green housecoat, brushed her fingers against its pattern of interlocking rosebuds, and unpinned her hair. She'd had it up too long, drawn away from her face for her morning at Crissys, and she'd never loosened it once the police came to take her to Kent. Now it ached at the scalp as she released it from its large sunflower hairslide, and she winced and felt moisture come to her eyes as she settled it round her face and her ears. She sat on the toilet, not to pee but instead to buy time.

What was there left to say to them? she wondered. She'd tried to return their father to her children for the last four years. What could she tell them now?

He'd said, "We've been apart more than long enough, Jean. We can get a divorce with no fault on either side."

"I been true to you, Kenny," had been her reply. She'd stayed across the kitchen, as far away from him as possible with the edge of the sink pressing hard into her back. It was the first time he'd used the word she'd been fearing since the day he left them. "I never did another bloke but you. Never. Not once in my life."

"I haven't expected you to be faithful to me. I never asked that once I moved out of here, did I?"

"I made vows, Kenny. I said till death. I said that whatever you wanted of me, I'd give you open-hearted. And you can't say I ever held back a thing.''

"I wouldn't say that.''

"Then you tell me why. And be straight with me, Kenny. No more of this rot 'bout finding the self of yourself. Let's get down to business. Who're you fucking on the side that you want to fuck legal and proper now?''

"Come on, girl. This isn't about fucking.''

"No? Then why've you gone all red at the ears? Who's it that you're doing the job on now? How 'bout Mrs. Whitelaw? She got you changing her oil twice a week?''

"Don't be daft, all right?''

"We went to a church, you and me. We said till death do us part.''

"We were seventeen years old. People change. They can't help it.''

"I don't change.'' She drew a breath against the feeling of rawness at the back of her mouth. The worst, she thought, was not knowing what you already knew, not having a name and a face towards which you could direct the force of your hatred. "I been true to you, Kenny. So you owe me truth in return. Who is it you're fucking now you're not fucking me?''

"Jean . . .''

"Only that's not putting it quite right, is it?''

"What's wrong between us isn't the sex part. It never was and you know it.''

"We got three kids. We got a life here. Least, we had one till Mrs. Whitelaw took it over.''

"This isn't about Miriam.''

"She's *Miriam* now? How long's she been Miriam? Is she Miriam in the light or is it just in the dark when you don't have to look at the piece of dough you're kneading?''

"For fuck's sake, Jean. Have a brain, won't you? I'm not sleeping with Miriam Whitelaw. She's a flipping old lady.''

"Then who? Tell me. Who?''

"You aren't listening to me. This isn't about sex.''

"Oh, too right. What is it, then? You taken to religion? You find someone you can sing hymns with on Sunday mornings?''

"There's been a gap between us where there shouldn't be. That's always been the case.''

"What gap? What?''

"You don't see it, do you? That's most of the trouble.''

She laughed, although even to herself the sound was high and nervous. "You're off your head, Kenny Fleming. You tell me one other couple who's got half what we've had since we was twelve years old."

He shook his head. He looked tired and resigned. "I'm not twelve years old any longer. I need something more. I need a woman I can share with. You and me . . . you and I . . . we're good in some ways but not in others. And not in the ways that count for something outside the bedroom."

Jeannie felt the edge of the sink bruising flesh and bone. She stood taller against it. "There's men out there would crawl across coals to have someone like me."

"I know that."

"So how'm I not good?"

"I didn't say you weren't good."

"You said you and me're good in some ways but not in others. How? Tell me. Now."

"Our interests. What we do. What we care about. What we talk about. What our plans are. What we want for our lives."

"We always had that. You know we did."

"We did at first. But we've grown apart. You see that. You just don't want to admit it."

"Who's telling you we didn't have it good? Is it her? Is Mrs. Whitelaw filling your head with this muck? Because she hates me, Kenny. She always has done."

"I've already told you this isn't about Miriam."

"She blames me for taking you away from school. She came to Billingsgate when I was pregnant with Jimmy."

"This's got nothing to do with all that."

"She said I'd ruin your life if you and me got married."

"That's in the past. Forget it."

"She said you'd be nothing if I let you leave school."

"She's our friend. She was only worried about us."

"Our *friend*, you say? She wanted me to give up my baby. She wanted me to kill it. She wanted me to die. She's always had it in for me, Kenny. She's always—"

"Stow it!" His hand hit the table. The ceramic salt shaker—shaped like a polar bear to match the panther pepper—fell to the floor, hitting a leg of the table. It cracked, and spilled salt in a silent dribble of white against the old green lino. Kenny picked it up. It broke in two pieces in his hand. More salt fell like bleached sand between his fingers. He said, look-ing at the salt, not at her, "You're dead wrong about Miriam. She's been good to me. She's been good to us. You. The kids."

"Then tell me who's better'n me for you."

He drew a pattern of squiggles in the salt. He brushed his hand across the pattern, flattened it out. He began to redraw. He said, "Hear me, girl. It's not about fucking," and he spoke to the salt and not to her. From the tone of his voice, she could see he'd made up his mind to tell the truth. From the set of his head and his shoulders she knew that the truth was going to be worse than her worst imaginings. "It's not about sex at all," he repeated. "Understand?"

"Oh," she said with a lightness she didn't feel. "So it's not about sex. You a priest now, Kenny?"

"All right. I've been to bed with her. Yes. We've been to bed. But it's not about sex. It's bigger than that. It's about . . ." He shoved the heel of his hand into the salt. He rubbed it back and forth. He scraped it against the broken edge of the shaker, lodging the salt loose and watching it fall and driving his hand back into it again. "It's about wanting," he said.

"And that's not about sex? Come on, Kenny."

He looked at her and she felt her fingers getting icy. She'd never seen his face so torn. "I've never felt like this before," he said. "I want to know her in every way that I can. I want to own her. I want to be her. That's what it's like."

"That's daft." Jeannie tried to sound scornful. She only sounded afraid.

"I've been reduced, Jean. Like I've been in a pot on the cooker and all of me's boiled away. What's left is this core. And the core is wanting. Her. Wanting her. I can't even think of anything else."

"You're talking rot, Kenny."

He turned his head away. "I didn't think you'd understand."

"But I expect she does. Miss Whoever-she-is."

"Yeah. She does."

"Who is it, then? Who's this her that you want to *be* so much?"

"What difference does it make?"

"It makes a difference to me. And you owe me the name. If it's over between us like you want it to be."

So he'd told her, saying only "Gabriella" in a low voice, repeating it on a breath with his head against his fists and the salt from the oilcloth speckling his wrists like tiny white freckles.

Jeannie didn't need to hear more. No surname was necessary. She felt as if he'd taken a cleaver to her like a butcher chops meat. She walked to the table, dazed. She said, "Gabriella Patten's who you want to know in every way? To own? To be?" She sank into a chair. "I won't let you do it."

"You don't see . . . you don't know . . . I can't explain what it's like." He tapped his fist to his forehead lightly, like he wanted her to peer right into his brain.

"Oh, I know what it's like. And I'll die first, Kenny, before I see you with her."

Only it hadn't happened that way. The dying had come. But they had the wrong corpse. Jeannie squeezed her eyes shut until she saw flicks of light against the back of her eyelids. When she knew she could speak in a normal voice if she had to—which she prayed she did not—she left the bathroom.

Sharon wasn't asleep. Jeannie cracked open her bedroom door and saw that she was sitting up in her bed next to the window. She was knitting. She hadn't put on a light. She was bent over like a hunchback, clicking needles together and twisting yarn, whispering, "Purl's like *this*. Knit's like this. Yes. And again." Across the blankets snaked the muffler she'd begun working on last month. It was meant for her dad, an out-of-season birthday present that Kenny would have worn to please his daughter, regardless of the weather, from the moment he opened the gift in late June.

When Jeannie pushed the door fully open, Sharon didn't look her way. Her small face was pinched with the effort at concentration, but since she didn't have her spectacles on, she was making a real hash of her work.

The spectacles lay on the bedside table next to the binoculars through which Sharon watched her birds. Jeannie picked them up, smoothed the pads of her fingers over the ear pieces, and thought about how old her daughter would have to be before she allowed her to start wearing lenses. She'd meant to ask Kenny about it once she'd discovered there were three yobs at the school who were ragging Sharon and calling her Frog Eyes. Not that the asking would have made any difference, because Jeannie knew what the answer would have been. Kenny'd have whisked Sharon off for the lenses at once, helped her learn how to use them, and made her go giggly at the thick-headedness of boys who only feel like toffs when they're poking fun at fourteen-year-old girls.

"Purl, purl, purl," Sharon whispered. "Knit, purl, purl, purl."

Jeannie offered her the spectacles. "Need these, Shar? You want the light? Can't see what you're doing in the dark like that, can you?"

Sharon shook her head furiously. "Knit," she said. "Purl, purl, purl." The needles made a sound like pecking birds.

Jeannie sat on the edge of her daughter's bed. She fingered the muffler. It was lumpy in the middle and misshapen on the edges. It was worse near the needles where tonight's work spewed forth in knots.

"Dad would of liked this, luv," Jeannie said. "It would of made him proud." She lifted her hand to touch her daughter's hair but finished the gesture by straightening the blankets. "You best try to sleep. You want to come in with me?"

Sharon shook her head. "Knit," she muttered. "Purl, purl, knit."

"Want me to stay here? If you scoot over, I can sit with you some." She wanted to say, "The first night's going t'be the worst, I think, when the hurting makes you want to punch your hand through the window." Instead she said, "P'rhaps we'll go to the river tomorrow. What you think of that? We'll try to see one of those birds you been looking for. What're they called, Shar?"

"Knit," Sharon whispered. "Knit, knit, purl."

"Odd name, it was. Sandwich something."

Sharon uncoiled more yarn from the ball. She twisted it round her hand. She didn't look at it, or even at her knitting. Her back was hunched over her work, but her eyes were vacantly fastened on the wall where she'd pinned up dozens of her bird sketchings.

"You want to go to the river, luv? Try to see some more birds? Take your sketch pad with us? Take a lunch as well?"

Sharon didn't reply. She merely eased herself onto her side, her back to her mother, and continued the knitting. Jeannie watched her for a moment. Her hand lingered over her, tracing the curve of her shoulder without touching it. She said, "Yeah. Well. That's a good idea. You try to sleep, luv," and went to her sons' room across the corridor.

It smelled of cigarette smoke, unwashed bodies, and dirty clothes. In one of the beds, Stan lay quietly, protected on all sides by a rank of stuffed animals set up to guard him. Cocooned in the middle of these, he slept with the covers round his ankles and his hand tucked into his pyjama bottoms.

"Wanks off every night, Stan does. He don't need a best friend. He's got his dong."

Jimmy's words came from the darkest corner of the room where the smell was strongest and where a fleeting red glow illuminated a fragment of lip and the knuckle of a finger. She left Stan's hand where it was and pulled up the blankets to cover him again. She said quietly, "How many times've we talked about smoking in bed, Jim?"

"Don't remember."

"You going t'be satisfied when you burn the house down?"

He snorted for reply.

She opened the curtains at the window and cranked at the casement to let in some fresh air. Moonlight fell across the brown carpet squares, making a path that led to the wreck of a clipper ship lying on its side with its three masts snapped off and a foot-size cavity smashed into its bow.

"What's happened here?" She bent to the model. It was a ruin of handcut and handstained balsawood, Jimmy's prized copy of the *Cutty Sark*. Months in the creation, it had been the pride of both father and son who'd spent hours and days at the kitchen table, designing, cutting, painting, gluing. "Oh no!" she cried softly. "Jim, I'm sorry. Did Stan—"

Jimmy sniggered. She looked up. The burning tobacco glowed and faded. She heard the smoke whistle out of his nose. "Stan didn't," he said. "Stan's too busy wanking to think of cleaning house. This lot's kid's stuff anyways. Who bloody needs it?"

Jeannie looked to the bookcase beneath the window. On the floor lay the ruins of the *Golden Hind*. Next to it *Gipsy Moth IV*. Beyond, *Victory* was tromped into bits, mixed in with the pieces of a Viking warship and a Roman galley.

"But you and Dad," Jeannie began uselessly. "Jimmy, you and Dad . . ."

"Yeah, Mum? Me 'n' Dad what?"

How odd, she thought, that these scraps of wood, filaments of string, and squares of cloth could make her want to cry. Kenny's death hadn't done it. Seeing his naked corpse hadn't done it. The popping lights and the questions from the journalists hadn't done it. She'd been utterly without emotion when she'd told Stan and Sharon that their father was dead, but now with her gaze taking in the wreck of these ships, she felt as broken as the ruins of them scattered on the carpet.

"This's what you had of him," she said. "These ships. They're you and Dad. These ships."

"The bugger's gone, i'n't he? No point to keeping reminders round the place. You ought to start mucking out this dump yourself, Mum.

Pictures, clothes, books. Old bats. His bike. Toss out the lot. Who needs it, anyway?"

"Don't talk like that."

"You don't reckon he collected keepsakes of us, do you?" Jimmy leaned forward, into the moonlight. He clasped his hands round his bony knees, flicking ash on the counterpane. "Wouldn't want reminders of the wife and kiddies at a crucial moment, would he, our dad? They might get in the way. Pictures of our mugs on the bedside table. That'd upset his love life right enough. A lock of our hairs in a brooch pinned onto his cricket togs. That'd damn well upset his bleeding game. One-a Sharon's bird drawings. One-a Stan's pet bears." The glow of his cigarette trembled like a firefly. "Or one-a your Dutch knickknacks that he used to poke fun at. How 'bout that stupid cow jug that pours out milk like it was being sick? He could use it in the morning with his cornflakes, couldn't he? Only when he poured the milk and thought about you, he'd look up and see someone else sitting there instead. No." He balanced on his elbow and stubbed out his cigarette on the side of a play skull that glowed in the dark. "He wouldn't want bits and pieces of his old life mixed up with his new. No. Never. Not our dad. No way."

From across the room, Jeannie could smell him. She wondered when it was that he had last washed. She could even smell his breath, foetid with the smoke of his cigarettes.

"He had pictures of you kids," she said. "You remember how he came to collect them, don't you? He put them in frames but the frames were wrong. Too big or too small. Mostly too big so Shar cut up paper to fill in the empty part. You helped. You chose the ones of yourself that you wanted him to have."

"Yeah? Well, I was a mutt then, wasn't I? Snot nosed and smarmy. Hoping Dad'd want us back if I licked his shoes good enough. Perishing joke, that is. What a rotter. I'm glad—"

"I don't believe that, Jim."

"Why? What's it to you, Mum?" His question was tense. He repeated it and added, "You sorry he's gone?"

"He was in a bad patch. He was trying to work things out in his head."

"Yeah. Aren't we all? Only we don't do our head working while we roger some slag, do we?"

She was glad for the dark. It hid and protected. But shadows worked both ways. While he couldn't clearly see her and thus couldn't know how his words were like nasty little fish hooks digging into her cheeks, she couldn't see him either, not the way a mother needs to see her son when there's a question to be asked and just about everything in the mother's life worth living rides on the answer he gives her.

But she couldn't ask it, so she asked another. "What're you trying to say?"

"I knew. All 'bout Dad. All 'bout blondie-from-a-bottle. All 'bout the great soul searching Dad was supposably doing while he humped her like a goat. Finding himself. What a two-faced turd."

"What he did with—" Jeannie couldn't say the name, not to her son. Affirming what he'd said by putting more into words was too much to ask of herself at the moment. She steadied herself by putting her hands into the pockets of her housecoat. Her right hand found a wadded tissue, her left a comb with missing teeth. "That had nothing to do with you, Jimmy. That was me and Dad. He loved you like always. Shar and Stan as well."

"Which is why we went on the river like he promised, right, Mum? We hired that cabin cruiser like he always said and sailed up the Thames. Saw the locks. Saw the swans. Stopped at Hampton Court and ran in the maze. Even waved at the Queen who was standing on the bridge in Windsor, just waiting for us to cruise by and doff our hats."

"He meant to take you on the river. You mustn't think he'd forgotten."

"And Henley Regatta. We saw that as well, didn't we? All tarted up in our dress-up clothes. With a hamper crammed with our favourite eats. Chips for Stan. Cocoa Pops for Shar. McDonald's for me. And when we were through, we went on the big birthday treat—Greek islands, the boat, just me and Dad."

"Jim, he needed to settle his mind. We'd been together since we was kids, Dad and me. He needed time to know if he wanted to go on. But to go on with me, with *me*, not with you. With you kids nothing was changed for Dad."

"Oh right, Mum. Nothing. And wouldn't she of been chuffed to have us lot hanging 'bout. There'd be Stan wanking in her spare room at the weekends and Shar pinning up bird pictures on her wallpaper and me getting motor grease on her rugs. She would of been dead keen to have us as step-kids. 'S matter of fact, I can't think she didn't tell Dad to bugger off till he guaranteed she'd get us as part of the bargain." He kicked off his Doc Martens. They hit the floor with a thud. He plumped up his pillow and leaned against the bed's headboard where he put his face into deepest shadow. "She must be in a real state right now, blondie-from-a-bottle. What you think, Mum? Dad's been chopped and that's too bad, isn't it, 'cause she can't have it off with him whenever she'd like. But the worst of the worst is that she don't get *us* as her step-kids now. And I bet she's real cut up 'bout that." He snickered quietly.

The sound sent a quiver the length of Jeannie's spine. Her left fingers sought the comb in her pocket and sank into the spaces where the teeth were missing. "Jimmy," she said, "I got something to ask you."

"Ask away, Mum. Ask anything. But I haven't rogered her, if that's what you want to know. Dad wasn't a bloke to share the goods."

"You knew who she was."

"Maybe I did."

Her right hand grasped the tissue. She began to ball it into pellets in her pocket. She didn't want to know the answer because she knew it already. Still she asked the question. "When he cancelled the boat trip, what did he tell you? Jim, tell me. What did he say?"

Jimmy's hand slithered out of the shadows. It reached for something next to the play skull. A flare followed a sound like *ssst*, and he was holding a lit match next to his pallid face. He kept his eyes on hers as the match burnt down. When the flame licked his fingers, he didn't wince. Nor did he answer.

Lynley finally found a spot in Sumner Place. Parking karma, Sergeant Havers would have called it. He wasn't so sure. He'd spent ten minutes cruising up and down the Fulham Road, circling South Kensington Station, and getting more acquainted than he would ever have dreamed possible with the restored Michelin building at Brompton Cross. He was about to give up and go home when he made a final pass into Sumner Place just in time to see an antique Morgan vacating a spot not twenty yards from where he was heading: Onslow Square.

The early morning was fine, dew-cool silence interrupted by the occasional *whoosh* of a vehicle on Old Brompton Road. He walked down Sumner Place, crossed near a small chapel at the bottom of the street, and made his way into Onslow Square.

All the lights save one were out in Helen's flat. She'd kept a lamp burning in the drawing room, just inside the small balcony that overlooked the square. He smiled when he saw it. Helen knew him better than he knew himself.

He went inside, climbed the stairs, let himself into the flat. She'd been reading before she had fallen asleep, he saw, because a book was open on the bedcovers, face down. He picked it up, tried and failed to read the title in the room's near darkness, set it on the bedside table, and used her gold bracelet to mark the page. He studied her.

She lay on her side, right hand beneath her cheek, lashes dark against her skin. Her lips were pursed, as if her dreams required concentration. A swirl of her hair curved from her ear to the corner of her mouth and when he brushed it off her face, she stirred but didn't wake. He smiled at this. She was the soundest sleeper he had ever known.

"Someone could break in, cart off all your belongings, and you'd never know," he'd said to her in complete exasperation when her sleep of the dead confronted his endless toss and turn of the quick. "For God's sake, Helen, there's something damned unhealthy about it. You don't fall asleep so much as lose consciousness. I think you ought to see a specialist about the problem."

She laughed and patted his cheek. "It's the benefit of having a completely uncluttered conscience, Tommy."

"Damn little good that'll do you if the building goes up in flames some night. You'd even sleep through the smoke alarm, wouldn't you?"

"Probably. What a ghastly thought." She looked momentarily sombre, then brightened with, "Ah. But you wouldn't, would you? Which does suggest that I ought to consider keeping you around."

"And do you?"

"What?"

"Consider it."

"More than you think."

"So?"

"So we ought to have dinner. I've some perfectly lovely chicken. New potatoes. *Haricots verts*. A *Pinot grigio* to swill."

"You've cooked dinner?" This was a change, indeed. Sweet vision of domesticity, he thought.

"I?" Helen laughed. "Heavens, Tommy, none of it's *cooked*. Oh, I looked and looked through a book at Simon's. Deborah even pointed out one or two recipes that didn't appear likely to tax my limited culinary talents. But it all seemed so complicated."

"It's only chicken."

"Yes, but the recipe asked me to dredge it. To *dredge*, for heaven's sake. Isn't that what they do in the fens? Aren't they always dredging the canals or something? How on earth does one go about doing that to a chicken?"

"Your imagination didn't tell you?"

"I don't even want to repeat what my imagination suggested about dredging. Your appetite would be forever destroyed."

"Which might not be a bad idea if I have expectations of eating anytime soon."

"You're disappointed. I've disappointed you. I'm sorry, darling. I'm utterly useless. Can't cook. Can't sew. Can't play the piano. No talent for sketching. Can't carry a tune."

"You're not auditioning for a role in a Jane Austen novel."

"Fall asleep at the symphony. Have nothing intelligent to say about Shakespeare or Pinter or Shaw. Thought Simone de Beauvoir was something to drink. Why do you put up with me?"

That was the question, all right. He had no answer.

"We're a pair, Helen," he said quietly into her sleep. "We're alpha and omega. We're positive and negative. We're a match made in heaven."

He took the small jewel box from his jacket pocket and set it on top of the novel on the bedside table. Because, after all, tonight was the night. Make the moment completely memorable, he'd thought. Make it shout *romance*. Do it with roses, candles, caviar, champagne. Have background music. Seal it with a kiss.

Only the last option was available to him. He sat on the edge of the bed and touched his lips to her cheek. She stirred, frowning. She turned onto her back. He kissed her mouth.

"Coming to bed?" she murmured, her eyes still closed.

"How do you know it's me? Or is that an invitation you'd extend to anyone who showed up in your bedroom at two in the morning?"

She smiled. "Only if he shows promise."

"I see."

She opened her eyes. Dark like her hair, in contrast with her skin, they made her look like the night. She was shadows and moonlight. "How was it?" she asked softly.

"Complicated," he said. "A cricketer. From the England team."

"Cricket," she murmured. "That ghastly game. Who can ever make sense of it?"

"Fortunately, that won't be a requirement of the case."

Her eyes drifted closed. "Come to bed, then. I miss you snoring in my ear."

"Do I snore?"

"No one's ever complained about it before?"

"No. And I should think . . ." He saw the trap when her lips slowly curved in a smile. "You're supposed to be more than half asleep, Helen."

"I am. I am. So should you be. Come to bed, darling."

"Despite—"

"Your chequered past. Yes. I love you. Come to bed and keep me warm."

"It's not cold."

"We'll pretend."

He lifted her hand, kissed the palm, curved the fingers round his. Her grasp was loose. She was falling back asleep. "Can't," he said. "I've got to be up too early."

"Pooh," she murmured. "You can set the alarm."

"I wouldn't want to," he said. "You distract me too much."

"That doesn't bode well for our future then, does it?"

"Have we a future?"

"You know we do."

He kissed her fingers and slipped her hand beneath the covers. In a reflex reaction, she turned on her side once again. "Sleep well," he said.

"Hmmm. Will. Yes."

He kissed her temple, rose, and headed for the door.

"Tommy?" It was little more than a mumble.

"Yes?"

"Why did you stop by?"

"I've left you something."

"For breakfast?"

He smiled. "No. Not for breakfast. You're on your own there."

"Then what?"

"You'll see."

"What's it for?"

A good question. He gave the most reasonable answer. "For love, I suppose." And life, he thought, and all of its messy complications.

"That's nice," she said. "Thoughtful of you, darling."

She rustled underneath the covers, burrowing for the optimum position. He stood in the doorway, waiting for the moment when her breathing deepened. He heard her sigh.

"Helen," he whispered.

Her breathing came and went.

"I love you," he said.

Her breathing came and went.

"Marry me," he said.

Her breathing came and went.

Having managed to fulfill his obligation to himself by the week's end as promised, he locked up and left her to dream her dreams.

CHAPTER
7

Miriam Whitelaw didn't speak until they had crossed the river, passing through the Elephant and Castle and making the turn into the New Kent Road. Then she stirred herself only to say faintly, "There's never been a convenient way to get out to Kent from Kensington, has there?" as if she meant to apologise for the bother she was causing them.

Lynley glanced at her in the rearview mirror, but he didn't respond. Next to him Sergeant Havers was hunched over, muttering into his car phone as she relayed the number plates and a description of Kenneth Fleming's Lotus-7 back to Detective Constable Winston Nkata at New Scotland Yard. "Put it on the PNC," she was saying. "And fax it to the district stations as well. . . . What? . . . Let me check." She raised her head and said to Lynley, "Want the media to have it?" And when he nodded, she said, "Right. That's okay. But nothing else for the moment.

Got it? . . . Fine." She replaced the phone and leaned back in her seat. She surveyed the congested street and sighed. "Where the dickens is everyone going?"

"Weekend," Lynley said. "Decent weather."

They were caught in a mass exodus from city to country, alternating between rolling along nicely and slowing to a sudden crawl. They had been on the road so far for forty minutes, weaving and inching their way first to the Embankment, then to Westminster Bridge, and from there to the continuously burgeoning urban mass that comprises south London. It promised to be a great deal more than forty additional minutes before they reached the Springburns in Kent.

They had spent the first hour of their day going through Kenneth Fleming's papers. Some of these were mixed with Mrs. Whitelaw's own, crammed into the drawers of a davenport in the morning room on the ground floor of the house. Others were folded neatly into his bedside table. Still others were in a letter holder on the work top in the kitchen. Among them, they found his current contract with the Middlesex county side, his former contracts documenting his cricket career in Kent, half a dozen bids for jobs for Whitelaw Printworks, a brochure about boating in Greece, a three-week-old letter verifying an appointment with a solicitor in Maida Vale—which Havers pocketed—and the information they were looking for about his car.

Mrs. Whitelaw attempted to help them in their search, but it was clear that her thought processes were muzzy at best. She wore the same sheath, jacket, and jewellery that she'd had on the previous night. Her cheeks and lips were colourless. Her eyes and nose were red. Her hair was rumpled. If she'd been to bed at all in the past twelve hours, she didn't appear to have reaped a single benefit from the experience.

Lynley gave her a second look in the mirror. He wondered how much longer she was going to hold up without a doctor's intervention. She pressed a handkerchief to her mouth—like her clothing, it appeared to be last night's as well—and with her elbow on the armrest, she kept her eyes closed for long periods. She had agreed to the trip to Kent immediately upon Lynley's making the request of her. But looking at her now, he began to think it was one of his less inspired ideas.

Still, it couldn't be helped. They needed her to examine the cottage. She would be able to tell them what, if anything, was missing, what was marginally odd, or what was altogether wrong. But her ability to produce that information for them depended upon her powers of observation. And visual acumen depended upon a mind that was clear.

"I don't know about this, Inspector," Sergeant Havers had muttered at him over the top of the Bentley in Staffordshire Terrace once they had tucked Mrs. Whitelaw into its back seat.

Neither did he. Less so now when in the mirror he watched the straining of cords in her neck and saw the glimmer of tears seep out like melting dreams beneath her eyes.

He wanted to say something to comfort the older woman. But he didn't know the words or how to begin to say them because he didn't altogether understand the nature of her grief. Her true relationship with Fleming was the great unknown that still had to be discussed, however delicately, between them.

She opened her eyes. She caught him watching her, turned her head to the window, and made a pretence of noting the view.

When they got beyond Lewisham and traffic loosened up, Lynley finally interrupted her thoughts. "Are you all right, Mrs. Whitelaw?" he asked. "Would you like to stop for a coffee somewhere?"

Without turning from the window, she shook her head. He gunned the Bentley into the right lane and passed an antique Morris with an ageing hippie at the wheel.

They drove on in silence. The car phone rang once. Havers answered it. She had a brief conversation with someone, consisting of "Yes? . . . What? . . . Who the hell wants to know? . . . No. You tell him we're not confirming at this end. He'll have to get his reliable source somewhere else." She hung up and said, "Newspapers. They're putting two and two together."

Lynley said, "Which paper?"

"Daily Mirror at the moment."

"Christ." And with a nod at the phone, "Who was that?"

"Dee Harriman."

A blessing, Lynley thought. No one was better at fending off journalists than the chief superintendent's secretary, who always diverted them with rapt questions about the state of one royal marriage or another royal divorce.

"What are they asking?"

"If the police would care to confirm the fact that Kenneth Fleming— who died as a result of a smouldering cigarette—wasn't a smoker in the first place. And if he wasn't a smoker, are we trying to suggest that the cigarette in the armchair was left there by someone else? And if so, who? . . . etc., etc. You know how it goes."

They passed a pantechnicon, a hearse, and an army lorry with soldiers riding on benches in the back. They passed a horse trailer and three caravans that crept along, snail-paced and snail-shaped. As they slowed for an upcoming traffic light, Mrs. Whitelaw spoke.

"They've been phoning me as well."

"The newspapers?" Lynley gave a look in the mirror. She'd turned away from the window. She'd switched from her spectacles to a pair of dark glasses. "When?"

"This morning. I had two calls before yours. Three afterwards."

"About the cigarette smoking?"

"About anything I might be willing to tell them. Truth or lie. I'm not certain they care. Just so long as it was something about Ken."

"You don't have to talk to them."

"I haven't talked to anyone." She went back to looking through the side window, saying, more to herself than to them, "What would be the point? Who could understand?"

"Understand?" Lynley fed her the question casually, all his attention ostensibly given to his driving.

Mrs. Whitelaw didn't immediately offer an answer. When she replied, her voice was quiet. "Who would have thought it," she said. "A young man of thirty-two—vital, virile, athletic, energetic—actually choosing to live not with some young creature firm of flesh and smooth of skin but with a dried-up old woman. A woman thirty-four years his senior. Old enough to be his mother. Ten years older, in fact, than his actual mother. It's an obscenity, isn't it?"

"More a curiosity, I should say. The situation's unusual. You see that, no doubt."

"I've heard the whispers and the titters. I've read the gossip. Oedipal relationship. Inability to break away from any primal tie, evidenced in his choice of living arrangements and his unwillingness to end his marriage. Failure to resolve childhood issues with his mother and consequently seeking another. Or on my part: Unwillingness to accept the realities of old age. Seeking a notoriety denied to me in my youth. Longing to prove myself through gaining control of a younger man. Everyone has an opinion. No one accepts the truth."

Sergeant Havers pivoted in her seat so that she could see Mrs. White-law. "We'd be interested in hearing the truth," she said. "We need to hear it, in fact."

"What does the sort of relationship I shared with Ken have to do with his death?"

"The sort of relationship Fleming had with every woman may have had a great deal to do with his death," Lynley answered.

She took up her handkerchief and watched her hands folding it over and over until it was a long, thin strip. She said, "I've known him since he was fifteen years old. He was a pupil of mine."

"You're a teacher?"

"Not any longer. Then. On the Isle of Dogs. He was a pupil in one of my English classes. I came to know him because he was . . ." She cleared her throat. "He was terribly clever. A real crack hand, the other children called him, and they liked him because he was easy with them, easy with himself, easy to be around. Right from the start, he was the sort of boy who knew who he was and didn't feel the need to pretend he was something else. Nor did he feel the need to rub other children's noses in the fact that he was more talented than they. I liked him for that enormously. For other things as well. He had dreams. I admired that. It was an unusual quality for a teenager to possess in the East End at that time. We struck up a pupil-teacher friendship. I encouraged him, tried to point him in the right direction."

"Which was?"

"Sixth Form College. Then university."

"Did he attend?"

"He did only a lower sixth year, in Sussex on a governor's scholar-ship. After that he came home and went to work for my husband at the printworks. Shortly after that, he married."

"Young."

"Yes." She unfolded the handkerchief, spread it against her lap, smoothed it out. "Yes. Ken was young."

"You knew the girl he married?"

"I wasn't surprised when he finally made the decision to separate. Jean's a good girl at heart, but she isn't what Ken should have ended up with."

"And Gabriella Patten?"

"Time would have told."

Lynley met the blank gaze of her dark glasses in the rearview mirror. "But you know her, don't you? You knew him. What do you think?"

"I think Gabriella is Jean," she said quietly, "with a great deal more money and a Knightsbridge wardrobe. She isn't . . . wasn't Ken's equal. But that's not strange, is it? Don't you find that most men rarely at heart want to marry an equal? It puts a strain on their strength of ego."

"You haven't described a man who appeared to be struggling with weakness of ego."

"He wasn't. He was struggling with man's propensity for recognising the familiar and repeating the past."

"And the past was what?"

"Marrying a woman on the strength of his physical passion for her. Honestly and naively believing that physical passion and the emotional rapture engendered by physical passion are both lasting states."

"Did you discuss your reservations with him?"

"We discussed everything, Inspector. Despite what the tabloids have on occasion suggested about us, Ken was like a son in my life. He *was*, in fact, a son in every way save the formalities of either birth or adoption."

"You have no other children?"

She watched a Porsche pass them, followed by a motorcyclist with long red hair streaming like banners from beneath an SS-shaped helmet. "I have a daughter," she said.

"Is she in London?"

Again, the long pause before she answered, as if the traffic they passed were giving her an indication of which words she should choose and how many. "As far as I know. She and I have been estranged for a number of years."

"Which must have made Fleming doubly important to you," Sergeant Havers noted.

"Because he took Olivia's place? I only wish it were that easy, Sergeant. One doesn't replace one child with another. It's not like owning a dog."

"But can't a relationship be replaced?"

"A new relationship can develop. But the cicatrix of the old one remains. And nothing grows on a cicatrix. Nothing grows through it."

"But it can become as important as a relationship that has preceded it," Lynley noted. "Will you agree with that?"

"It can become more important," Mrs. Whitelaw said.

They veered onto the M20 and began heading southeast. Lynley didn't make his next remark until they were spinning along comfortably in the far right lane.

"You've a great amount of property," he said. "The factory in Stepney, the house in Kensington, the cottage in Kent. I should guess you've other investments as well, especially if the printworks is a going concern."

"I'm not a wealthy woman."

"I dare say you're not straitened either."

"What the company makes is reinvested into the company, Inspector."

"Which makes it a valuable commodity. Is it a family business?"

"My father-in-law began it. My husband inherited it. When Gordon died, I took it over."

"And upon your death? Have you arranged for its future?"

Sergeant Havers, apparently seeing where Lynley was heading, shifted in her seat to give Mrs. Whitelaw her attention. "What does your will say about your fortune, Mrs. Whitelaw? Who gets what?"

She took off her sunglasses and slid them into a leather case, which she removed from her purse. She returned her regular spectacles to her nose. "My will is written to benefit Ken."

"I see," Lynley said thoughtfully. He saw Sergeant Havers reach in her shoulder bag and bring out her notebook. "Did Fleming know about this?"

"I'm afraid I don't see the point of your question."

"Might he have told someone? Have you told anyone?"

"It hardly matters now that he's dead."

"It matters a great deal. If that's why he's dead."

Her hand reached for her heavy necklace in much the same way she'd reached for it on the previous night. "You're suggesting—"

"That someone might not have appreciated the fact that Fleming was your beneficiary. That someone might have felt he'd used—" Lynley searched for a euphemism, "extraordinary means to win your affection and trust."

"That happens," Havers said.

"I assure you. It didn't happen in this case." Mrs. Whitelaw's words teetered between polite calm and cool anger. "As I said, I've known . . . I knew Ken Fleming from the time he was fifteen years old. He started out my pupil. Over time he became my son and my friend. But he was not . . . he was *not* . . ." Her voice wavered and she stopped herself until she could control it. "He was not my lover. Even though, Inspector, I am frankly still woman enough to have more than once wished myself a twenty-five-year-old girl with her life instead of her death ahead of her. A wish, I imagine you agree, that is not completely without its logic. Women are still women and men are still men, no matter their ages."

"And if their ages don't matter? To either of them?"

"Ken was unhappy in his marriage. He needed time to sort things out. I was happy to be able to give him that. First in the Springburns when he played for Kent. Then in my home when the Middlesex team offered him a contract. If that looks to people as if he were playing the gigolo with me, or as if I were attempting to put my gnarled claws into a younger man, it simply can't be helped."

"You were the brunt of gossip."

"Which was of no consequence to us. We knew the truth. You now know it as well."

Lynley wondered about that. He'd discovered long ago that the truth was rarely as simple as a verbal explanation made it out to be.

They exited the motorway and began to weave through the country roads towards the Springburns. In the market town of Greater Springburn, Saturday morning meant an open air market, which filled the square and clogged the streets with cars looking for spaces to park. They inched through the traffic and headed east on Swan Street, where ornamental cherry trees splashed blossoms the colour of candy floss onto the ground.

Beyond Greater Springburn, Mrs. Whitelaw directed them through a series of lanes sided by tall hedgerows of yew and blackberry brambles. They finally turned into a lane marked Water Street, and she said, "It's just along here," as they passed a line of cottages at the edge of an open field of flax. Just beyond this, they began to make a twisting descent towards a cottage that sat on a slight rise of land, surrounded by conifers and a wall, its drive closed off by crime scene tape. Two cars were drawn up to the wall, one a panda car and the other a metallic blue Rover. Lynley parked in front of the Rover, edging the Bentley part way into the cottage drive.

He surveyed the area—the hop field opposite, the scattering of old cottages farther along the lane, the distinctive cocked-hat chimneys of a line of oast roundels, the grassy paddock immediately next door. He turned to Mrs. Whitelaw. "Do you need a minute?"

"I'm ready."

"There'll be some interior damage to the cottage."

"I understand."

He nodded. Sergeant Havers hopped out and opened Mrs. White-law's door. The older woman stood still for a moment, breathing in the strong, medicinal scent of rape that made an enormous yellow coverlet on a slope of farmland farther along the lane. A cuckoo was calling some-where in the distance. Swifts were darting into the sky, wheeling higher and higher on scimitar wings.

Lynley ducked under the police tape, then held it up for Mrs. White-law. Sergeant Havers followed her, notebook in hand.

At the top of the drive, Lynley swung the garage door open and Mrs. Whitelaw stepped inside to verify that the Aston Martin within looked like Gabriella Patten's. She couldn't be absolutely certain, she told them, because she didn't know the number plates of Gabriella's car. But she knew Gabriella drove an Aston Martin. She'd seen it when the woman had come to Kensington to see Ken. This looked like the same car, but if asked to swear to it . . .

"That's fine," Lynley said as Havers noted the number plates. He asked her to look round the garage to see if anything was amiss.

There was little enough inside: three bicycles, two of which had flat tyres; one bicycle pump; an ancient three-pronged pitchfork; several bas-kets hanging from hooks; a folded chaise longue; cushions for outdoor furniture.

"This wasn't here before," Mrs. Whitelaw said in reference to a large sack of cat litter. "I don't keep cats." Everything else, she said, seemed to be in order.

They returned to the drive where they walked through the lattice-work gate and into the front garden. Lynley looked over its colourful abundance, not for the first time reflecting upon the universal obsession that his countrymen and women seemed to have with urging flora to burst from the soil. He always thought it was a direct reaction to the climate. Month upon month of dreary, wet, grey weather acted as a stimulus to which the only response was a starburst of colour the moment spring gave the remotest hint of appearing.

They found Inspector Ardery on the terrace behind the cottage. She was sitting at a wicker table beneath a grape arbour, talking into a cellular phone and using a biro to scribble aimless marks on a pad as she did so. She was saying pleasantly, "Listen to me, Bob, I don't exactly give a shit about your plans with Sally. I have a case. I can't take the boys this weekend. End of discussion . . . Yes. *Bitch* is exactly the epithet I'd choose as well. . . . Don't you bloody dare do that. . . . Bob, I won't be home, and you know it. Bob!" She folded the mouth piece closed. "Bastard," she muttered. She set the phone on the table, between a manila folder and a notebook. She looked up, saw them, and said without embarrassment, "Ex-husbands. A species apart. *Homo infuriatus.*" She rose, brought an ivory hairslide out of the pocket of her trousers, and used it to fasten her hair at the nape of her neck. "Mrs. Whitelaw," she said and introduced herself. She took several pairs of surgical gloves from her brief case and handed them round. "The dab boys have already come and gone, but I like to be careful all the same."

She waited until they had the gloves on before she ducked under the lintel of the kitchen door and led the way into the cottage. Mrs. Whitelaw hesitated just inside, fingering the lock that the fire brigade had broken to get inside. "What should I . . . ?"

"Take your time," Lynley told her. "Look round the rooms. Notice as much as you can. Compare what you see to what you know about the place. Sergeant Havers will be with you. Talk to her. Say anything that comes into your mind." He said to Havers, "Start above."

She replied, "Right," and led Mrs. Whitelaw through the kitchen, saying, "Stairway's this direction, ma'am?"

They heard Mrs. Whitelaw say, "Oh dear," when she saw the condition of the dining room. She added, "The smell."

"Soot. Smoke. Lots of this stuff'll probably have to go, I'm afraid."

Their voices faded as they climbed the stairs. Lynley took a moment to scrutinise the kitchen. The building itself was more than four centuries old, but the kitchen had been modernised to include new tiles on the work tops and floor, a leaf-green Aga, chrome fixtures at the sink. Glass-fronted cupboards held dishes and tinned goods. Window sills displayed pots of drooping maidenhair fern.

"We've taken what was in the sink," Inspector Ardery said as Lynley bent to inspect a double-bowled animal dish just inside the kitchen door. "It looked like dinner for one: plate, wineglass, water glass, one place setting of cutlery. Cold pork and salad from the fridge. With chutney."

"Have you come across the cat?" Lynley began to open and close the kitchen drawers.

"Kittens," she said. "There were two of them, according to the milkman. The Patten woman found them abandoned by the spring. We managed to locate them at one of the neighbours. They were wandering in the lane early Thursday morning. The kittens, not the neighbours. We've had some interesting news at that end of things, by the way. I've had some probationary DCs out interviewing the neighbours since yesterday afternoon.''

Lynley found nothing unusual in the drawers of cutlery, cooking utensils, and tea towels. He moved to the cupboards. ''What did the DCs hear?''

''It's what the neighbours heard, actually.'' She waited patiently until Lynley turned from the cupboard, his hand on the knob. ''An argument. A real screamer, from what John Freestone said. He farms the acreage that begins right across the paddock.''

''That's a good forty yards. He must have exceptional ears.''

''He was doing a fast-walk by the cottage. Around eleven Wednesday night.''

''Odd time for a stroll.''

''He's on a schedule of prescribed cardiovascular activity, or so he said. The truth is, Freestone may just have hoped to get a glimpse of Gabriella's evening ablutions. According to several accounts, she was well worth glimpsing and not overly particular about drawing the curtains when she began to undress.''

''And did he? Glimpse her, that is.''

''He heard a row. Male and female. But mostly female. Lots of colourful language, including some interesting and illuminating names for sexual activities and the male genitalia. That sort of thing.''

''Did he recognise her voice? Or the man's?''

''He said one woman's shrieking is about the same as another woman's shrieking to his way of thinking. He couldn't be sure who it was. But he did voice some surprise that 'that sweet woman would know setch lang'age.' '' She smiled wryly. ''I don't think he gets about much.''

Lynley chuckled and opened the first cupboard to see an orderly arrangement of plates, glasses, cups, and saucers. He opened the second cupboard. One packet of Silk Cut lay on the shelf in front of assorted tins of everything from new potatoes to soup. He examined the packet. It was still sealed in cellophane.

''Kitchen matches,'' he said more to himself than to Ardery.

''There were none,'' she said. ''There were book matches in the sitting room. And a packet of those long fireplace matches are on a shelf against the left wall of the dining room fireplace."

"A few of those couldn't have been chopped down to use round the cigarette?"

"Too thick."

Lynley absently passed the packet of Silk Cut from hand to hand. Ardery leaned against the Aga and watched him. "We have scores of dabs, for what they're worth. We've taken them off the Aston Martin as well, in hopes we can at least sort out Mrs. Patten's from the rest. We've got Fleming's, of course, so we can eliminate his."

"But that leaves whomever else she may have invited in for a chat at one time or another. Her husband's been here, by the way."

"We're trying to get a handle on local visitors right now. And the DCs are looking for someone else who may have heard the row."

Lynley set the cigarettes on the work top and went to the door that led into the dining room. It was exactly as Ardery had described it, except for the fact that the source of the fire—the armchair—was gone. She said, unnecessarily, that she had taken it to the lab for testing, and she began talking about fibres and rates of burning and potential accelerants while Lynley ducked beneath a beam, crossed a passageway that was the depth of two fireplaces, and entered the sitting room. Like the dining room, it was cluttered with antiques, all of them covered with a layer of soot. As he looked from nursing chairs to settees, from corner cupboards to chests, he decided that Celandine Cottage was a holding tank for whatever hadn't already been crammed into Mrs. Whitelaw's house in Staffordshire Terrace. At least she was consistent, he thought. No Danish modern in the country to contrast with English nineteenth century in the city.

A magazine lay open on a tripod table, revealing an article entitled "Getting It" and an accompanying photograph of a woman with glossy pouting lips and masses of raven hair. Lynley picked up the magazine and flipped it to its cover. *Vogue.*

Isabelle Ardery was watching him from the doorway, arms folded beneath her breasts. Her expression was unreadable, but he realised she wouldn't be altogether pleased with his invasion into territory that they'd mutually decided would be hers. He said, "Sorry. It's a compulsion of mine."

"I'm not offended, Inspector," she said steadily. "If our positions were reversed, I'd be doing the same."

"I imagine you'd rather have the case on your own."

"I'd rather have lots of things I'm not going to get."

"You're far more resigned than I." Lynley went to the narrow shelf of books and began tipping them out, then opening each, one after the next.

"I've had an interesting report from the DS who took Mrs. Fleming to identify the body," Inspector Ardery said. She added in a patient voice as Lynley opened a small writing desk and began to finger through the letters, brochures, and documents inside, "Inspector, we have catalogued the contents of the entire building. Outbuildings as well. I'll be only too happy to provide you with the lists." When Lynley raised his head, she said with a degree of professional dispassion that he had to admire, "It might save time, actually. Our crime scene boys have a reputation for being thorough."

He appreciated the control she maintained over her feelings, which were no doubt getting progressively more ruffled with every moment he spent doing what she had already directed her crime scene team to do. He said, "Knee jerk reaction. I'll probably start taking up the carpeting next." He gave a final scrutiny to the room, noting pictures in heavy gilt frames and a fireplace as large as the one in the dining room. He checked this. Its damper was closed.

"The dining room as well," Inspector Ardery said.

"What?"

"The damper. It was closed in the dining room fireplace. That's what you were checking for, isn't it?"

"Substantiation for murder," Lynley said.

"You've eliminated suicide?"

"Not a single indication of it. And Fleming didn't smoke." He headed out of the sitting room, dodging the low oak beams that served as lintels for the doorways. Inspector Ardery followed him outside to the terrace. "What did the DS report to you?" Lynley asked.

"She didn't ask a single pertinent question."

"Mrs. Fleming?"

"She insisted upon being called Cooper, not Fleming, by the way. She saw the body and wanted to know why it was coloured so pink. Once she heard it was carbon monoxide, she didn't ask a thing. When most people hear the words *carbon monoxide poisoning*, they assume exhaust fumes, don't they? Suicide committed in a garage with a car's motor providing the means. But even if they make that assumption, they still ask. Where? How? Why? When? Did he leave a note? She didn't ask a thing. She just looked at the body, agreed it was Fleming, and asked the detective sergeant to buy her a packet of Embassys please. That was it.''

Lynley let his eyes take in the back garden. Beyond it lay another paddock. Beyond the paddock, the field of rape blazed its colour back towards the sun like a mirror. "They'd been separated for years as I understand it. She may have been worn down. She may have reached the point where she didn't have an interest in him any longer. If that's the case, why bother with questions?''

"Women tend not to become that indifferent to their former husbands, Inspector. Not when there are children involved.''

He looked back at her. A faint wash of colour made hot spots high on her cheeks. "Accepted,'' he said. "But it could have been shock that kept her silent.''

"Accepted,'' she said. "But DS Coffman didn't think so. She's stood in before when wives have had to identify their husbands. Coffman thought something was off.''

"Generalisations are useless,'' Lynley pointed out. "Worse, they're dangerous.''

"Thank you. I'm quite aware of that. But when the generalisation is coupled with the facts and with the evidence at hand, I think you'll agree that the generalisation ought to be examined.''

Lynley noted her posture: arms still crossed. He noted the even tone of her voice and the directness of her contact with his eyes. He realised he was questioning her theories for the same reason he had felt compelled to crawl through the cottage inch by inch in order to ascertain that nothing had been missed. He didn't like what lay behind his instinct to distrust her. It was chauvinistic. If Helen knew he was struggling with the fact that this fellow officer of equal rank was a woman, she'd give him the tongue lashing he well deserved.

"You've found something,'' he said.

So happy you were able to deduce that much, her expression replied. She said, "This way.''

Feeling chagrined, he followed her across the grass towards the bottom of the garden. The garden was divided into two sections separated by a fence. Two-thirds of it was given over to lawn, flower beds, a gazebo fashioned of split chestnut rails, a bird house, a birdbath, and a small lily pond. The other third was a strip of lawn interrupted by pear trees and partially covered with a compost heap. It was to this farther section of the garden that Inspector Ardery strode, taking him to the northeast corner where a box hedge served as demarcation between the garden and the paddock that lay beyond it. The paddock itself was marked off by fencing of wooden poles with heavy wire running between them.

Inspector Ardery used a pencil, which she took from her pocket, to point to the pole just beyond the box hedge. "There were seven fibres here, at the top of the pole. Another caught on the wire. They were blue. Possibly denim. And here, you can still see it although it's rather faint, we had a footprint just beneath the hedge."

"Type of shoe?"

"We don't know at the moment. Round toe, distinct heel, thick sole. A dog's tooth pattern. It was the left foot. Driven deep as if someone jumped from the fence into the garden, landing mostly to the left. We've taken a cast."

"Were there no other prints?"

"None to speak of in this area. I've two constables out looking for others to match, but it's not going to be easy, considering the time that's passed since the death. We can't even be sure that this print has anything to do with Wednesday night."

"Still, it's a place to start."

"Yes. That's what I think." She pointed to the southwest and explained that there was a spring some ninety yards from the cottage. It bubbled into a stream along which a public footpath wound. The footpath was popular with the locals since it ultimately led to Lesser Springburn, about a ten-minute walk away. Although the path was heavily covered with last autumn's leaves and this spring's new growth of grass, it gave way now and again—particularly near stiles—to sections of uncluttered earth. There would be footprints at those points, but since more than a full day had elapsed between the actual death and the discovery of the body, if this footprint by the box hedge had been repeated elsewhere, no doubt others had obscured it since then.

"You're thinking someone walked in from Lesser Springburn?"

It was a possibility, she said.

"Someone local?"

Not necessarily, she explained. Just someone who knew where to find the footpath and where the footpath led. It wasn't particularly well marked in Lesser Springburn. It began behind a housing estate and ducked quickly into an apple orchard, so someone would have had to know what he was looking for in order to take the route in the first place. She admitted that she couldn't say for certain that this was the route the killer had chosen, but she had an additional constable in the village, attempting to ascertain if anyone saw movement or torchlight on the footpath on Wednesday night and if anyone else saw a strange vehicle parked anywhere at all in the environs.

"We also found a scattering of cigarette ends along here." She gestured to the bottom of the hedge. "There were six, all lying within three or four inches of each other. Not crushed out, but allowed to burn down. There were matches as well. Eighteen. Book matches, not kitchen."

"Windy night?" Lynley speculated.

"A nervous smoker with shaking hands?" she countered. She gestured towards the front of the house, in the direction of Water Street. "We tend to think whoever popped over the fence and the hedge here started out by hopping the wall and coming along the paddock from the street. It's all grass and clover so there weren't any footprints, but it makes more sense than to assume someone sneaked up the cottage drive, came through the gate, dashed across the lawn, and hid himself here to watch for a while. And the number of cigarettes does suggest a watcher, wouldn't you agree?"

"But not necessarily a killer?"

"Quite possibly a killer. Building up his courage."

"Or her courage?"

"Or hers. Yes. Naturally. It could have been a woman." She looked towards the cottage as Havers and Mrs. Whitelaw came through the kitchen door. She said, "The lab has the lot: fibres, matches, cigarette ends, cast of the print. We should start getting some results this afternoon." Her nod at Lynley indicated that this professional offering of information was at an end. She began to head back to the cottage.

"Inspector Ardery," Lynley said.

She paused, glanced back in his direction. Her hairslide slipped and she made a moue of disgust as she refastened it. "Yes?"

"If you have a moment, I'd like you to hear whatever my sergeant has to report. I'd appreciate your input."

She favoured him with another one of her disconcerting, unwavering observations. He was aware of how little he was probably benefiting from the scrutiny. She tilted her head towards the cottage. "Had I been a man, would you have done the same in there?"

"I think so," he said. "But I probably would have had the tact to be more surreptitious. I apologise, Inspector. I was out of line."

The eyes didn't waver. "Right," she said evenly. "You were."

She waited for Lynley to join her, and they crossed the lawn to meet Sergeant Havers. Mrs. Whitelaw remained at the wicker table, where she sat, put on her dark glasses, and fixed her attention upon the garage.

"None of her things seems to be missing," Havers told them quietly. "Aside from the armchair from the dining room, everything's exactly where it was last time she was here."

"When was that?"

She made reference to her notes. "The twenty-eighth of March. Less than a week before Gabriella moved in. She says the clothes upstairs are all Gabriella's. And a set of suitcases in the second bedroom are Gabriella's as well. Nothing of Fleming's is anywhere."

"It looks as if he didn't intend to stay that night," Inspector Ardery said.

Lynley thought of the cat bowls, the Silk Cut, the clothes. "It looks as if she didn't intend to leave, either. Not as a long-range plan, that is." He studied the cottage from where they stood, continuing reflectively, "They have a tremendous row, the two of them. Mrs. Patten grabs her handbag and charges into the night. Our watcher by the box hedge sees his opportunity—"

"Or her opportunity," Ardery said.

Lynley nodded. "And makes for the cottage. He lets himself inside. He's come prepared so it doesn't take long. He lights the incendiary device, tucks it into the armchair, and leaves."

"Locking up behind him," Ardery added. "Which means he had a key in the first place. It's a mortise lock."

Sergeant Havers gave her head a rough shake. "Have I missed something?" she asked. "A watcher? What watcher?"

Lynley gave her the facts as they crossed the lawn to rejoin Mrs. Whitelaw beneath the arbour. Like the rest of them, she'd not yet removed her surgical gloves, and her hands looked oddly cartoonish lying white and folded in her lap. He asked her who had keys to the cottage.

"Ken," she said, after a moment's thought. "Gabriella."

"Yourself?"

"Gabriella had mine."

"Are there any others?"

Mrs. Whitelaw raised her head to look at Lynley directly, although he couldn't read her expression behind the dark glasses. "Why?" she asked.

"Because it does appear that Kenneth Fleming was murdered."

"But you've said a cigarette. In the armchair."

"Yes. I've said that. Are there any other keys?"

"People loved this man. Loved him, Inspector."

"Perhaps not everyone. Are there other keys, Mrs. Whitelaw?"

She pressed three fingers to her forehead. She appeared to be considering the question, but giving the question consideration at this point suggested two possibilities to Lynley. Either she believed that answering would indicate her acceptance of the direction their thinking was taking them: that someone had hated Kenneth Fleming enough to murder him. Or she was temporising while she decided what her answer was likely to reveal.

"Are there other keys?" Lynley asked again.

Her reply was faint. "Not really."

"Not really? Either there are or there aren't additional keys."

"No one has them," she said.

"But they exist? Where are they?"

She lifted her chin in the general direction of the garage. "We've always kept a key to the kitchen door in the potting shed. Under a ceramic planter."

Lynley and the others looked in the direction she had indicated. No potting shed was visible, just a tall yew hedge with a break through which ran a brick path.

"Who knows about that key?" Lynley asked.

Mrs. Whitelaw caught her lower lip between her teeth, as if realising how odd her answer was going to sound. "I don't precisely know. I'm sorry."

"You don't know?" Sergeant Havers repeated slowly.

"We've kept it there for more than twenty years," Mrs. Whitelaw explained. "If work needed to be done while we were in London, the workmen could get in. When we came out at the weekends, if we forgot the key, there was the extra."

"We?" Lynley asked. "You and Fleming?" In her hesitation to respond, he saw how he had misinterpreted. "You and your family." He extended his hand to her. "Show us, please."

The potting shed abutted the rear of the garage. It was little more than a wooden frame with roof and sides made of sheets of polythene and shelves attached to the upright beams that formed the frame. Mrs. Whitelaw stepped past a ladder and dislodged dust from an upright, folded table

umbrella. She moved aside a beaten-down pair of men's shoes and indicated on one of the crowded shelves a yellow ceramic duck whose hol-
lowed-out back served as a planter.

"Under this," she said.

Sergeant Havers did the honours, lifting the duck carefully at bill and
tail with the tips of her gloved fingers. "Not a sausage," she reported. She
replaced the duck and looked beneath the clay pot next to it, then beneath a bottle of insect spray, and along the shelf until she'd moved every
object.

Mrs. Whitelaw said, "The key must be there," as Sergeant Havers
continued to search, but the tone of her voice indicated a protest given
largely because it was the expected response.

Lynley said, "I assume your daughter knows about the extra key."

Mrs. Whitelaw's shoulders seemed to stiffen. "I assure you, Inspector, my daughter would have had nothing to do with this."

"Did she know about your relationship with Fleming? You mentioned you've been estranged. Was it because of him?"

"No. Of course not. We've been estranged for years. It has nothing to
do—"

"He was like a son. Enough so that you altered your will in his
favour. When you made that alteration, did you cut your daughter out
entirely?"

"She hasn't seen the will."

"Does she know your solicitor? Is it a family firm? Might she have
learned about the will from him?"

"The idea's absurd."

"Which part?" Lynley asked mildly. "That she would know about
the will or that she would kill Fleming?"

Mrs. Whitelaw's colourless cheeks took on sudden colour, rising like
flames from her neck. "Do you actually intend me to answer that question?"

"I intend to get to the truth," he replied.

She removed her dark glasses. She hadn't her regular spectacles with
her, so there was nothing to replace the dark glasses with. It seemed a
gesture designed largely for its effect, a listen-to-me-young-man movement worthy of the schoolteacher she had once been.

"Gabriella also knew there was a key out here. I told her about it
myself. She may have told someone. She may have told anyone. She may
have *shown* anyone where it was."

"Would that make sense? You said last night that she came here for seclusion."

"I don't know what went on in Gabriella's mind. She enjoys men. She enjoys drama. If letting someone know where she was and where the key could be found heightened the possibility of a drama in which she could play the starring role, she would have told him. She probably would have sent out announcements."

"But not to your daughter," Lynley said, drawing her back into the line of fire even as he mentally acknowledged the fact that her description of Gabriella fitted hand-in-glove with Patten's description on the previous night.

Mrs. Whitelaw refused to be drawn into argument. She said with deliberate calm, "Ken lived out here for two years, Inspector, while he was playing for the Kent county side. His family stayed in London. They visited him here at the weekends. Jean, his wife. Jimmy, Stan, and Sharon, his children. They'd all know about the key."

And Lynley refused to let her sidestep. "When was the last time you saw your daughter, Mrs. Whitelaw?"

"Olivia didn't know Ken."

"But she no doubt knew about him."

"They'd never even met."

"Nonetheless. When did you see her last?"

"And if she had, if she knew about everything, it wouldn't have made a difference. She's always had contempt for money and material things. She wouldn't have cared a fig who was inheriting what."

"You'd be surprised how much people learn to care about goods and money when it comes down to it. When did you last see her, please?"

"She didn't—"

"Yes. When, Mrs. Whitelaw?"

The woman waited a stony fifteen seconds before she answered. "Ten years ago," she said. "Friday evening, the nineteenth of April, at the Covent Garden underground station."

"You've a remarkable memory."

"The date stands out."

"Why is that?"

"Because Olivia's father was with me that evening."

"Is that significant somehow?"

"It is to me. He dropped dead after our meeting. Now, if you don't mind, Inspector, I'd like to step into the air. It's rather close in here, and I wouldn't want to trouble you by fainting again.''

He stepped aside to let her pass. He heard her ripping off her surgical gloves.

Sergeant Havers passed the ceramic planter to Inspector Ardery. She looked about the potting shed with its sacks of soil and its dozens of pots and utensils. She muttered, ''What a mess. If there's fresh evidence in here, it's muddled up with fifty years of gubbins.'' She sighed and said to Lynley, ''What d'you think?''

''That it's time we tracked down Olivia Whitelaw,'' he said.

OLIVIA

We've had our dinner, Chris and I, and I've done the washing up, as usual. Chris is dead patient when it takes me three-quarters of an hour to do what he could do in ten minutes. He never says, "Give over, Livie." He never shuttles me to one side. When I break a plate or a glass or drop a pan on the kitchen floor, he lets me handle the mess of it by myself and he pretends not to notice when I curse and cry because the broom and the mop won't behave as I'd like. Sometimes in the night when he thinks I'm asleep, he sweeps up the crockery or glass that I've missed from the breakage. Sometimes he scrubs down the floor to take away the stickiness from where the pan spilled. I never mention the fact that he's done this, although I hear him at it.

Most nights before he goes to bed, he cracks open the door to my room to check on me. He pretends it's to see if the cat wants to go out, and I pretend to believe him. If he sees I'm awake, he says, "One last call for felines wishing to engage in further nightly ablutions. Any takers in here? What about you, Panda-cat?" I say, "She's settled in, I think," and he says, "Need anything yourself then, Livie?"

I do. Oh, I do. I'm need incarnate. I need him to shed his clothes in the light from the corridor. I need him to slide into my bed. I need him to hold me. I have a thousand and one needs that won't ever be fulfilled. They peel my flesh from my body one thin strip at a time.

Pride will go first, I was told. It'll seep as naturally as sweat from my pores, and it will begin this process the moment I recognise how much of my life is in the hands of others. But I fight that idea. I hold on to who I am. I summon the ever weakening image of Liv Whitelaw the Outlaw. I say to Chris, "No. I need nothing at all. I'm fine," and I sound to my own ears as if I mean it.

Sometimes quite late he says casually, "I'm going out for an hour or so. Will you be all right on your own? Shall I ask Max to pop over?"

I say, "Don't be daft. I'm fine," when I want to say instead, "Who is she, Chris? Where did you meet? Does she mind that you can't spend the night with her because you've got to come home to tend to me?"

And when he returns from those evenings and looks in on me before he goes to bed, I can smell the sex on him. It's thick and raw. I keep my eyes closed and my breathing even. I tell myself I have no rights here. I think, His life is his life and mine is mine I've known from the first there would be no point of real connection between the two of us he made that clear didn't he didn't he didn't he? Oh yes, oh yes. He made that clear. And I made it clear that that's the way I wanted it. Yes indeed, that was fine with me. So it doesn't really matter, does it, where he goes or who he sees? The least of what I feel is hurt. I tell myself all this as I listen to the water running and hear him yawning and know how she's made him feel this night. Whoever she is. However they met.

I give a laugh as I write this. I recognise the irony of my situation. Whoever would have thought that I'd find myself longing for any man, let alone this man who from the first did everything possible to illustrate the fact that he was not my type.

My type, you see, paid for what he got off me, in one way or another. Occasionally my type and I made a deal in advance for gin or for drugs, but mostly for cash. You can't be surprised by this piece of information because no doubt you understand that it is, after all, so much easier for one to leap downward than to climb upward in life.

I worked the streets because it was black and wicked, living on the edge. And the older the bloke, the better I liked it because they were the most pathetic. They wore business suits and cruised Earl's Court, pretending to be lost and in need of direction. Miss, I wonder can you tell me the quickest way to Hammersmith Flyover? to Parsons Green? to Putney Bridge? to a restaurant called . . . oh my dear, I seem to have forgotten the name of it. And they waited, lips curving hopefully, foreheads shining in the dome lights of their cars. They waited for a sign, a "Want business, love?" and a lean into an open window of their cars and a finger run from their ears to their jaw. "I can do what you like. Whatever you'd like. What d'you like, a lovely man like you? Tell Liv. She wants to make you feel good." They'd stutter and begin to sweat. They'd say tentatively, How much? My finger would travel downward on their bodies. "Depends on what you want. Tell me. Tell me every nasty thing you want me to do with you tonight."

It was all so easy. They had marginal imagination once their clothes were off and their hips were hanging like empty saddlebags round their waists. I'd smile and say, "Come on, baby. Come to Liv. Do you like this? Hmm? Does this feel nice?" And they'd say, "Oh my dear. Oh my goodness. Oh yes." And in five hours I'd make enough to pay a week's rent on the bedsit I'd found in Barkston Gardens and have enough left over to keep myself happy with a half-gram of coke or a bag of pills. The life was so easy I couldn't understand why every woman in London wasn't doing it.

Every now and again a younger bloke would come by and give me the look. But I stayed with the older types, the ones with wives who sighed and cooperated six or eight times a year, the ones who were tears-in-their-eyes grateful for someone who squealed and said, "Aren't *you* the dirty one? Who would've thought it to look at you?"

Naturally, all this was connected to my father's death. I didn't need nine or ten sessions with Dr. Freud to tell me as much. Two days after I received the telegram telling me Dad had died, I took on my first bloke over fifty years old. I enjoyed seducing him. I revelled in saying, "Are you a daddy? D'you want me to call you Daddy? What would you like to call me in return?" And I felt triumphant and somehow redeemed when I saw those blokes writhe, when I heard them gasp, when I waited for them to moan a name like Celia or Jenny or Emily. Hearing that, I knew the worst about them, which somehow allowed me to justify the worst about myself.

Such was the way I lived until the afternoon I met Chris Faraday some five years later. I was standing near the entrance to Earl's Court

Station, waiting for one of my regulars, a basset-faced estate agent with hair sprouting like wires from his nose. He had a predilection for pain and he always carried in the boot of his car various devices for administering it. Every Tuesday afternoon and Sunday morning, he'd say mournfully as I got into the car, "Archie was naughty yet again, my dear. How on earth shall we manage to punish him today?" He'd hand over the cash and I'd count through it and decide the going rate for handcuffing, nipple clamping, whipping, or terrorising him round the genital area. The money was good, but the level of amusement was starting to decline. He'd taken to calling me Mary Immaculate and asking me to call him Jesus. He'd been shrieking something along the lines of "This is my body which I offer to the Almighty in reparation for your sins" as I upped the pain, and the more I slapped, twisted, or squeezed, the more I clipped this little pincher or that little clamp on to his body, the more he loved it and the more he wanted. But although he happily paid in advance and even more happily drove off to the wife in Battersea afterwards, he was looking more and more to me like sudden heart failure waiting to happen, and I wasn't keen on finding myself with a smiling corpse on my hands. So when Archie didn't show at our appointed time of half past five that Tuesday, I was partly put out and partly relieved.

I was thinking about the loss in cash when Chris crossed the street in my direction. Archie had made his request in advance for once, and with gathering up the costumes and props—not to mention the time involved in dressing myself, undressing him, playing wrestle and tug and oh-no-you-don't-you-bad-little-boy, tying, handcuffing, and using the enema bag—I was losing enough on this one afternoon to keep me in coke for days. So I was cheesed off when I saw this skinny bloke with rips in the knees of his jeans dutifully walking in the zebra crossing as if the police would drag him to the nick should he step off the pavement anywhere else. On a lead he had a dog of a breed so mixed that the word *dog* itself seemed little more than a euphemism, and he appeared to be walking to accommodate himself to the animal's limping and lunging gait.

As he passed, I said, "That's the ugliest thing I've ever seen. Why don't you do the world a favour and keep it out of sight?"

He stopped. He looked from me to the dog, and slowly enough that I could tell he was making an unfavourable comparison. I said, "Where'd you get that thing, anyway?"

He said, "I pinched him."

I said, *"Pinched?* That? Well, you've got some odd taste, haven't you?'' because aside from having only three legs, half of the dog's head had no hair. Where the hair had been there were red sores just beginning to heal.

"He *is* a sad one to look at, isn't he?" Chris said, gazing reflectively at the dog. "But it wasn't his choice, which is the circumstance that rather touches me about animals. They can't make choices. So someone has to care enough to make the right choices for them."

"Someone should choose to shoot that thing, then. He's a blight on the landscape." I dug through my shoulder bag for my cigarettes. I lit one and pointed it at the dog. "So why'd you pinch him? Looking for an entry in an ugly mutt contest?"

"I pinched him because that's what I do," he said.

"What you do."

"Right." He lowered his eyes to the shopping bags round my feet. The costumes were in them, as well as some new supplies I'd bought for Archie's entertainment. "And what do you do?"

"I fuck for money."

"So encumbered?"

"What?"

He gestured to my packages. "Or are you taking a break from shopping?"

"Oh right. I look like I'm dressed for shopping, don't I?"

"No. You look like you're dressed for whoring, but I've never seen a whore hanging about with so many shopping bags. Won't you confuse the potential customers?"

"I'm waiting for someone."

"Who's failed to show."

"You don't know that, do you?"

"There're eight cigarette butts round your feet. They all have your lipstick round their filters. Terrible colour, by the way. Red doesn't suit you."

"You're some expert, are you?"

"Not in the field of women."

"In the field of mutts like that one, then?"

He looked down at the dog, which had sunk to the pavement, head on the single forepaw and eyes slowly closing. He squatted next to him and gently cupped his hand round the top of the dog's head. "Yes," he said. "In this I'm an expert. I'm the best there is. I'm like fog at midnight, no sight and no sound."

"What shit," I said, not because I thought so but because there was something all at once chilling about him and I couldn't put my finger on what it was. I thought, Puny little bean, bet he couldn't get it up for love or money. And once I thought that much, I had to know. I said, "Want business, then? Your mate there can watch for an extra five quid."

He cocked his head. "Where?"

I thought, Got you, and said, "Place called the Southerly on Glouces-ter Road. Room 69."

"Appropriate."

I smiled. "So?"

He straightened. The dog lumbered to his feet. "I could do with a meal. That's where we were heading, Toast and I. He's been on display at the Exhibition Centre, and he's knackered and hungry. And a spot grumpy as well."

"So it *was* an ugly dog contest after all. I wager he won."

"In a manner of speaking, he did." He watched me gather up my packages and said nothing more until I'd stowed them under my arms. "Right then. Come along. I'll tell you about this ugly dog of mine."

What an odd sight we were: a three-legged dog with his head ground up, a rake-thin young-communist-for-freedom type wearing ragged jeans and a kerchief round his head, and a tart in red spandex and five-inch black heels with a silver ring through her nostril.

I thought at the time that I was on my way to an interesting conquest. He didn't seem keen to have it off with me as we leaned against the outside brick ledge of a Chinese take-away, but I thought he'd come round in good time if I played it right. Blokes usually do. So we ate spring rolls and drank two cups of green tea apiece. We fed chop suey to the dog. We talked in the way people do when they don't know how far to trust or how much to say—where are you from? who are your people? where'd you go to school? you left university as well? ridiculous, wasn't it, all that cock?—and I didn't listen much because I was waiting for him to tell me what he wanted and how much he intended to pay for it. He'd pulled a wad of notes from his pocket to buy the food, so I judged him to be willing to part with a good forty quid. When after more than an hour, we were still at the chitchat stage, I finally said, "Look, what's it going to be?"

"Sorry?" he said.

I put my hand on his thigh. "Hand? Blow? In and out? Front or back? What d'you want?"

"Nothing," he said.

"Nothing."

"Sorry."

I felt my face get hot as my spine went tight. "You mean I've just spent the last ninety minutes waiting for you to—"

"We had a meal. That's what I told you this would be. A meal."

"You bloody well didn't! You said where and I said the Southerly on Gloucester Road. Room 69, I said. You said—"

"That I needed a meal. That I was hungry. So was Toast."

"Bugger Toast! I'm out something like thirty quid."

"Thirty quid? Is that all he pays you? What do you do for that? And how do you feel when it's over?"

"What's it to you? Fucking little worm. Give me the money or I'll raise bloody murder right here in the street."

He looked about at the people passing and seemed to consider the offer. "All right," he said. "But you'll have to work for it."

"I said I would already, didn't I?"

He nodded. "So you did. Come along then."

I followed in his wake, saying, "Hand is cheapest. Blow depends on how long it takes. You wear a rubber for in and out. More than one position and you pay extra. Clear?"

"Crystal."

"So where're we going?"

"My place."

I stopped. "No way. It's the Southerly or nowhere."

"Do you want your money?"

"Do you want your crumpet?"

We were at an impasse on West Cromwell Road, with dinnertime traffic whirling by us and pedestrians trying to get on their way. The smell of diesel fumes made my stomach churn uneasily round the grease from the spring roll.

"Look," he said. "I've got animals waiting to be fed in Little Venice."

"More like this thing?" I kicked my toe towards the dog.

"You don't need to be afraid. I'm not going to hurt you."

"As if you could."

"That's open to question, isn't it?" He started on his way, tossing over his shoulder, "If you want the money, you can come along or fight me for it on the street. The choice is yours."

"I'm not an animal then? I've got a choice?"

He gave me a bright grin. "You're more clever than you look."

So I went. I thought, What the hell. Archie wasn't going to show, and since I'd never done much more than pass through Little Venice, it seemed harmless enough to give it a closer look.

Chris led the way. He never bothered to see was I following. He chatted to the dog, who stood about as tall as his thigh. He patted his head and encouraged him to lope along, saying, "You're getting the feel of it, aren't you, Toast? In another month, you'll be a proper hound. You like the thought of that, don't you?"

I thought, I've got a daft one here. And I wondered how he liked his sex with a woman and if he'd want to do it like dogs since he seemed to be so fond of them in the first place.

It was dark by the time we reached the canal. We crossed the bridge and descended the steps to the towpath. I said, "It's a barge, then?" He said, "Yes. Not quite finished, but we're working on it."

I hesitated. "We?" I'd gone off doing groups the previous year. They weren't worth the money. "I never said I'd do more than one of you," I told him.

He said, "More than . . . ? Oh, sorry. I meant the animals."

"The animals."

"Yes. We. The animals and I."

Daft in spades, I thought. "Helping you out with the building, are they?"

"Work goes faster when the company is pleasant. You must find that true in your line of employment."

I squinted at him. He was making fun. Mr. Superior. We'd see who ended up sweating for whom. I said, "Which one is yours?"

He said, "The one at the end," and he led me to it.

It was different then from what it is today. It was barely halfway done. Oh, the outside was finished, which is why Chris was able to get the mooring in the first place. But the inside was all bare boards, chunks of wood, rolls of lino and carpet, and boxes upon boxes of books, clothes, model airplanes, dishes, pots and pans, and jumble. It looked like a job for the rag-and-bone man, as far as I could tell. There was only one clear space at the front end of the barge, and it was taken up by the *we* Chris had mentioned. Three dogs, two cats, half a dozen rabbits, and four long-tailed creatures Chris called hooded rats. All of them had something wrong with the eyes or the ears, with the skin, with the fur.

I said, "You a vet or something?"

"Or something."

I dropped my packages and looked about. There didn't appear to be a bed. Nor was there much available floor space. "Where exactly d'you plan for us to do it?"

He unhooked Toast's lead. The dog wandered to join the others, who were struggling up from the various blankets on which they lay. Chris stepped through what would be a future doorway and rooted on a cluttered work top for several bags of animal food: kibble for the dogs, pellets for the rats, carrot tops for the rabbits, something tinned for the cats. He said, "We can start over there," and nodded his head to the steps we'd just descended to get into the barge.

"Start?" I set down my packages. "What've you got in mind, anyway?"

"I've left the hammer on that beam just above the window. See it?"

"Hammer?"

"We should manage to get a fair amount done. You shift the wood and keep me supplied with boards and nails."

I stared at him. He was pouring out the animals' food, but I could swear he was smiling.

I said, "You bloody damn—"

"Thirty quid. I'll expect quality for that. Are you up to quality?"

"I'll show you quality, I will."

Which is how it began with Chris and me, working on the barge. All that first night I expected him to make a move. I expected him to make a move in the nights and days that followed. He never did. And when I decided to make the move myself, to get him steaming so that I could laugh and say, "Aren't you just like all the others after all," before I let him have me, he put his hands on my shoulders and held me at arm's length, saying, "That's not what this is about, Livie. You and I. I'm sorry. I don't mean to hurt you. But that's just not it."

Sometimes now late at night I think, He knew. He could feel it in the air, he could hear it in the way I breathed. Somehow he knew and he decided from the first to keep his distance from me because it was safer that way, because he'd never have to care, because he didn't want to love me, was afraid to love me, felt I was too much, thought I was too challenging. . . .

I hold on to those thoughts when he's out at night. When he's out with her. He was afraid, I thought. That's why nothing ever happened between us. You love and you lose. He didn't want that.

But that's giving myself more importance to Chris than I've ever had, and in my honest moments I know that. I also know that the greatest incongruity in my life is that I lived in defiance of my mother's dreams for me, determined to meet the world on my terms and not on hers, and I ended up in love with a man to whom she would have given me in the first place. Because he stands for something, does Chris Faraday. And that's just the sort of bloke Mother would have most approved of, since at one time, before all this became such a muddle of names, faces, desires, and emotions, Mother stood for something as well.

That's where she began with Kenneth Fleming.

She never forgot about him once he left school to do his duty by Jean Cooper. As I've said, she arranged to get him employment in Dad's print factory, working one of the presses. And when he organised a factory team to play cricket with other factory teams in Stepney, she encouraged Dad to encourage "the lads," as she called them, to have a measure of fun together. "It will make them a more cohesive group, Gordon," she told him when he informed us that young K. Fleming—Dad always referred to his employees by initial only—had approached him with the idea. "A cohesive group does, after all, work more effectively, doesn't it?"

Dad ruminated, jaws and mind working at once as we ate our roast chicken and our new potatoes. He said, "It can't necessarily be a bad thing. Unless, of course, someone gets hurt. In which case, he'll be off work, won't he? And wanting his sick pay. There's that to consider."

But Mother persuaded him to her way of thinking. "True, but exercise is healthy, Gordon. As is the fresh air. And the camaraderie among the men." Once the team was organised, she never went to a match to watch Kenneth play. Still, I imagine she thought she'd done something to give the boy some pleasure in the life of drudgery that she no doubt saw him leading in a marriage to Jean Cooper. They'd had their second child on the heels of the first, and it looked initially as if life's promise for them was going to be a baby a year and middle age descending before their thirtieth birthdays. So Mother did what she could and tried to forget the bright future that Kenneth Fleming's past had once presaged.

Then Dad died. Then things began.

At first, Mother left the handling of the printworks to a manager she'd hired. This wasn't much different from the way Dad had run the operation. He'd never been one for mixing it up with the ink-and-press lads, which is what he had learned to call them from his own father before the Second World War, so he ran the business from the antiseptic silence of his third-floor office and left the day-to-day management of print runs, machinery, and the distribution of overtime to a foreman who'd come up through the ranks.

Four years after Dad died, Mother retired from teaching. She still had a score of good works that she could have used to fill her diary each week, but she decided to cast about for something more challenging to engage her time and her interest. She was lonely, I think, and surprised to find herself so. The classroom and its attendant preparation and paperwork had given her a daily direction in life, and without it she was finally forced to consider the void. She and Dad had never been companions of the soul, but at least he'd *been* there, a presence in the house. Now he wasn't and she had nothing pressing that would allow her to ignore the solitude that confronted her without her teaching and without him. She and I were as estranged as we could possibly be—both intent upon never forgiving the other for sins committed and injuries inflicted. There was certainly no promise of grandchildren to dandle. There was only so much housework to be done. There were only so many meetings to attend. She needed more.

The printworks was the logical solution, and Mother took over its running with an ease that startled everyone. But unlike Dad, she believed in what she called a hands-on-with-the-lads approach. So she learned the business as an apprentice would have done, and in doing so she not only garnered the respect of the men who worked the floor, she also reestablished her tie to Kenneth Fleming.

I've enjoyed imagining what their first encounter must have been like, those nine years after he fell from grace. I've pictured it surrounded by the noise of the presses, the smell of ink and oil, and the sight of documents or pages of one sort or another flying along the line to be packed. I've seen Mother working her way from one machine to the next beneath those dim and dirty windows, at her elbow the foreman with a clipboard in his hand. He's shouting to be heard and she's nodding and asking pertinent questions. They stop by one of the presses. A man looks up, greasy overalls, a streak of oil in his hair, thick black crescents beneath his nails, a spanner in his hand. He says something like, "Goddamn machine's gone down again. We got to modernise or close this place," before he notices Mother. Pause for dramatic music. They are face to face. Mentor and pupil. All those years later. She says, "Ken." He doesn't know what to say, but he twists his wedding band round his filthy finger and somehow that says it all and more: It's been hell, I'm sorry, You were right, Forgive me, Take me back, Help me, Make a difference in my life.

Of course, that's probably not at all the way it happened. But happen it did. And it wasn't long before more notice was taken of Kenneth Fleming's talents and intelligence in seven months than had been taken in all the years he'd laboured in what the ink-and-press lads always referred to as the pit.

The first thing Mother wanted to know was what Kenneth meant by modernising the place. The second thing she wanted to know was how she could set him back on the track of making something special of his life.

The first reply he made directed her towards the world of word processing, computers, and laser printing. The second reply suggested that she keep her distance. No doubt Jean had something to do with the latter. She can't have been delirious with joy to know that Mrs. Whitelaw had made an unexpected reappearance at the borders of her life.

But Mother wasn't one to give up easily. She began by elevating Kenneth out of the pit and into part-time management, just to give him a taste of the what-might-be's. When he was successful—as he couldn't help be, considering his cleverness and that damnable affability Dad and I had heard about over the dinner table for months on end when he was a teenager—she began to make furrows in the long uncultivated field of his dreams. And over this lunch or that tea, after a discussion on the best way to handle a salary dispute or an employee grievance, she discovered that the dreams were still there, unchanged after nine years, three children, and day after day in the noise and the grime of the pit.

I can't think Kenneth readily revealed to Mother the fact that he still cherished the hope of watching that cherry-red ball soar beyond the boundary, of hearing the crowd's roar of approval as another six runs appeared on the scoreboard at Lord's next to the name K. Fleming. There he was, twenty-six years old, father of three, tied to a wife, the best hope of an education behind him, and all of it the fault of an evening when he'd assured Jean Cooper that nothing could happen the first time she had sex without taking her pills. He wouldn't have said, "I dream of playing for England, Mrs. Whitelaw. I dream of walking the length of the Long Room with the eyes of the MCC upon me and the bat in my hand. I dream of descending those steps from the Pavilion, of striding onto the wicket beneath a bright June sky, of seeing the wash of colours speckling the crowd, of facing the bowler, taking position, feeling the electrical surge of contact the length of my arm as my bat strikes the ball." He wouldn't have said that, Kenneth Fleming. He would have smiled, said, "Dreams are for little chaps, aren't they, Mrs. Whitelaw. My Jimmy has dreams. And Stan shall have them as well in a year or two when he's grown a little." But as for himself, he'd have waved dreams off. They weren't for the likes of himself, he'd say. At least not any longer.

But she would have worn him down over time, my mother. She'd have begun with "But surely there's something more you hope for, Ken, something beyond this printworks." He'd have said, "This place has been good to me, good for my family. I'm fine as I am." To which she would have confessed, perhaps, a dream of her own gone unfulfilled. Perhaps they'd have had a late evening chat over coffee when she said, "You know, this is silly . . . confessing it to one of my former pupils after all, confessing it to a man, to a younger man even . . ." and then she would have revealed a little something no one knew about her, a little something which she, perhaps, concocted on the spur of the moment just to encourage Kenneth to open his heart to her as he'd done as a boy.

Who knows how she managed it exactly. She's never given me all the facts. All I know is that, while it took her nearly a year to gain his confidence, gain it she did.

The marriage wasn't bad, he probably told her one evening when the factory was silent as the grave beneath them and they were working late. It hadn't even gone sour as one might have expected it to do, considering how it had come about. It was just . . . No, it wasn't fair to Jean. It felt like betrayal to talk about the girl behind her back. She did her best, did Jean. She loved him, loved the kids. She was a good mother. She was a good wife.

"But something is missing," Mother would have replied. "Is that the case, Ken?"

Perhaps he picked up a paperweight, unconsciously curving his fingers round it like a cricket ball. Perhaps he said, "I suppose I hoped for more," with a wry smile after which he added, "But I got what I purchased, didn't I?"

"Hoped for what?" Mother would have wanted to know.

He would have looked embarrassed. "It's nothing. It's foolishness and that's all." He would have packed up his belongings, ready to leave for the night. And in the end by the door where the shadows partially obscured his face, he would have said, "Cricket. That's what it is. Some idiot I am but I can't let go what it might have been like to play."

To push the issue further, Mother would have said, "But you do play, Ken."

"Not the way I might have," he'd have replied. "Not the way I wanted. We both know that, don't we?"

And those few phrases, the longing behind them, and most of all the use of that magical *we* gave my mother the opening she needed. To change his life, to change the lives of his wife and children, to change her own life, and to bring disaster upon us all.

CHAPTER
8

It was mid-afternoon when Lynley dropped Sergeant Havers at New Scotland Yard. They stood on the pavement near the Yard's revolving sign, speaking in low voices as if Mrs. Whitelaw could hear them from where she sat inside the Bentley.

Mrs. Whitelaw had told them she didn't know her daughter's current whereabouts. But a phone call to the Yard and two hours' wait had taken care of the problem. While they managed a late lunch at the Plough and Whistle in Greater Springburn, Detective Constable Winston Nkata checked the PNC in London. He also riffled through files, called in debts, spoke to mates at eight different divisions, and talked to several PCs at their collators' offices, encouraging them to dip into their reference files for a mention of Olivia Whitelaw's name. He reported back to Lynley via the car phone just as the Bentley was crawling across Westminster Bridge. One Olivia Whitelaw, Nkata said, was living in Little Venice, on a barge in Browning's Pool. "The lady in question did some lamppost-leaning round Earl's Court a few years back. But she was too quick to get stung, according to DI Favorworth. Great name, that, isn't it? Sounds like a tart himself. Anyway, if someone from vice showed up in the street, she knew it the minute her eyes locked on to him. Vice liked to ruffle her feathers a bit by having her down to the station for a chat whenever they could, but that was as far as they ever got with her."

She currently lived with a bloke called Christopher Faraday, Nkata said. There was nothing on him. Not even a traffic ticket.

Lynley waited until Sergeant Havers had lit her cigarette, taken two lungfuls, and exhaled the wispy, grey remnants of smoke into the cooling afternoon air. He looked at his pocket watch. It was nearly three o'clock. She would check in with Nkata, pick up a vehicle, and head out to the Isle of Dogs to see Fleming's family. With time to work on her report taken into consideration, she would need at least two and a half hours, possibly three to get everything done. The day was fast dissolving. The night was booking itself up with further obligations.

He said, "Let's try for half past six in my office. Sooner if you can make it."

"Right," Havers said. She took a final deep pull on her cigarette and headed towards the Yard's revolving doors, dodging a group of tourists who were wearily pondering a map and talking about "taking a taxi next time, George." When she disappeared inside, Lynley slid into the car and put it in gear.

"Your daughter's living in Little Venice, Mrs. Whitelaw," he said as they pulled away from the kerb.

She didn't comment. She hadn't moved the slightest degree since they'd left the pub where they'd had their silent, tense, and—at least on her part—little-eaten lunch. She didn't move now.

"You've never run into her? You've made no attempt to locate her throughout the years?"

"We parted badly," Mrs. Whitelaw said. "I had no interest in locating her. I've little doubt the feeling was mutual."

"When her father died—"

"Inspector. Please. I know you're doing your job . . ."

But and the accompanying protest went unsaid.

Lynley gave her a quick examination in the mirror. At this point, eighteen hours into her knowledge of Fleming's death, Miriam Whitelaw looked as if she'd been spiritually drawn and quartered, a decade older than she had appeared even that morning when Lynley had fetched her. Her wan face seemed to beg for mercy.

It was, Lynley knew, the perfect opportunity to press for answers while her ability to resist and avoid his queries wore thinner each moment. Every one of his colleagues in CID would have recognised that fact. And most of those same colleagues would have sought the advantage, hammering out questions and demanding answers until they had the ones they sought. But to Lynley's way of thinking, there was generally a point of diminishing returns in the questioning of those intimately connected to a murder victim. There was a point at which those intimately connected with the murder victim would say anything in order to bring a ceaseless interrogation to an end.

"Don't be soft, laddie," DI MacPherson would say. "Mairder is mairder. Go for the throat."

It never quite mattered whose throat was being gone for. Eventually, the right jugular vein would be hit.

Not for the first time, Lynley wondered if he had a hard enough core to be a policeman. The take-no-prisoners approach to conducting an investigation was anathema to him. But any other approach seemed to place him far too dangerously close to empathising with the living instead of avenging the dead.

He negotiated his way through the traffic near Buckingham Palace, getting stalled behind a tourist coach that was disgorging onto the pavement a large group of blue-haired women in polyester trousers and sensible shoes. He wove through the taxis in Knightsbridge, did some back-street navigating to avoid a traffic snarl south of Kensington Gardens, and finally emerged into the late afternoon shopping and pedestrian frenzy that was Kensington High Street. From there, it was less than three minutes to Staffordshire Terrace, where all was tranquil and a solitary little boy wobbled on a skateboard across the street from Number 18.

Lynley got out to help Mrs. Whitelaw from the car. She took his offered hand. Her own was cool and dry. Her fingers closed over his tightly, then moved to his arm as he led her to the steps. She leaned against him. She smelled faintly of lavender, powder, and dust.

At the door, she fumbled her key against the lock, scraping metal across metal until she was able to get it in. When she had the door opened, she turned to him.

She looked so unwell that Lynley said, "May I phone your doctor?"

"I'll be all right," she said. "I must try to sleep. I couldn't last night. Perhaps tonight. . . ."

"Wouldn't you like your doctor to prescribe something for you?"

She shook her head. "There's no medication to prescribe for this."

"Is there any message you'd like me to give your daughter? I'm going to Little Venice from here."

Her gaze drifted past him, over his shoulder, as if she was considering the question. Her mouth pulled down at the corners. "Tell her I'll always be her mother. Tell her Ken doesn't . . . Ken didn't change that."

Lynley nodded. He waited to see if she would say more. When she didn't, he went back down the steps. He'd opened the car door when he heard her say:

"Inspector Lynley?" He raised his head. She'd come to the edge of the top step. One of her hands was gripping the wrought-iron banister where a tendril of star jasmine wound about it. "I know you're trying to do your job," she said. "I thank you for that."

He waited until she had gone inside and closed the door behind her. Then he set off again, heading north as he had on the previous night beneath the planes and sycamores in Campden Hill Road. The distance from Kensington to Little Venice was considerably shorter than the trip to Hugh Patten's house in Hampstead had been. But that trip had been made after eleven at night when traffic was thin. Now the streets were clogged with vehicles. He used the time it took to inch through Bayswater to telephone Helen, but he ended up listening to her answering machine voice telling him she was out and inviting him to leave a message. He said, "Damn," as he waited for the infernal beep. He hated answering machines. They were just another indication of the social anomie plaguing these final years of the century. Impersonal and efficient, they reminded him how easy it was to replace a human being with an electronic device. Where once there had been a Caroline Shepherd to answer Helen's phone, cook her meals, and keep her life in order, now there was a tape cassette, take-away Chinese, and a weekly cleaning woman from County Clare.

"Hullo darling," he said when the beep finally sounded. And then he thought, Hullo darling and what? Did you find the ring where I left it? Do you like the stone? Will you marry me? Today? Tonight? Damn. He loathed these answering machines.

"I'm going to be tied up till this evening, I'm afraid. Shall we have dinner? Sometime around eight?" He paused idiotically as if expecting a reply. "Have you had a good day?" Another witless pause. "Look, I'll phone you when I get back to the Yard. Keep the evening free. I mean if you get this message keep the evening free. Because of course I realise you might not get this message at all. And if you don't, I can't expect you to hang about waiting for me to phone, can I? Helen, do you have something planned for the evening? I can't recall. Perhaps we can—"

A beep sounded. A computerised voice recited, "Thank you for the message. The time is three-twenty-one." The line disconnected.

Lynley cursed. He replaced the phone. He utterly despised those blasted machines.

Since the day had been a fine one, Little Venice still accommodated a good number of people who were taking the afternoon to explore some of London's canals. They floated along in tour boats and listened to their guides' commentaries and gossip to which they appreciatively murmured in response. They strolled along the pavement, admiring the bright spring flowers that grew in pots on the roofs and the decks of barges. They dawdled at the colourful railing of the Warwick Avenue bridge.

To the southwest of this bridge, Browning's Pool formed a rough triangle of oleaginous water, one side of which was lined with more barges. These were the wide, full-size, flat-bottomed crafts that had once been towed by horses through the system of canals that crisscrossed much of the south of England. In the nineteenth century, they had served as a means of transporting goods. Now they were stationary, and they acted as housing for artists, writers, craftsmen, and poseurs of the same.

Christopher Faraday's barge floated directly across from Browning's Island, an oblong of willow-studded land that rose from the centre of the pool. As Lynley approached it along the walkway bordering the canal, a young man in running gear overtook him. He was accompanied by two panting dogs, one of which loped along unsteadily on only three legs. While Lynley watched, the dogs dashed ahead of the runner and scrambled up the two steps and onto the barge to which he himself was heading.

When Lynley got there, the young man was standing on the deck, towelling the sweat from his face and neck, and the dogs—a beagle and the three-legged mixed breed who looked as if he'd seen the worse end of too many street fights with worthier opponents—were noisily slurping water from two heavy ceramic bowls, which sat on a stack of newspapers. The word *dawg* was painted on the beagle's bowl, the words *dawg two* on the mixed breed's.

Lynley said, "Mr. Faraday?" and the young man lowered the blue towel from his face. Lynley produced his warrant card and introduced himself. "Christopher Faraday?" he said again.

Faraday tossed the towel onto the waist-high roof of the cabin and moved to stand between Lynley and the animals. The beagle looked up from his water, jowls dripping. A low growl issued from his throat. "S'okay," Faraday said. It was difficult to tell whether he was speaking to Lynley or to the dog, since his eyes were on the former but his hand reached back to touch the head of the latter. This was scarred, Lynley noted, with a long-ago incision running from the crest of the head to between the eyes.

"What can I do for you?" Faraday said.

"I'm looking for Olivia Whitelaw."

"Livie?"

"I understand she lives here."

"What's up?"

"Is she at home?"

Faraday reached for the towel and slung it round his neck. "Go to Livie," he said to the dogs. And to Lynley as the animals obediently trotted to a glass gazebo-affair that topped the cabin and acted as its entry, "Just a minute, all right? Let me see if she's up."

Up? Lynley wondered. It was just after half past three. Was she still plying her trade at night that she had to sleep in the middle of the day?

Faraday ducked into the gazebo and descended some steps. He left the cabin door cracked open behind him. Lynley heard a sharp bark from one of the dogs, followed by the scratching of claws against linoleum or wood. He moved closer to the gazebo and listened. Hushed voices spoke.

Faraday's was barely distinguishable. ". . . police . . . asking for . . . no, I can't . . . you've got to . . ."

Olivia Whitelaw's became clearer and far more urgent. "I can't. Don't you see? Chris. Chris!"

". . . cool . . . be okay, Livie. . . ."

A sound of heavy shuffling followed. Papers crinkled. A cupboard slammed. Then another. Then a third. Moments later footsteps came to the door.

"Mind your head," Chris Faraday said. He'd donned the trousers of a tracksuit. They'd once been red but now were faded to the same rusty colour of his wiry hair. This was overly thin for a man his age, leaving a small, monk-like tonsure at the top of his head.

Lynley joined him in a long, dimly lit, pine-panelled room. It was partially fitted with carpet and partially floored in linoleum beneath a large workbench where the mixed-breed dog had gone to lie. On the carpet lay three enormous pillows. Near them sat a hotchpotch arrangement of five old and mismatched armchairs. One of these contained a woman, dressed neck to toe in black. Lynley would not have seen her at first had it not been for the colour of her hair, which acted as a beacon against the pine walls. It was an incandescent white-blonde, with an odd cast of yellow to it and roots the colour of dirty engine oil. It was hacked short on one side, grown out to beneath her ear on the other.

"Olivia Whitelaw?" Lynley said.

Faraday moved to the workbench and opened a panel of shutters approximately an inch. The resulting aperture cast light on the wood-panelled ceiling and allowed a diffused glow to fall upon the woman in the chair. She shrank from it and said, "Shit. Chris, go easy," and she reached slowly to the floor next to her chair and picked up an empty tomato tin from which she removed a packet of Marlboros and a plastic lighter.

When she lit her cigarette, her rings caught the light. They were silver, worn on every finger. They matched the studs that lined her right ear like chromium eruptions and acted as counterpoint to the large safety pin that slid through her left.

"Olivia Whitelaw. That's right. Who wants to know and why?" The cigarette smoke reflected the light. It created the sensation that an undulating veil of gauze hung between them. Faraday opened another panel of shutters. Olivia said, "That'll do. Why'n't you piss off somewhere?"

"I'm afraid he'll need to stay," Lynley said. "I'd like him to answer some questions as well."

Faraday pressed the button on a fluorescent lamp above the workbench. It shed a brilliant, white, and decidedly area-specific glow upon that small section of the room. At the same time it also served to create a fulgent diversion for the eyes, urging them away from the old armchair where Olivia sat.

There was a stool in front of the workbench, and Faraday chose to perch on this. Looking between them, Lynley's eyes would constantly be making the adjustment from brightness to shadow. It was a clever set-up. They'd managed it so quickly and effortlessly that Lynley wondered if it had been a what-to-do-when-the-rozzers-finally-arrive predetermined behaviour.

He chose the armchair closest to Olivia. "I've a message from your mother," he said.

The tip of her cigarette flared like a coal. "Yeah? Tra lah. Should I celebrate or something?"

"She said to tell you that she'll always be your mother."

Olivia observed him from behind the smoke, eyelids lowered and one hand keeping the cigarette at the ready, two inches from her mouth.

"She said to tell you Kenneth Fleming didn't change that."

Her eyes stayed on him. Her expression didn't alter at the mention of Fleming's name. "Am I supposed to know what that means?" she finally asked.

"Actually, I'm misquoting her. At first she said Kenneth Fleming doesn't change that."

"Well, I'm glad to know the old cow can still moo." Olivia sounded largely bored. Across the room Lynley heard Faraday's clothing rustle as he moved. Olivia didn't look in his direction.

"Present tense," Lynley said. *"Doesn't.* And then the switch to past. *Didn't.* She's been trading between the two since last night."

"Doesn't. Didn't. I know my grammar. And I also know Kenneth Fleming's dead, if that's what you're slithering towards."

"You've spoken to your mother?"

"I read the newspaper."

"Why?"

"Why? What sort of question is that? I read the newspaper because that's what I do when Chris brings it home. What do you do with yours? Cut it up in squares to use on your bum when you shit?"

"Livie," Faraday said from his workbench.

"I meant why didn't you telephone your mother?"

"We haven't spoken in years. Why should I have done?"

"I don't know. To see if there was something you could do to make her grieving a bit easier?"

"Something along the lines of 'sorry to hear your toyboy's had his ticket cancelled prematurely'?"

"So you knew that your mother had a relationship of some kind with Kenneth Fleming. Despite the years during which you haven't spoken."

Olivia pushed her cigarette between her lips. Lynley saw from her expression that she recognised how easily he had led her into the admission. He also saw her evaluating what else she had inadvertently revealed.

"I said I read newspapers," she replied. Against the chair, it seemed as if her left leg was vibrating, perhaps with cold—which it was not inside the barge—perhaps with nerves. "Their story's been rather hard to avoid for the past few years."

"What do you know of it?"

"Just what's been in the papers. He worked for her in Stepney. They live together. She's helped his career. She's supposed to be like his fairy godmother or something."

"The expression *toyboy* implies more than that."

"Toyboy?"

"The expression you used a moment ago. 'Her toyboy's had his ticket cancelled prematurely.' That suggests something beyond merely being a fairy godmother to a younger man, wouldn't you agree?"

Olivia flicked tobacco ash into the tomato tin. She brought the cigarette back to her mouth and spoke behind her hand. "Sorry," she said. "I've a nasty mind."

"Have you assumed from the first that they were lovers?" Lynley asked. "Or was there something more recent that gave you the impression?"

"I haven't assumed anything. I haven't been interested enough to assume. I'm just reaching the logical conclusion one generally reaches about what happens when a todger and a grumble—usually but not always unrelated to each other by blood or marriage—occupy the same space for a period of time. It's the birds and the bees. Hard cock and wet twat. I don't imagine I need explain it to you."

"It's rather unsettling, though, isn't it?"

"What?"

"The idea of your mother with a man so much younger. Younger than yourself or perhaps your own age." Lynley leaned forward, elbows on his knees. He aimed for a posture declaring this a move towards earnest conversation and in doing so managed to get a better look at her left leg. It was indeed vibrating, as was her right. But she didn't seem to be aware of the movement. "Let's be frank," he said with as much ingenuousness as he could manage. "Your mother isn't a particularly youthful sixty-six-year-old. Did you never ask yourself whether she was blindly and foolishly putting herself into the hands of a man who was after something rather more than the dubious pleasure of taking her to bed? He was a nationally known sportsman. Don't you agree that he could probably have had his pick of willing women less than half your mother's age? That being the case, what do you imagine he had in mind when he took up with your mother?''

Her eyes narrowed. She weighed his questions. ''He had a mother complex he was trying to work out. Or a grandmother complex. He liked them old and wrinkled. He liked them when they sagged. Or he only felt a bonk was truly worthwhile if the curlies were grey. Have it anyway you want. I can't explain the situation.''

''But weren't you bothered by it? If, in fact, that was the nature of their relationship. Your mother denies it, by the way.''

''She can say and do whatever she wants, far as I'm concerned. Her life is her life.'' Olivia gave a low whistle in the direction of a doorway that appeared to lead into a galley. ''Beans,'' she called. ''Get out here with you. What's he up to, Chris? Did you fold the laundry when you brought it home? If you didn't, he'll be sleeping in the middle of it.''

Faraday slipped off his stool. He touched her shoulder and disappeared round the doorway, calling, ''Beans! Come on. Hey! Damn it.'' Then he laughed. ''He's got my socks, Livie. This bloody animal is chewing on my socks. Let go, you mongrel. Here. Give me those.'' The sound of tussling followed, accompanied by a dog's playful growling. Under the workbench, the other dog raised his head.

''You stay there, Toast,'' Olivia said. She settled her shoulders against her chair when the dog obeyed. She looked pleased with the diversion she'd effected.

''If you reached one conclusion about your mother's relationship with Fleming,'' Lynley said, ''I can't think it would be difficult to reach another. She's a wealthy woman, when one considers her property in Kensington, Stepney, and Kent. And you and she are estranged.''

''So what?''

''Are you aware of the fact that your mother's will names Fleming as her chief beneficiary?''

''Should I be surprised?''

''Of course, she'll have to alter it now that he's dead.''

''And you're thinking I've hopes she'll leave her ducats to me?''

''Fleming's death makes that a possibility, wouldn't you say?''

''I'd say you misjudge the degree of animosity between us.''

''Between you and your mother? Or you and Fleming?''

"Fleming?" she repeated. "I didn't know the bloke."

"Knowing him wasn't necessary."

"For what?" She took a hard pull at her cigarette. "Are you leading up to suggesting that I had something to do with his death? Because I wanted my mother's money? What a fucking joke."

"Where were you on Wednesday night, Miss Whitelaw?"

"Where was I? Jesus!" Olivia laughed, but her laughter triggered a sharp spasm of some kind. She gave a choked gasp and jerked back into her chair. Her face quickly reddened and she dropped her cigarette into the tin, gulping out, "Chris!" and turning her head to one side, away from Lynley.

Faraday hurried back into the workroom. He said quietly with his hands on her shoulders, "Okay. Okay. Just breathe and relax." He knelt at her side and began kneading her legs as the beagle joined him and sniffed her feet.

A small black-and-white cat wandered into the workroom from the direction of the galley, mewling softly. Under the workbench, Toast began to struggle to his feet. Faraday said over his shoulder as he worked on Olivia, "No! Stay! You too Beans. Stay," and he clucked softly till the cat was within his reach. He scooped it off the floor and dropped it into Olivia's lap, saying, "Hang on to her, Livie. She's been messing round with the bandage again."

Olivia's hands dropped over the cat, but her head pressed back against the chair and she didn't look at the animal. Eyes closed, she was breathing deeply—in through her nose and out through her mouth—as if her lungs might at any moment forget how to work. Faraday continued to massage her legs. He said, "Better? Okay? Easing up now, is it?"

Finally she nodded. Her breathing slowed. Her head dropped and she gave her attention to the cat. She said in a strained voice, "This isn't going to heal if she doesn't wear a proper collar to keep her paws from it, Chris."

Lynley saw that what had first appeared to be part of the cat's white fur was really a bandage that looped round her left ear and covered her eye. "Cat fight?" he asked.

"She's lost the eye," Faraday said.

"It's quite a group you've got here."

"Yeah. Well. I look after the toss-outs."

Olivia laughed weakly. At her feet, the beagle's tail thumped happily against her chair, as if he understood and took part in some obscure joke.

Faraday drove his fingers into his hair. "Shit. Livie . . ."

"It doesn't matter," she replied. "Let's not start displaying our nasties here, Chris. The inspector isn't interested in them. Just in where I was on Wednesday night." She raised her head and looked at Lynley, continuing with "Where you were, too, Chris. I imagine he'll want to know that as well. Although the answer is quick and easy enough. I was where I always am, Inspector. Right here."

"Can someone corroborate that?"

"Unfortunately, I didn't know I'd be needing corroboration. Beans and Toast would be happy to oblige, of course, but somehow I doubt you're fluent in dog."

"And Mr. Faraday?"

Faraday rose. He rubbed at the back of his neck. He said, "I was out. A party with some blokes."

"Where was this?" Lynley asked.

"Clapham. I can give you the address if you want."

"How long were you gone?"

"I don't know. It was late when I got back. I drove one of the blokes home, up to Hampstead first, so it must have been round four."

"And you were asleep?" This to Olivia.

"I'd hardly be anything else at that hour." Olivia had returned to her earlier position, head resting against the back of the chair. Her eyes were closed. She was petting the cat, who was studiously ignoring her and rhythmically working her thighs into a suitable state for napping upon.

Lynley said, "There's an extra key to the cottage in Kent. Your mother indicates that you know about it."

"Does she?" Olivia murmured. "Well, that makes two of us, doesn't it?"

"It's gone missing."

"And I suppose you'd like to have a look round here for it? It's an honest desire on your part, but one requiring a warrant. Have you got one?"

"I imagine you know that can be arranged without too much difficulty."

Her eyes opened a slit. Her lips twitched with a smile. "Why is it I think you're bluffing, Inspector?"

"Come on, Livie," Faraday said with a sigh. And to Lynley, "We

don't have any key to any cottage. We haven't even been in Kent since
. . . Hell, I don't know.''

"But you have been there?"

"Out to Kent? Sure. But not to a cottage. I didn't even know there
was a cottage till you brought it up.''

"So you don't read the newspapers yourself. The ones you bring
home for Olivia to read.''

"I read them, yeah.''

"But you took no note of the cottage when you read the stories about
Fleming.''

"I didn't read the stories about Fleming. Livie wanted the newspapers. I fetched them for her.''

"Wanted the newspapers? Expressly wanted them? Why?"

"Because I always want them," Olivia snapped. She reached out and
circled Faraday's wrist with her hand. "Stop playing the game," she said
to him. "He only wants to trap us. He's looking to prove we snuffed
Kenneth Fleming. If he can do it before dinner tonight, he'll probably
have time to give his girlfriend a length. If he's got a girlfriend." She
pulled at Faraday's wrist. "Get my transport, Chris." And when he didn't
move at once, she said, "It's okay. It doesn't matter. Go on. Get it.''

Faraday went through the door to the galley and came back bearing a
three-sided aluminium walker. He said, "Beans, one side," and when the
dog had shuffled out of the way, he set it in front of Olivia's chair.
"Okay?" he said.

"Okay.''

She passed him the cat, who mewled in protest until Faraday placed
her on the tattered corduroy seat of another armchair. He turned back to
Olivia, who grasped the sides of the walker and began to hoist herself to
her feet. She gave a grunt and a heave, muttering, "Shit. Oh, fuck it,"
when she teetered to one side. She shook Faraday's protective hand from
her arm. Finally upright, she glared defiantly at Lynley.

"Some killer we've got here. Right, Inspector?" she demanded.

Chris Faraday waited inside the barge at the bottom of the steps. The
dogs milled next to him. They nudged their heads against his knees, mistakenly expecting to be taken on another run. In their minds, he had on

the proper clothes. He was standing beneath the door. He had one hand on the railing. As far as they were concerned, he was moments away from dashing up and out, and they meant to accompany him.

He was, in fact, listening to the sounds of the detective's departure and waiting for his heart to stop bludgeoning his chest. Eight years of training, eight years of what-to-do-when-and-if had not been enough to keep his body from threatening a most disastrous display of suzerainty over his mind. When he'd first looked upon the detective's warrant card, his bowels had grown so immediately loose that he'd been certain he wouldn't be able to contain himself long enough to get to a toilet, let alone long enough to sit through an interview with the appropriate air of insouciance. It was one thing to plan, to discuss, even to rehearse with one member or another of the governing core playing the part of the police. It was another thing to have it finally happen, despite their precautions, and to have crowd into one's mind in an instant a hundred and one suspicions about who had betrayed them.

He imagined he felt the barge dip as the detective stepped off it. He listened hard for the sound of footsteps receding on the path along the canal. He decided he heard them, and he climbed up to open the door, not so much to check whether the coast was clear but to let in air. This he breathed deeply. It tasted vaguely of diesel fumes and ozone, just a fraction fresher than the smoke-filled cabin. He sat on the second step from the top and considered what ought to be done next.

If he told the governing core about the detective's visit, they would vote to disband the unit. They'd done it before with lesser cause than a visit from the police, so he had no doubt they'd move to disband. They'd transfer him for six months to one of the lesser arms of the organisation and reassign all the members of his unit to other captains. It was the most sensible thing to do when a breach of security occurred.

But of course, this wasn't really a breach of security, was it? The detective had come to see Livie, not him. His visit had nothing at all to do with the organisation. It was merely coincidence that a murder investigation and the concerns of the movement had intersected at this arbitrary point in time. If he held fast, said nothing, and above all stuck to his story, the detective's interest in them would pass. It was passing already, in fact, wasn't it? Hadn't the inspector crossed Livie off his list of potential suspects the minute he saw what condition she was in? Certainly he had. He wasn't a fool.

Chris punched his right knuckles into his thigh and told himself roughly to stop mismanaging the truth. He had to report the visit from New Scotland Yard's CID to the governing core. He had to let them make the decision. All he could do was argue for time and hope they weighed his eight years of involvement with the organisation and five years as a successful assault captain before they took their vote. And if they voted to disband the unit, it couldn't be helped. He'd survive. He and Amanda would survive together. It might be all for the better, anyway. No more seeing each other on the sly, no more acting the part of business only, no more soldier and captain, no more anticipating being called up before the governing core for useless explanations and subsequent discipline. They would, at last, be relatively free.

Relatively. There was still Livie to consider.

"Think he went for it, Chris?" Livie's voice sounded slurred, the way it always sounded when she used up energy too quickly and hadn't had time to regain the strength required to command her brain.

"What?"

"The party."

He took a final, marginally bracing breath of the tainted air and eased his body three steps down the ladder. Olivia had plopped back into her armchair and flung her walker against the wall.

"The story will hold," Chris replied, but he didn't add that there were phone calls to make and favours to ask to ensure that it held.

"He's going to check on what you told him."

"We've always known that could happen."

"You worried?"

"No."

"Who's your first back-up?"

He watched her evenly and said, "Bloke called Paul Beckstead. I told you about him. He's part of the unit. He's—"

"Yeah. I know." She didn't challenge him to embellish the story. She would have done once. But she'd ceased her attempts to trip him up in a prevarication just about the same time she began making the first round of doctors' visits.

They watched each other from across the room. They were wary, like boxers summing up the opposition. Only in their cases, if the blows rained down, they would beat against the heart, leaving the exterior body untouched.

Chris went to the set of fitted cupboards on either side of the workbench. He liberated the posters and maps he'd quickly removed from the wall. He began to replace them: *Love Animals, Don't Eat Them; Save the Beluga Whale; 125,000 Deaths Each Hour; For Whatever Happens to the Beasts, Happens to Man: All Things Are Connected.*

"You could have told him the truth about yourself, Livie." He balled up some Blu-Tack between his thumb and forefinger, affixing it once again to a map of Great Britain that was divided not by countries and counties but by horizontal and vertical segments labelled as zones. "It would have got you off the hook at least. I've got the party but you've got nothing except being here alone, which doesn't look good."

She didn't reply. He heard her patting the arm of her chair and clicking her tongue for Panda, who, as always, ignored her. Panda always went Panda's own way. She was a real cat's feline, won over only when it suited her interests.

Chris said again, "You could have told him the truth. It would have got you off the hook. Livie, why—"

"And it would have run the risk of putting you right on it. Was I supposed to do that? Would you have done that to me?"

He pressed the map against the wall, saw it was crooked, straightened it. "I don't know."

"Oh come on."

"It's the truth. I don't know. Put to the same test, I just don't know."

"Well, that's okay, isn't it. Because I do know."

He faced her. He dug his hands into the pockets of his tracksuit trousers. Her expression made him feel impaled like a bug on the pinpoint of her belief in him. "Look," he said, "don't make me out as a hero here. I'll only disappoint you in the long run."

"Yeah. Well. Life's full of disappointments, isn't it."

He swallowed. "How're the legs now?"

"They're legs."

"Didn't look good, did that? It was bloody awful timing."

She smiled sardonically. "Just like a polygraph. Ask the question. Then watch her convulse. Get out the darbies and read her the caution."

Chris joined her, dropping into one of the other chairs, the one the detective had chosen, across from her. He stretched out his legs and touched the toe of his running shoe to the toe of her black thick-soled boot, one of two pairs she'd bought when she first thought that all she needed was more adequate and consistent support for her arches.

"We're a pair," he said, nudging his toe along her instep.

"How's that?"

"I was bricking it outside when he said who he was."

"You? No way. I don't believe it."

"It's true. I thought I was done for. Dead cert."

"That'll never happen. You're too good to get caught."

"I've never seen getting caught in the act as the way it would go."

"No? Then what?"

"Something like this. Something unrelated. Something that happens through chance." He saw her shoe was untied and he bent to tie it. Then he tied the other although it didn't need it. He touched her ankles and straightened her socks. She reached out and grazed her fingers from his temple to his ear.

"If it comes down to it, tell him," he said. He felt her hand drop abruptly. He looked up.

"Here, Beans," she said to the beagle who had placed his front paws on the ladder. "And you! Toast. C'mon, you two fleabags, the both of you. Chris, they're trying to get out. See to the door, okay?"

"You may need to, Livie. Someone may have seen you. If it comes down to it, you tell him the truth."

"My truth is none of his business," she said.

CHAPTER
9

"I already talked to the police in Kent," were Jean Cooper's first words when she opened the door of her house on Cardale Street and found herself looking at Sergeant Havers' identification. "I told them it was Kenny. I got nothing else to tell. And who're those blokes, anyway? Did you bring them with you? They weren't here before now."

"Media," Barbara Havers said in reference to three photographers who, upon Jean Cooper's opening the door, had begun clicking away with their cameras on the other side of the waist-high hedge that, growing just beyond a low brick wall, separated the front garden from the street. The garden itself was a depressing square of concrete bordered on three sides by an unplanted flower bed and decorated intermittently with plaster casts of coy little cottages, handpainted by someone with extremely limited talent.

"You lot buzz off," Jean shouted at the photographers. "There's nothing here for you." They continued to click and snap away. She punched her fists to her hips. "You listening to me? I said piss off."

"Mrs. Fleming," one of them hailed her. "The Kent police are claiming a cigarette caused the fire. Was your husband a smoker? We've a reliable source who says he wasn't. Will you confirm that? Can you give us a comment? Was he alone in the cottage?"

Jean's jaw clenched to harden her face. "I got nothing to say to you lot," she called back.

"We've a source in Kent who claims the cottage was being occupied by a woman called Gabriella Patten. That's Mrs. Hugh Patten. Are you familiar with the name? Would you care to comment?"

"I just *said* I got nothing—"

"Have your children been informed? How are they taking it?"

"You bloody well keep away from my children! If you ask any one of them a single question, I'll have your balls in a skillet. You understand?"

Barbara mounted the single front step. She said firmly, "Mrs. Fleming—"

"It's Cooper. *Cooper.*"

"Yes. Sorry. Ms. Cooper. Let me come in. They can't ask any more questions if you do, and the only pictures they can take won't interest their editors. Right, then? Can I come in?"

"Did they follow you here? Did they? Because if they did, I'm going to phone my solicitor and—"

"They were here already." Barbara aimed for patience but at the same time remained uncomfortably aware of the whir of power-driven cameras and her disinclination for being photographed elbowing her way into the putative grieving widow's home. "They were parked over on Plevna Street. Behind a lorry near the surgery. Their cars were hidden." She automatically added, "I'm sorry."

"Sorry," Jean Cooper scoffed. "Don't give me that. None of you lot's sorry about anything."

But she stepped back from the door and let Barbara into the sitting room of the small terraced house. She seemed to be in the process of some form of housecleaning, because several large black rubbish bags gaped half-filled on the floor and as she kicked these to one side to give Barbara access to a sagging three-piece suite, a hugely muscled man came down the stairs with three boxes stacked in his arms. He said with a laugh, "Great stuff that, Pook. But you ought t'said we was too busy wringing out our snot rags to talk to them now. Ooh. Please. Excuse me, copper, I can't converse at the moment cos I need to have myself another boo hoo." He hooted.

"Der," Jean said. "This's the police."

The man lowered the boxes. He looked more belligerent than embarrassed to have been caught speaking unguardedly. He gave Barbara a disbelieving scrutiny that quickly metamorphosed into a dismissive once over. *What a moo, what a minge bag,* his expression said. Barbara stared back. She held the man pinned with her vision until he thumped the boxes onto the floor near the doorway that led into the kitchen. Jean Cooper introduced him as her brother Derrick. She said to him, unnecessarily:

"She's here about Kenny."

"Is she?" He leaned against the wall and balanced on one foot with the other tipped on its toe in an odd dancer's position. He had unusually small feet for a man his size, made smaller looking by his capacious purple trousers, which were banded by elastic at the waist and the ankles and looked like something a harem dancer might wear. They appeared to be tailored to accommodate the tree-trunk size of his thighs. "What about him, then? You ask me, the naffing little creep finally got his comeuppance." He aimed his finger at his sister and cocked his thumb like a gun in her direction, although his performance seemed to be largely geared for Barbara's benefit. "Like I been saying all along, Pook, you lot're better off without the bleeding wanker. Mr. Effing K.F. Mr. Honeyarse taste so sweet when you kiss it. You ask me—"

"You got all Kenny's books, Der?" his sister asked pointedly. "There's more in the boys' room. But mind you check the insides for his name before you pack them. Don't take any of Stan's."

He folded his arms across his chest as well as he could, considering the girth of his pectorals and the limited range of motion caused by the bulge of his biceps. The position, while no doubt chosen to demonstrate dominance, merely emphasized the oddity of his physique. Through intensive weight training he'd managed to enlarge every part of his body except those whose size was predetermined by lack of muscle or the natural restrictions of skeletal growth. Hence, his hands, his feet, his head, and his ears seemed curiously delicate.

"You trying to get rid of me? 'Fraid I'll tell this sweet shitbag copper what a rude little prick you was married to?"

"That'll do," Jean said sharply. "If you want to stay, stay. But keep your mug shut because I'm just this close . . . just this close, Der . . ."

She held her thumb pinched to her index finger so that only the space between her nails was left. Her hand trembled. She buried it roughly into the pocket of her housecoat. "Oh bugger it all," she whispered, "all of it, *bugger* it."

Her brother's expression of insolent aggression vanished immediately. "You're dead knackered." He moved his mass from the wall. "You need a cuppa. You won't eat, fine. I can't make you do that. But you're having a cuppa and I'm standing over you till you drink every drop. I'll see to it, Pook." He went into the kitchen and started turning on water and slamming cupboards.

Jean began moving the half-filled rubbish bags nearer the stairway. She said, "Sit down, then," to Barbara. "Say what you've come to say. Then leave us be."

Barbara remained standing by an old television set while the other woman continued to shift the bags, lugging one to a deep cupboard beneath the stairway. There she pulled out a collection of scrapbooks and albums. She kept her attention fixed on their dusty covers, either in avoidance of Barbara or in avoidance of what the books and their pages displayed. They appeared to contain both photographs and news cuttings, but these had apparently been ill mounted inside because several pictures and several more articles fluttered to the floor as Jean transferred each large, dusty portfolio from the cupboard to the rubbish bag.

Barbara squatted to gather them. The headline of every article had the name Fleming highlighted in orange. They appeared to document the batsman's career. The photographs, on the other hand, chronicled his life. Here he was a child, there a grinning teenager with a contraband gin bottle raised in a salute, there a young father laughing as he swung a small boy by his hands.

Had the situation surrounding the man's death been different, Barbara would have said, "Wait. Please, Ms. Cooper. Don't throw these away. Hold on to them. You don't want them now because the pain's too raw. But you will eventually. Go slow here, won't you?" But any need she may have felt to offer those words of caution and sympathy diminished when she considered the possible implications behind a woman's holding on to so many mementoes of the man who had left her.

Barbara dropped pictures and cuttings into one of the bags. She said, "Did your husband tell you anything about this, Ms. Cooper?" and handed Jean one of the documents she'd removed from the davenport in Mrs. Whitelaw's house that morning. It was a letter from Q. Melvin Abercrombie, Esq., Randolph Ave., Maida Vale. Barbara had already memorised its brief contents, verification of an appointment with the solicitor.

Jean read the letter and handed it back. She returned to her packing. "He had a meet with a bloke in Maida Vale."

"I can see that, Ms. Cooper. Did he tell you about it?"

"Ask him. The bloke. Mr. Nibhead Ashercrown or whoever he was."

"I can phone Mr. Abercrombie for the information I need," Barbara said. "Because a client is generally frank with his solicitor when he begins the process of divorce, and a solicitor is generally more than happy to be frank with the police when that client's been murdered." She saw Jean's hands close tightly round the edges of an album. Bull's-eye, she thought. "There are papers to be filed and others to be served, and no doubt this bloke Abercrombie knows exactly how far your husband got doing what. So I could phone him for the information, but when I find out, I'll only return to talk to you again. And the press will no doubt still be outside, snapping away and wondering what the coppers are on to and why. Where are your children, by the way?"

Jean stared at her defiantly.

"They know their father is dead, I take it?"

"They aren't new potatoes, Sergeant. What the hell do you think?"

"Do they also know that their father had recently asked you for a divorce? And he *had* asked you, hadn't he?"

Jean inspected the torn corner of one of the picture albums. With her thumb, she smoothed the rent in the artificial leather.

"Tell her, Pook." Derrick Cooper had come to the kitchen doorway, a box of P.G. Tips in one hand and in the other a mug decorated with Elvis Presley's famous sneer-smile. "What difference does it make? Tell her. You don't need him. You never needed him."

"Which is just as well, isn't it, him being dead." Jean raised her pale face. "Yes," she said to Barbara. "But you knew the answer already, didn't you, 'cause he would of told the old crow that he gave me the word and the crow would of been only too chuffed to pass the news on to everyone in London, especially if it could make me look bad which is what she's been working at for the last sixteen years."

"Mrs. Whitelaw?"

"Her and who else."

"Trying to make you look bad? Why?"

"I wasn't ever good enough to marry her Kenny." Jeannie snorted a laugh. "Like Gabriella was?"

"Then you knew he intended to marry Gabriella Patten?"

She shoved the album she was holding into one of the bags. She looked about for more employment, but nothing seemed to be at hand. She said, "These need binding up, Der. Where'd you put the wire? Is it still upstairs?" And she watched him plod up to the first floor in reply.

"Did your husband tell your children about the divorce?" Barbara asked. "Where are they, by the way?"

"Leave them out of this," Jeannie said. "Leave them bloody well alone. They've had enough. Four years of enough and it's going no further."

"I understand your son had a holiday planned with his father. Boating in Greece. They were supposed to leave last Wednesday evening. Why didn't they go?"

Jean pushed herself off the floor and walked to the sitting room window where she took a packet of Embassys from the sill and lit one.

"You got to quit that shit," her brother said as he lumbered down the stairs and flipped a roll of wire onto one of the bags. "How many times I got to tell you that, Pook?"

"Yeah," she said. "Right. But now's not exactly the moment. Weren't you making tea? I heard the kettle shut off."

He scowled and disappeared into the kitchen. Water poured and a spoon clinked energetically round a cup. He returned with the tea. He set it on the window-sill and dropped onto the sofa. He assumed a position with legs crossed at the ankles on the coffee table, which communicated his intention of remaining throughout the rest of the interview. Let him, Barbara thought. She returned to previously cultivated ground.

"Your husband had told you he wanted a divorce? He'd told you he intended to remarry? He told you he'd be marrying Gabriella Patten? Did he tell your children all this? Did you tell them?"

She shook her head.

"Why not?"

"People change their minds. Kenny was people."

Her brother groaned. "That shitbag wasn't people. He was a fucking star. He was writing his legend and you lot here was a finished chapter. Why'n't you ever see that? Why'n't you just let go?"

Jean shot him a look.

"You could of found somebody else by now. You could of gave your kids a real dad. You could of—"

"Shut your face, Der."

"Hey. Watch who you're talking at."

"No. You watch. You can stay if you want, but just shut up. About me, 'bout Kenny, 'bout everything. Okay?"

"Listen." He jutted his chin at his sister. "Know what your problem is? What it always was. You don't want to face what you never want to face. That bloody sod thought he was God Almighty with the rest of us born just to lick his arse and you can't see it, can you?"

"You're talking rot."

"You still can't see it. He walked out on you, Pook. He found a nicer bit of pussy to play with. You knew it when it happened and still you waited for him to have enough of her and come catting back home."

"We had a marriage. I wanted to keep it."

"You had something, all right." His small acorn-shaped eyes slit shut when he smirked. "You was the doormat and he was the boots. Did you like getting tramped on?"

Jean stubbed out her cigarette as carefully as if the ashtray were a piece of Belleek and not what it was, a bit of shell-shaped tin. "Enjoy saying that?" she asked in a low voice. "Make you feel like somebody? Make you feel big?"

"I'm only saying what you need to hear."

"You're only saying what you been wanting to say since you was eighteen years old."

"Oh shit. Don't be daft."

"When you first knew Kenny was ten times the man you ever hoped to be."

Derrick's biceps grew taut. He dropped his legs to the floor.

"Bugger that rot. Bugger it. Bug—"

"All right," Barbara said. "You've made your point, Mr. Cooper."

Derrick's eyes snapped to her. "What's it to you?"

"You've said enough. We've got the message. Now I'd like you to leave so that I can talk to your sister."

He rose in a surge. "Who the hell you telling to shove off here?"

"You. I'm telling you. I thought that was clear. Now can you find the door yourself or do you need my assistance?"

"Oooh, just listen to her. I'm shitting my knickers."

"Then I'd walk carefully if I were you."

His face flamed. "You shit-eating slag. I'll—"

"Der!" Jean said.

"Piss off out of here, Cooper," Barbara said quietly, "because if you don't, I'll have you in the nick so fast that you won't have time to impress the screws by flexing."

"You snot-nosed piece of—"

"But I'll put a week's pay on most of the lags liking you just fine."

An ugly vein popped out on his forehead. His chest expanded. His right arm dropped back. His elbow bent.

"Try me," Barbara said, moving onto the balls of her feet. "Try me. Please. I've ten years of Kwai Tan and I'm itching to use them."

"Derrick!" Jean put herself between Barbara and her brother. He was breathing in a way that reminded Barbara of a water buffalo she'd once watched at the zoo. "Derrick," Jean said again. "Go easy. She's a cop."

"Don't mean bugger all."

"You do what she says. Derrick! You hear? Derrick!" She grabbed his arm and shook it.

His eyes seemed to unglaze. They moved from Barbara to his sister. "Yeah," he said. "I hear." He raised a hand as if to touch his sister's shoulder, but he lowered it before he made contact with her.

"You go home," she said and touched her forehead to his arm. "I know you mean good, but we got to talk alone, her and me."

"Mum and Dad're broke up 'bout this," he said. "Kenny."

"That's no surprise."

"They always liked him, Pook. Even after he left. They always took his side."

"I know that, Der."

"They thought it was you. I said it wasn't fair to think like that when they didn't know what's what, but they'd never listen. Dad'd say, What in hell's name d'you know about having a successful marriage, you twit."

"Dad was cut up. He didn't mean to talk nasty."

"They always called him *son*. Son, Pook. Why? I was their son."

Jean smoothed her hand against his hair. "You go on home, Der. Things'll be all right. Go on. Okay? Through the back, though. Don't let those wallies out front get at you."

"I ain't afraid of them."

"No need giving them something to write about. Go out the back, okay?"

"Drink your tea."

"I will."

She sat on the sofa as her brother went into the kitchen. A door opened and closed. Then a moment later, a gate in the back garden creaked on rusty hinges. Jean cradled the mug of tea in her hands.

"Kwai Tan," she said to Barbara. "What's that?"

Barbara found that she was still on her toes. She came down off them and began to breathe normally. "Haven't a clue. I think it's a way to cook chicken."

She reached in her shoulder bag for her cigarettes. She lit, smoked, and wondered when the last time it was that a burning carcinogen had tasted this good. ASH be damned. She was owed this fag. She dodged two rubbish bags and made her way to one of the chairs of the three-piece suite. She sat. The cushion was so old and so thin that it felt as if it were filled with bird shot. "Did you speak to your husband any time on Wednesday?"

"Why would I?"

"He was supposed to take your son boating. They were supposed to leave Wednesday evening. The plans got changed. Did he phone to tell you?"

"It was for Jimmy's birthday. That was the promise, leastways. Who knows if he meant it?"

"He meant it," Barbara said. Jean looked up sharply. "We found the plane tickets in one of his jackets in Kensington. And Mrs. Whitelaw told us that she helped him pack and watched him put his gear in the car. But somewhere along the line, his plans got changed. Did he tell you why?"

She shook her head and drank from the mug of tea. Barbara noticed that it was one of those trick mugs on which the picture changed when the liquid heated it. Young Elvis sneer-smiling had altered to the bloated Elvis of his later years, satin-garbed and warbling into a microphone.

"Did he tell Jimmy?"

Jean's hands closed round the mug. Elvis disappeared beneath her fingers. She watched the level of the tea rise from right to left as she tilted the mug back and forth. She finally said, "Yeah. He talked to Jimmy."

"When was this?"

"I don't know what time."

"You don't need to be exact. Was it morning? Afternoon? Just before they were supposed to be leaving? He was going to drive here and fetch the boy, wasn't he? Did he phone shortly before he was to arrive?"

She lowered her head farther, giving closer scrutiny to her tea.

Barbara said, "Go back through the day mentally. You got up, got dressed, perhaps got the children ready for school. What else? You went to work. You came home. Jimmy was packed for the trip. He was unpacked. He was ready. He was excited. He was disappointed. What?"

The tea continued to hold her attention. Although her head was still lowered, Barbara could see from the movement of her chin that she was chewing on the inside of her lower lip. Jimmy Cooper, she thought with a stirring of interest. What might the rozzers at the local substation have to say when they heard the name?

"Where *is* Jimmy?" she asked. "If you can't tell me anything about this Greece trip and his father—"

Jean said, "Wednesday afternoon." She raised her head as Barbara tapped cigarette ash into the tin shell. "Wednesday afternoon."

"That's when he phoned?"

"I took Stan and Shar to the video shop so they could each have a film for when Jimmy left with their dad. So they wouldn't feel bad they weren't going as well."

"This was after school, then."

"When we got home, the trip was off. Round half four."

"Jimmy told you?"

"He didn't need to tell me. He'd unpacked. All his gear was slung about his room."

"What did he say?"

"That he wasn't going to Greece."

"Why?"

"I don't know."

"But he knew. Jimmy knew."

She lifted the tea and drank. She said, "I expect some cricket business came up and Kenny had to see to it. He was hoping to be chosen for England again."

"But Jimmy didn't say?"

"He was cut up. He didn't want to talk."

"Still, he felt let down by his dad?"

"He'd been dead keen on going and then it was off. Yeah. He was let down."

"Angry?" When Jean glanced her way sharply, Barbara said in easy explanation, "You mentioned that he hadn't unpacked so much as thrown his clothes about the room. That sounds like temper to me. Was he angry?"

"Like any kid would be. No different from that."

Barbara stubbed out her cigarette and took her time about considering whether to light another. She rejected the idea. "Does Jimmy have a means of transportation?"

"Why'd you need to know that?"

"Did he stay home Wednesday night? Stan and Shar had their videos. He had his disappointment. Did he stay home with you or go out and do something to cheer himself up? He was cut up, you said. He'd have probably wanted something to lift his spirits."

"He was in and out. He's always in and out. He likes to mess about with his mates."

"And Wednesday night? He was with his mates then? What time did he come home?"

Jean placed her mug of tea on the coffee table. She pushed her left hand into the pocket of her housedress and seemed to find something to grasp inside. Out on the street, a woman's voice shrilled, "Sandy, Paulie, teatime! Come inside before it gets cold."

"Did he come home at all, Ms. Cooper?" Barbara asked.

"Course he did," she said. "I just don't know the time, do I? I was asleep. The boy has his own key. He comes and he goes."

"And he was here in the morning when you got up?"

"Where else would he be? In the dust bin?"

"And today? Where is he? With his mates again? Who are they, by the way? I'll need their names. Especially the ones he was with on Wednesday."

"He's taken Stan and Shar off somewhere." She indicated the rubbish bags with a dip of her head. "So they wouldn't have to see their dad's things packed."

"I'm going to need to talk to him eventually," Barbara said. "It would be easier if I could see him now. Can you tell me where he's gone?"

She shook her head.

"Or when he'll return?"

"What could he say that I can't?"

"He could tell me where he was Wednesday night, and what time he got home."

"I don't see what help that would be to you."

"He could tell me what his conversation with his father was all about."

"I've said already. The trip was off."

"But you haven't said why."

"What does *why* matter?"

"*Why* tells us who might have known Kenneth Fleming was going to Kent." Barbara watched for Jean Cooper's reaction to the statement. It was subtle enough, a mottling of skin where her floral housedress exposed a pale triangle of chest. The colour climbed no higher. Barbara said, "I understand you spent weekends out there when your husband first played on the county side. You and the children."

"What if we did?"

"Would you drive out yourself to the cottage? Or would your husband come to fetch you?"

"We'd drive out."

"And if he wasn't there when you arrived? Had you your own set of keys to let yourself in?"

Jean's back straightened. She crushed her cigarette out. "I see," she said. "I know what you're saying. Where was Jimmy on Wednesday night? Did he ever come home? Was he in a temper over his holiday being spoiled? And if you don't mind my asking, could he have pinched a set of keys to the cottage, popped out to Kent, and killed his own dad?"

"It's an interesting question," Barbara noted. "I wouldn't mind in the least if you commented on it."

"He was home, *home*."

"But you can't say what time."

"And there isn't any bloody keys for anyone to pinch. There never was."

"So how did you get into the cottage when your husband wasn't there?"

Jean was caught up short. She said, "What? When?"

"When you used to go to Kent at the weekends. How did you get in if your husband wasn't there?"

Jean gave an agitated pull at the collar of her dress. The action seemed to calm her because she raised her head and said, "There was a key always kept in a shed, back of the garage. We used that to get in."

"Who knew about that key?"

"Who knew? What difference does it make? We all bloody knew. All right?"

"Not quite. The key's gone missing."

"And you think Jimmy took it."

"Not necessarily." Barbara lifted her bag from the floor and slung it to her shoulder. "Tell me, Ms. Cooper," she said in conclusion, knowing the answer without having to hear it, "is there anyone who can verify where you were on Wednesday night?"

Jimmy paid for the crisps, the Cadbury bars, the Hob Nobs, and the Custard Cremes. Earlier, at the bottom of the stairs where the fruit vendor had his stall at Island Gardens Station, he'd pinched two bananas, a peach, and a nectarine while some old cow with too much pink scalp and too little blue hair kept whining about the price of sprouts. As if anyone with sense would eat those filthy green gobs in the first place.

He had plenty of money to pay for the fruit. Mum had passed him ten quid that morning and said to give Stan and Shar a treat somewhere nice. But bananas, peaches, and nectarines didn't qualify as treats and even if that hadn't been the case, his act of petty theft had been a matter of principle. The fruit vendor was a first-class toe-rag, always had been, always would be. "Flipping yobs," he'd mutter whenever some of the blokes from school would pass too close to his naffing tomatoes. "Stop poncing round here. Get some decent employment, you miserable louts." So it was a matter of honour among the blokes from George Green Comprehensive to nick as much fruit and veg as possible from the freaking jack.

But Jimmy had no grudge against the old bugger who ran the Island Gardens refreshment caff. So when they trotted over to the squat building at the edge of the green, when Shar asked for crisps and a chocolate bar, and when Stan pointed silently to the Hob Nobs and the Custard Cremes, Jimmy shoved a five-quid note across the counter willingly, not knowing at first how to respond when the old boy said, "Nicest sort of a day for an outing, dearie, isn't it?" and patted his hand. At first Jimmy thought the old bloke was a fairy trying to pull him with the hope of doing a brown behind the counter when no one was looking. But then he looked at him closer when the old man handed him the change from his purchases and he realised from the goopy screen of white across his eyes that the poor sod was nearly blind. He'd seen Jimmy's hair, but he'd heard Sharon's voice. He thought he was flirting with a local bird.

They'd already had two egg sandwiches and a sausage roll riding on the docklands train from Crossharbour down to the river. It wasn't a long trip—two stations was all—but they'd had enough time to wolf down their food and wash it back with two Cokes and a Fanta orange. Shar had said, "I don't think we're s'pose to eat on the train, Jimmy." Jimmy said, "So don't if you're scared," and bit off a hunk of sandwich that he chewed with an open mouth right next to her ear. "Munch, munch, munch," he'd said with his mouth full of bread and his teeth coated yellow with egg. "Eat too slow and end up in Borstal. Here they come to get us. Shar, here they come!" She'd giggled and unwrapped her sandwich. She'd eaten half and saved the rest.

He squinted at her now from one of the tables at the Island Gardens caff. Dimly he could see that she'd taken the two slices of bread apart, carefully wiped the egg off with a paper napkin, and at the moment she appeared to be making a line of crumbles along the embankment wall some thirty yards from where he sat. When the bread was in place, she scurried back across the lawn and took her binoculars from their leather case.

"Too many people," Jimmy said. "You won't see nothing but pigeons, Shar."

"There's gulls on the river. Plenty of gulls."

"So what? Gull's a gull."

"No. There's gulls, and then there's gulls," she said obscurely. "You got to be patient."

She took a small, prettily bound notebook from her knapsack. She opened it and neatly printed the date on the top of a new page. Jimmy looked away. Dad had given the notebook to her at Christmas, with three more bird books and a smaller but more powerful pair of binoculars. "These are for some *serious* watching," he'd said. "Shall we try them out, Shar? We can take them to Hampstead and see what's flying round the heath one day. Want to do that?"

She'd said, "Oh yes, Dad," with a shining face and she'd waited serenely as first the days then the weeks went by, always confident that Dad would do what he said.

But something last October had changed him, making his word worth nothing, turning him edgy whenever they saw him, filling him with the need to pop his knuckles, to walk to windows, and to jump for the telephone whenever it rang. One day he acted like a single wrong word was enough to put him into a lather. The next he was completely buzzed up, like he'd scored a century without even trying. It had taken Jimmy a few weeks and some detective work to sort out what had happened to change his father so much. But once he knew what that "what happened" was, he also knew that nothing in their unconventional family life was ever going to be the same.

He shut his eyes for a moment. He concentrated on the sounds. The gulls screaming, the tapping of footsteps on the path behind the caff, the chatter of trippers come to ride the lift down to the Greenwich foot tunnel, the scrape of metal as someone tried to crank open one of the grimy umbrellas that stood among the outdoor tables.

"See, there's black-headed gulls and herring gulls and glaucous gulls and all sorts of gulls," his sister was saying companionably. She was polishing her spectacles on the hem of her jumper. "But I've been looking for a kittiwake lately."

"Yeah? What's that? Don't sound like a bird to me." Jimmy opened the packet of Stan's Hob Nobs and popped one into his mouth. On the lawn at the far side of a circular flower bed abloom with reds, yellows, and pinks, Stan was attempting to be both bowler and batsman in a single-man cricket match, tossing the ball up, swinging at it wildly, generally missing, and yelling when he hit it, "That's a four, that's a four. You saw it, didn't you?"

"A kittiwake is almost exclusively sea-going," Shar informed Jimmy. She returned her spectacles to her nose. "They rarely come inshore except to scavenge from fishing boats. In summer—like it almost is now, right?—they nest on cliffs. They make these sweet little nest cups out of mud and bits of string and weeds and they attach them to rocks."

"Yeah? So why're you looking for a kitti-whatever here?"

"Kittiwake," she said patiently. "Because of how unusual it would be to see one. It'd be a real coup." She lifted her binoculars and scanned the embankment wall where several gulls—unintimidated by the passersby and the afternoon loungers who sat on the benches—were attending to the crumbs she'd left them.

"Kittiwakes have blackish brown legs," she said. "They have yellow beaks and dark eyes."

"That sounds like every gull in the world."

"And when they fly, they bank quite wildly and cut the waves with their wing tips. That's especially how you tell what they are."

"Ain't no waves here, Shar, in case you didn't notice."

"Well, of course, I know that. So we won't see them bank. We'll have to rely on other visual stimuli."

Jimmy went for another Hob Nob. He reached into the pocket of his windcheater and brought out his cigarettes. Without looking away from her binoculars, Sharon said, "You oughtn't to smoke. You know it's bad. It gives you cancer."

"What if I want cancer?"

"Why would you want cancer?"

"Quicker way out of this place."

"But it gives other people cancer as well. It's called passive smoking. Did you know? The way it works is if you keep smoking, we could die from breathing it, me and Stan. If we're round you enough."

"So maybe you don't want to be round me. No big loss to either of us, is it?"

She lowered the binoculars and set them on the table. The lenses of her spectacles magnified her eyes. "Dad wouldn't of wanted you to smoke," she said. "He was always after Mummy to stop."

Jimmy's fingers closed round his packet of JPS. He heard the paper crinkle as he crushed it.

"D'you think if she'd stopped smoking . . ." Sharon gave a delicate cough like she was clearing her throat. "I mean, he asked so many times. He said, 'Jean, you got to quit it with the fags. You're killing yourself. You're killing us all.' And I used to wonder—"

"Don't be daft, all right?" Jimmy said harshly. "Blokes don't leave their wives cos they smoke fags. Jesus, Shar. What a dimwit."

Sharon gave her attention to the notebook open on the table. Gently, she flipped back a few pages to earlier in the year. She ran her finger over the sketch of a brown bird with subtle orange markings. Jimmy saw the neat label *nightjar* written beneath it.

"Was it because of us, then?" she said. "Because he didn't want us? D'you think that's it?"

Jimmy felt a circle of cold growing round him. He ate another Hob Nob. He took the purloined fruit from his windcheater and laid it on the table in front of them. His stomach felt like it was filled with stones, but he took the nectarine and bit into it with a kind of fury.

"Then why?" Sharon asked. "Did Mummy do something bad? Did she find another bloke? Did Dad stop loving—"

"Shut up about it!" Jimmy pushed himself to his feet. He strode towards the embankment, calling over his shoulder, "What difference does it make? He's dead. Just shut up."

Her face crumpled but he turned away. He heard Shar call after him, "And you ought to wear your specs, Jimmy. Dad would of wanted you to wear your specs." He kicked savagely at the grass. Stan ran to join him. He dragged his cricket bat behind him like a rudder.

"Did you see how I hit it?" Stan asked. "Jimmy, did you see?"

Jimmy nodded numbly. He hurled his nectarine into the flower bed and reached for his cigarettes only to realise he'd left them on the table. He walked to the wall where the pigeons and gulls picked among the crumbs that Sharon had left them. He leaned against it. He looked down at the river.

"Will you bowl for me, Jimmy?" Stan asked eagerly. "Please? I can't bat proper unless someone bowls."

"Sure," Jimmy told him. "A minute. Okay?"

"Okay. Sure." Stan ran back to the lawn, calling, "Shar, watch us. Jimmy's goin' to bowl."

Which is, of course, what Dad wanted him to do. *You've got a fine arm, Jim. You've got a Bedser arm on you. Let's go down to the pitch. You bowl. I bat.*

Jimmy stopped himself from shrieking into the air. He grasped the wrought-iron railing that ran along the top of the embankment wall. He leaned his forehead against it and closed his eyes. It hurt too much. To think, to talk, to try to understand . . .

Did Mummy do something bad? Did she find another bloke? Did Dad stop loving her?

Jimmy hit his forehead against the wrought-iron balusters. He clenched them so hard that they felt like they were melting through his flesh and becoming his bones. He forced his eyes open and looked at the river. The tide was turning. The water was turbid. The current was swift. He thought about the rowing club on Saundersness Road, about the boat launch where the coarse pebbles giving onto the Thames were always strewn with Evian bottles, Cadbury wrappers, cigarette ends, used condoms, and rotting fruit. You could walk right into the river there. No wall to climb over, no fence to scale. *Danger! Deep Water! No Swimming!* were the warnings mounted on the lamppost that stood at the entrance to the launch. But that's what he wanted: danger and deep water.

Across the river, if he squinted hard, he could just make out the classical domes of the Royal Naval College, and he could use his imagination to fill in the rest: the pediments and columns, the noble facade. Just to the west of these buildings, the *Cutty Sark* stood in dry dock and although they weren't massive enough for him to make out from the north bank of the river, he could visualise the clipper's three proud masts and the ten miles of ropes that made up her rigging. On the Australian wool run, she'd never been beaten by another ship. She'd been built as a tea-clipper to sail from China, but when the Suez Canal opened, she'd had to adapt.

That's what life was about, right? Adapting. That's what Dad would have called matching one's bowling to the pitch.

Dad. Dad. Jimmy felt like glass was cutting his chest. He felt on fire. He wanted to be gone from this place, but more than that he wanted to be gone from this life. Not Jimmy any longer, not Ken Fleming's son, not an older brother who was supposed to do something to make things easier for Sharon and Stan, but a rock sitting in somebody's garden, a fallen tree in the country, a footpath through the woods. A chair, a cooker, a picture frame. Anything but who and what he was.

"Jimmy?"

Jimmy looked down. Stan was at his elbow, tentatively pinching the navy windcheater between his fingers. Jimmy blinked at the upturned face and the hair that flopped across his forehead and dipped into his eyes. Stan's nose wanted blowing, and having nothing proper to use for the job, Jimmy took the hem of his T-shirt and wiped it across his brother's upper lip.

"That's disgusting, that is," he said to Stan. "Can't you feel it dripping out? No wonder all the sprogs think you're such a twit."

"I ain't," he said.

"You could of fooled me."

Stan's cheeks drooped. His chin began to dimple the way it always did when he was trying not to cry.

"Look," Jimmy said with a sigh, "you got to blow your nose. You got to keep yourself up. You can't wait for somebody to do it for you. There won't always be somebody around, will there?"

Stan's eyelids quivered. "There's Mum," he whispered. "There's Shar. There's you."

"Well, don't go depending on me, all right? Don't depend on Mum. Don't depend on no one. See to yourself."

Stan nodded and drew a quivering breath. He raised his head and looked out at the river, his nose reaching only to the top of the wall. "We never got to go sailing. We won't sail now, will we? Mum won't take us. Cos if she takes us it'd remind her of him. So we won't sail, will we? Will we, Jimmy?"

Jimmy turned from the water with burning eyes. He took the cricket ball from his brother's hand. He gazed over the lawn of Island Gardens and saw that the grass was far too long to make a proper pitch. Even if it had been decently clipped, the ground was uneven. It looked like moles had started a roadworks under the trees.

"Dad would of taken us to the nets," Stan said, as if reading Jimmy's thoughts. "You remember when he took us to the nets that time? He said to those blokes, 'This one here'll be a star bowler for England one day and this one'll bat.' You remember that? He said to us, 'Okay, you toffs, show us your stuff.' He played wicket keeper and he shouted, 'A googly. Come on. We want to see a proper googly, Jim.' "

Jimmy's fingers closed round the hard leather ball. *Off break with leg break*, he could hear his father shouting. *Go for it. Now. Bowl with your head, Jimmy. Come on. With your head!*

Why, he wondered. What was the point? He couldn't be his father. He couldn't re-do what his father had done. He didn't even want to. But to be with him, to feel his arm tighten round his shoulders and his cheek press briefly against the top of his head. He would bowl for that. Googlies, off breaks, leg breaks, chinamen. Fast, medium, or slow. He would loosen his shoulders, stretch his muscles, and practise the run-up and the follow-through until he was ready to drop. If that's what it took to please him. If that's what it took to bring him home.

"Jimmy?" Stan tugged on his elbow. "You want to bowl for me now?"

Across the lawn, Jimmy could see Shar's form still in place in front of the caff. But she was standing now, the binoculars to her face, following the flight of a grey-white bird from east to west, along the river. He wondered if it was the kittiwake gull. For her sake, he hoped so.

"The ground's no good," Stan was saying. "But you could just maybe toss it. That'd be okay with me. Could you toss it, Jimmy?"

"Yeah," he said. He strode past the sign that announced *no ball games* in big black letters on white. He led the way to the smoothest patch of lawn, twenty yards long beneath the mulberry trees.

Stan scampered after him, bat on his shoulder. "Wait'll you see," he said. "I'm getting pretty good. I'll be as good as Dad someday."

Jimmy swallowed hard and tried to forget that the ground was too soft and the grass was too long and it was too late to be as good as anyone. "Take guard," he said to his little brother. "Let's see what you can do."

CHAPTER
10

Detective Constable Winston Nkata sauntered into Lynley's office, his suit jacket slung over his shoulder, contemplatively rubbing the hair's width scar that ran across his coffee skin like the shape of a scythe from his right eye to the corner of his mouth. It was a memento of his street days in Brixton—chief battle counsel of the Brixton Warriors—received at the hands of a rival gang member who was currently doing hard time at the Scrubs.

"I have been living the life today." Nkata affectionately laid his jacket over the back of a chair in front of Lynley's desk. "First Shepherd's Market eyeing some fine ladies. Then on to Berkeley Square for a nice little crawl through the Cherbourg Club. It get any better than this when I make sergeant?"

"I wouldn't know," Havers said, fingering the material of his jacket experimentally. He was clearly modelling himself sartorially after the detective inspector for whom they both worked. "I've spent the afternoon on the Isle of Dogs."

"Sergeant of my Dreams, you have not yet met the right people."

"Obviously."

Lynley was talking on the phone to their superintendent at his home in north London. They were going over the rota list, with Lynley informing his superior officer which detective constables would be pulled off what remained of their weekend leave to assist in the murder investigation.

Superintendent Webberly said to him, "And what're you doing about the press, Tommy?"

"Considering how best to use them. They're hot enough on the story."

"Go careful with that. They like a good whiff of scandal, the bastards. See to it you're not the one to give them the crumb that prejudices the case."

"Right." Lynley rang off. He rolled his chair a few inches away from his desk and said, "Where are we, then?" to Nkata and Havers.

"Patten's clean as an ankle-biter after a bath," Nkata told them. "He was at the Cherbourg Club on Wednesday night, playing some fancy card game in a private room with the big punters. He didn't leave till the milk-floats were floating next morning."

"They're sure it was Wednesday?"

"Members sign in on a chit. Chit's kept six months. All the doorman had to do was finger through last week's lot and there he was, Wednesday night, with a guest of the female persuasion. Even if they hadn't had the chits, I'd say they'd remember Patten well enough."

"Why?"

"According to a dealer I chatted up, Patten drops one or two thousand quid at the tables every month or so. Everyone knows him. It's a case of 'Come in, sit down, and what can we get you to make you happy while we're bleeding you dry.' "

"He said he was winning on Wednesday night."

"So he was and so the dealer said. But he's usually paying it out, not taking it in. He's a drinker too. Keeps a flask on him. There's no drinking in the games room, from what I was told, but the dealer's been instructed to look the other way when he takes a nip."

"Who were the other big punters in the room that night?" Havers asked.

Nkata consulted his notebook. This was maroon and minuscule, and he generally wrote in it using a matching mechanical pencil with which he produced a delicate microscopic script at odds with his large and lanky frame. He recited the names of two members of the House of Lords, an Italian industrialist, a well-known QC, an entrepreneur whose businesses included everything from film making to take-away foods, and a computer wizard from California who was in London on holiday and more than willing to pay the two-hundred-fifty-quid temporary membership fee to say he'd been fleeced in a private casino.

"Patten's play wasn't even interrupted during the evening,"Nkata said. "He went down once round one in the morning to pop his lady into a taxi, but even then he just patted her bum, handed her over to the doorman, and got back to the game. And that's where he stayed."

"What about Shepherd's Market," Lynley said. "Did he go there for action afterwards?"

Once a well-known red-light district, Shepherd's Market was a short walk from Berkeley Square and the Cherbourg Club. Although it had undergone a renaissance in recent years, one could still wander through its network of pleasant pedestrian walkways past its wine bars, its florists, and its chemists' shops, and make the sort of eye contact with a lone, loitering woman that led to sex for hire.

"Might have," Nkata replied. "But the doorman said Patten was driving his Jag that night and he had it brought round when he was ready to leave. He'd've walked to the market. No hope of getting a parking space otherwise. Course he could've cruised through, picked up a flash-tail, and took her home. But that's not where Shepherd's Market fits in." Nkata savoured the moment of announcement by leaning back in his chair and giving his facial scar another caress. "God bless the clamp," he said with devotion. "And the clampers and the blessed clampees. The clampees, especially, in this case."

Havers said, "What's that got to do with—"

"Fleming's car," Lynley said. "You've found the Lotus."

Nkata smiled. "You're quick, man. I'll say that for you. I must stop thinking that you made DI fast 'cause your face is so pretty."

"Where is it?"

"Where it oughtn't be, according to the clampers who were good enough to lock up its tyre. It's on a stretch of double yellow. On Curzon Street. Sitting there like it was begging to get clamped."

"Hell," Havers groaned. "In the middle of Mayfair. She could be anywhere."

"No one's phoned about having the clamp removed? No one's paid the fine?"

Nkata shook his head. "Car wasn't even locked. The keys were sitting on the driver's seat as well. Like she was inviting someone to nick it." He seemed to find a speck on his tie, because he frowned and flicked his fingers against the silk. "If you ask me, there's one mare out there in a boil over something, and her name's Gabriella Patten."

"She could have been just in a rush," Havers said.

"Not leaving the keys like that. That's no rush. That's premeditation. That's 'How am I best gonna put the little bastard's cobblers in a real tight squeeze?'"

"No sign of her anywhere?" Lynley asked.

"I rang bells and knocked doors from Hill Street to Piccadilly. If she's there, she's gone to ground and no one's talking about it. We could set someone to watch the car, if you want."

"No," Lynley said. "She has no intention of going back for it now. That's why she left the keys. Have it impounded."

"Right." Nkata jotted a pinhead-size note in his book.

"Mayfair." Havers dug in her trousers pocket and brought out a packet of shortbreads, which she ripped open with her teeth. She shook one into her hand and passed the packet round. She munched thoughtfully. "She could be anywhere. A hotel. A flat. Somebody's town house. She knows he's dead by now. Why won't she come forward?"

"I say she's glad about it," Nkata offered to a page in his notebook. "He got what she wanted to give him herself."

"The chop? But why? He wanted to marry her. She wanted to marry him."

"Surely you have been boiling enough to want to kill someone you don't truly want dead," Nkata said. "You get steaming and say, 'I could *kill* you, man, I wish you were dead' and you mean it at the time. You just don't 'xpect someone to come along like the good-bad fairy and grant your wish."

Havers pulled at her earlobe, as if considering Nkata's words. "There may be a group of good-bad fairies on the Isle of Dogs, then." She told them what she had learned, underscoring Derrick Cooper's antipathy for his brother-in-law, Jean Cooper's weak alibi for the night in question—"In bed asleep from half past nine onward without a sprat able to corroborate, sir"—and Jimmy's disappearance after the cancellation of the boating holiday. She said, "His mum declares he was there the next morning, tucked into his bed like Christopher Robin, but I've a fiver that says he never made it home, and I talked to three blokes at the Manchester Road substation who say he's been heading for Borstal since he was eleven."

Jimmy was a troublemaker, the police had told her. Graffiti at the rowing club, window breaking at the old Brewis Transport building not a quarter of a mile away from the police station itself, pinching cigarettes and sweets near Canary Wharf, knuckling anybody he considered someone's blue-eyed boy, trespassing behind the walls of the new yuppie housing down by the river, once punching a hole in the wall of his fourth form classroom, doing a bi- or tri-weekly bunk from school.

"Hardly the sort of thing to be underscored on the daily charge sheet," Lynley noted drily.

"Right. I see that. Your possible thug-in-the-making that could still be turned round if someone took him on. But there was one thing more that interested me about him." She munched on another shortbread as she flipped through her notebook. It was larger than Nkata's, a Ryman's purchase with a wrinkled, blue cardboard cover and a spiral binding. Most of the pages were dog-eared. Several were stained with mustard. "He was a fire raiser," she said as she chewed. "When he was . . . bloody hell . . . where did I . . . Here it is. When he was eleven, our Jimmy started a fire in the waste bin at the junior school in Cubitt Town. In the classroom, by the way, during lunch. He was feeding some science texts into the blaze when he was found."

"Had something against Darwin," Nkata murmured.

Havers snorted. "Headmaster phoned the police. A magistrate got involved. Jimmy had to see a social worker for . . . let's see . . . ten months after that."

"Did he continue with the fires?"

"It appears to be a one-time thing."

"Possibly associated with his parents' separation," Lynley noted.

"And another fire could be associated with their divorce," Havers added.

"Did he know the divorce was pending?"

"Jean Cooper says not, but she would do, wouldn't she? The kid's got *means* and *opportunity* written all over him, and she bloody well knows it, so she's not likely to help us write *motive* as well."

"And what is the motive?" Nkata asked. "You divorce my mum, I set fire to your cottage? Did he even know his dad was there?"

Havers shifted gears with ease. "It may have nothing to do with the divorce at all. He could have been in a temper because his dad had cancelled their holiday. He talked to Fleming on the phone. We don't know what they said. What if he knew Fleming was going to Kent? Jimmy might have got out there somehow, he could have seen his dad's car in the drive, he could have heard the argument that this bloke—what was his name, Inspector, the farmer who was walking by the cottage?"

"Freestone."

"Right. He could have heard the same argument that Freestone heard. He could have seen Gabriella Patten leave. He could have popped inside and regressed to an eleven-year-old's act of retaliation."

"You've not talked to the boy?" Lynley asked.

"He wasn't there. Jean wouldn't tell me where he'd gone. I had a drive round the length of the A1206, but I'd still be there hunting if I'd tried every street." She popped another shortbread into her mouth and ran her hand through her hair, ruffling it messily. "We need more manpower on this one, sir. I'd at least like someone on Cardale Street who could give us the word when the kid turns up. And he's going to eventually. He's got his brother and sister with him right now. Or so his mum said. They can't stay out all night."

"I've put some calls out. We'll have help." Lynley leaned back in his chair and felt the restless need for a cigarette. Something to do with his hands, his lips, his lungs. . . . He obliterated the thought by writing *Kensington, Isle of Dogs,* and *Little Venice* next to the list of DCs who were even at this moment being given the word by Dorothea Harriman that the bad luck of being on rota had just fallen their way.

Havers glanced at his notepad. "So?" she said. "What about the daughter?"

Handicapped, he told her. Olivia Whitelaw couldn't walk unaided. He went on to explain what he'd seen of the muscle contortions she'd had and what Faraday had done to ease them.

"Palsy of some kind?" Havers asked.

This appeared to be something that was affecting only her legs. A disease, perhaps, rather than a congenital condition. She hadn't said what it was. He hadn't asked. Whatever she was suffering from had hardly—at that moment, anyway—seemed germane to Kenneth Fleming's death.

"At that moment?" Nkata asked.

"You've got something," Havers said.

Lynley was looking at the names of the DCs, deciding how to divide them and how many to send to each location. "Something," he said. "It may be nothing, but it makes me want to double-check. Olivia Whitelaw claims she spent all of Wednesday night on the barge. Faraday was out. Now, if Olivia was to have left Little Venice, it would have been something of a production. Someone would have had to carry her. Or she'd have had to use the walker. In either case, the going would be slow. So if she went out Wednesday night once Faraday took off, someone may have noticed."

"But she couldn't have killed Fleming, could she?" Havers protested. "She could have hardly got round the cottage garden if she's as bad off as you say."

"She couldn't have done it alone." He drew a circle round the words *Little Venice.* He followed up with an arrow pointing to them as well. "She and Faraday keep a stack of newspapers under the dogs' water dishes on the deck of the barge. I had a look at them before I left. She and Faraday have bought every available broadsheet today. And all of the tabloids."

"So what?" Havers said, playing devil's advocate. "She's practically an invalid. She'd want to read. She'd send her boyfriend out to fetch the papers."

"And every one of the papers was open to the same story."

"Fleming's death," Nkata said.

"Yes. It made me wonder what she's looking for."

"But she didn't know Fleming, did she?" Havers asked.

"She claims she didn't. But if I were a betting man, I'd put money on the fact that she certainly knows something."

"Or wants to know something," Nkata said.

"Yes. There's that as well."

There was one more thread to be woven into the fabric of the investigation, and the fact that it was nearly eight o'clock on a Saturday night didn't obviate their obligation to see to it. But it would only take two of them. So once DC Nkata had shrugged into his jacket, carefully brushed at its lapels, and jauntily set off in pursuit of whatever Saturday night pleasures he'd been keeping on hold, Lynley said to Sergeant Havers, "There's one more thing."

She was in the act of lobbing her balled-up shortbread wrapper into his waste bin. She lowered her arm and sighed. "There goes dinner, I suppose."

"In Italy they rarely dine before ten o'clock, Sergeant."

"Jesus. I'm living *la dolce vita* and I didn't even know it. Do I have time to get a sandwich, at least?"

"If you're quick about it."

She set off in the direction of the officers' canteen. Lynley picked up the phone and punched in Helen's number. Eight double rings and he was listening to her answering machine for the second time that day. She couldn't get to the phone; if the caller cared to leave a message. . . .

He didn't care to leave a message. He cared to talk to her. He waited impatiently for the blasted beep.

He said pleasantly through gritted teeth, "I'm still working, Helen. Are you there?" He waited. Surely she was just screening her phone calls, waiting for his. She was in the drawing room. It would take her a moment to get to the machine. She was just now gliding to her feet, floating into the kitchen, flipping on the light, reaching for the phone, getting ready to murmur, "Tommy darling," expectantly. He waited. Nothing. "It's nearly eight," he said as he wondered where she was and fought an unsuccessful battle against feeling aggrieved that she wasn't sitting in her flat waiting for him to phone and outline their evening's ever more quickly eroding plans. "I thought I'd be able to wrap this up earlier, but that's not going to be the case, I'm afraid. I've another call to make. I can't say what time I'll be done. Half past nine? I'm not sure. I'd rather you didn't hang about waiting for me at this point. Except obviously you haven't done that, have you?" He winced as this last slipped out. Pique was its undercurrent. He went hastily on. "Listen, I'm awfully sorry this weekend's got so damnably cocked up, Helen. I'll be in touch with you as soon as I know—"

The machine's android voice thanked him for his message, recited the time—which he already knew—and disconnected.

He said, "God*damn* it," and slammed the phone home.

Where was she at eight o'clock on a Saturday night when she was supposed to be with him? When they had planned to be together the entire weekend? He considered the possibilities. There were her parents in Surrey, her sister in Cambridge, Deborah and Simon St. James in Chelsea, an old school chum who'd just exchanged contracts for a house in a fast-becoming-chi-chi neighbourhood in Fulham. And then there were her erstwhile lovers as well, but he preferred not to think that one of them had coincidentally come skulking out of her past at the very weekend when her future was supposed to be settled.

"Damn," he said again.

"My very thought," Havers said as she sauntered into his office, sandwich in hand. "Another Saturday evening when I could have crammed myself into something made of spandex and sequins to frug like a maniac—does anyone still do the frug, by the way? Did anyone ever do it?—and here I am, nose to the grindstone, teeth sinking into something the canteen is calling a *croque-monsieur.*"

Lynley examined the sandwich she was extending to him. "It looks like grilled ham."

"But if they give it a French name, they can charge more for it, son. Just you wait. Next week we'll be grubbing up with *pommes frites* and paying mightily for the pleasure." She chewed like a chipmunk, both cheeks bulging, as Lynley returned his spectacles to his jacket pocket and fished out his car keys. "We're off, then?" she said. "Where to?"

"Wapping." He led the way, saying, "Guy Mollison's made his statement to the media. It was on the radio news this afternoon. 'A tragedy for England, a brilliant batsman cut off in his prime, a real blow to our hopes of regaining the Ashes from the Aussies, a cause for serious thought among the selectors.' "

Havers stuffed into her mouth the last triangle of the first half of her sandwich. She said, past the food, "That's an interesting point, isn't it, sir? I hadn't thought before now. Fleming was sure to be chosen for England again. Now he'll have to be replaced. So somebody's fortunes are on the definite rise."

They cruised up the ramp from the underground parking. Havers gave a longing glance towards the Italian restaurant to the north of the Yard as Lynley turned into Broadway and passed the green at the end of the street where the street lamps were suddenly illuminated, filtering light through the tall plane trees and settling it against the Suffragette Scroll.

They drove in the direction of Parliament Square. At this time of evening, the ranks of tourist coaches were gone, so Winston Churchill's statue was left to gaze broodingly towards the river in peace.

They headed north just before Westminster Bridge, making the turn into Victoria Embankment and spinning along the river. They were driving against the traffic now, and once they passed the catwalk structure of Hungerford Footbridge, the road they were on led towards the City where no one would be going on a Saturday night. They had gardens on one side, the river on the other, and ample time to consider what the post-war architecture on the river's south bank was doing to demolish the city skyline.

"What do we know about Mollison?" Havers asked. She'd finished the other half of her sandwich and was digging something out of her trousers pocket. It was a roll of breath mints. Using her thumb, she prised one out and handed the roll to Lynley saying in the spurious bright voice of an overworked air hostess, "Care for a sweet after your meal, sir?"

He said, "Thanks," and popped a mint into his mouth. It tasted dusty, as if she'd picked up a partially unwrapped roll from the floor somewhere and decided she couldn't let it go to waste.

She said, "I know he plays for Essex when he's not playing for England, but that's the extent of it."

"He's been playing for England for the last ten years," Lynley told her. He went on to disclose the additional facts about Mollison that he'd gathered in a phone conversation with Simon St. James, friend, forensic scientist, and cricket aficionado nonpareil. They'd spoken at teatime, with several interruptions as St. James added fourth and fifth lumps of sugar to his cup, to the background accompaniment of his wife's strenuous objections. "He's thirty-seven—"

"Not too many good years at the wicket left, then."

"—and married to a barrister called Allison Hepple. Her father has in the past been a team sponsor, by the way."

"These blokes keep popping up everywhere, don't they?"

"Mollison's a Cambridge graduate—Pembroke College—with a rather undistinguished third in natural science. He played cricket at Harrow and then got a Blue at the University. He continued playing once he'd completed his studies."

"Sounds like education was just an excuse to play cricket."

"It seems that way."

"So he'd have the team's best interests at heart, whatever they are."

"Whatever they are."

Guy Mollison lived in a section of Wapping that had undergone considerable urban renewal. It was a part of London in which enormous

Victorian warehouses loomed over the narrow cobbled streets along the river. Some were still in use, although one glance at a lorry on which *Fruit of the Loom Active Wear* blazed in bright letters told the partial story of Wapping's metamorphosis. This was no longer the teeming, crime-ridden dockland where shouting lumpers jostled each other on gangplanks, man-handling everything from lampblack to tortoiseshell. Where once the wharves and the streets overflowed with bales, barrels, and sacks, rejuve-nation reigned. Eighteenth-century oglers of convicted pirates, con-demned to be chained at low water and to drown in the ebb and flow of three tides near the Town of Ramsgate pub, had become twentieth-cen-tury young professionals. They lived in the warehouses and the wharves themselves, which, listed as historical buildings, could not be torn down and replaced with the south bank behemoths that hulked like monoliths from Royal Hall in Southwark to London Bridge.

Guy Mollison's home was in China Silk Wharf, a six-storey building of cinnamon brick that stood at the juncture of Garnet Street and Wap-ping Wall. Its Cerberus was a porter who, when Lynley and Havers ar-rived, was standing guard in a desultory fashion, plonked down in front of a miniature television set in an office the size of a packing crate that opened into the locked, brick-floored entry to the wharf.

"Mollison?" he said when Lynley rang the bell, produced his warrant card, and identified his destination. "You wait right here, the both of you. Got it?" He pointed to a spot on the floor and retreated to his office—Lynley's warrant card in hand—where he picked up the phone and punched a few numbers to the accompaniment of the television audi-ence's howl of merriment at the sight of four game show contestants crawling through large barrels of red gelatin.

He returned with the warrant card and what seemed to be a forkful of jellied eel, his evening snack. He said, "Four seventeen. Fourth floor. Turn left from the lift. And mind you check out with me when you leave. Got it?"

He gave a nod, pitchforked the eel into his mouth, and sent them on their way. They found that the directions to Mollison's flat were unneces-sary, however. When the lift doors purred open on the fourth floor, En-gland's captain was waiting for them in the corridor. He stood leaning against the wall opposite the lift, with his hands balled into the pockets of his wrinkled linen trousers and his feet crossed at the ankles.

Lynley recognised Mollison from his signature feature: the nose twice broken on the cricket pitch, flattened at the bridge and never set properly.

He was ruddy faced from exposure to the sun, and freckles splattered along the deep V of his receding hairline. Beneath his left eye, a bruise the size of a cricket ball—or a fist, for that matter—was beginning to turn from purple to yellow along its edges.

Mollison extended his hand, saying, "Inspector Lynley? Maidstone police said they'd asked Scotland Yard to have a look at things. You're it, I take it."

Lynley shook. Mollison's grip was strong. "Yes," he said and introduced Sergeant Havers. "You've been in touch with Maidstone?"

Mollison gave Sergeant Havers a nod as he said, "I've been trying to get something definite out of the police since yesterday night, but they're good at fencing off enquiries, aren't they?"

"What sort of information are you looking for?"

"I'd like to know what happened. Ken didn't smoke, so what's this nonsense about an armchair fire and a cigarette? And how can an armchair fire and a cigarette turn to 'possible homicide' within twelve hours?" Mollison settled back against the wall. This was brick, painted white, and he lounged against it with the overhead light striking his dust-coloured hair and streaking it with gold. "Frankly, I expect I'm reacting to the fact that I still can't manage to believe he's dead. I'd spoken to him only on Wednesday evening. We chatted. We rang off. Everything was right as rain. Then this."

"It's the phone call we'd like to talk to you about."

"You know we talked?" Mollison's features sharpened. Then he seemed to relax with the words, "Oh. Miriam. Of course. She answered. I'd forgotten." He slipped his hands into his pockets again and slid a half inch down the wall, as if he intended to remain there for a while. "What can I tell you?" He looked from one to the other ingenuously, as if he saw nothing strange in the fact that their conference was taking place in the corridor.

"May we go to your flat?" Lynley asked.

"That's rather rough," Mollison said. "I'd like to handle things out here, if we can."

"Why?"

He cocked his head in the general direction of his flat, saying in a lowered voice, "My wife. Allison. I'd like not to upset her if I can avoid it. She's eight months pregnant and not feeling up to snuff. Things are rather dicey."

"She knew Kenneth Fleming?"

"Ken? No. Well, to speak to him, yes. They made casual chit-chat if they saw each other at a drinks party or something."

"Then I assume she's not in shock over his death?"

"No. No. Nothing like that." Mollison grinned and gently knocked his head against the wall in a self-deprecating manner. "I'm a worrier, Inspector. This is our first. A boy. I don't want things to go wrong."

"We'll keep that in mind," Lynley said pleasantly. "And unless your wife has some information she'd like to share with us regarding Fleming's death, she doesn't even need to stay in the room."

Mollison quirked his mouth as if to say more. He used his elbows to push himself away from the wall. "Right then. Come along. But mind her condition, won't you?"

He led them down the corridor to the third door, which he swung open upon an enormous room with oak-framed windows overlooking the river. He called out, "Allie?" as he crossed the birch floor and made for a sitting area that formed three sides of a quadrangle. The fourth side comprised glass doors that stood open to reveal one of the wharf's original landing planks where goods had once been hoisted up into the warehouse.

A strong breeze was riffling the pages of a newspaper, which lay open on a coffee table in the sitting area. Mollison closed the doors, folded the newspaper, said, "Sit down if you like," and called his wife's name again.

A woman's voice responded, "In the bedroom. Are you through with them, then?"

"Not quite," he said. "Shut the door so we don't disturb you, darling."

In reply, they heard her footsteps, but instead of shutting herself off, Allison moved into the room, with one hand holding a sheaf of papers and the other pressed into the small of her back. She was hugely pregnant, but she didn't seem to be unwell, as her husband had suggested. Rather, she appeared to be caught in the middle of work, with spectacles perched on the top of her head and a biro clipped on to the collar of her smock.

"Finish with the brief," her husband said. "We don't need you here." And then with an anxious look at Lynley, "Do we?"

Before Lynley could reply, Allison said, "Nonsense. I don't need coddling, Guy. I quite wish you'd stop it." She set her papers on a glass dining table that stood between the sitting area and the kitchen behind it. She removed her spectacles and unclipped her biro. "Would you like something?" she asked Lynley and Havers. "A coffee perhaps?"

"Allie. Cripes. You know you're not supposed to—"

She sighed. "I wasn't planning to have one myself."

Mollison grimaced. "Sorry. Hell's bells. I'll be glad when it's over."

"You're certainly not alone." His wife repeated her offer to Lynley and Havers.

"I could do with a glass of water," Havers said.

"Nothing for me," said Lynley.

"Guy?"

Mollison asked for a beer and fastened his eyes on his wife as she lumbered into the kitchen where recessed lighting gleamed down on speckled granite work tops and brushed chrome cupboards. She returned with a can of Heineken and a water goblet in which floated two slivers of ice. She placed both on the coffee table and lowered herself into an over-stuffed chair. Lynley and Havers took the sofa.

Mollison, ignoring the beer he'd asked for, remained standing. He went to the doors he'd previously shut and opened one of them. "You're looking flushed, Allie. Bit close in here, isn't it?"

"It's fine. I'm fine. Everything's fine. Drink your beer."

"Right." But instead of joining them, he squatted next to the open door where a wicker basket stood in front of a pair of potted palms. He reached into the basket and brought out three cricket balls.

Lynley thought of Captain Queeg and half expected to see him begin rolling them round his palm, despite their size.

"Who's going to replace Ken Fleming on the team?" he asked.

Mollison blinked. "That presupposes Ken would have been chosen to play for England another time."

"Would he have been chosen?"

"What's that got to do with anything?"

"I don't know at the moment." Lynley recalled additional information St. James had given him. "Fleming replaced a chap called Ryecroft, didn't he? Wasn't that just before the winter tour? Two years ago?"

"Ryecroft chipped his elbow."

"And Fleming took his place."

"If you want to call it that."

"Ryecroft never played for England again."

"He never got his form back. He doesn't play for anyone any longer."

"You were at Harrow and Cambridge together, weren't you? You and Ryecroft?"

"What's my friendship with Brent Ryecroft got to do with Fleming? I've known him since I was thirteen years old. We were at school together.

We played cricket together. We were best man for each other at our weddings. We're friends."

"You've been his advocate as well, I dare say."

"When he could play, yes. But he can't now, so I'm not. That's an end to it." Mollison straightened, two balls in one hand, one in the other. He juggled them expertly for a good thirty seconds before he went on, looking through them to say, "Why? Are you thinking I got rid of Fleming to get Brent back on to the England team? That's a lousy proposition. There're a hundred players better than Brent at this point. He knows it. I know it. The selectors know it."

"Did you know Fleming was going to Kent on Wednesday night?"

He shook his head, concentrating on the balls in the air. "As far as I knew, he was taking off on a holiday with his boy."

"He didn't mention that he'd cancelled the trip? Or postponed it?"

"He didn't give a hint in that direction." Mollison leaped forward as a ball got beyond him. It clattered to the floor and bounced onto a carpet the colour of sea foam, which served as boundary for the sitting area they were in. It rolled to Sergeant Havers. She picked it up and placed it deliberately on the sofa beside her.

Mollison's wife, at least, read the message clearly. "Sit down, Guy," she said.

"Can't," he replied with a boyish smile. "I'm up. All this energy. Got to work it off."

Allison said to them with a weary smile, "When the baby arrives, he'll be my second child. Do you want the beer or not, Guy?"

"I'll drink it. I'll drink it." He juggled two balls instead of three.

"What are you so nervous about?" his wife asked. She added, with a tiny grunt as she adjusted her position to face Lynley more directly, "Guy was here on Wednesday night with me, Inspector. That's why you've come to talk to him, isn't it? To check on his alibi? If we get to the facts straightaway, we can put the conjectures to rest." She curved her hand round her stomach, as if to emphasise her condition. "I don't sleep well any longer. I doze when I can. I was up most of the night. Guy was here. If he'd left, I would have known. And if I somehow miraculously slept through his departure, the porter would not have done. You've met the night porter, I take it?"

"Allison, cripes." Mollison finally pitched the balls back to their wicker basket. He strode to one of the other chairs, sat, and popped the top on his beer. "He doesn't think I killed Ken. Why would I, in the first place? I was just talking bosh."

"What was your row about?" Lynley asked. He didn't wait for Mollison to counter with "What row?" He went on to say, "Miriam Whitelaw heard the beginning of your conversation with Fleming. She said you mentioned a row. You said something about forgetting the row and getting on with things."

"We had a dust-up during a four-day match last week at Lord's. Things were tense. Middlesex needed ninety-one with eight wickets in hand. They had to work like the devil to win. One of their better batsmen had gone out with a fractured finger, so they weren't a particularly happy group. I made a remark after the third day, out in the car park, about one of their Paki players. It had to do with the play, not the man, but Ken didn't want to see it that way. He took it as racist. Things went from there."

"They had a fight," Allison clarified calmly. "Out in the car park. Guy got the worst of it. Two bruised ribs, the black eye."

"Odd that it didn't make the papers," Havers noted. "Tabloids being what they are."

"It was late," Mollison said. "No one was about."

"Just the two of you were there?"

"That's it." Mollison gulped his beer.

"You didn't tell anyone afterwards you'd brawled with Fleming? Why's that?"

"Because it was stupid. We'd had too much to drink. We were acting like thugs. It's not something either one of us wanted to get round."

"And you made peace with him afterwards?"

"Not straightaway. That's why I phoned on Wednesday. I assumed he'd be selected for the England team this summer. I assumed as much about myself. As far as I was concerned, we didn't need to be living in each other's knickers for things to go smoothly when the Aussies arrive, but we needed at least to be at ease with each other. I'd made the remark in the first place. I thought it wise if I also made peace."

"What else did you talk about on Wednesday night?"

He set the beer on the table, leaned forward, and clasped his hands loosely between his legs. "The Aussie spin bowler. The condition of the pitches at the Oval. How many more centuries we can expect from Jack Pollard. That sort of thing."

"And during that conversation, Fleming never mentioned he was heading to Kent that night?"

"Never."

"Or Gabriella Patten? Did he mention her?"

"Gabriella Patten?" Mollison cocked his head in perplexity. "No. He didn't mention Gabriella Patten." He looked so directly at Lynley as he spoke that the very earnestness of his gaze gave him away.

"Do you know her?" Lynley asked.

Still the eyes remained firm. "Sure. Hugh Patten's wife. He's sponsoring the test match series this summer. But you must have dug up that information by now."

"She and her husband are living apart at the moment. Are you aware of that?"

A quick shift of the eyes towards his wife and Mollison returned his gaze to Lynley. "I didn't know. I'm sorry to hear it. I'd always got the impression she and Hugh were crazy about each other."

"You saw a lot of them?"

"Here and there. Parties. The occasional test matches. Some of the winter tour. They follow cricket pretty closely. Well, I suppose they would, wouldn't they, since he sponsors the team." Mollison lifted his beer, drained the can. He began to use his thumbs to cave in the side. "Is there another?" he asked his wife, and then said, "No. Stay. I'll get it." He sprang to his feet and went to the kitchen where he rooted through the refrigerator, saying, "D'you want something, Allie? You didn't have enough dinner to keep a gnat going. These chicken legs look decent. Want one, darling?"

Allison was directing a thoughtful gaze upon the dented beer can that her husband had left on the coffee table. He called her name again when she didn't respond. She said, "I'm not interested, Guy. In food."

He rejoined them, using his thumb to flick open his Heineken. "Sure you don't want one?" he asked Lynley and Havers.

Lynley said, "And the county matches?"

"What?"

"Did Patten and his wife attend those as well? Did they ever watch an Essex match, for example? Do they have a side they favour when England isn't playing?"

"They back Middlesex, I should guess. Or Kent. The home counties. You know."

"And Essex? Did they ever come to watch you play?"

"Probably. I couldn't swear to it. But like I said, they follow the game."

"Recently?"

"Recently?"

"Yes. I was wondering when you last saw them."

"I saw Hugh last week."

"Where was this?"

"At the Garrick. For lunch. It's part of what I do: keeping the current team sponsor happy to be the team sponsor."

"He didn't tell you about his separation from his wife?"

"Hell, no. I don't know him. I mean I know him, but it's a formal sort of thing. Sports talk. Who looks good to open the bowling against the Aussies. How I plan to set the field. Who the selectors are thinking of choosing for the team." He raised his beer, drank.

Lynley waited until Mollison had lowered the beer before asking, "And Mrs. Patten. When did you last see her?"

Mollison looked at an enormous Hockney-like canvas that hung on the wall behind the sofa, as if it were a large desk calendar on which he was examining how he had spent his days. "I don't remember, to tell the truth."

"She was at the dinner party," Allison said. "The end of March." When her husband appeared nonplussed by the information, she added, "The River Room. The Savoy."

"Cripes. What a memory, Allie," Mollison said. "That was it. The end of March. A Wednesday—"

"Thursday."

"A Thursday night. That's right. You wore that purple African thing."

"It's Persian."

"Persian. That's right. And I—"

Lynley stopped Gingold and Chevalier before they got to the refrain. He said, "You haven't seen her since then? You haven't seen her since she's been living in Kent?"

"In Kent?" His face was blank. "I didn't know she was in Kent. What's she doing in Kent? Where?"

"Where Kenneth Fleming died. The very cottage in fact."

"Cripes." He swallowed.

"When you spoke to him on Wednesday evening, Kenneth Fleming didn't tell you he was heading out to Kent to see Gabriella Patten?"

"No."

"You didn't know he was having an affair with her?"

"No."

"You didn't know he had been having an affair with her since the previous autumn?"

"No."

"That they were planning to divorce their spouses and marry?"

"No. No way. I didn't know any of that." He turned to his wife. "Did you know this stuff, Allie?"

She'd been watching him throughout Lynley's questioning. She said without a change of expression, "I'm hardly in a position to know."

Mollison said, "I thought she might have said something to you. In March. At the dinner."

"She was there with Hugh."

"I meant in the cloakroom. Or something."

"We had no time alone. And even if we had, revealing that you're fucking someone outside your marriage isn't generally cloakroom conversation, Guy. Among women, that is." Her face and her tone belied her choice of vocabulary. All three served to pin her husband's eyes on hers. A silence played among them, and Lynley let it stretch out. Beyond the open door, a boat on the river sounded a single blast of its horn. As if this was the cause, a current of chill air gusted into the room. The breeze susurrated the palm fronds and feathered away from her cheeks the strands of hazelnut hair that had escaped the peach ribbon that bound it at the base of Allison's neck. Guy stood hastily and closed the door.

Lynley rose as well. Sergeant Havers shot him an are-you-crazy-his-wicket's-as-sticky-as-it's-going-to-get look. She reluctantly dug her way out of the overstuffed sofa. Lynley took out his card. He said, "If anything else comes to mind, Mr. Mollison," and when Mollison turned from the door, he handed the card over to him.

"I've told you everything," Mollison said. "I don't know what else . . ."

"Occasionally something jogs the memory. A chance remark. An overheard conversation. A photograph. A dream. Telephone me if that happens to you."

Mollison shoved the card into the breast pocket of his shirt. "Sure. But I don't think—"

"If it happens," Lynley said. He nodded to Mollison's wife and ended the interview.

He and Havers didn't speak until they were in the lift, gliding down to the entry where the porter would release the doorlocks and let them out into the street. Havers said, "He's dancing a jig with the truth."

Lynley said, "Yes."

"Then why aren't we up there pinning him to the wall?"

The lift doors *shooshed* open. They stepped out into the entry. The porter came out of his office and marched them to the door with the formality of a prison guard releasing convicts. Lynley said nothing as they went out into the night.

Havers lit a cigarette as they walked towards the Bentley. She said, "Sir, why aren't we—"

"We don't need to do what his wife can do for us," was Lynley's reply. "She's a barrister. There's a blessing in that."

At the car, they stood on opposite sides. Lynley gazed in the direction of the Prospect of Whitby where a few pub regulars had spilled into the street. Havers puffed away on her cigarette, bulking up on the nicotine before the long drive home.

"But she won't be on our side," Havers said. "Not with a baby due. Not if Mollison's involved."

"We don't need her on our side. We just need her to tell him what he forgot to ask."

Havers stopped the cigarette midway to her mouth. "Forgot to ask?"

" 'Where's Gabriella now?' " Lynley said. "The fire was in Gabriella's lodgings. The coppers have got one corpse they're nosing round, but that corpse is Fleming. So where the hell is Gabriella?" Lynley disarmed the car's security system. "Interesting, isn't it?" he said as he opened the door and slid inside. "All the things people reveal by saying nothing."

CHAPTER
11

The beer garden of the Load of Hay tavern was aswarm with life. Fairy lights glittered from the trees and made a coruscating rooftop above the drinkers, shining on the bare arms and long legs of those celebrants of the ever-warming May weather. Unlike the previous evening, however, Barbara did not give a passing thought to joining them as she cruised past. She still hadn't yet imbibed her weekly pint of Bass, she still hadn't spoken to a soul in her neighbourhood aside from Bhimani at the grocery, but it was half past ten and she'd been up too long with too little sleep to bolster her. She was knackered.

She took the first parking space she found, next to a mound of rubbish bags, which bled weeds and grass cuttings onto the pavement. It was in Steele's Road, directly beneath an alder whose reaching branches stretched high above the street and promised a prodigious speckling of bird droppings by morning. Not that bird droppings mattered all that much, when one considered the condition of the Mini. Indeed, if her luck held, Barbara thought, there might be enough guano to plug up the holes that currently freckled the car's rusting bonnet.

She picked her way through the rubbish bags to the pavement and trudged in the direction of Eton Villas. She yawned, rubbed the soreness from her shoulder, and vowed to dump out the contents of her bag and do some committed jettisoning of her belongings. What was in the damn thing anyway, she wondered as she lugged it towards her home. It felt as if she were hauling round a load of bricks. It felt, in fact, as if she'd stopped by Jaffri's Fine Groceries, picked up another two bags of ice, and tucked them in with the rest of her belongings.

Her footsteps halted at the mental picture her mind created of Jaffri's and ice. Bloody hell in sodding spades, she thought. She'd forgotten about the refrigerator.

She picked up her pace. She rounded the corner to Eton Villas. She hoped against hope and prayed against prayer that gran's son's son had managed to figure things out for himself when he made the long drive from Fulham to Chalk Farm in that open-back lorry of his. Barbara hadn't told him exactly where to deliver the refrigerator, incorrectly assuming that she would be home when he arrived. But since she hadn't been, surely he would have asked someone for direction. He wouldn't have left it sitting on the pavement, would he? And no way would he have simply dropped it in the street.

He'd done neither, she found, when she got to the house. She went up the drive, skirted a late model red Golf, pushed through the gate, and saw that gran's son's son had managed—with or without assistance, she was never to know—to manoeuvre the refrigerator across the lawn in front of the house and down four narrow concrete steps. Now it stood, half-wrapped in a pink blanket with one leg sinking into a delicate mound of chamomile that grew between the flagstones in front of the ground-floor flat.

"Wrong," Barbara fumed. "Wrong, wrong, wrong. You flaming absolutely unforgivable *twit.*"

She kicked at a flagstone and set her shoulder against the rope that held the pink blanket in place. She gave a grunt and a shove and tested the weight she would have to heave to get the refrigerator back up the four steps, shoo it along the side of the house, and shift it into her cottage at the bottom of the garden. She managed to raise one side two inches, but the effort sank the other side deeper into the chamomile, which, no doubt, the resident of the ground-floor flat was growing for a crucial medicinal need that would now go wanting because of gran's son's more-than-useless son.

She said, "Bloody bleeding hell," and gave the refrigerator another heave. It sank another inch. She heaved once more. Once more it sank. She said, "Stuff it," with as much energy as she had used in the heaving, and she plunged her hand into her shoulder bag and brought forth her cigarettes. Disgruntled, she went to a wooden bench that stood in front of the french doors of the ground-floor flat. She sat down and lit up. She observed the refrigerator through the smoke and tried to decide what to do.

A light went on above her head. One of the french doors opened. Barbara turned to see the same small, dark girl who had been laying plates on the table for dinner the previous night. She wasn't in a school uniform this time, however. She was in a nightgown, long and perfectly white with a flounce at the hem and a drawstring at the neck. Her hair was still in plaits.

"Is it yours, then?" the girl asked solemnly, using one toe to scratch the opposite ankle. "We've been wondering about that."

Barbara looked beyond her for the rest of *we*. The flat was dark save for a rod of light that extended from an open doorway in the back.

"I forgot it was going to be delivered," Barbara said. "Some idiot bloke delivered it here by mistake."

"Yes," the girl said. "I saw him. I tried to tell him that we didn't want a refrigerator, but he wouldn't listen. We've got one already, I told him, and I would've let him in to see for himself only I'm not supposed to let anyone in when Dad's not home and he wasn't home yet. He's home now, though."

"Is he?"

"Yes. But he's asleep. That's why I'm talking low. So I don't wake him. He brought chicken for dinner and I made courgettes and we had *chapatis* and then he fell asleep. I'm not supposed to let anyone in when he's not home. I'm not supposed to even open the door. But it's all right now, isn't it, because he's home. I can shout if I need him, can't I?"

"Sure," Barbara said. She flicked a wedge of ash onto the neat flag-stones and when the girl's dark eyes followed its descent with a thought-ful frown, Barbara slipped one trainer-shod foot over and casually ground the ash to a smudge of grey-black. The girl observed this and sucked on her lip.

Barbara said, "Shouldn't you be in bed?"

"I don't sleep well, I'm afraid. I mostly read till I can't keep my eyes open. I have to wait till Dad falls asleep before I turn on my light, though, because if I turn on my light while he's still awake, he comes into my room and takes the book away. He says I should count backwards from one hundred to fall asleep, but I think it's so much nicer to read, don't you? Besides, I can count backwards from one hundred faster than I can fall asleep and when I get to zero, what am I supposed to do?"

"That's a problem, all right." Barbara peered beyond the child again, into the flat. "Isn't your mum here, then?"

"My mum's visiting friends. In Ontario. That's in Canada."

"Yeah. I know."

"She hasn't sent me a postcard yet. I expect she's busy, which is what happens when one visits friends. Her name's Malak, my mum. Well, that's not her real name, is it? It's what Dad calls her. Malak means angel. Isn't that pretty? I wish it was my name. I'm Hadiyyah, which I don't think is nearly as pretty as Malak. And it doesn't mean angel."

"It's a nice enough name."

"Have you got a name?"

"Sorry. It's Barbara. I live round the back."

Hadiyyah's cheeks formed little pouches as she smiled. "In that sweet little cottage?" She clasped her hands to her chest. "Oh, I wanted us to live there when we first moved here except it's far too small. It's just like a play house. Can I see it?"

"Sure. Why not? Sometime."

"Can I see it now?"

"Now?" Barbara asked blankly. She was beginning to feel a shade uncomfortable. Wasn't this how things began just before an innocent suspect was charged with committing a vile crime against a child? "I don't know about now. Shouldn't you be in bed? What if your dad wakes up?"

"He never wakes up before morning. Ever. Only if I have a nightmare."

"But if he heard a noise and woke up and you weren't here—"

"I'll be here, won't I?" She offered an elfin smile. "I'll just be at the back of the house. I could write him a note and leave it on my bed in case he wakes up. I could tell him I've just gone round to the back. I could tell him that I'm with you—I'll even use your name, I'll say I'm with Barbara —and that you'll bring me back when I've seen the cottage. Don't you think that would do?"

No, Barbara thought. What would do would be a long hot shower, a fried egg sandwich, and a cup of Horlicks, because a single strip of grilled ham and a dollop of cheese with a fancy French name didn't count for dinner. And afterwards, what would also do, if she could keep her eyes opened, would be quarter of an hour's literary discovery of exactly what Flint Southern had throbbing for Star Flaxen in those sculpted blue jeans he was wearing.

"Some other time." Barbara slipped the strap of her bag on to her shoulder and heaved herself from the wooden bench.

"I expect you're tired, aren't you?" Hadiyyah said. "I expect you're dragging."

"Right."

"Dad's like that when he gets home from work. He flops onto the sofa and can't move for an hour. I bring him tea. He likes Earl Grey tea. I can make tea."

"Can you?"

"I know how long to seep it. It's all in the seeping."

"The seeping."

"Oh yes." The little girl had her hands still clasped at her chest as if she held a talisman between them. Her great dark eyes were so beseeching that Barbara wanted to tell her brusquely to toughen up, to get used to life. Instead, she flipped her cigarette to the flagstones, crushed it out with the toe of her trainer, and put the butt in the pocket of her trousers.

"Write him a note," she said. "I'll wait."

Hadiyyah's smile was beatific. She spun. She darted into the flat. The slash of light widened as she went into the room at the back. In less than two minutes, she returned.

"I stuck the note on my lamp," she confided. "But he probably won't wake up. He doesn't, usually. Unless I have a nightmare."

"Right," Barbara said and headed for the steps. "It's this way."

"I know the way. I do. I do." Hadiyyah skipped ahead. Over her shoulder she called, "Next week's my birthday. I'll be eight years old. Dad says I can have a party. He says I can have chocolate cakes and strawberry ice cream. Will you come? You don't need to bring a present at all." She shot away without waiting for an answer.

Barbara noted that she still didn't have on shoes. Great, she thought. The kid would get pneumonia and she'd be to blame.

She caught Hadiyyah up at the patch of lawn that lay between the main house and Barbara's cottage. Here, the child had paused to right an overturned tricycle. "It belongs to Quentin," she said. "He's always leaving his stuff outside. His mum goes quite distracted and shouts at him from the windows, but he never listens. I expect he doesn't know what she wants from him, don't you?"

She didn't wait for an answer. She pointed to a collapsible canvas chaise longue and after that to a white plastic table and two matching chairs. "That's Mrs. Downey's. She lives in the bed-sit. Have you met her? She's got a cat called Jones. And those're the Jensens'. I don't much like them—the Jensens, that is—but you won't say, will you?"

"Mum's the word at this end."

Hadiyyah's nose wrinkled. "You're sort of cheeky, aren't you? Dad doesn't like me to be cheeky with people. You got to be careful when you meet him, okay? It's important that he likes you. So that you can come to the party. The party's for my birthday. It's—"

"Next week. Right."

Barbara led the child to her front door and fished in her bag for the key. She unlocked the door and flipped on the ceiling light. Hadiyyah stepped past her.

"How sweet!" she exclaimed. "It's perfect. It's like a doll's house." She dashed into the middle of the room and twirled about. "I wish we lived here. I wish. I wish."

"You'll get dizzy." Barbara set her bag on the work top. She went to fill the kettle.

"I won't," Hadiyyah answered. She twirled three more times and then stopped and staggered. "Well, perhaps a bit." She looked about. She rubbed her hands down the sides of her nightgown. Her glance flitted from one object to another. She finally said with studied formality, "You've made it quite nice here, Barbara."

Barbara stifled a smile. Hadiyyah was hovering between good manners and questionable taste. Everything in the room had either made the trip from her parents' home in Acton or been dug up in a jumble sale. If the former was the case, the article was smelly, tattered, gouged, or abused. If the latter was the case, the article was functional and little else. The only piece of furniture that she had allowed herself to purchase new was the day-bed. This was wicker, its mattress covered by a line of motley pillows and a bedspread decorated in an Indian print.

Hadiyyah skipped to the bed and inspected a framed photograph that stood on the table next to it. She bounced from foot to foot so much that Barbara was tempted to ask her if she needed the loo. Instead, she said, "That's my brother. Tony."

"But he's little. Like me."

"It was taken a long time ago. He died."

Hadiyyah frowned. She looked over her shoulder at Barbara. "How sad. Are you sad about it still?"

"Sometimes. Not always."

"I'm sad sometimes. There's no one hereabouts to play with and I don't have any brothers and sisters. Dad says being sad is okay if I examine my soul and decide it's an honest feeling inside me. I'm not quite sure how to examine my soul. I tried to do it by looking in the mirror, but it made me feel all queer when I looked for too long. Have you ever done that? Looked in the mirror and felt all queer?"

Barbara laughed wearily in spite of herself. She dragged the bucket out from beneath the sink and examined its meagre contents. "Most days," she said. She scooped out two eggs and put them on the counter. She reached inside her bag for her cigarettes.

"Dad smokes. He knows he shouldn't, but he does. He stopped for a whole two years because Mummy didn't like it. But he's taken it up again and she'll be quite miffed with him when she comes home. She's—"

"In Canada."

"Right. I told you that already, didn't I? Sorry."

"That's okay."

Hadiyyah bounced to Barbara's side and inspected the empty spot in the kitchen. "That's for the fridge," she announced. "You mustn't worry about the fridge, Barbara. When Dad gets up tomorrow, he'll move it back here for you. I'll tell him it's yours. I'll say you're my friend. Is that all right? If I say you're my friend? It's a good idea, you know, if I say that. Dad'll be only too happy to help out my friend."

Eagerly she waited, on one foot with hands clasped behind her, for Barbara's response. Barbara gave it and wondered what she was letting herself in for. "Sure. You can say that."

Hadiyyah beamed. She whirled across the room to the fireplace. She said, "And this is sweet too. Do you think it works? Can we toast marshmallows in it? Is this an answer machine? Look. You've had a call, Barbara." She reached out towards it on its shelf by the fireplace. "Shall we see who—"

"No!"

Hadiyyah yanked her hand back. She sidled quickly away from the machine. "I oughtn't to have . . ." She looked so chastened that Barbara said, "Sorry. I didn't mean to snap."

"I expect you're tired. Dad snaps sometimes when he's specially tired. Shall I make you some tea?"

"No. Thanks. I've got the water on. I'll make it myself."

"Oh." Hadiyyah looked about, as if seeking further employment of some kind. Seeing none, she murmured, "I ought to be off, then."

"It's been a long day."

"Yes, it has, hasn't it?" Hadiyyah moved towards the door and Barbara noticed for the first time that the tiny hairbows that tied up her plaits were white. She wondered if the little girl changed them each time she changed her clothes. "Well," she said at the door. "Good night, Barbara. It was a pleasure to meet you."

"Likewise," Barbara said. "Hold on for a moment, and I'll walk you back." She poured hot water into her tea mug and dunked a bag into it. When she turned to the door, the girl was gone. She called, "Hadiyyah?" and walked out into the garden.

She heard her call, "Good night, good night," and saw the flutter of her white nightgown against the house as she scampered back the way she had come. "Don't forget the party. It's—"

"For your birthday," Barbara said quietly. "Yes. I know." She waited until she heard the sound of the ground-floor flat's door shutting. She went back to her tea.

The answering machine beckoned her, a reminder of the second obligation she'd failed to meet that day. She didn't need to listen to the message to know who it was. She picked up the phone and dialled Mrs. Flo's number.

"Why, we were just having a nice cup of Bourn-vita," Mrs. Flo said when she answered. "And a little snack of marmite toast. Mum's taken to cutting the bread into bunny shapes—Haven't you, dear? Yes, that's very sweet, isn't it?—and we just slip it into the toaster as easy as anything and keep our eyes on it so it doesn't burn."

"How is she?" Barbara asked. "I'm sorry I didn't get out there today. I got called out on a case."

There was the sound of shuffling, of footsteps on lino, of Mrs. Flo saying to someone, "You'll watch that closely for a moment, won't you, dear? Yes, stand right next to it like that. Well done. You know what to do if it starts to smoke, don't you? Can you tell me, dear?"

Mumbling came in response. Muted giggles followed. Mrs. Flo said,

"You're being the naughty one tonight, aren't you?" And then with the word, "Barbie?" the timbre of her voice changed, not so much with mood but as if she'd gone into a smaller room.

Out of the kitchen and into the passage, Barbara thought. She felt a moment of disquiet.

"I've just got back from work," Barbara said. "Has something . . . How's Mum?"

"You work far too hard, my dear," Mrs. Flo said. "Are you eating well? Taking care of yourself? Getting enough sleep?"

"I'm doing fine. Everything's fine. I've got a refrigerator sitting outside my neighbour's flat instead of inside my kitchen, but other than that, nothing's changed in my life. How's Mum, Mrs. Flo? Is she better?"

"She's had another grumbly tummy most of the day, so she was off her food, which worried me a bit. But things are looking brighter now. She's missing you, though." Mrs. Flo paused. Barbara could picture her standing in the dark passage that led to the kitchen. She'd be wearing one of her spotless shirtwaisters with one of her many flower-shaped brooches pinned at the throat. The tights on her legs would match some colour in the dress and her flat-soled shoes would be buffed to perfection. Barbara had never seen her attired otherwise. Even when she worked in the garden, Mrs. Flo dressed as if expecting the Princess Royal to drop by for tea.

"Yes," Barbara said, "I know. Hell. I'm so sorry."

"You're not to worry and you're not to feel guilty," Mrs. Flo said firmly. Her voice was warm. "You're doing the best that you can. Mum's nearly right as rain at the moment. Her temperature's still up a degree, but we've got her eating her marmite toast."

"She can't survive on that."

"She'll do very well on it for the present, dear."

"May I talk to her?"

"Of course. She'll be happy as a little lark when she hears your voice." Her own voice changed again as she went back into the kitchen, saying past the mouthpiece of the receiver, "We've a special phone call here, dearies. Who do you suppose is phoning especially to talk to her mummy? Mrs. Pendlebury, *what* are you doing with that jam? Here, dear, it goes on *top* of the toast. Like that. Yes. Very nice, dear."

A moment passed. Barbara tried not to think of marmite toast, of jam, of food of any kind. Her mother wasn't well, she had failed to visit her, and all she could think of was cramming something remotely edible between her lips. What kind of daughter was she?

"Doris? Dorrie?" Mrs. Havers' voice quavered uncertainly at the other end of the line. "Mrs. Flo says there's no blackout any longer. I said we must cover the windows so the Germans can't find us, but she said there's no need. There isn't any war. Did you know? Has Mummy uncovered the windows at home?"

"Hello, Mum," Barbara said. "Mrs. Flo told me you'd had a bad day yesterday and today as well. Is your stomach in a rumble?"

"I saw you with Stevie Baker," Mrs. Havers said. "You thought I didn't, but I saw you, Dorrie. He had your dress rucked up and your knickers pulled down. You were making a sausage roll with him."

"Mum," Barbara said. "This isn't Auntie Doris. She died, remember? During the war?"

"But there isn't any war. Mrs. Flo said—"

"She meant the war ended, Mum. This is Barbara. Your daughter. Auntie Doris is dead."

"Barbara." Mrs. Havers repeated the name so thoughtfully that Barbara could visualise the wheels of her disintegrating brain painfully creaking in her head. "I don't know that I recall . . ." She'd be twisting the telephone cord in her fingers as her confusion grew. Her glance would be darting round Mrs. Flo's kitchen as if the key to comprehension were hidden there.

"We lived in Acton," Barbara said gently. "You and Dad. Me. Tony."

"Tony. I've a picture upstairs."

"Yes. That's Tony, Mum."

"He doesn't come to see me."

"No. Well, you see . . ." Barbara suddenly felt how tight was her grip on the telephone receiver, and she forced herself to loosen it. "He's dead as well." As was her father. As was virtually everyone else who had once formed the circumference of her mother's small world.

"Is he? How did he . . . ? Did he die in the war like Dorrie?"

"No. Tony was too young for that. He was born after the war. A long time after."

"So a bomb didn't hit him?"

"No. No. It was nothing like that." Far worse, Barbara thought, far less merciful than a split second of flash, fire, and flame and an endless hurtle into eternity. "He had leukaemia, Mum. It's when something goes wrong with the blood."

"Leukaemia. Oh." Her voice brightened. "I don't have that, Barbie. Just a grumbly tummy. Mrs. Flo wanted me to eat soup this noon, but I couldn't. It didn't want to go down. But I'm eating now. We've made marmite toast. And we've blackberry jam. I'm eating the marmite. Mrs. Pendlebury is eating the jam.''

Barbara sent a mental thanks heavenward for the moment of lucidity and grasped it quickly before her mother faded out again. "Good. That's very good for you, Mum. You need to eat to keep up your strength. Listen, I'm dead sorry I wasn't able to make it out today. I got called onto a case last night. But I'll try to get out there before next weekend. Okay?''

"Will Tony come as well? Will Dad come, Barbie?''

"No. Just me.''

"But I haven't seen Dad in ever so long.''

"I know, Mum. But I'll bring you a treat. Remember how you were talking about New Zealand? The holiday to Auckland?''

"Summer's winter in New Zealand, Barbie.''

"Good. That's right. That's excellent, Mum.'' It was odd, Barbara thought, the facts remembered, the faces forgotten. Where did information come from? How was it lost? "I've got the brochures for you. You'll be able to start putting the holiday together next time I come out. We can do it together, you and I. How does that sound?''

"But we can't take a holiday if there's a blackout, can we? And Stevie Baker won't want you to go off without him. If you make sausage rolls with Stevie Baker, something bad will happen, Dorrie. I saw his sausage, you know. I saw where he put it. You thought I was playing jacks in the kitchen, but I followed you. I saw how he kissed you. You took your knickers off yourself. And then you lied to Mummy about where you'd been. You said you and Cora Trotter'd been rolling bandages. You said you were practising for when you were going to be a Wren. You said—''

"Barbie?'' Mrs. Flo's soft voice. Overpowering it, in the background, Mrs. Havers was continuing her recitation of her sister's adolescent sins. "She's getting a bit agitated, dear. Not to worry, however. It's the excitement of your phoning. She'll settle right down once she has a touch more Bourn-vita and toast. And then it's a brush of her teeth and off to bed. She's already had her bath.''

Barbara swallowed. It never got easier. She always braced herself for the worst. She knew what to expect in advance. But every once in a while —every third or fourth conversation with her mother—she felt part of her strength giving way, like a sandstone cliff too long beaten by the ocean.

"Right,'' Barbara said.

"I don't want you to worry.''

"Right," Barbara said.

"Mum knows you'll come to see her when you can."

Mum knew nothing of the kind, but it was generous of Mrs. Flo to make the remark. Not for the first time, Barbara wondered from what remarkable source Florence Magentry took her presence of mind, her patience, and her essential goodness. "I'm on a case," she told her again. "Perhaps you read about it or saw it on the news. That cricketer. Fleming. He died in a fire."

Mrs. Flo clucked sympathetically. "Poor soul," she said.

Yes, Barbara thought. Indeed. Poor soul.

She rang off and went back to her tea. On the work top, the sand-coloured shells of the eggs had begun to sweat with pinpricks of moisture. She picked one of them up. She rolled it the length of her cheek. She didn't feel much like eating any longer.

Lynley made sure the door to Helen's flat was locked as he left. He spent a moment reflecting upon the brass knob and matching dead bolt. She wasn't at home. As far as he could tell from the fact that the post hadn't been retrieved, she hadn't been home for most of the day. So, like a bumbling, amateur sleuth, he'd roamed through her flat, looking for clues that would explain her disappearance.

The dishes in the kitchen sink were from breakfast—why Helen couldn't manage to slide one cereal bowl, one coffee cup, one saucer, and two spoons into the dishwasher would eternally remain a mystery to him —and both *The Times* and the *Guardian* bore the appearance of having been unfolded and read. All right. So she hadn't been in a rush to leave, and no unknown circumstances had upset her to a degree that made her unable to eat. The reality was that he had never actually known Helen to lose her appetite as the result of anything, but at least it was a place to start: no rush to leave and no major catastrophe.

He went to her bedroom. The bed was made—support for the no-rush-to-leave theory. Her dressing table was as precisely arranged as it had been on the previous evening. Her jewellery box was closed. A silver-based scent bottle stood slightly out of line from the rest and Lynley removed its stopper.

He wondered how ill it boded that she'd applied scent before leaving the flat. Did she always wear it? Did she have it on last night? He couldn't recall. He felt a vague sense of unease as he wondered if his not recalling was as evil an omen as might be Helen's wearing scent for the first time in weeks. Why did women wear scent, after all? To lure, to heighten interest, to arouse, to invite?

The thought made him stride to the wardrobe and begin fingering through her clothes. Gowns, frocks, trousers, suits. If she was meeting someone, surely her manner of dress would reveal the sex, if not the identity. He began considering the men who had once been her lovers. What had she worn when he'd seen her with them? It was a question without answer. It was a hopeless task. He couldn't remember. He found himself becoming distracted by the cool-water touch against his cheek of a satin nightgown, which hung on the inside of the wardrobe door.

Insanity, he thought. No, inanity. He shoved the wardrobe door closed in disgust. What was he becoming? If he didn't get himself under control, he'd soon find himself kissing her jewellery or caressing the soles of her unworn shoes.

That was it, he thought. Jewellery. The bedside table. The ring. The jewel box wasn't there, where he had placed it last night. Nor was it in the table's drawer. Nor was it among her other jewellery. Which meant that she was wearing the ring, which meant that she agreed, which meant that certainly she'd gone to her parents to give them the news.

She'd have to spend the night there, so she'd have taken a suitcase. Of course, that was it. Why hadn't he grasped the truth at once? He hastily checked in the corridor cupboard to verify his conclusion. Another dead end. Her two suitcases were there.

Back in the kitchen, he saw what he had seen at first and had willed himself to ignore. Her answering machine was blinking furiously. It looked as if she'd had a score of calls during the day. He told himself he wouldn't stoop that low. If he started in with invading her answering machine, he'd soon find himself next steaming open her letters. The long and short of it was that she was out, she had been out all day, and if she intended to return any time soon, she was going to manage it without him standing in the bushes like a lovelorn Romeo waiting for the light.

So he left her flat and drove home to Eaton Terrace, dropping down Sydney Street and weaving his way to the silent white-porticoed neighbourhoods of Belgravia. He told himself that he was exhausted anyway, that he was famished, that he could do with a whisky.

"Evening, m'lord. Rather longish day for you." Denton greeted him at the door, under his arm a stack of precisely folded white towels. Although he was wearing his usual jacket and trousers, he had already donned his bedroom slippers, Denton's subtle way of illuminating an *off-duty* sign. "Expected you round eight."

They both looked at the grandfather clock ticking sonorously in the entry. Two minutes to eleven.

"Eight?" Lynley said blankly.

"Right. Lady Helen said—"

"Helen? Has she phoned?"

"Hasn't needed to phone."

"Hasn't needed . . . ?"

"She's been here since seven. Said you'd left her a message. Said she'd got the impression you'd be home near eight. So she popped round and had dinner waiting for you. It's gone off, I'm afraid. You can only expect so much longevity when it comes to pasta. I tried to warn her off cooking it before you got here, but she wasn't having any advice from me."

"Cooking?" Lynley looked vaguely in the direction of the dining room at the rear of the house. "Denton, are you telling me that Helen cooked dinner? Helen?"

"As ever was and I don't want to get into what she did to my kitchen. I've put it right." Denton shifted the towels to his other arm and headed for the stairway. He jerked his head upward. "She's in the library," he said and began climbing the stairs. "Shall I make you an omelette? Believe me, you won't be wanting the pasta unless you plan to use it for a door-stop."

"Cooking," Lynley repeated to himself in wonder. He left Denton waiting for an answer. He made his way to the dining room.

At this point, three hours after it was meant to be consumed, the meal looked like the plastic dinner displays one sees in the windows of restaurants in Tokyo. She'd assembled a concoction of fettuccine and prawns, with wilted side salads, limp asparagus, a sliced baguette, and red wine. This last had been uncorked but not poured. Lynley filled the glasses at the two places laid. He gazed at the meal.

"Cooking," he said.

He was intrigued by the thought of what the food might actually taste like. As far as he knew, Helen had never assembled an entire meal—unassisted—in her life.

He picked up his glass of wine and circled the table, eyeing each dish, each fork, each knife. He sipped the wine. When he'd made a complete circuit of the dining room, he took a fork and caught three strands of fettuccine between its tines. Certainly, the food was stone cold and probably beyond the redemption of a microwave, but still he could get an idea. . . .

"Christ," he whispered. What in God's name had she put into the sauce? Tomatoes, to be sure, but had she actually used tarragon in place of parsley? He chased the pasta down with a hefty swallow of wine. Perhaps it was just as well that he'd arrived home three hours too late to savour the culinary delights spread out on his table.

He picked up the second glass and left the dining room. At least they had the wine. And it was a decent claret. He wondered if she had picked it out herself or if Denton had unearthed it from the wine stock for her.

The thought of Denton made Lynley smile. He could imagine his valet's horror—and his attempt to conceal it—as Helen created havoc in his kitchen, no doubt airily brushing aside his suggestions with a "darling Denton, if you confuse me any further, I shall make a ghastly muddle of things. Have you any spices, by the way? Spices are the secret of an excellent spaghetti sauce, I understand."

The fine difference between a herb and a spice would have been lost on Helen. She would have wielded nutmeg and cinnamon over her brew with as much gusto as she flung in thyme and sage.

He climbed the stairs to the first floor where the library door was cracked open just enough to let a thread of light fall upon the carpet. She was sitting in one of the large, wingback chairs near the fireplace with the glow from a reading lamp creating an aureole of light round her head. At first glance, she seemed to be intently studying a book that was open upon her lap, but as Lynley approached her, he saw in reality that she was asleep, her cheek on her fist. She had been reading Antonia Fraser's *The Six Wives of Henry VIII*, which was not exactly the auspicious augury Lynley had been looking for from her. But when he glanced at the wife whose biography she was currently perusing and saw it was Jane Seymour, he decided to interpret this as a positive sign. Further inspection, however, showed that she was in the midst of the ludicrous trial of Anne Boleyn, Seymour's predecessor, which boded ill. On the other hand, the fact that she had fallen *asleep* in the midst of the trial of Anne Boleyn could be interpreted as . . .

Lynley shook himself mentally. It was ironic, really, when he thought about it. Through most of his adult life, with only one exception, he'd held the upper hand with women. He'd gone his own way and if the path they were taking happened to intersect his, that was well and good. If not, he had rarely felt a mourner for the amorous loss. But with Helen, his entire *modus operandi* had been set upon its ear. In the sixteen months since he'd first admitted to himself that he'd somehow managed to fall in love with a woman who'd been one of his closest friends for nearly half his life, he'd become completely turned round. He went from one moment believing that he understood women completely to the next moment despairing of ever making the slightest degree of headway into his own profound ignorance. In his blackest periods, he found himself longing for what he liked to describe as "the good old days" when women were born and bred to be wives, consorts, mistresses, courtesans, or anything else that required of them complete submission to the will of the male. How convenient it would have been, really, to present himself at the home of Helen's father, to lay out his claim for her affections, perhaps even to barter for a dowry, but above all to end up with her, free from having to worry in the least about her wishes in the matter. Had marriages only still been arranged, he could have had her first and worried about winning her later. As it was, the wooing and winning were grinding him down. He was not—had never been—a particularly patient man.

He set her wineglass upon the table next to her chair. He removed the book from her lap, marked the place, and closed it. He squatted in front of her and covered her free hand with his. The hand turned, and their fingers twined. His own closed over an unexpected, unyielding, projecting object and he dropped his glance to see that she was wearing the ring he'd left her. He raised her hand and kissed the palm.

At this, she finally stirred. "I was dreaming of Catherine of Aragon," she murmured.

"What was she like?"

"Unhappy. Henry didn't treat her very well."

"Unfortunately, he'd fallen in love."

"Yes, but he wouldn't have discarded her if she'd only provided him with a living son. Why are men so awful?"

"That's a leap."

"From Henry to men in general? I wonder." She stretched. She noted the wineglass he was holding. "I see you've found your dinner."

"I have. I'm sorry, darling. If I'd known—"

"It doesn't matter. I gave Denton a taste of it and from the expression on his face—which, to his credit, he did try to hide—I could tell I hadn't exactly scaled a culinary Himalaya. He was good about letting me use the kitchen, though. Did he describe the chaos I reduced it to?''

"He was remarkably circumspect."

She smiled. "If you and I marry, Denton will certainly divorce you, Tommy. How could he possibly endure my burning the bottoms off all his pots and pans?''

"Is that what you did?"

"He *was* circumspect, wasn't he? What a lovely man." She reached for her wineglass and slowly twirled it by its stem. "It was only one pot, actually. And a small one at that. And I didn't burn the bottom entirely off. You see, the recipe called for sautéing garlic and I set it to sauté and got distracted by the phone—it was your mother, by the way. If the smoke alarm hadn't gone off, you probably would have come home to rubble instead of''—she waved her hand in the general direction of the dining room, *"fettuccine à la mer avec les crevettes et les moules."*

"What did Mother have to say?"

"She extolled your virtues. Intelligence, compassion, wit, integrity, moral fibre. I asked about your teeth, but she wasn't terribly helpful there.''

"You'd have to talk to my dentist. Shall I give you his number?''

"Would you do that?''

"And more. I'd even eat *fettuccine à la mer avec les crevettes et les moules."*

She smiled again. "I had a taste of it myself. Lord, it was dreadful. I'm hopeless, Tommy.''

"Have you eaten?''

"Denton took mercy upon me at half past nine. He whipped up something with chicken and artichokes that was absolute heaven. I bolted it down at the kitchen table and swore him to secrecy on the subject. But there's more of it left. I saw him stow it away in the refrigerator. Shall I reheat it for you? Surely I can do that much without burning down the house. Or have you had dinner somewhere already?''

He told her that he hadn't, that every moment he'd expected to bring an end to the day's work, but that at every juncture the investigation had simply kept extending itself. He admitted he was famished, he drew her to her feet, and they descended the stairs. They avoided the dining room and its steadily solidifying *fettuccine à la mer* and went instead to the basement kitchen. Helen rooted through the refrigerator while

Lynley watched. He felt absurdly comforted in some childish way by the sight of her shifting through jars and plastic bags to pull forth a container in triumph. What was this all about, he wondered, this sudden feeling of total complacency? Was it the ring and the fact that she had chosen to wear it? Was it the promise of a moderately decent meal? Or was it her behaviour, bustling about his kitchen, acting so decidedly wifely towards him, bringing plates from cupboards, taking cutlery from drawers, dumping the chicken and artichokes into a stainless steel pot, setting the pot into the microwave, smacking its door shut with an air of—

"Helen!" Lynley leapt across the kitchen before she had a chance to turn the microwave on. "You can't put metal in there."

She looked at him blankly. "Why ever not?"

"Because you can't. Because the metal and the microwaves will . . . Hell, I don't know. I just know you can't."

She studied the machine. "Goodness. I wonder . . ."

"What?"

"That must be what happened to mine."

"You put metal in it?"

"I actually didn't think of it as metal. One doesn't, you know."

"What? What was it?"

"A tin of vichyssoise. I've never cared for it cold, you see. And I thought, Let me just pop it in the microwave for a minute or two. That was that. It boomed, hissed, fizzled, and died. I remember thinking, No wonder they serve it cold, but I thought it was the soup. I never actually connected the tin itself to the booming, hissing, and fizzling." Her shoulders drooped and she sighed. "First the fettuccine. Now this. I don't know, Tommy." She twisted the ring on her finger. He put his arm round her shoulders and kissed her temple.

"Why do you love me?" she asked. "I'm utterly without hope and completely without promise."

"I wouldn't say that."

"I ruin your dinner. I destroy your pots."

"Nonsense," he said and turned her to him.

"I nearly blow up the kitchen. Lord, you'd be safer with the IRA."

"Don't be absurd." He kissed her.

"Left to my own devices, I shall probably burn down this house and all of Howenstow as well. Can you imagine the horror of that. Have you tried?"

"Not yet. But I will. Momentarily." He kissed her again, drawing her closer this time, teasing her mouth and lips with his tongue. She fitted him naturally, and he marvelled at the entire miraculous, antipodal nature of male-female sexuality. Angle for curve, rough for smooth, hard for soft. Helen was a wonder. She was everything he wanted. And the moment after he had something to eat, he'd prove it to her.

Her arms slipped round his neck. Her fingers moved languorously into his hair. Her hips pressed against his. He felt simultaneously hot in the groin and dizzy in the head as two appetites battled for control of his body.

He couldn't actually remember the last time he'd managed to have a well-balanced, strength-producing meal. It had been at least thirty-six hours, hadn't it? He'd had a single boiled egg and a slice of toast this morning, but that hardly counted when one considered the number of hours that had passed since then. He really ought to eat. The chicken and artichokes were sitting on the work top. The concoction would take less than five minutes to reheat. Five more to devour. Three to wash up if he didn't want to leave the remains for Denton. Yes. Perhaps that was the best idea. Food. Less than fifteen minutes and he'd be right as rain, he'd be strong as an ox, he'd be fit as a fiddle. He groaned. Jesus. What was happening to his mind? He needed sustenance. This very instant. Because if he didn't eat, he couldn't possibly . . .

Helen's hands drifted down his chest, unbuttoning as they went. They dropped to his trousers and teased his belt loose.

"Has Denton gone to bed, darling?" she whispered against his mouth.

Denton? What had Denton to do with anything?

"He won't be wandering into the kitchen, will he?"

The kitchen? Did she actually mean them to . . . No. No. She couldn't mean that.

He heard the sound of his zip being lowered. A veil of black gauze seemed to fall before his eyes. He thought about the likelihood of his passing out from hunger. Then her hand was against him and whatever blood was left in his head seemed to pound elsewhere.

He said, "Helen. I haven't eaten in hours. Frankly, I don't know if I'll even be able to—"

"Nonsense." She brought her mouth back to his. "I expect you'll do just fine."

He did.

OLIVIA

My legs have been cramping. I've dropped four pencils in the last twenty minutes, and I haven't had the energy to pick them up. I just take another out of the tin. I keep writing onwards and try to ignore what my handwriting's evolved to over the past few months.

Chris came through a moment ago. He stood behind me. He rested his hands on my shoulders and kneaded my muscles in the way I love. He put his cheek against the top of my head. "You don't have to write it all at one go," he said.

I said, "That's just what I've got to do."

"Why?"

"Don't ask. You know."

He left me alone. He's in the workroom now, crafting a hutch for Felix. "Six feet long," he told me. "Most people don't understand how much room a rabbit needs." He usually works with music playing, but he's kept both the radio and the stereo off because he wants me to be able to think and write clearly. I want as much as well, but the telephone rings and I hear him catch it. I hear the way his voice goes soft. It's gentle round the edges, like brandy if brandy were composed of sound. I try to ignore it, the "Yes . . . No . . . No real change . . . I won't be able to . . . No . . . No, it isn't that at all . . ." A long terrible silence after which he says, "I understand," in a voice that hurts me with the way it aches. I wait for more, telltale whispered words like *love*, like *want*, *miss*, and *if only*, telltale sounds like sighs. I strain to hear even as I recite the alphabet backwards in my head to block out his voice. I hear him say, "Only patience," and the words get fuzzy on the paper before me. The pencil slips and falls to the floor. I reach for another.

Chris comes into the galley. He plugs in the kettle. He takes a mug from the dresser, tea from a cupboard. He places his hands on the work top and lowers his head as if he's examining something there.

I feel my heart beating inside my throat and I want to say, "You can go to her. You can go if you like," but I don't because I'm afraid he'll do it.

It hurts too much to love. Why do we expect it to be so wonderful? Love's misery on misery. It's like pouring acid into one's heart.

The kettle boils and clicks off. He pours the water. He says, "Want a cuppa, Livie?" and I say, "Ta. Yes."

He says, "Oolong?"

I say, "No. Have we got any Gunpowder?"

He rattles through a cupboard for the tin. He says, "I don't know how you abide this stuff. It doesn't taste like anything but water to me."

"One needs a subtle palate," I say. "Some tastes are more delicate than others."

He turns. We look at each other a while. We say in silence all the things we can't take the chance of saying aloud. Finally, he remarks, "I ought to finish that hutch. Felix'll want a place to doss tonight."

I nod, but my face feels tight. When he passes me, his hand brushes near my arm and I want to catch it and press it to my cheek.

I say, "Chris," and he pauses behind me. I breathe and it hurts rather more than I expect. I say, "I'm probably going to be at this thing for a good few hours longer. If you'd like to go out . . . take the dogs for a final run or something . . . pop into the pub."

He says quietly, "I expect the dogs're all right."

I look at this yellow lined pad, the third I've started since beginning the writing. I say, "It can't be much longer now. You know."

He says, "Take your time."

He goes back to work. He says to Felix, "Now tell me, son, would you like a western or eastern exposure in your new accommodation?" and the hammering begins, quick blows, one-two for each nail. Chris is strong and skilled. He doesn't make mistakes.

I used to wonder why he took me on. "Was I a whim of the moment?" I'd asked him. Because it didn't make sense to me that he'd pick up a whore, buy her two cups of coffee and a spring roll, take her home, put her to work at carpentry, and end up inviting her to stay when he had no intention—not to mention no desire—of screwing her. At first I thought he meant me to whore for him. I thought he had a habit to support and I kept waiting for the sight of needles, spoons, and packets of powder. When I said, "What's this all about anyway," he said, "What's what all about?" and looked round the barge as if my question referred to it.

"This. Here. Me. With you."

"Is it supposed to be about something?"

"A bloke and a girl. Together they're usually about something, I'd say."

"Ah." He shouldered a board and cocked his head. "Where's the hammer taken itself off to?" And he'd set to work and set me to work as well.

While we were finishing the barge, we dossed on two Lilos, to the left of the stairs, at the opposite end from the animals. Chris slept in his underwear. I slept in the nude. Sometimes in the early morning, I threw the covers off and lay on my side so that my breasts looked fuller. I pretended to sleep and waited for something to happen between us. I caught him watching me once. I caught his eyes slowly wandering the length of my body. I saw him look reflective. I thought, This is it. I stretched to arch my back in what I knew from experience was a lissome movement.

He said, "You've remarkable musculature, Livie. Do you exercise regularly? Are you a runner?"

I said, "Hell." Then, "Yeah. I suppose I can run when I have to."

"How fast?"

"How'm I supposed to know?"

"How do you feel about the dark?"

I reached out and played my hand down his chest. "Depends on what's going on in it, actually."

"Running. Jumping. Climbing. Hiding."

"What? Playing war games?"

"Something like that."

I slipped my fingers into the waistband of his underpants. He caught my hand in his.

"Let's see," he said.

"What?"

"If you're good at something besides this."

"Are you queer? Is that it? Are you undersexed or something? Why don't you want to do it?"

"Because that's not how it's going to be between us." He rolled off the Lilo and got to his feet. He reached for his blue jeans and shirt. He was dressed in less than a minute, his back to me and his neck bent so that I could see the knob at the nape where he looked most vulnerable. "You don't have to be that way with men," he said. "There are other ways of being."

"Being what?"

"Who you are. Of value. Whatever."

"Oh, right." I sat up, pulling the blanket round me. Through the stacks of timber and the unfinished framing of the interior of the barge, I could see the animals at the other end. Toast was awake and chewing on a rubber ball, as was a beagle Chris called Jam. One of the rats was running on the exercise wheel inside the cage. It made an odd sound like the *rat-a-tat-tat* of machine-gun fire heard at a distance. "So go ahead," I said.

"With what?"

"The lecture you've been so hot to give me. Only you'd better be careful because I'm not like them." I flung my arm towards the animals. "I can walk out of here any time I like."

"Why don't you?"

I glared at him. I couldn't answer. I had the bed-sit in Earl's Court. I had regular clients. I had daily opportunity to expand my business out on the street. As long as I was willing to do anything and to try everything, I had a steady source of income. So why did I stay?

At the time I thought, It's because I intend to show you what's what. Before this is over, little bean, I'll have you baying at the moon, I'll see you so randy that you'll be grovelling at my feet just to lick my ankle.

And to do that, of course, I had to stay with him on the barge.

I grabbed my clothes from the floor between the Lilos. I stuffed myself into them. I folded my blanket. I ran my hand through my hair to comb it. "All right," I said.

"What?"

"I'll show you."

"What?"

"How fast I can run. How far. And whatever else you've a fancy to see."

"Climbing?"

"Fine."

"Crouching?"

"Fine."

"Slithering on your stomach?"

"I expect you'll find I'm expert at that."

He coloured. It was the first and only time I ever managed to embarrass him. He toed a piece of wood to one side. He said, "Livie."

I said, "I wasn't going to charge you."

He sighed. "It's not because you're a whore. It's got nothing to do with that."

"It has," I said. "I wouldn't be here in the first place if I wasn't a whore." I climbed up to the deck. He joined me. The day was grey, and the wind was blowing. Leaves scratched along the surface of the towpath. Even as we stood there, the first of the rain began to dimple the surface of the canal. "Right," I said. "Run, climb, crouch, slither." And I set off, with Chris following close behind, to show him exactly what I could do.

He was testing my skills. It's obvious to me now, but at the time I assumed he was devising strategies to keep himself from caving in to me. You see, I didn't know he had any outside interests then. For the first several weeks that we were together, he worked on the barge, he met with clients who needed his expertise in renovating their houses, he cared for his animals. He stayed in at night, reading mostly, although he listened to music and fielded dozens of phone calls that I assumed—from his businesslike tone and the many references he made to both city and ordnance maps—were related to his work with plaster and wood. He went out for the first time at night some four weeks after he'd taken up with me. He said he had a meeting to attend—he said it was a monthly do he had with four chaps he had been at school with, and in a way it was, as I found out later—and he told me he wouldn't be back late. He wasn't. But then he went out a second night that week and then a third. On the fourth he didn't get back till three and when he came in, he woke me up with his clatter. I asked him where he'd been. He answered, "Too much to drink" and he fell onto his Lilo and into a stuporous sleep. A week later, he began the process again. He was meeting with his mates, he said. Only this time on the third night out, he didn't come back at all.

I sat on the deck with Toast and Jam, and I waited for him. As the hours passed, my worry about him began to curdle. I said to myself, All right, two can play at this game. I dressed in spandex, spangles, black stockings, and heels. I made my way to Paddington. I picked up an Australian film editor who was working on a project at Shepperton Studios. He wanted to go to his hotel, but that didn't suit. I wanted him on the barge.

He was still there—asleep and splayed naked with one arm crooked to cover his eyes and one hand on my head where it rested against his chest—when Chris finally returned, quiet as a housebreaker, at half past six the next morning. He opened the door and came down the steps with his jacket in his arms. For a moment I couldn't see him clearly against the light. I squinted, then stretched quite happily when I saw the familiar halo of his hair. I yawned and ran my hand down and up the Australian's leg. The Australian groaned.

I said, "Morning, Chris. This's Bri. An Aussie. Lovely, isn't he?" And I turned to minister to him, increasing the volume of Brian's groans. He accommodated me further by moaning, "Not again. I can't. I'll be shooting blanks, Liv." As far as I could tell, he hadn't opened his eyes.

Chris said, "Get rid of him, Livie. I need you."

I waved him off and continued with Brian, who said, "Wha'? Who?" and struggled to his elbows. He grabbed a blanket, which he threw across his lap.

"This's Chris," I said. I nuzzled Brian's chest. "He lives here."

"Who is he?"

"No one. He's Chris. I told you. He lives here." I pulled at the blanket. Brian held on to it. With the other hand he began feeling round the floor for his clothes. I kicked them away, saying, "He's busy. We won't be bothering him. Come on. You liked it well enough last night."

"I've got the point," Chris said. "Get him out of here."

And then there was another sound, a low whine, and I saw that Chris wasn't holding his jacket at all. It was an old brown blanket with its piping ripped away, wrapped round something large. Chris carried it through the barge to the far end where the animals were. The galley was finished now, as were the animals' space, and the loo, so I couldn't tell what he was doing up there. I heard Jam bark.

Chris called over his shoulder, "Have you at least fed the animals?

Have you taken the dogs out?'' Then, ''Oh hell. Forget it.'' And much more quietly, ''Here. It's all right. You're all right. You're fine,'' in a gentle voice.

We stared in the direction he'd gone. Brian said, ''I'll shove off.''

I said, ''Right,'' but my eyes were on the door to the galley. I struggled into a T-shirt. I heard Brian clump up the steps. The door closed behind him. I went through the galley to Chris.

He was bent over the long work top in the animals' space. He hadn't turned on the light. Weak morning sun filtered through the window. He was saying, ''You're all right. You are. You are,'' in a tender voice. ''Rough night, wasn't it? But it's over now.''

I said, ''What've you got?'' and looked over his shoulder. ''Oh good God,'' I said, my stomach lurching. ''What's happened? Were you drunk? Where's he come from? Did you hit him with a car?''

That's all I could think of when I first saw the beagle, although if I'd been less woozy from drink, I would have understood that the sutures running from between the dog's eyes to the back of his head were not recent enough to be indicators of emergency surgery performed in the night. He lay on his side, drawing slow breaths with great spaces between them. When Chris touched the back of his fingers to the dog's jaw, his tail flopped weakly.

I grabbed Chris's arm. ''He looks awful. What'd you *do* to him?''

He glanced at me and for the first time I saw how white he was. ''I pinched him,'' he said. ''That's what I do.''

''Pinched? That . . . ? From . . . ? What in God's name's the matter with you? Did you break into a vet's?''

''He wasn't at a vet's.''

''Then where—''

''They removed part of his skull to expose his brain. They like to use beagles because the breed is friendly. It's easy to gain their confidence. Which, of course, is what they need before—''

''They? Who? What're you talking about?'' He was frightening me, just as he had done the night I first met him.

He reached for a bottle and a box of cotton wool. He daubed the sutures. The dog looked up at him with sad, cloudy eyes and ears that clung, drooping, to his wreck of a skull. Chris took a delicate pinch of the beagle's skin between his thumb and index finger. When he let it go, the skin stayed in place, pinched.

"Dehydrated," Chris said. "We need an IV."

"We haven't *got*—"

"I know that. Watch him. Don't let him get up." He went to the galley. Water ran. On the work top the dog's eyes drooped closed. His breathing slowed. His paws began to twitch. Beneath his lids, his eyes seemed to flick back and forth.

"Chris!" I called. "Hurry!"

Toast was up, nudging at my hand. Jam had retreated to a corner where he chewed at a piece of rawhide.

"Chris!" And then when he came back to the animals with a fresh bowl of water, "He's dying. I think he's dying."

Chris set the water down and bent to the dog. He watched him, resting a hand on his flank. "He's sleeping," he said.

"But his paws. His eyes."

"He's dreaming, Livie. Animals dream, you know, just like us." He dipped his fingers in the water, held them to the beagle's nose. It quivered. The dog cracked open his eyes. He lapped the drops from Chris's fingers. His tongue was nearly white. "Yes," Chris said. "You take it this way. Slow. Easy." He dipped his hand in the water again, held it again, watched the dog lick it again from his hand. The dog's tail *tip-tapped* against the work top. He coughed. Chris stood by him patiently, feeding him the water. It took forever. When he was done, he gently lowered him to a nest of blankets on the floor. Toast hobbled over to snuffle round the edges of the blankets. Jam stayed where he was, chewing away.

I was saying, "Where've you been? What's happened? Where'd you get him?" when a man's voice called from the other end of the barge, "Chris? Are you here? I only just now got the message. Sorry."

Chris called over his shoulder, "In here, Max."

An older bloke joined us. He was bald, with an eye patch. He was impeccably dressed in a navy suit, white shirt, speckled tie. He carried a black bag of the sort doctors use. He glanced at me, then at Chris. He hesitated.

"She's all right," Chris said. "This is Livie."

The bloke nodded at me and immediately dismissed me. He said to Chris, "What've you managed?"

Chris said, "I've got this one. Robert's got two others. His mum has a fourth. This one was the worst."

"Anything else?"

"Ten ferrets. Eight rabbits."

"Where?"

"Sarah. Mike."

"And this one?" He squatted to look at the dog. "Never mind. I can see." He opened his bag. "Take the others out, why don't you?" he suggested with a nod at Toast and Jam.

"You aren't going to put him down, are you, Max? I can look after him. Just give me what I need. I'll see to it."

Max looked up. "Take the dogs out, Chris."

I picked their leads from the nails on the wall. "Come on," I said to Chris.

He would go no farther than the towpath. We watched the dogs wander its length towards the bridge. They sniffed along the wall, stopped frequently to christen it. They rambled to the water and barked at the ducks. Jam shook off, ears flapping wildly, like he was wet. Toast did the same, lost his balance, came down hard on his shoulder, popped up again. Chris whistled. They turned, began to lope in our direction.

Max joined us. Chris said, "Well?"

"I'll give it forty-eight hours." Max snapped his bag closed. "I've left you pills. Feed him boiled rice and minced lamb. Half a cup. We'll see what happens."

"Thanks," Chris said. "I'm going to call him Beans."

"I'd call him damn lucky."

Max fondled Toast's head as the dogs returned to us. He gave a gentle tug to Jam's ears. "This one's ready for a home," he said to Chris. "There's a family in Holland Park."

"I don't know. We'll see."

"You can't keep them all."

"I'm aware of that."

Max glanced at his watch. "Quite," he said. He fished in his pocket. The two dogs yelped and danced back a few steps. He smiled and tossed them each a biscuit. "Get some sleep," he said to Chris. "Well done." He nodded to me a second time and headed in the direction of the bridge.

Chris took his Lilo into the animals' space. He spent the morning sleeping next to Beans. I kept Toast and Jam with me in the workroom where, while they tussled over a squeaky toy, I tried to organise the boxes, the tools, and the timber. I periodically took messages from the phone. These were all cryptic, like: "Tell Chris it's yes on Vale of March kennels," "Waiting on Laundry Farm," "Fifty doves at Lancashire P-A-L,"

"Nothing on Boots yet. Still waiting for word from Sonia." By the time Chris rose at a quarter past twelve, I'd come to understand what I'd been too thick to see before.

I was assisted by the BBC radio news, which reported what the Animal Rescue Movement had carried out in Whitechapel on the previous night. When Chris came into the workroom, someone was being interviewed, saying, ". . . have callously destroyed fifteen years' medical research through their blind stupidity," in an outraged voice.

Chris stopped in the doorway, a cup of tea in his hand. I examined him. "You pinch animals," I said.

"That's what I do."

"Toast?"

"Yes."

"Jam?"

"Right."

"The hooded rats?"

"And cats and birds and mice. The occasional pony. And monkeys. Lots of monkeys."

"But . . . but that's against the law."

"Isn't it."

"So why're you . . ." It was inconceivable. Chris Faraday, most compliant of citizens. Who was he, anyway? "What're they doing to them? To the animals? What?"

"Whatever they want. Electric shock, blinding, fracturing skulls, ulcerating stomachs, severing spinal cords, setting them afire. Whatever they want. They're only animals. They can't feel pain. Despite having a central nervous system like the rest of us. Despite having pain receptors and neural connections between those receptors and the nervous system. Despite . . ." He rubbed the back of his hand across his eyes. "Sorry. I'm preaching. It was a long night. I've got to see to Beans."

"Is he going to live?"

"If I have anything to do with it."

He stayed with Beans all day and all night. Max came back the next morning. They had a terse conference. I heard Max say, "Listen to me, Christopher. You can't—" and Chris interrupt with, "No. I will."

In the end, Chris won because he was willing to compromise: Jam went happily off to the home Max had found for him in Holland Park; we kept Beans. And when the barge was completed, it became a halfway house for other animals snatched in the darkness, the hub from which Chris expertly wielded his clandestine power.

Power. When we saw the pictures of what happened at the river last Tuesday afternoon, Chris said it was time that I told the truth. He said, "You can stop all this, Livie. You have the power." And how odd it was to hear those words because that's just exactly what I always wanted.

In that, I suppose, I am more like my mother than I care to be. While I was learning to attend to the animals, sitting in on my first meetings of the Movement, and establishing myself in a form of employment that could be useful to our ends—I was the lowest grade of technician at the London Zoo's animal hospital—Mother was setting in motion her plans for Kenneth Fleming. Once she knew he had a secret dream of playing cricket for England, she had access to the fissure she was looking for in his marriage to Jean Cooper. It would have been incomprehensible to Mother that Kenneth and Jean might have been not only compatible but also happy with each other and with the life they'd managed to make for themselves and their children. Jean was, after all, Kenneth's intellectual inferior. She did, after all, trap him into a marriage to which he, after all, had submitted himself in the name of duty-and-responsibility but certainly not in the name of love. In Mother's eyes, he was yoked to a plough that had long ago become mired in the mud. Cricket would be the means by which he was freed.

She moved neither hastily nor mindlessly. Kenneth was still a member of the factory's cricket team, so she began by attending their matches. At first the men were put off by her appearance, deck chair in hand and sun hat on her head, at the edge of their playing field in Mile End Park. She was "Ma'am" to the lads from the pit, and both they and their families gave her a wide berth.

Mother wasn't put off by this. She was used to it. She knew that she was an imposing figure in her summer sheaths with their matching shoes and handbags. She also knew that a great deal more than Hyde Park, Green Park, and the City of London separated her life and experience from those of her employees. But she was confident of winning them over eventually. At each match, she mingled somewhat longer with the players' wives. She spoke to their children. She made herself at once one of them and one step removed: shouting, "Oh, well played! Well *played*!" from the sidelines next to the tea urn and the biscuits which she always took with her, commenting at the tea interval, after the match, or later at work upon an especially good inning. The players and their families grew to accept and even to anticipate her presence. Eventually, she established regular team meetings, and she encouraged strategising, scouting other teams, and seeking advice.

She even made inroads on Jean Cooper's misgivings over her presence at the matches. She knew that a key to Kenneth's future lay in garnering Jean's trust, and she set about proving herself worthy of it. She professed herself interested in the schooling of the two older children. She immersed herself in conversations about the health and development of the youngest one, a three-year-old called Stan who was slow to talk and who toddled unsteadily when he should have moved solidly on his feet. "Olivia was just like Stan at that age," Mother confided. "But by the time she was five, I couldn't hold her in one place and I would have needed a muzzle to keep her from talking." Mother laughed gently at her long-ago anxieties. "How we worry over them, don't we?" A nice touch, that *we*.

So that unfortunate day at Billingsgate Market years before might never have occurred between Jean and Mother. In the place of invective slipped discussions over the cost of child care, over Jimmy's remarkable resemblance to his dad, over Sharon's maternal instincts and how she began demonstrating them the very day Jean brought little Stan home from hospital. Mother stayed away from any topic that might have caused Jean to feel her inferiority. If they were to be co-conspirators in Kenneth's personal renaissance, they had to be equals. Jean would eventually have to agree to the previously unthinkable, and Mother was wise enough to know that her agreement could only be won if Jean thought in part that the idea was her own.

I've wondered if Mother laid her plans systematically or if she allowed her scheme to follow an organic pattern. I've also wondered if she decided how she wanted things to be the moment she saw Kenneth Fleming in the pit. What's so remarkable and so audacious about her machinations is that they seem—even now, to me, who knows the truth —unquestionably natural, a sequence of events that cannot be explored from any direction with the hope of finding a Machiavelli at their root.

Where did it first come from, the idea that the factory cricket team needed a captain? From logic, of course. From a gentle and perplexed question dropped here or there: Tell me now, England's team have a captain, haven't they? The county sides have captains, haven't they? In fact the cricket first eleven at every school in the country must have a captain. Perhaps the lads from Whitelaw Printworks should have a captain as well.

The lads cast about for a choice and selected their foreman. Who better to set the field than the same chap who oversaw their workdays? But then again, perhaps that wasn't such a good idea after all. The skills that went into managing the pit at Whitelaw Printworks weren't exactly suited to the cricket pitch, were they? And even if they were, a certain distinction should be made between time spent on the job and time spent in pleasure, and how could that distinction be made if the foreman at work became the foreman at play? Wouldn't it be a fine idea for the foreman just to be one of the lads on the team rather than the team leader? Wouldn't it go further to advance employee bonhomie if the foreman were the lads' equal in this endeavour?

Yes, yes. The lads saw it that way and the foreman saw it no differently. They cast about for a second choice, someone who knew the game, who'd played it in school, someone who inspired performance on the pitch, either as batsman or as bowler. They had a decent two bowlers: Shelby the compositor and Franklin, who kept the machinery up and running. And they had a stellar batsman: Fleming, who worked one of the presses part time and worked management as well. Well, what about Fleming? Would he do? If they chose him, neither Shelby nor Franklin would have occasion to think the team considered the other a better bowler. Why not give Fleming a go?

So Kenneth became team captain. There was no money involved and just about the same amount of prestige. But that didn't matter, because the entire point was to whet his appetite for the game, to make him start longing more intensely for the what-could-have-beens, and to inveigle him away from the dismal what-weres.

To no one's surprise, least of all Mother's, Kenneth made a great success of his position as captain. He set the field with wisdom and precision, switching players from one position to another until he had them where they performed the best. He saw the game as a science rather than as an opportunity for popularity among the lads. His own performance was always the same. With a bat in his hand, Kenneth Fleming was magic.

He never played cricket for its potential for public adulation. He played cricket because he loved the game. And that love showed, from the deliberation with which he took guard at the crease to the grin that cracked across his face a second after he hit the ball. So he was first to agree with enthusiasm when an old gent called Hal Rashadam, who'd come to three or four matches, offered his services as the team's coach. For a lark, Rashadam said. Love the game, I do. Used to play it myself when I was able. Always want to see it played c'rrec'ly.

A coach for a factory cricket team? Who'd ever heard of such a thing? Where had he come from, anyway? The lads had seen him on the edge of the playing field, leaning back on his heels, pulling on his chin, nodding, talking to himself now and again. They'd thought he was one of the neighbourhood loonies and dismissed him as such among themselves. So when Rashadam approached after a particularly sticky match against a tyre company from Haggerston and offered his thoughts about how they played, the lads' inclination was to tell him to be about his business.

It was Mother who said, "Wait a moment, gentlemen. There's something . . . What is it you're talking about, sir?" And she no doubt said it so ingenuously that not one of them guessed how long it had taken her to persuade Hal Rashadam into giving the lads from Whitelaw Printworks—and particularly one lad among them—a serious look. Because make no mistake, Mother was behind Rashadam's presence, as anyone with a brain would have known once he introduced himself and Kenneth Fleming said, "Rashadam. *Rashadam?*" He struck his forehead and laughed. "Crikey," to his teammates, "you loobies. Don't you know who this is?"

Harold Rashadam. Are you familiar with the name? You wouldn't be if you don't follow the game with the sort of passion Kenneth Fleming had. Rashadam was taken out of cricket some thirty years ago by a bad shoulder that refused to heal properly. But when he played a brief two years for Derbyshire and for England, he'd made his mark as an outstanding all-rounder.

People believe what they want to believe, and it seemed that the Whitelaw Printworks lads wanted to believe that Hal Rashadam happened upon their team on a visit to whoever on earth he might have known in the environs of Mile End Park. Just strolling by, he told them, and they lapped up the information like cats after cream. They also wanted to believe that he was, as he said, offering his services as a coach gratis, out of love for the game and nothing more. Retired, he said, Got time on my hands, love to have something to take my mind off these old bones, don't you know. Beyond that, they wanted to trust in the fact that Rashadam was interested in the group, not in an individual, and that the group would benefit from his presence in some obscure way only marginally related to cricket in the first place.

Mother encouraged them. She said, "Let us think about it, if you please, Mr. Rashadam," to his offer, and she met with the lads and played the role of Lady Caution, saying, "Is he really who he says? And who was this Rashadam when he was somebody?"

Someone did the research for her, unearthing old newspaper clippings, procuring a copy of *Wisden Cricketers' Almanack* so that she could see for herself. Mother transmogrified from Lady Caution to Lady Interest, no doubt inwardly thrilled to see how keen Rashadam's appearance at Mile End Park had made Kenneth Fleming.

How would she have met Rashadam? You're wondering that, aren't you? You're asking how on earth Miriam Whitelaw, former schoolteacher, could have pulled an ace cricketer out of the hat?

You must consider the years of her life that she gave to volunteer work and what those years meant in terms of contacts she had, people she knew, organisations that owed her one favour or another. A friend of a friend was all she needed. If she could get someone like Rashadam to visit Mile End Park on a Sunday afternoon, to stroll along the playing field behind the spectators and their deck chairs and their picnic lunches, Kenneth Fleming's talents would do the rest. She was sure of it.

Naturally, there was money involved. Rashadam wouldn't have done any of it out of the goodness of his heart, and Mother wouldn't have asked that of him. She was a businesswoman. This was part of business. He would have named an hourly sum to visit, to talk with, and to coach. She would have paid.

And you're wondering why. I can hear you ask. Why would she go to the trouble? Why make the sacrifice?

Because it was neither trouble nor sacrifice to Mother. It was simply what she wanted to do. She no longer had a husband. Her relationship with me had been mutually destroyed. She needed Kenneth Fleming. Call him what you want: a focus for her attention and concern, a potential recipient of her affection, a cause that could be fought for and won, a man to replace the one who had died, a child to replace the one she'd expunged from her life. Perhaps she felt she'd failed him when he was her pupil ten years earlier. Perhaps she saw their renewed relationship as an opportunity not to fail him a second time. She'd always believed in his potential. Perhaps she was merely seeking a way to prove herself right. I don't know exactly what she was thinking, hoping, dreaming, or planning when she began. I believe her heart was in the right place, though. She wanted the best for Kenneth. But she also wanted to be the one who said what that *best* would be.

So Rashadam joined the factory team. It wasn't long before he singled out Kenneth for special attention. This attention took place at first in Mile End Park, with Rashadam working on Kenneth's skill with the bat. But within two months, the old cricketer suggested they book a few sessions in the nets at Lord's.

More privacy there, after a fashion, he would have informed Kenneth Fleming. We don't want scouts from any other team having a look at what we're developing here, do we?

So to Lord's they went, on Sunday mornings at first, and you can imagine what it probably felt like to Kenneth Fleming when the door to the indoor cricket school closed behind him and he heard the crack of bats hitting balls and he heard the *whoosh* of balls being bowled. What he must have felt as he walked along the netted enclosures: nerves making his stomach quiver, anxiety making his palms become damp, excitement obscuring any question he might have asked about why Hal Rashadam was spending so much time and so much energy with a young man whose real future lay not with cricket—Good God, he was already twenty-seven years old!—but on the Isle of Dogs, in a terraced house, with a wife and three children, in Cubitt Town.

And what of Jean, you ask? Where was she, what was she doing, and how was she reacting to the attention Kenneth was getting from Rashadam? I imagine she didn't notice at first. Initially the attention was subtle. When Kenneth came home and said, "Hal thinks this" or "Hal says that," she no doubt nodded and noticed how her husband's hair was getting lighter with the exposure to the sun, how his skin looked healthier than it had in years, how his movements were more agile than they'd ever been before, how his face radiated an enthusiasm for living that she'd forgotten he once possessed. All this would have translated to desire. And when they were in bed and their bodies were working rhythmically together, the least important question to ponder was where this ardour for cricket was going to lead them, not to mention what potential for unhappiness lay in one man's simple love for a sport.

OLIVIA

I imagine Kenneth Fleming kept his deepest and most heart-felt wish a secret from his wife, born as it was from the midnight joining of hope and fantasy. It had little enough to do with their everyday lives. Jean's time would have been taken up with her homemaking, her children, her job at Billingsgate Market. She probably would have scoffed at the idea of Kenneth's ever doing anything more than making a name for himself at Whitelaw Printworks and perhaps becoming plant manager someday. This doubt of hers wouldn't have grown from an inability or unwillingness to believe in her husband. It would have grown from a practical examination of the facts at hand.

It seems to me that Jean had always been the level-headed partner between them. Remember that she had been the one to question having sex without the protection of the pill so many years ago, and she had been the one to announce her pregnancy and decide to keep the baby and get on with her life regardless of Kenneth's own decisions in the matter.

So it seems reasonable to conclude that she would have been fully capable of realistically evaluating the facts when Hal Rashadam first walked into their lives: Kenneth was fast approaching his twenty-eighth birthday; he'd never played cricket other than in school, with his children, or with the lads; there was a drenched-in-tradition course one took when one hoped eventually to play for England.

Kenneth hadn't followed this course. Oh, he'd taken the first step and played at school, but that was the limit of his involvement.

Jean would have gently scoffed at the very idea of Kenneth's playing professionally. She would have said, "Kenny, luv, you got your head in the clouds." She would have teased and asked him how long he expected to have to wait for the England captain and the national selectors to come round and watch the test match of the century between Whitelaw Printworks and Cowper's Guaranteed Rebuilt Appliances. But in doing that, she would have reckoned without my mother.

Perhaps it was at Mother's suggestion that Kenneth didn't mention his dreams to Jean. Or perhaps Mother said, "Does Jean know about all this, Ken dear?" when he first told her what was in his heart. If he said no, perhaps she said wisely, "Yes. Well, some things *are* best left unmentioned, aren't they?" and in doing so established the first of the adult bonds between them.

If you know the history of Kenneth Fleming's rise to fame and fortune, then you know the rest of the story. Hal Rashadam bided his time while he coached Kenneth privately. Then he invited the committee head of the Kent county side to watch a session in the nets. The head's interest was piqued enough to make him willing to come to a match in Mile End Park where the lads from Whitelaw Printworks were taking on East London Tool Manufacturers, Ltd. At the end of the match, introductions were made between Kenneth Fleming and the gent from Kent. Kent said, "Care to come out for a Guinness?" And Kenneth accompanied him.

Mother took care to keep her distance. In inviting the committee head of the Kent county side to watch the match, Rashadam was acting under Mother's aegis, but no one was to know that. No one was to think that there was a Greater Plan at work.

Over their pints of Guinness, Kent's captain suggested that Kenneth come to a practise session and give their side a look-over. This he did, with Rashadam in attendance on a Friday morning when Mother said, "You go ahead to Canterbury, Ken. You can make up the time later. It's not a problem at all," and hoped for the best. Rashadam told him in advance to wear his playing clothes. Kenneth asked why. Rashadam said, "Just do it, lad." Kenneth said, "But I'll feel a total fool." Rashadam said, "We'll see who feels the fool when the day is over."

And when the day was over, Kenneth had his place in the Kent county side, in defiance of tradition and "the way things are done." It was just forty-eight hours short of eight months since Hal Rashadam had first watched the lads from Whitelaw Printworks at play.

There were only two problems associated with Kenneth's playing in the Kent side. The first was the pay: it was just over half what he made at the printworks. The second was his home: the Isle of Dogs was too far from the playing and practise field in Canterbury, especially for a novice about whom the team would have had doubts. According to the captain, if he wanted to play for Kent, he needed to move to Kent.

Essentially, then, Phase One in Mother's plan for Kenneth was completed. The need to move to Kent constituted Phase Two.

Kenneth would have shared each moment of the unfolding drama with my mother. First, because they worked closely together in the hours he spent in management. Second, because it was through what he no doubt saw as her generosity and her unfailing faith in him that he'd had the offer to play in a county side in the first place. But what, he probably asked her as well as himself, could he do about the problems associated with playing in the Kent county side? He couldn't move the family to Kent. Jean had her job at Billingsgate Market, which would be ever more crucial to the family's survival if he were to accept this opportunity. Even if he could ask her to make the long commute—and he couldn't, he wouldn't, there was no question of that—he wouldn't have her driving from Canterbury to East London in what went for the middle of the night, driving an old car that could break down and leave her stranded in the middle of nowhere. It wasn't thinkable. Besides, her entire family was on the Isle of Dogs. The children's mates were there as well. And there was still and always the problem of money. Because even if Jean continued her job at Billingsgate Market, how could they survive on that when he would be making less than what he made at the printworks? There were far too many financial considerations involved. The expense of a move, the expense of finding a suitable place to live, the expense of the car . . . There was simply not enough money.

I can picture the conversation between them, Kenneth and my mother. They're in the third-floor office that she'd made over from my father's to hers. She's reading a set of contracts while on the desk a blue-edged white porcelain teapot emits a shimmering plume of Earl Grey steam. It's later in the evening—sometime near eight o'clock—when the building has settled into stillness, and five immigrant custodians are wielding brooms, mops, and rags among the motionless machinery in the pit.

Kenneth comes into the office with another contract for Mother to look over. She takes off her glasses and rubs her temples. She's shut off the overhead lights in the office because they give her a headache. Her desk lamp throws shadows like giant handprints against the walls. She says, "I've been thinking, Ken."

He says, "I've done the estimate on the job for the Ministry of Agriculture. I think we'll get it." He hands the paperwork to her.

She places the estimate on the corner of her desk. She pours herself another cup of tea. She fetches a second cup for him. She's careful not to return to her chair. She won't ever sit behind the desk while he's in the office, because she knows to do so is to define the gulf in their relationship.

"What I've been thinking of," she says, "is you. And Kent."

He raises his hands and drops them in a what's-there-to-discuss gesture. He looks resigned.

Mother says, "You've not given them an answer yet, have you?"

"Been putting it off," he says. "I've a fancy to hold on to the dream as long as I can."

"When do they need to know?"

"End of the week is when I said I'd phone."

She pours his tea. She knows how he takes it—with sugar but no milk—and she hands him the cup. There's a table at one side of the office where the shadows are deepest, and she leads him to this and tells him to sit. He says he ought to be off, Jean will be wondering what's happened to him, they've a family dinner to attend at her parents' house, he's late already, she's probably taken the kids and gone on without him. . . . But he makes no move to depart.

Mother says, "She's an independent one, your Jean."

"She's that," he acknowledges. He stirs his tea but he doesn't drink it at once. He sets the cup on the table and sits. He's lanky—more so than he was as a boy—and he seems to fill up a room in ways other men don't. Something vibrates off him, some sort of curious life force akin to restless energy but more than that.

Mother notices this. She's attuned to him. She says, "Is there absolutely no chance she might find work in Kent?"

"Oh, she could do," he replies. "But she'd have to work in a shop. Or a caff. And she'd not make enough to offset our expenses."

"She has no . . . real skills, Ken?" Naturally, Mother knows the answer to that question. But she wants to make him say it himself.

"Job skills, you mean?" He gives the cup a turn in its saucer. "Just what she's learned at the caff at Billingsgate."

Little enough is the real answer. As is *She's waited on tables, filled out bills, rung up charges on the till, made change.*

"Yes. I see. That makes things tricky, doesn't it?"

"It makes things impossible."

"It makes things . . . shall we say difficult?"

"Difficult. Tricky. Impossible. Dicey. They all add up to one sum, don't they? You don't need to remind me. I've made my own bed."

Which is probably not the allusion Mother would have chosen. Which is probably why she goes quickly on before he can complete it.

"Perhaps there's another road to consider, one that doesn't involve quite so much disruption in your family's life."

"I could ask for a chance in Kent. I could make the commute and prove it isn't a problem. But as for the money . . ." He pushes the tea-cup away. "No. I'm a big lad, Miriam. Jean's put away her childhood dreams and it's time I did the same with mine."

"Is she asking that of you?"

"She says we got to consider the kids, what's best for them, not what's best for ourselves. I can't argue with that. I could leave the printworks and run back and forth to Kent for years and still end up with nothing much to show for it. She asks is it worth the risk when nothing is guaranteed."

"And if something were guaranteed? Your job here, for instance."

He looks thoughtful. He considers Mother in that frank way of his, eyes steady on her face as if he'd read her mind. "I couldn't ask you to hold my job open. That wouldn't be fair to the other men. And even if you did that much for me, there's too many other difficulties to scramble over."

She goes to her desk. She returns with a notebook. She says, "Let's list them, shall we?"

He protests, but only half-heartedly. As long as he has someone to dream his dreams with after hours, it doesn't feel quite as if he's letting them go. He says that he needs to phone Jean, to tell her he'll be later still. And while he's off tracking down his wife and family, Mother sets to work, listing and counter-listing and arriving at the conclusion she'd no doubt arrived at the moment she saw him first hit the ball beyond the boundary in Mile End Park. Oxford was lost to him, true enough. But the future was still open in another way.

They talk. They toss ideas back and forth. She suggests. He objects. They argue fine points. They finally leave the printworks and go down to Limehouse for a Chinese meal, over which they continue to thrash with the facts. But Mother holds an ace that she's been careful not to display too soon. Celandine Cottage in the Springburns. And Kent.

Celandine Cottage has been in our family since somewhere round 1870. For a time, my great-grandfather used it to house his mistress and their two children. It passed to my grandfather, who retired there. It passed to my father, who let it out to a succession of farmworkers until such a time as it became trendy to have a weekend getaway in the country. We used it occasionally when I was a teenager. It was currently unoccupied.

What if, Mother suggested, Kenneth used Celandine Cottage as a base of operation? That would take care of his need to be in Kent. What if he renovated what needed renovating at the cottage, gardened what needed gardening, painted what needed painting, plastered what needed plastering, and otherwise made himself useful to the place? That would take care of his need to pay rent. What if he worked at the printworks when he was able and compiled bids for printing jobs on his own time? Mother would pay him for doing so, and that would take care of at least part of his money troubles. What if Jean and the children stayed in place on the Isle of Dogs—where Jean could keep her job, where the children would have their extended family as well as their mates nearby—and Kenneth brought them to the country at the weekends? That would minimise the disruption in their lives, keep the family together, and give the children the opportunity to romp in the fresh air. This way, if Ken didn't have a real chance of making his way in the world of professional cricket, at least he would have tried.

Mother was Mephisto. It was her finest moment. Except that she meant well. I do believe that she truly meant well. Most people do, at heart, I think. . . .

Chris calls out, "Livie, have a look at this," and I scoot my chair back and cant my head to see round the galley door into the workroom. He's finished the hutch. Felix is exploring it. He gives a hesitant hop and a sniff. Another hop.

"He needs a garden to scuff about in," I note.

"Quite. But since we haven't got a garden, this will have to do until his lodgings change." Chris watches Felix hop inside and go to the water bottle where he drinks. The bottle rattles against the cage like the clicking of rail carriages against a track.

"How do they know to do that?" I ask.

"What? Drink out of a bottle?" He returns nails to their appropriate containers by size. He puts away his hammer and neatly sweeps sawdust from the workbench into a bin. "Process of observation and exploration, I should guess. He susses out the new digs, bumps into the water bottle, explores it with his nose. But he's been in a hutch before, so he probably knows what to find inside anyway."

We watch the rabbit, I from my chair in the galley, and Chris from his position in front of the workbench. At least Chris watches the rabbit. I watch Chris.

I say, "It's been quiet lately, hasn't it? Telephone hasn't rung for days."

He nods. We both ignore the phone call he's received only an hour ago because we both know what I'm talking about. Not social calls, not business calls, but ARM calls. He runs his hand along the top front edge of Felix's hutch, finds a spot that's rough, applies sandpaper to it.

"Is there nothing in the works, then?" I ask.

"Just Wales."

"What's up?"

"Beagle kennels. If our unit takes them on, I'll be gone a few days."

"Whose decision?" I ask. "Whether to take it, that is."

"Mine."

"Then take it."

He looks at me. He wraps the sandpaper round his finger. He tightens it, loosens it, examines the tube he's created and rolls it back and forth on his palm.

"I can cope," I say. "I'll be fine. I'll be perfect. Ask Max to drop by. He can walk the dogs. We'll play cribbage afterwards."

"We'll see."

"When do you have to decide?"

He replaces the sandpaper. "There's time."

"But the beagles . . . Chris, are the kennels getting ready to ship them?"

"They're always getting ready for that."

"Then you must—"

"We'll see, Livie. If I don't take it, someone else will. Don't worry. The dogs won't go to a lab."

"But you're the best of the lot. Especially with dogs. And they'll be looking for disturbance, the kennel owners, if the puppies are getting old enough to be shipped. Someone good needs to go. The best needs to go."

He clicks off the fluorescent light above the workbench. Felix rustles round in his hutch. Chris comes into the galley.

"Look. You don't need to watch over me," I say. "I hate that. It makes me feel like such a freak."

He sits and reaches for my hand. He turns it in his. He scrutinises my palm. He bends the fingers closed. He watches me open them. We both know how I concentrate to make the movement smooth.

When my fingers are unbent, he covers my hand so that it's completely enclosed by both of his. He says, "I've two new members in the unit, Livie. I'm not certain they're ready for something like Wales. And I won't risk the dogs to feed my ego." His hands press mine. "That's what it is. It has nothing to do with you. Or with this. All right?"

"New members?" I say. "You never said." I would have known at one time. We would have talked it over.

"I must have forgotten. They've been with me for about six weeks now."

"Who?"

"A chap called Paul. His sister. Amanda."

He holds my gaze so unflinchingly that I realise she's the one. Amanda. Her name seems to hang between us like a vapour.

I want to say, "Amanda. How pretty a name." I want to go on breezily with, "She's the one, isn't she? So tell me about it. How did you fall in love? How long was it before you took her to bed?"

I want him to say, "Livie" and look uncomfortable so that I can go on with, "But aren't you breaking a few of your rules?" as if I couldn't be less bothered with the knowledge. I want to say, "Doesn't the organisation forbid involvement? Isn't that what you always said to me? And since members of a unit—not to mention members of the entire bleeding group —know only the Christian names of other members, doesn't that put a crimp in your love affair? Or have you two exchanged more than just bodily fluids? Does she know who you are? Have the two of you made plans?"

If I say all that and say it quickly enough, I don't have to picture the two of them together. I don't have to wonder where they do it or how. I don't have to think of it if I can only force myself to ask the questions and to put him on the defensive.

But I can't. One time I would have done, but I seem to have lost the part of me that could leap from out of nowhere, snarling and trying to wound.

He's watching me. He knows that I know. One word from me and we can have the discussion he has no doubt promised Amanda that we'll have. "I'll tell her about us," he probably whispers when they've finished and their bodies are slick with that blend of loving each other and sweat. "I'll tell her. I will." He kisses her neck, her cheek, her mouth. Her leg shifts and locks round his. He says, "Amanda," or "Mandy," against her mouth in place of a kiss. They doze.

No. I won't think of them like that. I won't think of them at all. Chris has a right to his life, just as I've had a right to mine. And I broke enough of the organisation's rules myself while I was an active member.

Once I proved myself physically to Chris's satisfaction—running, climbing, jumping, sliding, slithering, and doing whatever else he commanded—I began to attend the open meetings of the educational branch of ARM. These were held in churches, schools, and community centres where antivivisectionists from half a dozen organisations pressed information upon the local citizenry. Through this means, I came to know the hows and the whats of animal research: what Boots was doing in Thurgarton, what factory farms are like, how many mongrels at Laundry Farm were alleged to be stolen pets, the neurotic behaviour of caged minks in Halifax, the number of biological suppliers who breed animals for labs. I became familiar with the moral and ethical arguments on both sides of the issue. I read what I was given. I listened to what was said.

I wanted to be part of an assault unit from the first. I'd like to claim that one look at Beans the morning he arrived at the barge was enough to win me over to the cause. But the truth is that I wanted to be part of an assault unit not because I believed so passionately in saving the animals but because of Chris. What I wanted from him. What I wanted to demonstrate about myself to him. Oh, I didn't admit that, naturally. I told myself that I wanted to be in a unit because the activities surrounding the animals' liberation seemed to be filled with tension, with the terror of being caught in the act, and—most importantly—with an unbelievable heady exhilaration when an assault was carried off without a hitch. I'd been off the streets for some months at this point. I felt restless, in need of a decent dose of the sort of excitement provided by the unknown, by danger and a hair's-breadth escape from danger. Taking part in an assault seemed just the ticket.

The assault units consisted of specialists and runners. The specialists paved the way—infiltrating the target weeks in advance, filching documents, photographing the subjects, mapping out the environment, discovering alarm systems and ultimately deactivating them for the runners. The runners carried out the actual assault at night, led by a captain whose word was law.

Chris never made an error. He met with his specialists, he met with the governing core of ARM, he met with his runners. One group never saw the other. He was the liaison among us all.

My first assault with the unit took place nearly a year after Chris and I met. I wanted it sooner, but he wouldn't allow me to short circuit the process that everyone else went through. So I worked my way up through the organisation and I kept my sights set on battering through what I believed were Chris's defences against me. No doubt you see how ignoble I was.

My first assault was made upon a study of spinal cord injuries taking place in a red-brick university two hours from London where Chris had had a specialist in place for seven weeks. We arrived in four cars and a mini-van, and while the sentries moved forward to eliminate the security lights, the rest of us crouched in the shelter of a yew hedge and listened to Chris's final instructions.

Our primary goal was the animals, he told us. Our secondary goal was the research. Liberate the first. Destroy the second. But only move on to the secondary goal if and when the first was achieved. Take all animals. The decision would be made later as to which of them could be kept.

"Kept?" I whispered. "Chris, aren't we here to save them all? We aren't going to return any of them, are we?"

He ignored me and pulled down his ski mask. The moment the security lights blinked off, he said, "Now," and sent in the first wave of the unit: the liberators.

I can still see them, head-to-toe black figures moving in the darkness like dancers. They glided across the courtyard, using the deeper shadows of the trees for protection. We lost sight of them as they bled round the side of the building. Chris held a torch beam on his watch while a girl called Karen shielded the light with her hands.

Two minutes went by. I watched the building. A pinpoint of light made an eyeblink from a ground-floor window. "They're in," I said.

"Now," Chris said.

I was in the unit's second wave: the transporters. Equipped with carriers, we dashed across the courtyard, low to the ground. By the time we reached the building, two of the windows were open. Hands reached for us, pulled us inside. It was someone's office, filled with the shapes of books, folders, a word processor and printer, graphs on the walls, charts. We slipped out of it and into a corridor. A light winked once to our left. The liberators were already in the lab.

The only sounds were our breathing, the snap of cages being opened, the weak cry of the kittens. Torches flicked on and off, just enough to verify that an animal was in a cage. The liberators shifted cats and kittens. The transporters darted back to the open window with the cardboard carriers. And the receivers—the final wave of the unit—raced silently with the carriers back to the cars and the mini-van. The entire operation was designed to take less than ten minutes.

Chris came in last. He carried the paint, the sand, and the honey. As the transporters melted back into the night, joining the receivers at the cars, he and the liberators destroyed the research. They allowed themselves two minutes among the papers, the graphs, the computers, and the files. When time was up, they slid back out the window and dashed across the courtyard. The window was closed behind them, locked as it had been before. While we waited at the edge of the courtyard—sheltered again by the hedge—the sentries materialised round the side of the building. They slipped into the deeper darkness near the trees. They moved from shadow to shadow until they rejoined us.

"Quarter of an hour," Chris whispered. "Too slow."

He jerked his head and we followed him between the buildings and back to the cars. The receivers had already put the animals in Chris's mini-van and gone on their way.

"Tuesday night," Chris said in a low voice. "Practical manoeuvres." He climbed into the van. He peeled off his mask. I followed. We waited until the remaining cars drove off in different directions. Chris started the van. We headed southwest.

"Great, great, *great*," I said. I leaned over. I pulled Chris towards me. I kissed him. He righted himself and kept his eyes on the road. "That was great. That was something. God! Did you see us? Did you *see* us? We were flaming invincible." I laughed and clapped my hands. "When do we do it again? Chris, answer. When do we do it again?"

He didn't reply. He stepped down hard on the accelerator. The mini-van zoomed forward. Behind us, the cardboard carriers slid back a few inches. Several kittens mewed.

"What're we going to do with them? Chris, answer. What're we going to do with them? We can't keep them all. Chris, you aren't planning to keep them all, are you?"

He glanced at me. He looked back at the road. The lights from the dashboard made his face appear yellow. A roadsign for the M20 loomed in the headlamps. He guided the van to the left towards the motorway.

"Have you homes lined up already? Are we going to deliver them this morning, like the milk? Oh, but let's keep one. She'll be a souvenir. I'll call her Break-in."

He winced. He looked like something was pinching him behind his eyes.

I said, "Did you get hurt? Did you cut yourself? Did you hurt your hands? Shall I drive? I'll drive. Chris, pull over. Let me drive."

He stepped harder on the accelerator. I watched the needle on the speedometer creep higher. The kittens cried.

I twisted in my seat and pulled one of the carriers towards me, saying, "Okay, you. Let's see what we've got."

Chris said, "Livie."

"Who are you? What's your name? Are you glad to be out of that nasty old place?"

Chris said, "Livie."

But I already had the top open and I was scooping the little ball of fur into my hand. I could see the kitten was a tabby, grey-brown and white with overlarge ears and eyes. I said, "Oh, you're a sweet one," and rested the kitten on my lap. He mewled. His little claws caught at my leggings. He began to crawl towards my knees.

Chris said, "Put him back," just at the moment that I noticed the kitten's back legs. They dangled, useless and twisted, behind him. His tail hung limp. A long thin incision ran along his spine, held together by blood-crusted metal sutures. Towards his shoulders the incision oozed pus that matted against the fur.

I felt myself recoil. "Shit!" I said.

Chris said, "Put him back in the carrier."

"I . . . What's he . . . What's been done . . . ?"

"They've broken his spinal cord. Put him back."

I couldn't. I couldn't bring myself to touch him. I pressed my head against the back of the seat.

"Take him off me," I said. "Chris. Please."

"What did you think? What in hell did you think?"

I squeezed my eyes closed. I felt the tiny claws against my skin. I saw the kitten against the back of my eyelids. They burned. My face burned. The kitten mewled. I felt his small head brush my hand.

"I'm going to be sick," I said.

Chris swerved into a layby. He got out, slammed the door, came round to my side. He yanked my door open. I heard him curse.

He scooped the kitten off me and pulled me out of the van. He said, "What'd you think this was? A game? What'd you think this was, for God's sake?"

His voice was high and tight. The sound of it rather than what he said made me open my eyes. He looked like I felt: punched in the gullet. He cradled the kitten against his chest.

"Come here," he said. He walked to the rear of the van. "I said come here."

"Don't make me—"

"Goddamn it. Come here, Livie. Now."

He flung the rear door open. He began to tear at the carriers' tops. "Look," he said. "Livie. Come here. I'm telling you to look."

"I don't need to see."

"We've got broken spinal cords."

"Don't."

"We've got open brains."

"No."

"We've got skull-mounted plugs and—"

"Chris!"

"—electrodes sutured into muscles."

"Please."

"No. Look. *Look.*" And then his voice broke. And he leaned his forehead against the van. And he started to cry.

I watched. I couldn't move to him. I heard his weeping and the cries of the animals blend together. I could think of nothing but being at least a hundred miles away from this narrow layby in the darkness with a cool breeze blowing from the distant channel. His shoulders quaked. I took a step towards him. I knew in that instant that there was no redemption if I did not look. At the half-shaven and thoroughly broken bodies, the shriv-elled limbs, the swelling and the sutures, the clots of dried blood.

I went hot then cold. I thought about my words. I considered all the things I didn't know. I turned away. I said, "Here, Chris. Give him to me." I loosened Chris's fingers, took the kitten, and held him cradled in my hands. I put him back in his carrier. I closed the tops of the others. I shut the van door and grasped Chris's arm. "Here," I said and led him to the passenger's seat.

When we were both inside, I said, "Where's Max waiting for us?" because I now knew what he'd kept to himself throughout planning the assault, throughout carrying it off. "Chris," I asked again, "where're we to meet Max?"

So we put them down, those kittens and cats, one by one. Max administered the injections. Chris and I held them. We held them against our chests so that the last thing each little animal felt was a human heart beating steadily against him.

When we were finished, Max gripped my shoulder. "Not the initia-tion you were expecting, was it?"

I shook my head numbly. I laid the final little body in the box that Max had ready for the purpose.

"Well done, girlie," Max said.

Chris turned and went out into the early morning. It was just before dawn, the moment when the sky hasn't decided between darkness and light, so both exist simultaneously. To the west the sky was shrouded, dove grey. To the east, it was feathered with rose-edged clouds.

Chris was standing next to the mini-van, his hand on its roof curled into a fist. He watched the dawn.

I said, "Why do people do what they do?"

He shook his head blindly. He got into the van. On the way back to Little Venice, I held his hand. I wanted to comfort him. I wanted to make things right.

When we got back to the barge, Toast and Beans met us at the door. They whimpered and rustled round our legs.

"They want a run," I said. "Shall I take them?"

Chris nodded. He threw his rucksack into a chair and headed for his room. I heard his door close.

I took the dogs out and we loped and gambolled along the canal. They chased a ball, tussling with each other and growling, racing to drop the ball at my feet then dashing ahead with a happy yelp to fetch it again. When they'd had enough and the morning was beginning to stir with school children and commuters on their way to work, we wandered back to the barge. It was dark inside, so I opened the shutters in the workroom. I fed and watered the dogs. I crept quietly along the passageway and paused outside the door to Chris's room. I tapped against it. He didn't answer. I tried the knob and went in.

He was lying on the bed. He'd taken off his jacket and his shoes, but he still wore the rest of his clothes: black jeans, black pullover, black socks with a hole at the heel of the right one. He wasn't asleep. Rather he was gazing, unblinking, at a photograph that stood among the books on his bookshelf. I'd seen it before. Chris and his brother at five and eight years old. They were kneeling in the muck and grinning happily, their arms slung over the neck of a baby donkey. Chris was dressed as Sir Galahad. His brother was dressed like Robin Hood.

I tipped my knee against the edge of the bed. I put my hand on his leg.

He said, "Odd."

"What?"

"That. I was supposed to become a barrister as well. Like Jeffrey. Have I told you?"

"Only that he's a barrister. Not the other."

"Jeff's got ulcers. I didn't want them. I want to make change, I told him, and this isn't the way to go about it. Change happens from working within the system, he said. I thought he was wrong. But I was."

"You weren't."

"I don't know. I don't think so."

I sat on the edge of the bed. "You weren't wrong," I said. "Look how you've changed me."

"People change themselves."

"Not always. Not now."

I lay next to him, my head sharing his pillow, my face close to his. His eyelids dropped. I touched my fingers to them. I traced his sandy lashes. I grazed the pockmarks that peppered his cheekbones.

"Chris," I whispered.

Other than closing his eyes, he hadn't moved. "Hmm?"

"Nothing."

Have you ever wanted someone so much that you ache between the legs? That's what it was like. My heart beat just like it always beat. My breathing didn't alter. But I was throbbing and sore. I felt the need for him burn like a hot ring pressing into my body.

I knew what to do: where to place my hands, how to move, when to loosen his clothes and rid myself of my own. I knew how to arouse him. I knew exactly what he would like. I knew how best to make him forget.

OLIVIA

The ache climbed my body like a white-hot shaft. And I had the power to obliterate the pain. All I needed to do was go back to the past. Be a young swan floating on the Serpentine, be a cloud in the sky, be a doe in the forest, be a pony running wild in the wind of Dartmoor. Be anything that allowed me to perform without feeling. Make any one of the hundred moves I'd once indifferently made for money, and the ache would dissolve with Chris's surrender.

I did nothing. I lay on his bed and I watched him sleep. By the time the pain climbed my body to arrive in my throat, I'd admitted the worst to myself about love.

I hated him at first. I hated what he had brought me to. I hated the woman he had proven to me that I could become.

I swore then that I'd eradicate emotion, and I began the process by taking on every bloke I could find. I had them in cars, in squats, in underground stations, in parks, in pub toilets, and on the barge. I made them bark like dogs. I made them sweat and weep. I made them beg. I watched them crawl. I heard them gasp and howl. Chris never reacted. He never said a word, until I began to go to work on the blokes who were part of our assault unit.

They were such easy pickings. Sensitive to begin with, they felt the excitement of a successful assault as much as I did. They received the suggestion of a post-assault celebration like the innocents they were. They said initially, "But we're not supposed to . . ." and "Actually, it's my understanding that outside the structure of the organisation's regular activities, we aren't allowed . . ." and "Gosh, we can't, Livie. We gave our word. About getting involved." To which I said, "Pooh. Who's going to know? I'm not going to tell anyone. Are you?" To which they replied, with a heavy blush climbing their peach-skin cheeks, "I wouldn't tell. Of course not. I'm not that sort." To which I said in all wide-eyed innocence, "What sort? I'm only talking about having a drink together." To which they would stammer, "Of course. I didn't mean . . . I wouldn't presume to think . . ."

I took them to the barge, these blokes. They said, "Livie, we can't. At least not here. If Chris finds out, we're finished." I said, "You let me worry about Christopher," and I closed the door behind us. "Or don't you want to?" I said. I locked my fingers round the buckles of their belts and pulled them forward. I lifted my mouth to theirs. "Or don't you want to?" I asked and insinuated my fingers into their jeans. "Well?" I said against their mouths as I hooked one arm round their waists. "Do you or don't you? Better make up your mind."

What mind they had left at that point was targeted on a single thought, which wasn't much of a thought in the first place. We fell onto my bed and kicked off our clothes. I liked it best if they were vocal because things got properly noisy then, and as noisy as possible was how I wanted it.

I was doing two of them one early morning after an assault when Chris intervened. White-faced, he walked into my room. He grabbed one bloke by the hair and the other by the arm. He said, "You're gone. Finished," and he shoved them down the passageway towards the galley. One of them said, "Hey! Aren't you being rather a hypocrite, Faraday?" The other yowled. "Out. Take your gear. Get out," Chris said. When the barge door slammed on them and the bolts flew home, Chris returned to me.

I lounged on my bed and lit a cigarette, indifference personified.

"Spoilsport," I pouted. I was naked, and I made no move for either blanket or robe.

His fingers curled tightly into his palms. He didn't appear to breathe. "Put your clothes on. *Now.*"

"Why? Are you throwing me out as well?"

"I've no intention of being so bloody easy on you."

I sighed. "What're you in such a twist about? We were just having fun."

"No," he said. "You were just having at me."

I rolled my eyes and dragged on my cigarette.

"If you destroy the whole unit, will that satisfy you? Will that be enough amends on my part?"

"Amends for what?"

"For not wanting to shag you. Because I don't. I haven't ever, and I don't propose to start no matter how many dimwits in London stuff you. Why can't you accept that? Why can't you just let us be as we are? And for Christ's sake put on some clothes."

"If you don't want me and you haven't ever and you don't intend to start wanting me now, what's it to you if I'm dressed or not? Are you getting heated up?"

He went to the clothes cupboard and pulled out my robe. He threw it at me. "I'm getting heated, yes, but not the way you want."

"I'm not the one who wants," I pointed out to him. "I'm the one who takes."

"And that's what you're doing with all these blokes, is it? Taking what you want? Don't make me laugh."

"I see one I fancy. I have him. That's it. What's the problem with that? Does it bother you?"

"Does it bother *you?*"

"What?"

"To lie? To rationalise? To play a role? Come on, Livie. Start facing who you are. Start dealing with the truth." He walked out of my room, calling, "Beans, Toast, let's go."

I stayed where I was and I hated him.

Start facing who you are. Start dealing with the truth. I can still hear him saying that. And I wonder how he's facing who he is and dealing with his truths each time he meets with Amanda.

He's breaking the organisation's rules, just as I did. What sort of rationalisation has he developed to excuse himself? I have little doubt that he's got a rationalisation ready for their involvement. He may call it *future wife* or *the test of loyalty* or *it's bigger than we are* or *she needs my protection* or *I was seduced* or *I finally met the woman to risk everything for*, but he's definitely developed some slick justification that he'll trot out to vindicate himself once ARM's governing core demands an accounting.

I suppose I sound cynical, totally without sympathy for his situation, bitter, vindictive, holding dear to the hope that he'll get caught with his trousers dropped. But I don't feel cynical, and I'm not aware of that hot little stone of indignation sizzling between my breasts when I think of Chris and her. I don't feel compelled to make accusations. I merely think it's wise to assume that most people rationalise at one time or another. Because what better way is there to avoid being answerable other than to rationalise? And no one really *wants* to be answerable, not when things get sticky.

It's for the best was Mother's rationalisation. Only a fool would have walked away from what she offered Kenneth Fleming: Celandine Cottage in Kent, part-time employment at the printworks during the months that the county sides played, full-time employment in the winter. She had anticipated all possible objections that Jean might have raised to the plan, and she presented her offer to Kenneth in such a way that every objection was taken into account. It was a win-win for everyone concerned. All Jean had to agree to was Kenneth's move to Kent and a part-time marriage.

"Think of the possibilities," Mother would have said to Kenneth, hoping that he carried the message back to Jean. "Think of playing for England eventually. Think of everything that could mean to you."

"Facing the finest players in the world," Kenneth would have mused, with his chair tilted back and his eyes going soft as he saw in his mind a batsman and a bowler facing each other on the playing field at Lord's.

"As well as travel, celebrity, endorsements. Money."

"That's counting chickens."

"Only if you don't believe in yourself as I believe in you."

"Don't believe in me, Miriam. I let you down once."

"Don't let's talk of the past."

"I could let you down again."

She would have rested her fingers lightly for a moment against his wrist. "Far more serious is the fact that you could let yourself down. And Jean. And your children."

You can fill in the rest. Phase Two concluded on schedule. Kenneth Fleming went to Kent.

I don't need to tell you of Kenneth's success. The newspapers have been recounting the story ever since his death. Directly Kenneth died, Hal Rashadam said in an interview that he'd never seen a man "more designed by God's beneficence and wisdom to play this game." Kenneth had an athlete's body and natural talent. He was only waiting for someone who knew how to put the two together.

Effecting this union of body and talent required time and effort. It wasn't enough to practise with and play in the Kent county side. For Kenneth to reach his highest potential, he would need a programme that combined diet, body building, exercise, and coaching. He would need to observe the best players in the world whenever and wherever they were available to him. He would succeed only by knowing what he was up against and going them one better . . . in physical condition, in skill, in technique. He had to overcome the twin disadvantages of age and inexperience. This would take time.

Tabloid journalists have speculated that the demise of Kenneth's marriage to Jean Cooper followed an age-old pattern. Hours and days spent in pursuit of the dream meant hours and days away from Jean and the children. The father-at-the-weekend plan fell apart as soon as Kenneth and Jean discovered exactly how much time was going to be necessary to reach optimum fitness, to hone his batting skills, to study the opposition as well as the other potential challengers for the England team. As often as not Jean and the children would faithfully make the trek out to Kent at the weekend only to discover that husband-and-father was to be Saturday in Hampshire and Sunday in Somerset, and when he wasn't off either playing, practising, or watching, he was training. When he wasn't training, he was fulfilling his obligations to Whitelaw Printworks. So the traditional explanation for the chasm that began to sink into the Fleming marriage revolves round the deserted but still demanding wife and the absent husband. But there was more to it than that.

Imagine it, if you will. This period in Kent represented the first time in his life that Kenneth Fleming had ever been truly on his own. He'd gone from his parents' house to that brief year at school and from school to marriage, and now he was experiencing freedom. It wasn't a freedom without obligation, but for the first time the obligations he had were directly related to the attainment of a dream, not merely to the grubbing for money. He needn't even feel guilty about striving to attain this dream, since its attainment meant the future betterment of his family. So he could give himself single-mindedly to the pursuit of professional cricket, and if he loved being liberated from his wife and children, that was in reality a happy and unexpected by-product of the larger scheme of things.

I imagine he felt a little odd when he moved to Celandine Cottage, especially the first night. He would have unpacked his belongings and cooked himself a meal. In eating it, he would have felt the stillness press against him, so foreign to everything he knew. He would have phoned Jean but she and the children would have gone out for a meal, a special treat to divert their thoughts from the terraced house now empty of Kenny-and-Dad. He would have phoned Hal Rashadam to review their schedule only to hear that Rashadam was dining with his daughter and her husband that night. Finally, when the need for some sort of human contact was beginning to string out his nerves, he would have phoned Mother.

"I'm in," he would have said, trying not to look at the windows and the black endless night smeared against them.

"I'm so glad, my dear. You have everything you need?"

"I suppose. Yes. I have. I suppose."

"What is it, Ken? Is something wrong with the cottage? Is something amiss? You had no trouble getting in?"

"No trouble. It's just . . . Nothing. Only . . . I'm blithering on. Sound like I'm going mental, don't I?"

"What? What is it? Tell me."

"I didn't expect to feel . . . out of sorts, somehow."

"Ill?"

"I keep waiting to hear Stan banging his ball against the wall in the sitting room. I keep waiting to hear Jean shout at him to stop. It's odd they're not here."

"It's natural that you should miss them. Don't be hard on yourself."

"I s'pose I do miss them."

"Of course you do. They're a large part of your life."

"It's just that I phoned them and . . . Hell. I shouldn't be weeping on your shoulder about this. You've been good to me. To all of us. Giving me this chance. It might change our lives."

Changing their lives was part of the plan. That night on the telephone, Mother would have advised him to take things slowly, to get used to the cottage and the countryside, to enjoy the opportunity that had fallen his way.

"I'll keep in close touch with Jean," she would have said. "I'll stop by tomorrow after work and see how she and the children are coping. I know that won't make you miss them less, but will it at least set your mind at rest?''

"You're too good to us."

"I'm happy to do whatever I can."

Then she would have advised him to take a cup of coffee or a brandy out into the garden and to look up where stars unlike anything he could see in London were creating pyrotechnics in the sky. Get a good night's sleep, she would have counselled. Throw yourself into work in the morning. There's plenty to do, not only in cricket but at the cottage.

He would have followed her advice as he always had done. He would have carried the brandy outside, not only a glass but the bottle as well. He would have sat on the uncut lawn, on the part that slopes towards the lane. He would have poured his drink and looked up at the stars. He would have heard the noises the country makes at night.

A horse nickering from the paddock next door, crickets calling from field and verge, a tawny owl *kee-veck*ing as the night's hunt began, a church bell sounding from one of the Springburns, the *whoosh* and rattle of a distant train. Not silent at all, he would have thought with surprise.

He would have rested back on his elbows and poured his drink. He would have downed the first one quickly and poured another. His mood would have lifted. He would have lain back on the lawn, crooked his arm behind his head, and realised that his life was his own.

Actually, I don't think it really happened that quickly, all in the first night. It was probably a more seductive process in which the duties of training, practising, and scouting combined with a burgeoning sense of licence. What was initially strange ultimately became welcome. No bickering children, no wife whose conversation got rather tedious and repetitive at times, no job to drag himself off to in the morning, no neighbours' arguments to listen to through thin walls, no dinners with the in-laws to try to avoid. He found that he liked the independence. Liking it, he wanted more of it. Wanting more of it, he set himself on a collision course with Jean.

He would have made excuses at first, to explain why he couldn't see them at a weekend here and there. Pulled a muscle in my back that's laid me flat, luv. Got an estimate for the printworks that I must attend to. Torn up the kitchen and the bathroom, I have; I'm setting them right for Mrs. Whitelaw. Rashadam's insisting I dash up to watch a match in Leeds.

During these weekends without his family, he would have found he got on just fine. If he went to a party that Kent was sponsoring, he would have drunk the drinks, chatted up the other players, their wives and girl-friends, and made what he probably told himself was a fair and objective assessment of the prospect of Jean's fitting in with this group. He may even have given her a chance early on, watching how and if she interacted with the others, judging her movement along the edges of the crowd as unease rather than caution and reticence, reaching the convenient conclu-sion that an exposure to the superficial conversation of the women and the bantering of the men was going to take the mickey out of his wife if he wasn't careful to shield her.

So he had indisputable reasons why he couldn't see his family as regularly as he wanted. Once Jean began to question and to challenge him, once she pointed out to him that his responsibilities as a father extended beyond the money he was able to pass her way, he would have needed to come up with something better. Once Jean went for the jugular and began making demands that threatened his liberty, he would have decided to tell her a form of the truth designed to hurt her the least.

He made this decision, no doubt, with the delicate assistance of his primary confidante, my mother. She must have supported him well through his time of uncertainty. Kenneth was trying to evaluate his situa-tion: I don't know how I feel any longer. Do I love her? Do I want her? Do I want this marriage? Am I feeling this way because I was trapped for so many years? Did Jean trap me? Did I trap myself? If I'm meant to be married, why is it I feel like I've finally come alive since we've been apart? How can I feel this way? She's my wife. They're my children. I love them. I feel like a bastard.

How reasonable for Mother to suggest a period apart, especially since they were apart in the first place: You need to sort things through, my dear. Your life's in a muddle, and that shouldn't come as a terrible shock. Look at the changes you've faced in just a few short months. Not only you, but Jean and the children as well. Give yourselves some time and some space to decide who you are. You've never had the opportunity to do that in all these years, have you? Either of you?

Clever to phrase it that way. It wouldn't be Kenneth who needed to "think things through." It would be both of them. No matter that Jean didn't find it essential to think anything through, least of all whether she wanted to continue in her marriage. Once Kenneth decided that a period on their own would clarify who they were and what, if anything, they could be to each other in the future, the die was cast. He was already out of the house. Jean could demand that he return, but he didn't need to do so.

"Things've happened so fast," he probably told her. "Can't you give me a few weeks to suss out who I am? To sort through how I feel?"

"About what?" she demanded. "Me? The kids? What rubbish is this, Kenny?"

"It's not you. Not the kids. It's me. I'm out of sorts."

"Isn't that convenient. Balls, Kenny. Balls. You want a divorce? Is that what this is all about? You too much the milksop to say it direct?"

"Get off it, luvvie. You're off your nut. Did I mention divorce?"

"Who's at the bottom of this? You tell me, Kenny. You seeing someone? Is that what you're too spineless to tell me?"

"What're you thinking, girl? Jesus. Hell. I'm not seeing anyone. I don't want to see anyone."

"Then why? *Why?* Damn you, Kenny Fleming."

"Two months, luv. That's all I ask."

"I got no choice, have I? So don't turn this into a bleeding game, *asking* for two months."

"Don't cry. There's no need. It'll worry the kids."

"And *this* flaming won't? Not seeing their dad? Not knowing if we're a family or not? That won't worry the kids?"

"It's selfish. I know."

"Damn bloody right."

"But it's what I need."

She had no choice but to agree. They wouldn't see each other much while he thought things through. The two months he asked for stretched to four, the four to six, the six to ten, the ten to twelve. One year eased its way into two. He faced, no doubt, a moment of indecision about his living circumstances when he fell out with the Kent cricket committee and made the move to play for Middlesex instead, but by the time Kenneth Fleming attained his dream, by the time the national selectors tapped Middlesex's new and foremost batsman to play for England, his marriage was a formality only.

For reasons that remain unclear to me, he didn't press for a divorce. Nor did she. Why not? you ask. Because of the children? For a sense of security? To keep up appearances? I only know that when he moved back to London in order to be close to the Middlesex playing field not far from Regent's Park, he didn't move back to the Isle of Dogs. Instead, he moved into my mother's house in Kensington.

The location was, after all, very nearly perfect. A hop up Ladbroke Grove, a skip across Maida Vale, a jump the length of St. John's Wood Road and there was Lord's Cricket Ground, where Middlesex play.

The situation was ideal. Mother was rattling round that enormous house on Staffordshire Terrace with bedrooms to spare. Kenneth needed a place to live that wasn't so expensive that he couldn't afford to continue to help out his wife and children.

The bond between Kenneth and my mother was already in place. She was one-third mascot, one-third inspiration, and one-third source of inner strength to him. When he shared with her the difficulties surrounding his decision to cease playing for Kent and to join Middlesex, he would also have shared his reluctance to return to his old way of life. To which reluctance she would have responded gravely, "Does Jean know this, Ken?" To which he would have said, "I haven't told her yet." To which Mother would have made the cautious recommendation, "Perhaps you need to let your lives unfold gradually. Let nature take its course. What if . . . This may sound rather impulsive, but what if you moved in with me for a while? While you see what direction your life's going to take. . . ." Because it was closer to Lord's, because he wouldn't yet be making the money that would allow the family to pull up stakes, because because because. "Would that be of help to you, my dear?"

She gave him the words. No doubt he used them. The end was the same no matter how it was effected. He moved in with my mother.

And while she was devoting herself to Kenneth Fleming's welfare, I was working at the zoo in Regent's Park.

I remember thinking, You want truth, Chris? I'll show you truth, after that morning in my bedroom. I thought, He thinks he knows me, the stupid berk. He doesn't know sod all.

I set about proving how little he knew. I worked at the zoo, first mucking round with the maintenance staff and eventually picking up a job at the animal hospital where I had access to their data bases, which eventually proved invaluable and heightened my standing with the organisation when ARM decided it was time to track where surplus animals were being shipped. I involved myself more devotedly with ARM. If Chris could love animals, I could love them more. I could prove my love more. I could take bigger risks.

I requested assignment to a second assault unit. "We're too slow," I said. "We're not doing enough. We're not quick enough. If you allow some of us to cross between units, we can double our activities. Perhaps even triple them. Think of the number of animals we can save." Request denied.

So I began to push our own unit to do more. "We're sitting back on our arses. We're getting complacent. Come on. Come on."

Chris watched me with a wary eye. He'd spent enough time round me to have the right to wonder what my ulterior motives were. He kept waiting for them to emerge.

Had we been involved in something less gut-wrenching, those motives would have emerged within weeks. It's ironic now that I think of it. I heightened my activities in the organisation with the intent of making Chris see who I really was so that he would have to fall in love with me so that I could screw him and then reject him and walk away filled with jubilation at the fact that I didn't care. I intended to use the liberation activities cold-bloodedly, with no more concern about the fate of the animals than I would have had for the fate of the men I used to pick up off the street. I ended up with my heart feeling as if someone had cut it into strips with a pair of rusty secateurs.

It wasn't a process that happened quickly. I felt neither a dent nor a fissure in the armour of my indifference at the dry lick from the tongue of the first beagle pup I rescued from a lab studying stomach ulcers. I just handed him over to the transporter, moved to the next cage, and kept myself focussed on the need for speed and silence.

When I finally cracked, it wasn't over scientific experimentation at all, but rather over an illegal puppy farm that we raided in Hampshire, not far from the Wallops.

Have you heard of these places? They breed dogs for volume and profit. They're always in isolated locations, sometimes run out of what otherwise appear to be working farms.

This puppy farm had come to our attention because one of our runners on a visit to Mum and Dad in Hampshire had been poking round a car boot sale, and he'd come upon a woman with puppies. Had two dogs at home, she claimed a touch too earnestly, both whelped at once, crawling in puppies at the moment I am, willing to sell them for next to nothing, pure as pure could be the whole flipping lot of them. Our runner didn't like the look of the woman or the dispirited look of the puppies. He followed her home, on a winding, dipping, pencil sketch of a road that dwindled down to two ruts with oil-streaked grass growing between them.

"She's got them in a barn," he told us. He pressed his palms together and held them like he was praying as he talked. "There're cages. Stacked on each other. There's no light. No ventilation."

"Sounds like a case for the RSPCA," Chris noted.

"That could take weeks. And even if they moved against her, the thing is . . ." He directed a solemn look round the group. "Listen. This woman needs to be dealt with permanently."

Someone raised the problem of logistics. This wasn't a lab deserted at night. This was where someone lived, a mere fifty yards away from the barn in which the animals were kept. What if the dogs barked, as they undoubtedly would? Wouldn't the farm owner set up the alarm? phone the police? make after us with a shot gun?

She might do, Chris acknowledged. He decided to recce the location himself.

He went to Hampshire alone. When he returned, all he would say is, "We'll do it next week."

I said, "Next week? Chris, that's not enough time. That puts everyone at risk. That—"

He said, "Next week," and brought out a plan of the farm. He assigned the sentries to deal with the problem of Mrs. Porter, the owner, remarking that she wouldn't be likely to phone the police and bring the law down upon herself for running the puppy farm in the first place. But she might do something else. The sentries would need to be prepared to head her off. He told us to bring along surgical masks and right then I should have known how bad it was going to be.

We arrived at one in the morning. The sentries slipped to guard both entrances to the farmhouse, one on the yard and the other facing a perfect front garden and the crater-filled lane. When the flicker of their lights told us the sentries were in position, we liberators prepared for the dash to the barn. For once, Chris would accompany us. No one dared ask why.

We found the first dead animal in a pen just outside the barn. In the circle of light Chris flashed upon him, we could see that he'd once been a spaniel. Now he was bloat, but the bloat seemed to shift in an undulating pattern in the beam from Chris's torch. These were the maggots. His companion in the pen was a golden retriever matted with mud and faeces. This dog struggled to his feet. He wobbled back into the wire fence.

"Shit," someone murmured.

The retriever set up the alarm we'd been expecting.

"Go," Chris said. "Pass over this one."

We heard the shouting from the farmhouse once we were inside the barn. But it fast became merely an auditory backdrop to what we found within. We all had torches. We switched them on. Excrement was everywhere. Our feet sucked and plopped as we sank into hay that lay over the muck.

Animals whimpered. They were crammed into cages the size of shoe boxes. These were stacked one on top of the other so that dogs beneath lived in the waste of dogs above. Under the cages lay three black rubbish bags. One spilled out its contents into the muck: four dead terrier puppies tossed in among wet hair, faeces, and rotting food.

No one spoke, which was usual. What wasn't usual was that one of the chaps began to weep. He stumbled against the side of a stall. Chris said urgently, "Patrick, Patrick, don't fade on me, mate." And to me, "Give the signal," as he moved to the cages.

The dogs began to yip. I went back to the barn door and flashed the light to the transporters waiting beneath the hedgerow that lined the property. At the farmhouse, the sentries were struggling with Mrs. Porter. She'd made it as far as her front step where she shouted, "Police! Help! Police!" before one of the sentries whipped her arms behind her and the other gagged her. They dragged her back into the house. The interior lights went black.

The transporters thundered across the farmyard and into the barn. One of them slipped in the muck and fell. The dogs began to howl.

Chris zipped along the line of cages. I ran to join the others working the opposite side of the barn. Even in the limited light of my torch, I could still see, and I felt vertigo sweep over me. There were puppies everywhere but they weren't the sweet little things one sees on calendars at Christmas. These Yorkies and Shelties, these retrievers and spaniels had ulcerated eyes, open sores. Parasites crawled through hairless patches of their flesh.

One of the older blokes began cursing. Two of the women were crying. I was trying not to breathe and trying to ignore the alternating waves of heat and cold that kept washing over me. A ringing in my ears did much to drown out the sound of the animals. But in the abject terror that the ringing might stop, I began reciting everything I could remember from *The Bad Child's Book of Beasts*. I'd done the yak, the polar bear, and the whale when I got to the final cage. In it lay a small Lhasa apso. I put my gloved fingers between the bars, muttering as much as I could remember from the rhyme about the Dodo. It began with something about walking around. Something about taking the sun and the air.

I flipped open the cage, concentrating on the rhymes. They had to match *around* and *air*. I couldn't think what they were.

I reached for the dog, but I sought the words. Something something ground? Lah lah la bare? What was it? What was it?

I pulled the dog towards me. Round? Sound? Dodo not there? Somehow I had to put the rhyme together because if I didn't, I'd start crumbling, and I couldn't face that. I didn't know what to do to prevent it except to move on quickly to another rhyme, one more familiar, one whose words I couldn't forget. Like "Humpty Dumpty."

I lifted the dog and caught sight of her right back foot. It dangled uselessly from a strip of flesh. In the flesh were the unmistakable punctures and grooves of canines. As if she'd tried to chew her own foot off. As if the dog occupying the cage below had tried to chew it off for her.

My vision narrowed to a pinpoint of light. I cried out but made no sound that could have been either a word or a name. The dog felt lifeless resting against me.

All round me was movement, smudges of black as liberators moved animals and tried not to breathe. I gulped for air but couldn't find enough.

"Here, let me take it," someone said at my elbow. "Livie. Livie. Give me the dog."

I couldn't let go. I couldn't move. All I could do was feel myself melting, like a great blaze was burning away my flesh. I began to weep.

"Her foot," I cried.

After all I'd seen in my time with ARM, it hardly seems sensible that a dog's foot dangling on a strip of dead flesh would be what broke me. But it did. I felt the rage course through me. I felt helplessness drag me under like quicksand. I said, "Enough." And I was the one to grab the petrol can from the doorway where Chris had left it.

He said, "Livie, keep away."

I said, "Get that dog from the pen. Outside. Get it. I said *get it*, Chris. Get it." And I began sloshing the petrol around the interior of that hellhole. When the last dog had been taken and the last cage had been tumbled to the floor, I lit the match. The flames burst up like a geyser and never had I seen such a beautiful sight as fire.

Chris pulled me by the arm or I might have stayed inside and gone up with the interior of that wretched barn. Instead I stumbled out, made sure the retriever had been rescued from the pen, and ran for the lane. I kept saying, "Enough." I kept trying to wipe from my mind the image of that single pathetic dangling little foot.

We stopped at a phone box in Itchen Abbas. Chris rang the emergency number and reported the fire. He came back to the mini-van.

"That's more than she deserves," I said.

"We can't leave her tied up. We don't want murder on our consciences."

"Why not? She's got it on hers."

"That's what makes us different."

I watched the night streak by. The motorway loomed ahead, a gash of grey concrete splitting open the land.

"It isn't fun any longer," I said to my reflection in the passenger's window. I felt Chris looking at me.

"You want out?" he asked.

I closed my eyes. "I just want it to end."

"It will," he said.

We shot onto the motorway.

CHAPTER
12

The rustling of the bedclothes awakened him, but Lynley kept his eyes shut for a moment. He listened to her breathing. How odd, he thought, that he should find joy in such an unadorned thing.

He turned on his side to face her, carefully so that he shouldn't wake her. But she was awake already, lying on her back with one leg drawn up and her eyes studying the acanthus leaves that looped in plaster across the ceiling.

He found her hand beneath the covers and locked her fingers in his. She glanced at him, and he saw that a small vertical line had formed between her eyebrows. With his other hand, he smoothed it away.

"I've realised," she said.

"What?"

"You diverted me last night, so I never had an answer to my question."

"As I recall, you diverted me. You promised chicken and artichokes, didn't you? Wasn't that why we trekked down to the kitchen?"

"And it was in the kitchen that I asked you, wasn't it? But you never answered."

"I was occupied. You occupied me."

A smile feathered her mouth. "Hardly," she said.

He laughed quietly. He leaned over to kiss her. He traced the curve of her ear where her hair fell away.

"Why do you love me?" she asked.

"What?"

"That was the question I asked you last night. Don't you remember?"

"Ah. That question." He rolled onto his back and joined her in looking at the ceiling. He held her hand against his chest and considered the elusive why of loving.

"I can't match you in either education or experience," she pointed out. He lifted a doubting eyebrow. She smiled fleetingly. "All right. I can't match you in education. I have no career. I'm not even gainfully employed. I have no wifely skills and fewer wifely aspirations. I'm very nearly frivolity personified. Our backgrounds are similar, if it comes to that, but what does similarity in background have to do with giving your heart to another?"

"It had everything to do with marriage at one time."

"We're not talking about marriage. We're talking about love. More often than not, those two are mutually exclusive and entirely different subjects. Catherine of Aragon and Henry VIII were married and look what happened to them. She had his babies and got to make his shirts. He catted round and used up six wives. So much for similarity in background."

Lynley yawned. "What else could she expect, marrying a Tudor? Richmond's own son. She was establishing a genealogical link to primeval slime. Cowardly. Penurious. Murderous. Politically paranoid. And with damned good reason for the latter."

"Oh dear. We're not heading towards the line of succession and the Princes in the Tower, are we, darling? That takes us somewhat off the track."

"Sorry." Lynley raised her hand and kissed her fingers. "Get me anywhere close to Henry Tudor and I become a bit rabid."

"It's a very good way to avoid the question."

"I wasn't avoiding. Merely temporising while I thought."

"And? Why? Why do you love me? Because if you can't either explain or define love, perhaps it's better to admit that real love doesn't exist in the first place."

"If that's the case, what do we have, you and I?"

She made a restless movement, akin to a shrug. "Lust. Passion. Body heat. Something pleasant but ephemeral. I don't know."

He raised himself on one elbow and observed her. "Let me make certain I understand. We ought to consider that this is a relationship grounded in lust?"

"Aren't you willing to admit that's a possibility? Especially if you consider last night. How we were."

"How we were," he repeated.

"In the kitchen. Then the bedroom. I admit that I was the instigator, Tommy, so I don't mean to suggest that you're the only one who might be absorbed by the chemistry and blind to the reality."

"What reality?"

"That there's nothing beyond chemistry between us in the first place."

He stared at her long before he moved or spoke. He could feel the muscles of his abdomen tighten. He could sense that his blood was beginning to heat. It wasn't lust this time that he was starting to feel. But it was a passion all the same. He said calmly, "Helen, what in God's name is the matter with you?"

"What sort of question is that? I merely want to point out that what you think of as love might be a flash in the pan. Isn't that a wise possibility to ponder? Because if we were to marry and then discover that what we felt for each other had never been more than—"

He threw back the covers, got out of bed, and struggled into his dressing gown. "Listen to me for once, Helen. Hear this clearly from beginning to end. I love you. You love me. We marry or we don't. That's the long and short of it. All right?" He strode across the room and muttered imprecations under his breath. He pulled back the curtains to fill the room with the bright spring sunlight that was blazing down on the back garden of his town house. The window was already partially open, but he threw the sash fully up and took in deep breaths of the morning air.

"Tommy," she said. "I merely wanted to know—"

"Enough," he said and thought, Women. *Women*. The twists of their minds. The questions. The probing. The infernal indecision. God in heaven. Monkhood was better.

A hesitant tap sounded against his bedroom door. Lynley snapped, "What is it?"

"Sorry, m'lord," Denton said. "There's someone here to see you."

"Someone . . . What time is it?" Even as he asked the question, Lynley strode to the table next to the bed and snatched up the alarm clock.

"Nearly nine," Denton said as Lynley simultaneously read the time and cursed soundly. "Shall I tell him—"

"Who is it?"

"Guy Mollison. I told him he ought to phone the Yard and talk to whoever's on duty, but he insisted. He said you'd want to hear what he has to say. He said to tell you he remembered something. I told him to leave his number, but he said that wasn't on. He said he had to see you. Shall I put him off?"

Lynley was already heading in the direction of the bath. "Give him coffee, breakfast, whatever he likes."

"Shall I tell him—"

"Twenty minutes," Lynley said. "And phone Sergeant Havers for me, will you, Denton? Tell her to get over here as soon as she can." He cursed again for good measure and firmly shut the bathroom door behind him.

He'd already bathed and was in the midst of shaving when Helen joined him.

"Don't say another damn word," he said to her reflection in the mirror as he whipped the razor against his lathered cheek. "I'm not up to dealing with any more nonsense. If you can't accept marriage as the normal consequence of love, we're finished. If this—" with a jerk of his thumb towards the bedroom—"is merely about having a good hot grind as far as you're concerned, then I've had it. All right? Because if you're still too bloody minded to see that— Ouch! God*damn* it." He'd nicked himself. He grabbed a square of tissue and pressed it to the spot of blood.

"You're going too fast," she said.

"Don't give me that. Don't you bloody give me that. We've known each other since you were eighteen years old. Eighteen. *Eighteen.* We've been friends. We've been lovers. We've been . . ." He shook the razor at her reflection. "What are you waiting for, Helen? What are you—"

"I meant the shaving," she interjected.

Half-masked in lather, he stared at her blankly. "The shaving," he repeated.

"You're shaving too quickly. You'll cut yourself again."

He lowered his gaze to the razor in his hand. It, too, was covered with lather. He thrust it under the tap and let the water wash over it and its speckling of ginger whiskers.

"I'm too much of a distraction," Helen noted. "You said so yourself on Friday night."

He knew where she was heading with her statement, but for a moment he didn't try to block her path. He pondered the word *distraction:* what it explained, what it promised, and what it implied. He finally had the answer. "That's the whole point."

"What?"

"The distraction."

"I don't understand."

He finished his shaving, rinsed his face, and dried it on a towel she handed him. He didn't answer until after he had slapped his cheeks with lotion. "I love you," he said to her, "because when I'm with you, I don't have to think about what I otherwise would be forced to think about. Twenty-four hours a day. Seven days a week."

He pushed past her into the bedroom and began tossing his clothes onto the bed. "I need you for that," he said, as he dressed. "To temper my world. To offer me something that isn't black or foul." She listened. He threw on his clothes. "I love coming home to you and wondering what I'll find. I love having to wonder. I love having to worry you might blow up the house with the microwave because when I worry about that, in those five or fifteen or twenty-five seconds that I'm worrying, I don't have to think of whose murder I'm trying like the devil to investigate, how that murder was committed, and who's responsible for it." He went in search of a pair of shoes, saying over his shoulder, "That's the way of it, all right? Oh, there's lust involved. Passion. Body heat. Whatever you will. There's plenty of lust, always has been, frankly, because I enjoy taking women to bed."

"Women?"

"Helen, don't try to trap me, all right? You know what I mean." Under the bed, he found the shoes he was seeking. He thrust his feet into them and tied the laces so tight that pain shot into his knees. "And when the lust I feel for you wears off—as it's going to, eventually—I suppose I'll find myself left with the rest. All those distractions. Which just happen to constitute the reason I love you in the first place."

He went to his serpentine chest of drawers where he shoved the brush through his hair four times. He crossed back to the bathroom. She still stood by the door. He put his hand on her shoulder and kissed her, hard.

"That's the story," he said to her. "Beginning to end. Now decide what you want and have done with it."

Lynley found Guy Mollison in the drawing room that overlooked Eaton Terrace. Denton had thoughtfully provided the cricketer with entertainment as well as coffee, croissants, fruit, and jam: Rachmaninoff was soaring from the stereo. Lynley wondered who had made the choice of music and decided it had to be Mollison. Left to his own devices, Denton opted for show stoppers from musicals.

Mollison was leaning over the coffee table, cup and saucer in hand, reading *The Sunday Times*. This was spread open next to the tray upon which Denton had laid out his meal. He wasn't reading an article about sports, however, as one might expect of the longtime captain of England's national team in advance of a test match with Australia, but about Fleming's death and the investigation. Particularly, Lynley saw as he passed the table on his way to silence the stereo, he was perusing an article that bore the now outdated headline "Cricket Car Sought."

Lynley pulled the plug on the music. Denton stuck his head in the doorway. "Got your breakfast, m'lord. In here? The dining room?"

Lynley winced inwardly. He hated the use of the title in any situation related to his work. He said brusquely, "Here. Did you track down Sergeant Havers?"

"She's on her way. She was at the Yard. Said to tell you the blokes are on the beat. That make sense to you, does it?"

It did. Havers had taken it upon herself to assign the DCs he'd pulled off rota. The move was irregular—he would have preferred to talk to them himself—but the fact that she had assumed the responsibility was due to his own failure to set the alarm before falling into bed with Helen the previous night.

"Yes. Thank you. It makes perfect sense." As Denton vanished,

Lynley turned to Mollison, who had risen to watch the exchange with undisguised interest.

"Who are you?" he asked. "Exactly."

"What?"

"I saw the coat of arms by the doorbell, but I thought it was a joke."

"It is," Lynley said. Mollison looked as if he was going to argue the point. Lynley poured the cricketer another cup of coffee.

Mollison said slowly, more to himself than to Lynley, "You showed the porter some police identification last night. At least that's what he told me."

"You weren't misinformed. Now what can I do for you, Mr. Mollison? I understand you have some information for me."

Mollison cast a glance round the room as if evaluating its contents and matching them to what he knew or didn't know of a policeman's pay. He looked suddenly wary. He said, "I'd like to have a look for myself, if you don't mind. At your identification."

Lynley fished out and handed over his warrant card. Mollison examined it. After a long scrutiny, he was apparently satisfied because he handed the card back and said, "All right, then. I like to be careful. For Allison's sake. We get all kinds prying into our lives. It tends to be part of things when you have a name."

"Doubtless," Lynley said drily. "As to your information?"

"I wasn't altogether truthful with you last night, not about everything. I'm sorry about that. But there are certain things . . ." He chewed on the nail of his index finger. He gave a grimace, made a fist, and dropped his hand to his thigh. "It's this," he announced. "Some things I can't say in front of Allison. No matter the legal consequences. Understand?"

"Which is why you initially wanted to conduct our interview in the corridor instead of in the flat."

"I don't like to upset her." Mollison picked up his cup and saucer. "She's eight months along."

"You mentioned that last night."

"But I could tell when you saw her . . ." He set his coffee down, undrunk. "Look, I'm not telling you what you don't know already: The baby's fine. Allison's fine. But anything upsetting could really cock things up at this point."

"Between the two of you."

"I'm sorry I stretched the truth when I said she wasn't well, but I

couldn't think of any other way to keep you from talking in front of her."
He began on the fingernail again. He indicated the newspaper with a nod
of his head. "You're looking for his car."

"Not any longer."

"Why not?"

"Mr. Mollison, is there something you want to tell me?"

"Have you found it? The Lotus?"

"I thought you were here to offer information."

Denton entered, another tray in his hands. He'd apparently decided
that heroic measures needed to be taken after last night's *fettuccine à la
mer:* He'd prepared cornflakes and bananas, eggs and sausages, grilled
tomatoes and mushrooms, grapefruit and toast. He'd thoughtfully provided a rose in a vase and a pot of Lapsang Souchong as well. As he was
laying the meal out, the doorbell rang.

"That'll be the sergeant," he said.

"I'll get it."

Denton was right. Lynley found Havers on the doorstep.

"Mollison's here." He closed the door behind her.

"What's he given us?"

"So far, nothing but excuses and evasion. He's betrayed a passing
interest in Rachmaninoff, however."

"That must have warmed your heart. I hope you crossed him off
your list of suspects straightaway."

Lynley smiled. He and Havers passed Denton, who offered coffee
and croissants to which Havers said, "Coffee. I'm dieting this hour."

Denton guffawed and went on his way. In the drawing room, Mollison had moved from the sofa to the window where he stood taking
squirrel bits from his fingernails and their surrounding skin. He nodded a
hello to Havers as Lynley went back to his breakfast. He didn't say anything until Denton had returned with another cup and saucer, poured
coffee for Havers, and left again.

Then Mollison said, "Are you looking for his car?"

"We've found it," Lynley said.

"But the paper said—"

"We like to stay one step ahead of the papers when we can," Havers
remarked.

"And Gabbie?"

"Gabbie?"

"Gabriella Patten. Have you spoken to her?"

"Gabbie." Lynley mused over the diminutive as he tucked into his cornflakes. He'd never managed to get a proper meal last night. He couldn't remember when food had tasted so fine.

"If you've found the car, then—"

"Why don't you tell us what you've come to tell us, Mr. Mollison?" Lynley said. "Mrs. Patten is either a primary suspect in or a material witness to a homicide. If you know where she is, you'd do well to share the information. As, no doubt, your wife has already told you."

"Allison isn't to be involved in this. I told you that last night. I meant it."

"Indeed."

"If I can have your assurance that what I say to you will go no further." Mollison nervously played his thumb along his index finger, as if testing the texture of his skin. "I can't talk to you unless you give me an assurance."

"I'm afraid that's not possible," Lynley said. "But you can phone a solicitor if you'd like."

"I don't need a solicitor. I haven't done anything. I just want to make certain that my wife . . . Look, Allie doesn't know . . . If she somehow discovered that . . ." He spun back to the window and stared out at Eaton Terrace. "Shit. I was just helping out. No. I was just *trying* to help out."

"Mrs. Patten?" Lynley set his cornflakes down and went on to the eggs. Sergeant Havers slid her cover-creased notebook out of her bag.

Mollison sighed. "She phoned me."

"When?"

"Wednesday night."

"Before or after you talked to Fleming?"

"After. Hours after."

"What time?"

"It must have been . . . I don't know . . . shortly before eleven? Shortly after? Something like that."

"Where was she?"

"A call box in Greater Springburn. She and Ken had had a bust-up, she said. Things were finished between them. She needed somewhere to go."

"Why did she phone you and not someone else? A female friend, perhaps."

"Because Gabbie hasn't any female friends. And even if she had, she phoned me because I was the reason for the bust-up in the first place. I owed her, she said. And she was right. I did."

"Owed her?" Havers asked. "She'd done you favours?"

Mollison turned back to them. His ruddy face was taking on an ugly flush that had begun on his neck and was climbing rapidly. "She and I . . . At one time. The two of us. You know."

"We don't," Havers said. "But why don't you tell us?"

"We had some laughs together. That sort of thing."

"You and Mrs. Patten were lovers?" Lynley clarified and when Mollison's hue deepened, he said, "When was this?"

"Three years ago." He returned to the sofa and took up his coffee cup. He drained it like a man who was desperate for something to give him strength or to calm his nerves. "It was such a stupid thing to do. It nearly cost me my marriage. We . . . well, we misread each other's signals."

Lynley speared a hunk of sausage on the end of his fork. He added egg. He ate and impassively watched Mollison watching him. Sergeant Havers wrote, her pencil steadily scratching against the paper of her notebook.

Mollison said, "It's like this. When you've got a name, there are always women who decide they fancy you. They want . . . They're interested in . . . They have these fantasies. About you. I mean, you're part of their fantasy. They're part of their fantasy as well. And they generally won't rest until they've had an opportunity to see how close their fantasy comes to the truth."

"So you and Gabriella Patten boffed each other like rattlesnakes." Havers was cut-to-the-chase incarnate. She even looked at her Timex in case her point escaped Mollison's comprehension.

Mollison scowled at her, a look that said, What could you possibly know? But he went on. "I thought she wanted what the others . . ." He grimaced once again. "Listen. I'm not a saint. If a woman makes me an offer, I'm likely to take it. But it's just an hour of laughs on the side. I always know that. The woman always knows that."

"Gabriella Patten didn't know that," Lynley said.

"She thought that when she and I . . . when we . . ."

"Boffed each other," Sergeant Havers prompted.

"The difficulty was that things continued," Mollison said. "I mean we did it more than once. I should have cut her off when I first realised that she was making more out of the—the affair . . . than she should have.''

"She had expectations of you,'' Lynley said.

"I didn't understand at first. What she wanted. Then when I did, I was just so caught up in . . . in her. She's . . . How can I say this so that it won't sound so blasted . . . There's something about her. Once you've had her . . . I mean, once you've experienced . . . Then things become . . . Oh hell. This sounds awful." He dug a crumpled handkerchief from his pocket and passed it over his face.

"So she shivers your timbers," Havers said.

Mollison looked at her blankly.

"She makes the earth move."

Still no response.

"She's a hot tamale between the sheets."

"Now listen here," Mollison began, a hot one himself.

"Sergeant," Lynley said mildly.

Havers said, "I was only trying to—"

He lifted an eyebrow. Try less, it told her. She grumbled herself back into position, pencil at the ready.

Mollison shoved his handkerchief back into his pocket. "When I knew what she really wanted, I thought I could play the affair along for a while. I didn't want to give her up."

"And exactly what did she want?" Lynley asked.

"Me. I mean, she wanted me to leave Allie so that she and I could be together. She wanted marriage."

"But she was married to Patten at the time, wasn't she?"

"Things were sour between them. I don't know why."

"She never said?"

"I didn't ask. You don't. I mean, if it's just for a laugh—the bedroom business—you don't actually enquire about the state of your partner's marriage. You just assume things could be better, but you don't want to get involved in something messy, so you keep everything light. Drinks. Perhaps a meal when time allows. Then . . ." He cleared his throat.

Havers' mouth formed the words *You boff each other*, but she didn't say them.

"So all I know is that she wasn't happy with Hugh. I mean she wasn't . . . How can I put this without sounding . . . She wasn't happy with him sexually. He wasn't always able to . . . He didn't . . .

When they did it, she never . . . I mean, I only know what she told me and I realise that since she told me while we were in the middle of it, she might have been lying. But she said she'd never actually . . . you know. With Hugh."

"I think we understand," Lynley said.

"Quite. Well, that's what she told me. But as I said, she told me while we were doing it ourselves, so . . . You know how women can be. If she wanted me to feel like I was the only one who'd ever . . . And she was good at that. I did feel that way. Only I didn't want to marry her. She was something on the side. A diversion. Because I love my wife. I love Allie. I worship her. The rest of this is just the kind of thing that happens when you have something, like a name."

"Does your wife know about the affair?"

"That's how I got out of it, actually. I had to confess. It upset Allison like hell—and I'm still sorry for that, mind you—but at least I was able to end things with Gabbie. And I swore to Allison that I'd never have anything to do with Gabbie again. Aside from the times I had to see her with Hugh. When the England team and potential sponsors met."

"A promise you haven't kept, I take it?"

"You're wrong about that. Once we ended the affair, I never saw Gabbie again without Hugh. Until she phoned on Wednesday night." He looked to the floor miserably. "And then she needed my help. So I gave it to her. And she was . . . she was grateful."

"Need we ask how she demonstrated her gratitude?" Havers asked politely.

"Damn," Mollison whispered. He blinked rapidly. "It didn't happen on Wednesday night. I didn't see her then. It was Thursday afternoon." He lifted his head. "She was upset. She was practically hysterical. It was my fault. I wanted to do something to help. It just happened between us. I'd rather Allie didn't know."

"The nature of the help you gave her Wednesday night," Lynley said. "You supplied her a place to stay?"

"In Shepherd's Market. I have a flat there with three other blokes from Essex. We use it when we . . ." He dropped his head again.

"Want to boff someone besides your wives on the sly," Havers said tiredly.

Mollison didn't react. He merely said with equal tiredness, "When she phoned on Wednesday night, I told her I'd arrange for her to use the flat."

"How did she get in?"

"We keep the keys there. In the building. With the porter. So that our wives . . . You know."

"And the address?"

"I'll have to take you there. I'm sorry, but she won't let you in otherwise. She won't even answer the door."

Lynley got to his feet. Mollison and Havers did likewise. Lynley said, "Your row with Fleming. The one you phoned him about on Wednesday night. It had nothing to do with the Pakistani player on the Middlesex side, did it?"

"It had to do with Gabbie," Mollison said. "That's why Ken went out to the Springburns to see her."

"You knew he was going."

"I knew."

"What happened out there?"

Mollison's hands were at his sides, but still Lynley could see his thumbs picking at the skin round his nails. "Gabbie'll have to tell you that," he replied.

What Mollison was willing to add to his story was the cause of his fight with Kenneth Fleming. He'd manufactured the tale about the Pakistani player for Allison's benefit, he said. Had they only conducted the interview in the corridor at China Silk Wharf on the previous evening, he would have been forthright. But he couldn't venture honesty in Allison's presence. It too much ran the risk of taking them in the direction of a disclosure about Thursday afternoon. Besides, the row about the Pakistani player was what he'd used to explain away his injuries to his wife when the fracas occurred in the first place.

They headed in the direction of Mayfair, rolling through Eaton Square where the central gardens were a wash of colour supplied by everything from pansies to tulips. As they made the turn into Grosvenor Place and buzzed along the buff wall that sheltered Buckingham Palace Gardens from the scrutiny of the curious, Mollison continued.

What happened between him and Fleming, he said, did indeed happen after the third day of the four-day match between Middlesex and Kent. And it did happen in the car park at Lord's. But it started in the bar—"the one in the Pavilion . . . behind the Long Room . . . no doubt the bartender can verify the story if you like"—where Mollison and Fleming, along with six or seven other players, were having a friendly drink together.

"I was drinking tequila," he said. "It's a stealthy little bugger, the way it hits you. It goes to your head before you know what's happened. Your tongue gets looser than it ought. It gets looser faster. So you say things to blokes that you'd otherwise never say."

He'd heard rumours, Mollison told them, just the odd word dropped now and again linking Fleming to Gabriella Patten. He never heard or saw anything first hand himself—"They were careful about that, but then that's Gabriella's way. She doesn't advertise the fact when she's taken a lover"—but when their affair began to head in the direction of marriage, they relaxed their vigilance. People saw. People speculated. Mollison heard.

He didn't know exactly what it was that prompted him to speak, Mollison told them. He hadn't . . . well, he hadn't *done* anything with Gabriella for the last two years. When their own affair had ended—okay, okay, when he'd confessed his sins to Allison so that he'd had to end the affair or lose his wife—he'd felt relieved and utterly recommitted to his marriage, and that feeling had lasted about two months during which time he was absolutely faithful to Allison. No playing around with anyone at all, not even for laughs. But after that, he began to miss Gabbie. He missed her so much that half the time with Allison he didn't even want to . . . He tried to pretend but there are some things a bloke can't fake. . . . Well, they knew what he meant, didn't they? He consoled himself with the thought that Gabbie probably missed him as well. He thought she would do, wouldn't she, because Hugh always drank like a sailor on leave, which made him a disaster between the sheets. And she wasn't having it off with anyone else. At least he didn't think she was. After a time, the soreness of missing her wore off a fraction. He had a few laughs with other women, which made his performance with Allie all the stronger, which allowed him to talk himself into believing that his fling with Gabbie had been just that, good fun while it lasted but still a fling.

And then he heard the speculation about Fleming. Ken's living circumstances had always been bizarre, but he—Mollison—had assumed that in the long run Fleming would return to his wife when he'd worked out of his system whatever he needed to work out of his system. That's what blokes generally did, wasn't it? But when word went round that Fleming had taken on a pricey solicitor to sort through his situation and to draw up paperwork, and when equal word went round that Hugh and Gabriella Patten were no longer occupying space beneath the same roof, and when he himself saw an affectionate exchange between Fleming and Gabriella on the concourse at Lord's not a stone's throw away from the Pavilion where *anyone* might have seen them. . . . Well, Mollison was no fool, was he?

"I was jealous," he admitted. He had directed Lynley to a narrow, cobbled street that formed the south boundary of Shepherd's Market. They parked in front of a pub called Ye Grapes, heavily hung with ivy. They got out of the car and he leaned against it, apparently determined to finish his tale before taking them to the leading female character in it. Sergeant Havers continued making notes of their conversation. Lynley crossed his arms and listened impassively.

"I could have had her myself—married her, I mean—and I hadn't wanted her," Mollison said. "But now that someone else had her—"

"Dog in the manger," Havers said.

"That's what it was. That and the tequila and being forced to remember what it had been like when she and I were together. And having to think about her doing all that with another bloke. Especially a bloke I knew. I began to feel what a fool I'd been to miss her so badly. She'd probably gone from me to someone else straightaway. I was probably just one in a line of her lovers with Fleming at the end, the wally she'd caught."

So he'd made a remark in the form of a question that day after the cricket match. It was crude, it demonstrated a familiarity with Gabriella that bore the unmistakable ring of authenticity. He'd rather not tell them what it was, if they didn't mind. He wasn't very pleased with the nasty passion that had inspired it, nor with the lack of gallantry that had allowed him to say it in the first place.

"Ken went completely blank at first," Mollison said. "It was as if we were talking about two different people." So he drove the point home with an allusion to the number of cricketers who'd had a share of what Gabriella Patten was willing to pass round the table.

Fleming left the bar, but he didn't leave Lord's. When Mollison got out to the car park, the other man was waiting.

"He jumped me," Mollison said. "I don't know if he was defending her honour or just letting me have it. In either case, he caught me off guard. If the groundsman hadn't come along to pull him off, I'd probably be the murder you're investigating right now."

"And Wednesday night when you spoke to him," Lynley said. "What was that actually about?"

"I told you the truth about my motivation, at least. I wanted to apologise. We were probably going to play together when the team was chosen for the Ashes test matches. I wanted no bad blood between us."

"What was his reaction to that?"

"He said it didn't matter, that it was forgotten, that in any case he was going to sort through the muddle with Gabbie that night."

"He no longer seemed bothered?"

"I expect he was bothered to the bone. But I was the last person he'd let know that, wasn't I?" Mollison pushed his way off the car. "Gabbie can tell you how bothered he was. She can show you as well."

He led them to Shepherd Street, a few yards from where they had parked the Bentley. There, across from a florist with a window filled with irises, roses, narcissi, and carnations, he pressed the bell for a flat marked by the number 4 and no other identification. He waited for a moment and pressed two more times. Like husband, like wife, Lynley thought sardonically.

After a moment, the sound of static flickered from the small metal speaker next to the panel of buttons. Guy said into it, "It's Guy."

A moment passed before the door buzzed. He pushed it open, saying to Havers and Lynley, "Don't be rough with her. You'll see there isn't any need."

He led them down a corridor to the rear of the building and up a short flight of stairs to a mezzanine. Off this, a door stood slightly off the latch. Mollison pushed it open, saying, "Gabbie?"

"In here," was the response. "Jean-Paul is taking his aggressions out on me. Ouch! Be careful. I'm not made of rubber."

In here was the sitting room round the corner from the entry. Its overstuffed furniture had been pushed against the walls in order to accommodate a massage table. On this a lightly tanned woman lay upon her stomach. She was petite but voluptuously proportioned, her nudity partially cloaked by a sheet. Her head was turned away from them towards windows that overlooked a courtyard.

"You didn't phone first," she said in a sleepy voice as Jean-Paul— garbed from his turban to his toes in white—worked on her right thigh. "Hmm. That's wonderful," she whispered.

"I couldn't."

"Really. Whyever not? Is the dread Allison being a bother again?"

Mollison's face flamed. "I've brought someone," he said. "You need to talk to him, Gabbie. I'm sorry."

The head—capped by a billowing of hair the colour of harvested wheat—slowly turned in their direction. The blue eyes with their heavy fringe of dark lashes went from Mollison to Havers to Lynley and remained on the last. She winced as Jean-Paul's industrious fingers found a muscle in her thigh that had not as yet submitted to his efforts. She said, "And who exactly are these someones you've brought?"

"They've got Ken's car, Gabbie," Mollison said. His thumbs played nervously along his fingers. "They've been looking for you. They've already started to comb Mayfair. It's better for us both if—"

"You mean it's better for you." Gabriella Patten's eyes were still on Lynley. She lifted one foot and rotated it. Perhaps seeing this as direction, Jean-Paul grasped it and began his work, from toes, to ball, to arch. "Lovely," she murmured. "You reduce me to softened butter, Jean-Paul."

Jean-Paul was all business. His hand moved up her leg, from there to her thigh. *"Vous avez tort,"* he said in brusque disagreement. "Feel this, Madame Patten. How tense it is become in an instant. Like twisted stone. More than before. Much more. And here and here." He clucked disapproval.

Lynley felt his lips twitch in a smile that he did his best to control. Jean-Paul was more efficient than a polygraph.

Abruptly, Gabriella shook the masseur's hands from her body. She said, "I think I've had enough for today." She flipped over, sat up, and swung her legs off the table. The sheet dropped to her waist. Jean-Paul hastily draped her shoulders with a large, pristine white towel. She took her time about using it as a sarong. As Jean-Paul collapsed the massage table and began moving the furniture back into position, Gabriella strolled to a gate-legged table not two feet from where her visitors stood. On this a heavy glass bowl held an array of fruit. She selected an orange and dug manicured fingernails into its skin. The scent of its flesh fairly leapt into the air. She began to peel it away. She said in a quiet voice to Mollison, "Thank you, Judas."

Mollison groaned. "Come on, Gabbie. What were the options?"

"I don't know. Why don't you ask your personal barrister? I'm sure she'd be more than willing to advise you."

"You can't stay here forever."

"I didn't want that."

"They need to talk to you. They need to know what happened. They need to get to the bottom of things."

"Do they? And when did you decide to play the little copper's nark?"

"Gabbie, just tell them what happened when Ken got to the cottage. Tell them what you told me. That's all they want to know. Then they'll be off."

Gabriella stared defiantly at Mollison for a long moment. She finally dropped her head and gave her attention to the orange. A segment of its peel slipped out of her hand, and she and Mollison bent simultaneously to retrieve it. He reached it first. Her hand closed over his. "Guy," she said in an urgent voice.

"It'll all work out," he said gently. "I promise. Just tell them the truth. Will you do that?"

"If I talk, will you stay?"

"We've already been through that. I can't. You know."

"I don't mean afterwards. I mean now. While they're here. Will you stay?"

"Allison thinks I've gone to the sports centre. I couldn't tell her where . . . Gabbie, I've got to get back."

"Please," she said. "Don't make me face this alone. I won't know what to say."

"Just tell them the truth."

"Help me tell it. Please." Her fingers moved from his wrist to his arm. "Please," she repeated. "I won't take long, Guy. I promise you."

It seemed as if Mollison tore his eyes from her only through an effort of will. He said, "I can't spare more than half an hour."

"Thank you," she replied on a breath. "I'll put on some clothes." She brushed past them and disappeared into a bedroom, shutting the door behind her.

Jean-Paul let himself out discreetly. The others made their way farther into the sitting room. Sergeant Havers went to one of two chairs that sat beneath the courtyard windows. She plopped down, heaved her shoulder bag to the floor, and balanced one brogue-shod foot on the opposite knee. She caught Lynley's gaze and rolled her eyes heavenward. Lynley smiled. The sergeant had done an admirable job of controlling herself thus far. Gabriella Patten was the sort of woman Havers would have preferred to swat like a fly.

Mollison went first to the fireplace where he fingered the silk leaves of an artificial aspidistra. He examined himself in the mirrored wall. Then he went to the recessed bookshelves and ran his finger along a collection of paperbacks heavily devoted to Dick Francis, Jeffrey Archer, and Nelson DeMille. He bit at his fingernails for a few moments before swinging round to Lynley.

"It's not what it looks like," he said impulsively.

"What isn't?"

He canted his head towards the doorway. "That bloke. The fact that he was here. It makes her look bad. But it doesn't mean what you think."

Lynley wondered what conclusion Mollison assumed he had drawn from Gabriella's brief but affecting performance. He decided to opt for silence and see where Mollison's verbal ruminations took him. He wandered to the window and inspected the courtyard where two small birds dipped and bobbed along the edge of a fountain.

"She cares."

"About what?" Havers asked.

"About what happened to Ken. She's acting like she doesn't because of Wednesday night. Because of what he said to her. Because of what he did. She's hurt. She doesn't want to show it. Would you?"

"I think I'd tread carefully in a murder investigation," Havers said, "especially if I was the last known person to have seen the corpse before it was a corpse."

"She didn't *do* anything. She just got out fast. And she had cause for that, if you want to know the truth."

"That's what we're looking for."

"Good. Because I'm quite prepared to tell it."

Gabriella Patten had rejoined them. She stood framed in the sitting room doorway, clothed in black leggings, a thin-strapped top printed with tropical flowers, and a diaphanous black overjacket that billowed as she moved to the sofa. She unfastened the delicate gold buckles of the black sandals she was wearing and slipped the sandals from her feet. These— pedicured, with toenails painted to match the pink of her fingernails—she curled beneath her as she took position in a corner of the sofa and cast a fleeting smile in Mollison's direction.

He said, "Do you want anything, Gabbie? Tea? Coffee? A Coke?"

"It's enough that you're here. It's going to be tortuous, having to live through it again. Bless you for staying." She placed the flat of her palm to the sofa next to her. She said, "Will you?"

In reply, Mollison pushed off from the bookshelves and sat what appeared to be a calculated eight inches from her, close enough to communicate his support while at the same time just beyond her reach. Lynley wondered which of them was supposed to receive the message implied by those eight inches: the police or Gabriella Patten herself. She seemed oblivious of it. Straightening her shoulders and her spine, she turned her attention to the others with a shake of the soft curls that fell to her shoulders.

"You want to know what happened on Wednesday night," she said.

"It's a good place to start," Lynley replied. "But we may venture beyond it."

"There's little enough to tell. Ken drove out to the Springburns. We had an ugly row. I left. I have no idea what happened after that. To Ken, that is." She rested her head against her hand—temple upon fingertips, upper arm stretched along the back of the sofa—and watched Sergeant Havers riffle through her notebook. "Is that necessary?" she asked.

Sergeant Havers continued to riffle. She found the page she wanted, she licked the tip of her pencil, she began to scribble.

"I said—" Gabriella began.

"You had a row with Fleming. You left," Havers murmured as she wrote. "What time was this?"

"Do you have to take notes?"

"It's the best way to keep everyone's story straight."

Gabriella looked to Lynley to intervene. He said, "As to the time, Mrs. Patten?"

She hesitated, frowning, her attention still on Havers as if wishing to telegraph her unhappiness with the fact that her words would be rendered immortal by the sergeant's pencil. "I can't tell you exactly. I didn't look at a clock."

"You phoned me sometime round eleven, Gabbie," Mollison prompted. "From the call box in Greater Springburn. So you must have had the row before then."

"What time did Fleming arrive to see you?" Lynley asked.

"Half past nine? Ten? I don't know exactly because I'd been for a walk and when I got back, there he was."

"You didn't know he was coming?"

"I thought he was going to Greece. With that—" she rearranged the draping black overjacket carefully, "with his son. He'd said it was James's birthday and he was trying to put things right with him, so they were heading to Athens. And from there to a boat."

"Trying to put things right with him?"

"There was considerable anomie between them, Inspector."

"I beg your pardon?"

"They didn't get on."

"Ah." Lynley saw Havers' mouth work round *anomie* as she diligently wrote. God only knew what she would make of the malapropism when she constructed her report. "What was the source of this . . . anomie?" he asked.

"James couldn't adjust to the fact that Ken had left his mother."

"Fleming told you as much."

"He didn't need to. James was hostility itself towards his father, and it doesn't require a background in child psychology to understand why. Children always cling to the tenebrous hope that their separated parents will reunite." She touched her palm to her chest in emphasis. "I represented the interloper, Inspector. James knew about me. He knew what my presence in his father's life implied. He didn't like that, and he let his father know he didn't like it in any way he could."

Havers said, "Jimmy's mother says he didn't know his father intended to marry you. She says none of the kids knew."

"Then James's mother is prevaricating," Gabriella said. "Ken told the children. He told Jean as well."

"As far as you know."

"What are you suggesting?"

"Were you present when he told his wife and children?" Lynley asked.

"I had no desire to publicly revel in the fact that Ken was ending his marriage to be with me. Nor did I have a need to be present to verify the fact that he'd informed his family."

"But privately?"

"What?"

"Did you revel in it privately?"

"Until Wednesday night, I was mad about him. I wanted to marry him. I would be guilty of prevarication myself if I said I wasn't pleased to know that he was taking steps in his personal life to bring us together."

"How did Wednesday night change things?"

She turned her head so that the fingers on her temple were now at her brow. "There are certain things that, when said between a man and a woman, inflict irreparable damage upon a relationship. I'm sure you understand."

More matter with less art was what Lynley thought. What he said was, "I'm going to have to ask you to be specific, Mrs. Patten. Fleming arrived at half past nine or ten. Did the row begin immediately or did he lead up to it in some way?"

She raised her head. A perfect circle of colour the size of a ten pence coin had appeared in each of her cheeks. "I don't see how a detail-by-detail regurgitation of the evening is going to make any difference to what came afterwards."

"We'll judge that for ourselves," Lynley said. "Did the row begin immediately?"

She made no reply. Mollison said, "Gabbie, tell him. It's all right," with some urgency. "It doesn't make you look bad."

She gave a quick, breathy laugh. "That's because I didn't tell you all of it. I couldn't, Guy. And to have to tell it all now . . ." Her fingers passed over her eyelids, and her lips trembled convulsively beneath the shelter of her hand.

"Would you like me to leave?" Mollison offered. "Or I could wait in the other room. Or outside—"

She leaned towards him, reached for his hand. He moved an inch closer to her. "No," she said. "You're my strength. Stay. Please." She held his hand in both of hers. She took a deep breath. "All right," she said.

She'd been out for a long walk, she told them. It was part of her routine, two long walks a day for aerobic exercise, one in the morning and one in the evening. On this evening, she'd made a partial circuit of the Springburns, covering at least six miles at a brisk, steady pace. She arrived back at Celandine Cottage to find Ken Fleming's Lotus sitting in the drive.

"As I said, I thought he'd gone to Greece with James. So I was surprised to see his car. But I was happy as well because we hadn't been together since the previous Saturday night and, prior to that moment of realising he'd come out to Kent on a whim, I'd had no hope of seeing him before his return from Greece on Sunday night."

She entered the cottage, calling his name. She found him upstairs in the loo. He was kneeling on the floor, going through the rubbish. He'd already done the same in the kitchen as well as in the sitting room, and he'd left the waste bins overturned behind him.

"What was he looking for?" Lynley asked.

That's what Gabriella wanted to know, and Fleming wouldn't tell her at first. He wouldn't say a word, in fact. He simply tore through the rubbish and when he was done, he stormed into the bedroom and ripped the counterpane and the covers from the bed. He examined the sheets. Then he went downstairs to the dining room, took the liquor bottles from the antique washstand that held them, lined them up on the table, and studied the level of the liquid in each. After he was done—with Gabriella continually asking him what he was looking for, what was wrong, what had happened—he returned to the kitchen and pawed through the rubbish another time.

"I asked him if he'd lost something," Gabriella said. "He repeated the question and laughed." Then he got to his feet, kicked the rubbish to one side, and grabbed her arm. He demanded to know who had been there. He said Gabriella had been alone since Sunday morning, it was now Wednesday night, she couldn't have actually been expected to survive four entire days without a good dose of slavering male companionship— she'd never done that before, had she?—so who had provided it? Before she could answer or protest her innocence, he flew out of the cottage and stalked through the garden to the compost heap where he began digging through that as well.

"He was like a madman. I've never seen anything like it before. I begged him to at least tell me what he was looking for so that I could help him find it, and he said. . . ." She lifted Mollison's imprisoned hand to her cheek and closed her eyes.

"It's okay, Gabbie," Mollison said.

"It isn't," she whispered. "His face was so twisted I wouldn't have known him. I backed away. I said, 'Ken, what is it? What *is* it? Can't you tell me? You've got to tell me,' and he—he leaped up. He soared right off the ground."

Fleming recited the time they'd been apart, saying, Sunday night, Monday night, Tuesday night, Gabriella. Not to mention the mornings and the afternoons in between. That gave her plenty of time, he declared. Gabriella asked him time for what, for *what*? He laughed and said she'd had quite enough time to service all of Middlesex and half of Essex as well. And she was a wily one, wasn't she? She'd have destroyed the evidence, if there was evidence in the first place. Because perhaps she didn't ask the others to make the same accommodation to her puling need for protection and security as she had asked of Fleming. Perhaps the others were enjoying the rewarding plunge into her excessively cooperative minge without the hindrance of latex between them. Is that what it was, Gabriella? Ask Ken to use condoms to keep him thinking what a cautious little lover our Gabriella is while all the time you're passing it out to the others with no such demand?

"So he'd been going through the rubbish. . . . He'd actually been *looking* for . . . As if I . . ." Gabriella faltered.

"I think we get the picture." Havers tapped her pencil against the sole of her brogue. "Did you have the row outside?"

That's where it began, Gabriella told them. First Fleming accused and Gabriella denied, but her denials only enraged him further. She told him that she refused to discuss such ludicrous accusations, and she returned to the cottage. He followed. She tried to lock him out but, of course, he had his own key. So she went through to the sitting room and tried unsuccessfully to wedge the door closed by propping a chair beneath its handle. The effort was useless. Fleming bashed the door open by using his shoulder. The chair slid to the floor. He was inside. Gabriella retreated to a corner with one of the fire irons in her hand. She warned him not to come near. He disregarded her.

"I thought I could strike him," she said. "But when it came down to it, all I could imagine was the blood and the bone and what he would look like if I actually did it." She hesitated as Fleming approached her. She warned him off again. She raised the fire iron. "And then suddenly he became quite rational," she told them.

He apologised. He asked for the fire iron. He promised he wouldn't hurt her. He said he'd heard rumours. He'd been told things, he confessed, and they'd been swarming round inside his skull like hornets. She asked what things, what rumours? She asked to be told so that she could at least defend herself or explain. He asked if she would, if she would explain, if he told her a name would she tell him the truth?

"There was something so pitiful about him," Gabriella said. "He seemed helpless and broken. So I set down the fire iron. I told him I loved him and that I'd do anything to help him through whatever it was he was going through."

He said Mollison, then. He wanted to know about Mollison first. She repeated the word *first*. She asked him what he meant by *first*. And that single word set him off again.

"He fancied that I'd had a score of lovers. I didn't much like his accusations. So I made some nasty ones of my own. About him. About Miriam. He reacted to that. The row escalated from there."

"What prompted you to leave?" Lynley asked.

"This." She swept the heavy mass of hair from her shoulders. On either side of her neck bruises lay like watery ink stains against her skin. "I actually thought he was going to kill me. He was wild."

"In defence of Mrs. Whitelaw?"

No. He laughed Gabriella's accusations off as an utter absurdity. His real concerns lay in Gabriella's past. How many times had she been unfaithful to Hugh? With whom? Where? How did the couplings come about? Because don't tell me it's only Mollison, he warned. That answer isn't on. I've spent the last three days asking around. I've got names. I've got places. And the best you can do for yourself right now is just to make sure the names and places match.

"I'm at fault for that," Mollison said. With his free hand, he brushed Gabriella's hair back into place. His gesture hid her bruises once again.

"As am I." Gabriella lifted Mollison's hand a second time and spoke against it. "Because after you and I ended, I was distraught, Guy. I did exactly what he accused me of doing. Oh, not everything because who would have had the time to do all the things he wanted to believe that I managed to do. But I did some of it, yes. And with more than one lover. Because I was desperate. Because my marriage was a joke. Because I missed you so much that I wanted to die, so what did it matter what happened to me anyway?"

"Oh Gabbie," Mollison said.

"I'm sorry." She dropped their hands to her lap. She raised her head and gave him a tremulous smile. Mollison lifted his free hand to her cheek. A single tear trailed down it. He brushed it away.

Havers broke into the tender scene. "So he was choking you, right? You broke away and made a run for it."

"Yes. That's what happened."

"Why'd you take his car?"

"Because it was blocking mine."

"He didn't run after you?"

"No."

"How'd you get his keys?"

"Keys?"

"To the car."

"He'd left them on the work top in the kitchen. I took them to stop him from following me. Then, when I got out to the drive, I saw that the

Lotus was in the way. So I took his car. I never heard from him or saw him after that."

"And the kittens?" Lynley asked.

She looked at him, nonplussed. "Kittens?"

"What did you do with them? I understand you have two."

"Oh God, I've quite forgotten about the kittens. They were sleeping in the kitchen when I left for my walk earlier." She looked genuinely stricken for the first time. "I was supposed to take care of them. I made a bargain with myself when I found them by the spring. I promised I wouldn't abandon them. And then I ran off and—"

"You were terrified," Mollison told her. "You were running for your life. You can't be expected to think of every ramification of what you were doing."

"That's not the point, is it. They were helpless and I left them because all I could think about was myself."

"They'll turn up somewhere," Mollison said. "Someone's got them, if they weren't at the cottage."

"Where did you go when you left?" Lynley asked.

She said, "I drove directly to Greater Springburn. I telephoned Guy."

"How long a drive is that?"

"Fifteen minutes."

"So your row with Fleming lasted more than an hour?"

"More than . . . ?" Gabriella looked at Mollison in confusion.

"If he arrived at half past nine or ten and if you didn't phone Mollison until after eleven, we have more than an hour to account for," Lynley said.

"Then we must have quarrelled that long. Yes, I suppose we did."

"You did nothing else?"

"What's that supposed to mean?"

"There was a packet of Silk Cut in a kitchen cupboard at the cottage," Lynley said. "Are you a smoker, Mrs. Patten?"

Mollison moved restlessly on the sofa. "You can't be thinking that Gabriella—"

"Do you smoke, Mrs. Patten?"

"No."

"Then whose cigarettes are those? We've been told Fleming didn't smoke."

"They're mine. I used to smoke, but I've been off them for nearly four months. For Ken's sake, mostly. It's what he wanted. But I always keep a packet nearby just in case I need them. I find it's easier to resist them if they're in the next room. It doesn't feel quite so much like denial that way."

"So you didn't have another packet? Opened already?"

She looked from Lynley to Havers. She went back to Lynley. She seemed to put the question in context. She said, "You aren't thinking I killed him. You aren't thinking I set some sort of fire. How could I have done? He was there. He was raging. Do you think he might have paused for a while and stepped aside and let me . . . What is it that I'm supposed to have done?"

"Do you have a packet of cigarettes here as well?" Lynley asked. "To make it easier to keep resisting?"

"I've a packet. Unopened. Would you like to see it?"

"Before we leave. Yes." Gabriella bridled at this, but Lynley went on. "Once you phoned Mollison and made the arrangements for this flat, what happened next?"

"I got in the car and drove here," she said.

"Did anyone meet you here?"

"At the flat? No."

"So no one can actually verify the time you arrived."

Her eyes flashed angrily at the implication. "I woke the porter. He gave me the key."

"And does he live alone? The porter?"

"What does that have to do with anything, Inspector?"

"Did Fleming end your relationship on Wednesday night, Mrs. Patten? Was that part of the row? Were your personal plans for a new marriage junked?"

"Now wait a minute," Mollison said hotly.

"No, Guy." Gabriella released Mollison's hand. She shifted her position. Her legs were still beneath her, but she faced Lynley now. Indignation made her speech stiff. "Ken ended the relationship. I ended the relationship. What does it matter? It was over. I left. I phoned Guy. I came to London. I arrived around midnight."

"Can someone confirm that? Besides the porter," who, Lynley thought, would probably be only too happy to verify anything Gabriella claimed.

"Oh yes indeed. Someone else can confirm."

"We'll need the name."

"And believe me, I'm happy to give it. Miriam Whitelaw. We spoke on the phone not five minutes after I walked into this flat." Her face flashed with a smile of triumph when she read the momentary surprise on Lynley's.

Double alibi, he thought. One for each of them.

CHAPTER

13

Sergeant Havers stood outside the Bentley in Shepherd's Market, splitting a blueberry muffin in two. While Lynley was phoning the Yard, she had paid a visit to the Express Café, returning with two steaming styrofoam cups, which she placed on the car's bonnet, and a paper bag from which she drew forth her mid-morning snack.

"Bit early for elevenses, but what the hell," she remarked, offering Lynley a portion.

He waved her off with a "Mind the car for God's sake, will you, Sergeant?" He was listening to Constable Nkata's report, which so far consisted of how the DCs assigned to the Isle of Dogs and Kensington were managing to avoid speaking to the press who, in Nkata's words, were "hanging on the slack like a flock of crows waiting for road kill." There was nothing of burning import to relay at the moment from either location or from Little Venice, where another team of DCs was delving into

the Wednesday night movements of Olivia Whitelaw and Chris Faraday.
"Whole family's home in Cardale Street, though," Nkata said.

"The boy as well?" Lynley asked. "Jimmy?"

"Far as we know."

"Good. If he leaves, tail him."

"Will do, 'Spector." The sound of rustling came over the wire, as if
Nkata was juggling papers close to the receiver. He said, "Maidstone
phoned in. A bird, saying you're to phone her when you can."

"Inspector Ardery?"

More rustling. "Right. Ardery. Tell me, she as foxy as she sounds?"

"She's too old for you, Winston."

"Hell. Isn't that always the story?"

Lynley rang off and joined Havers on the pavement. He tasted the
coffee she'd brought him. "Havers, this is foul."

His sergeant said past a mouthful of muffin, "But it's wet."

"So is motor oil, but I prefer not to drink it."

Havers munched and raised her cup in the direction from which they
had come. "So what d'you think?"

"That's the question of the hour," Lynley said. He reflected upon
their interview with Gabriella Patten.

"We can verify the phone call with Mrs. Whitelaw," Havers said. "If
she did phone Kensington around midnight on Wednesday, she did it
from the flat since the porter verifies the time she picked up the key.
Which puts her out of the running. She couldn't be in two places at once,
could she, setting a fire in Kent and having a friendly little chat with Mrs.
Whitelaw in London. I expect that's beyond even Gabriella's powers."

But she had others, as they both had seen. And she had no apparent
reluctance to use them.

"I'll stay here for a while," Guy Mollison had confided without no-
ticeable embarrassment at the conclusion of the interview when he
stepped with Lynley and Havers onto the mezzanine and pulled the door
partially shut behind him. "She's had a rough time of it. She needs a
friend. If I can do that much . . . Well, I'm at fault here. If I hadn't
started the trouble with Ken in the first place . . . It's just that I owe her.
You know." He looked back over his shoulder at the door. His tongue
slipped out, wetted his lips. "She's broken up about his death. She'll want
someone to talk to. You can see that."

Lynley wondered at the man's capacity for self-delusion. It was remarkable to think that they'd actually witnessed the same performance.

From her position on the sofa—head and shoulders thrown back, hands folded—Gabriella had told them of her conversation with Miriam Whitelaw and what led up to it.

"The woman's an utter hypocrite," she said. "She was butter-wouldn't-melt whenever she saw Ken and I together. But she hated me, she didn't want him to marry me, she thought I wasn't good enough for him. No one was good enough for Ken as far as Miriam was concerned. No one but Miriam, that is."

"She denies they were lovers."

"Of course they weren't lovers," Gabriella asserted. "But it wasn't for want of her trying, believe me."

"Fleming told you this?"

"He didn't need to tell me. All I had to do was to watch. How she looked at him, how she treated him, how she hung on his words. It was nauseous. And behind his back, there she was, always picking away. At me. At us. All in the name of having only Ken's best interests at heart. And everything—all of it—done with that treacly little smile on her face. 'Gabriella, do forgive me. I don't intend to make you self-conscious . . .' and off she'd go."

"Self-conscious about what?"

" 'Are you sure that's the word you want to use, dear?' " She did a fair imitation of Mrs. Whitelaw's soft voice. " 'Don't you mean *me* instead of *I*? What an intriguing . . . ah . . . point of view you're expressing. Have you read much on the subject? Ken's a verbacious reader, you know.' "

Lynley doubted Miriam Whitelaw would have ventured into manufacturing words, but he got the general idea. Gabriella's mimicry continued.

" 'I'm sure that, when you and Ken marry, you'll want it to be a lasting match, won't you? So you won't mind my pointing out to you the importance of a man and woman meeting on an intellectual plane, as well as on a physical one.' " Gabriella shook back her mass of hair, an agitated movement in which she uncovered her bruises once again. "She knew he loved me. She knew he wanted me. She couldn't bear the thought of Ken feeling something for another woman, so she had to demean it. 'Of course, you know that ardour isn't lasting. There has to be something more between lovers if a relationship is going to stand the test of time. I'm sure you and Ken have come to terms with this already, haven't you, dear?

He won't want to make the same unfortunate mistake with you that he made with Jean.' "

If that's what she said to Gabriella's face, then what did the police imagine Mrs. Butter-Wouldn't-Melt was saying behind Gabriella's back? To Ken? All of it, Gabriella declared, would have been proclaimed so gently, with such care, with no indication that Mrs. Whitelaw felt anything other than maternal concern for a young man she'd known since he was fifteen years old.

"So when I got to London, I phoned her," Gabriella said. "She'd spent so much time trying to break us apart, I thought she'd like to know she was finally successful."

"How long did this conversation last?"

"Just long enough for me to tell the bitch she'd got what she wanted."

"And the time?"

"I've already said. Around midnight. I didn't check, but I'd driven in from Kent directly so it couldn't have been any later than half past twelve."

Which also, Lynley knew, could be verified by checking with Mrs. Whitelaw. He took another drink of his coffee, grimaced, and poured the remaining contents into the gutter where it formed a suspiciously pinguid pool. He tossed the cup into a litter bin and returned to the car.

"Well?" Havers said. "So, if Gabriella's out of it, who's looking good now?"

"Inspector Ardery's got something for us," Lynley replied. "We need to talk to her."

He got into the car. Havers followed, leaving a trail of muffin crumbs like Hansel's sister. She slung the door closed and balanced both coffee and muffin on her knees as she fastened her seat belt, saying, "One thing's cleared up, for me at least."

"What's that?"

"What I've been thinking about since Friday night. What, I reckon, you meant when you said Fleming's death wasn't a suicide, a murder, or an accident: Gabriella Patten as potential murder victim. She's out of the picture. Wouldn't you agree?"

Lynley didn't answer at once. He pondered the question, idly watching as a well-coiffed woman in a suspiciously body-clinging black dress passed the Bentley and took up a casual stance against a street lamp not far from Ye Grapes. She arranged her face into a mask that managed to convey sensuality, ennui, and hardened indifference simultaneously.

Havers followed the direction of Lynley's gaze. She sighed. "Oh hell. Shall I telephone vice?"

Lynley shook his head and turned the ignition key, although he didn't put the car in gear. "It's early in the day. I doubt she'll get much custom."

"She must be desperate."

"I dare say she is." He rested his hand on the gear stick thoughtfully. "Perhaps desperation's the key in all this."

"To Fleming's death, you mean? And it's Fleming's death—premeditated and all—that we're onto, isn't it, sir? It's not Gabriella's." Havers took a gulp of coffee and warmed to her subject before he had a chance to disagree. "Here's how it works. There were only three people who may have wanted her dead and who also knew where Gabriella was on Wednesday night. But the problem is that all three potential killers have iron-clad alibis."

"Hugh Patten," Lynley said meditatively.

"Who from all accounts was exactly where he said he was, at the gaming tables in the Cherbourg Club."

"Miriam Whitelaw."

"Whose alibi was unconsciously corroborated by Gabriella Patten not ten minutes ago."

"And the last?" Lynley asked.

"Fleming himself, broken on the wheel of his discoveries about her unsavoury past. And he happens to have the best alibi of all."

"So you're discounting Jean Cooper. And the boy. Jimmy."

"For Gabriella's potential death? They didn't know where she was. But if Fleming was our intended victim from the first, we've a whole new cricket match, haven't we? Because Jimmy *must* have known his father intended to push forward with the divorce. And he spoke to his father that same afternoon. He may have known where Fleming was headed. The way I see it, Fleming had hurt the boy's mother, he'd hurt the boy himself, he'd hurt the boy's brother and sister, he'd made promises he wasn't willing to keep—"

"You're not suggesting Jimmy murdered his father because of a cancelled boat trip, are you?"

"The cancelled boat trip was just a symptom. It wasn't the disease. Jimmy decided they'd all had enough exposure to it, so he took himself out to Kent on Wednesday night and administered the only medicine he knew that would cure it. He even fell back on a past behaviour at the same time. He set a fire.''

"Rather a sophisticated means of murder for a sixteen-year-old, wouldn't you say?''

"Not at all. He's set fires before—"

"One."

"One that we know of. And the fact that the cottage fire was so obviously set suggests a lack of sophistication, not the opposite. Sir, we need to get our hands on that kid.''

"We need something to work with first.''

"Like what?''

"Like a single piece of hard evidence. Like a witness who can place the boy at the scene on Wednesday.''

"Inspector . . .''

"Havers, I see your point, but I'm not going to play an early hand in this. Your reasoning about Gabriella is sound: The people who may have wanted her dead and knew where she was all have alibis while the people with motives but without alibis didn't know where she was. I accept all that.''

"Then—"

"There are other points you're not considering.''

"Such as?''

"The bruises on her neck. Did Fleming inflict them? Did she inflict them herself to support her story?''

"But someone—that bloke out for a walk, that farmer—he heard the row. So there's corroboration for her story. And she herself made the best point of all. What was Fleming supposed to be doing while she crept round the cottage setting up the fire?''

"Who put out the cats?''

"The cats?''

"The kittens. Who put out the kittens? Fleming? Why? Did he know they were there? Did he even care?''

"So what are you saying? Fleming was killed by a man-hating animal lover?''

"There's that to consider, isn't there?'' Lynley put the car in gear and pointed it towards Piccadilly.

.   .   .

From the deck of the barge, where the mid-morning sun had at last managed to scrape the top of the trees and was finally streaming band after band of comforting heat against his aching muscles, Chris Faraday watched the two policemen and felt his stomach go numb. They weren't dressed like cops—one in a leather jacket and blue jeans, the other in cotton trousers and an open-necked shirt—so under other circumstances, Chris might have talked himself into believing they were anyone from casual day trippers to Jehovah's Witnesses doing their witnessing along the canal. But under these circumstances, watching them climb aboard one barge after another, seeing barge owners' heads swivel in his direction and then rapidly look away after catching sight of him, Chris knew who the men were and what they were doing. Their job was to question his neighbours and to gather either corroboration for or a conflicting account of his movements on Wednesday night, and they were employing a professional and systematic approach. It also happened to be a conspicuous one, designed to rattle his nerves if he managed to catch sight of it.

Success, he mentally saluted them. His nerves were appropriately rattled.

There were steps to be taken, phone calls to be made, and reports to be given. But he couldn't summon the will to do anything. This has nothing to do with me, he kept telling himself. But the truth was it had everything to do with him and had done for the last five years, since the evening he'd picked Livie off the street and mentally designated her rehabilitation and regeneration his personal challenge. Fool, he thought. Pride goeth and here at last was the fall.

He dug his fingers into the angry muscles at the base of his skull. They were bunched into knots, like a tangle of wires. They were responding in part to the sight of the police but also in part to a night without sleep.

Misery and irony make for nasty bedfellows, Chris decided. Not only had they kept him awake, but they were turning his life into a waiting game. The very fact of them, creeping round the boundaries of his consciousness, had caused him to open his eyes this morning, to fasten them on the knot holes in the pine ceiling of his bedroom, and to feel like a Puritan being tested for witchcraft, with a weight like an anvil sitting squarely on his chest. He must have slept, but he couldn't remember having actually done so. And the sheets and blankets—so twisted that they looked and felt like laundry just come out of a washing machine—

gave mute testimony to the thrashing round that had taken the place of slumber.

He'd grunted with the pain of first movement. His neck and shoulders felt frozen in position, and while he needed to pee so badly that his dick was practically seeking out the toilet without his assistance, his back was sore and his limbs were weary. Getting out of bed loomed like a project he couldn't hope to complete in less than a month.

What had got him up was the thought of Livie, the *this must be what it's like for her* that sent equal proportions of energy and guilt swirling through his system. He'd groaned, flopped from his back to his side, and stuck his feet out of bed to test the room's temperature. A soft tongue licked his toe. Beans was lying on the floor, patiently waiting for breakfast and a run.

Chris dropped his hand over the side of the bed, and the beagle cooperatively slithered forward on the floor, putting his head within petting distance. Chris smiled. "Good boy," he murmured. "How 'bout a cup of tea? Are you here to take my order for breakfast? I'll have eggs, toast, a rasher of bacon—not too crisp, mind you—and a bowl of strawberries on the side. Got that, Beans?"

The dog's tail thumped. He offered a pleasurable whine in reply. Livie's voice called from across the corridor, "Chris, you up? You up yet, Chris?"

"Getting," Chris said.

"You slept late."

She hadn't sounded reproachful. She never sounded reproachful. But still he'd felt reproached.

"Sorry," he said.

"Chris, I didn't mean—"

"I know. It's nothing. Just a bad night." He swung himself out of bed. He sat for a moment, his head in his hands. He tried not to think but failed, as he had failed for most of the night.

What a monumental howl the fates must be having with all this, he'd thought. He'd lived his entire life thus far without giving in to impulse. He'd only deviated from that mode of living once. And now, because of that single moment when he'd first seen Livie waiting for her regular Sunday afternoon trick with those shopping bags of sexual gewgaws at her feet, because of that instant when he'd wondered idly if her hard brittle edges could possibly be smoothed, he was going to pay. One way or another, if he couldn't think of a direction in which he could lead the police, he was heading for consequences the likes of which he'd never once dreamed of. And it was such a bloody joke at the bottom of it all. Because, for the very first time, he was guilty of nothing . . . and guilty of everything.

"Shit," he'd moaned.

"You all right, Chris?" Livie called. "Chris, you all right?"

He'd scooped his pyjama bottoms from the floor and thrust his legs into them. He'd gone to her room. He could tell from the placement of the walker that she'd tried to get herself out of bed, and he felt another rush of guilt. "Livie, why didn't you call me?"

She offered him a wan smile. She'd managed to put all of her jewellery on—except for the nose ring, which lay on a copy of something called *Hollywood Wives*. He frowned at the book and not for the first time wondered at her capacity for wallowing in the tasteless and the insignificant. She said as if in answer, "I'm picking up pointers. They have hours and hours of acrobatic sex."

"I hope they enjoy it," Chris said.

He sat on her bed and eased Panda to one side as the dogs crowded into the room. They moved restlessly from the bed to the chest of drawers to the clothes cupboard that gaped open and spit a cascade of black in the direction of the floor.

"They're wanting their run," Livie said.

"Spoiled little beggars. I'll take them in a minute. You ready, then?"

"Right."

She grasped his arm and he swept back the covers, pivoted her body, dropped her legs to the floor. He placed the walker in front of her and raised her to her feet.

"I can cope with the rest," she said and began the torturous progress towards the loo, inching forward, lifting the walker, dragging her feet in the only semblance of walking she could manage now. She was getting worse, he realised and he wondered exactly when it had happened. She could no longer put her feet squarely down. Instead, she walked—if her sluggish movement could be called that—on whatever happened to hit the floor first, be it ankle, arch, heel, or toe.

He still needed the toilet himself. He could have been and gone in the time it would take her just to make it from her room to the loo. But he stayed where he was on the edge of her bed and made himself wait. It was little enough punishment, he decided.

He'd left her in the galley, doing her part to make their breakfast, which consisted of pouring cornflakes into bowls and spilling a quarter of the contents onto the floor. He'd taken the dogs for their run and returned with *The Sunday Times*. She'd dipped her spoon into her bowl in silence and begun to read the paper. He'd been holding his breath every time she opened a newspaper from Thursday evening onwards. He'd kept thinking, She'll notice, she'll begin to question, she isn't a fool. But thus far she had neither noticed nor questioned. So caught up was she in what was in the paper that she hadn't yet noticed what was not.

He'd left her running her finger along the print for a story about the search for a car. He'd said, "I'll be on deck. Give a shout if you need me," and she'd made a vague murmur in response. He'd climbed the stairs, unfolded a fading canvas chair, plopped into it with a wince, and tried to think and not to think simultaneously. To think what to do. Not to think what he'd done.

He'd been mulling the possibilities and sun-soaking his weary muscles for an hour when he first spotted the police. They were on the deck of the Scannels' barge, the one closest to the Warwick Avenue bridge. John Scannel stood in front of an easel. His wife posed, semi-recumbent and seven-eighths nude, on the roof of the barge's cabin. Along the path, Scannel had already lined previous depictions of his wife's ample curves for potential collectors to snap up for a bargain, and he'd no doubt harboured the mistaken hope that the two men who joined him were connoisseurs of the cubism he favoured.

Chris had watched, only idly attentive. But when Scannel looked in his direction and then leaned confidingly towards his visitors, Chris's interest had quickened. From that point on, he observed the men's progress from one barge to the next. He watched his neighbours talk, he imagined he heard them, and he listened to the nails pounding into his coffin.

The police wouldn't interview him, and he knew it. They would carry their report back to their superior, that bloke with the twenty-quid haircut and the bespoke suit. Then, no doubt, the inspector would come to call again. Only this time his questions would be specific. And if Chris wasn't able to answer them convincingly, there'd be hell to pay everywhere, without a doubt.

The cops moved on. And on again. They finally climbed aboard the barge nearest to Chris's, so close at this point that Chris could hear one of them clear his throat and the other rap quietly on the closed door of the cabin. The Bidwells inside—a drunken novelist and a self-deluding erstwhile mannequin who still believed that the cover of *Vogue* was within her reach if she only managed to drop two stone—wouldn't be stirring for at least another hour. And once rudely awakened by the police or by anyone else for that matter, they'd be none too cooperative either. There was, at least, a mercy in that. Perhaps the Bidwells would inadvertently buy him some time. Because time was what he needed if he was successfully to negotiate the mire of the last four days and escape without sinking up to his neck.

He waited until he heard Henry Bidwell growling, "Wha' the bloody . . . Whizzit, damn you?" from behind the cabin door. He didn't wait to hear the cops' reply. He picked up his mug of tea—scummed over and long since gone undrinkable—and said, "Beans, Toast," to the dogs, who, like him, were taking advantage of the sun. They scrambled to their feet and clattered off the roof of the cabin. Their eager, cocked heads said, "Run? Walk? Eat? What?" and their whipping tails indicated their willingness to cooperate in whatever he suggested. "Below," he said. Toast limped instead for the side of the barge. Ever the willing sheep, Beans followed. Chris said, "No. Not now. You've had one run already. Go to Livie. *Go.*" Despite Chris's words, Toast put his one front paw on the side of the barge, preparatory to leaping out onto the steps, from there to the pathway, and from there, doubtless, to Regent's Park. Chris said, "Hey," sharply and pointed to the cabin. Toast thought it over and decided to obey. Beans followed. Chris brought up the rear.

Livie was where he'd left her, at the table in the galley. Their cereal bowls still sat among the banana peels, the teapot, the sugar, and a jug of milk. The Sunday newspaper was still spread out in front of her, open to the page she'd been perusing more than an hour earlier. And she still appeared to be perusing it, because her head was bent to it, her forehead rested in one hand, and the fingers of the other with their line of silver rings curved round the first word of the headline: *Cricket*. The only change, in fact, that Chris could see was the presence of Panda who had sprung to the table, finished off the milk and soggy cornflakes in one bowl, and was in the midst of lapping up the remains in the other. The cat crouched happily in front of it, eyes closed with bliss, tongue working furiously against the sure moment when she'd be caught.

"You!" Chris snapped. "Panda! Get off!"

Livie jerked spasmodically. Her hands flew out, crashing against the dishes, and one bowl slid off the table while the other upended. Its remaining milk, bananas, and cereal spattered the cat's front paws. Panda did not appear disconcerted. She set to licking.

"Sorry," Chris said. He went for the dishes as the cat leapt soundlessly to the floor and scooted down the corridor and out of punishment's way. "Were you asleep?"

There was something peculiar about her face. Her eyes didn't look focussed, and her lips were pale.

"You didn't see Pan?" Chris said. "I don't like her on the table, Livie. She goes after the dishes, and it's not very—"

"Sorry. I wasn't paying attention." She smoothed her hand over the newspaper, brought it away smudged with ink, and began returning the pages to their original order. She gave much attention to this. She rearranged, she lined up the corners, she folded, she halved, she stacked. He watched her. Her right hand began to tremble, so she dropped it to her lap and went on with her left.

"I'll see to that," he said.

"Some of the pages got wet. From the milk. I'm sorry. You've not read it yet."

"It's okay, Livie. It's just a paper. What's it matter? I can get another if I need one." He scooped up her bowl. She'd been mostly playing with her cereal earlier during breakfast and from what he could see, she'd never got beyond playing with it the morning long. Sodden cornflakes and ever-darkening banana slices marked the trajectory of the cereal bowl she'd upended. "Still not hungry?" he asked. "Shall I make you an egg? Would you like a sandwich? Or what about tofu? I could do a salad with that."

"No."

"Livie, you've got to eat something."

"I'm not hungry."

"Hungry doesn't matter. You know you've got to—"

"What? Keep up my strength?"

"For a start. Yes. It's not a bad idea."

"You don't want that, Chris."

Slowly, he turned from dumping the limp cereal and the gelatinous bananas into the rubbish. He examined her pinched features and her pasty skin, and he wondered why she was choosing this moment to strike out at him. True, his behaviour this morning had been deficient—his lie-in had been at her expense—but it wasn't like Livie to accuse without facts at her fingertips. And she didn't have facts. He'd been careful enough to see to that. "What's going on?" he asked her.

"When my strength goes, I go as well."

"And you think that's what I want?"

"Why wouldn't you?"

He set the bowls in the sink. He returned to the table for the sugar and the milk jug. He placed them on the work top. He went back to her. He sat across the table. Her left hand was balled into a loose fist and he reached to cover it with his own, but she pulled away. Then he saw. For the first time, her right arm was fibrillating. The muscles were quivering from her wrist to her elbow up to her shoulder. A coolness passed over him at the sight, as if a cloud had not only covered the sun but also invaded the cabin as well, bringing with it the distinct sensation of heavy, dank air. Shit, he thought. And he told himself to keep his voice all business.

"How long has that been going on?" he asked.

"What?"

"You know."

She moved her left hand and watched its fingers close round the bend of her right elbow, as if by the gaze of her eyes and the inadequate pressure she was able to apply, she could master the muscles. She kept her vision fixed on her arm, on her fingers and their feeble attempt to obey whatever message her brain was sending them.

"Livie," he said. "I want to know."

"What's it matter how long? What difference does it make?"

"I'm involved here, Livie."

"But not for long."

He read the many meanings behind her statement. They spoke of his future, her future, the decisions she'd made, and more than that, the real reason she'd made them. For the first time since she'd come into his life, Chris felt a surge of real fury. And as it rushed from his chest to the tips of his fingers, his mental half seemed to leave his body, seemed to float towards the ceiling where it lingered, looking down on the two of them, tittering and saying, This is why, this is why, simpleton, fool.

"So you lied," he said. "It had nothing to do with the barge at all. With the size of the doors. With needing a wheelchair."

She moved her fingers from her elbow to her wrist.

"Did it?" he demanded. "That wasn't why, was it?" He reached across the table to grab her, but she jerked away. "How long? Come on, Livie. How long has it been in your arm?"

She watched him for a moment, as wary as any one of the animals he'd rescued. She picked up her right hand with her left. She cradled them both against her chest. She said, "I can't work any longer. I can't cook. I can't clean. I can't even fuck."

"How long?" he said.

"Not that the last has ever bothered you, has it?"

"Tell me."

"I suppose I could give you some decent head if you'd let me. But the last time I tried, you weren't having it, remember? From me, that is."

"Shove that crap, Livie. What about the left arm? Is it there as well? Goddamn it, you can't use a bloody wheelchair and you know it. So why the hell—"

"I'm not a member of the team. I've been replaced. It's time I cleared out."

"We've had this discussion before. I thought we worked through it."

"We've had lots of discussions."

"Then we'll have one more, but it'll be brief. You're getting worse. You've known that for weeks. You don't trust me to cope. That's the case, isn't it?"

The fingers of her left hand were working ineffectually against her right arm, which she'd dropped once again to her lap. Cramps were no doubt beginning to grip the muscles, but she no longer possessed the strength to soothe them. Her head dropped towards her right shoulder as if the movement would somehow relieve pain. Her features contorted, and she finally said, "Chris," in a voice that fractured upon his name. "I'm so scared."

In an instant, he felt his anger fade. She was thirty-two years old. She was face to face with her own mortality. She knew death was approaching. She also knew exactly how it would take her.

He pushed away from the table and went to her. He stood behind her chair. He put his hands on her shoulders, then dropped them so that he could clasp them together and rest them against her skeletal chest.

Like her, he knew how it would be. He'd gone to the library and rooted out every book, every scientific journal, every newspaper or magazine article that offered even a flicker of illumination. So he knew that the progress of degeneration began in the extremities and moved ruthlessly upward and inward like an invading army that took no prisoners. The hands and feet went first, the arms and the legs rapidly followed. When the disease finally reached her respiratory system, she would feel shortness of breath and the sensation of drowning. She could then choose between immediate suffocation or life on a ventilator, but in either case the end result was the same. One way or the other she was going to die. Either soon or sooner.

He bent and pressed his cheek to her chopped-up hair. Its scent was pungent with sweat. He should have washed it for her yesterday, but the visit from Scotland Yard had chased from his mind any thought that didn't specifically relate to his own immediate, personal, and delitescent concerns. Rotter, he thought. Bastard. Swine. He wanted to say, "Don't be scared. I'll be with you. Right to the end," but she'd already taken that option out of his hands. So instead, he whispered, "I'm scared as well."

"But not with my cause."

"No. Not with."

He kissed her hair. Beneath his hands, he felt her chest heave. Then her body shuddered.

"I don't know what to do," she said. "I don't know how to be."

"We'll work it out. We always have."

"Not this time. It's too late for that." She didn't add what he already knew. Dying made everything too little and too late. Instead she pulled her quivering arm firmly against her body. She straightened her shoulders and then her spine. "I need to go to Mother," she said. "Will you take me there?"

"Now?"

"Now."

CHAPTER
14

It was half past two when Lynley and Havers arrived at Celandine Cottage for the second time. The only alteration from the previous day appeared to be the absence of gawkers at the edge of the property. In their place, five young female riders on horseback picked their way along the lane—booted, helmeted, with riding crops in their hands. But these girls didn't appear the least interested in the police tape that bound off Celandine Cottage. They walked their horses directly by it without a glance.

Lynley and Havers stood by the Bentley and watched them pass. Havers smoked in silence and Lynley gazed at the chestnut poles that rose behind the hedgerow across the lane. Strings running from these poles to the ground would offer support for hops in the coming weeks. But at the moment strings and poles together looked like denuded tepees in a systematically arranged—but nonetheless abandoned—American Indian village.

They were waiting for the arrival of Inspector Ardery. After four phone calls, made as they zigzagged from Mayfair southeast to Westminster Bridge, Lynley had tracked her down in the restaurant of a country house hotel not far from Maidstone. She'd said when he identified himself, "I've brought my mother out to lunch, Inspector," as if the mere sound of his voice had acted as an unspoken and completely unauthorised reprimand against which she felt she had to defend herself. She added, "It's her birthday," in a testy tone and, "I did phone you earlier," to which he replied, "I realise that. I'm returning the call." She had wanted to give him her information over the phone. He had demurred. He liked to have the reports in hand, he told her. It was a quirk of his. Besides, he wanted to have a look at the crime scene again. They'd tracked down and spoken to Mrs. Patten, and he wanted to verify the information she'd given them. Couldn't Ardery herself do the verifying? the inspector had asked him. She could do, but he'd rest more easily if he once again examined the cottage first hand. If she didn't mind . . .

Lynley could tell that Inspector Ardery minded a great deal. He couldn't blame her. They'd set up the ground rules on Friday evening, and he was trying to bend them, if not attempting to violate them altogether. Well, the transgression couldn't be helped.

Whatever pique she may have been feeling, Isabelle Ardery had it successfully hidden when she braked her Rover and climbed out of it ten minutes after their arrival. She was still attired in lunching-with-Mother: a gauzy bronze dress belted at the waist, five gold bangles on her wrist, matching hoop earrings. But she was all business, saying, "Sorry," in reference to the delay, "I had a call from the lab that they'd identified the cast of the footprint. I thought you might want to have a look at that as well, so I stopped by to pick it up. And ended up getting cornered by the *Daily Mirror*'s chief Mr. Smarm. Could I confirm, if I would, the fact that Fleming was found completely nude with his hands and his feet tied to the bedposts in Celandine Cottage? Would I be willing to go on the record as stating that Fleming had drunk himself into a stupor? If the *Mirror* conjectured that Fleming was diddling two or three of the wives of sponsors of the England cricket team, would their story be inaccurate? A simple yes or no is all we need, Inspector." She slammed the Rover's door and walked to the boot, which she opened with a yank. "What slugs," she said, and then as she raised her head from the boot, "Sorry. I'm going on a bit."

"We're dealing with them in London as well," Lynley said. "What's your approach?"

"We generally tell them whatever will be useful to us."

She took out a cardboard box. She shut the boot. She balanced the box on her hip. She looked at him and cocked her head, as if with interest or perhaps speculation. "Do you really? I've never told them a thing. I loathe symbiosis between press and the police."

"So do I," Lynley replied. "But it serves us sometimes."

She shot him a sceptical look and made her way to the crime scene tape, which she ducked under. They followed her through the white rail gate and up the drive. She led them towards the back of the cottage, to the table beneath the grape arbour. Here, she set down the box. Lynley could see that inside were a sheaf of papers, a set of photographs, and two plaster casts. Of these latter, one formed a complete footprint, the other a partial.

He said as she reached in to begin unpacking, "I'd like to have another look inside the cottage first, if you don't mind, Inspector."

She paused with the partial print in her hands. "You do have the photographs," she reminded him. "As well as the report."

"As I said on the phone, I have additional information. Which I'd like to confirm. With your cooperation, of course."

Her eyes moved from him to Havers. She returned the plaster cast to its box. It was clear that she was engaged in a mental skirmish with herself: whether to oblige a fellow officer, whether to protest further. She finally said, "Right," and she pressed her lips together as if to keep herself from further comment.

She removed the police lock from the cottage door and stepped back for them to enter. Lynley nodded his thanks. He went first to the sink where, opening the cupboard beneath it, he verified with Inspector Ardery that Maidstone's crime scene team had, as he expected, taken the rubbish with them. They were searching for anything with a connection to the incendiary device, she told him. All the rubbish had been carted off. Why did he want the rubbish?

Lynley related Gabriella Patten's story about Fleming's search through the waste bins. Ardery listened, her eyebrows drawn together pensively and her hand at her collarbone. No, she told him when he was done, there had been no rubbish left on the floor anywhere. Not in the kitchen. Not in the loo. Not in the sitting room. If Fleming had dumped rubbish out in anger, he'd replaced it all when he had time to cool off. And he'd been scrupulous enough about doing so, she added. There hadn't been a scrap left anywhere on the floor.

"He could have come to his senses once Gabriella'd left," Havers pointed out to Lynley. "It's Mrs. Whitelaw's cottage. He probably wouldn't want to trash it, no matter his rage."

That was a possibility, Lynley conceded. He asked about any cigarette ends in the rubbish, telling Ardery about Gabriella Patten's claim that she'd stopped smoking. Ardery confirmed. There had been no ends, no burnt matches either. He slipped into an inglenook where a pine table stood. Beneath it sat a wicker animal basket. He squatted to examine it and scraped from its cushion a few strands of fur.

"Gabriella Patten claims the kittens were inside when she left," he said. "In this basket, I should guess."

"Well, they got out somehow, didn't they?" Ardery said.

Lynley moved through the dining room and along the short passage that led to the sitting room. There, he examined the front of the door. Gabriella had used the word *bash* to describe how Fleming had managed to get into the sitting room where she'd tried to hide herself from his wrath. If that word was accurate, there would be evidence to support it.

Like the rest of the house, the door was painted white, although also like the rest of the house, it now bore a jet patina of soot. Lynley brushed this off at shoulder height. He did the same round the knob. There was no evidence of force.

Ardery and Havers came to join him, Ardery saying with what appeared to be a deliberate show of patience, "We've got a match on most of the fingerprints, Inspector," as Havers checked the fireplace for the fire irons Gabriella had claimed to have used to defend herself. A set was there, a poker that hung from a stand with a brush, a miniature shovel, and tongs. She said, "On these as well? Have you checked these for prints?"

"We've checked everything for prints, Sergeant. I believe the information you want is in the report I've brought with me."

Lynley was closing the sitting room door to study its other side. He used his handkerchief to wipe away soot. He said, "Ah. Here it is, Sergeant," and Havers joined him.

Beneath the knob, a thin, serrated line of discolouration marred the white wood for perhaps eight inches. Lynley ran his fingers along it, then turned from the door to the rest of the room.

"She said she used a chair," Havers said, and together they examined each of them.

The chair in question was yet another of Mrs. Whitelaw's nursing chairs, upholstered in bottle-green velvet and sitting beneath a hanging corner cupboard. Havers pulled it away from the wall. Lynley immediately saw the uneven ridge of white against the darker walnut that rimmed the top of the chair and ran down its sides. He placed the chair beneath the knob of the door. The smear of white matched up to the serrated line. "Confirmed," he said.

Inspector Ardery stood by the fireplace. She said, "Inspector, if you'd told me what you were looking for in the first place, my crime team could have saved you this trip."

Lynley stooped to scrutinise the carpet in the vicinity of the door. He found a minute rip that lined up with the direction that the chair would have travelled had someone forced it away from the doorknob beneath which it had leaned. Additional confirmation, he thought. At least in part, Gabriella Patten had been telling the truth.

"Inspector Lynley," Ardery said again.

Lynley stood. Every inch of the other officer's body was communicating affront. Their agreement had been easily enough reached: she would handle Kent, he would handle London. They would meet intellectually— and physically as well, if it came down to it—somewhere in between. But getting to the truth behind Fleming's death wasn't as simple as that, as he well knew. The nature of the investigation was going to call for one of the two of them to become subordinate, and he could see that Ardery didn't like the idea of subordination being assigned to her.

He said, "Sergeant, would you give us a moment?"

Havers said, "Right," and disappeared in the direction of the kitchen. He heard the outer door close behind her as she left the cottage.

Ardery said, "You're pushing things, Inspector Lynley. Yesterday. Today. I don't appreciate it. I've got the information for you. I've got the reports. I've got the lab working overtime. What more do you want?"

"Sorry," he said. "I don't mean to press in."

"Sorry worked yesterday. It's not good enough this afternoon. You intend to press. You intend to keep pressing. I want to know why."

He gave fleeting thought to whether he should attempt to unruffle her feathers. It couldn't be easy for her, exercising her profession in a field dominated by men who probably questioned her every movement and doubted her every opinion and report. But to placate her now seemed condescending. He knew he wouldn't have bothered had she been a man. So, to his way of thinking, the fact that she wasn't shouldn't enter into their discussion now.

He said, "The point isn't who does what or who investigates where. The point is finding a killer. We agree on that, don't we?"

"Don't patronise me. What we agreed to was a clear delineation of your responsibility as opposed to mine. I've kept to my side of the bargain. What's happened to yours?"

"This isn't a contractual situation, Inspector. Our predetermined boundaries aren't as clear as you'd like them to be. We have to work together or we won't work at all."

"Then perhaps you need to redefine what working together is going to mean. Because as far as I can see at the moment, I'm working for you, at your pleasure and behest. And if that's the way it's going to be, then I'd appreciate your clarifying the point right now so that I can decide what steps I'm going to take to give you the headroom you appear to need."

"What I need is your expertise, Inspector Ardery."

"I find that difficult to believe."

"And I won't be getting it if you ask your CC to remove you from the case."

"I didn't say—"

"We both know the threat was implicit." He didn't add the other adjective, *unprofessional.* He never much cared for the way that word was bandied about whenever one officer came into conflict with another. Instead he said, "We all work differently. We have to make accommodations for each other's style. Mine is to hound each piece of information. I don't intend to step on toes when I do it, but that happens sometimes. It doesn't mean I think my colleagues can't do their jobs. It just means I've learned to trust my own instincts."

"More than anyone else's, obviously."

"Yes. But if I'm wrong then I've only myself to blame and only my own mess to clean up."

"I see. How convenient."

"What?"

"How you have your professional commitments arranged. Your colleagues make accommodation for you. You make no accommodation for them."

"I didn't say that, Inspector."

"You didn't have to, Inspector. You made it fairly clear. You're to hound information in any way you choose. I'm to provide it when and if it meets your needs."

"That's arguing your role is unimportant," Lynley said. "I don't believe that. Why do you?"

"Beyond that," she continued as if he hadn't spoken, "I'm to offer no opinion and make no objection to whatever direction you choose to take. And if that direction requires me to be at your beck and call, I'm to accept it, like it, and keep my mouth shut like a good little woman, no doubt."

"This isn't a male-female problem," Lynley said. "It's one of approach. I've brought you away from your Sunday afternoon to serve my needs and I apologise for that. But we're beginning to gather some information that may break the case open, and I'd like to follow up on it while I can. The fact that I choose to follow up on it personally has nothing to do with you. It's not a statement about your competence. It is, if anything, a statement about mine. I've offended where I didn't mean to. I'd like to get past that and move on to have a look at what you've gathered since yesterday. If I may."

She had clasped her arms in front of her as they were speaking. Lynley could see the pressure she was applying with her fingertips. He waited for her to conclude whatever inward battle she was engaged in, and he tried to keep his impatience from showing and his face as noncommittal as possible. There seemed no purpose in offending her further. Both of them knew that the advantage was his. A single phone call from him and the Yard would take whatever political steps were necessary to either neutralise her or remove her from the case. Which, he felt, would be rather a waste as she seemed to be quick, intelligent, and able.

Her grip loosened on her arms. She said, "All right." Lynley didn't know what she was agreeing to and guessed she was agreeing to nothing save making the next move, which was to lead him back through the cottage and out the kitchen door where Sergeant Havers was lounging in one of the chairs under the arbour. Wisely, Lynley saw, she hadn't touched anything in Inspector Ardery's box of evidence and reports. And her face was a perfect study of disregard as they joined her.

Ardery once again removed the plaster casts of the footprints from the box, as well as the reports and the photographs. She said, "We've identified the shoe. The pattern on the sole is fairly distinctive."

She handed the complete cast to Lynley. It duplicated the entire sole of a shoe. Around the edges ran markings that resembled a dog-tooth cornice. Indentations in the plaster, they would be raised portions on the shoe sole itself. Extending diagonally across the shoe bottom from one cornice to another was a second series of indentations, like slashes. These motifs were repeated on the heel. It was, Lynley saw, a distinctive design.

"Doc Martens," Ardery said.

"Walking shoes? Boots?"

"They appear to be boots."

"Good for exercising one's right to xenophobia," Havers remarked. "Have a little march through Bethnal Green. Stomp on some faces with those nice metal tips."

Lynley set the second cast next to the first. The second depicted the toe end of the shoe and perhaps three inches of the sole. He could see they'd been made by the same boot. One of the cornice markings along the left edge was misshapen, as if it had been irregularly worn down or partially chopped off with a knife. This misshapen mass appeared in both casts and was not, Ardery told them, a normal feature of the shoes themselves.

"The complete cast is from the bottom of the garden," Ardery said. "It marked the spot where someone came over the fence from the paddock next door."

"And the other?" Lynley asked.

She gestured towards the west. "There's a public footpath that runs above the spring. It goes to the village, Lesser Springburn. There's a stile perhaps three-quarters of the way into the village. The print was there."

Lynley ventured a question she wasn't going to like. It bore too much the unspoken message that she and her team might have missed something along the way. "Will you show us?"

"Inspector, we've combed the village. We've spoken to everyone there. Believe me, the report—"

"Is probably far more complete than any I might write," Lynley said. "Nonetheless, I'd like to have a look for myself. If you don't mind."

She was well aware of the fact that they didn't need either her permission or her presence if they chose to have a wander down a public footpath. Lynley could read that understanding in her expression. Although his request had implied equality, at the same time it suggested doubt about her thoroughness. It was up to her to choose which meaning she would comprehend.

"Very well," she said. "We can go into the village and have a look round there. It's only a ten-minute walk from here."

The footpath began at the spring, a bubbling pool some fifty yards from Celandine Cottage. The path was well trodden. It rose gently above the stream that flowed from the pool, on one side edging first a series of paddocks and then an orchard in which untended apple trees—blooming pink and white like a snowfall at sunset—were being fatally overgrown with the creeping pestilence of old man's beard. On the other side of the path, blind nettles mixed with blackberry brambles, and the white sprays of cow parsley rose above ivy which climbed the oaks, the alders, and the willows. Most of the trees along the path and the stream were in leaf, and the distinctive *prree* answered by a strong clear whistle indicated the presence of both warbler and thrush.

In spite of her shoes—heeled sandals that brought her to Lynley's height—Inspector Ardery moved along the footpath briskly. She brushed by hedges and brambles, ducked round branches, and spoke over her shoulder as she went. "We've an identification of the fibres we found on the split-rail fence at the bottom of the garden. It's denim. Standard blue jeans. Levi Strauss."

"That narrows things down to seventy-five percent of the population," Havers noted quietly.

Lynley fired a monitory look at his sergeant, who was following a few yards in his wake. Having garnered the inspector's cooperation, however grudging such cooperation might be, he wasn't about to risk it with one of Havers' spontaneous but nonetheless ill-timed remarks. She caught his expression and mouthed the word *sorry*.

Ardery either did not hear the remark or chose to ignore it. She said, "There was oil on the fibres as well. We've sent them to analysis to be certain, but one of our older blokes had a good long look under the microscope and he says it's motor oil. I tend to believe him. He was working in forensic before we had chromatographs to give us all the answers, so he generally knows what he's looking at."

"What about the cigarette ends?" Lynley asked. "The one used in the cottage and the others in the garden."

"We don't have identification yet." Ardery hurried on, as if anticipating Lynley's conclusion that there was some sort of problem requiring his insistence that part of her evidence be assigned for analysis to someone more capable at New Scotland Yard. "Our man's heading back today from Sheffield. He was speaking at a conference. He'll get the cigarettes tomorrow morning, and once he's got them in hand it won't take long."

"There's nothing preliminary to go on?" Lynley asked.

She said, "He's our expert. We could give you guesswork, but it would be only that. There are eight different points of identification on a cigarette end, and I vastly prefer my man to mark them all for us rather than to catch one or two of them myself, make a stab at the brand, and be incorrect.''

She had come to a rail fence that bisected the footpath. She paused at the lichenous extended board that constituted its simple stile. ''Here,'' she said.

The earth round the stile was softer than that on the path. It presented a maze of footprints, most of them blurred by additional prints that had fallen on top of them. Ardery's team had been lucky, indeed, to find anything that matched the print at Celandine Cottage. Even a partial seemed miraculous.

''It was towards the edge,'' Ardery said, as if in response to Lynley's thought. ''Here, where the bits of plaster are.''

Lynley nodded and looked beyond the fence. Perhaps 150 yards to the northwest, he could see the rooftops that designated the boundary of Lesser Springburn. The path was clearly marked, a beaten track that veered away from the stream, crossed a railway track, skirted an orchard, and dipped into a small housing estate.

They climbed over the stile. At the housing estate, the path finally widened to allow them to walk three abreast, with the back gardens of neat houses lined up on either side of them. They came out into the housing estate itself, a curve of identical detached dwellings with brick exteriors, squat chimneys, bay windows, and gabled roofs. The three detectives were the object of some interest here, for the street was lively with children skipping rope, two men-of-the-house hosing down cars, and a modified cricket match being played by a group of small boys.

''We've made the circuit here,'' Ardery said. ''No one saw anything out of the ordinary on Wednesday night. But they'd have been indoors when he passed.''

''You've decided on *he*,'' Lynley said.

''The brand of shoe. Its size. The depth of the print at Celandine Cottage. Yes,'' she said, ''I'd say we're looking for a *he*.''

They emerged onto the Springburn Road at the bottom of the village. To their right, the narrow high street twisted up a modest acclivity between a row of ancient thatched bungalows and a line of shops. Directly in front of them, a secondary lane occupied by a rank of timber-framed cottages led to a church. To their left, a pebbled drive gave way to the car park of the Fox and Hounds pub. From where he stood, Lynley could see that a common lay beyond the pub, with oaks and ashes casting long mid-afternoon shadows against the lawn. A tangle of thick, untended shrubbery grew along its edge. Giving a glance to both the high street and the lane that led to the church, Lynley made his decision and headed for this.

The shrubbery didn't present an unbroken border. There were occasional gaps in the growth, which connected the pub car park to the edge of the common, and the detectives stepped through one of these, beneath a natural archway that grew from an oak.

Another cricket match was going on at the south end of the lawn. It was a village match by the look of it. The players were adults garbed in traditional if individual white and the spectators sat in deck chairs, round which children shrieked and darted, frequently causing one of the umpires to shout, "Donna, for God's sake, get those little blighters off the pitch."

Lynley and his companions attracted no attention since the shrubbery grew along the common's northeast boundary. The ground was rough here, hard uneven earth across which ivy grew in irregular patches, its tendrils creeping not only along the ground but also up a sagging expanse of wooden fence. Along this fence, rhododendrons flourished, their branches nodding heavily under the weight of enormous heliotrope blooms. The occasional holly bush reached out spiny-leafed branches among the rhododendrons, and Sergeant Havers went to look at these as Lynley inspected the ground and Ardery watched.

"One of our crime-team blokes spoke to Connor O'Neil," Ardery said. "He owns the pub. He was working the taps on Wednesday night along with his son."

"Did he give us anything?"

"He said they finished up around half past twelve. Neither of them saw a strange car in the car park when they locked up. There were no cars left but their own, in fact."

Lynley said, "That's no surprise, is it?"

"We checked this site as well," Ardery continued firmly. "As you can see, Inspector, the ground's beaten down. It isn't the proper consistency for taking a print."

Lynley could see she was right. The vacant spots where ivy didn't grow were littered with last year's disintegrating leaves. Beneath them the ground was packed solid, like a stretch of cement. It wouldn't be capable of taking an impression of anything, be it footprint, tyre print, or the killer's signature.

He straightened. He looked back the way they had come. The shrubbery was, he believed, the most logical place to hide a vehicle if, indeed, a vehicle had been used at some stage of the crime. It gave on to the car park, which in its turn gave on to the lane that led to the footpath. The footpath steered the walker to within fifty yards of Celandine Cottage. All that was required of the killer they sought was a working knowledge of the local environment.

On the other hand, hiding a vehicle wasn't completely necessary if the killer acted in concert with someone else. A driver could have paused momentarily at the Fox and Hounds, let off a killer who faded down the lane that led to the footpath, and merely spent an hour or more driving round the countryside until the fire was set and the starter returned. That suggested not only long-term collusion but also an intimate knowledge of Fleming's movements on the day of his death. Two people, rather than one, would have had to possess a vested interest in his demise.

"Sir," Sergeant Havers said. "Have a look at this."

Lynley saw that Havers had inched along the rhododendrons and holly. She was squatting at the point where the shrubbery last made contact with the pub's car park. She was brushing some fallen leaves to one side and lifting a tendril of ivy from among perhaps a dozen that reached into an oblong patch of earth.

Lynley and Ardery joined her. Over her shoulder, Lynley could see what she had found, a rough circle of packed earth some three inches in diameter. It was stained darker than the rest of the ground, coffee coloured as opposed to the hazel surrounding it.

Havers used her fingers to snap off the tendril she was holding. She grunted her way to her feet, shoved her hair off her forehead, and held the tendril out for Lynley's inspection. "Looks like some kind of oil to me," she said. "It's dripped onto three of these leaves as well. See? Here's some. And more there. And there."

"Motor oil," Lynley murmured.

"That's what I'd say. Just like the oil on the blue jeans." Havers indicated the Springburn Road. "He'd have come along there, killed the engine and the lights, and coasted along the edge of the lawn. Parked here. Slipped through the shrubbery and the car park, making for the footpath. Taken the path to the cottage. Jumped the wall into the paddock next door. Waited at the bottom of the garden for the coast to clear."

Ardery said quickly, "You can't think we wouldn't have found tyre prints, Sergeant. Because if a car actually drove across the lawn—"

"Not a car," Havers said. "A motorbike. Two tyres, not four. Lighter than a car. Less likely to leave a trail. Easy to manoeuvre. Easier to hide."

Lynley felt reluctant to accept this scenario. "A motorbike rider who then smoked six or eight cigarettes to mark his place at Celandine Cottage? How does that play, Sergeant? What kind of killer leaves a calling card?"

"The kind of killer who doesn't expect to get caught."

"But anyone with the least knowledge of forensics would know the importance of not leaving evidence," Lynley said. "Any evidence. Of any kind."

"Right. So we're looking for a killer who foolishly assumed this killing wasn't going to look like a killing in the first place. We're looking for someone who was thinking primarily of the end product here: Fleming's death. How to bring it off and what there was to be gained, not how it might be investigated afterwards. We're looking for someone who thought that cottage—crammed with antique bloody *firewood*, Inspector —would go up like a torch once that cigarette burned down far enough in the armchair. In his mind there wouldn't be evidence. There wouldn't be a cigarette end. There wouldn't be the remains of matches. There wouldn't be anything but rubble. And what, he would think if he did pause to think, would the police be able to make of rubble?"

A cheer went up from the spectators of the cricket match. The three detectives swung about. The batsman had hit the ball and was dashing for the other set of stumps. Two fielders were racing across the outfield. The bowler was yelling. The wicket keeper was throwing one of his gloves to the ground in disgust. Obviously someone had forgotten a cardinal rule of cricket: No matter what, always try for the catch.

"We need to talk to that boy, Inspector," Havers said. "You wanted evidence. The Inspector here has provided us with it. Cigarette ends—"

"Which have yet to be identified."

"Denim fibres stained with oil."

"To be substantiated by the chromatograph."

"Footprints which have already been identified. A shoe sole with a distinctive marking. And now this." She gestured to the ivy he held. "What more do you want?"

Lynley didn't reply. He knew how Havers would react to his answer. It wasn't more that he wanted. It was less, far less.

Inspector Ardery, he saw, was still staring at the ground beyond Sergeant Havers where the oil stain made its circular splodge. Her face was vexed. She said quietly, more to herself than to them, "I told them to check for prints. We didn't have the word yet about oil on the fibres."

"It doesn't matter," Lynley said.

"No. It does. If you hadn't insisted . . ."

Havers' resigned look asked Lynley if she should make herself scarce a second time. Lynley lifted a hand to tell her to stay where she was. He said, "You can't be expected to anticipate evidence."

"That's my job."

"This oil may mean nothing. It may not be the same as that on the fibres."

"Damn it," Ardery said more to herself than to them. She spent nearly a minute watching the cricket match—the same two batsmen were relentlessly continuing to try the marginal skills of the opposing side—before her features settled once more into a semblance of professional disinterest.

"When this is all over," Lynley said with a smile as her eyes met his once again, "I'll have Sergeant Havers relate some of my more interesting errors in judgement on the job."

Ardery's head raised fractionally. Her response was cool. "We all make errors, Inspector. I like to learn from mine. This sort of thing won't happen again."

She moved away from them, in the direction of the car park, saying, "Is there more you'd like to see in the village?" She did not wait to hear his response.

Havers took the tendril of ivy from his hand. She bagged the individual leaves. "Speaking of errors in judgement," she said meaningfully and followed Ardery into the car park.

CHAPTER
15

Jeannie Cooper poured boiling water over the P. G. Tips and watched the teabags bob to the surface like buoys. She took a spoon, stirred, and put the lid on the pot. She'd deliberately chosen the special tea-set this afternoon, the one with the pot shaped like a rabbit, with carrot cups and lettuce leaf saucers. It was the pot she always used when the kids were ill, to cheer them up and make them think of something besides an achy ear or a stomach gone peculiar.

She set the pot on the kitchen table where earlier she'd removed the old red oilcloth, spreading out in its place a green cotton tablecloth speckled with violets. On top of this she'd already laid the rest of the tea-set: lettuce leaf plates and the bunny-shaped milk jug with its matching sugar bowl. On the rabbit-family platter in the centre of the table, she'd stacked the liver paste sandwiches. She'd cut off the crusts, alternated the sandwiches with plain bread and butter, and surrounded the lot with Custard Cremes.

Stan and Sharon were in the sitting room. Stan was watching the telly, across whose screen a giant eel was swimming hypnotically to the rhythm of a background voice saying, "The habitat of the moray eel . . ." while Sharon bent over her bird notebook, using coloured pencils to fill in the markings on a gull she'd sketched yesterday afternoon. Her glasses had slipped to the end of her nose and her breathing was laboured and loud, like she had a bad head cold.

"Tea's ready," Jeannie said. "Shar, fetch Jimmy."

Sharon raised her head and snuffled. She used the back of her hand to push her spectacles into place. She said, "He won't come down."

"You don't know that, do you? Now fetch him like I said."

Jimmy had spent the day in his bedroom. He'd wanted to go out earlier, around half past eleven that morning. He'd slouched into the kitchen with his windcheater on, opened the fridge, and pulled out the remains of a take-away pizza. This he rolled up, wrapped in tinfoil, and stuffed into his pocket. Jeannie watched him from the sink where she turned from washing the breakfast dishes. She said, "What're you about then, Jim?" to which he replied with the single word *nothing*. She said that it looked to her like he was planning on going out. He said what if he was? He wasn't about to hang round the house all day like a two-year-old. Besides, he had plans to meet a mate at Millwall Outer Dock. What mate is that, Jeannie had wanted to know. Just a mate, that's all, he said. She didn't know him and she didn't need to know him. Was it Brian Jones, Jeannie had asked next. Jimmy had said, Brian Jones? Who the hell . . . He didn't know any Bri—Then he'd recognised the trap. Jeannie remarked with innocence that he remembered, didn't he, Brian Jones . . . from Deptford? Him Jimmy was with all day on Friday instead of going to school?

Jimmy had shoved the refrigerator door closed. He'd headed for the back door, saying he was off. Jeannie had said that he best come have a look out the window, first. She had said she meant it and if he knew what was good for him, he was to do like she asked.

He'd stood with one hand on the doorknob and his eyes shifting uneasily from her to the cooker and back to her. She said for him to come. She wanted him to see. He'd asked what, with that curl of the lip which she always wanted to slap from his face. She'd said he was just to come here, Jim. He was to have a good long look outside.

She could tell the boy thought her request was a trick, so she moved away from the window to give him room. He sidled across the floor as if expecting her to pounce upon him, and he looked out the window as she had bidden.

He'd seen the reporters. It was hard to miss them, lounging against their Escort across the street. He'd said, So what, they were there yesterday, to which she'd replied, Not there, Jim. He was to look in front of the Cowpers' house, she told him. Who did he think those blokes were, the ones sitting in the black Nova? He'd shrugged, indifferent. She'd said, The police. So he could go out if he wanted, she told him. But he wasn't to expect to be going out alone. The police would follow him.

He'd grappled with this information physically as well as mentally, his hands clenching into fists at his side. He'd asked what the police wanted. She'd told him they wanted to know about his dad. About what happened to him. About who was with him on Wednesday night. About why he died.

And then she waited. She watched him watching them, the police and the reporters. He tried to look uncaring, but he couldn't fool her. There were subtle signs that gave him away: the rapid shift of weight from one foot to the other, one fist driven into the pocket of the jeans. He threw his head back and lifted his chin and demanded to know who gave a shit anyway, but he shifted his weight uneasily once more, and Jeannie could imagine that his palms were sweating and his stomach was quivering like jelly.

She found herself wanting to be the victor in this situation, wanting to ask him casually if he still planned to go out and about on this fine Sunday morning. She found herself wanting to press the issue, to open the door, to bid him be on his way just to force him to admit to his grief, to his fear, to a need for her help, to whatever the truth was, to anything. But she'd kept silent, remembering at the last moment—and with a clarity that cut—just what it was like to be sixteen years old and facing a crisis. She let him leave the kitchen and pound up the stairs, and she hadn't invaded his privacy since.

Now, as Sharon climbed up to fetch him, Jeannie said to Stan, "Into the kitchen. Look sharp, all right? Time for tea." He didn't reply. She saw that he was scouring the inside of his nose with his little finger, and she said, "You! Stan! That's disgusting! Stop it!" and the finger was hastily removed. Stan ducked his head and thrust his hands well beneath his arse. Jeannie said in a gentler voice, "Come on with you, luv. I've made us some tea."

She directed him to the sink to wash while she poured the tea into their carrot cups. He came to her side and mumbled, "Got the special plates today, Mum," and he slipped his hand—still damp from the washing—into hers.

She said, "Yeah. I thought we could do with some cheering up."

"Jimmy coming downstairs?"

"I don't know. We'll see."

Stan pulled his chair away from the table and plopped onto it. He chose a Custard Creme, a slice of buttered bread, and a liver paste sandwich for his plate. This latter he opened, holding each half flat in either of his palms. He said, "Jimmy was cryin' last night, Mum."

Jeannie's interest quickened, but she said only, "Cryin's natural. Don't you go hard on your brother over that."

Stan licked the liver paste from the bread. "He d'n't think I heard him cos I didn't say. But I heard all right. He had his head in the pillow and he was hitting the mattress and saying, fuck it, just fuck it." Stan shrank back as Jeannie lifted a quick disciplinary hand. "It's what I *heard*, Mum. I'm not saying it myself."

"Well, mind that you don't." Jeannie filled the other cups. "What else?" she asked quietly.

Having divested it of its liver paste, Stan was chewing the bread. "More naughty words."

"Such as?"

"Bastard. Fuck it, just fuck it, you bastard. That's what he said. While he was crying." Stan licked the liver paste from the bread slice in his other palm. "I 'spect he was crying about Dad. I 'spect he was talking about Dad as well. He broke them sailing boats of his, did you know?"

"I saw that, Stan."

"And he said fuck you fuck you fuck you, when he did it."

Jeannie sat opposite her youngest child. She closed her thumb and index finger round his thin wrist. She said, "You aren't telling tales to tell tales, are you, Stan? That's a nasty habit if you are."

"I wouldn't—"

"Good. Because Jimmy's your brother and you're meant to love him. He's in a bad patch now, but he'll come round all right." Even as she said it, Jeannie felt the spear, the one that kept up the pressure beneath her left breast without ever once breaking the skin. Kenny had been in a bad patch as well, a patch that started out bad and only got worse.

"Jimmy says he doesn't want any bleeding tea. Only he didn't say *bleeding*. He said something else." Shar fluttered into the kitchen like one of her birds, with sheets of drawing paper for wings. She pushed Jimmy's plate, cup, and saucer to one side and smoothed the paper on top of the tablecloth. She picked up a sandwich delicately and took a ladylike bite as she surveyed her work, a bald eagle soaring above pine trees, with the pine trees so small that the eagle looked like he was a second cousin to King Kong.

"He said *fucking*, didn't he?" Stan pinched the edges of his bread and butter, scalloping them.

"That's enough of that word," Jeannie said. "And wipe your mouth. Shar, see to your brother's table manners, please. I'll see to Jim."

She rummaged in the cupboard next to the sink and brought out a chipped plastic tray. It had been a long ago wedding present to her and Kenny, lime green decorated with sprays of forget-me-nots. Just the thing, she had thought, for passing round scones and sandwiches at tea. She'd never used it for that, however, just for lugging one meal after another upstairs, catering to a child with a cold or flu. She put Jimmy's teacup on it, adding sugar and milk the way he liked it. She picked among the sandwiches, the bread and butter, and the Custard Cremes.

"Don't he have to come down, Mum?" Stan asked as she headed for the stairs.

"Doesn't," Shar corrected absently as she added more colour to the wings of her eagle.

"Cos you always say that if we're not feeling grumpy, we got to eat down here," Stan persisted.

"Yeah," Jeannie said. "Well, Jim feels grumpy. You said so yourself."

Shar had not closed Jimmy's bedroom door completely behind her, so after saying, "Jim?" Jeannie used her bum to push the door open. "I brought you your tea."

He'd been sitting on his bed, his back against the headboard, and as she walked into the room with the tray, he stuffed something under the pillow and followed this action with hastily sliding shut the drawer of the bedside table. Jeannie pretended to ignore both movements. She'd been through that drawer more than once in the past few months. She knew what he kept there. She'd spoken to Kenny about the photographs, and he'd been concerned enough to come by the house when Jimmy was at school. He'd gone through them himself, careful to keep them in the order Jimmy had them arranged, sitting on the edge of his oldest boy's bed with his long legs stretched out against the worn carpet squares. He'd given a chuckle at the sight of the women, at their choice of clothing or the lack thereof, at their positions, at their pouting expressions, at the spread of their legs and the arch of their backs and the size of their perfectly, unnaturally proportioned breasts. He'd said, "It's nothing to worry over, Jean." She'd asked him what in the hell he meant. His son had a drawerful of dirty pictures and if that wasn't something to worry over, could he tell her what was? Kenny'd said, "These aren't dirty. They aren't pornography. He's curious, that's all," and he'd added, "I can find you some of the real stuff if you want to have something to worry over." The real stuff, he told her, featured more than one subject—male and female, male and male, adult and child, child and child, female and female, female and animal, male and animal. He said, "It's nothing like this, girl. This is what young blokes look at while they're still wondering what it's like to feel a woman beneath them. It's natural, it is. It's part of growing up." She asked him if he'd had pictures like these—pictures he hid away from his family like a nasty secret—if it was so much a part of growing up. He'd replaced the photographs carefully and shut the drawer. "No," he said after a moment and not looking at her when he said it. "I had you, didn't I? I didn't have to wonder what it would be like when it finally happened. I always knew." Then he'd turned his head and smiled and she'd felt like her heart was flooding open. How he'd make her feel, that Kenny Fleming. How always always he could make her feel.

She spoke past the ache in her throat. "I've done some liver sandwiches for you. Move your legs, Jim, so I can put the tray down."

"I tol' Shar. I ain't hungry." His voice was defiant, but his eyes were wary. Still, he moved his legs as his mother had asked, and Jeannie grasped on to this as a hopeful sign. She set the tray on the bed, near his knees. He was wearing a pair of filthy jeans. He hadn't removed his windcheater or his shoes, as if he still expected to be going out when the police grew tired of watching the house. Jeannie wanted to tell him how unlikely it was that the police would grow weary of maintaining surveillance. There were dozens of them, hundreds, perhaps thousands, and all they had to do was keep replacing each other out on the street.

"I forgot to say ta for yesterday," Jeannie said.

Jimmy shoved his fingers back through his hair. He looked at the tray without reacting to the sight of the special tea-set. He looked back at her.

"Stan and Shar," she said. "Keeping them busy like you did. It was good of you, Jim. Your dad—"

"Bugger him."

She took a steady breath and continued. "Your dad would of been real proud to see you acting so good to your brother and sister."

"Yeah? What did Dad know about acting good?"

"Stan and Shar, they'll be looking to you now. You got to be like a dad, 'specially to Stan."

"Stan'd do better to look after himself. He depend on anyone, he'll just get himself bashed."

"Not if he depends on you."

Jimmy adjusted his position, backing up closer against the headboard, to ease his spine or to get distance from her. He reached for a half-smashed packet of cigarettes and screwed one into his mouth. He lit it and blew the smoke through his nostrils in a quick, fierce stream.

"He don't need me," Jimmy said.

"Yeah, Jim, he does."

"Not while he's got his mum to look after him. I'n't that the case?"

He spoke with a surly challenge in his voice, as if a hidden message existed in the statement and the subsequent question. Jeannie tried and failed to read the message. "Little boys need a man to look up to."

"Yeah? Well, I don't expect to be round here much longer. So if Stan needs someone to wipe his nose and keep his hands off his dick when the lights go out, it ain't going t'be me. Got it?" Jimmy leaned forward and flicked ash into the lettuce leaf saucer beneath the carrot cup.

"Where you planning on going, then?"

"I don't know. Somewheres. Anywheres. It don't matter much so long as it's not here. I hate this place. I'm that sick of it."

"What about your family?"

"What about them? Huh?"

"With your dad gone—"

"Don't talk about him. What's it matter where that poncey bloke is? He was gone already, before he got the chop. He wasn't never coming back. You think Stan and Shar expected him to show up on the porch one day, asking them could he please move home?" he barked and brought his cigarette to his mouth. His fingers were nicotine-stained yellow-orange. "You were the only one liked to think that, Mum. The rest of us, we knew Dad wasn't coming back. And we knew about her. From the very first. We even met her. Only we all decided to never say about it because we didn't want you to feel no worse."

"You met Dad's—"

"Yeah. We met her all right. Twice or three times. Four. I don't know. With Dad looking at her and her looking at Dad and both of'm trying to act all innocent, calling each other *Mr.* Fleming and *Mrs.* Patten, like they wasn't going to stick each other like pigs the minute we was gone.'' He returned to his cigarette, puffing furiously. Jeannie could see that the cigarette shook.

"I didn't know that," she said. She moved away from the bed and went to the window. She looked, unseeing, at the garden below. Her hand went to the curtains. Washing, she thought. They needed washing. "You should of told me, Jim."

"Why? Would you of done something different?"

"Different?"

"Yeah. You know what I mean."

Jeannie turned reluctantly from the window. "Different how?" she asked.

"You could of divorced him. You could of done that much for Stan."

"For Stan?"

"He was four years old when Dad left, wasn't he? He would of got over it. And when he did, he'd still have his mum. Why'n't you think about that?" He knocked more ashes into the saucer. "You think things were cocked up proper before this, Mum. But they're cocked up worse now."

In the stuffy room, Jeannie felt a chill gust of air wash over her, as if a window had been opened somewhere nearby. "You best talk to me," she told her son. "You best tell me the truth."

Jimmy shook his head and smoked.

"Mummy?" Sharon had come to stand in the bedroom door.

"Not now," Jeannie said. "I'm talking to your brother. You can see that, can't you?"

The girl took a half step back. Behind her glasses, her eyes looked froggish, overlarge and bulging out like she might lose them altogether. When she didn't leave, Jeannie bit out the words, "Did you hear me, Shar? Are you going deaf as well as blind? Go back to your tea."

"I . . ." She looked over her shoulder in the direction of the stair-way. "There's . . ."

"Spit it out, Shar," her brother said.

"Police," she said. "At the door. For Jimmy."

.   .   .

As soon as Lynley and Havers had climbed out of the Bentley, the reporters had leapt from their semi-recumbent positions against a Ford Escort. They waited only long enough to make certain Lynley and Havers were heading towards the Cooper-Fleming house. At that point, as if on automatic pilot, they had begun firing questions. They seemed to have no expectation of these questions' being answered, merely a need to ask them, to get in the way, and thus to make the presence of the fourth estate felt.

"Any suspects?" one had shouted.

And another, ". . . located Mrs. Patten yet?"

And a third, ". . . in Mayfair with the keys on the seat. Will you confirm that for us?" as the cameras clicked and whirred.

Lynley had ignored them and had rung the doorbell as Havers observed the Nova down the street. "Our blokes are over there," she said quietly, "playing it for intimidation, it looks like."

Lynley saw them himself. "No doubt they've rattled a few nerves," he remarked.

The door had swung open and they faced a young girl with thick spectacles on her nose, breadcrumbs at the corners of her mouth, and a scattering of spots on her chin. Lynley had shown his identification and asked to speak to Jimmy Fleming.

The girl had said, "Cooper, you mean. Jimmy? You want Jimmy?" and without waiting for a reply, she left them on the front step and thundered up the stairs.

They had let themselves inside, into a sitting room where a television featured a great white shark slamming its snout against the bars of a cage in which a hapless scuba diver floated, gesticulated, and photographed the creature. The sound was turned low. No one appeared to be watching. As they observed it in silence, a small boy's voice said, "That's like *Jaws*, that fish. I saw it on a video at my mate's house once."

Lynley saw that the boy was speaking from the kitchen where he'd scooted his chair out from the table in order to put it in line with the sitting room door. He was having his tea, swinging his feet against the chair legs and munching on a biscuit of some sort.

"You a detective?" he asked. "Like Spender? I used to see that on the telly."

"Yes," Lynley said. "Something like Spender. Are you Stan?"

The boy's eyes widened, as if Lynley had displayed a preternatural knowledge that had to be reckoned with. "How'd you know that?"

"I saw a photograph of you. In your father's bedroom."

"At Mrs. Whitelaw's house? Oh, I been there lots. She lets me wind her clocks. Except the one in the morning room doesn't get wind. Did you know that? She said her grandfather stopped it the night Queen Victoria died and he never started it again."

"Are you fond of clocks?"

"Not 'specially. But she's got all sorts of thingummies in her house. All over the place. When I go there, she lets me—"

"That'll do, Stan." A woman stood on the stairs.

Havers said, "Ms. Cooper, this is Detective Inspector—"

"I don't need his name." She descended to the sitting room. She said without looking in his direction, "Stan, take your tea to your room."

"But I'm not feeling grumbly," he said anxiously.

"Do like I said. Now. And shut the door."

He scrambled off his chair. He filled his hands with sandwiches and biscuits. He scurried up the stairs. A door closed somewhere above.

Jean Cooper crossed the room and turned off the television where the great white shark was displaying what appeared to be half a dozen rows of jagged teeth. She took a packet of Embassys from the top of the set, lit one, and swung round to face them.

"What's this?" she asked them.

"We'd like to talk to your son."

"You were just doing that, weren't you?"

"Your older son, Ms. Cooper."

"And if he's not home?"

"We know that he is."

"I know my rights. I don't have to let you see him. I c'n ring a solicitor if I want."

"We don't mind if you do that."

She flipped a curt nod at Havers. "I told you everything, didn't I? Yesterday."

"Jimmy wasn't home yesterday," Havers said. "It's a formality, Ms. Cooper. That's all."

"You didn't ask to talk to Shar. Or Stan. Why's Jimmy the only one you want?"

"He was supposed to go on a sailing trip with his father," Lynley said. "He was supposed to leave with his father on Wednesday night. If the trip was formally cancelled or perhaps postponed, he may have spoken to his father. We'd like to talk to him about that." He watched her roll the cigarette restlessly between her fingers before she took another drag on it. He added, "As Sergeant Havers said, it's just a formality. We're speaking to anyone who might know anything about your husband's final hours."

Jean Cooper flinched from his last statement, but it was just a blink of her eyes and a fractional shrinking away from the words. "It's more than formality," she said.

"You can stay while we talk to him," Havers said. "Or you can phone for a solicitor. Either way, it's your right since he's under age."

"You keep that in mind," she said. "He's sixteen years old. Sixteen. He's a boy."

"We know that," Lynley said. "If you'll fetch him for us."

She said over her shoulder, "Jimmy. Best you talk to them, luv. Get it over with quick."

The boy had obviously been listening at the top of the stairs, just out of sight. He came down slowly, his body slumped, his shoulders curved inward and his head cocked to one side.

He didn't make eye contact with anyone. He ambled to the sofa and dropped onto it. His chin touched his chest and his legs stretched out before him. His position gave Lynley ample opportunity to examine his feet. He was wearing boots. Their soles bore a pattern identical to the cast Inspector Ardery had made in Kent, down to the misshapen bit of dog-tooth cornice.

Lynley introduced himself and Sergeant Havers. He took one of the armchairs of the three-piece suite. Havers took the other. Jean Cooper joined her son on the sofa. She scooped a metal ashtray from the coffee table and placed it on her knees.

"Need a fag?" she asked her son quietly.

He said, "Nah," and flipped his hair away from his shoulders. She reached out as if to assist him with this, but then seemed to think better of the idea and pulled back her hand.

Lynley said, "You spoke to your father on Wednesday."

Jimmy nodded, eyes still focussed somewhere between his knees and the floor.

"What time was this?"

"Don't remember."

"Morning? Afternoon? Your flight to Greece was scheduled for the evening. He would have phoned before that."

"Afternoon, I guess."

"Close to lunch? Close to tea?"

"I took Stan to the dentist," his mother said. "Dad must of phoned then, Jim. Round four o'clock or half past."

"Does that seem right?" Lynley asked the boy. He rolled his shoulders in silent response. Lynley took it for affirmation. "What did your father say?"

Jimmy pulled at the thread that was unravelling the hem of his T-shirt. "Something to see to," he said.

"What?"

"Dad said he had something to see to." The boy's answer was underscored with impatience. *Stupid pigs* was implied in the tone.

"That day?"

"Yeah."

"And the trip?"

"What about it?"

Lynley asked the boy what had happened to their plans for the boat trip. Had they been postponed? Were they cancelled altogether?

Jimmy appeared to think this question over. At least that's what Lynley took from the shifting of the boy's eyes. He finally told them that his father had said the trip would have to be put off for a few days. He'd phone him in the morning, he said. They'd lay out new plans then.

"And when he didn't phone you in the morning," Lynley said, "what did you think?"

"Didn't think nothing. That was Dad, wasn't it? He said he was going to do lots of things that he never did. Boat trip was one of them. I didn't care. I didn't want to go in the first place, did I?" To emphasise his final question, he dug the heel of his boot into the beige carpet. It must have been something he did quite often, because the carpet was worn and sooty coloured where he was sitting.

"And what about Kent?" Lynley asked.

The boy gave a sharp tug to the thread on the hem of his shirt. It broke off. His fingers sought another.

"You were out there on Wednesday night," Lynley said. "At the cottage. We know you were in the garden. I'm wondering if you went in the house as well."

Jean Cooper's head shot up. She'd been in the act of tapping ash from her cigarette, but she stopped and reached for her son's arm. He pulled away from her, saying nothing.

"Do you smoke Embassys like your mother, or were the cigarette ends we found at the bottom of the garden from some other brand?"

"What is this?" Jean demanded.

"The key from the potting shed's gone missing as well," Lynley said. "If we search your bedroom—or have you empty your pockets—will we find it, Jimmy?"

The boy's hair had begun to slither forward on his shoulders as if it lived a life of its own. He allowed it to do so, screening his face.

"Did you follow your father to Kent? Or did he tell you he was going there? You said he told you he had things to sort out. Did he tell you the things had to do with Gabriella Patten, or did you just assume that?"

"Stop it!" Jean mashed out her cigarette and slammed the metal ashtray onto the coffee table. "What're you going on about, you? You got no right to come into my house and talk to my Jim like this. You got no shred of proof. You got no witness. You got no—"

"On the contrary," Lynley said. Jean snapped her mouth shut. He leaned forward in his chair. "Do you want a solicitor, Jimmy? Your mother can phone for one, if you like."

The boy shrugged.

"Ms. Cooper," Havers said, "you can phone for a solicitor. You might want to do that."

But Jean's previous threat to do so had apparently been attentuated by her anger. "We don't need a naffing solicitor," she hissed. "He's done nothing, my Jim. Nothing. *Nothing.* He's sixteen years old. He's the man of this family. He sees to his brother and sister. He has no interest in Kent. He was here Wednesday night. He was tucked in bed. I saw to it myself. He—"

"Jimmy," Lynley said, "we've made casts of two footprints that are going to match the boots you're wearing. They're Doc Martens, aren't they?" The boy gave no response. "One print was at the bottom of the garden where you came over the fence from the paddock next door."

"This is rubbish," Jeannie said.

"The other was on the footpath from Lesser Springburn. At the base of that stile near the railway tracks." Lynley told him the rest: the denim fibres that no doubt would match the knee rips of the jeans he was wearing, the oil on those fibres, the oil in the shrubbery near Lesser Springburn's common. He willed the boy to react in some way. To shrink away from the words, to attempt to deny them, to give them something—however tenuous—to work with. But Jimmy said nothing.

"What were you doing in Kent?" Lynley asked.

"Don't you talk to him like this!" Jean cried. "He wasn't in Kent! He wasn't ever!"

"That's not the case, Ms. Cooper. I dare say you know it."

"Get out of this house." She jumped to her feet. She placed herself between Lynley and her son. "Get out. The both of you. You've had your say. You've asked your questions. You've seen the boy. Now get out. Out!"

Lynley sighed. He felt doubly burdened—by what he knew, by what he needed to know. He said, "We're going to have to have answers, Ms. Cooper. Jimmy can give them to us now or he can come along and give them to us later. But either way, he's going to have to talk to us. Would you like to phone your solicitor now?"

"Who d'you work for, Mr. Fancy Talk? Give me the name. It's him I'll phone."

"Webberly," Lynley said. "Malcolm Webberly."

She seemed taken aback at Lynley's cooperation. She narrowed her eyes and scrutinised him, perhaps wavering between standing her ground and making for the telephone. *A trick*, her expression said. If she left the room to make the call, they'd have her son alone and she knew it.

"Does your son have a motorbike?" Lynley asked.

"Motorbike proves nothing."

"May we see it, please?"

"It's a piece of rust. Wouldn't take him as far as the Tower of London. He couldn't of got to Kent on that bike. He couldn't."

"It wasn't in front of the house," Lynley said. "Is it in the back?"

"I said—"

Lynley rose. "Does it leak oil, Ms. Cooper?"

Jeannie clasped her hands in front of her in what could have been taken as an attitude of supplication. She began to twist one within the other. When Havers rose from her chair as well, Jean looked from one of them to the other, as if she were considering flight. Behind her, her son moved, pulling in his legs, shoving himself to his feet.

He shambled into the kitchen. They heard him open a door that squeaked on unoiled hinges. Jean cried, "Jim!" but he didn't answer.

Lynley and Havers followed him, with his mother close on their heels. When they joined him, he was pulling open the door of a small shed at the bottom of the garden. Next to it, a gate gave way into what appeared to be a walk that ran between the houses on Cardale Street and those on the street behind them.

As they watched, Jimmy Cooper wheeled his motorbike out of the shed. He straddled the seat, started the bike, let it idle, then shut it off. He did it all without looking at any of them. Then he stood to one side—right arm clasping left elbow, weight on left hip—as Lynley squatted to examine the machine.

The motorbike was as Jean Cooper had said, largely rust. Where it wasn't rust, it had once been red, but the colour had oxidized over time, leaving dull patches that, mixing with the rust, looked like scabs. The engine itself still ran, however. When Lynley started it himself, it turned over without difficulty and rumbled without misfiring once. He shut the engine off and set the bike on its kickstand.

"I told you," Jean said. "It's a heap of rust. He drives it round Cubitt Town. He knows he isn't to take it anywhere else. He does errands for me. He goes to see his grandma. Down by Millwall Park. He—"

"Sir." Sergeant Havers had been squatting on the bike's other side, examining it. Now she lifted a finger, and Lynley saw the oil dotting the end of it like a blood blister. "It's got a leak," she added unnecessarily, and as she did another drop of oil fell from the engine onto the concrete of the path where Jimmy had parked it.

He should have felt a sense of vindication, but instead Lynley felt only regret. At first he couldn't understand why. The boy was surly, uncooperative, and filthy, a probable young thug who'd been asking for trouble for years. He'd found it now, he'd be put out of commission, but that last fact gave Lynley absolutely no pleasure. A moment's consideration told him why. He'd been Jimmy's age when he first fell out with one of his parents. He knew what it felt like to hate and to love an incomprehensible adult with equal force.

He said heavily, "Sergeant. If you will," and he walked to the gate and studied its wood as Havers read Jimmy Cooper the official caution.

CHAPTER
16

They took him out the front, which gave the reporters and their companion photographers plenty of grist for tomorrow's newspapers, all of it to be craftily moulded to reveal as much as possible through innuendo while still protecting the rights of everyone involved. The moment Lynley opened the door and motioned Jimmy Cooper out before him—with the boy's head lolling forward like a marionette's and his hands clasped in front of him as if he already wore handcuffs—a shout of excitement erupted from the small band of journalists. They thrust their way between the cars parked along the kerb, tape recorders and notebooks in hand. The photographers began to fire off pictures as the reporters barked questions.

"An arrest, Inspector?"

"This the oldest boy?"

"Jimmy! You, Jim! Have a statement, lad?"

"What's this about? Jealousy? Money?"

Jimmy ducked his head to one side. He muttered, "Bugger you lot," and staggered when his toe caught on an uneven piece of pavement in the front garden. Lynley grabbed him by the arm to steady him. The cameras blazed to catch the moment.

"You lot clear out!" The shriek came from the doorway where Jean Cooper stood with her other children looking out from beneath her obstructing arms. The cameras flashed in her direction. She pushed Stan and Sharon into the sitting room, out of range. She ran out of the house and snatched Lynley's arm. The cameras snapped and whirred.

"You leave him," Jean cried.

"I can't do that," Lynley said to her quietly. "If he won't speak to us here, we have no choice. Would you like to come as well? It's your right, Ms. Cooper. He's under age."

She rubbed her hands down the sides of her oversize T-shirt. She cast a look back towards the house where her other two children stared at them from the sitting room window. She no doubt considered what might happen should she leave them alone, within reach of the press. She said, "I got to phone my brother first."

Jimmy said, "I don't want her to come."

"Jim!"

"I said." He shook back his hair, realised his error when the photographers rapidly caught his unshielded face, lowered his head again.

"You got to let me—"

"No."

Lynley was aware of the fodder they were providing the reporters, who were listening as eagerly as they were taking notes. It was too soon for their newspapers to run a story that included Jimmy's name, and their editors—governed by the Contempt of Court Act—would make certain not to print an identifiable photograph that could prejudice a trial and land them all in the nick for two years. But still the papers would be sure to use what they could, when they could, so he said quietly, "Phone your solicitor if you'd like, Ms. Cooper. Have him meet us at the Yard."

"What d'you think I am? A piece of fluff from Knightsbridge? I don't *have* a bleeding . . . Jim! Jim! You let me come."

Jimmy looked at Lynley for the first time. "I don't want her. I won't talk with her there."

"Jimmy!" His mother said his name in a wail. She spun and stumbled back into the house.

The reporters acted the part of Greek chorus again.

"Solicitor? Then he's a definite suspect."

"Will you confirm that, Inspector? Is it safe to assume—"

"Is Maidstone Constabulary cooperating completely?"

"Have you the autopsy report yet?"

"Come on, Inspector. Give us something, for God's sake."

Lynley ignored them. Havers swung open the gate. She pushed past them and made room for Lynley and the boy. The reporters and photographers dogged them down the street to the Bentley. When their questions continued to go ignored, they merely increased their volume, shifting in subject matter from "Do you have a statement?" to "Kill your dad, boy?" The noise brought neighbours into gardens. Dogs started to bark.

Havers said, "Jesus," under her breath and, "Mind your head there," to Jimmy as Lynley opened the back door of the car. As the boy slid inside and the photographers pressed round the window to record every nuance of expression on his face, Jean Cooper burst through them. She waved a Tesco's bag in her hand. Lynley stiffened. Havers said, "Watch it, sir!" and moved forward as if she would intercede.

Jean flung a reporter to one side. She snarled, "Sod you," at another. She thrust the bag at Lynley. "You listen to me. You hurt my son . . . You bloody even touch him . . ." Her voice quavered. She pressed her knuckles against her mouth. "I know my rights," she said. "He's sixteen years old. You don't ask him one question without a solicitor. You don't even ask him to spell his name." She leaned over and shouted through the raised window of the Bentley. "Jimmy, you don't talk to no one till the solicitor comes. You hear that, Jim? You don't talk to no one."

Her son stared straight ahead. Jean cried out his name. Lynley said, "We can arrange the solicitor at our end, Ms. Cooper. If that would be of help."

She straightened and flung her head back in a movement not unlike her son's. She said, "I don't fancy your kind of help." She pushed back through the reporters and photographers. She broke into a run as they began to follow.

Lynley handed the Tesco's bag to Havers. They were heading north on Manchester Road before she opened it. She said, ploughing through it, "One change of clothes. Two pieces of bread and butter. Sailing book of some sort. Pair of glasses." She shifted in her seat and said as she offered these last to Jimmy, "D'you want the specs?"

He stared at her in answer, offered her an expression of "Get knot-ted," then looked away.

Havers popped the glasses back into the bag, put it on the floor, and said, "Right, then," as Lynley picked up the car phone and punched in the number for New Scotland Yard. He tracked down Detective Constable Nkata in the incidents room where the background noise of telephones and conversation told him that at least some of the officers he'd called off rota to work the weekend had returned from their investigations into the Wednesday night movements of the case's primary suspects. He said, "What do we have?"

Nkata said, "Kensington's in. No change there, man. She's staying clean, your Mrs. Whitelaw."

"What's the report?"

"Staffordshire Terrace's lined with conversions. You know that, 'Spector?"

"I've been in the street, Nkata."

"Every conversion, it has six, seven flats. Every flat, it has three, four occupants."

"This is beginning to sound like the DC's lament."

"All I mean here, man, is that that woman's clean. We talked to every Jack and Dick we could find in every flipping flat. No one in Staf-fordshire Terrace could say they'd seen her go anywhere in the last week."

"Which doesn't say much for their powers of observation, does it? Since she went somewhere with us yesterday morning."

"But if she's trekking out to Kent at midnight or thereabouts, she is using her car to get there, right? She's not asking a taxi to pop her out and wait while she sets a fire. She's not taking a bus. She's not taking the train. Not at that hour. And that's where she's clean."

"Go on."

"Her car's parked in a garage behind the house, in a mews called—here it is—Phillips Walk. Now, according to our blokes was out there this morning, Phillips Walk is nine-tenths conversions these days."

"Mews cottages?"

"Right. Bumping up against each other like tarts at King's Cross. With windows above and windows below. All open Wednesday night 'cause the weather was fine."

"I take it that no one saw Mrs. Whitelaw leave? No one heard her car start?"

"And on Wednesday night, baby in the cottage opposite her garage was up past four in the morning, being sick on his mummy's shoulder. Mummy would've heard the car since she spent the night pacing in front of the windows trying to settle the nip down. Nothing, though. So unless Mrs. Whitelaw levitated out of there off her roof, she's clean, 'Spector. Sorry if that's a spanner."

"No matter," Lynley said. "The news doesn't surprise me. She's already been given an alibi by another of the principals."

"You like her for the killer?"

"Not particularly. But I've always been partial to tying up loose ends." He finished the call by telling Nkata to have an interrogation room ready and to let the press office know that a sixteen-year-old boy from the East End was going to be assisting the police in their enquiries. He replaced the phone and they made the rest of the journey to New Scotland Yard in silence.

The journalists on the Isle of Dogs had obviously phoned whatever colleagues they had hanging about Victoria Street, because when Lynley pulled into the entrance of New Scotland Yard in Broadway, the Bentley was immediately surrounded. Among the jostling crowd shouting questions and thrusting cameras towards the backseat, the television news media were also represented by aggressive cameramen who shouldered through the others.

Havers muttered, "Holy hell," as Lynley said, "Lower your head, Jim," and inched the car towards the kiosk and the entry to the underground parking. They gained the kiosk at the cost of a hundred or more photographs and countless feet of video footage, which would no doubt appear on every television station by the day's end.

Through it all, Jimmy Cooper didn't react other than to avert his head from the cameras. He betrayed neither interest nor trepidation as Lynley and Havers escorted him to the lift and then through one corridor after another where a press officer hurried along with them for a minute, notebook in her hand, saying unnecessarily considering the gauntlet they'd just run, "The announcement's gone out, Inspector. A boy. Age sixteen. The East End," with a quick glance at Jimmy. "Anything else safe to add at this point? The boy's school? Number of brothers and sisters? Veiled allusions to the family? Anything from Kent?"

Lynley shook his head. The officer said, "Right. Our phones are ringing like fire alarms. You'll give me more when you can, won't you?"

She faded away without receiving an answer.

Constable Nkata met them at the interrogation room, where the tape recorder was set and the chairs were arranged, two on each side of a metal-legged table, two backed against the facing walls. He said to Lynley, "You want his dabs?" to which Lynley replied, "Not yet." He indicated which chair he wished the boy to take. "May we chat for a moment, Jimmy? Or would you prefer to wait for your mother to send a solicitor?"

Jimmy slumped into the chair, hands picking at the hem of his T-shirt. "Don't matter."

Lynley said to Nkata, "Let us know when he gets here. We'll be chatting till then."

Nkata's expression told Lynley the message had been received. They'd get what they could from the boy before his solicitor arrived to muzzle him indefinitely.

Lynley flipped the record switch on the tape machine, gave the date and the time, and indicated the persons present in the interrogation room: himself, Sergeant Barbara Havers, and James Cooper, the son of Kenneth Fleming. He said again, "Would you like a solicitor present, Jimmy? Shall we wait?" and when the boy shrugged, Lynley said, "You're going to need to answer."

"I don't need no naffing solicitor, all right? I don't want one."

Lynley sat opposite the boy. Sergeant Havers went to one of the chairs against the wall. Lynley heard the scratch of a match being lit and smelled the cigarette smoke a second later. Jimmy's eyes rested hungrily if briefly on Havers, and then flitted away. Lynley mentally saluted his sergeant. Her habit sometimes served them well. He said, "Smoke if you want," to the boy. Sergeant Havers flipped her matches onto the table. "Need a fag?" she asked Jimmy. He shook his head once. But his feet moved restlessly on the floor and his fingers continued to pluck at his shirt.

"It's rough talking in front of your mother," Lynley said. "She means well, but she's a mother, isn't she? They like to hang on to a chap. They like to hang about."

Jimmy wiped a finger beneath his nose. His glance went to the matchbook, dropped away.

"They don't tend to give one much privacy either," Lynley continued. "At least mine never did. And they have a hell of a time recognising when a boy's become a man."

Jimmy raised his head long enough to brush his hair from his face. He used the movement to steal a look at Lynley.

Lynley said, "It makes sense that you wouldn't want to talk in front of her. I should have seen that at once because God knows I wouldn't have wanted to do any talking in front of my mother. She doesn't give you much space to move about, does she?"

Jimmy scratched his arm. He scratched his shoulder. He went back to picking at his shirt.

"What I'm hoping," Lynley said, "is that you can help us clear a few details off the slate. You aren't under arrest. You're here to help. We know you were in Kent, at the cottage. We're assuming you were there on Wednesday night. We'd like to know why. We'd like to know how you got there. We'd like to know what time you arrived and what time you left. That's it. Can you give us some help?"

Behind him, Lynley heard Havers inhale, then the smoke from her cigarette wafted more strongly towards them. Once again, Lynley carefully laid out the evidence that supported the boy's presence in Kent. He ended with, "Did you follow your dad?"

Jimmy coughed. He lifted the front legs of the chair a half inch or so.

"Was it a guess on your part that he'd be going there? He said he had some things to see to. Did he sound upset? Anxious? Did that tell you he was going out to meet with Gabriella Patten?"

Jimmy lowered the chair legs.

Lynley said, "He'd seen a solicitor recently. About divorcing your mother. She would have been upset about that. You may have seen her crying and wondered why. She may have talked to you. She may have told you—"

"I did it." Jimmy finally looked up. His hazel eyes were bloodshot, but they met Lynley's directly. He said, "I did it. I chopped the sodding bastard. He deserved to die."

Behind them, Lynley heard Sergeant Havers stir. Jimmy pulled his hand from his pocket and dropped a key onto the table. When Lynley made no remark, the boy demanded, "Tha's what you want, isn't it?" He pulled cigarettes from his other pocket, a squashed packet of JPS from which he managed to extricate one, partially broken. He lit it with Sergeant Havers' matches. He needed four tries to make his fingers work the knob of sulphur against its striking pad.

"Tell me about it," Lynley said.

Jimmy smoked deeply, holding the cigarette with his thumb and index finger. "Thought he was a toff, did Dad. Thought he could do anything."

"Did you follow him to Kent?"

"I followed him everywhere. Whenever I wanted."

"On the bike? That night?"

"I knew where he lived. I been there before. Bugger thought he could say anything and make things all right. No matter how much crap we took off him."

"What happened that night, Jimmy?"

He went to Lesser Springburn, Jimmy said, because his father had lied to him and he wanted to catch him in the lie and throw the lie in that rotten bastard's face. He'd said that they had to postpone their holiday because he had cricket business to attend to, urgent business that couldn't be put off. Something to do with the test matches, the Ashes, an England bowler, a friendly match somewhere. . . . Jimmy didn't remember and he didn't care to because he hadn't believed the lie for a moment.

"It was her," he said. "Her out in Kent. She'd phoned him and said she wanted to fuck him a good one like he'd never had before, she wanted to give him something to remember whiles he was in Greece with me, and he couldn't wait to do it. That's how he was when it came to her. Randy. Like a dog."

He didn't go directly to Celandine Cottage, Jimmy said, because he wanted to take them both by surprise. He didn't want to risk them hearing the bike. He didn't want to chance that they'd see him on the drive. So he overshot the turn from the Springburn Road and went on to the village. He parked behind the pub, where he shoved the bike into the shrubbery at the edge of the common. He hiked along the footpath.

"How did you know about the footpath?" Lynley asked.

They'd been there as kids, hadn't they? When their dad first moved out there while he played for Kent. They'd go at the weekend. He and Shar would explore. They both knew about the path. Everyone knew about the path.

"And that night?" Lynley asked. "At the cottage?"

He jumped the wall next to the cottage, he explained, the one that gave onto the paddock that belonged to the farm just to the east. He'd sidled along it till he came to the corner of the property belonging to Celandine Cottage. There he'd climbed the fence and leapt over the hedge to land at the bottom of the garden.

"What time was this?"

He didn't know. It was after time was called at the pub in Lesser Springburn, though, because there hadn't been no cars in the car park when he got there. He stood at the bottom of the garden, he said, and he thought about them.

"Who?" Lynley asked.

Her, he said. The blonde. And his dad. He hoped they were enjoying their fuck, he said. He hoped they were sweating over it proper because he decided then and there that it was going to be their last.

He knew where the extra key was kept, in the potting shed under the pottery duck. He fetched it. He unlocked the kitchen door. He set the fire in the armchair. He sprinted back to his motorbike and set off for home.

"I meant them both to die." He smashed his cigarette into the ashtray and spat a shred of tobacco onto the table. "I'll get that cow later. See if I don't."

"How did you know your father was there? Did you follow him when he left Kensington?"

"Didn't need to, did I? I found him all right."

"Did you see his car? Parked in front of the cottage? Or in the drive?"

Jimmy looked incredulous. His father's car was more precious to him than his flaming dick, Jimmy told them. He wouldn't of left it outside, not with a garage standing right there. The boy dug in his packet of cigarettes and managed to rescue another mangled one. This one he lit without any difficulty. He saw his father through the kitchen window, he said, before he put out the lights and went upstairs to do her.

Lynley said, "Tell me about the fire itself. The one in the armchair."

What about it? Jimmy wanted to know.

"Tell me how you set it."

He used a cigarette, he said. He lit it. He stuck it in the bleeding chair. He ducked out through the kitchen and made for home.

"Take me step by step through it, if you will," Lynley asked. "Were you smoking a cigarette at the time?"

No. Of course he wasn't smoking it at the time. What did the cops think? That he was some sort of wally?

"Was it like these? A JPS?"

Yeah. That's right. A JPS.

"And you lit it?" Lynley asked. "Will you show me, please?"

Jimmy inched his chair away from the table. He said sharply, "Show you what?"

"How you lit the cigarette."

"Why? You never light a fag or something?"

"I'd like to see you do it if you will."

"How the hell you expect I lit it?"

"I don't know. Did you use a lighter?"

"Course not. Matches."

"Like these?"

Jimmy jutted his chin in Havers' direction, his expression a look of you-can't-trip-me-up. "Those're hers."

"I realise that. What I'm asking is if you used a book of matches since you didn't use a lighter."

The boy dropped his head. He fixed his attention on the ashtray.

"Were the matches like these?" Lynley asked again.

"Sod you," he muttered.

"Did you take them with you or use matches from the cottage?"

"He deserved it," Jimmy said, as if he were speaking to himself. "He bloody deserved it and I'll get her next. You just see if I don't."

A tap sounded on the door of the interrogation room. Sergeant Havers went to it. A murmur of conversation ensued. Lynley observed Jimmy Cooper in silence. The boy's face—what Lynley could see of it—was hardened into an expression of indifference, as if poured into a mould and set into concrete. Lynley wondered what degree of pain, guilt, and sorrow was required to effect such studied nonchalance.

"Sir?" Havers spoke from the doorway. Lynley went to join her. Nkata was standing in the corridor. "Little Venice and the Isle of Dogs are reporting in," she said. "They're in the incidents room. Shall I suss things out?"

Lynley shook his head. To Nkata, "Get the boy something to eat. Take his prints. See if he'll hand over the shoes voluntarily. I expect he will. We'll need to get something for a DNA sample as well."

"Tha's going to be dicey," Nkata said.

"Has his solicitor arrived?"

"Not yet."

"Then see if you can get him to volunteer before we release him."

Havers interjected quickly with, "Release him? But sir, he's just bloody told us—"

"Once his solicitor's got him," Lynley continued as if she hadn't spoken.

Nkata concluded the thought. "We got trouble."

"Work quickly. But, Nkata—" this as the DC set his shoulder against the door—"keep the boy calm."

"Got it."

Nkata slipped into the interrogation room. Lynley and Havers headed for the incidents room. It had been set up not far from Lynley's office. Maps, photographs, and charts hung on the walls. Files were scattered across desks. Six detective constables—four male, two female—had stationed themselves at telephones, at filing cabinets, and at a circular table spread with newspapers.

Lynley said, "Isle of Dogs," as he entered the room, flinging his jacket over the back of a chair.

One of the female DCs replied, a telephone balanced on her shoulder as she waited for someone to answer on the other end. "The boy comes and goes all night long, just about every day of the week. He's got a motorbike. He exits through the back and makes a hell of a row riding it along the path between the houses, gunning the engine, sounding the horn. Neighbours couldn't swear he was out on Wednesday night since he's out most nights and one night sounds pretty much like the other. So maybe he was, maybe he wasn't, with the odds on maybe he was."

Her partner, a male DC dressed in faded black jeans and a sweat shirt with the arms cut off, said, "He's a real yob, though. Rows with the neighbours. Roughs up littler blokes. Talks back to his mum."

"What about his mother?" Lynley said.

"Works at Billingsgate Market. Leaves for the job round three-forty in the morning. Gets home round noon."

"Wednesday night? Thursday morning?"

"She never makes a sound other than to start her car," the female DC said. "So the neighbours couldn't give us much on her when we asked about Wednesday. Fleming was a regular visitor, though. Everyone we talked to verified that."

"To see the children?"

"No. He showed up in the afternoons around one, when the kids weren't home. He generally stayed two hours or more. He'd been there earlier in the week, by the way. Maybe Monday or Tuesday."

"Was Jean at work on Thursday?"

The female DC used the phone to gesture with. "I'm working on that. I can't rouse anyone who can tell us, so far. Billingsgate's closed till tomorrow."

"She said she was home on Wednesday night," Havers said to Lynley. "But there's no one to corroborate because she was by herself except for the kids. And they were asleep."

"What about Little Venice?" he asked.

"Gold," one of the other DCs said. He was sitting at the table with his partner, both of them dressed for simultaneous day tripping and blending into the environment. "Faraday left the barge somewhere around half past ten on Wednesday night."

"He admitted that much yesterday."

"Add this to it, sir. Olivia Whitelaw was with him. Two different neighbours noticed them going because it's evidently something of a production, getting Whitelaw off the barge and up to the street."

"Did they speak to anyone?" Lynley asked.

"No, but the trip was an odd one for two reasons." He used his thumb for the first, his index finger for the second. "One, they didn't take their dogs, which isn't the norm according to everyone we talked to. Two—" and here he smiled, showing a wide gap between his front teeth, "according to a bloke called Bidwell, they didn't come tripping home till half past five the next morning. Which is when he himself came tripping home from an art show in Windsor that turned into a drinks party that turned into what Bidwell called 'a blooming bleeding blessed bacchanal but mum's the word to the wife, you blokes.' "

"Now that's an interesting turn of events," Havers said to Lynley. "A confession on one hand. A set of lies where no lies are necessary on the other. What d'you suppose we've got here, sir?"

Lynley reached for his jacket. "Let's ask them," he said.

Nkata and a second DC stayed to man the telephones, with directions to hand Jimmy Cooper over to his solicitor once he arrived. The boy had surrendered his Doc Martens at Nkata's request, had suffered through having his fingerprints and his photograph taken. To the casual solicitation of a few strands of hair, he'd lifted one shoulder wordlessly. He either didn't fully understand the implication of what was happening to him, or he didn't care. So the hairs were harvested, placed in a collection bag, and labelled.

It was well after seven when Lynley and Havers cruised over the Warwick Avenue bridge and turned into Blomfield Road. They found a space to park at the base of one of the elegant Victorian villas overlooking the canal, and they walked quickly along the pavement, descending the steps to the path that led to Browning's Pool.

No one was on the deck of Faraday's barge although the cabin door stood open and the sound of either a television or a radio combined with cooking noises came from below. Lynley rapped against the wooden gazebo and called out Faraday's name. The radio or television was hastily muted on the words ". . . to Greece with his son, who celebrated his sixteenth birthday on Friday . . ."

A moment later, Chris Faraday's face appeared below them in the cabin. His body blocked the stairway. His eyes narrowed when he saw it was Lynley. "What is it?" he said. "I'm cooking dinner."

"We need to clarify a few points," Lynley said, stepping down unbidden from the deck onto the stairs.

Faraday held up a hand as Lynley began to descend. "Hey, can't this wait?"

"It won't take long."

He blew out his breath, then stepped to one side.

Lynley said, "I see you've been decorating," in reference to a collection of posters that hung haphazardly on the pine walls of the cabin. "These weren't here yesterday, were they? This is my sergeant, Barbara Havers, by the way." He examined the posters, dwelling particularly on a curious map of Great Britain and the unusual manner in which it had been divided into sectors.

"What is this?" Faraday said. "I've dinner on. It's going to burn."

"Then you might want to turn the fire down a bit. Is Miss Whitelaw here? We'll want to speak with her as well."

Faraday looked as if he wanted to argue, but he turned on his heel and disappeared into the galley. From beyond it, they could hear a door opening and the murmur of his voice. Hers rose in answer, saying, "Chris! What? Chris!" He said something more. Her answer was lost when the dogs began barking. More noise followed: the rattling of metal, the shuffling of a body, the clicking of canine nails on a linoleum floor.

Within two minutes, Olivia Whitelaw had joined them, half-dragging, half-walking, her weight on the walker and her face haggard. Behind her, Faraday moved round the kitchen, banging pot lids and pots, slamming cupboards, ordering the dogs out of the way with an accompanying and angry, "Ouch!" and "God*damn* it!" to which Olivia said, "Have a care, Chris," without removing her attention from Havers, who was wandering along the wall and reading the posters.

"I was having a lie down," Olivia told Lynley. "What do you want that can't wait till later?"

"Your story's not clear on last Wednesday night," Lynley said. "Apparently, there are some details you've forgotten."

"What the hell?" Faraday came out of the galley, the dogs at his heels and a dish-cloth in his hands, which he was drying. He lobbed it onto the dining table where it landed onto one of the plates laid for dinner. He went to Olivia's side and when he would have helped her into one of the chairs, she said brusquely, "I can cope," and lowered herself. She flung the walker to one side. The beagle dodged it with a yelp. He joined the mongrel in an investigation of Sergeant Havers' brogues.

"Wednesday night?" Faraday said.

"Yes. Wednesday night."

Faraday and Olivia exchanged a look. He said, "I've already told you. I went to a party in Clapham."

"Yes. Tell me more about that party." Lynley rested his weight against the arm of the chair opposite Olivia's. Havers chose the stool next to the workbench. She crackled through her notebook to find a pristine page.

"What about it?"

"Who was the party for?"

"It wasn't for anyone. It was just a group of blokes getting together to blow off steam."

"Who are these blokes?"

"You want their names?" Faraday rubbed the back of his neck as if it was stiff. "Right." He frowned and began a slow recitation of names, hesitating now and then to add something along the lines of, "Oh right. Bloke called Geoff was there as well. I'd not met him before."

"And the address in Clapham?" Lynley asked.

It was on Orlando Road, he told them. He went to the workbench and pulled an old address book from among a collection of large battered volumes. He fingered through the pages, then read off the address, saying, "Chap called David Prior lives there. You want his number?"

"Please."

Faraday recited it. Havers jotted it down. He shoved the address book among the other volumes and returned to Olivia, where he finally sat in the chair next to hers.

"Were there women at that party as well?" Lynley asked.

"It was stag. The women wouldn't have fancied it much. You know. It was one of those sorts of parties."

"Those sorts of parties?"

Faraday glanced uneasily at Olivia. "We watched some films. It was just some blokes getting together, drinking, making noise, and having a lark. It didn't mean anything."

"And no women were present? None at all?"

"No. They wouldn't have wanted to watch that stuff, would they?"

"Pornography?"

"I wouldn't go that far. It was more artistic than that, actually." Olivia was looking at him steadily. He grinned and said, "Livie, you know it was nothing. *The Naughty Nanny. Daddy's Little Girl. Bangkok Buddha.*"

"Those were the films?" Havers clarified, pencil poised.

Seeing she intended to write them down, Faraday willingly recited the rest although the pits on his cheeks took on a deeper hue as he did so. He said when he'd completed the list, "We got them in Soho. There's a video rental on Berwick Street."

"And no women were there," Lynley said. "You're sure of that? At no time during the evening?"

"Of course I'm sure. Why do you keep asking?"

"What time did you get home?"

"Home?" Faraday gave Olivia a querying look. "I told you before. It was late. I don't know. Sometime after four."

"And you were alone here?" Lynley said to Olivia. "You didn't go out. You didn't hear Mr. Faraday return?"

"That's right, Inspector. So if you don't mind, can we have our dinner now?"

Lynley left his chair and sauntered to the window where he adjusted the shutters and gave a long scrutiny to Browning's Island a short distance across the pool. He said, looking out, "There were no women present at the party."

Faraday said, "What is this? I've told you that already."

"Miss Whitelaw didn't go?"

"I think I still count as a woman, Inspector," Olivia said.

"Then where were you and Mr. Faraday heading at half past ten on Wednesday night? And more importantly, where were you coming from when you returned around five the next morning? If, of course, you weren't at the . . . You did say it was a stag party?"

Neither of them spoke for a moment. One of the dogs—the three-legged mongrel—lurched to his feet and limped in Olivia's direction. He placed his misshapen head on her knee. Her hand dropped to it but lay flaccid there.

Faraday looked neither at the police nor at Olivia. Instead, he reached for the walker that Olivia had flung to one side. He righted it, ran his hand along its aluminium framework. Finally, he directed a look at Olivia. Clearly, the decision to clarify the situation or to lie further lay with her.

She said under her breath, "Bidwell. That snoop." She swung her head to Faraday. "I've left my fags by the bed. Will you . . . ?"

"Right." He seemed happy enough to be out of the room, even for the brief time it would take him to fetch her cigarettes. He returned with Marlboros, a lighter, and a tomato tin with half its label missing. This last he placed between her knees. He shook out a cigarette and lit it for her. She spoke to them without removing it from her mouth. When it needed to have its ash dislodged, she let this heedlessly fall onto her black jersey.

"Chris took me out," she said. "He went on to the party. He fetched me when the party was over."

"Out," Lynley said. "From ten at night until five the next morning?"

"That's right. Out. From ten at night till five in the morning. Probably more like half past five, which Bidwell would have no doubt been delighted to tell you had he been sober enough to read his watch correctly."

"You were at a party yourself?"

A laugh gusted from her nose. "While the men were getting sweaty watching porn, the women were elsewhere, having a bake-off of their chocolate gateaux? No, I wasn't at a party."

"Then where were you, please?"

"I wasn't in Kent, if we're heading back in that direction."

"Can someone confirm where it is that you were?"

She inhaled and peered at him through the smoke. It veiled her as effectively as it had done yesterday, perhaps more so now because she was so insistent about keeping the cigarette in her mouth.

"Miss Whitelaw," Lynley said. He was weary. He was hungry. It was getting late. They'd bandied the truth round long enough. "Perhaps we'd all be more comfortable having this conversation elsewhere." At the workbench Havers snapped her notebook closed.

"Livie," Faraday said.

"All right." She stubbed her cigarette out and fumbled with the packet. It slipped from her fingers and fell to the floor. She said, "Leave it," when Faraday would have picked it up. "I was with my mother," she told Lynley.

Lynley wasn't sure what he had expected to hear, but this wasn't it. He said, "Your mother."

"Right. You've met her, no doubt. Miriam Whitelaw, woman of few but eternally correct words. Number 18 Staffordshire Terrace. The mouldy, old Victorian relic. That's the house, not my mother, by the way. Although she does come in a fine second in the mould and old department. I went to see her at half past ten on Wednesday night, when Chris set off for the party. He fetched me the next morning on his way home."

Havers opened her notebook once again. Lynley could hear her pencil scratching furiously against the paper.

"Why didn't you tell me this earlier?" he asked. The larger question remained unasked: Why hadn't Miriam Whitelaw herself told him earlier?

"Because it had nothing to do with Kenneth Fleming. His life, his death, his anything. It had to do with me. It had to do with Chris. It had to do with my mother. I didn't tell you because it was none of your business. She didn't tell you because she wanted to protect my privacy. What little I have left."

"No one has privacy in a murder investigation, Miss Whitelaw."

"Oh balls. What pompous, arrogant, narrow-minded shit. Do you trot that line out for everyone? I didn't know Kenneth Fleming. I never even met him."

"Then I'd assume you'd be eager to clear yourself of any suspicion. His death, after all, removes every obstruction to your inheriting your mother's fortune."

"Have you always been such a bleeding fool or is this an act for my benefit only?" She raised her head to look at the ceiling. He could see her blink. He watched her throat work. Faraday put his hand on the arm of her chair, but he didn't touch her. "Look at me," she said. It sounded as if she spoke through her teeth. She lowered her head and met Lynley's eyes. "Just bloody look at me and use your brains. I don't give a shit about my mother's will. I don't care about her house, her money, her stocks, her bonds, her business, her anything. I'm dying, all right? Can you deal with that fact, no matter how much it destroys your precious case? I'm dying. *Dying.* So if I had it in mind to knock off Kenneth Fleming and weasel back into my mother's will, what in God's name would be the point? I'll be dead in eighteen months. She'll be alive another twenty years. I'm not inheriting anything, from her or anyone. Not anything. Got it?''

She'd begun to tremble. Her legs were jitterbugging against her chair. Faraday murmured her name. She snapped, "No!" without a clear reason. She held her left arm against her body. Her face had taken on a sheen during their interview, and it seemed to glisten more brightly. "I went to see her on Wednesday night because I knew Chris had the party to go to and couldn't come with me. Because I didn't want Chris to come with me. Because I needed to see her alone.''

"Alone?" Lynley asked. "Weren't you running the chance that Fleming would have been there?"

"He didn't count as far as I was concerned. I couldn't bear the thought of Chris seeing me grovel. But if Kenneth saw, if he was in the room even, I thought it might increase my chance for success. The way I saw it, Mother'd be only too happy to act the role of Lady Forgiveness and Mother Compassion in front of Kenneth. She wouldn't think of chucking me into the street if he was there.''

"And when he wasn't there?" Lynley asked.

"I found it didn't matter. Mother saw . . ." Olivia twisted her head towards Faraday. He seemed to believe that she needed encouragement because he nodded at her and his expression was gentle. "Mother saw me. Like this. Maybe worse than this because it was later, at night, and I'm worse at night. And it turned out that I didn't need to grovel. I didn't need to ask her for anything.''

"That's why you'd gone to see her in the first place? To ask for something?''

"Yes. That's why."

"What?"

"It has nothing to do with this. With Kenneth. With his death. With anything but me and my mother. And my father as well.''

"Nonetheless, it's a final point. We'll need it. I'm sorry if it's difficult for you.''

"No. You're not sorry." She moved her head from side to side in slow negation. She looked too weary to fight him any longer. "I requested," she said. "Mother agreed.''

"To what, Miss Whitelaw?"

"To mix my ashes with my father's, Inspector.''

CHAPTER
17

Barbara Havers was experiencing that God's-in-His-heaven feeling as she reached the serving platter an instant before Lynley and speared the last hoop of *calamari fritti*. She lingered over the satisfying decision as to which sauce she would use for the squid's submersion: marinara, virgin olive oil and herbs, or garlic and butter. She chose the second, wondering which of them was virgin, the olive or the oil. And, for that matter, how either one of them could possibly be a virgin in the first place.

When Lynley had first suggested sharing the *calamari* to start, she'd said, "Good idea, sir. *Calamari* it is," and gazed at the menu with an attempt at arranging her features into something that might communicate the appropriate degree of sophistication. Her most significant experience with Italian food had been the occasional plate of *spaghetti bolognese* bolted down in one café or another where the spaghetti came from a packet and the bolognese from a tin, and both were slopped onto a plate where a ring of rust-coloured oil quickly seeped from the food like an invitation to permanent dyspepsia.

There had been no *spaghetti bolognese* on the menu here. Nor had there been an English translation of anything else. One could probably have obtained an English menu for the asking, but that would mean revealing one's ignorance before one's superior officer who spoke at least three bloody languages that Barbara was aware of and who perused the menu with great interest and asked the waiter just how *stagionato* the *cinghiale* was and what process was used to age it. So she ordered blithely away, mangling pronunciations, affecting an aura of experience, and praying she wasn't requesting octopus.

Calamari came close, as she discovered. True, it didn't look like squid. No tentacles gestured companionably to her from the platter. But had she known what it was when she agreed to share it with Lynley, she would have pleaded an allergy to all things having appendages that were even remotely capable of suction.

Her first taste of it reassured her, however. Her second, third, and fourth—moving among the dipping sauces with ever increasing enthusiasm—convinced her that she'd been leading a far too sheltered gastronomic existence. She was making a decided inroad into the artful arrangement of delicate hoops when she first realised that Lynley was hardly keeping pace. She soldiered on, effecting her final prandial ace in triumph and waiting for Lynley to remark upon either her appetite or her table manners.

He did neither. He was watching his fingers tear a piece of *focaccia* into bits, as if with the intention of scattering the resulting crumbs along the edge of the planter that marked the perimeter of Capannina di Sante, a restaurant that sat a few steps off Kensington High Street and offered— along with a putative but obscure connnection to an eating establishment of the same name in Florence—the Continental experience of *al fresco* dining whenever the capricious London weather permitted it. Through some process of avian telepathy, six small brown birds had gathered the moment Lynley removed the bread from its wicker serving basket and dropped it onto his plate. Now they hopped expectantly from the planter's edge to the well-trimmed junipers growing within it, each fastening a bright, beseeching eye on Lynley, who seemed oblivious of them.

Barbara popped the last hoop of *calamari* into her mouth. She chewed, savoured, swallowed, sighed, and anticipated *il secondo*, soon to come. She'd chosen it solely for the complexity of its name: *tagliatelle fagioli all'uccelletto.* All those letters. All those words. However they were supposed to be pronounced, she was sure the dish had to be the chef's masterwork. If it wasn't, *anatra albicocche* would follow. And if she found she didn't care for that—whatever it was—she had little doubt that Lynley's dinner would go mostly uneaten, and be passed her way. At least, that's how things were shaping up so far.

"Well?" she said to him. "Is it the food or the company?"

He said, apropos of nothing as far as she could tell, "Helen cooked for me last night."

Barbara reached for another piece of *focaccia* and ignored the birds. Lynley had put on his spectacles to read a wine label and he nodded for the waiter to pour.

"And the grub was so memorable you can't bear to eat here? Lest the taste of food drive the memory away? You made a vow that nothing would cross your lips unless it came from her hands? What?" Barbara asked. "How much of that squid did you have, anyway? I thought this was supposed to be a celebration. We've got our confession. What else do you want?"

"She can't cook, Havers. Although I imagine she might manage an egg. If she boiled it."

"So?"

"So nothing. I was merely reminded."

"Of Helen's cooking?"

"We had a disagreement."

"Over her cooking? That's bloody sexist, Inspector. Is she going to sew buttons and darn socks for you next?"

Lynley returned his spectacles to their case, slipped the case into his pocket. He picked up his glass and considered the colour of the wine before he drank.

"I told her to decide," he said. "We move forward or we end it. I'm tired of begging and I'm finished with limbo."

"And did she decide?"

"I don't know. I haven't spoken to her since. I hadn't even thought of her, in fact, until just now. What do you think that means? Have I a chance of recovery when she breaks my heart?"

"We all recover when it comes to love."

"Do we?"

"Recover from sexual love? Romantic love? Yeah. But as far as the other goes, I don't think we ever recover from that." She paused as the waiter removed and replaced plates and cutlery. He poured more wine for Lynley, more mineral water for her. "He says he hated him, but I don't believe that. I think he killed him because he couldn't stand how much he loved him and how much it hurt to watch him choose Gabriella Patten over him. Because that's the way Jimmy would have seen it. That's the way kids always see these things. Not only as a rejection of their mums but as a rejection of themselves as well. Gabriella took his dad—"

"Fleming had been out of the house for years."

"But it was never permanent until now, was it? There was always hope. Now hope was dead. And to make things worse, to make the rejection feel even more complete, his dad was postponing Jimmy's birthday holiday. And why? To go to Gabriella."

"To end their relationship, according to Gabriella."

"But Jimmy didn't know that. He thought his dad was running out to Kent to boff her." Barbara lifted her glass of mineral water and pondered the scenario she'd created. "Wait. What if that's the key?" She asked the question more of herself than of him. Lynley waited cooperatively. Their second courses arrived. Fresh cheese was offered, Romano or Parmesan. Lynley chose the Romano. Barbara followed his lead. She tucked into her pasta, tomatoes, and beans. Not what she would have expected from the name. But not at all bad. She threw on some salt.

"He knew her," she said, twirling the *tagliatelle* somewhat inexpertly on the edge of her plate. The waiter had thoughtfully provided her with a large spoon, but she hadn't a clue how she was supposed to use it. "He saw her. He'd been round her, hadn't he? Sometimes with his dad. But other times . . . Other times suppose not. Dad would go off with the other two kids, leaving Jimmy with her. Because Jimmy was the hard nut, wasn't he? The other two might have been easy to win over, but Jimmy wasn't. So she'd play up to him. Fleming would even encourage her to do so. She was going to be the boy's step-mum one day. She'd want him to like her. Fleming'd want him to like her. It was important that he like her. She'd want him, in fact, to more than like her."

"Havers, you can't be suggesting she seduced that boy."

"Why not? You saw her yourself this morning."

"What I saw was that she had Mollison to win over and not a great deal of time to do it."

"D'you think that come-on was for Mollison's benefit? What about for yours? A little glimpse of what you were going to miss out on because you happened to be a cop on a case. But what if you weren't? Or what if you phoned her later this evening and said you needed to come round to talk and get a few more facts straight? D'you think she wouldn't like to test her power on you?'' Lynley slid the tines of a fork into a scampi. He ate without reply. "She likes to pull men, sir. Her husband told us, Mollison told us, she as much as told us herself. How could she have resisted the chance to pull Jimmy if the chance came along?''

"Frankly?'' Lynley asked.

"Frankly.''

"Because he's repellent. Unwashed, unhygienic, probably infested with body lice, and possibly a carrier of disease. Herpes, syphilis, gonorrhoea, warts, HIV. Gabriella Patten might enjoy exercising her sexual prowess over men, but she didn't strike me as entirely mindless. Her first concern in any situation would be taking excellent care of Gabriella Patten. We've heard that, Havers. From her husband, from Mrs. Whitelaw, from Mollison, from Gabriella herself.''

"But you're thinking of Jimmy *now*, Inspector. What about then? What about before? He can't have always been such a sleazo. It had to start somewhere.''

"And the loss of his father from the family isn't enough of a start for you?''

"Was it enough of a start for you? Or your brother?'' Barbara saw him lift his head quickly and knew that she'd gone too far. "Sorry. I was out of line there.'' She went back to her pasta. "He says he hated him. He says he killed him because he hated him because he was a bastard and deserved to die.''

"You don't see that as sufficient motive?''

"I'm just saying there's probably more to it and the more to it is probably Gabriella. She wouldn't have a clue how to win him over as his future step-mum, but she'd have plenty of tricks up her sleeve or down her blouse. So let's say she did it. Half because she gets a kick out of seducing a teenager. Half because it's the only way she can think to get Jimmy on her side. Only she gets him too much on her side. He wants in where his dad's been playing. He's in a lather of sexual jealousy and when he sees the chance, he pops off Dad and expects to have Gabriella for himself.''

"That doesn't take into account the fact that he thought Gabriella was in the cottage as well,'' Lynley pointed out.

"So he says. And he would do, wouldn't he? It would hardly do for us to know he was giving Dad the chop because he wanted in bed with his mum-to-be. But he *knew* his dad was there for a fact. He saw him through the kitchen window."

"Ardery hasn't given us his footprints by the window."

"So? He was in the garden."

"At the bottom of the garden."

"He was in the potting shed. He could have seen his father from there." Barbara paused in the act of twirling her pasta. She could see how difficult it would be to gain weight eating this sort of food every day. The effort to get it from plate to mouth was enormous. She evaluated the expression on Lynley's face. It was shuttered, too shuttered. She didn't like it. She said, "You're not backing away from the kid, are you? Come on. We've got a confession, Inspector."

"An incomplete confession."

"What did you expect on a first go with him?"

Lynley slid his plate towards the centre of the table. He glanced at the planter where the birds still waited hopefully. He threw them a palmful of crumbs.

"Inspector . . ."

"Wednesday night," Lynley said. "What did you do after work?"

"What did I . . . ? I don't know."

"Think about it. You left the Yard. Were you alone? With someone? Did you drive? Take the underground?"

She thought about it. "Winston and I went for a drink," she said. "The King's Arms."

"What did you have?"

"Lemonade."

"Nkata?"

"I don't know. Whatever he usually has."

"After that?"

"I went home. Had something to eat. Watched a film on the telly. Went to bed."

"Ah. Good. What film? What time did you watch it? When did it begin? When did it end?"

She frowned. "It must have been after the news."

"Which news? Which station?"

"Hell, I don't know."

"Who was in the film?"

"I didn't catch the credits. No one special. Except maybe one of the Redgraves, one of the younger ones. And that's only a maybe."

"What was it about?"

"Something to do with mining? I don't know exactly. I fell asleep."

"What was it called?"

"I don't remember."

"You watched a film and you don't remember the name, the plot, or any of the actors?" Lynley asked.

"Right."

"Astonishing."

She bristled at his tone, at its dual implication of inherent superiority and conciliatory understanding. "Why? Was I supposed to remember? What's this all about?"

Lynley nodded at the waiter to remove his plate. Barbara shovelled a last slithering forkful of *tagliatelle* into her mouth and waved her own plate off as well. The waiter prepared the table for their main courses, adding cutlery.

"Alibis," Lynley said. "Who has them. Who hasn't." He took another piece of *focaccia* and began to crumble it as he'd done with the first. Five more birds had joined the original six dancing along the edge of the planter. Lynley tossed them crumbs, oblivious of the fact that he wasn't endearing himself to either the other diners or the restaurant manager, who glowered at him from the doorway.

Their main courses arrived, and Lynley took up his knife and fork. But Barbara didn't give her food a glance, instead carrying on the discussion as steam rose from her plate in an aromatic plume. "You're completely daft and you know it, Inspector. We don't need to look at anyone's alibi. We've got the boy."

"I'm not convinced."

"So let's get to the bottom of him. Jimmy's given a confession. Let's run with it."

"An incomplete confession," Lynley reminded her.

"So let's get it complete. Let's pick the yob up again, drag him back to the Yard. Grill him. Have at him. Keep up the pressure till he tells the whole story from start to finish."

Lynley slid a wedge of *cinghiale* on to his fork. He gave his attention to the birds as he chewed. They were simultaneously patient and persistent, hopping from the junipers to the edge of the planter. Their presence alone bent his will to theirs. He threw them more crumbs. He watched them fall to. One of them captured a chunk of bread the size of a thumbnail and greedily flew off with it, perching on the drip course above a window across the street.

"You'll only encourage them," Barbara finally said. "They can fend for themselves, you know."

"Can they?" Lynley asked contemplatively.

He ate. He drank. Barbara waited. She knew he was sifting through the facts and the faces. There was little point in arguing with him further. Still, she felt compelled to add as calmly as she could, considering the strength of her feelings in the matter, "He was there, in Kent. We've got the fibres, the footprints, and the oil from the bike. We've got his dabs now and they're on their way to Ardery. All we need is the brand of that cigarette."

"And the truth," Lynley said.

"Jesus Christ, Inspector! What more do you want?"

Lynley nodded at her plate. "Your food's getting cold."

She looked down at it. Some kind of fowl in some kind of sauce. The fowl was crispy. The sauce was amber. She poked tentatively at the former with her fork and wondered what it was that she'd ordered.

"Duck," Lynley said, as if reading her mind. "With apricot sauce."

"At least it's not chicken."

"Decidedly not." He continued eating. Near them, other diners chatted. Waiters moved silently, pausing to light candles as the evening drew on. "I would have translated," he said.

"What?"

"The menu. You only needed to ask."

Barbara sliced into the duck. She'd never eaten duck before. The flesh was darker than she'd expected. "I like to take chances."

"When chances aren't necessary?"

"It's more fun that way. Spice of life and all. You know what I mean."

"But only in restaurants," he said.

"What?"

"Taking chances. Running a risk. Following your instincts."

She set her fork down. "So I'm Sergeant Plod. So there's room for that. Somebody has to use reason occasionally."

"I don't disagree."

"Then why are you avoiding Jimmy Cooper? What the bleeding hell's wrong with Jimmy Cooper?"

Once more he attended to his food. He checked the basket, obviously in a search for more bread to give to the birds, but they'd eaten it all. He drank his wine and, with a glance in the direction of the waiter, brought him hastily to their table to pour another glassful and disappear. That Lynley was using all this time to make a decision about the next direction they'd take was clear to Barbara. She schooled herself to hold her tongue, to keep to her place, and to accept what that decision was. When he spoke, she found it difficult to believe that she'd actually prevailed.

"Have him back at the Yard at ten tomorrow morning," Lynley said. "Make sure his solicitor's with him."

"Yes, sir."

"And tell the press office we're bringing in the same sixteen-year-old for a second go-round."

Barbara felt her jaw drop. She closed it abruptly. "The press office? But they'll let out the word and those flaming journalists—"

"Yes. That's right," Lynley said thoughtfully.

"Where's his shoes?" was the first question Jeannie Cooper asked when Mr. Friskin ushered Jimmy into the house. She asked it in a high tight voice because from the moment the Scotland Yard detectives had driven off with her son, her insides had begun to squash in on themselves and her hearing had faded in and out so that she could no longer gauge how she sounded. She'd frightened both Sharon and Stan, who'd first clung to her arms and then run from the sitting room when she shook them off violently, saying only, "No. No! *No!*" in an ever rising voice that they mistakenly believed was directed towards them. Stan had thudded up the stairs. Shar had flown into the back garden. Jeannie had left them both in whatever refuge they'd managed to find. She herself had paced.

The only positive action she'd taken in the first quarter of an hour after Jimmy's departure was to pick up the phone and ring the only person she knew who could possibly help them at this point. And while she hated to do it because Miriam Whitelaw was the well-spring of every drop of anguish Jeannie had experienced in the last six years since Mrs. Whitelaw had re-entered Kenny's life, she was also the single person Jeannie knew who could pull a solicitor out of the air at half past five on a Sunday afternoon. The only question was whether Miriam Whitelaw would consider doing so for Jimmy.

She had done, saying only, "Jean. My God," in a grief-stricken voice when Jeannie had first identified herself over the phone. "I can't believe . . ." Jeannie knew she couldn't do with Miriam's tears, with the thought of weeping and all it implied of the hair-tearing grief she could not feel, would not allow herself to feel, so she said abruptly, "They've taken Jim to Scotland Yard. I need a solicitor," and Miriam had provided one.

Now this solicitor stood before her, one step behind and to the left of Jimmy and she said again, "Where's his shoes? What of they done to his shoes?"

The Tesco's bag was dangling from her son's right hand, but it didn't bulge enough to contain the Doc Martens. She looked to his feet a second time, for no reason except to reassure herself that her eyes hadn't deceived her, that he wore only a pair of socks that might have been either grimy white or permanently grey.

Mr. Friskin—whom Jeannie had expected to be middle-aged, stoop-shouldered, charcoal-suited, and bald but who was actually young and lithe, with a bright floral tie pulled askew against his blue shirt and a mane of dark hair that swept off his face and down to his shoulders in the manner of a romance novel hero—answered for her son, but not the question she'd asked. He said, "Mrs. Cooper—"

"Ms."

"Sorry. Yes. Jim spoke to them before I arrived. He's given the police a confession."

Her vision went stark white, then black, like lightning struck in the room. Mr. Friskin kept talking about what would happen next and how Jimmy wasn't to step a foot outside this house or say a word to anyone not a member of the family without his solicitor right beside him. He said something about understandable duress and added the words *juvenile* and *intimidation* and went on with something about the requirements of the Judges Rules, but she didn't catch it all because she was wondering if she'd actually gone blind like that saint in the Bible except that he'd done just the reverse, hadn't he? Hadn't he been struck all at once with sight? She couldn't remember. It probably hadn't happened anyway. The Bible was mostly nonsense.

From the kitchen a chair scraped against the lino and Jeannie knew that her brother, who had no doubt listened to every word Mr. Friskin had uttered, was lumbering to his feet. Hearing this, she regretted having rung her parents' flat the second hour into Jimmy's visit to Scotland Yard. She'd smoked, she'd paced, she'd gone to the kitchen window and watched Shar huddle like a beggar at the base of the fractured concrete bird bath outside, she'd listened to Stan being sick three times in the loo, and she'd finally broken as much as she would allow herself to break.

She hadn't spoken to either of her parents because their love for Kenny was a frightening thing and in their eyes it was always her fault that Kenny had ever asked in the first place for time and space from his marriage in order to sort out a life which they believed didn't need any sorting. So she'd asked for Der and he'd come in a flash, spewing the exact amount of rage, disbelief, and vows for revenge that she needed to hear someone make against the sodding police.

Her vision cleared as Der said, "What? You gone loony, Jim? You talked to them blighters?"

Jeannie said, "Der."

Der said, "Oy! I thought you was supposed to be there to shut up his mug," to Mr. Friskin. "I'n't that the point of having a poncey mouthpiece in the first place? How d'you earn your lolly?"

Obviously used to dealing with clients in emotional twists, Mr. Friskin explained that Jimmy had apparently wanted to talk. He had even talked freely, it seemed, from Mr. Friskin's insistence on monitoring the tape the police had made of the proceedings. There had been no coercion whatsoever evident—

"You dimwit, Jim!" Der lunged into the sitting room. "You squawked to those wankers on *tape?*"

Jimmy said nothing. He stood in front of Mr. Friskin like his backbone was slowly melting. His head hung on his neck, his stomach was a cave.

Der said, "Oy! I'm talking to you, dickhead."

Jeannie said, "Jim, I told you. I *told* you. Why'nt you listen to me?"

Mr. Friskin said, "Ms. Cooper, believe me. It's early yet," to which Der roared, "Early! I'll show you what's early. You were s'posed to keep his gob shut tight and now we hear he's spilled his whole guts. What're you good for, anyways?" He swung on Jeannie. "What's the matter with you, Pook? Where'd you find this ponce? And *you*—" this to Jimmy, pushing past his sister to loom over the boy, "what of you got in your head? Beans? Fish guts? What? You don't talk to cops. You don't ever talk to cops. What'd they scare you with, shitface? Borstal? The Scrubs?''

Jimmy didn't even look like a person, Jeannie thought. He looked like a dirty blow-up doll with the air seeping out of him from a pin prick somewhere. He just stood there mute and let himself be battered, like he knew it would end sooner if he didn't reply.

She said, "You eat something, Jim?"

Der said, "Eat? Eat? Eat?" each time louder. "He i'n't going to eat till we get some answers. And we'll get them right now." He grabbed the boy's arm. Jimmy whipped forward like a doll filled with straw. Jeannie saw the heavy muscles on her brother's arm flex. "Talk to us, yobbo." Der peered into Jimmy's face. "Talk to us like you talked to the cops. Talk now and talk good."

"This isn't accomplishing anything," Mr. Friskin said. "The boy's been through an ordeal that most adults have difficulty recovering from."

"I'll show *you* a deal," Derrick snarled, flipping his head up into Mr. Friskin's face.

The solicitor didn't so much as flinch. He said quietly and with utterly polite reason, "Ms. Cooper, make a decision for us, please. Who would you like to handle your son's case?"

Jeannie said, "Der," in admonishment. "Let Jim be. Mr. Friskin knows what's best."

Derrick dropped Jimmy's arm like it was made of slime. "Stupid bugger," he said. Spittle from the first word hit Jimmy's cheek. The boy winced, but he didn't lift a hand to wipe the spittle away.

Jeannie said to her brother, "Go on up to Stan. He's been puking like a drunk since Jimmy went off." Out of the corner of her eye, she saw her older son raise his head at that, but he'd lowered it again by the time she turned to him.

Der said, "Yeah. Right," and cast a sneer at both Jimmy and Mr. Friskin before he trudged up the stairs, shouting, "Stan! Oy! You still got your head in the toilet?"

Jeannie said, "Sorry," to Mr. Friskin. "Der doesn't always think before he blows off."

Mr. Friskin made noises like it was an everyday thing to have the uncle of a suspect breathing in his face like a bull that was going for the matador's cape. He explained that Jimmy had handed over his Doc Martens at the request of the police, that he'd allowed himself to be finger-printed and photographed, that he'd given them several strands of his hair.

"Hair?" Jeannie's eyes went to the matted mess on her son's head.

"They're either matching it to samples from within the cottage or using it for DNA typing. If it's the first, their specialists can do it within hours. If it's the second, we've bought ourselves a few weeks."

"What's it all mean?"

They were building a case, Mr. Friskin told her. They didn't have a complete confession yet.

"But they got enough?"

"To hold him? To charge him?" Mr. Friskin nodded. "If they want to."

"Then why'd they let him go? Is that the end of it, then?"

No, Mr. Friskin told her. That wasn't the end. They had something up their sleeves. She could rest assured that they would be back. But when that happened, he'd be with Jimmy. There was no chance the police would talk to the boy alone again.

He said, "Have you any questions, Jim?" and when Jimmy slung his head to one side in place of reply, Mr. Friskin handed Jeannie his card, said, "Try not to worry, Ms. Cooper," and left them.

When the door closed behind him, Jeannie said, "Jim?" She reached for the Tesco's bag and took it, laying it on the coffee table with deliberate care as if it contained pieces of hand-blown glass. Jimmy stayed where he was, weight on one hip, right arm moving to clasp left elbow. His toes curled against the floor like his feet were cold. "Want your slippers?" she asked him. He lifted a shoulder and dropped it. "I'll heat you some soup. I got tomato with rice, Jim. You come with me."

She expected resistance, but he followed her into the kitchen. He'd just sat at the table when the back door opened with a screech and Shar came in. She closed the door and stood with her back to it, hands reaching behind her to hold on to the knob. Her nose was red and her specs were smudged in big half circles along the bottom. She gazed at her brother, wide eyed and wordless. She gulped and Jeannie saw her lips quivering, saw her mouth the word *Dad* but fail to say it. Jeannie nodded her head in the direction of the stairway. Shar looked as if she meant to disobey, but at the final moment when a sob burst from her, she fled the kitchen and hurtled up the stairs.

Jimmy slumped in his chair. Jeannie opened the tin of soup and dumped it into a pan. She set the pan on the cooker, fumbled about with a knob, and failed on two attempts to produce the required flame. She muttered, "Damn." She knew that this moment with her son was precious. She understood that the slightest glitch in moving this precious moment forward might be all that was required to demolish it entirely. And it couldn't be demolished. Not until she knew.

She heard him stir. The chair pushed on the lino. She said hastily, "Got to get a new cooker sometime, huh?" to try to keep him with her. And, "It'll be ready in a tick now, Jim," when she thought he would leave. But instead of leaving, he went to a drawer. He brought out a box of matches. He lit one, held it to the burner, and produced the flame. The match burnt down between his fingers like it had done on Friday night. Only unlike Friday night, she was closer to him, so when the flame sizzled down the wood to his skin, she was near enough to blow it out.

He was taller than her now, she realised. Soon he'd be as tall as his dad. It didn't seem that long ago that she'd been able to look down into his upturned face, even less long ago that they were eye to eye. And now she lifted her chin to see him. He was only part boy and larger part man.

"Cops didn't hurt you?" she asked. "They didn't mess you about?" He shook his head. He turned to go but she grasped his wrist. He tried to pull away. She held firm.

Two days of agonising were enough, she decided. Two days of inwardly saying, *No I won't, no I can't,* had gained her no information, no understanding, and more than that, no peace of mind. She thought, How did I lose you, Jimmy? Where? When? I wanted to be strong for all of us, but I only ended up pushing you away when you needed me. I thought if I showed how much I could take the hurts of what happened and not fall to bits, the three of you'd learn to take the hurts as well. But that's not how it was, was it, Jimmy? That's not how it is.

And because she knew that she'd finally reached a degree of understanding she'd not had before, she found the courage. "Tell me what you told the police," she said.

His face looked like it hardened, round the eyes first, then the mouth and the jaw. He didn't attempt to pull away again, but he directed his attention from her to the wall above the cooker where for years had hung a framed piece of needlepoint. It was faded now and spotted with grease, but you could still read the words that scrolled across the green-and-white background of cricketers and wicket: *The match ain't over when the over is over*, a joke-present for Kenny from his mother-in-law. Jeannie realised she should have removed it long ago.

"Tell me," she said. "Talk to me, Jimmy. I did things wrong. But I did them for the best. You got to know that, son. And you got to know that I love you. Always. You got to talk to me now. I got to know about you and Wednesday night."

He shuddered, so strong it felt like a spasm went from his shoulders down to his toes. Tentatively, she firmed her grip on his wrist. He didn't pull away a second time. She moved her hand from his wrist, to his arm, to his shoulder. She ventured a touch against his hair.

"You tell me," she said. "You talk to me, son." And then she added what she had to add but didn't believe for a moment and didn't know how to begin to accomplish, "I won't let nothing hurt you, Jim. We'll get through this somehow. But I need to know what you told them."

She waited for him to ask the logical question: *Why?* But he didn't. The tomato soup sent up wafts of fragrance from the cooker, and she stirred it without looking, her eyes fixed on her son. Fear, knowledge, disbelief, and denial all thrashed inside her like food gone bad, but she tried to keep them from showing on her face and from echoing in the tone of her voice.

"When I was fourteen, I first started messing about with your dad," she said. "I wanted to be like my sisters and they messed about with blokes regular enough so I thought why shouldn't I do the same, I'm as good as them any day of the week." Jimmy kept his gaze on the needle-point. Jeannie stirred the soup and went on. "We had our fun, we did, only my dad found out because your auntie Lynn told him. So Dad took off his belt one night when I got home from messing with Kenny and he made me take off every stitch I was wearing and he beat me proper while the family watched. I didn't cry. But I hated him. I wanted him dead. I would of been glad if he'd dropped on the spot. Maybe I would of done something myself to help him along."

She reached for a bowl from the cupboard. She ventured a glance at her son as she ladled soup from the pot into the bowl. "Smells good, this. You want toast with it, Jim?"

His expression was something between wary and confused. She wasn't describing it like she wanted to, that mix of rage and humiliation that made her for a single blind instant will her father to die a thousand times. Jimmy didn't understand. Perhaps because their rages were different, hers a brief firestorm, his a single smouldering coal that burned on and on.

She took the soup to the table. She poured him milk. She made him toast. She laid the meal out and gestured him to it. He stayed where he was by the cooker.

She made the only remark there was left to make, one she didn't believe, but one she had to persuade him to accept if she was ever to know the truth. "What matters is what's left of us," she said. "You and me, Stan and Shar. That's how it is, Jim."

He looked from her to the soup. She motioned to the bowl welcomingly and sat at the table herself, in a place that would put her opposite him should he decide to join her. He wiped his hands along the seams of his blue jeans. His fingers curled.

"Bastard," he said conversationally. "He started fucking her last October, and she kept him running round proper, she did. He said they were just friends because she was married to that rich bloke, but I knew, didn't I? Shar would ask him when he was coming home, and he'd say in a while, in a month or two, when I know who I am, when I know how things are. He'd say don't you worry about nothing, luv. But all the time, he meant to have her when he could. He'd put his hand on her bum when he thought no one was looking. If he hugged her, she'd rub up against his cock. And all the time you could tell what they really wanted which was for us to be gone so that they could do it."

Jeannie wanted to stop up her ears. This wasn't the recitation she had been seeking. But she forced herself to listen. She kept her face blank and said to herself that she didn't care. She already knew, didn't she, and this portion of the truth could not touch her further.

"He wasn't Dad any longer," Jimmy said. "He was only in a twist about her. She'd phone and he'd be off to sniff her up. She'd say leave me be, Ken, and he'd punch his fist into walls. She'd say I need or I want and he'd rush right there, doing whatever'd make her happy. And when he was through with her, he'd—" Jimmy stopped himself but kept staring at the soup, as if he saw the history of the tired affair playing out in the bowl.

"And when he was through with her . . ." Jeannie spoke past the spear-pain that she'd grown to know well.

Her son gave a derisive snort. "You know, Mum." He finally came across the kitchen and sat at the table, opposite her. "He was a liar. He was a bastard. And a bleeding cheat." He dipped his spoon into the soup. He held it at the height of his chin. He met her eyes for the first time since coming home. "And you wanted him dead. You wanted him dead more 'n anything, Mum. We both know that, don't we?"

OLIVIA

From where I'm sitting, I can see the glow of Chris's reading light. I can hear him turn pages every so often. He ought to have gone to bed long ago, but he's reading in his room, waiting for me to finish my writing. The dogs are with him. I can hear Toast snoring. Beans is chewing on a rawhide bone. Panda came in to keep me company half an hour ago. She started off in my lap, but now she's curled on the dresser in her special place—on top of the day's post, which she has rearranged to her liking. She pretends to be asleep, but she isn't fooling me. Every time I flip another sheet of the pad, her ears turn my way like radar.

I lift the mug from which I drank my Gunpowder tea, and I examine the speckling of leaves that managed to escape the strainer. They've arranged themselves into a pattern that resembles a rainbow overhung with a bolt of lightning. I touch my pencil tip to the lightning to straighten it, and I wonder what a fortune teller would make of such a combination of auspicious and inauspicious signs.

Last week when Max and I were playing poker—using dog kibble to make our wagers—he set his cards facedown on the table, leaned back in his chair, and running his hand over his bald pate, said, "It's a dunghill, girlie. No doubt about that."

"Hmm. Precisely."

"But there are distinct advantages to a dunghill, you know."

"Which I imagine you're about to reveal."

"Used properly, dung helps flowers grow."

"As does bat guano, but I'd rather not roll around in it."

"Not to mention crops. It enriches the soil from which life springs."

"I'll treasure that thought." I moved my cards about, as if a new arrangement would change the single pair of fours to something better.

"Knowing when, girlie. Have you thought about the power of knowing when?"

I said, throwing two kibbles between us for my ante, "I don't know when. I know how. There's a difference."

"But you've more idea than most."

"What kind of satisfaction is there supposed to be in that? I'd be glad to trade knowledge for ignorance and bliss."

"What would you do differently, if you were ignorant like the rest of us?"

I fanned out my cards and wondered about the statistical possibility of rejecting three of them and ending up with a full house. Slim to none, I decided. I discarded. Max dealt. I rearranged. I decided to bluff. I flicked six more kibbles onto the table between us, saying, "Okay, baby. Let's play."

"Well?" he asked. "What would you do? If you were ignorant like the rest of us."

"Nothing," I said. "I'd still be here. But things would be different because I could compete."

"With Chris? Why in God's name would you ever feel the need—"

"Not with Chris. With her."

Max puffed out his lips. He picked up his cards. He rearranged them. At last he looked over the tops of them at me, his single eye unusually bright. He had the kindness not to feign lack of knowledge. "I'm sorry," he said. "I didn't know you were aware. He doesn't mean to be cruel."

"He isn't being cruel. He's being discreet. He's never even mentioned her name."

"Chris cares for you, girlie."

I shot him a look that said, "Wither, you berk."

He said, "You know I'm speaking the truth."

"That doesn't exactly make despair go down easier. Chris cares for the animals as well."

Max and I looked long and hard at each other. I could tell what he was thinking. If he'd spoken the truth, so had I.

I never thought it would be this way. I thought I'd stop wanting. I thought I'd give up. I thought I'd say, "Well, that's that, isn't it," and accept this rotten poker hand without trying to shift the cards. But I've managed nothing more than hiding hunger and anger. I realise this is more than I would have managed at one time, but it's small enough cause for celebration.

One stumble. That's what started the descent. One minor stumble just a year ago as I was getting out of the mini-van. At first I put it down to being in a hurry. I opened the van door, took a step, and stumbled trying to negotiate the distance from the level of the street to the height of the kerb. Before I realised what had happened, I was sprawled on the pavement with a cut on my chin, tasting blood where my teeth had sunk into my lip. Beans was sniffing my hair in some concern, and Toast was nosing through the oranges that had rolled from my grocery bag into the gutter.

I thought, "Clumsy oaf," and pushed myself to my knees. Everything felt bruised but nothing felt broken. I pressed the arm of my jersey to my chin, brought it away streaked with blood, and said, "Damn." I gathered up the oranges, told the dogs to come along, and picked my way down the steps to the tow path along the canal.

When I was crossing the workroom that night with the dogs leaping round, eager for their nighttime run, Chris said, "What've you done to yourself, Livie?"

"Done?"

"You're limping."

I'd taken a fall, I told him. It was nothing much. I must have pulled a muscle.

"You won't want to run, then. Have a rest. I'll take the dogs out when I finish here."

"I can cope."

"You're sure?"

"I wouldn't say so if I wasn't."

I climbed the stairs and went out. I spent a few minutes gingerly stretching. Nothing actually hurt, which seemed rather odd, because if I'd pulled a muscle, torn a ligament, or broken a bone, I'd feel it, wouldn't I? I felt nothing, other than the limp itself when it occurred each time I tried to move my right leg.

I must have looked like Toast that night, attempting to jog along the canal with the dogs in front of me. All I could manage was the short distance to the bridge. When the dogs scrambled up the steps to head as usual down Maida Avenue towards Lisson Grove and the Grand Union Canal, I called them back. They hesitated, clearly confused, caught between tradition and cooperation.

"Come on, you two," I said. "Not tonight."

And not any night that succeeded it. The next day my right foot wasn't working properly. I was helping the zoo's ultrasound team move their equipment into a tapir's enclosure where they were going to monitor her pregnancy. I had the bucket of apples and carrots. The team had the trolley with the machine. One of them said to me, "What's gone wrong with you, Livie?" which was the first indication I had that I was dragging my foot behind me in a movement that looked like step-shuffle-bob-step.

What caused me disquiet was the fact that both times—with the limp and with the foot dragging—I'd not realised I was doing it.

"Could be a pinched nerve," Chris said that night. "That'd cut off feeling." He took my foot in his hand and turned it right and left.

I watched his fingers probe. "Wouldn't it feel worse if it was nerves? Wouldn't it tingle or ache or something?"

He lowered my foot to the floor. "Could be something else."

"What?"

"We'll speak to Max, shall we?"

Max tapped against the sole and the ball of my foot. He ran a wheel with tiny serrations along my flesh and asked me to describe what I felt. He pulled at his nose and knocked his index finger against his chin. He suggested we take ourselves to a doctor.

He said, "How long has it been like this?"

I said, "Nearly a week."

He talked about Harley Street, a specialist there, and the need to have some definitive answers.

"What is it?" I asked. "You know, don't you? You don't want to say. God, is it cancer? D'you think I've got a tumour?"

"A vet has no real expertise in human disease, girlie."

I said, "Disease. *Disease*. What is it?"

He said he didn't know. He said it looked to him like something might be affecting my neurons.

I recalled Chris's amateur diagnosis. "Pinched nerve?"

Chris murmured, "Central nervous system, Livie."

The walls seemed to shimmy in my direction. "What?" I asked. "Central nervous system? What?"

Max said, "The neurons are cells: body, axon, and dendrites. They conduct impulses to the brain. If they're—"

"A brain tumour?" I grasped his arm. "Max, d'you think I've got a brain tumour?"

He squeezed my hand. "What you've got is a case of the panics," he said. "You need to have some tests and put your mind at ease. Now, what about that game of chess we left unfinished, Christopher?"

Max sounded breezy but when he left that night, I heard him talking to Chris on the tow path. I couldn't make out any of the words, just the single time he said my name. When Chris came back inside to fetch the dogs for their final run, I said, "He knows what the problem is, doesn't he? He knows it's serious. Why won't he tell me? I heard him talking about me. I heard him tell you. You tell me, Chris. Because if you don't—"

Chris came to my chair and held my head against his stomach for a moment, his hand warm against my ear. He jiggled me playfully. "Hedgehog," he said. "You're getting too prickly. What he said was that he can ring some friends to ring some friends to get you in quick to see this Harley Street bloke. I told him to go ahead and make the calls. I think that's best. Okay?"

I pulled away. "Look at me, Chris."

"What?" His face was composed.

"He told you something else."

"What makes you think that?"

"Because he called me Olivia."

Chris shook his head in exasperation. He tilted mine. He bent and brushed a kiss against my lips. He'd never kissed me before. He's never kissed me since. The dry, fleeting pressure of his mouth against mine told me more than I wanted to know.

I began the first round of visiting doctors and taking tests. They started with the simple things: blood and urine. They moved on to general X-rays. From there, I was treated to the science fiction experience of sliding into what looked like a futuristic iron lung for an MRI. After studying the results—with me sitting in a chair across the desk in an office so richly panelled it looked like a movie set and Chris waiting in reception because I didn't want him to be there when I heard the worst—the doctor said only, "We're going to have to do a spinal tap. When shall I arrange it?"

"Why? Why don't you know now? Why can't you tell me? I don't want any more tests. And least of all that. It's horrible, isn't it? I know what it's like. The needles and the fluid. I don't want it. Nothing more."

He tapped his fingers together, resting his hands on the ever-growing file of my test results. "I'm sorry," he said. "It's necessary."

"But what do you *think?*"

"That you're going to have to have this test. And then we'll see how everything adds up."

People with money probably have this sort of test in some posh private hospital with flowers in the corridors, carpet on the floor, and music playing. I had it courtesy of the National Health. A medical student performed it, which didn't give me a lot of confidence perhaps because of the fact that his supervisor was standing over him issuing instructions in medical mumbo jumbo that included incisive questions such as, "Excuse me, but exactly which lumbar vertebra are you targetting there, Harris?" Afterwards, I lay in the required position—flat on my back, head downwards—and tried to ignore the rapid pulse that seemed to beat along my spine, and tried to ignore the sense of foreboding I'd had in bed this very morning when the muscles in my right leg had begun to vibrate as if they had a will of their own.

I put it down to nerves.

The final test occurred several days later, in the doctor's examining room. There, seating me on a table that was covered with leather as soft as the centre of a baby's palm, he put his hand on the ball of my right foot.

"Push," he said.

I did what I could.

"Push again."

I did.

He held out his hands for my own. "Push."

"This isn't about my hands."

"Push."

I did.

He nodded, made some notations on the papers in my file, nodded again. He said, "Come with me," and took me back to his office. He disappeared. He returned with Chris.

I felt my hackles rise and said, "What's this?" but instead of answering, he gestured not to the chairs opposite his desk but to a sofa that stood beneath a darkly hued painting of a country scene: enormous hills, a river, hulking trees, and a girl with a leafy switch herding cows. Among all the details of that late morning in Harley Street, how odd it is that I still remember that painting. I only glanced at it once.

He drew a wingback chair over to join us. He brought along my file although he didn't refer to it. He sat, placed the file on his lap, and poured some water from a decanter on the coffee table between us. He held the decanter up, offering. Chris said no. I was parched and said yes.

"It appears to be a disorder called amyotrophic lateral sclerosis," the doctor said.

Tension left me like water breaking through a dike. A disorder. Hallelujah. A disorder. A *disorder*. No disease after all. Not a tumour. Not a cancer. Thank God. Thank God.

Next to me on the sofa, Chris stirred and leaned forward. "Amyo—what?"

"Amyotrophic lateral sclerosis. It's a disorder affecting the motor neurons. It's usually shortened to ALS."

"What do I take for it?" I asked.

"Nothing."

"Nothing?"

"There are no drugs available, I'm afraid."

"Oh. Well, I s'pose there wouldn't be. Not for a disorder. What do I do to take care of it, then? Exercise? Physical therapy?"

The doctor ran his fingers along the edge of the file as if to straighten papers inside that were already perfectly lined up together. "Actually, there is nothing you can do," he said.

"You mean I'm going to limp and twitch for the rest of my life."

"No," he said, "you won't do that."

There was something in his voice that made my stomach push my breakfast in the direction of my throat. I tasted the nasty flavour of bile. There was a window just next to the sofa, and through the translucent curtains I could see the shape of a tree, still bare-branched although it was late April. Plane tree, I thought needlessly, they always take the longest to leaf, no abandoned bird nests in it, how nice it would be to climb in summer, I never had a tree house, I remember the conkers growing at the side of the stream in Kent . . . and playing conkers, with the chestnut whistling like a cowboy's lariat above my head.

"I'm terribly sorry to tell you this," the doctor said, "but it's—"

"I don't want to know."

"Livie." Chris reached for my hand. I pushed him off.

"I'm afraid it's progressive," the doctor said.

I could tell he was watching me, but I was watching the tree.

It's a disorder that affects the spinal cord, he said slowly so that I would understand, and the lower brain stem, and the large motor neurons of the cerebral cortex. It results in the progressive degeneration of motor neurons as well as the progressive weakening and ultimate wasting of muscles.

"You don't know I've got it," I said.. "You can't be sure."

I could seek a second opinion, he told me. In fact, he suggested I do so. He went on to talk about the evidence he'd gathered: the results of the spinal tap, the general loss of muscle tone, the weakness of my muscular response. He said the disorder usually affects the hands first, moving up the forearms and the shoulders and attacking the lower extremities later. In my case, however, it seemed to be proceeding in the opposite direction.

"So I could have something else," I pointed out. "So you can't be sure, can you?"

He agreed that no medical science was ever exact. But then he said, "Let me ask you this. Have you had any fibrillation of the muscles in your leg?"

"Fib—what?"

"Rapid twitching. Vibrations."

I turned back to the window. We'd put the conkers on strings, we'd swung them in the air, the sound they'd made was *whssst . . . whssst . . . whssst*, we'd pretended to be American cowboys, we'd lassoed calves with conkers instead of with ropes.

"Livie?" Chris said. "Have your muscles—"

"It doesn't mean anything. And anyway, I can beat it. I can get cured. I need to exercise more."

So that's what I did at first. Rapid walking, climbing stairs, lifting weights. I thought, Muscular weakness is all it is. I'll pull through this. I've pulled through everything else, haven't I? Nothing's got me down for long, and this won't, either.

I continued to go on assaults, fired by fear and anger. I would prove them wrong, I told myself. I would make my body perform like a machine.

For five months Chris allowed me to maintain my position as a liberator until the first night I slowed the unit down. Then he moved me to sentry, saying, "No arguments, Livie," when I shouted, "You can't! You're making me a laughing stock! You aren't giving me a chance to build back my strength. I want to be in, with you, with the rest. *Chris!*" He said I needed to face the facts. I said I'd show him facts, I would, and I took myself off to the teaching hospital to gather them through another round of tests.

The results were the same. The atmosphere in which I received them was different. No posh office this time, but a cubicle off a busy corridor down which trolleys were rolled with grim-reaper frequency. When the doctor shut the door, turned her chair to face me, and sat with her knees practically touching mine, I knew.

She dwelt upon what bright spots there were, although she called ALS a disease and did not use the more palatable word, *disorder*. She said my condition would worsen steadily, but slowly, *slowly*, she stressed. My muscles would first become weak, then they would atrophy. As the nerve cells in the brain and spinal cord degenerated, they would begin sending irregular impulses to the muscles in my arms and legs, which would fibrillate. The disease would progress from my feet and legs, from my hands and arms, inward, until I was completely paralysed. However, she stressed in her motherly voice, I would always keep control of my bladder and sphincter. And my intelligence and awareness would never be affected, even in the terminal stages of the disease when it advanced to my lungs and caused them to atrophy as well.

"You mean I'll know exactly how disgusting I am," I said.

She said, placing the tips of her fingers on my kneecap, "You know, Olivia, I seriously doubt Stephen Hawking thinks of himself as disgusting. You know who he is, don't you?"

"Stephen Hawking? What's he got to do with . . . ." I backed my chair away. I'd seen him in newspapers. I'd seen him on the telly. The electric wheelchair, the attendants, the computerised voice. "That's ALS?" I said.

The doctor said, "Yes. Motor Neuron Disease. It's marvellous to think how he's defied the odds all these years. Anything's possible and you mustn't forget it."

"Possible? What?"

"To live. The progress of this disease is generally eighteen months to seven years. Tell Hawking that. He's survived more than thirty."

"But . . . like that. In a chair. Hooked up . . . I can't. I don't want—"

"You'll astonish yourself with what you want and what you can do. Wait and see."

I had to leave Chris once I knew the worst. I wouldn't be able to hold my own round the barge, and I didn't intend to stay on and become a charity case. I went back to Little Venice and starting shoving my things in rucksacks. I'd go back to Earl's Court and find a bed-sit. I'd keep my job in the zoo as long as I could and once I couldn't manage that, there'd be something else. Did a bloke care if he was screwing a tart whose legs couldn't lock round his arse any longer? whose feet couldn't walk in those five-inch heels? Whatever happened to Archie and his whips and his leather? It'd been several years. Would he still like it if his Mary Immaculate smacked him into an ecstatic frenzy while she was under a sentence of death? Would he like it better, in fact, if he knew? We would see.

I was writing Chris a note at the table in the galley when he came home. He said, "Got a sizable project in Fulham that should set us up properly for a while. One of those mansion flats. You should see the rooms, Livie. They're . . ." He paused at the galley door. He lowered a roll of sketches to the table. "What's this, then?" He straddled a chair and touched his foot to one of my rucksacks. "You taking in laundry or something?"

"I'm clearing off," I said.

"Why?"

"It's time. We're going separate ways. Have been for ages. No use keeping the corpse unburied till it rots. You know." I stabbed a full stop onto the last sentence I was writing and poked the pencil among the others in their new potatoes tin. I shoved the note his way and pushed myself to my feet.

He said, "So it's true."

I jerked the first rucksack onto my shoulders. "What?"

"ALS."

"What if it is?"

"You must have been told today. That's why . . . this." He read the note. He folded it carefully. "You've misspelled *inevitable*. It's got an *a* in it."

"Whatever." I scooped up the second rucksack. *"A* or *i* don't change the facts, do they? A bloke and a girl can't live together like this without things falling apart eventually."

"Inevitable was what you said in the note."

"You've got your work and I've got—"

"ALS. That's why you're clearing off." He put the note in his pocket. "Odd, Livie. I never saw you for a quitter."

"I'm not quitting anything. I'm just leaving. This isn't about ALS. It's about you and me. What I want. What you want. Who I am. Who you are. It's not going to work."

"It's been working for more than four years."

"Not for me it hasn't. It's . . ." I hooked one arm into the second rucksack and one arm into the third. I caught sight of my reflection in the galley window. I looked like a hunchback with saddlebags. "Listen, it's not normal, living like this. You and me. It's freaky. Like being in a sideshow. Come see the celibates. I feel like I'm in a convent or something. It isn't life, this. I can't cope with it, okay?"

He used his fingers to count off the points as he responded. "Freaky. Sideshow. Celibate. Convent. Have you ever read *Hamlet?"*

"What's *Hamlet* got to do with the price of cheese?"

"Someone says something about protesting too much."

"I'm not protesting a flaming thing."

"Laying out too many arguments or denials," he explained. "And they don't make sense. Especially when one considers the fact that you've never been celibate for more than a week."

"That's a rotten lie!" I dropped the rucksacks from my arms. I heard the click of dog nails against the linoleum as Beans came in from the workroom to give the sacks a sniff-over.

"Is it?" Chris reached for an apple from a bowl on the dresser and polished it idly against his worn flannel shirt. "What about the zoo?"

"What *about* the zoo?"

"You've been there—what is it?—nearly two years? How many of those blokes have you done it with?"

I felt the heat surge into my face. "You've got some cheek."

"So you haven't been celibate. So we can rest that argument. And the one about the convent as well."

I shook off the third rucksack and dropped it with the others. Beans thrust his nose beneath the rucksack's flap. He made a sound like *blubbersnarf* as he found something to his liking. I pushed him away. "You listen," I began, "and you listen good. There's nothing wrong with liking sex. There's nothing wrong with wanting it. I like it and I want it and—"

"Which leaves us with sideshow and freak," he said.

My mouth gaped. I snapped it shut.

"Don't you agree?" he asked. "We're using the process of elimination here, Livie."

"You calling me a freak?"

"You said celibate, convent, sideshow, and freak. We've dismissed the first two. Now we're examining the others. We're looking for the truth."

"Well, I'll give you truth, Mr. Shrivelcock Faraday. When I meet a bloke who likes it like I do and wants it as well, then we do it. We have a good time. And if you want to condemn me for something as natural as breathing, then go ahead and condemn and enjoy yourself. But you'll have to do your judging without an audience because I'm sick to death of your holier-than-thou's, so I'm clearing out."

"Because you can't abide living with a freak?"

"Hallelujah. The lad's finally got it right."

"Or because you're afraid that you'll become one yourself and end up discovering that *I* can't abide it?"

I countered with a laugh. "No chance of that. There's nothing wrong with me. We established that. I'm one hundred percent woman who likes having it off with one hundred percent man. That's been the case from the first, and I'm not ashamed to admit it to anyone."

He bit into his apple. Toast showed up and put his nose on Chris's knee. Beans nudged one of my rucksacks along the floor.

"Good rebuttal if I was referring to sex," Chris said. "But as I'm not, you've lost the advantage."

"This isn't about ALS," I said patiently. "This is you and me. And our differences."

"Part of which is ALS, as you'll no doubt agree."

"Oh balls." I waved him off. I squatted to fasten the buckle of the rucksack where Beans had done his exploring. "Believe what you want. Whatever goes easier on your ego, okay?"

"You're projecting, Livie."

"What's that supposed to mean?"

"That it's a far sight easier on your ego to leave now, rather than run the risk of seeing what happens between us when the disease starts getting worse."

I leapt, with a stumble, back to my feet. "It's not a disease. It's a bloody disorder."

He turned his apple in his fingers, three bites taken from it. I saw he'd eaten his way into a bruise. The pith was mud-coloured. It looked inedible. He took a bite directly from the damaged spot. I shuddered. He chewed.

"Why don't you give me a chance?" he asked.

"To what?"

"Prove myself. Be your friend."

"Oh please. Don't get smarmy. That makes my skin crawl." I wrestled into the straps of the rucksacks again. I went to the table where my shoulder bag lay, spilling its contents. I shoved them inside. "Play-act at sainthood with someone else," I said. "Go back to Earl's Court. Find yourself another tart. But leave me alone." I began to pull the shoulder bag from the table. He leaned forward and circled his fingers round my arm.

"You still don't get it, do you?"

I tried to jerk away but he held me firm. "What?"

"Sometimes people love each other just to love each other, Livie."

"And sometimes people go parched from spitting at the moon."

"Hasn't anyone ever loved you without expectation? Without demanding something in return?"

I pulled away from him but still I couldn't loosen his grip. My flesh would bruise where his fingers held me. I'd find their marks in the morning.

"I love you," he said. "I admit it's not the way you want to be loved. It's not the way you think of men and women loving and being together. But it's love all the same. It's real and it's there. Most of all, it's there. And the way I see it, that kind of love is enough to get us through. Which is a far sight more than you can expect to get from some bloke you find on the street."

He released me. I raised my arm to my breasts, held it between them. I rubbed where his fingers had been. I stared at him, my back beginning to ache with the burden of the rucksacks, the muscles in my right leg beginning to twitch. He went back to his apple, finished it off in three bites. He let Toast sniff the core and reject it before he tossed it across the galley and into the sink.

"I don't want you to leave," he said. "You challenge me. You get on my nerves. You make me better than I am."

I walked to the sink. I fished out his apple core. I threw it in the rubbish.

"Livie. I want you to stay."

Through the window I could see the street lamps casting their lights onto the water of the pool. In the floating ovals of illumination, the trees from Browning's Island were sketched. I looked at my watch. It was nearly eight. By the time I battled my way to Earl's Court, it would be almost nine. My right leg was beginning to quake.

"I'll be like a rag doll," I mumbled. "Like an overcooked marrow with arms and legs."

"Would you walk out if it was me?"

"I don't know."

"I do."

I heard him get up from the table and cross the galley. He removed the rucksacks from my body. He dropped them to the floor. He put his arm round my shoulders. He put his mouth against my hair.

"The love's different," he said, "but the fact of it's the same."

So I stayed. I kept up my programme of exercise and weight-lifting. I saw healers who suggested that I was suffering from a cyst, developing a mass, failing to mobilise energy, reacting to a negative atmosphere. When in the first year, the disease hadn't progressed beyond my legs, I told myself that, like Stephen Hawking, I was going to beat the odds in my own peculiar way. I felt confident of that fact and I remained buoyed by it until the day I looked down at a grocery list and saw what my fingers were doing to my handwriting.

I don't tell you all this in a play for your sympathy. I tell you all this because while having ALS is a curse, it's also the reason I know what I know. It's the reason I know what no one else knows. Except my mother.

There was gossip aplenty when Kenneth Fleming moved in with Mother in Kensington. Had Kenneth not begun his career playing for England with such a humiliating performance at Lord's, it might have taken ages for the tabloids to suss out what his living circumstances were. But when he achieved that memorable and mortifying golden duck, he fixed the attention of the cricket world upon himself. When that happened, Mother came under scrutiny as well.

It did make good press: the thirty-four years that stretched between the cricketer and his patron. What was she to him? they wanted to know.

Was she his real mother, having sent him off to adoption at birth, only to track him down in her old age when she was lonely? Was she his aunt, choosing him from among myriad East End nieces and nephews to be the recipient of her largess? Was she a fairy godmother with money on her hands, a woman who searched through the boroughs of London to find a promising life over which she waved her magic wand? Was she a new patron of the England team, one who took her responsibilities to heart by means of intimate involvement in the ostensibly troubled lives of the players? Or was it perhaps something a trifle nasty? An Oedipal thing on the part of Kenneth Fleming to which Miriam Whitelaw's Jocasta responded with more enthusiasm than was wise?

Where did each of them sleep? the press wanted to know. Did they live in the house together, alone? Were there servants who might reveal the true story? daily help who made not two beds but one? If they had separate bedrooms, were they on the same floor? And what did it mean that Miriam Whitelaw never missed a match that Kenneth Fleming played?

Since the real story couldn't possibly be as interesting as the speculation, the tabloids stuck with the speculation. It sold more copies. Who wanted to read about an erstwhile English teacher and her favourite pupil in whose life she had become involved? That wasn't nearly as intriguing as the titillating insinuations suggested by a photograph of Kenneth and Mother, emerging from the Grace Gate under a single umbrella, his arm round her shoulders, her smiling face held up to his.

And what of Jean? You may already know. She talked to the press rather more than she should have done, at first. She was an easy target for both the *Daily Mirror* and the *Sun*. Jean wanted Kenneth back at home, and she thought that the press would help her put him there. So there were pictures of her at work in the café at Billingsgate Market, pictures of the kids on the way to school, pictures of the family sans Dad sitting round the red oilcloth-covered kitchen table with their bangers and mash on a Saturday evening, pictures of Jean awkwardly bowling to Jimmy who had dreams—she confided—of being just like his dad. "Where's Ken?" some of the tabloids demanded while "Left Behind and Heartbroken" declared the others. "Too Good for Her Now?" queried *Woman's Own* as *Woman's Realm* pondered "What To Do When He Leaves You for Someone Who Looks Like His Mum."

Through it all, Kenneth held his tongue and concentrated on cricket.

He made periodic visits to the Isle of Dogs, but whatever he said to Jean about her dealings with the press, he said them in private. His life-style may have been unconventional, but "It's for the best at the moment" was all he ever went on record saying.

What and how things were between Kenneth and Mother during this time, I can only surmise. I can fill in the blanks of the tabloids' speculations, naturally, with details like the sleeping arrangements: different bedrooms but on the same floor and with a door adjoining them because Kenneth took over what once had been my great-grandfather's dressing chamber, which was actually the second largest bedroom in the house. There was nothing questionable in that. Those few guests we'd had had always slept in that room. With details like who was in the house with them: no one, with the exception of a Sri Lankan woman who came in to clean and do the laundry twice a week. But the rest, like everyone else, I can only guess at.

Their conversation would have been multifaceted. When Mother was facing a decision at the printworks, she would have solicited Kenneth's advice, presented theories and considerations to him, listened closely to what he had to say. When Kenneth saw Jean and the kids, he would have talked about them, about his decision to remain apart from them, about why he hadn't asked for a divorce. When the England team travelled out of the country, he would have reported to her the details of his journey, telling her about the people he'd met and the sights he'd seen. If she'd read a book or seen a play, she'd have revealed her reactions. If he'd developed an interest in national politics, he would have shared this interest with her.

However it happened, they grew close, Kenneth Fleming and my mother. He called her his best mate in the world, and the months he lived with her merged into a year and the year into two years and all the while they ignored the gossip and the speculation.

When I first heard about them, it was through the newspapers. I didn't much care because I was hot and heavy with ARM, and ARM was hot and heavy into raising as much of the devil as could be raised at Cambridge University. Nothing could have given me more pleasure than becoming a clot in the bloodstream of that pinch-nosed place, so when I read about Mother and Kenneth, I shrugged them off and used the newspaper to wrap potato peelings in.

When I thought about it later, I concluded that Mother was engaged in some active replacing. First it seemed that she was replacing me. She and I hadn't had contact in years, so she was using Kenneth as a surrogate child, one with whom her mothering skills could be a success. Then, frankly, as speculation was fueled by the silence of the principals themselves, I began to think she was replacing my father. It seemed ludicrous initially, the thought of Mother and Kenneth going at it under cover of darkness, with him trying to ignore all the places where she bagged and sagged and her trying to keep him hard enough to complete the act to their mutual satisfaction. But after a while, when Kenneth's name was connected to no other, it was the only explanation that made any sense. As long as he stayed married to Jean, he could fend off the attentions of women his age, using, "Sorry but I'm a married bloke," as an excuse. Which would keep him free from entanglements that might threaten his real entanglement with Mother.

She was, as he said himself, his very best mate. How difficult would it have been for best mate to transform to bed mate on an evening when the intimacy of their conversation called for an intimacy of another kind?

He would have looked across the drawing room at her and felt desire and horror at desire. Jesus, she could be my mum, he would have thought.

She would have received his look with a smile and a softening of her face and a heartbeat pulsing at the tips of her fingers. "What is it," she would have wanted to know. "Why have you fallen silent?"

"Nothing," he would have said and touched his palm to his forehead in a quick wiping movement. "It's only . . ."

"What?"

"Nothing. Nothing. It's daft."

"Nothing you say is daft, my dear. Not to me."

" 'My dear,' " he would have mocked. "Makes me feel like a child, that does."

"I'm sorry, Ken. I don't think of you as a child."

"Then what? What do you . . . How do you think of me?"

"As a man, of course."

She would have looked at the clock. She would have said, "I think I'll go up. Are you staying down for a while?"

He would have got to his feet. "No," he would have said, "I'm going up as well. If that's all right . . . with you, Miriam."

Ah, that hesitation between *right* and *with you*. If it hadn't been there, his meaning would have gone misunderstood.

Mother would have passed him, paused, briefly twined her fingers in his. "It's perfectly all right," she would have said. "Perfectly, Ken."

Best mate, soul mate, thirty-year-old bed mate. For the very first time, Mother had what she wanted.

OLIVIA

It was Max who first brought up the subject of telling Mother. Ten months after the diagnosis, we were eating Italian just down the road from Camden Lock Market where Max had spent an hour pawing through boxes of what appeared to be jumble posing as antique clothing in that large warehouse where they display everything from gum machines to velvet settees. He'd been looking for a pair of suitably tattered plus fours to use in an amateur theatrical that he was directing, whether as a prop or a costume he wouldn't say. "Can't disclose company secrets, boys and girls," he declared. "You must see the production for yourselves." I'd been using a cane for some time now—which didn't much please me—and I tired more quickly than I would have liked. When I tired, my muscles fibrillated. Fibrillation often led to cramps. Which is what I was experiencing by the time my spinach lasagna was set in front of me, steaming aromatically and bubbling with cheese.

When the first cramp formed that rocklike knot just below and behind my right knee, I gave a little grunt, put my hand to my eyes, and bit down hard, teeth into teeth. Chris said, "Bad, is it?"

I said, "It'll pass."

The lasagna continued to steam and I continued to ignore it. Chris pushed back his chair and began the massage, which was the only thing that ever provided relief.

"Eat your meal," I said.

"It'll be there when I'm done."

"I can cope, for God's sake." The spasms intensified. They were the worst I'd ever had. It felt like my entire right leg was being gnarled. And then my left leg began to fibrillate for the very first time. "Shit," I whispered.

"What is it?"

"Nothing."

His hands moved expertly. The other leg's vibrating began to increase. I stared at the table. The cutlery shimmered. I tried to think of other things.

"Better?" he said.

What a bloody laugh. I said in a tight voice, "Thank you. That's enough."

"Are you sure? If there's pain—"

"Piss off, all right? Eat!"

Chris dropped his hands, but he didn't turn away. I could imagine him counting from one to ten.

I wanted to say sorry. I wanted to say, "I'm afraid. It's not you. I'm afraid, I'm afraid." Instead I concentrated on sending impulses from my brain to my legs. Imaging, my latest healer had called it. Practise mental pictures, that's the ticket, you'll see. My mental pictures were two legs calmly and smoothly crossing, covered in black stockings, finished off by high heels. The cramps and fibrillations continued. I clenched my fists at my forehead. My eyes were squeezed shut so hard that tears dribbled from their corners. Screw it, I thought.

Across the table from me, I could hear that Max had begun to eat. Chris hadn't moved. I could feel the accusation behind his silence. I probably deserved it, but that couldn't be helped.

"Goddamn it, Chris. Stop staring at me," I said from between my teeth. "You're making me feel like a two-headed baby."

He turned then. He picked up his fork and thrusted it into a twisted mass of pasta and mushrooms. He twirled the fork too savagely and ended up hoisting a ball-of-yarn mound of pasta towards his mouth. He dropped the mess back into his plate.

Max was chewing rapidly and moving his eye from Chris to me to Chris to me. It was a cautious, bird-like look. He put down his fork. He dabbed at his mouth with a paper napkin printed, as I recall, with the words *Evelyn's Eats*, which was odd considering that we were in a restaurant called the Black Olive.

He said, "Girlie, have I mentioned? I read about your mum again last week in our local lemon-hued rag."

I made an effort and picked up my fork. I stabbed it into the lasagna. "Yeah?"

"Quite the woman, your mum seems to be. The situation's a speck unusual, of course—her and that cricket bloke—but she seems the proper lady, if you ask my opinion. It's odd, though."

"What?"

"You've never mentioned her much. Considering her growing notoriety, I find that a bit . . . peculiar, shall we say?"

"There's nothing peculiar in it, Max. We've been out of touch."

"Ah. Since when?"

"Since a long time." I took a deep breath. The vibration continued, but the cramps were beginning to ease. I looked at Chris. "Sorry," I said in a low voice. "Chris, I don't mean to be . . . how I am. Like this. Like any of this." He waved me off but said nothing. I went on uselessly with, "Oh shit, Chris. Please."

"Forget it."

"I don't mean to . . . When things get . . . I get . . . I stop being myself."

"It's okay. You don't need to explain. I—"

"Understand. That's what you're going to say. For God's sake, Chris. You don't need to be such a martyr on the spit all the time. I wish you'd—"

"What? Smack you? Walk out? Would you feel better then? Why the hell do you keep trying to push me?"

I threw down my fork. "Jesus. This is nowhere."

Max was drinking from the single glass of red wine he allowed himself daily. He took a sip, held it on his tongue for five seconds, then swallowed appreciatively. "You're attempting the impossible, you two," he noted.

"I've been saying that for years."

He ignored my comment. "You're not going to be able to handle this alone," he said to Chris, and to both of us, "You're fools to think so," and to me, "It's time."

"What's time? What?"

"She needs to be told."

It wasn't exactly tough to put this remark next to his earlier questions and comments. I bridled. "She doesn't need to know anything from me, thank you."

"Don't play games, girlie. Game-playing's unbecoming. This is terminal business we're dealing with here."

"So send her a telegram when I've dropped off the hooks."

"You'd treat your mother that way?"

"Tit for tat. She'll recover. I did."

"Not from this."

"I know I'm going to die. There's no need to remind me."

"I wasn't speaking of you but of her."

"You don't know her. Believe me, the woman has resources louts like us only dream about. She'll pass off my passing off like it was rainwater she was shaking from her Burberry brolly."

"Perhaps," he said. "But that's discounting the possibility that she could be of help."

"I don't need her help. I don't want it either."

"And Chris?" Max asked. "If he does? Both need and want? Not now, but later, when things get rough? As you know they will?"

I picked up my fork. I dug into the lasagna and watched the cheese ooze between the tines like vanilla toffee.

"Well?" Max said.

"Chris?" I said.

"I can cope," he replied.

"That's that, then." But as I lifted my fork to my mouth, I saw the look that Max and Chris exchanged, and I knew they'd already spoken about Mother.

I hadn't seen her in more than nine years. During the time that I was on the game near Earl's Court, it had been unlikely that our paths would ever cross. Despite her renown for social good works, Mother had never been one to involve herself with elevating the hearts and souls of the city's flesh peddlers, and that being the case, I'd always known I was safe from the potential unpleasantness of running into her. Not that I would have cared much had I done so. But it would have put a crimp in my business to have had a middle-aged harpy at my heels.

Since leaving the street life, though, I'd placed myself in a more precarious situation with regard to Mother. There she was in Kensington. There I was fifteen minutes away in Little Venice. I would have liked to forget about her existence entirely, but the truth is that there were weeks when I never left the barge by daylight without wondering if I would see her somewhere along my route to the zoo, to the grocer's, to inspect a flat needing Chris's attention, to the lumberyard to pick up supplies for finishing and fixing up the barge.

I can't explain why I still thought of her. I hadn't expected to. Rather I had expected the bridge between us to remain thoroughly burned. And it *was* burned physically. I'd burned my half that night at Covent Garden. She'd burned her half with the telegram informing me of Dad's death and cremation. She hadn't even left me a grave to visit in privacy, and that, in my mind, was as unforgivable as the means by which she'd informed me of his dying. So I had no intention that my world should ever again intersect with hers.

The only thing I wasn't able to do was excise Mother from memory and thought. I'm not sure anyone can accomplish that when it comes to a parent or a sibling. The tie that binds one to immediate family can be cut, but the severed ends of it tend to flutter in one's face on windy days.

Naturally, when Mother and Kenneth Fleming became the subjects of heavy journalistic speculation some two years ago, those ends began fluttering in my face more often than I would have liked. It's difficult to explain how I felt, now and again seeing her picture and his in the *Daily Mail*, which one of the technicians religiously brought to the zoo's animal hospital to read while she was enjoying her elevenses each day. I'd see the photographs over her shoulder. Sometimes I'd catch a glimpse of the headline. I'd look away. I'd take my coffee to a table near the windows. I'd drink it down fast with my eyes on the tree-tops. And I'd wonder why my stomach felt queer.

I originally thought that I'd seen nothing more than proof that she'd carried her lifetime of good works to their logical conclusion by making fact out of theory like a competent social scientist. The hypothesis had always been that, given the appropriate set of opportunities, the disadvantaged could reach the same heights of glory as did the advantaged. It had nothing to do with birth, blood, genetic predispositions, or familial role models. *Homo sapiens* wanted to succeed by virtue of being *Homo sapiens* in the first place. Kenneth Fleming had been the subject of her study. Kenneth Fleming had proved her theory true. So what was it to me?

How I hate to admit it. How juvenile and questionable it really seems. I can't even relate it without embarrassment.

In keeping Kenneth Fleming in her home, Mother had confirmed my long-held belief that she preferred him to me and had always wished that he were her child. Not just at that point in time when it was reasonable to think that she'd be more than eager to find a replacement for the street slime she'd encountered near Covent Garden Station. But long before that, when I was still at home, when Kenneth and I were both fifth formers at our respective state schools.

When I first saw their photographs in the newspapers, when I first read the stories, beneath my brittle veneer of what's-the-old-cow-up-to-this-time, lay the unprotected skin of rebuff. Beneath that thin skin, the reaction to rejection festered like a boil.

Hurt and jealousy. I felt them both. And I suppose you're wondering why. We'd been estranged for so many years, my mother and I, why should I care that she'd taken into her home and her life someone who could play the role of her adult-child? I hadn't wanted to play that role, had I? Had I? *Had I?*

You don't quite believe me, do you? Like Chris, you think I'm protesting too much. You're deciding it wasn't hurt or jealousy at all that I felt, aren't you? You're labelling it fear. You're reasoning that Miriam Whitelaw isn't going to live forever, and there must be quite an inheritance involved when she pops off: the house in Kensington and all its contents, the printworks, the cottage in Kent, God only knows how many investments . . . Isn't that the real reason, you're wondering, that Olivia Whitelaw's stomach did flip-flops the first time she realised what Kenneth Fleming's presence in her mother's life might really mean? Because the truth is that Olivia wouldn't have had much of a legal leg to stand on had her mother decided to leave everything she possessed to Kenneth Fleming. Olivia had, after all, removed herself from her mother's life in a rather terminal fashion some time in the past.

Perhaps you won't believe me, but I don't actively recall those concerns being part of what I felt. My mother was only sixty years old when she became reinvolved with Kenneth Fleming at the printworks. She was in perfect health. I had no real thought of her dying, so I had no real thought of how she intended ultimately to dispose of her possessions.

Once I got used to the idea of Mother and Kenneth together—more, once the oddity of their situation began to strike people when Kenneth continued to do nothing to alter his marital status—my hurt dissolved first to incredulity. She's over sixty years old, I would think. What's she planning on happening between them? Incredulity fast faded to derision. She's making a howling fool of herself.

As time went on and I began to see that Kenneth and Mother's arrangement suited them fine, I did my best to ignore the two of them. Who gave a hoot if they were mother-son, best mates, lovers, or the biggest cricket freaks ever known to mankind? They could do what they wanted, as far as I was concerned. They could have their fun. They could wiggle and wag in the nude in front of Buckingham Palace, for all that I cared.

So when Max suggested that it was time to tell Mother about ALS, I said no. Put me into hospital, I said. Find me a nursing home. Put me on the street. But don't tell that old twat anything about me. Is that clear? Is it? *Is* it?

Nothing was said about Mother after that. But the seed had been planted, which may have been Max's intention in the first place. If that's so, he'd planted the seed in the cleverest fashion: Don't tell your mother for her sake, girlie. That isn't the point. If you're going to tell her, do it for Chris.

Chris. At the end of things, what is it that I wouldn't do for Chris?

Exercise, exercise. Walking. Lifting weights. Climbing endless stairways. I *would* be the random victim to beat this disease. I would beat it in the most fantastic manner. I wouldn't do it like Hawking, a brilliant razor mind confined within an immobilised body. I'd take my mind under complete control, name it master of my body, and triumph over the quakes, the cramps, the weakness, the shakes.

The initial progress of the disease was slow. I dismissed the fact that I'd been told to expect this, and instead I took the disease's relative inactivity as a sign that my programme of self-recovery was proving effective. Look look, my every stumble-bumble step announced, the right leg's no worse, the left leg's unaffected, I've got this sod ALS by the curlies and I don't intend to let him go. But there was no real change in my condition. This period was merely an interlude, a time of irony when I allowed myself to believe I could stop the ebb of the tide by wading into the sea and politely asking the water if it wouldn't be willing to stick around.

My right leg became loose flesh that dangled from bone. And underneath it hung muscles that twisted, tightened, fought with each other, tied themselves into knots, and loosened into strips of gristle again. I asked why. Why, if the muscles still move, if they still cramp and twist, why why why won't they do what I want, when I make the demand? But that, I was told, is the nature of the disease. It's like a high tension electrical wire that's been damaged in a storm. Electricity still runs through it, sparks shoot out randomly, but the energy produced is useless.

And then my left leg began to go. From the time of the first fibrillations in the restaurant near Camden Lock, there was no real yielding of the disintegration. It was slow, true, a minor weakness that became ever slightly more pronounced as the weeks went by. But there was no denying that the disease was advancing. Fibrillation increased, building strength from the vibrations until they evolved into agonising cramps. When this occurred, exercise became out of the question. One couldn't walk, climb stairs, or lift weights when one was concentrating on managing pain without beating one's head into rotting grapefruit against the nearest wall.

Through it all, Chris said nothing. By that, I don't mean to say he was mute. He kept me apprised of how the assault unit was managing without me, he talked about his renovation work, he solicited advice about dealing with sticky situations among the governing core of ARM, he chatted about his parents and his brother and made plans for us to make another trek to Leeds to see them.

I knew that Chris would never be the one to bring up ALS. I had made the decision to start using a cane. I had made the decision when it was time for a second cane. I could see that the next step was going to be a walker so that I could drag myself more efficiently from bedroom to loo, from loo to galley, from galley to workroom to bedroom again. But after that, when the walker began putting demands on my endurance that I could no longer meet, I would be forced into a wheelchair. And it was the wheelchair I feared—the wheelchair I still desperately fear—and all that the wheelchair implies. But these were things that Chris would never speak of because the disease was mine, not his, and the decisions that went along with fighting the disease were mine, not his, as well. So if these pending decisions were going to be discussed, I was the one who was going to have to introduce the topic.

When I began to use the aluminium walker, to wrestle my way from the workroom into the galley, I knew it was time. The effort at movement with the walker brought sweat out in great patches down my back and beneath my arms. I tried to tell myself that the only problem was one of getting used to this new form of mobility, but to get used to a new form of mobility I was expecting myself to build upper-body strength in a situation in which strength was draining from me a teaspoon at a time. It became apparent that Chris and I would have to talk.

I'd been using the walker for less than three weeks when Max came to spend an evening with us. It was in early April, this very year, on a Sunday evening. We'd had dinner together, and we were sitting on the deck of the barge watching the dogs play-act at brawling on the roof of the cabin. Chris had carried me up the stairs, Max had lit my cigarette, both had pulled at non-existent forelocks, made sweeping bows, and disappeared below to fetch blankets, brandy, glasses, and the bowl of fruit. I heard the murmur of their voices: Chris saying, "No, nothing really," and Max saying, "Seems weaker." I turned away from the sound of them as best I could and concentrated on the canal, the pool, and Browning's Island.

It was hard to believe that I'd been here five years, coming and going, establishing myself at the zoo, moving animals in and out, alternately fighting with and loving Chris. There had been moments when I'd acknowledged the safety and the peace of this place, but never before had each element of Little Venice meant to me what it meant that night. I took all of it in in great gulps, like air. The one strange willow on Browning's Island that, dissimilar to the others, leans like a reckless schoolboy over the water, drooping branches within an inch of the pier. The row of citrus-coloured barges whose owners sit on the decks when the evening's pleasant and nod and wave as we run the dogs by. The red and green wrought-iron of the Warwick Avenue bridge and the great row of white houses that line the avenue that leads to the bridge. And in front of those houses, the ornamental cherry trees are beginning to bloom, and the wind stirs the blossoms like angel's hair and they float to the pavement and form palettes of pink. Birds scatter the petals. They dart from Warwick Avenue to the canal. There they flitter from tree to towpath in a search for bits of string, small twigs, hair from which to fashion their nests. . . . How could I leave this place?

Then I heard their voices again.

". . . difficult, you know . . . She calls it our trial by fire . . . doing her best to understand . . ."

And Max's reply: ". . . whenever you need to get away, you know."

And Chris: "Thanks. I know. It makes things more bearable."

I studied the water, how the outline of the canal trees and the buildings beyond them zigzagged in the ripples, how a goose plopping into the pool from the island caused an ever-widening circle of undulations that ultimately reached but did not move the barge. I felt no betrayal in the fact that Chris and Max were talking about me, about her whose name I still didn't know, about the miserable situation we found ourselves in. It was time I did some talking about myself.

They returned with the brandy, the glasses, the fruit. Chris wrapped a blanket round my legs and, with a smile, tapped his fingers gently against my cheek. Beans leaped off the cabin's roof to the deck, eager at the prospect of food. Toast pranced along the edge of the roof, whining and waiting for someone to lift him down.

"He's being a baby," Chris said as Max made a move to lower Toast to the deck. "He can manage well enough."

"Ah, but he's a sweet wee beastie," Max said as he set Toast next to Beans. "That being the case, I don't mind the trouble."

"So long as he doesn't get used to being catered to," Chris said. "He'll become too dependent if he knows someone's willing to do for him what he can do for himself. And that, my friend, will be the ruination of him."

"What?" I asked. "Dependence?"

Max took his time about cutting up an apple. Chris poured the brandy and sat at my feet. He pulled Beans down next to him and rubbed the tender spot he called "the area of supreme puppy ecstasy" just underneath the beagle's floppy ears.

"It is," I said.

"What?" Chris asked. Max fed a quarter of the apple to Toast.

"Ruination. You're right. Dependence leads to ruination."

"I was just blithering about nothing, Livie."

"It's like a fishing net," I said. "You've seen them, haven't you? The kind boats lay out on the surface of the water to catch a school of mackerel or something. That's what ruination is, a net. It doesn't just snag and destroy the dependent one. It catches everyone else as well. All the little fishes swimming blithely along with the single fish who's dependent in the first place."

"That's rather an elastic metaphor, girlie." Max plunged his knife into another apple quarter and held it out to me. I shook my head.

"It suits," I said. I looked at Chris. He held my gaze. His hand stopped rubbing beneath the beagle's ears. Beans nudged his fingers. Chris dropped his eyes.

"If all those fish swam apart from one another, they'd never be caught," I said. "Oh, perhaps one or two of them, even ten or twelve. But not the whole school. That's what's so sad about the fact that they stay together."

"It's instinct," Chris said. "That's how they operate. Schools of fish, flocks of birds, herds of animals. It's all the same."

"Except for people. We don't need to operate on instinct. We can reason things through and do what's best to protect our fellows from our own ruination. Don't you agree? Chris? Well?"

He began to peel an orange. I could feel the rich oil of its scent on the back of my tongue as I drew a breath. He began to divide the orange into sections. He handed me one. Our fingers touched as I took it. He turned his head and examined the water as if he was searching for debris.

Max said, "There's some sense to what you're saying, girlie."

Chris said, "Max," in a cautious tone.

Max said, "It's a question of responsibility. How far are we responsible for the lives that have meshed with our own?"

"And for the ruination of those lives," I said. "Especially if we turn a blind eye to what we can do to prevent the ruination."

Max fed the rest of his apple to the dogs—a quarter to Beans, a quarter to Toast. He set upon another with his paring knife. This time he peeled it, starting at the top and striving to achieve a single spiral. We watched him, Chris and I. The knife slipped three-quarters of the way through the project, slitting through the peel, which fell to the deck. The three of us observed it against the boards, a ribbon of red marking a failed attempt at perfection.

"So I can't," I said. "You see that, don't you?"

"What?" Chris asked.

We watched the dogs sniff at and then reject the apple peel. They wanted the real thing, Beans and Toast. The sweet pith of the fruit, not the biting sharp taste of the skin.

"What?" Chris repeated. "Can't what?"

"Be responsible."

"For what?"

"You know. Come on, Chris."

I watched him closely. He had to feel relief at my words. I wasn't his wife, wasn't even his lover, had never been either, had never been promised that I might be either. I was five years later the tart he'd picked off the street across from Earl's Court Exhibition Centre as he'd passed by with a ruined dog on a lead. I had held my own as his barge mate. I had made a contribution to our living circumstances. But the time that I was going to be able to continue doing so was fast running out. Both of us knew it. So I watched him and waited to see an indication that he recognised the moment when his deliverance was at hand.

And yes, I suppose I wanted him to protest. I imagined him saying, "I can cope. We can cope. We always have done. We always will do. We're bound together, you and I are, Livie. We're in it till the end."

Because he'd said it before in rather different words when it was easier, when the ALS wasn't quite as bad as it was fast becoming. Then we could talk bravely about how it would be, but we didn't have to face it because it wasn't how-it-would-be at the moment. But this time, he said nothing. He pulled Toast to him and scrutinised a rough patch between the dog's eyes. Toast enjoyed the attention and brushed his tail happily against the deck.

"Chris?" I said.

"You're not my ruination," he answered. "Things're tough, that's all."

Max pulled the cork from the brandy bottle and topped up our glasses although we'd none of us touched a drop yet. He rested his big hand on my knee for a moment. He squeezed. The pressure said, Take heart, girlie, go on.

"My legs are getting weaker. The walker's not enough."

"You need to get used to it. Build up your strength."

"My legs'll be like cooked spaghetti, Chris."

"You're not practising enough. You're not using the walker as much as you could."

"I won't be able to stand in another two months."

"If your arms are in shape, then—"

"Goddamn it, *listen.* I'm going to need a wheelchair."

Chris made no reply. Max rose, rested his hips against the roof of the cabin. He drank from his brandy. He set the glass on the cabin roof and fished in his pocket for the stub of a cigar. He put it into his mouth, unlit.

"So we'll get a wheelchair," Chris said.

"And then what?" I asked.

"What?"

"Where do I live?"

"What do you mean? Here. Where else?"

"Don't be so daft. I can't. You know it. You built it, didn't you?"

Chris looked blank. "I can't stay here," I said. "I won't be able to get about."

"Of course you—"

"The doorways, Chris."

I'd said all I could. The walker, the wheelchair. He didn't need to know any more than that. I couldn't talk about the vibrations that had started in my fingers. I couldn't mention how a biro had begun to slide wildly across the paper like leather soles against polished wood when I tried to write. Because that told me that even the wheelchair I dreaded and loathed would serve me only a few precious months before ALS made my arms as useless as my legs were becoming.

"I'm not ill enough yet for a nursing home," I told him. "But I'm getting too ill to stay here."

Max tossed his cigar stub—still unlit—into the tomato tin. He stepped past the dogs who sprawled on either side of Chris and came round to the back of my chair. I felt his hands on my shoulders. Warmth and pressure, the faint indication of a massage. He saw me as noble and saintly, did Max, the best of English womanhood on the fade, a disease-ridden sufferer releasing her beloved into living a life of his own. What rubbish. I was hovering directly between hollow and nothing.

"We'll move, then," Chris said. "Find digs where you can get about easy in a chair."

"Not from your home," I said. "We won't do that."

"I can let the barge easier than anything, Livie. Probably for more than we'd pay for a flat. I don't want you—"

"I've already phoned her," I said. "She knows I want to see her. She just doesn't know why."

Chris raised his head to look behind me. I kept perfectly still. I summoned the presence of Liv Whitelaw the Outlaw to see me through the lie without a crack in composure.

"It's done," I said.

"When are you going to see her?"

"When I think it's time. We left it at the I'd-like-to-get-together-with-you-if-you-can-bear-it stage."

"And she's willing?"

"She's still my mother, Chris." I crushed out my cigarette and shook another into my lap. I held it between my fingers without lifting it to my mouth. I didn't want to smoke it as much as I wanted something to do until he responded. But he said nothing. It was Max who replied.

"You've made a proper decision, girlie. She's a right to know. You've a right to her help."

I didn't want her help. I wanted to work at the zoo, to run along the canal with the dogs, to melt like shadows into labs with the liberators, to drink to our victories with Chris in pubs, to stand at the window of that flat where the assault team meet near Wormwood Scrubs and look at the prison and thank God I was prisoner of nothing any longer.

"It's done, Chris," I repeated.

He circled his arm round his legs, resting his head on his knees. "If that's your decision," he said.

"Yeah. Well. It is," I lied.

CHAPTER
18

Lynley chose Bach's *Brandenburgischen Konzerte* Number One because the music reminded him of childhood, of making a carefree run across the park at his family home in Cornwall, racing his brother and sister towards the old woodland that protected Howenstow from the sea. Bach didn't make demands as Lynley found that the Russians did. Bach was froth and air, the perfect companion to engaging in thoughts having nothing at all to do with his music.

Lynley swirled the last of the whisky in his glass and noted how the amber turned to gold when the light struck it. He drank it down, enjoyed the heat of it against the back of his throat, and placed the glass next to the decanter on the cherrywood table beside his chair. Violins and French horns were chasing one another in the Bach concerto. Lynley's thoughts were doing much the same within his skull.

He and Sergeant Havers had separated after their dinner in Kensington, Havers catching the tube in the high street to return to her car and

New Scotland Yard, Lynley paying another visit to Staffordshire Terrace. It was an evaluation both of this visit and of his own disquiet for which the concerto served as background.

Miriam Whitelaw had led him once again up the stairs and into the drawing room where a single brass floor lamp shed a cone of light upon a wingback chair. The lamp did virtually nothing to eliminate the drawing room's enormous caverns of darkness, and Miriam Whitelaw faded easily into the gloom, dressed in a black tunic and trousers. It didn't appear as if she had taken him to this part of the house by deliberate design, however, knowing he intended to question her and seeking darkness to hide from him. On the contrary, it appeared as if she'd been sitting there herself prior to his arrival because she murmured, "I can't seem to deal with the light any longer. The moment I see it, my head begins to pound and then a migraine comes and then I'm useless. Which is what I don't want to be."

She had moved slowly but with sure knowledge of the room's plethora of furniture, and she switched on a fringed lamp just beyond the piano. And then another on a gate-leg table. None of the bulbs were bright, so the light remained muted, glowing much as the gaslamps must have done in her grandfather's time. She said, "The darkness helps me to pretend. I've been sitting here imagining sounds." She seemed to read the question from the shadows where Lynley stood because she went on quietly with, "I always first heard Ken before I saw him when he came home. The garage door slamming shut. His footsteps on the flagstones in the garden. The kitchen door opening. I've been imagining that. Those sounds. Hearing him come home. Not actually being here, you see, not in the room with me, not even in the house because that isn't possible, is it? But arriving. The sounds he made. Because somehow if I can force them to exist again in my head, it seems to me that he won't be gone."

She had returned to a chair where, Lynley saw, an old cricket ball lay tangent to a Persian pillow. She sat and cupped her hands round the ball in a position so natural that Lynley realised she must have been doing that in the semi-darkness before his arrival, just sitting with the ball in her hands.

She had said, "Jean phoned late this afternoon. She said you'd taken Jimmy. Jimmy." Her hands trembled and she grasped the ball more firmly. "I find I've finally become too old, Inspector. I don't understand anything any longer. Men and women. Husbands and wives. Parents and children. All of it. I don't understand."

Lynley had used the opening to ask her why she hadn't told him about her own daughter's visit to her on the night of Fleming's death. For a moment she said nothing. Silence magnified the ticking of the grandfather clock. Finally, she murmured in what sounded like defeat, "Then you've spoken to Olivia."

He said he'd spoken to Olivia twice and since she'd lied the first time about where she'd been on the night that Fleming died, he wondered what else she might be lying about. Or her mother for that matter, who, as it turned out, had lied as well.

"I made a deliberate omission," Mrs. Whitelaw said. "I did not lie." She went on to tell him, much as her daughter had done although far more quietly and with greater resignation, that the visit had nothing to do with the case, that discussing it with him would have violated Olivia's right to privacy. And Olivia had that right, Mrs. Whitelaw asserted. That right was one of the few things she did have left.

"I've lost them both. Ken . . . Ken now. And Olivia . . ." She brought the cricket ball to her breasts and held it there as if it helped her to continue. "Olivia soon. And in a way so brutal that when I think about it . . . which I can barely bring myself to do . . . to be stripped of control over her body, to be stripped of her pride, but every moment until she breathes her last to be completely *aware* of that inhuman stripping . . . Because she was so proud, my Olivia, she was so haughty, she was a wild thing that raged through my life for years until I couldn't bear her any longer and blessed the day she finally pushed me far enough to break with her completely." She seemed on the verge of losing her composure, but she reined herself back. "No, I didn't tell you about Olivia, Inspector. I couldn't. She's dying. It was bad enough to have to talk about Ken. To talk about Olivia as well. . . . I couldn't bear it."

She would have to bear it now, Lynley had thought. And he'd asked her why Olivia had come to see her. To make peace, Mrs. Whitelaw told him. To ask for help.

"Which will come to her far more easily now that Fleming's gone," Lynley pointed out.

She'd turned her head into one of the projecting wings of the chair, saying with great weariness, "Why won't you believe me? Olivia had nothing to do with Ken's death."

"Perhaps not Olivia herself," Lynley said and waited for her reaction. It was a motionless one, head still turned into the side of the chair, hand still holding the cricket ball to her breast. Nearly a minute of silence ticked by on the grandfather clock before she asked him what he meant.

So he had told her what he still was mulling over now as he sat in his drawing room in Eaton Terrace, what he had been mulling over during his dinner with Sergeant Havers: Chris Faraday had been gone that entire Wednesday night, as had Olivia. Did Mrs. Whitelaw know that?

No. She didn't.

Lynley didn't add Faraday's alibi for Mrs. Whitelaw. But it was Faraday's alibi that had caused Lynley's disquiet since he and Havers had first left the barge.

It had been too like a recitation, Faraday's story of where he had been and what he had done on Wednesday night. He'd run through it with barely a hesitation. The list of party-goers, the list of films they'd hired, the name and address of the video shop. The very ease of Faraday's account of his evening smacked of something well prepared in advance. Especially his memory of the films themselves, not big screen Hollywood productions with stars as familiar as one's breakfast cereal, but small-time pornography like *Betty Does Bangkok* or *Wild in the Woolly* or whatever else Faraday had called them. And how many had he listed so effortlessly? Ten? Twelve? Sergeant Havers would have argued that they could check out the shop if Lynley had trouble with the veracity of Faraday's story. But Lynley had no doubt the shop's records would show that the films had indeed been hired out that night, either by Faraday himself or by one of the chaps on the list of party-goers he'd recited. Which was the whole point in the first place. The alibi was too perfectly constructed.

"Olivia's boyfriend?" Mrs. Whitelaw had said. "But why have you taken Jimmy? Jean said you took Jimmy."

For questioning only, Lynley told her. Sometimes it helped one's memory of events when one was asked to recall them at New Scotland Yard. Were there any other events of Wednesday night that Mrs. Whitelaw herself would now like to relate? Anything she'd left out of their earlier conversations?

No, she had told him. There was nothing. He knew everything now.

He'd said nothing further until they stood at the front door where the light in the entry shone directly into her face. He paused with his hand on the doorknob, affecting a sudden recollection, and turned back to her to say, "Gabriella Patten. Have you heard from her?"

"I haven't spoken to Gabriella in weeks. Have you found her?"

"Yes."

"Is she . . . How is she?"

"Not what I expected of a woman who's just lost the man she intended to marry."

"Well," she said. "That's Gabriella, isn't it?"

"I don't know," Lynley said. "Is it Gabriella?"

"Gabriella wasn't worth Ken's shoe scrapings, Inspector," Mrs. Whitelaw said. "I only wish Ken had been able to see that for himself."

"Would he be alive had he done so?"

"I believe he would."

In the greater light of the entry he'd seen that she'd recently cut herself high on the forehead. A plaster followed the line of her hair. A drop of blood—grumous, dark brown like a cancerous mole—had seeped through the gauze. She raised her fingers and grazed them against the plaster, saying, "It was easier."

"What?"

"Causing myself this kind of pain. Rather than facing the other."

Lynley nodded. "It usually is."

He sank further into his chair in the Eaton Terrace drawing room. He stretched out his legs and gave a speculative glance to the whisky decanter standing next to his glass. He rejected the urge, if only for the moment, steepling his fingers beneath his chin and staring at the pattern in the Axminster carpet. He thought about the truth, half-truths, and lies, the beliefs we cling to, those we publicly espouse, and the frightening juggernaut that love can become when it is felt too wildly, when its once-reciprocated passion is rejected, or when it goes completely unreturned.

Murder was not generally the sacrifice exacted by the force of blind love. Surrendering the self to the person and to the will of another took many other forms. But when one's headlong capitulation to obsession grew deadly, the consequence of unseeing devotion was catastrophe.

If that had been the case with Kenneth Fleming's murder, then his killer had loved and hated him in equal parts. And ending his life had been a way for the killer to effect a marriage with the victim, forcing an indissoluble bond between body and body, between soul and soul, linking each to the other permanently in death in a manner that could not have been achieved in life.

Except all of this, Lynley realised, begged the question of Gabriella Patten. And Gabriella Patten—who she was, what she did, and what she said—could not be avoided if he was ever to get to the truth.

The drawing room door swung open slightly and Denton peered

round it. When his glance met Lynley's, he side-stepped into the room and padded on slippered feet to Lynley's chair. He lifted the decanter from the table, his expression saying, "More?" Lynley nodded. Denton poured the whisky and replaced the decanter among the others on the breakfront cabinet. Lynley smiled at this subtle management of his alcohol intake. Denton was smooth, no question of that. There would be little chance of dipsomania as long as he was around.

"Anything else, my lord?" Denton raised his voice to be heard. Lynley signalled to him to lower the stereo's volume. Bach receded to a pleasant background lilt.

Lynley asked the question he didn't need to ask, already knowing the answer from his valet's silence on the subject. "Lady Helen hasn't phoned?"

"Not since she left this morning." Denton assiduously saw to a speck of lint on his sleeve.

"Which was when?"

"When?" He considered the question by lifting his eyes to the Adam ceiling as if the answer to Lynley's question resided there. "Around an hour after you and the sergeant took off."

Lynley picked up his glass and swirled the whisky while Denton removed a handkerchief from his pocket and ran it unnecessarily along the top of the cabinet. He went on to use it on one of the decanters. Lynley cleared his throat and made his next question casual. "How did she seem to you?"

"Who?"

"Helen."

"Seem?"

"Yes. I think we've clarified my question. How did she seem?"

Denton frowned thoughtfully, but he was making too much of portraying himself as Mr. Contemplation. "How did she seem . . . Well . . . Let me think. . . ."

"Denton, get on with it if you will."

"Yes. It's just that I couldn't quite—"

"Spare me. You know we had a row. I don't accuse you of listening at key holes, but as you arrived hard upon its heels, you know we were engaged in a disagreement. So answer my question. How did she seem?"

"Well, actually, she seemed the same as always."

At least, Lynley thought, he had the kindness to look regretful as he imparted the information. But Denton wasn't one to read nuances from a

woman, as any examination of his heavily chequered love life would at-
test. So Lynley went on with "She wasn't in a temper? She didn't
seem . . ." What was the word he wanted? Thoughtful? Disheartened?
Determined? Exasperated? Wretched? Anxious? Any one of them could
apply at this point.

"She seemed like herself," Denton said. "She seemed like Lady
Helen."

Which was, Lynley knew, to seem unruffled. Which was, in its turn,
Helen Clyde's forte. She wielded composure as usefully as if it were a
Purdey shotgun. He'd been caught in the line of fire more than once with
her, and her consistent refusal to stoop to a show of temper infuriated
him.

To hell with it, he thought, and drank down his whisky. He wanted
to add, To hell with her, but he couldn't do so.

"Will that be all, then, my lord?" Denton asked. His face had composed itself into a blank and he'd altered his voice to an irritating demonstration of your-every-wish and all the etceteras.

"For Christ's sake. Leave Jeeves in the kitchen," Lynley said. "And
yes, that's all."

"Very good, my—"

"Denton," Lynley said.

Denton grinned. "Right." He returned to Lynley's chair and deftly
appropriated the whisky glass. "I'll pop off to bed now. How'd you like
your eggs in the morning, then?"

"Cooked," Lynley said.

"Not a bad idea."

Denton adjusted the Bach concerto to its previous volume and left
Lynley to his music and to his thoughts.

Lynley had each of the morning's newspapers spread out across his
desk, and he was leaning over them in the process of evaluating their
contents when Superintendent Malcolm Webberly joined him. He was
accompanied by the acrid scent of cigar smoke, which preceded him by
several feet. Indeed, without looking up from his newspapers and before
his superior officer spoke, Lynley murmured, "Sir," in greeting as he
compared the *Daily Mail*'s page one coverage of the murder investigation
to the story's position in *The Times* (page three), the *Guardian* (page

seven), and the *Daily Mirror* (front page with a half-page accompanying photograph of Jean Cooper dashing to Lynley's car with the Tesco's bag in her hand). He still had the *Independent*, the *Observer*, and the *Daily Telegraph* to peruse, and Dorothea Harriman was out doing her best to unearth copies of the *Sun* and the *Daily Express*. So far all of the newspapers were walking the fine line dictated by the Contempt of Court Act. No clear picture of Jimmy Cooper. No mention of his name in connection with the heretofore unidentified sixteen-year-old boy who was "helping the police with their enquiries." Just a careful recitation of details, presented in such an order that anyone with a modicum of intelligence could read between the lines for the facts.

Webberly came to his side. With him, the smell. It permeated his suit jacket and wafted off him in waves. Lynley had no doubt that the superintendent still reeked of it after he'd bathed, brushed his teeth, gargled with mouth wash, and scrubbed his hair.

"Who's controlling the information flow?" Webberly asked.

"I am," was Lynley's reply.

"Don't cock things up." Webberly picked up the *Daily Mirror*, gave it a look, muttered, "Carrion eaters," and dropped it back onto Lynley's desk. He struck a match. Lynley raised his head as Webberly applied it to a half-burnt cigar he had removed from his jacket pocket. Lynley looked pained and went back to his papers.

Webberly moved restlessly round the office. He fingered a stack of folders. He took a copy of a PSI report from the filing cabinet. He replaced it. He sighed. He finally said, "See here, lad. I'm bothered." Lynley raised his head again. Webberly went on. "You've got a pack of newshounds barking at the press office and a second pack prowling round outside. That seems intentional, if you ask me. So where's it all heading? I ask, mind you, because Hillier's going to want to know if he and his latest Henry Poole happen to arrive while the pack's still baying for a fox. They may go after him as well, lad, which as I don't need to remind you, is a situation we'd do well to head off before it happens."

There was truth in that. Sir David Hillier was Chief Superintendent and he liked his CID to work like a well-oiled machine: efficiently, cost effectively, and as silently as possible. The presence of the press would suggest to Hillier a cog in the works or at least in the making. He wouldn't be pleased.

"It's to be expected," Lynley said, folding *The Times* and replacing it with the *Independent*. "Fleming was a sportsman, a national figure. One can't expect an investigation into his murder to go unaccompanied by numerous queries from the press.''

A noxious cloud of smoke ballooned between him and his newspapers. Lynley coughed discreetly. Webberly ignored him.

''You mean that's what I'm to tell Hillier,'' the superintendent said.

''If he asks.'' Lynley leafed open the *Independent* and said, ''Ah,'' at the sight of the photograph on page three. The shape of Jimmy Cooper's head was framed in the window of the Bentley. And in the reflection on the glass winked the discernible and unmistakable silver letters on the revolving sign in front of the Yard.

Looking over his shoulder, Webberly sighed. ''I don't like this, lad. If you aren't careful, you'll sink your own case before it gets to court.''

''I'm taking care,'' Lynley replied. ''But it's a matter of basic chemistry, whether we like it or not.''

''Meaning?''

''If you increase the pressure, you alter the temperature,'' Lynley said.

''That's liquids, Tommy. These are people. They don't boil.''

''You're right. They break.''

With a breathless ''I've managed to get the lot, Detective Inspector Lynley,'' Dorothea Harriman whipped into the office, a final stack of newspapers over her arm. She said, ''*Sun, Express*, yesterday's *Telegraph*, yesterday's *Mail*,'' and with a pointed look at Webberly, ''Sigmund Freud smoked twelve cigars a day. Did you know that, Superintendent Webberly? He ended up with cancer in the roof of his mouth.''

''But I'll wager he died with a smile on his face,'' Webberly retorted.

Harriman rolled her eyes expressively. ''Anything else, Detective Inspector Lynley?''

Lynley considered telling her to stop using his full title, but he knew that the directive would be useless. ''That's it, Dee.''

''Press office wants to know if you plan to speak to the reporters this morning. What shall I tell them?''

''That I'll leave the pleasure to my higher-ups today.''

''Sir?'' Sergeant Havers appeared in the doorway, in a crumpled brown suit that looked as if it had also once served hard time as a dish cloth. The contrast between her and Webberly's secretary—neatly turned out in cream crepe with black piping unmarred by newsprint despite her recent expeditions for Lynley—was wince-producing. ''We've got the boy.''

Lynley glanced at his watch. Four minutes after ten. "Fine," he said, removing his glasses. "I'll be along directly. Is his solicitor with him?"

"A bloke called Friskin. He's saying our Jimmy has nothing more to offer the police at this time."

"Is he?" Lynley took his jacket from the back of his chair and the Fleming files from beneath the newspapers. "We'll see about that."

They set off to the interview room, dodging DIs, clerks, secretaries, and messengers along the corridors, Havers bobbing along quickly at Lynley's side. She was referring to her notebook and ticking off items as she related them to him. Nkata was checking the video shop in Berwick Street, and another DC was snooping round Clapham where the Wednesday-night stag party was allegedly held. There was still no word from Inspector Ardery about her forensic team's evaluation of the evidence. Should Havers phone Maidstone and rattle the cage?

"If we don't hear something by noon," Lynley said.

"Right," Havers said and hurried on her way to the incidents room.

At the interview room, Friskin was on his feet the moment Lynley opened the door. He strode to meet him, saying, "I'd like a word, Inspector," and stepped into the corridor where a file clerk nearly ran into him. "I've serious reservations about your interview with my client yesterday. Judges Rules require a civilian adult be present. Why weren't those rules adhered to?"

"You've heard the tape, Mr. Friskin. The boy was offered a solicitor."

Friskin's grey eyes narrowed. "How far do you honestly expect to take that ridiculous confession in a court of law?"

"At the moment, I'm not concerned with a court of law. I'm concerned with getting to the bottom of Kenneth Fleming's death. His son is connected to that death—"

"Circumstantially. Circum*stan*tially only. You haven't one piece of hard evidence to place my client inside that cottage on Wednesday night and you bloody well know it."

"I'd like to hear what he has to say about his movements and his whereabouts on Wednesday night. So far we've got an incomplete story. As soon as he completes it, we'll know where to go. Now may we proceed or would you like to discuss it further?"

Friskin blocked the door by putting his hand on the knob. "Tell me, Inspector. Are you responsible for this morning's gauntlet as well? Don't look at me as if you don't understand. The press went after my car like feeding sharks. They'd been told we were coming. Who's throwing out the chum?''

Lynley unhooked his pocket watch and flipped it open. ''They won't print anything that could cause themselves trouble.''

Friskin stabbed a finger into his face. ''Don't think I'm a fool, Inspector Lynley. You play it that way and I'll see to it you don't get another word from the boy. You can attempt to intimidate a teenager, if you wish, but hear me well. You won't intimidate me. Have I made myself clear?''

''Perfectly, Mr. Friskin. Now may we begin?''

''As you bloody wish.'' Friskin shoved the door open and stalked back to his client.

Jimmy was slouched where he had been slouched yesterday, picking at the unravelling hem of the same T-shirt he'd been wearing then. Everything about him was the same as it had been before, with the exception of his shoes. He now wore a pair of unlaced trainers in place of the Doc Martens, which had been taken for evidence.

Lynley offered him a drink. Coffee, tea, milk, juice. Jimmy flipped his head to the left as refusal. Lynley switched on the tape recorder, gave the time, the date, and the people present as he took his own chair.

''Let me be clear,'' Mr. Friskin said, seizing the advantage adroitly. ''Jim, you needn't say anything more. The police are giving you the impression that they're in charge because they've brought you here. That's to frighten you. That's to make you believe they've got the upper hand. The truth is that you haven't been arrested, charges haven't been brought, you've only been cautioned. And there is a distinct legal difference between each one of those conditions. We're here to assist the police and to cooperate to the extent that we deem appropriate, but we're not here at their behest. Do you understand? If you don't want to talk, you don't need to talk. You don't need to tell them anything.''

Jimmy's head was down but he gave what went for a nod. Having said his piece, Friskin yanked loose his floral tie and leaned back in his chair. ''Then go ahead, Inspector Lynley,'' he said, but his expression declared that the inspector would do well to keep his expectations at ground level or below.

Lynley reviewed everything that Jimmy had told them on the previous day. The phone call from his father, the excuses Fleming had made, the motorbike ride out to Kent, the pub's empty car park, the footpath to Celandine Cottage, the key from the potting shed. He went over the story

Jimmy had told them about setting the fire itself. He concluded with, "You said the cigarette was a JPS. You said you put it in an armchair. That's as far as we got. Do you recall that, Jim?"

"Yeah."

"Then let's return to the lighting of the cigarette," Lynley said.

"Wha' about it, then?"

"You said you lit it with a match."

"Yeah."

"Tell me about that please."

" 'Bout what?"

"The match. Where did it come from? Did you take matches with you? Or did you stop somewhere along the way to get matches? Or were they in the cottage?"

Jimmy rubbed his finger beneath his nose. He said, "Wha's it matter?"

"I'm not sure it matters at all," Lynley said easily. "It probably doesn't. But I'm trying to complete a mental picture of what happened. That's part of my job."

Friskin said, "Have a care, Jim." The boy pressed his mouth closed.

Lynley said, "Yesterday when you had a cigarette in here, you used four matches to light it. Do you remember that? I'm wondering if you had that difficulty in the cottage on Wednesday night. Did you light it with one match? Did you use more?"

"I c'n light a fag with one match. I'm not a spas, am I?"

"So you used one match. From a book? From a box?" The boy shifted in his chair without answer. Lynley took a different tack. "What did you do with the match when you had the JPS lit? And it was a JPS, wasn't it?" A nod. "Good. And the match? What happened to it?"

Jimmy's eyes flicked from side to side. Remembering the facts, altering them, fabricating them as he went along. Lynley couldn't yet tell. The boy finally said with a smile pulling at the corners of his mouth, "Took it with me, I did. In my pocket."

"The match."

"Sure. I didn't want to leave evidence, see?"

"So you lit the cigarette with a single match, put the match in your pocket and did what with the cigarette?"

"Do you want to answer that, Jim?" Mr. Friskin interjected. "It isn't necessary. You can keep silent."

"Nah. I c'n tell him. He knows anyways, don't he?"

"He doesn't know anything you don't tell him."

Jimmy worked this one over. Friskin said, "May I have a moment with my client?" Lynley reached forward to switch the tape machine off.

Jimmy said before Lynley's hand hit the *stop* button, "Look, I lit the bloody fag and I put it in the chair. I tol' you that yesterday."

"Which chair was this?"

"Jim, go easy," Mr. Friskin cautioned.

"What d'you mean, which chair?"

"I mean which chair in which room?"

Jimmy twisted his hands into the hem of his T-shirt. He lifted the front legs of his chair an inch off the floor. He said under his breath, "Fucking cops," and Lynley continued with, "We've got the kitchen, the dining room, the sitting room, the bedroom. Where exactly was the chair that you set on fire, Jim?"

"You know which chair it was. You saw it yourself. What're you asking me all this bloody crap for?"

"On which side of the chair did you place the cigarette?"

He made no reply.

"Did you place it on the left or was it on the right? Or was it in the back? Or beneath the cushion?"

Jimmy rocked in his chair.

"And what happened to Mrs. Patten's animals, by the way? Did you see them in the cottage? Did you take them with you?"

The boy slammed his chair back to the floor. He said, "You listen. I did it. I chopped Dad good and I'll get her next. I told you that much. I won't say nothing more."

"Yes, you did say that much yesterday." On the table, Lynley opened the file he'd carried from his office. From the photographs Inspector Ardery had supplied, he found a single enlargement of the armchair in question. It filled the frame with only the scalloped edge of a window curtain hanging above it. "Here," Lynley said. "Does this jog your memory?"

Jimmy hurled a sullen glance at it, saying, "Yeah, tha's it," and began to move his eyes away. They stopped, however, at the corner of a photograph that triangled out from beneath the others. In it, a hand dangled limply over the side of a bed. Lynley saw Jimmy swallow as his eyes locked on to the sight of that hand.

Lynley inched the photograph from the pile, watching the expressions flit across the boy's face as his father's body slowly came into view.

The hand, the arm, the shoulder, then the side of the face. Kenneth Fleming might have been sleeping save for the deadly flush of his skin and the delicate roseate froth that bubbled from his mouth.

Jimmy was held by the photograph as if it were the stare of a cobra. His hands twisted once again in his T-shirt.

Lynley said quietly, "Which chair was it, Jim?"

The boy said nothing, eyes imprisoned by the picture. Outside the room, work noises ricocheted round the corridor. Inside, the tape machine clicked softly as the tape kept turning in its cassette.

"What happened on Wednesday night?" Lynley asked. "From start to finish. We need the truth."

"I told you. I did."

"But you're not telling me everything, are you? Why is that, Jimmy? Are you afraid?"

"Of course, he's afraid," Friskin said angrily. "Put that photograph away. Turn off the machine. This interview has ended. Now. I mean it."

"Do you want to end the interview, Jimmy?"

The boy managed at last to force his eyes from the picture. He said, "Yeah. I said what I said."

Lynley pressed the *stop* button. He made much of gathering the photographs together, but Jimmy wouldn't look at them again. Lynley said to Friskin, "We'll be in touch," and left the solicitor to usher his client through the reporters and photographers who by this time no doubt lay in wait at every entrance and exit to New Scotland Yard.

He met Sergeant Havers—toasted crumpet in one hand, plastic cup in the other—on his way to his office. She said past a bulging cheekful of crumpet, "Billingsgate verifies. Jean Cooper was at work Thursday morning. Right on time."

"Which was?"

"Four A.M."

"Interesting."

"But she's not there today."

"No? Where is she?"

"Downstairs from what reception tells me. Raising holy hell and trying to get past security. You done with the kid?"

"For now."

"He's still here?"

"He's just left with Friskin."

"Too bad," Havers said. "Ardery phoned in."

She waited until they'd got to his office before she passed along Inspector Ardery's information. The oil on the ivy leaves from Lesser Springburn's common matched the oil on the fibres found at the cottage. And both matched the oil from Jimmy Cooper's motorbike.

"Fine," Lynley said.

Havers went on. Jimmy Cooper's fingerprints matched the prints on the duck from the potting shed, but—and this was interesting, sir—there appeared to be none at all inside the cottage, none on the window-sills, none on the doors. None of Jimmy's at least. There were plenty of others.

Lynley nodded. He tossed the Fleming files onto his desk. He opened the next set of newspapers that he'd not yet examined and reached for his glasses.

"You're not looking surprised," Havers remarked.

"No. I'm not."

"Then I suppose you won't be surprised by the rest."

"Which is?"

"The cigarette. Their expert got in at nine this morning. He's made the identification, done the photographs, and finished his report."

"And?"

"B and H."

"Benson and Hedges?" Lynley swung his desk chair round towards the window. The pedestrian architecture of the Home Office confronted him, but he didn't see that as much as he saw the application of flame to a tube of tobacco, followed by one face after another, followed by a cirrus of smoke.

"Definitely," Havers said. "B and H." She set her plastic cup on his desk and took the opportunity to flop into one of the chairs in front of it. "That cocks things up for us properly, doesn't it?"

He didn't respond. Instead he began yet another mental assessment of what they knew about motive and means, trying to match them with opportunity.

"Well?" Havers said after nearly a minute passed without his reply. "It does, doesn't it? Doesn't the B and H cock things up?"

Lynley watched a flock of pigeons rocket from the roof of the Home Office into the sky. They formed themselves into a shape like an arrowhead and soared as one in the direction of St. James's Park. It was feeding time. The footbridge that passed over the park's lobster-shaped lake would be lined with tourists, hands outstretched with seeds for the spar-rows. The pigeons meant to have their share.

"Indeed," Lynley said as he watched the birds fly, zeroing in on their destination because they always and only had a single purpose behind their flight. "It certainly puts a new spin on things, Sergeant."

CHAPTER
19

Jeannie Cooper followed Mr. Friskin's Rover in the blue Cavalier that Kenny had bought for her last year, the first and only item she'd accepted from his cricket largess. He'd brought it round one Tuesday afternoon, saying into her stubborn refusal to accept it, "I don't want you carting the kids round in that Metro, Jean. It's nothing but a breakdown waiting to happen, and if it blows on the motorway, the lot of you'll be stranded." She'd said stiffly, "We can cope if we're stranded. You needn't think Mrs. Whitelaw's phone is going to ring some night with me on the line asking you to come fetch us." To which he'd said in that quiet way of his, flipping the car key from one hand to the other and boring into her eyes with his so that she couldn't look away no matter how much she wanted to, "Jean, it isn't about you and me, this car. It's about them. The kids. So you take it. You tell them whatever you want about how you got it. I don't mind what you tell them. Don't mention my name if that's what you want. I'm only looking to keep them safe."

Safe, she thought, and a hard angry laugh that bubbled on the fringes of hysteria burst from her mouth like the promise of a serious eruption to come. Kenny wanted to keep them safe, all right. She choked back the cry that wanted to follow the laugh. No, she said to herself. She wouldn't give anyone the flaming satisfaction of seeing her break another time. Not after yesterday afternoon with those cameras clicking in her face and the reporters like jackals, circling fast and sussing her out, waiting for a show of weakness to record. Well, they'd got their show and they'd mashed it across the front of the paper and that was all she intended to give the bastards.

She'd fought her way through them at New Scotland Yard with a face like a clam shell. They'd shouted their questions and fired off their cameras, and while she reckoned they'd had themselves a fine time with her Crissys smock and her cap and the splattered apron she hadn't bothered to remove in her haste to be gone once Mr. Friskin had phoned her at Billingsgate Market with the news that the police were wanting Jimmy once again, she hadn't given them anything else. Just the outside woman who went to work and came home to her kids. The rest of her the reporters and photographers didn't see. And if they didn't see, they could not touch.

They navigated the congestion at Parliament Square, and Jeannie kept as close as she could to Mr. Friskin's Rover, with the half-formed and unarticulated design of somehow protecting her son this way. Jimmy had refused to ride with her. Instead, he had ducked into Mr. Friskin's car before either his mother or his solicitor had the chance to speak to him or to each other. Jeannie asked, "What's happened? What of they done to him?"

Mr. Friskin responded with only a grim "We're playing police games at the moment. It's par for the course."

"What games?" she'd asked. "What's happened? What d'you mean?"

He said, "They'll be trying to grind us down. And we'll be trying to maintain our position."

That's all he would say because the herd of journalists came thundering down on them. He muttered, "They'll be after Jim again. No, not the media—" this as her attention flew to the approaching newspeople. "They'll be after him as well, but I meant the police."

"What'd he say?" she demanded, feeling sweat break out in a band along the back of her neck. "What'd he *tell* them?"

"Not now." Mr. Friskin had hopped into the car and started it with a roar. He spun away and left her to elbow through the throng to the Cavalier. She'd opened the door and locked herself inside. The cameras recorded her every move, but the pictures would show no word or glance of acknowledgement to the questions, and no reaction on the face to the media frenzy over a son being questioned about the murder of his father.

And still she was no closer to learning what he had told the police than she had been after their conversation in the kitchen on the previous night.

You wanted him dead more 'n anything, Mum? We both know that, don't we?

Long after he had left her sitting across from his bowl of soup, observing the skin form on the top of it, forcing herself to wonder how it was that tomato soup formed a skin when it cooled while other soups didn't, Jimmy's two questions bounced in her head like rubber echoes. She did what she could to drive the questions away, but nothing—no prayer, no evocation of the sight of her husband, the faces of her children, the memory of their once-whole family sitting down to have a Sunday joint of beef —could keep her from hearing Jimmy's questions, the conspiratorial, sly tone in which he asked them, or the answers that came to her, as immediate as they were completely contradictory.

No. I didn't want him dead, Jimmy. I wanted him with me for the rest of my life. I wanted his laughter, his breath on my shoulder when he slept, his hand on my thigh at night when we talked about the day, the sight of him snapping a newspaper open and falling into a story the way a sky diver falls out of a plane. I wanted the smell of his skin, the sound of him shouting, "Move that ball, Jimmy! Come on, think like a bowler, son," the touch of him squeezing the back of my neck like he did every night when he got home from the printworks, the vision of him at the sea with Stan on his shoulders and Shar at his side and the binoculars passed among them in a search for birds, and the taste of him that was purely him. I wanted him, Jimmy. And to want him like that and to have him like that was to want him and have him alive, not dead.

But she was there, wasn't she? Seeing what I saw. Lolling like a cat with cream in what was mine. She stood between us and what was meant to be—Kenny coming home, Kenny singing like a hyena every morning in the bath, Kenny leaving his trousers in a heap at night and his shoes and socks at the bottom of the stairs, Kenny climbing into bed and turning me to him and pressing our legs and our stomachs together. So long as she stood between me and Kenny, between Kenny and his family, between Kenny and what was meant to be, there was no hope, Jim. And so long as she stood there, I wanted him dead. Because if he was dead—truly dead—I wouldn't ever have to think of Kenny and her.

How could she tell him this, Jeannie wondered. Her son wanted *yes*'s and *no*'s. They made sense out of life. They were the great untanglers. To lay all this before him would be to ask him to make a leap into adulthood that he couldn't yet make. Far easier just to say, No, no, I never wanted that, Jim. Far easier to make fast and loose with the facts. But as she followed the Rover along the Thames and tried vainly to read what was happening between the solicitor and her son in the other car as they made their way home, Jeannie knew she would not lie to Jimmy, any more than she could tell him the truth.

In Cardale Street, the journalists were finally gone and it seemed, at least for the moment, that none of them had decided to make the long trek back to the Isle of Dogs. Obviously, there was more scope for stories in hanging about Scotland Yard right now. Still, Jeannie had little doubt that they would be back with their notebooks and their cameras the very instant the journey seemed profitable. The trick was going to be to make it unprofitable. The only way to achieve this seemed to be to stay in the house and keep away from the windows.

Mr. Friskin followed Jeannie inside. Jimmy pushed past them and headed for the stairs. When Jeannie called his name he didn't stop, and the solicitor said kindly, "Best to let him go, Ms. Cooper."

She felt desperately tired, useless as a dried-out sponge, and completely alone. She'd sent Stan and Shar off to school this morning, but now she wished she hadn't done. With them in the house, there'd at least be someone's lunch to fix. She knew without completely understanding why or how she knew that if she fixed lunch for Jimmy, he wasn't going to eat it. For some reason, this realisation filled her with new despair. She could offer her son nothing of what he either needed or wanted. No food to strengthen him, no family to support him, no father to guide him.

She knew she should have done things differently. But as she watched Jimmy's trainers disappear up the stairs, she couldn't have said what things or how.

"He wouldn't say last night," she said to Mr. Friskin. "What's he told them?"

Mr. Friskin related it all to her, what she already knew and had tried to deny since the moment the two police officers had walked into Crissys on Friday afternoon and identified themselves as having come from Kent. Each fact felt like a death blow to her, despite Mr. Friskin's efforts to relate them kindly. "So he's confirmed a number of their suspicions," the solicitor concluded.

"What's that s'posed to mean?"

"That they're going to press forward to see what else they can get from him. He isn't telling them everything they want to know. That much is obvious."

"What d'they want to know?"

He spread out his hands and showed them as empty. "For them to tell me what they're looking for would be for them to place me on their side, and I'm not on their side. I'm on yours. And Jim's. It's not over yet, although I expect they may wait twenty-four hours or longer to let the boy worry about what's going to happen next."

"Is it going to get worse, then?"

"They like to push, Ms. Cooper. They're going to push. It's part of their job."

"So what d'we do?"

"We do our jobs as well as they do theirs. We play the game."

"But he's told them more than he told them when they were here, at the house," Jeannie said. "Can't you stop him?" She could hear the desperation in her voice and she tried to control it, not so much out of pride at this point but mostly out of fear of what desperation might indicate to the solicitor about the truth. "Because if he keeps telling them . . . If you let him just talk . . . Can't you make him hush?"

"It isn't like that. I've advised him and I'll continue to advise him, but there's a point at which the rest is up to Jim. I can't gag him if he wants to talk. And . . ." Here Mr. Friskin hesitated. He looked like he was sorting through his words carefully, which wasn't the kind of behaviour Jeannie expected a solicitor to have to engage in. Words came out of them slippery and easy, like eels out of traps, didn't they? "He does appear to *want* to talk to them, Ms. Cooper," Mr. Friskin said. "Can you think why?"

He wants to talk to them, wants to talk to them, wants to talk. She could hear nothing else. Dazed by the revelation, she felt her way to the telly where her cigarettes lay. She dug one out and a flame shot up in front of her face like a rocket launched from Mr. Friskin's lighter.

"Can you?" he asked. "Can you think why he wants to talk to them?"

She shook her head, using the cigarette, the inhaling, the very activity of smoking, as a reason not to speak. Mr. Friskin regarded her evenly. She waited for him to ask another question or to offer an expert opinion of his own to explain Jimmy's unaccountable behaviour. He did neither. He merely held her in an eye lock that had the effect of saying, Can you can you can you, Ms. Cooper, as good as if he was saying it himself. Still, she remained mute.

"The next move is up to them," he said finally. "When it happens, I'll be there. Until then . . ." He removed his car keys from the pocket of his trousers and went to the door. "Phone me if you think there's anything we need to discuss."

She nodded. He was gone.

She stayed by the telly like an automaton. She thought of Jimmy in the interview room. She thought of Jimmy wanting to talk.

"Kids are all a bit odd," Kenny had said to her one afternoon in the bedroom, sprawled out on the bed with his right leg cocked like it was forming the number four with his left. The curtains were drawn against the midday sun which still filtered through them, altering the colour of their bodies. Kenny's was tawny, corded with muscles that sculpted his skin, and he lay against the pillows with one arm crooked behind his head, looking like he meant to stay forever. Which he did not. Which she knew he did not. He ran his hand up her spine and circled his fingers in gentle massage at the base of her neck. "Don't you remember what we were like at that age?"

"You talked to me then," she replied. "He won't."

"That's 'cause you're his mum. Lads don't talk to their mums."

"Who d'they talk to, then?"

"Their birds," and he leaned forward to kiss her shoulder. He murmured against it as his mouth marked a path from her shoulder to her neck, "Their mates as well."

"Yeah? And their dads?"

His mouth stopped moving. It didn't speak and it didn't kiss. She put her hand on his calf, rubbing her thumb along the muscle that arced from beneath his knee.

"He needs his dad, Kenny."

She could feel him leaving her, like his spirit was fading even while his body was still as water at the bottom of a well. He was close enough to her that his breath was a ghost kiss against her skin, but the Kenny of him was an ebbing tide.

"He has his dad."

She said, "You know what I mean. Here. At home."

He sat up and swung his legs off the bed. He reached for his pants and his trousers and began to dress. She listened to the clothes sliding over his skin, thinking how each piece served to armour him from her better than mail. The act of his dressing and the when of his doing it comprised his answer to her unspoken request. She couldn't bear the hurt of it.

She said, "I love you. My heart feels so full when you're here." She felt the bed give a heave as he lifted himself from it. "We need you, Kenny. And it's not just me I'm thinking of. It's them."

"Jean," he said. "It's hard enough for me to—"

"And you want me to make it easy for you, right?"

"I'm not saying that. I'm saying it's not as simple as packing my bags and moving home."

"It could be that simple if you wanted it to be."

"For you. Not for me."

She took a breath that caught.

He said, "Don't cry, girl. Come on. Jean."

She ducked her head, and she hiccupped to keep the sob from breaking. She said, "Why d'you come round here, Kenny? Why d'you keep coming round? Why'n't you just let *go*?"

He came to stand before her. His fingers lifted and released fine strands of her hair. He didn't answer the question. She didn't require an answer. What he needed was here, within these walls. But what he wanted was elsewhere and he hadn't found it.

Jeannie ground her cigarette into the shell ashtray and dumped the ashes and stubs into the kitchen rubbish. She removed her Crissys cap and apron, placing the former on the table between the panther pepper pot and the palm-leaf holder for paper napkins, hanging the latter over one of the chairs where she smoothed it carefully into pleats like she was planning to wear it tomorrow.

A collection of *should have*'s took up residence in her mind, each one of them declaring how changed their circumstances might have been at the moment had she only had the foresight to act differently. The largest and the loudest of the *should have*'s was the one that badgered her about Kenny. It was simple enough. She'd been listening to it every day and every night for the last four years. She should have known what to do to hang on to her husband.

The root of every trouble they'd experienced was with Kenny's departure from Cardale Street. Trouble had started small, with the death of Jim's multicoloured mongrel, flip-flopped and crushed beneath the wheels of a lorry on Manchester Road not a week after Kenny had packed his bags. But it had grown like a cancer. And when she thought about those troubles now—from the death of Bouncer, to the fire Jimmy had set at his school, to Stan's bed wetting and nightly masturbation, to Shar's blind devotion to her birds, to all the ways her children had been shouting out for her notice and failing to get it and giving up about wanting it or needing it in the first place—she wanted to lay the blame at Kenny's door. Because he was their father. He had responsibilities here. He'd been a willing partner in creating three lives, and he had no right to walk out on those lives or on his duty to safeguard them. But even as she wanted to lay blame on her husband, the primary *should have* returned once again to remind Jeannie where the strongest measure of guilt and accountability truly belonged. She should have known what to do to hang on to her husband. Because if she had done, all the troubles of the last four years would never have descended upon her family in the first place.

She finally felt ready to climb the stairs. Jimmy's door was closed and she opened it without knocking. Jimmy was lying on his bed, face down into the pillow like he was trying to smother himself. One of his hands scrabbled at the counterpane while the other curved round the stubby bed-post. His arm was jerking like it wanted to pull him to the headboard and crush his skull, and the toes of his trainers dug into the bed, first one then the other, in a mimicry of running.

"Jim," she said.

Hands and feet stopped moving. Jeannie thought of what she wanted to say and what she needed to say, but all she managed to say was, "Mr. Friskin says they'll want to talk to you again. He says maybe tomorrow. But maybe, he says, they'll make you wait. Did he tell you that as well?"

She saw his hand tighten on the bed-post.

"Seems like Mr. Friskin knows what's what," she said. "Don't you think?"

She walked into the room, pausing to pick up one of Stan's teddy bears and set it among the others against the headboard. Then she went to Jimmy's bed. She sat on the edge of it and felt the sudden rigidity of her son's body shoot through the mattress like an electrical current. She was careful not to touch him.

"He said . . ." Jeannie smoothed her hand along the front of her smock, pressing her palm against a wrinkle that ran from the waistband to the hem. She thought she'd ironed this smock at two in the morning when she'd finally given up the idea of sleeping, but perhaps she hadn't done. Perhaps she'd ironed one and put on another. That would be typical of how her mind and her body had taken to working, on auto-pilot, just going through the motions.

"I was sixteen," she said, "when you were born. You know that, Jim? I thought I knew everything. I thought I could be a proper mother without nobody telling me what I was s'posed to do to be one. It comes natural to women, is what I thought. Bloke gets a girl pregnant and her body changes and so does the rest of her with it. I didn't want no one telling me how to be a mum to my little boy because I *knew*, see. I decided it'd be just like an advert, with me spooning cereal into your mouth and your dad hanging about in the background taking snapshots of how happy we were. I decided to make another baby fast as well because I reckoned kids aren't s'posed to grow up alone and I wanted to do things the way a mum's s'posed to do them. So we had you and then we had Shar and then we were eighteen years old, me and your dad."

Jimmy made a sound into the pillow, but it was inarticulate, more a mewl than a word.

"But I didn't know, see. That was the problem. I thought you had a baby and you loved him and he grew up and had babies of his own. I didn't think about other parts: the talking to him and listening to him, scolding him when he's done wrong, not flying off the handle when you want to scream and smack his bum for doing what you told him a hundred times not to do. I thought of Father Christmas and seeing his face in a bonfire's light on Guy Fawkes Day. We'll have such good times, I thought. I'll be such a good mummy. And I know it all already, I do, because I have my mum and dad for models so I know exactly what kind of parent I don't want to be."

She inched her hand across the counterpane, leaving it resting close to his body. She could feel the warmth of him even though she didn't touch him. She hoped he could feel the same from her.

"I guess what I'm saying's that I didn't do right, Jim. I thought I knew everything so I didn't want to learn. What I'm saying is that I'm a failure, Jim. But I want you to know that I didn't mean to be."

His body was still tense, but it didn't seem quite so rigid as it had before. And she thought she saw his head turn a fraction.

She said, "Mr. Friskin told me what you said to them. But he said there's more that they want to know. And he asked me something, too,

Mr. Friskin. He said . . .'' She found it was no easier than it had been the first time she'd attempted to say it. Only this time there was nothing else to do but to plunge forward and hear the worst in response. "He said that you wanted to talk to them, Jim. He said that you wanted to tell them something. Won't you . . . Jim, won't you tell me what it is? Won't you trust me that much?''

His shoulders then his back began to quake.

"Jim?''

Then his entire body was quivering. He pulled on the bed-post. He scrabbled with the counterpane. He dug into the bed with his toes.

"Jimmy," his mother said. "Jimmy. Jim!''

He turned his head and gasped for a breath. Which is when Jeannie saw that her son was laughing.

Barbara Havers hung up the phone, crammed the last bourbon biscuit into her mouth, chewed energetically, and sloshed down a mouthful of tepid Darjeeling. So much for afternoon tea, she thought. Wasn't employment at New Scotland Yard just another variation on nutritional bliss?

She grabbed her notebook and headed for Lynley's office. She didn't find him behind his desk, however. Instead, she encountered Dorothea Harriman making yet another newspaper delivery. This one was today's *Evening Standard*. Her face bore an expression communicating both her disapproval of and distaste for this chore, but it seemed more directed to the reading material itself than to being charged with the task of procuring it for Lynley. Two other offending tabloids dangled at arm's length from her body. She placed them on the floor next to Lynley's chair and neatly followed up with the others she'd brought him that morning until only the *Evening Standard* remained on his desk.

"Ghastly things." Harriman spoke with a toss of her head, every bit as if she didn't avidly thumb through those same papers on a daily basis, looking for the latest and most lubricious gossip on the royal family. "I can't think what he wants them for in the first place.''

"It's to do with the case," Barbara said.

"The case?" Harriman's tone of voice suggested how absurd she thought this line of reasoning was. "Well, I hope he knows what he's doing, Detective Sergeant Havers.''

Barbara shared the sentiment. As Harriman took herself off in answer to Webberly's distant roar of "Harriman! Dee! Where's the flaming Snowbridge file," Barbara sauntered over to Lynley's desk for a look. Head dangling so that his hair obscured his face, hands hanging limp at his sides, Jimmy Cooper graced the front page. As did Mr. Friskin, who was speaking urgently into the boy's ear. It was impossible to tell whether the picture came from yesterday's visit to the Yard or today's, since Jimmy's T-shirt and blue jeans seemed as permanently attached to his body as his skin and since Barbara hadn't seen—and hence was not able to judge by— Mr. Friskin's apparel on either visit. She read the caption and saw that the paper was connecting the picture to this morning's visit and using it as an illustration for an accompanying article whose headline read: "Yard Pushing Forward on Cricket Murder."

Barbara scanned the first two paragraphs. Lynley, she saw, was reeling information out to the press with consummate skill. There were plenty of *allegedly*'s and several mentions of *an unconfirmed report* and *sources well placed within Scotland Yard*. Barbara pulled on her lower lip as she read and wondered at the efficacy of this approach. Like Harriman, she hoped Lynley knew what he was doing.

She found him in the incidents room, where copies of the photographs of Fleming's body and the crime scene had been posted on a bulletin board. He was staring at them as one of the DCs spoke on the phone about additional surveillance on the Cardale Street residence and a departmental secretary typed at a word processor. Another DC was on the phone to Maidstone, saying, "If you'll have her phone DI Lynley as soon as the autopsy . . . Yeah . . . Right . . . Okay. Got it."

Barbara joined Lynley, who was sipping from a plastic cup with an unopened packet of Jaffa Cakes at his fingertips. She eyed the biscuits longingly, decided she didn't need to add any more useless blubber to her frame this afternoon, and sank into a chair.

"Q-for-Quentin Melvin Abercrombie," she said by way of introducing her topic. "Fleming's solicitor. I just got off the phone with him." Lynley raised an eyebrow although he didn't take his eyes from the photographs. "Okay. I know. You didn't tell me to phone. But once Maidstone identified those cigarettes . . . I don't know, sir. It seems to me that we need to start hedging a few bets round here."

"And?"

"And I think I've got something you might want to know."

"About the Fleming-Cooper divorce, I take it."

"According to Abercrombie, he and Fleming filled out the petition for divorce three weeks ago this Wednesday. Abercrombie delivered the petition to Somerset House on Thursday and Jean was scheduled to receive her copy and something called the acknowledgement of service form by the following Tuesday afternoon. Abercrombie says that Fleming was hoping to get the divorce on grounds of a two-year separation, which of course was really a four-year separation—as we already know—but all that's needed legally is two years apart. Following?"

"Perfectly."

"If Jean agreed to end the marriage, Fleming could have had the whole divorce process signed, sealed, and delivered within five months and he'd be free to marry right afterward, which according to Abercrombie, he was hot to do. But he also thought Jean might fight the proceedings, which is what he told Abercrombie and which is why, according to Abercrombie, Fleming wanted to deliver Jean's copy of the petition to her personally. He couldn't do that—it has to come from the divorce registry—but he told Abercrombie that he wanted to take a copy to her to prepare her for what was coming. To sugar-coat it, I suppose. Still with me?"

"And did he?"

"Take her an unofficial copy of the petition?" Barbara nodded. "Abercrombie thinks so, although like a typical solicitor he wouldn't swear to the fact since he didn't see the papers pass from Fleming's hands to hers with his own eyes. *But* he got a message from Fleming on his machine that Tuesday evening and in the message Fleming said that Jean had the papers and that it was looking like she was going to fight it."

"The divorce?"

"Right."

"Was he willing to go into open court with her?"

"Abercrombie said he didn't think so because in the message Fleming made an allusion to having to wait another year—to make it five years they've been apart—in order to get a divorce without Jean's consent to it. He didn't want to have to do that because, Abercrombie says, he was hot as a pepper to get on with his life—"

"As you've already mentioned."

"Quite. But he wanted even less to fight it out in open court and have everyone's name and dirty linen in the paper."

"Especially his own, no doubt."

"And Gabriella Patten's."

Lynley gave his plastic cup a half turn on the table, saying, "So how does all this constitute hedging our bets, Sergeant?"

"Because of how it all fits together. Are you familiar with divorce laws, sir?"

"Having never managed so much as a marriage . . ."

"Right. Well, I had a crash course from Q. Melvin on the phone." She underlined each step as she related it to him. First the solicitor and the client filled out a petition for dissolution of the marriage. Then the petition was filed with the divorce registry, who forwarded a copy of it along with an acknowledgement of service form to the respondent. The respondent had eight days to verify receipt of the paperwork by filling in the acknowledgement of service form and returning it to the court. And then the rest of the wheels of the process began to roll.

"Which is what's so interesting," Barbara said. "Jean received her copy of the petition on the Tuesday in question, and she had eight days to acknowledge having got it. But as things turned out, she never had to acknowledge having got it, so the process of divorcing never had to begin."

"Because on the same day that the acknowledgement of service form was due back in court, Fleming died in Kent," Lynley said.

"Right. On the very same day. Now how's that for a flipping coincidence." Barbara went to look at the pictures, particularly a close-up of Fleming's face. The murdered dead, she thought, never do look as if they're sleeping. It's only in fantasies that the police gaze upon them and reflect upon the poignant beauty of a life cut off prematurely. "Should we bring her in?" she asked. "Because it does explain why—"

"What a day, what a day." Detective Constable Winston Nkata swung into the room with his jacket slung over his shoulder and a lamb samosa steaming in his hand. "Have you any idea how many video shops're in Soho? I tell you, man, I have seen each one of them inside and out, upside and down." He took a mountain lion's bite from his samosa and, having garnered their attention, he flipped a chair round backwards and dropped onto it, leaning his elbows on its back and using the samosa to emphasise his remarks. "But the end result was the end result, no matter how many catalogues I forced these innocent eyes to wander through. And let me tell you, 'Spector, my dear mum is going to do some serious talking to you about what you had her youngest boy sifting through today."

"I believe you had the name of the shop," Lynley said drily. "There wasn't a need to make this an extended pornographic expedition, was there?''

Nkata took another bite of the samosa. Barbara felt her stomach rumbling in response to the scent of the meat. Oh, to be back on the streets, she thought, with access to food unprocessed, unpreserved, and more than likely unhealthy.

"Got to be thorough, man. When promotion time comes, you think of Nkata behind those letters DS.'' His jaws worked the meat like a pile driver forcing steel into the ground. "Here's the situation, though it took some doing to get it from the shop bloke 'cause, as he kept saying in my ear when he wasn't trying to blow in it—which is a story I'll save for another time—''

"Thank you,'' Lynley said fervently.

"—seems like most blokes out there don't much like it broadcast to the fuzz when they're hiring skin films. Not that it's illegal, mind you. But it puts a dent in the reputation. Course in this case, there was nothing to worry about since the blokes in question never hired those films.'' He took a last bite and licked the pastry crumbs from his fingers. "Now, why is it I'm thinking that news doesn't surprise you?''

"Do the films even exist?'' Barbara asked.

"Oh my yes. Every one of them, though according to the shop bloke *Wild in the Woolly* has been hired so often it's like watching gymnastics in a snow storm.''

Barbara said to Lynley, "But if Faraday or one of his mates didn't hire them last Wednesday . . .'' She gave the pictures of Fleming another glance. "What's this got to do with Jimmy Cooper, sir?''

"Now I'm not saying Faraday's mate didn't hire them at all,'' Nkata added hastily. "I'm saying he didn't hire them that night. On other nights—'' Here, he removed his notebook from his jacket pocket. He wiped his fingers on a spotless white handkerchief before he applied them to the pages of his book. He opened to a page that was marked with a thin red ribbon and read off a list of dates going back more than five years. Each one was connected to a different video shop, but the list was cyclical in nature, repeating itself after all the shops had been used once. There was, however, no set period of time between each date. "In'eresting, that bit of detective work. Wouldn't you say?''

"Nice initiative, Winston,'' Lynley acknowledged. The constable ducked his head in a show of spurious humility.

One of the telephones rang and was answered. The DC manning it spoke in a hushed voice. Barbara thought about Nkata's information. Nkata himself went on.

"Unless they just worked up a fondness for this p'rticular set of films, seems to me like these blokes're arranging a permanent group alibi for themselves. Memorise a list of films for when the cops come round asking questions, right? Only detail that changes from one time to the next is the shop the films came from, and that's easy enough to remember, isn't it, once you're told the name."

"So someone sifting through the records of a single shop wouldn't see the same films hired over and over," Barbara said meditatively.

"Which'd be like putting the alibi in neon. Which is what they didn't want to do."

"They," she said.

"Faraday's stag party," Nkata said. "Looks to me like whatever they're into, these blokes, they're into together."

"But not last Wednesday."

"Right. Whatever Faraday was into that night, he was into it alone."

"Sir?" The DC who had answered the phone turned from his desk into the room. He said, "Maidstone's faxing the autopsy over, but there's not much to add. Asphyxiation from carbon monoxide. And enough alcohol in his system to drop a bull."

"There's a bottle of Black Bush on the bedside table." Barbara gestured to the photographs. "A glass as well."

"From the blood alcohol level," the DC said, "it's a good bet that he passed out well before the fire was lit. Slept right through it, in a manner of speaking."

"If you got to go," Nkata remarked, "it's not a bad way."

Lynley rose. "Except that he didn't."

"What?"

"Have to go." He picked up his now empty cup and his unopened packet of Jaffa Cakes. The former he pitched into the rubbish. The latter he looked at with indecision before making up his mind and tossing them to Havers. "Let's find him," he said.

"Faraday?"

"Let's see what he can trot out next about last Wednesday night."

She hurried after him, saying, "But what about Jean Cooper? What about the divorce?"

"She'll still be there when we're through with Faraday."

CHAPTER
20

A telephone call located Chris Faraday. He wasn't in Little Venice but working instead in Kilburn, in a lock-up midway down a mews called Priory Walk. This wasn't much more than an alleyway, sided by abandoned buildings with boarded windows and graffiti-covered, dingy brick walls. Aside from a Ladbrokes on the corner and a Chinese take-away next door to it called Dump-Ling's Exotic Foods, the only truly booming enterprise in the area appeared to be the Platinum Gym and Aerobic Studio, whose "especially designed cushioned flooring which reduces impact to your knees and ankles" was at the moment bearing the weight and the sweating gyrations of a veritable herd of after-work aerobic enthusiasts. A vocal by Cyndi Lauper encouraged them whenever their instructor paused in her relentless counting to take a breath.

Faraday's lock-up was directly opposite this gym. Its corrugated metal door was three-quarters closed, but a dusty green van was drawn up next to it, and as they approached, Lynley and Havers could see a pair of trainer-shod feet moving from one side of the lock-up to the other.

Lynley slapped his hand against the corrugated door, called out, "Faraday?" and ducked beneath it. Havers followed.

Chris Faraday swung round from a workbench that dropped down from one of the walls. On it, various rubber moulds lay amid bags of plaster and metal tools. Five elaborate pencil sketches rendered on onionskin paper were pinned above this. They represented coffering, various cove mouldings, and other ceiling ornamentations. They were Adam-like in their delicacy, but at the same time bolder than Adam, as if designed by someone without the slightest hope of ever having a ceiling upon which he could mount them.

Faraday saw Lynley evaluating them. "After a while you see enough of Taylor, Adam, and Nash, and you find yourself thinking, 'This looks easy, I could have a bash at plaster myself.' Not that there's much call for new designs. But everyone's always looking for someone with talent for repairing the old ones."

"These are good," Lynley said. "Innovative."

"Innovative doesn't cut it if you haven't got a name. And I haven't got a name."

"As what?" Lynley asked.

"As anything other than a fixer."

"There's a place for fixers, as you've no doubt found."

"Not one I want to occupy forever." Faraday used the pad of his index finger to test the consistency of the plaster that was setting in one of his moulds. He wiped his finger on his stained blue jeans and slung a plastic bucket up from the floor. He carried this to a concrete tub at the far end of the lock-up and began sluicing water into it. He said over his shoulder, "You haven't come here to talk about ceilings. What can I do for you?"

"You can tell me about last Wednesday night. The truth this time, if you please."

Faraday sloshed water in the bucket. He scrubbed at it with a metal brush that he took from a shelf above the tub. He poured the water off and rinsed the bucket out. He brought it back to the workbench and set it next to a bag of plaster. His feet left a trail through the white dust that powdered the floor of the lock-up. His prints mixed with others already there.

"I've got the distinct impression of intelligence from you," Lynley said. "Both times we've met. You must have known we would check on your story, so I've been wondering why you told it in the first place."

Faraday settled against the workbench. His mouth played in and out with a bubble of air as he apparently considered the various answers he might give at this point. "I didn't have any choice," he finally said. "Livie was there."

"And you'd told her you'd gone to a stag party?" Lynley asked.

"She thought I'd talk about going to a stag party."

"That's an intriguing distinction, Mr. Faraday."

There was a tall stool on wheels tucked beneath the workbench. Faraday rolled this out and straddled its seat. Sergeant Havers made a place for herself on the top step of a three-step ladder, settling in with notebook in hand, while Lynley remained where he was. The lighting in the lock-up, unlike the lighting he had encountered during his visits to the barge, benefited Lynley this time. It came both from the street and from a fluorescent tube above the workbench, and it shone directly into Faraday's face.

"Obviously," Lynley said, "we're going to need an explanation. Because if you weren't at a stag party and were merely using it as a cover for something else, it does seem more likely that you would have cooked up something less easy for the police to verify. As I've already said, you must have known we'd check into it as soon as you gave us the names of the films and the video shop."

"If I'd said anything else . . ." Faraday rubbed his fingers into his neck. "What a mess," he muttered. "Look, what I was up to has to do with Livie and me. It has nothing to do with Fleming. I didn't know him. I mean, I knew he lived in Kensington all right, with Livie's mother. But that was it. I'd never met the bloke. Neither had Livie."

"Then I imagine you'll have no difficulty relating the facts of last Wednesday night to us. If they have nothing to do with Fleming's death."

Sergeant Havers made meaningful noises with the pages of her notebook. Faraday looked in her direction.

"Livie believed that the stag party story would check out," Faraday said. "Under different circumstances, it would have done. So she was expecting me to talk about the party and if I hadn't done, it would have led her to know something that would hurt her. I didn't want to hurt her, so I gave you the story she expected to hear. That's it."

"I take it, then, that you use the stag party as a regular alibi."

"I'm not saying that."

"Sergeant?" Lynley said. Havers began reading off the list of video shops that Nkata had given them, as well as the dates upon which the films had been rented throughout the last five years. She'd recited only three years back before Faraday stopped her.

"I get the point. But I'm not talking about it, okay? The stag party story has nothing to do with what you've come to see me about in the first place."

"Then what does it have to do with?"

"Not with Wednesday night and not with Fleming, if that's what you're hoping. So do you want me to talk about Wednesday or not? Because I will, Inspector—and the story'll check out—but I'll only tell it if you agree to back off about the rest." When Lynley started to respond, Faraday interrupted with, "And don't tell me the police don't make deals when it comes to the truth. You and I both know that you do it all the time."

Lynley pondered his options but realised there was little point in carting Faraday off to New Scotland Yard for a show of police muscle and a taped session in the interview room. All the other man had to do was phone a solicitor and maintain his silence and Lynley would find himself with no more information than he'd been able to garner from his previous interviews with the fixer.

"Go on," he said evenly.

"You'll back off about the rest?"

"I've said I'm interested in Wednesday night, Mr. Faraday."

Faraday dropped his hand to the surface of the workbench where his fingers sought one of the rubber mouldings. "All right," he said. "Livie thinks I was out on Wednesday night, doing something that I needed a solid cover story for. That's what I told her, and since she already knew the cover story, I didn't have much choice but to trot it out for you when you came round. But the fact is—" He jiggled the rubber moulding. He stirred on his seat. "The fact is that I was with a woman on Wednesday night. She's called Amanda Beckstead. I spent the night at her flat in Pimlico." He looked at Lynley with some measure of defiance in his expression, as if expecting to be judged and readying himself for the judgement. He seemed to feel compelled to add, "Livie and I aren't lovers, in case you think I'm betraying her. We never were. I just don't want to hurt her by making her think I need something she would like to give me herself but can't. I don't expect you to understand what I'm talking about, but I'm telling you the truth."

Faraday finished the sentence with his colour high. Lynley didn't point out to him that there was more than one form of betrayal. Instead he said merely, "Amanda Beckstead's address and phone number?"

Faraday recited them. Sergeant Havers scribbled them into her notes. Faraday added, "Her brother lives there as well. In Pimlico. He knows I was with her. He'll confirm. The neighbours can probably do the same."

"You left her rather early in the morning, if our account of your return is accurate."

"Livie expected me to show up around five to fetch her from her mother's. So that's what I did. Although as things turned out, I needn't have made such a rush of it. She and her mother were still going great guns over breakfast."

"Arguing?"

Faraday's expression was surprised. "Hell no. Burying the hatchet, I guess you'd call it. They'd been separated since Livie was twenty-two, so they had a lot of ground to cover with each other and not a lot of time to cover it in. From what I could tell, they'd been up all night talking."

"About what?"

Faraday shifted his attention to the rubber mould nearest his fingers. He smoothed his thumb against the side.

"May I assume," Lynley said, "that they were covering topics other than the ultimate disposition of Olivia's ashes?"

"It wasn't anything to do with Fleming," Faraday said.

"Then you should have no qualms about telling us."

"That's not quite it, Inspector." He raised his head and fastened his eyes on Lynley. "It's to do with Livie herself. And it ought to come from her, not from me."

"I find there's a great deal of energy being expended on protecting Olivia Whitelaw. Her mother protects her. You protect her. She protects herself. Why do you think that is?"

"I'm not expending energy on protecting Livie."

"The act of denial requires energy, Mr. Faraday. As do evasions and outright lies."

"What the hell are you suggesting?"

"That you're being less than forthright with the facts."

"I told you where I was on Wednesday night. I told you who I was with. I as much as told you what we were doing. That's my part of the story and the rest you're going to have to get from someone else."

"So you do know what they were talking about. All night."

Faraday cursed on an expelled breath. He got up from his stool and paced across the room. Outside, Cyndi Lauper at the Platinum Gym had given way to Metallica at maximum volume. Faraday strode to the door of the lock-up and slammed it to the cement floor. The howling guitars faded slightly.

"I can't cope much longer. Livie knows it. I know it. I've managed to hang on this long mostly because I've been able to scrape together a few hours now and again to see Amanda. She's been . . . I don't know. I guess she's been my lifeline. Without her I think I would have chucked the whole thing long ago."

"The whole thing?"

"Coping with Livie and ALS. That's what she's got. Motor Neuron Disease. From this point on, she's going to get a whole lot worse." He moved restlessly from the workbench to a stack of old mouldings that lay against the far wall of the lock-up. He poked at these with the toe of his trainer, and when he continued to speak, he did so to the floor rather than to Lynley. "When she can't use the walker any longer, she's going to need a wheelchair. After that a ventilator and a hospital bed. When she gets to that point, she can't stay on the barge. She could go into a nursing home, but she doesn't want that and I don't want that for her. The more we thought about the situation and wrestled with solutions, the more we kept coming up with her mother. And going home to her mother. That's why Livie went to see her on Wednesday."

"To ask her mother about moving home?"

Faraday nodded. He kicked at the pile of old mouldings. Three of them broke, coughing a gust of powder onto his jeans. He brushed the powder off. It was a useless gesture. The white dust of it was everywhere.

"Why didn't the two of you simply tell me this to begin with?" Lynley asked him.

"I've already told you," he said. "Or at least I've tried. Can't you see what's going on? She's living with dying. She loses ground every day. She and her mother'd had nothing to do with each other for years and there Livie was, having to crawl back in order to ask her mother for help. You think that was easy for Livie? She has a lot of pride. The whole situation put her through hell. So if she didn't feel like relating every detail of that night to you, I wasn't about to make her. It seemed to me like she told you enough anyway. What more did you want from her?"

"The truth," Lynley said. "Which is what I want from everyone involved."

"Well, you've got the truth now, haven't you?"

Lynley wondered. Not so much about whether he had the truth or not but about Faraday himself. He'd seemed forthright enough once he'd made up his mind to cooperate, but there was no way to overlook one salient aspect of their interview with him. As long as he'd been relating the facts of his own behaviour on Wednesday night, he'd stayed in the glare of the fluorescent light. But once his story shifted to Olivia, he'd sought the shadows. Light and shadows seemed to be recurring themes in Lynley's encounters with Faraday and the Whitelaw women. He found he couldn't ignore the nagging question that asked why these three individuals kept seeking the dark.

Lynley insisted upon driving her home. Once Barbara told him that she'd suffered the torments of the Northern Line that morning rather than exposing herself to the aggravation of constipated traffic, he noted the fact that Kilburn was no great distance from Belsize Park below which the neighbourhood of Chalk Farm made a diagonal slash between Camden Lock and Haverstock Hill. It would be ludicrous, he said into her protests, to return her to the Yard when a ten-minute drive would take her to her doorstep. When she tried to argue, he said that he wasn't hearing any idiotic arguments, Havers, so did she want to direct him to her house or did she want him to drive round blindly with the hope of stumbling upon it by chance?

Barbara had managed to keep him away from the grim realities of her home in Acton for the three and a half years of their partnership. But she could tell by the set of his jaw that she wasn't going to be successful in arguing for the nearest tube station this evening. Especially since the nearest station was on the wrong line entirely and would require an extended romp changing trains at Baker Street and an even longer romp doing the same at King's Cross. It was a good forty minutes by train or ten minutes by car. She grumbled about it, but she gave him directions with a show of good grace.

In Eton Villas, Lynley surprised her by pulling the Bentley into a vacant space and shutting off the engine. She said, "Thanks for the lift, sir. What's on for tomorrow morning?" and opened her door.

He did likewise. He stepped into the street and took a moment to scrutinise the surrounding houses. The street lamps clicked on in the midst of his observation, highlighting in a pleasant fashion the Edwardian buildings beneath them. He nodded. "Nice area, Sergeant. Quiet."

"Right. So what time d'you want—"

"Let's see your new digs." Lynley slammed his door.

See? she thought. Her chest filled with a bellow of protest, but she managed to control it. She said, "Uh, sir?" and thought of his own digs in Belgravia. Gilt-framed oil paintings, porcelains on the mantelpieces, silver glinting in the breakfront cupboards. Eaton Terrace was a far cry from Eton Villas, despite the homophonic coincidence of their names. Holy hell, she thought and hastened to say, "Oh, gosh. It's not much, Inspector. It's not anything, in fact. I don't think you—"

"Nonsense." And he was striding up the drive.

She followed him saying, "Sir . . . sir?" but saw it was useless when he pushed open the gate and began heading for the front steps. Still she tried with, "It's just a cottage. No, that's not right. It's not even a cottage. It's more like a shed. Sir, the ceiling's not high enough for you. Really. If you go inside, you'll feel like Quasimodo in less than a minute."

He followed the path in the direction of the front door. She threw in the towel and said, "Balls," to herself and then to him, "Inspector? Sir? It's this way. Round the back."

She led him along the side of the house, trying to recall in what condition she'd left the cottage upon her departure that morning. Underwear hanging over the kitchen sink? Bed made or unmade? Plates off the table? Crumbs on the floor? She couldn't remember. She fumbled for her keys.

"Unusual," Lynley said behind her as she searched through her shoulder bag. "Is this intentional, Havers? Part of the overall design for convenient modern living?"

She looked up and saw that her little neighbour Hadiyyah had at last seen to it that her promise was kept. The pink-draped refrigerator that as late as this morning had still been sitting on the flagstones in front of the ground-floor flat had now been moved and was standing to one side of Barbara's own front door. A note was sellotaped to the top. Lynley handed it to Barbara. She ripped it open. In the diffused light shining from one of the windows at the back of the house, she saw a delicate script that resembled calligraphy more than it did cursive. Someone had written: *Unfortunately unable to place refrigerator within your cottage as door was locked. Terribly sorry*, and then signed, as if with disgust at the beauty of the script, two names of which only the initial few letters were legible. T-a-y on the first name. A-z on the second.

"Well, thank you Tay Az," Barbara said. She related the ballad of the misplaced appliance to Lynley. She finished with, "So I assume Hadiyyah's father moved it back here for me. Nice of him, wasn't it? Although I don't suppose he's much liked having it as a conversation piece outside his front door for the last two days. When I get the chance . . ." She flipped on the lights and gave the cottage a swift inspection. A pink bra and a pair of knickers speckled with green dots were slung over a cord that ran between two cupboards above the kitchen sink. She hastily buried them in a drawer with the cutlery before she switched on a light next to the day-bed and returned to the door. "It's really not much. You'll probably— Sir, what are you doing?"

It was a needless question, for Lynley had put his shoulder to the refrigerator and was in the process of moving it. Barbara had visions of oily grime soiling his elegant suit. She said, "I can manage that. Really. I'll do it in the morning. If you'll . . . Inspector, come on. D'you want a drink or something? I've got a bottle of . . ." What the hell did she have a bottle of, she wondered as Lynley continued to heave the refrigerator from one leg to another, walking it towards the door.

She went to assist him, taking up a position on the other side. They moved it easily enough across her small terrace and had only a few minutes' discussion over how best to waltz it across the threshold and into the kitchen without having to remove the front door in the process. When they finally had the refrigerator in position, its flex plugged into the socket, its motor whirring with only an occasional ominous wheeze, Barbara said, "Terrific. Thank you, sir. If we get the sack over this Fleming business, we can always go into removals next."

He was taking in the hotchpotch of her belongings, one part Camden Lock, three parts Acton, and a good fifteen parts jumble sale. Like a compulsive bibliophile, he went to the bookshelves. He chose a volume at random, then another. She hastily said, "Junk reading. It takes my mind off work."

He replaced the volume, and picked up the paperback on the table next to her bed. He put on his spectacles and read its back cover. "Do people always live happily ever after in these books, Sergeant?"

"I don't know. The stories stop short of the ever-after part. But the sex scenes are diverting. If you like that sort of thing." Barbara winced as he read the title—*Sweet Southern Comfort*—and made an observation of the book's obvious artwork. Bloody hell, she thought. She said, "Sir. Sir, d'you want something to eat? I don't know about you, but I never got a proper lunch today. What about some food?"

Lynley carried the novel to one of the two chairs that were tucked beneath the dining table. He said, as he read, "I wouldn't mind that, Havers. What have you got?"

"Eggs. And eggs."

"I'll have eggs then."

She said, "Right," and rustled for the bucket beneath the kitchen sink.

She wasn't much of a cook because she never had the time or the energy to devote to practising. So as Lynley leafed through *Sweet Southern Comfort*, pausing every few pages to read, to harrumph, and once to say, "Good Lord," she threw together what she hoped would pass for an omelette. It was slightly burned and slightly lopsided, but she filled it with cheese and onions and a single tomato that was languishing in the bucket atop a mayonnaise jar, and she produced toast from four slices of decidedly stale—but thankfully not mouldy—whole wheat bread.

She was pouring hot water into a teapot when Lynley got to his feet. "Sorry. I'm not much of a guest. I ought to be helping. Where's your cutlery, Sergeant?"

She said, "Drawer next to the sink, sir," and carried the teapot to the table. She was saying, "This isn't much, but it'll have to—" when she suddenly remembered and crashed the teapot down. She dashed back to the kitchen just as Lynley was sliding the drawer open. She reached past him and snatched up her pants and bra.

He raised an eyebrow. She stuffed the underwear into her pocket. "Such a shortage of drawer space," she said airily. "I hope you don't mind P. G. Tips. I don't have Lapsang Souchong."

He picked out two knives, two forks, and two spoons from the tangled metallic maze of the drawer. He said, "P. G. Tips is fine," and took the cutlery to the table. She followed with the plates.

The omelette was on the rubbery side, but Lynley cut into it, forked it up, said, "This looks excellent, Sergeant," and ate. She'd used the excuse of setting the table to remove *Sweet Southern Comfort* to the far reaches of the cottage, but he didn't seem to notice the novel's absence.

Instead, he seemed thoughtful. Extended reflection wasn't in her line, so after a few minutes of mutual silent forking, chewing, and swallowing, Barbara began to feel restive and finally said, "What?"

"What?" he asked in reply.

"Is it the food, the atmosphere, or the company? Or is it the sight of my underwear? They were clean, by the way. Or was it the book? Did Flint Southern do the deed with Star Whatsername? I can't remember."

"They didn't appear to take off their clothes," Lynley said, after a moment's pondering. "How is that possible?"

"Editorial error. So I guess they did it?"

"So I would assume."

"Right. Good. I don't need to read the rest. Which is just as well. Flint was getting on my nerves."

They went on with their meal. Lynley spread blackberry jam on a triangle of toast, graciously ignoring the flecks of butter that speckled the fruit from previous meals. Barbara watched him, uneasy. It was unlike Lynley to withdraw into a lengthy reflection when he was with her. Indeed, she couldn't remember a time during their partnership when he hadn't shared with her every permutation of his thought process as they worked through a case. His willingness to sift through his ideas and to encourage her own was a quality in him that she had greatly admired and had ultimately come to take for granted. That he would abjure now what was most essential in their working relationship was out of character in him and disheartening to her.

When he didn't pursue the opening she'd given him, she ate more omelette, lathered butter onto her toast, and poured herself another cup of tea. She finally said, "Is it Helen, Inspector?"

The mention of Helen seemed to rouse him moderately into saying, "Helen?"

"Right. You remember Helen. About five feet seven inches. Chestnut hair. Brown eyes. Good skin. Weighs something like eight and a half stone. You've been sleeping with her since last November. Is this ringing a bell?"

He smoothed more jam across his toast. "It's not Helen," he said. "Any more than it's not always Helen at one level or another."

"That's an illuminating response. If not Helen, what?"

"I was thinking about Faraday."

"What? His story?"

"Its expediency bothers me. It begs to be believed."

"If he didn't kill Fleming, he's going to have an alibi, isn't he?"

"It's rather convenient that his is so solid when everyone else's is sketchy at best."

"Patten's is as solid as Faraday's," she countered. "For that matter, so is Mollison's. So is Mrs. Whitelaw's. So is Olivia's. You can't actually be thinking that Faraday's got this Amanda Beckstead, her brother, and her neighbours all willing to perjure themselves for his benefit. Besides, what did he stand to gain if Fleming died?"

"He doesn't profit directly."

"Then who does?" Barbara answered her own question a moment after she asked it. "Olivia?"

"If they managed to get Fleming out of the way, it would be even more certain that Olivia's mother would take her back. Don't you agree?"

Barbara sank her knife into the jar of jam and smeared her toast liberally. "Sure," she said. "After losing Fleming, Mrs. Whitelaw would probably be ripe for the emotional picking."

"So—"

Barbara lifted her purple-stained knife to stop him. "But facts are still facts no matter how much we'd like to massage them to fit our theories. You know as well as I do that Faraday's story is going to check out. I'll do my duty and track down Amanda and Co. tomorrow morning, but five quid says that everyone I talk to has a tale matching Faraday's point for point. Amanda and her brother might even be able to add someone we can phone to verify everything further. Like a pub with a talkative barman, where Amanda and Faraday swilled pints of Guinness till time was called. Or a neighbour who heard one of them upchucking on the stairs. Or someone who banged on the ceiling and complained how much the bedsprings were creaking while they boffed each other from midnight till dawn. Sure, Faraday didn't tell the truth at first, but his reasons make sense. You've seen Olivia. She's making the big slide into oblivion. If you were in Faraday's position, would you want to hurt her if you didn't have to? You seem to be assigning him some sinister design when all that's going on is a realistic protection of someone who's dying."

Barbara sat back in her chair and took a breath. It was the longest speech she'd ever made in his presence. She waited for him to react to it.

Lynley finished his tea. She poured him another cup. He stirred it absently without adding either sugar or milk, and he used his fork to chase round a last particle of tomato on his plate. It was obvious to her that he wasn't persuaded by her line of reasoning, and she couldn't understand why.

She said, "Face it, Inspector. What Faraday's said is going to check out. Now, we can keep worrying the story if we want to. We can even assign three or four DCs to find out what Faraday's really up to when he uses the stag party alibi to cover his arse. But at the end of the day, we won't be any closer to Fleming's killer than we were in the morning. And it's Fleming's killer we're after here. Or has our focus shifted while I was blinking?"

Lynley crossed his empty plate with his fork and knife. Barbara went to the kitchen where she fetched a bowl of slowly decomposing grapes. She rescued those that still appeared edible and took them back to the table with a hunk of cheddar from which she peeled away a fine down of mould.

"Here's what I think," she said. "I think we need Jean Cooper in the interview room. We need to ask her why she hasn't been exactly forthcoming with helpful information. About her marriage. About Fleming's visits to her. About the divorce petition and its interesting timing. We need to pick her up and keep her at the Yard for a good six hours. We need to give her a proper grilling for once. We need to wear her down."

"She won't venture into Scotland Yard without a solicitor, Havers."

"What difference does that make? We can deal with Friskin or whoever else she decides to bring with her. The point is to shake her up, Inspector. Which, as far as I'm concerned, is the only way we're ever going to get to the truth. Because if she hasn't been shaken up so far—with her son being paraded like a sacrificial goat before the press—then she's not going to be shaken up till we put the thumbscrews to her personally." Barbara carved herself some cheese and ate it with the last of her toast. She grabbed a handful of grapes and said, "Yeow!" when their sour taste shot across her tongue and into her throat. She removed the bowl with, "Sorry. *Bleah.* So much for that."

Lynley cut a slice from the cheddar, but rather than eat it, he merely used his fork to lace it with a geometric decoration of tiny holes. When Barbara was at the point of despairing that he would reply to her suggestion—which, to her way of thinking, was the next and only logical move in the investigation—he nodded as if he and his thoughts had arrived at a point of compromise.

"Sergeant, you're right," he said. "And the more I think of it, the more I'm convinced. Shaking up is what's called for."

"Good," she said. "So do we pick Jean up or have her—"

"Not Jean," he said.

"Not . . . Then who?"

"Jimmy."

"Jimmy? *Jimmy?*" Barbara felt the need to do something to keep herself from levitating with pure aggravation. She grasped the edges of her chair seat. "Sir, she's not going to break over Jimmy. Friskin will have told her today that Jimmy's not giving us the facts we want. She'll tell Jimmy to hold the line. If he hangs on and keeps clapping his mouth when we get too close to pinning him down, he's home free and he's got to know it. So does she. I'm telling you, sir, Jean Cooper is not going to be shaken up over Jimmy. And she's not going to break over Jimmy either."

"Have him there around noon," Lynley said.

"But why waste our time carting him in again? The press'll be all over us, not to mention how Webberly and Hillier will react. We won't gain a thing. And we'll end up losing more time in the bargain. Sir, listen to me. If we nab Jean, we're back on track. We've got something to work with. If we stick with Jimmy, we won't shake Jean up at all."

"You're right about that," Lynley said. He balled up his paper napkin and tossed it on the table.

"Right about what?"

"Shaking up Jean Cooper."

"Great. So if I'm right—"

"But it's not Jean Cooper I want to shake up. Have Jimmy there at noon."

Lynley took a deliberately circuitous route home. He was in no hurry. He had no reason to believe that a message from Helen Clyde would be waiting—he understood her well enough by now to know how little she would have liked his attempt to force her hand on the previous morning—and even if that hadn't been the case, he sometimes found that removing himself from a location in which he was expected to think actually allowed him to think with more clarity than he could muster either at home or in his office. For this reason on more than one occasion, he'd ducked out of New Scotland Yard in the middle of an investigation and cut through the underground station to make the five minutes' walk to St. James's Park. There he would follow the path that encircled the lake, where he admired the pelicans, listened to the squawking inhabitants of Duck Island, and waited for his mind to clear. So this night, instead of driving southwest towards Belgravia, he dropped down to Regent's Park. He drifted round the Outer Circle then the Inner Circle, and finally ended up spinning along Park Road where a turn to the west took him without thinking to the entrance of Lord's Cricket Ground.

Lights were on in the concourse, temporary lights set up by workmen doing repairs to a drain outside the Pavilion. When Lynley ducked inside the Grace Gates and began to pace in the direction of the stands, a security guard stopped him. After Lynley showed him his warrant card and mentioned the name Kenneth Fleming, the guard appeared ready to settle in for a natter.

He said, "Scotland Yard, are you? Close to breaking the case? And if you break it, then what? You ask me, we ought to bring back the gallows. Take care of this bloke proper. Do it in public." He pulled on his tubular nose and spat on the ground. "He was a fine chap, Fleming. Always had a kind word. Asked after the wife and the children, he did. Knew every one of us blokes by name. You don't find that often. That's quality, that is."

Lynley murmured, "Indeed." The guard seemed to accept this as encouragement. He looked as if he was about to warm to his topic, so Lynley asked him if the stands were open.

"Not much to see in there," the guard replied. "Most of the lights 's off. You need them switched on?"

No, Lynley told him and nodded as the guard waved him on his way.

He knew there would be very little point in bathing the grounds, the playing field, or even the stands with light. Both yesterday evening and all of today had illustrated to him that the essential key to unlocking the truth in the death of Kenneth Fleming was not going to be a piece of evidence—a hair, a match, a note, a footprint—that one could examine in the artificial lights of a cricket ground or even a laboratory and subsequently present in a court of law as irrefutable proof of a killer's identity. Rather, the key to bringing the case to a close was going to be something far more ethereal, a verification of guilt that rose from a single soul's unwillingness to keep silent and that same soul's inability to bear the weight of injustice.

Lynley made his way into one of the stands and walked down the dark aisle to the barrier that divided spectators from field. He rested his elbows on this barrier and let his vision wander from the Pavilion on his left to the shadowy circus-tent awnings that loomed over the Mound Stand on his right, from the square of tarmac at the far end of the field that led one into the nursery grounds to the field itself, a barely perceptible slope of seventeen pitches. In the darkness, the scoreboard was a rectangular shadow etched with ghostly letters, and the gently curving rows of white seats fanned out like cards lying against an ebony table.

Here Fleming had played, Lynley thought. Here at Lord's he'd lived his dream. He'd batted with a combination of joy and skill, making effortless centuries as if he believed he was owed a hundred runs whenever he took guard. His bat, his name, and his portrait as well might all have one day been collected in the Long Room, placed among those of Fry and Grace. But that possibility, as well as the promise that his skill once made to the future of the sport, had died along with Fleming in Kent.

It was the perfect crime.

From years of investigating murders, Lynley knew that the perfect crime was not one in which there was no evidence, since such a creature could no longer exist in a world where also existed gas chromatography, comparison microscopes, DNA typing, computer enhancement, lasers, and fibre-optic lamps. Rather in this day the perfect crime was one in which none of the evidence collected at the scene could be attached—beyond the law's required shadow of a doubt—to the killer. There might be hairs on the corpse, but their presence could be easily explained away. There might be fingerprints in the room with the body, but they would be found to belong to another. A questionable presence in the vicinity, a chance remark overheard prior to or after the commission of the crime, an inability to say with certainty where one was at the moment of murder . . . These constituted mere circumstantial data, and in the hands of a good defence counsel, they were about as significant as dust motes.

Every killer worth his salt knew this fact. And Fleming's killer was no exception.

In the quiet darkness of Lord's Cricket Ground, Lynley admitted to himself exactly where the investigation stood after seventy-two hours. They had no hard, usable evidence that could be indisputably attached to one of their suspects at the same time as it was intimately connected to the murder itself. On the one hand, they had cigarette ends, footprints, fibres, two sets of oil stains—one on the fibres, one on the ground—and a confession. On the other hand, they had a burnt-out chair, half a dozen match ends, and what remained of a single Benson and Hedges cigarette.

Beyond that, they had a crucial key to the kitchen door in Jimmy Cooper's possession, an argument overheard by a farmer out for an evening's walk, a car park brawl at the cricket ground, a divorce petition due to be acknowledged, and a love affair brought to an unhappy end. But every concrete object in their possession, as well as the testimony collected so far, acted as a tile in what promised to remain a mosaic forever incomplete.

And it was what they didn't have that gave Lynley pause, that coursed him back through time to the library of his family home in Cornwall where a fire flickered ochroid light against the library walls and the rain beat on the leaded windows in steady waves. He lay on the floor, head pillowed in his arms. His sister curled round a cushion nearby. Their father sat in his wingback chair and read the tale both children knew by heart: the disappearance of a winning race horse, the death of its trainer, and the deductive powers of Sherlock Holmes. It was a story they'd heard times beyond counting, the first one they requested whenever their father made one of his infrequent offers to read to them aloud. Each time as the earl approached the story's peak moment, their sense of anticipation grew. Lynley would sit up. Judith would clutch the cushion to her stomach. And when the earl cleared his throat and said to Sherlock Holmes in Inspector Gregory's deferential voice, " 'Is there any point to which you would wish to draw my attention?' " Lynley and his sister would chime in with the rest: Lynley saying, " 'To the curious incident of the dog in the night-time,' " while Judith countered with mock confusion, " 'The dog did nothing in the night-time," and both of them shouting in happy finale: " 'That was the curious incident.' "

Only in this case of Kenneth Fleming, the dialogue between Holmes and Gregory would have been altered, from the dog in the night-time to the suspect's statement. Because that's where Lynley's attention was drawn: to the curious incident of the suspect's statement.

The suspect in question had said absolutely nothing.

Which was—at the end of things—what was so curious.

CHAPTER
21

"Let's go back to the moment you opened the cottage door," Lynley said. "Remind me again. Which door was it?"

Jimmy Cooper lifted a hand to his mouth and ripped a sliver of flesh from his finger. They'd been in the interview room for more than an hour, and during that time the boy had managed to draw blood twice, neither time apparently feeling any pain.

Lynley had kept Friskin and Jimmy Cooper waiting in the interview room for forty-seven minutes. He wanted the boy as much on edge as was possible when he finally joined them, so he'd allowed solicitor and client to simmer in the sauce of their own anticipation while they were forced to listen to efficient-police-business-as-usual going on outside in the corridor. There was no question that Friskin was astute enough to have informed his client of the ploy that the police were using in making them wait, but Friskin had no real control over the boy's psychological state. It was Jimmy's neck on the line, after all, not his solicitor's. Lynley was depending upon the boy's ability to realise that fact.

"Are you intending to bring charges against my client?" Mr. Friskin sounded testy. He and Jimmy had once again run the media gauntlet between Victoria Street and Broadway, and the solicitor didn't appear to be enjoying the experience. "We're happy to cooperate with the police, as I believe our presence here has indicated from the first, but if you've no intention of bringing charges, don't you agree that Jim might be better off spending his time in school?"

Lynley didn't bother to point out to Friskin that the George Green Comprehensive had given Jimmy over to the ministrations of Social Services and the truancy officers during Autumn term. He knew that the solicitor's protest was more a matter of form than of substance, an overt illustration of support for his client designed to gain his confidence.

Friskin continued. "We've raked over the same facts at least four times. A fifth time isn't going to change them."

"Can you clarify for me which door it was?" Lynley asked again.

Friskin made much of sighing in disgust. Jimmy shifted his weight from buttock to buttock. "I already said. The kitchen."

"And you used the key . . . ?"

"From the shed. I already told you that too."

"Yes. You've said as much. I merely want to make certain we've got the facts completely straight. You put the key in the lock. You turned the key. What happened next?"

"What d'you mean what happened next?"

"This is ridiculous," Friskin said.

"What's s'posed to happen?" Jimmy asked. "I opened the naffing door and I went inside."

"How did you open the door?"

"Shit!" Jimmy shoved his chair away from the table.

"Inspector," Friskin interposed. "Is this sojourn into the minutiae of door opening absolutely necessary? What's the point? What are you after from my client?"

"Did the door swing open once you turned the key?" Lynley asked. "Or did you have to push it?"

"Jim . . ." Friskin cautioned, as if suddenly realising where Lynley was heading.

Jimmy jerked a shoulder away from the solicitor, perhaps his way of telling Friskin to shove off. "Course I pushed it. How else d'you open a door?"

"Fine. Tell me how."

"How what?"

"How you pushed it."

"I just gave it a shove."

"Below the knob? Above the knob? On the knob? Where?"

"I don't know." The boy slouched in his chair. "Above I guess."

"You gave it a shove above the doorknob. The door opened. You went inside. Were the lights on inside?"

Jimmy furrowed his brow. It was a question Lynley hadn't asked before. Jimmy shook his head.

"Did you switch them on?"

"Why would I?"

"I expect you'd have wanted to find your way about. You would have needed to locate the armchair. Did you have a torch with you? Did you light a match?"

Jimmy appeared to mull over the options—switching on the lights, carrying a torch, striking a match—and what each of the options might imply. He finally settled on saying, "I couldn't take a torch on my motorbike, could I?"

"Then you used a match?"

"I didn't say that."

"Then you switched on the lights?"

"I might of. For a second."

"Fine. Then what?"

"Then I did what I already said I did. I lit the bloody fag and I stuffed it in the chair. Then I left."

Lynley nodded thoughtfully. He put on his spectacles and removed the photographs of the crime scene from a manila folder. He sifted through them, saying as he perused them, "You didn't see your father?"

"I already said—"

"You didn't speak to him?"

"No."

"You didn't hear him moving about in the bedroom above?"

"I *told* you all that."

"Yes. You did." Lynley laid the pictures out. Jimmy kept his eyes averted. Lynley made much of studying them. He finally raised his head and said, "You left the way you had come? Through the kitchen?"

"Yeah."

"Had you left the door opened?"

Jimmy's right hand snaked to his mouth. His index finger slipped between his front teeth and he was chewing before he seemed to realise it. "Yeah. I guess."

"It was open?" Lynley asked sharply.

Jimmy shifted gears. "No."

"It was shut?"

"Yeah. Shut. It was shut. Shut."

"You're certain about this?"

Friskin leaned forward. "Exactly how many more times is he going to have to—"

"And you slipped in and slipped out with no impediments?"

"What?"

"No difficulties. You encountered nothing. No one."

"I said that, di'n't I? I said it ten times."

"Then what happened to the animals?" Lynley asked. "Mrs. Patten said that the animals were inside when she left."

"I didn't see no animals."

"They weren't in the cottage?"

"I'm not saying that."

"You've said you watched the cottage from the bottom of the garden. You've told me you saw your father through the kitchen window. You've said you saw when he went up to bed. Did you also see him open the door? Did you see him put the kittens out?"

Jimmy's face declared that he realised the questions were some sort of trick. But he clearly couldn't fathom what the nature of the trick was. "I don't know, see. I don't remember."

"Perhaps your father put them out before you arrived. Did you notice the kittens in the garden somewhere?"

"Who cares a sod about them bleeding cats?"

Lynley rearranged the photographs. Jimmy's glance dropped to them and quickly darted away.

"This is a waste of everyone's time," Friskin said. "We're not making any progress, and we have no hope of making progress unless and until you have something new to work with. When you do, Jim will be more than willing to cooperate with your questions, but until that time—"

"What did you wear that night, Jimmy?" Lynley asked.

"Inspector, he's already told you—"

"A T-shirt, as I recall," Lynley said. "Is that right? Blue jeans. A pullover. The Doc Martens. Anything else?"

"Underpants and socks." Jimmy smirked. "Same 's I got on right now."

"And that's all."

"That's it."

"Nothing else?"

"Inspector—'

"Nothing else, Jimmy?"

"I said. Nothing else."

Lynley removed his glasses and laid them on the table, saying, "That's intriguing, then."

"Why?"

"Because you left no fingerprints, so I'd assumed you wore gloves."

"I didn't touch nothing."

"But you've just explained how you touched the door to shove it open. Yet it didn't bear your fingerprints. On the wood, on the knob, inside, outside. The kitchen light switch had no prints of yours either."

"I wiped them off. I forgot. Tha's right. I wiped them off."

"You wiped your prints off and yet managed to leave all the other prints on? How did you orchestrate that?"

Friskin straightened in his chair and looked sharply at the boy. Then he turned his attention to Lynley. He kept silent.

Jimmy shuffled his feet beneath his chair. He pounded the toe of his trainer into the floor. He too said nothing.

"And if you managed the feat of wiping your prints off at the same time as you preserved all the others, why did you then leave your fingerprints on the ceramic duck in the potting shed?"

"I did what I did."

Friskin said, "May we have a moment, Inspector?"

Lynley began to rise.

"I don't need no moment!" Jimmy said. "I told you what I did. I said it and said it. I got the key. I went inside. I put the fag in the chair."

"No," Lynley said. "That's not what happened."

"It is! I told you and told you and—"

"You've told us how you imagined it happened. Perhaps you've told us how you would have carried it off had you been given the opportunity. But you haven't told us how it was done."

"I have!"

"No." Lynley stopped the tape recorder. He removed the cassette and replaced it with one from their previous session. It was pre-set at the spot he'd selected earlier that morning, and he punched the button and let it play. Their voices issued from the speakers.

"Were you smoking a cigarette at the time?"

"What d'you think? I'm some sort of wally?"

"Was it like these? A JPS?"

"Yeah. Tha's right. A JPS."

"And you lit it? Will you show me, please?"

"Show you what?"

"How you lit the cigarette."

Lynley shut off the machine, removed the tape, replaced it with the cassette from this current session. He punched *record*.

"So?" Jimmy said. "I said what I said. I did what I did."

"With a JPS?"

"You heard it, di'n't you?"

"Yes. I heard it." Lynley rubbed his forehead, then dropped his hand to observe the boy. Jimmy had tilted his chair onto its back legs and was rocking it. Lynley said, "Why are you lying, Jim?"

"I never—"

"What don't you want us to know?"

The boy continued to rock. "Hey, I *told* you—"

"Not the truth. You haven't told me that."

"I was there. I said."

"Yes. You were there. You were in the garden. You were in the potting shed. But you weren't in the cottage. You didn't kill your father any more than I did."

"I did. Bastard. I gave it to him good."

"The day your father was murdered was the same day that your mother was supposed to acknowledge his petition for divorce. Did you know that, Jim?"

"He deserved to die."

"But your mother didn't want to divorce. If she'd wanted that, she would have served him with her own petition two years after he'd left his family. That's legal desertion. She would have had grounds."

"I wanted him dead."

"But instead she held on for four years. And she may have thought she was finally going to win him back."

"I'd kill him again if I got the chance."

"Would she have reason to think that, Jim? After all, your father had continued to visit her throughout those years. When you kids weren't home. Did you know that?"

"I did it. I *did.*"

"I dare say her hopes may still have been strong. If he continued to seek her out."

Jimmy dropped the legs of his chair to the floor. His hands twisted inside his T-shirt, stretching the material in the direction of his knees. He said, "I *told* you." And his meaning was clear: Bugger off. I'm not saying nothing else.

Lynley rose. "We won't be bringing charges against your client," he said to Mr. Friskin.

Jimmy's head flew up.

"But we'll want to talk to him again. Once he's had a chance to recall exactly what happened last Wednesday night."

Two hours later, Barbara Havers was giving Lynley her report into the Wednesday-night movements of Chris Faraday and Amanda Beckstead. Amanda, she told him, lived in a conversion on Moreton Street. There were neighbours above and neighbours below, a friendly group who acted as if they spent all of their waking hours monitoring one another's business. Amanda confirmed that Chris Faraday had been with her.

"It's a rather difficult situation because of Livie," she'd said in a soft, composed voice, her right hand curved gently round her left. She'd been on her lunch hour from the animal grooming and photography studio that she and her brother ran in Pimlico, and she'd agreed to a chat with the detective sergeant so long as she was able to eat her cheese sandwich and drink her bottle of Evian at the same time. They'd walked to Pimlico Gardens and Shrubbery at the edge of the river, where they sat not far from the statue of William Huskisson, a nineteenth-century statesman rendered in stone and attired in a toga and what appeared to be riding boots. Amanda didn't seem to notice the incongruity of Huskisson's apparel, nor did she seem bothered by the wind that was picking up off the river or the cyclonic howl of traffic tearing along Grosvenor Road. She merely sat in an easy lotus position on the wooden bench and spoke earnestly as she attended to her lunch.

"Livie and Chris have lived together for some years," she said, "and it hasn't seemed right for Chris to move on now that Livie's so ill. I've suggested we might try to live communally, my brother, Chris, Livie, myself. But Chris doesn't want that. He says Livie wouldn't be able to deal with it if she knew he and I wanted to be together. She'd insist on going into a home, Chris says, because that's what she's like. He doesn't want that. He feels responsible for her. So we're left as we are." They'd scraped together what time they could over the past few months, she told Barbara, but they'd never been able to manage much more than four hours alone. Wednesday had been their first opportunity to have an entire night because Livie had made arrangements to see her mother and she wasn't expecting Chris to return for her until the morning. Amanda said frankly, "It's just that we wanted to sleep together. And wake up together. It was more than having sex. It was being connected in ways more important than having sex. Do you understand what I mean?"

She'd looked so sincere that Barbara had nodded, as if the experience of sleeping with a man were right up her alley. Quite, she'd thought. Being connected to some bloke. I understand how that feels. Ab-so-bloody-lutely and without a doubt.

At the conclusion of her report, Barbara said to Lynley, "So I see it this way. Either Fleming's death is a conspiracy involving most of Moreton Street, or Amanda Beckstead is telling the truth. I cast my vote with the second option. What about you?"

Lynley was standing at his office window, hands in his pockets, attention directed down towards the street. Barbara wondered if the reporters and photographers had dispersed. She said, "So what did you get from the yobbo this time round?"

"More inadvertent verification that he didn't murder his father."

"He's holding tight on everything else?"

"At the moment."

"Bollocks." She pulled out a stick of Juicy Fruit and folded it into her mouth. She said, "Why don't we just pick her up? What's the point of going through the back door like this?"

"The point is evidence, Sergeant."

"We'll get the evidence. We've already got motive. We've got means and opportunity. We've got enough to haul her in and have at least one decent go at her. The rest'll fall into place after that."

Lynley shook his head slowly. For a long time he gazed at the street below, then at the sky, which was grey as a battleship, as if spring had decided on a sudden moratorium. "The boy has to name her," he finally said.

Barbara tried to believe she'd misheard him. She popped her chewing gum in exasperation. It was so unlike Lynley to take this mincing-on-tiptoes approach that she wondered, with a twinge of disloyalty, if his habitual indecision about his future with Helen Clyde was finally beginning to seep into his work. "Sir." She aimed for a tone of comradely patience. "Isn't that an unrealistic expectation of a sixteen-year-old boy? She's his mother, after all. They may not get on, but if he names her as his father's killer, don't you see what he'll be doing to himself? And don't you think he *knows* what he'll be doing to himself?"

Lynley pensively fingered his jaw. Barbara felt encouraged enough to continue.

"He'll be losing both parents inside of a week. Do you actually imagine him doing that? Do you expect him to turn his sister and his brother—not to mention himself—into legal orphans? Wards of the court? Isn't that asking a hell of a lot? Isn't that trying to break him more than he needs to be broken?"

"It may be, Havers," Lynley said.

"Good. Then—"

"But, unfortunately, breaking Jimmy Cooper that much is exactly what we need if we're to get to the truth."

Barbara was about to argue her own point further when Lynley looked past her and said to the doorway, "Yes, Dee. What is it?"

Dorothea Harriman adjusted one of the frills of her silk jabot. She was a vision in blue this afternoon. "Superintendent Webberly is asking for you and Detective Sergeant Havers," Harriman said. "Shall I tell him you've just left?"

"No. We'll come along."

"Sir David's with him," Harriman added. "Sir David's called for the meeting, in fact."

"Hillier," Barbara groaned. "God spare us. Sir, it'll be at least two hours if he builds up a head of steam. Let's duck out while we can. Dee can make our excuses."

Harriman dimpled. "More than happy to do it, Detective Inspector. He's in charcoal, by the way."

Barbara sank deeper into her chair. Sir David Hillier's charcoal suits were legendary at New Scotland Yard. Perfectly tailored, creased like

newly forged axe blades wherever creases were needed, otherwise un-
wrinkled, unfrayed, and unmarred, they were what Hillier donned whenever he wanted to project the power of his position as Chief
Superintendent. He was always "Sir David" when he arrived in Victoria
Street wearing charcoal. On any other day, he was simply "the Guv."

"Are they in Webberly's office?" Lynley asked.

Harriman nodded and led the way.

Both Hillier and Webberly were seated at the circular central table in
Webberly's office, and the subject Hillier clearly wished to discuss covered every inch of the table-top, spread out as if perused rapaciously by an
inexperienced actor seeking journalistic approbation after opening night.
This morning's newspapers. And, from what Barbara could ascertain from
a quick glance as Hillier made much of getting to his feet in the presence
of a member of the opposite sex, the chief superintendent had got his
hands on yesterday's as well.

"Inspector, Sergeant," Hillier said.

Webberly heaved himself from the table and moved behind them to
shut the door. The superintendent had enjoyed more than one cigar so far
this day, and the atmosphere in his office was fusty, the room overhung
with a layer of smoke.

Hillier used a gold pencil in a sweeping gesture to take in the newspapers on the table. The photographs from this morning's selection featured
everything from Mr. Friskin using his arm to shelter Jimmy's face from
the photographers to Jean Cooper pushing her way through a jostling
crowd of reporters as she tried to make her way to her car. Additionally,
however, readers' appetites for information had today been fed with a
broader array of pictures than those depicting the principals in the case.
The *Daily Mail* was running what appeared to be a photo-essay on the life
and times of Kenneth Fleming, complete with pictures of his former
home on the Isle of Dogs, his family, the cottage in Kent, the printworks
in Stepney, Miriam Whitelaw, and Gabriella Patten. The *Guardian* and
the *Independent* were going for a more intellectual approach, using a
graphic of the crime scene. And the *Daily Mirror*, the *Sun*, and the *Daily
Express* were running interviews with sponsors of the England team, Guy
Mollison, and the captain of the Middlesex side. But the largest number
of column inches—in *The Times*—had been devoted to the issue of the
growing crime rate among teenagers, leaving the reader to conclude what
veiled allusions the newspaper was making by running such a story in
conjunction with features on the murder of Fleming. No prejudice here,

the story declared, but heavy use of the word *alleged* didn't deter the paper from honing its story on the possibility of an unnamed sixteen-year-old's guilt.

Hillier used his pencil a second time, to indicate two chairs opposite his own. When Barbara and Lynley sat cooperatively, he paced to the bulletin board across the room by the door and made much of examining the departmental notices that were hanging there. Webberly wandered over to his desk, but instead of sitting, he leaned his barrel-sized bum against the window-sill and stripped open a cigar.

"Explain," Hillier said. He spoke to Webberly's bulletin board.

"Sir," Lynley said.

Barbara glanced Lynley's way. His tone was even but not deferential. Hillier wouldn't like that.

The chief superintendent continued, employing a modulation of voice that suggested he was engaged in a verbal contemplation. "I spent my morning most curiously. Half in fending off the editors of every major daily in the city. Half on the phone with former and future sponsors of the England cricket team. I experienced a less-than-gratifying meeting with the deputy commissioner and went on to partake of an indigestible lunch at Lord's Cricket Ground with seven members of the MCC. Are you perceiving a pattern in these activities, Lord Asherton?"

Next to her, Barbara could feel Lynley bristle at the use of his title. She could sense the effort it cost him not to take Hillier's bait.

He said with perfect equanimity, "There's understandable anxiety on every front that we close this case. But that's generally the situation when a public figure is murdered. Don't you agree . . . Sir David?"

Touché, Barbara thought. Still, she cringed inwardly in anticipation of Hillier's reply.

As he turned to them, Hillier's face, always florid, seemed more so, a crimson contrast to his full grey hair. If they were going to play at bandying about titles, he stood to be the loser and all of them knew it. He said, "I don't need to tell you that it's been six days since Fleming was murdered, Inspector."

"But only four days since we've had the case."

"And as far as I can tell," Hillier continued, "you've spent most of your time trekking back and forth from the Isle of Dogs in unnecessary pursuit of a sixteen-year-old boy."

"Sir, that's not quite accurate," Barbara said.

"Then tell me different," Hillier said with a smile that seemed to aim for deliberate insincerity. "Because although I read the newspapers, that's not my preferred method of obtaining information from my subordinate officers."

Barbara began rooting through her shoulder bag for her informal notes. She saw Lynley's hand move on the arm of his chair and knew he was telling her not to bother. A moment later, she understood why when Hillier continued with:

"According to this lot," with a manicured hand waved in the direction of the papers, "you've a confession on your hands, Inspector. I've discovered this morning that that precise information has been leaked throughout this building as well as to the street. I imagine you not only damn well know that but intended it from the first. Am I right?"

"I wouldn't argue with that conclusion," Lynley said.

Hillier obviously wasn't pleased with this response. He said, "Then hear me. Some serious concerns are being voiced at every level about the competency of this entire investigation. And with damned good reason."

Lynley looked towards Webberly. "Sir?"

Webberly worked the cigar from one side of his mouth to the other. He dug his index finger into the frayed collar of his shirt. As it was Hillier's job to run interference between CID and every other department that might get in the way of CID, it was Webberly's job to run interference between Hillier and Webberly's divisional detectives. He had failed in this objective today, and he obviously didn't like to be reminded of that fact, even by so simple a word as *sir*. Besides, he knew what that one-syllable question implied: Whose side are you taking? Do I have your backing? Are you willing to adopt a dicey position?

Webberly said gruffly, "I'm behind you, lad. But the Chief Super"— Webberly had never once called Hillier Sir David—"needs something to work with if we're going to ask him to liaise with the public and the higher-ups."

"Why haven't you brought charges against this boy?" Hillier demanded, apparently satisfied with the position that Webberly had taken.

"We're not ready for that."

"Then why the hell have you led the press office into releasing information designed to be interpreted as if an arrest is imminent? Is this some sort of game whose rules only you are privy to? Are you aware of how the facts of this investigation are being interpreted, Inspector? By everyone from the deputy commissioner to the ticket sellers on the underground?

'If the police have a confession, if they have the evidence, why aren't they moving?' How would you have me answer that?''

"By explaining what you already know: that an admission of guilt doesn't constitute a viable confession," Lynley said. "We have the one from the boy. We don't have the other."

"You trot him into the Yard. You get nowhere with him. You trot him back home. You engage in the process a second and third time to no avail. With reporters following like dogs on your heels. And with the end result being that you—and by inadvertent connection the rest of us—look incompetent for being unable—or is it unwilling, Inspector?—to make a positive move. It looks as if you're being played for a fool by a simple-minded sixteen-year-old who needs a bath."

"That can't be helped," Lynley said. "And frankly if it doesn't bother me, Chief Superintendent Hillier, I can't understand why it bothers you."

Barbara lowered her head to hide her wince. Out of line, she thought. Lynley might have vastly outranked Hillier in the aristocracy game, but at New Scotland Yard there was a pecking order that had nothing to do with the blueness of one's blood or the manner in which one received a title: via the New Year's list or by right of birth.

As Hillier's face took on the colour of ripe plum skin, he said, "I'm responsible, damn you. That's why it bothers me. And if you can't bring this case to a timely close, then perhaps we need another DI on it."

"That's your decision, of course," Lynley said.

"One that I'll be more than happy to make."

"If you aren't bothered by the additional loss in time, then make it."

"David," Webberly interceded quickly in a voice that was underscored with entreaty as well as with admonition. It said, Step back, let me handle this. Hillier gave him a bare second's look of acknowledgement. "No one's suggesting replacing you, Tommy. No one's questioning your competence. But we've some uneasiness over the procedure. You're taking an irregular path in dealing with the press, and that's bound to get some notice."

"As I intend," Lynley said.

Hillier added, "May I point out to you that historically there's been nothing gained by conducting an enquiry into a murder by means of the media?"

"That's not what I'm doing."

"Then regale us with an explanation of what you're doing, if you please. Because from what I can see"—another semi-circular sweep of the gold pencil to indicate the newspapers—"whenever Detective Inspector Lynley sneezes, the press is informed just in time to say, 'God bless.' "

"That's an unintentional by-product of—"

"I don't want excuses, Detective Inspector. I want the facts. You may be enjoying your moment in the sun, but bear in mind that you're a bloody small cog in this operation and easy enough to replace. Now tell me what the hell is going on."

Out of the corner of her eye, Barbara could see Lynley's hand at rest on the arm of his chair. His ring and little fingers pressed into the worn fabric, but that was the only indication he gave of experiencing a reaction to Hillier's assault.

In a steady voice and without removing his gaze from the chief superintendent, Lynley related the facts of the case. Where he needed Barbara to interject a comment, he merely said, "Havers," without looking her way. When he was finished—having covered everything from Hugh Patten's presence at the Cherbourg Club on the night of Fleming's death to Amanda Beckstead's corroboration of Chris Faraday's whereabouts—he delivered a *coup de grace* that even Barbara would never have expected to hear him utter.

"I know the Yard would like the case closed," he said, "but the truth of the matter is that, despite our best efforts and all the manpower available, we might not be able to close it."

Barbara waited for Hillier to have a stroke. Lynley appeared to have no qualms about causing one, for he continued.

"We have nothing concrete to give to the prosecutors, I'm afraid."

"Explain yourself," Hillier said. "You've just spent four days and God only knows how many hours of manpower trailing suspects and collecting physical evidence. You've just taken twenty minutes to recount both for me."

"But at the end of trailing suspects and collecting evidence, I still can't positively identify the killer because there's no direct link between killer and evidence. I'm not prepared to ask a prosecutor to argue the guilt of someone I can't prove culpable of committing a crime in the first place. I'd be laughed out of court if I tried. And even if that weren't the case, I couldn't live with myself if I sent someone to the dock without believing him guilty."

Hillier had grown more and more stiff-bodied as Lynley continued.

He said, "And God forbid that we should ask you to do something that would make you incapable of living with yourself, Inspector Lynley."

"Yes," Lynley said in reply quite evenly. "I shouldn't care to have that asked of me. Again. Chief Superintendent. Once is enough in any career. Wouldn't you agree?"

They engaged each other in a lengthy duel of eyeball warfare. Lynley crossed one leg over the other as if settling in for a long postponed but much needed verbal brawl.

Barbara was thinking, Are you out of your flaming box? as Webberly said, "That'll do, Tommy." He lit his cigar. He puffed forth enough smoke to make breathing hazardous. "We've all got professional skeletons dangling somewhere. No need to rattle them out at the moment." He lumbered round his desk to join them at the table where he used his cigar as a pointer in much the same way Hillier had used his pencil. He said to Lynley in reference to the papers, "You've climbed out on a limb with all this. Who's going down with you if it breaks?"

"No one."

"You keep it that way." He tipped his head towards the door to dismiss them.

Barbara did her best not to shoot from her seat. Lynley followed her at a leisurely pace. When they were both in the corridor with the door swinging shut behind them, Hillier snapped, "Glib little fanny rat," in a volume guaranteed to carry. "Christ, how I'd love to—"

"You have done already, haven't you, David?" Webberly asked.

Lynley, Barbara saw, seemed unperturbed by Hillier's opprobrium. He was checking the time on his pocket watch. She looked at her own watch. It was half past four.

She said, "Why'd you say that, Inspector?"

He headed towards his office. When he didn't reply, she said, "Why'd you tell Hillier we might not be able to close the case?"

"Because he wanted the truth and that's it."

"How can you say that?" Barbara demanded. Lynley continued to walk, side-stepping a clerk who was rolling a trolley of tea urns and coffee pots in the direction of one of the incidents rooms. He appeared to disregard her question. "We haven't talked to her yet," Barbara pressed on. "I mean *really* talked to her. We haven't tried to push her. We know more now than we knew when I had her alone on Saturday, and it only makes sense that we see her again. Ask her what Fleming wanted all those times he came to see her. Ask her about the divorce petition. Ask her about acknowledging the divorce petition and what it means that she doesn't have to acknowledge it now. Ask her for the terms of Fleming's will and how the will stands now that he died with her his legal and only wife. Get a warrant to search her house and her car. Look for matches. Look for Benson and Hedges. Sir, we don't even need a complete cigarette. A seal from the package would do for a start."

Lynley reached his office. Barbara followed him inside. He was flipping through the Fleming paperwork, which was beginning to assume mountainous proportions. Transcripts of interviews, background checks, reports on surveillance, photographs, evidence, autopsy information, and a stack of newspapers that was reaching waist height.

Barbara felt impatience creeping down her limbs. She wanted to pace. She wanted to smoke. She wanted to grab the paperwork from his hands and force him to listen to reason. She said, "If you don't talk to her now, Inspector, you're playing right into Hillier's hands. He'd love to stamp *dereliction of duty* across your next performance evaluation. He's in a real muck-sweat over you because he knows the day's coming when you're going to outrank him and he can't stand the thought of calling you *Guv.* As if he ever would." She drove her fingers into her hairline and yanked hard on her hair. "Time's wasting," she said. "Each day that we don't make a move is a day that makes moving just that much harder. Time gives people a chance to cook up alibis. It gives them an opportunity to embellish their stories. Worse, it gives them a chance to think."

"Which is what I want," Lynley said.

Barbara gave up the effort of respecting his tediously smoke-free environment. She said, "Sorry. I'm about to punch my arm through the wall." She lit up a cigarette and retreated to the doorway where she could blow the smoke into the corridor. She pondered what he'd said.

From what she could see, Inspector Lynley had been doing far too much thinking about this case. Despite his lofty speech to the contrary at dinner on Sunday night, he'd abandoned his usual mode of operation, giving up on gut instinct at the very point in the case when instinct should be carrying him forward. In an odd reversal of their positions, it seemed to Barbara that she was the one who was operating on instinct now while he was the one who for some reason had decided to plod, unwilling even to begin to lift the right foot from the ground unless the left foot was in place solidly from heel to toe. She couldn't understand the change in him. He wasn't afraid of censure from the higher-ups. He had no need of this employment in the first place. If they chose to sack him, he'd clean out his desk, take the pictures from the walls of his office, collect his books, turn in his warrant card, depart for Cornwall, and never look back. So why was he being so hesitant now? What the flaming hell did he want to think about? What the flaming hell was there *left* to think about?

She allowed herself a mental curse and made it a gratifying one. Then she said, "So how much time do you need?"

"For what?" He was assembling the newspapers inside a box.

"For your thinking. How much time do you need to think?"

He set a copy of *The Times* on top of the *Sun*. A lock of blond hair fell against his forehead and he swept it back with an index finger. He said, "You've misunderstood. I'm not the one who needs time to think."

"Then who does, Inspector?"

"I thought it was obvious. We're waiting for the killer to be identified by name. And that takes time."

"How much more, for Christ's sake?" Barbara demanded. Her voice rode the scale, and she tried to control it. He's lost it, she thought. He's gone right over the ruddy edge on this one. "Inspector, I don't want to tread where you'd rather not have me, but is there the slightest possibility that Jimmy's—" she desperately sought a neutral word, couldn't find a decent one, and settled on, "Jimmy's conflict with his mother strikes too close to home? Is there a chance that you're giving him and Jean Cooper so much elbow room because . . . well, because you've been there before, in a manner of speaking?" She inhaled quickly on the cigarette, tapped ash to the floor, and surreptitiously spread it round in the guise of dust.

"In what manner of speaking?" Lynley enquired pleasantly.

"You and your mum. I mean, for a time you were . . ." She sighed and blurted it out. "You and she were at odds for years, weren't you? So perhaps you're seeing too much of you and your mum whenever you think about Jimmy and his. I mean . . ." She kicked the heel of her right brogue into the instep of her left. She was digging her grave and although she knew it, she couldn't quite decide how to put down the shovel. "Maybe you're thinking that with time you'd have been capable of something Jimmy Cooper can't manage, sir."

"Ah," Lynley said. He finished stacking the newspapers in the box. "You're wrong about that."

"So you agree that even you would have balked at naming your mother in a murder case?"

"I'm not saying that, although it's probably the truth. What I'm saying is you're wrong about what I'm thinking. And about who in this case needs to manage what."

He lifted the box of newspapers. She picked up the accompanying stack of files. He headed for the door and she trailed behind him, unsure where they were taking this lot but ready to tag along to see.

"Then who?" she asked. "Who needs to manage what?"

"Not Jimmy," Lynley said. "It never was Jimmy."

CHAPTER
22

Jeannie Cooper took her time about folding the last article of laundry. It wasn't so much that the job of folding an eight-year-old's pyjama top was a difficult one. It was, instead, that once the laundry was finished, Jeannie would have no additional excuse for not joining her children in the sitting room where for the last half hour they'd been watching a chat show on the telly.

In the kitchen stuffing clothes into the washer-dryer, Jeannie strained to hear conversation among them. But they were as silent as mourners at a wake.

Jeannie couldn't exactly recall if this was how her children had always watched television. She didn't think so. She seemed to remember the occasional shout of protest when one or the other of them switched the channels, the occasional laugh at an ancient Benny Hill sketch. She seemed to remember questions asked by Stan and answered by Jimmy and countered with mild disagreement from Shar. But even in clouded memory Jeannie realised that all of these reactions and exchanges between her children had taken place outside the realm of her own experience, like dreams in which she was an observer but in which she played no active part. And that, she saw with a slow dawn of understanding, had been fairly much the way that she had approached being a mother since Kenny had left her.

During the past few years, she'd used the idea of getting on with things as a way to avoid her children. Getting on with things meant that she went to work at Crissys as always, rising at quarter past three, leaving the house before four, arriving home at midday in time to go through the motions of motherhood such as asking was there school work to be done for the morning. She saw to having their clothes washed proper. She made the meals. She kept up the house. She told herself that she did right by them as a proper mum by doing her duty: hot meals on the table, church on occasion, a Christmas tree strung with fairy lights, Easter Sunday with Gran, money to play on the video games. But even as she made these efforts at a normal life, she knew that she too had committed the sin of desertion against her children, just like Kenny. Only she'd committed it more insidiously than Kenny. For while her living body had remained in place in Cardale Street—allowing her children to believe they still had one parent present whose love was constant—the heart and soul of her had fled like feathers in the wind the very same day that Kenny left.

Loving her husband more than the three lives created by that love was the ugly secret which Jeannie had long kept closed up inside. She mostly ignored it. Because first of all she couldn't bear the burning pain that moved quite regularly from between her breasts to between her legs where she ached for him whenever she heard or read his name or listened to his voice on the telephone. And because second of all, she knew that loving a man in excess of the children she had borne that man was a sin so grave and so unnatural that she could not expect redemption no matter how long she attempted to pay for committing it.

She'd believed that the least she could do was to keep her children from knowing. She promised herself they weren't ever to realise how she felt every day like a fresh used milk bottle, all empty inside but with a film remaining, reminding her what the contents had been. So she went through the motions of mothering, promising herself she wouldn't let her kids down and cause them more pain like their dad.

But despite her efforts at playing the role she'd decided she was supposed to play, Jeannie now saw that the end had been that she'd caused her kids as much grief as their dad had done, because her mulish commitment to getting on with things had required an equal getting on from them. If she was to go through the motions of being mother, without once owning up to the desolation she felt at Kenny's departure, then her kids could go through the motions of being kids in the very same fashion. They'd all muddle through it together that way, their behaviour declaring—despite what they felt—that if Dad was gone, if he didn't want them, if he wasn't coming back, then to hell with him.

She put Stan's pyjamas on top of the final stack of laundry and picked it up. She hesitated at the foot of the stairs. Stan was on the floor between the sofa and the coffee table, pressing his cheek against Jimmy's knee. Shar was shoulder-to-shoulder with her brother, holding the sleeve of his T-shirt between her fingers. They were losing him, they knew they were losing him, and the sight of them clinging to him as if clinging alone could prevent that loss made Jeannie's eyes smart so bad that she wanted to snap at their heads and fling them apart.

"Kids," she said, but it came out too sharp.

Shar looked quickly in her direction, as did Stan. Stan's arm tightened round Jimmy's leg. Jeannie knew they were armouring themselves, and she wondered when they'd learned so much from simply hearing the tone of her voice. She altered it and said with a gentleness that felt born from exhaustion and despair, "I got us fish fingers and chips for tonight. Cokes as well."

Stan's face brightened. He said, "Cokes!" and looked up expectantly at his brother. Cokes were a treat, but Jimmy gave no reaction to the news, although Shar said with grave courtesy, "Cokes're real nice, Mummy. Shall I do the table?"

"You do that, luv," Jeannie said.

She carried the laundry upstairs. She took her time about replacing everything in its appropriate drawer.

In the boys' room she rearranged Stan's platoon of teddy bears. She made orderly the books and the comic books on their wrought-iron shelves. She picked up a shoelace. She folded a jersey. She plumped up the pillows on both boys' beds. Doing something was what counted. Keep moving, keep doing, don't think, don't question, and most of all don't wonder why.

Jeannie sat abruptly on the edge of Jimmy's bed.

"The police claim that he's lying to them," Mr. Friskin had told her. "They're saying he wasn't in the cottage but that's not an unchanging situation, believe me. I assure you that they intend to keep at him."

Jeannie had grasped eagerly at this frail thread of hope. "But if he's lying—"

"They *claim* that he's lying. There's a fine distinction between what they claim to us and what they actually know when we're not there. The police use dozens of tricks to get suspects to talk, and we have to be wary that this may be one of them."

"What if it isn't? What if it's true that he lied from the first and they know it? Why would they want to keep at him?"

"For one logical reason. I assume they expect he can name the killer."

Horror came over her like a rush of sickness, pushing from her stomach up to her throat.

"That's my best guess on what they're up to," Mr. Friskin said. "It's a reasonable conclusion for them to reach. They're assuming, from his admitted presence at the scene last Wednesday, that he must have seen the arsonist. They're carrying that assumption further to include the fact that he knows who the arsonist is. They're doubtless concluding that he's assuming responsibility so that he doesn't have to sneak on someone else."

She was able to manage only the single word "Sneak."

"We frequently see this sort of recalcitrance on the part of teenagers, Mrs . . . Ms. Cooper. Although admittedly, it's usually the product of an unwillingness to betray one of their peers. But that tendency of young people to hold their tongues might well have become somewhat skewed in Jimmy. Because of his—pardon me for saying it quite this way—but because of his circumstances, who knows exactly where his loyalties lie?"

"What's that mean?" she asked. " 'Because of his circumstances'?"

The solicitor studied the tops of his shoes. "If we're to assume the boy's lying betrays an unwillingness to sneak and nothing else, then we have to examine his life for the sort of close social ties that encourage this predilection for holding one's tongue no matter the cost. Ties like those formed at school with good mates. But if there are no deep social ties and thus no way he may have learned this behaviour, then we have to assume the boy's lying represents something else altogether."

"Like what?" Jeannie asked although her lips and mouth felt dry when she said it.

"Like protecting someone." Mr. Friskin moved his study of his shoes to a study of her face. Seconds ticked their way towards a minute, and Jeannie felt their passage in the pulse that was beating in her temples.

The police would be back, Mr. Friskin finally told her. The best that she could do for her son right now would be to encourage him to tell them the truth when they came. She saw that, didn't she? Didn't she see that the truth was their only hope of removing the police and the media from Jimmy's life? Because he didn't really deserve to have them hounding him like this indefinitely, did he, Ms. Cooper? Certainly the boy's very own mother would agree with that.

Jeannie pressed her hand along the brown zigzagging design of the counterpane on Jimmy's bed. She could still hear Mr. Friskin's grave voice: *It's really the only way, Ms. Cooper. Encourage the boy to tell the truth.*

And even if he told the truth, what then? she wondered. How would telling the truth ever serve to obliterate the reality of having gone through this hell in the first place?

She had told her son on the previous night that she'd failed as a mother, but Jeannie saw now that the statement was nothing but self-serving twaddle because when she'd made it, she hadn't really believed it at all. She'd merely said it as a means of getting the boy to talk to her, hoping he'd say, No, you ain't been bad, Mum, you been through a rough patch like all of us have, I understand that, I always did. And the talk between them would grow from there. Because that's what children were supposed to do. Talk to their mums if their mums were proper. But even the solicitor who'd known Jeannie and her children a mere forty-eight hours had recognised the nature of the relationship between mother and this particular child. For he'd said she was to encourage her son to tell the truth, but he hadn't suggested that she make any attempt to have Jimmy tell the truth to her.

Tell the truth to your solicitor, Jim. Tell it to the police. Tell it to those reporters who keep nipping at your heels. Tell it to strangers. But don't give a thought to telling it to me. And once you tell it, Jimmy . . . And once you tell what you saw and what you know to people who don't care a stuff for what you're suffering, to people who only want to end this case so they can go home straightaway and put supper in their stomachs. . . .

No, she thought. It wasn't going to happen like that. She was his mother. In spite of everything—and because of everything—no one had a duty to the boy but her.

She went back down the stairs. Shar was in the kitchen. She was replacing the oilcloth with their Christmas tablecloth, one edged in holly with a wreath in the centre and Father Christmas ho-hoing in all four corners. Stan and Jim were still watching the telly where a beaky-nosed man with an unshaven face was going on about some film he'd just made, talking like he had a plum in his mouth.

"Bloody poof, he is, i'n't he, Jim?" Stan giggled and punched his brother on the knee.

Jeannie said, "Watch your mouth. Help your sister with the table," and went to turn the television off. She said to Jimmy, "Come with me," and added in a gentler tone as he shrank into the sofa, "Come on, Jim luv. We're just going out back." They left Shar meticulously laying fish fingers out on a cooking sheet and Stan shaking frozen chips into a pan.

"Shall I do a green salad as well, Mummy?" Shar asked as Jeannie opened the door to the garden.

"C'n we have baked beans?" Stan added.

"You make what you want," Jeannie told them. "You call us when things're ready."

Jimmy preceded her down the single concrete step to the garden. He ambled to the birdbath and Jeannie joined him, setting her cigarettes and a matchbook on the broken edge.

"Have a fag if you want," she told her son.

He picked at a jagged section of the birdbath where a chunk of it had long ago fallen off. He made no move towards the cigarettes.

"Course, I wished you wouldn't smoke," Jeannie said, "but if you want, it's okay for now. Me, I wished I never started smoking. P'rhaps I can give it up when all this's over."

She looked round the pitiful excuse for a garden: one broken birdbath, one concrete slab with beds of scraggly pansies running along its edges. She said, "It'd be nice to have a proper garden, don't you think, Jim? P'rhaps we can make this dunghill into a real showplace. When all this's over. If we take out this old concrete and put in a lawn, some pretty flowers, and a tree, we could sit out here when the weather's fine. I'd like to do that. I'd want your help, though, with the work. I couldn't cope with it on my own."

Jimmy's hands went into the pockets of his jeans. He brought out his own cigarettes and matches. He lit one and laid the packet and the matches next to her own.

Jeannie felt the hunger strike her when she smelled the smoke. It worked through her nerves like they were being pulled tight. But she didn't reach for her own cigarettes. Instead, she said, "Oh ta, Jim. That's nice of you. I will," and took one of his. She lit it, coughed, and said, "Cor, we both got to get off the weed, huh? P'rhaps we can do it together. I help you. You help me. Afterwards. When this is over."

Jimmy flicked ash into the empty birdbath.

"I can use the help," she said. "You probably can use the help as well. 'Sides, we don't want Shar and Stan to start smoking. We got to set an example. We could even make these here our last fags if we wanted. We got to take care of Shar and Stan."

He let out breath and smoke. It sounded like a snort. He was scoffing at her words.

She answered the scoff. "Shar and Stan need you."

His head was turned towards the wall that separated their garden from their neighbour's, so she couldn't see his expression although she heard him well enough when he muttered, "They got you."

"Sure they got me," Jeannie said. "I'm their mum and I'll always be here. But they need their older brother as well. You see that, don't you? They need you here, now more'n ever. They're going to look to you now that . . ." She saw the pitfall. She made her voice strong and forced herself on. "They're going to need you special now that your dad's—"

"I said they got you." Jimmy's voice was terse. "They got their mum."

"But they need a man as well."

"Uncle Der."

"Uncle Der's not you. He loves them, yeah, but he doesn't know them like you do, Jim. And they don't look to him like they look to you. A brother's different from an uncle. A brother's more close. A brother's right there all the time so he can look out for them. That's important. Looking out for them. For Stan. For Shar." She licked her lips and inhaled the acrid tobacco smoke. She was fast running out of harmless words.

She ventured round the side of the birdbath so that she was facing him. She took a final drag from the cigarette and crushed what was left of it beneath the sole of her shoe. She saw his eyes dart warily in her direction, and when their glances met, she finally asked gently, "Why're you lying to the cops, luv?"

He moved his head. He took such a long drag from his cigarette that Jeannie thought he'd smoke it straight to the end in one long gasp.

"What'd you see that night?" she asked softly.

"He deserved to die."

"Don't say that."

"I'll say what I want. I got the right. I don't care that he's dead."

"You care. You do. You loved your dad like nobody on earth, and no lie you tell's going to change that, Jimmy."

He spat a shred of tobacco onto the ground. He followed it with a heavy glob of grey-green sputum. Jeannie refused to let him derail her.

She said, "You wanted Dad home as bad 's I did. Maybe worse'n I did because there wasn't a pricey blonde slag that was standing between you and him like there was standing between him and me. So there was nothing that made you all bollixed up about how you felt and whether you really wanted him back in the first place. Maybe that's why you're lying now, Jim. To me. To Mr. Friskin. To the cops." She saw a muscle suddenly tighten in his jaw. She felt them hovering on the edge of what needed to be said and she went on with "Maybe you're lying cos it's easier to lie. Did you ever think that? Maybe you're lying cos it's easier than having to go through the hurt of knowing Dad's gone forever this time."

Jimmy tossed his cigarette to the ground and let it smoulder there. He said, "That's it. You got it dead right, Mum," and he sounded too relieved for Jeannie's liking.

He began to reach for his packet of JPS. Jeannie got to the cigarettes before he did and closed her hand round them as well as round her own. She said, "But maybe it *is* like Mr. Friskin said."

"Mummy?" Shar called from the kitchen door.

Jim blocked Jeannie's view of the house. She ignored her daughter, saying instead in a lower voice, "You listen to me, Jim."

"Mummy?" Shar called again.

"You got to tell me why you're lying. You got to tell me the truth right now."

"I already told it."

"You got to tell me exactly what you saw." She reached for him across the birdbath, but he jerked back. "If you tell me that, if you tell me, Jim, then we can think what to do next, you and me."

"I *tol'* the truth. A hundred times. Nobody wants to know it."

"Not the whole truth. That's what you got to tell me now. So we can think what to do. Because we can't think what to do so long as you—"

"Mummy!" Shar called.

Stan wailed, "Jimmy!"

Jim spun round in the direction of the door. Jeannie stepped past the birdbath and grasped his elbow.

Jim said, "Hell!"

Jeannie said, "No."

And Inspector Lynley gently disengaged Shar and Stan from hanging on to his arms. From the kitchen he said, "We have a few more questions."

And Jimmy bolted.

Lynley wouldn't have thought the boy could have moved so fast. In the time it took Lynley to finish his sentence, Jimmy wrenched himself from the grasp of his mother and dashed to the bottom of the garden. He didn't bother with the gate. Instead he flung himself at the wall and, with a yelp, he leaped over it. His footsteps began pounding along the path between the houses.

His mother cried, "Jimmy!" and headed after him.

Lynley called over his shoulder, "He's on the run towards Plevna Street. Try to cut him off," to Sergeant Havers. He shoved his way past the other two children and set off in pursuit of the boy as Havers ran back through the sitting room and out the front door.

Jean Cooper had wrested the garden gate open by the time Lynley reached her. She clutched his arm, shouting, "Leave him be!" Lynley broke her hold and shot after the boy. She followed, crying out her son's name.

Jimmy was racing along the narrow concrete path between the houses. He tossed one look back over his shoulder, then increased his speed. A bicycle leaned against a garden gate one house from the end of the walk, and as he flew by this, he flung it onto the path behind him and vaulted onto the cyclone fencing that edged the top of the brick wall which marked the path's far boundary on Plevna Street. He scrambled over this and dropped out of sight.

Lynley cleared the bicycle with a jump and tore to a wooden gate in the wall that the boy had ignored. It was locked. He sprang for a handhold on the cyclone fence. Beyond the wall, he heard Havers shout. Then the sound of footsteps drummed against the pavement. Too many footsteps.

He pulled himself up and over and dropped to the pavement in time to see Havers flying up Plevna Street in the direction of Manchester Road, trailed by three men, one of whom bore two cameras. He said, "God-*damn*," and took up the chase, dodging a cane-wielding pensioner and a pink-haired girl eating Indian take-away on the kerb.

It was a ten-second effort to pass the journalists. Another five seconds caught him up to Havers.

"Where?" he asked.

She pointed and kept running and Lynley saw him. He'd jumped another fence that bordered a park on the corner of Plevna Street. He was ripping along a curved brick path, set in the direction of Manchester Road.

"Fool to go that way," Havers panted.

"Why?"

"Manchester substation. Quarter mile along. Towards the river."

"Phone them."

"Where?"

Lynley pointed ahead to the corner of Plevna Street and Manchester Road where a squat brick building bore two red crosses and the red word *surgery* along a white cornice. Havers ran towards it. Lynley raced round the park's perimeter.

Jimmy emerged through the park gates onto Manchester Road and sprinted south. Lynley shouted his name and as he did so, Jean Cooper and the journalists rounded the curve of Plevna Street and joined him.

The journalists cried out, "Who's—" and "Why're you—" while the photographer lifted one of his cameras and began to shoot. Lynley again set off after the boy. Jean Cooper shrieked, "Jimmy! Stop!"

Jimmy bent into the run with more determination. The wind was blowing in from the east, and when Manchester Road veered slightly to the west, he was easily able to lengthen the distance between himself and his pursuers. He was running wildly with his feet flying outward and his head tucked low. He passed an abandoned warehouse and started to swerve towards the street as he approached a florist's shop where a green-smocked elderly woman was in the process of moving containers of flowers from the pavement indoors. The woman gave a startled cry as Jimmy hurled himself past her. In response an Alsatian charged out of the shop.

The dog howled in a fury, launched itself at the boy, and locked teeth round the sleeve of his T-shirt.

Lynley thought, Thank God, and slowed his pace. Some distance behind him, he heard the boy's mother screaming Jimmy's name. The flower seller dropped a bucket of narcissi onto the pavement, shouting, "Caesar! Down!" and dragging at the Alsatian's collar. The dog released Jimmy just as Lynley yelled, "No! Hold him there!" And when the woman turned round with her hand dug into the Alsatian's fur and an expression of fear and perplexity on her face, Jimmy streaked away.

Lynley thudded through the narcissi as the boy broke to the right thirty yards ahead of him. He scaled yet another fence and disappeared into the grounds of the Cubitt Town junior school.

Not even winded, Lynley thought in amazement. The boy was either propelled by terror or a distance runner in his spare time.

Jimmy tore across the school-yard; Lynley followed him over the fence. Heavy construction was underway on a new addition to the dun brick school, and Jimmy bolted through this, weaving through piles of bricks, stacks of timber, and hills of sand. The school day was over by at least two hours, so there was no one in the yard to impede his progress, but as he approached the farthest building beyond which lay the playing fields, a caretaker sauntered out of the weathered double doors, caught sight of him, and gave a yell. Jimmy was past him before the man had a chance to act. Then he saw Lynley, shouted, "What's this?" and planted himself directly in the path that Jimmy had taken.

"Hold on here, Mister." The night watchman barred the way, arms akimbo. He looked beyond Lynley to Manchester Road where Jean Cooper was dropping over the fence, with the journalists not far behind her. He shouted, "You! Stay where you are! These grounds is closed!"

Lynley said, "Police."

The caretaker said, "Prove it."

Jean staggered up to them. "You . . ." She grasped Lynley's jacket. "You leave him . . ."

Lynley thrust the watchman to one side. Jimmy had gained another twenty yards in the time Lynley had lost. He was halfway across the playing fields, rushing in the direction of a housing estate. Lynley set off again.

The caretaker yelled, "Hey! I'm ringing the police!"

Lynley could only pray he would do so.

Jean Cooper stumbled along behind him. She was sobbing, but for breath and not with tears. She said, "He's going . . . He's home. Going home. Can't you see?"

Jimmy was indeed circling back in the direction of Cardale Street, but Lynley was unwilling to believe he'd be such a fool as to run directly into a trap. The boy had looked behind him more than once. Surely he would have seen that Sergeant Havers wasn't with those who were trailing him.

He gained the far side of the playing field. It was bordered with a hedge. He crashed right through it, but he lost several seconds when he stumbled and fell to his knees on the other side.

Lynley's chest felt banded round with heat. He hoped the boy would stay where he was. But as Lynley closed the gap between them, Jimmy surged to his feet and stumbled on.

He raced across a vacant lot where a burnt-out car sat on rotting tyres amid empty wine bottles and rubbish. He burst from the lot onto East Ferry Road, and dashed to the north in the direction of his home. Lynley heard the boy's mother crying out, "I told you!" but even as she cried, Jimmy darted across the road, dodged a motorcycle rider who skidded and slid to miss him, and flung himself up the stairway to Crossharbour Station where even now a blue train from the Docklands Railway was sliding to a halt on the elevated tracks.

Lynley stood no chance. The doors of the train were closed on the boy and the train itself was pulling out of the station as Lynley thundered onto East Ferry Road.

"Jimmy!" his mother screamed.

Lynley fought to catch his breath. Jean Cooper reeled to a stop against him. Behind them, the journalists were fighting through the hedge. They were shouting as much at each other as they shouted at Lynley.

"Where's he going?" Lynley asked.

Jean shook her head. She gasped for breath.

"How many stations are left on the line?"

"Two." She dragged her hand across her brow. "Mudchute. Island Gardens."

The railway line was straight, Lynley saw, running parallel to East Ferry Road. "How far to Mudchute?"

Jean dug her knuckles into her cheek.

"How far?" he demanded.

"A mile? No, less. Less."

Lynley gave the train a last look as it disappeared. He couldn't run it by foot. But Cardale Street emptied into East Ferry Road sixty yards to the north, and the Bentley was sitting in Cardale Street. There was a slight chance. . . .

He ran in the direction of the car. Jean Cooper followed hard behind him. She was crying, "What're you going to do? Leave him be. He's done nothing. He's got nothing more to tell."

In Cardale Street, Sergeant Havers was leaning against the Bentley. She looked up at the sound of Lynley's approach.

"Lose him?" she asked, as Lynley gasped, "The car. *Go.*"

She clambered inside. Lynley started the Bentley with a roar. Stan and Shar darted out of the house, their mouths forming cries that went unheard over the engine, and as Shar fumbled with the latch on the front gate, Jean Cooper rounded the corner and waved them back.

Lynley stomped on the accelerator and swung from the kerb. Jean Cooper leapt into the path of the car.

Havers cried, "Watch it!" and grabbed on to the dashboard as Lynley slammed on the brakes and swerved to miss her. Jean pounded her fist against the car's bonnet, then stumbled along its side and pulled open the back door. She fell inside, gulping, "Why . . . why'n't you *leave* him? He's done nothing. You *know* that. You—" Lynley took off.

They careened round the corner and sped south on East Ferry Road. They whizzed past the journalists who were limping breathlessly in the opposite direction, towards Cardale Street. Above them and just to the west of the road, the tracks for the Docklands Railway ran, making a clean line for Mudchute.

"Did you get the Manchester Road substation?" Lynley's words came out in fits and starts.

"They're on it," Havers said.

"Police?" Jean cried. "More police?"

Lynley sounded the horn at a lorry in front of them. He swung into the right lane and shot past it. The fashionable housing of Crossharbour and Millwall Outer Dock gave way to the dingy brick terraces of Cubitt Town, where flags of laundry fluttered from clotheslines strung width-wise across narrow back gardens.

Jean's hand clutched the back of Lynley's seat as they veered round an old Vauxhall that puttered along the road like a hedgehog. Her voice was insistent when she demanded, "Why'd you ring the police? You're the police. We don't need them. He's only—"

"There!" Sergeant Havers' arm shot out in the direction of Mudchute, where the land rose away from the road in knolls created over generations from the silted mud of the Millwall docks. Jimmy Cooper was scurrying up one of these knolls, scrambling southeast.

"He's going to his gran's," Jean asserted as Lynley pulled to the edge of the road. "In Schooner Estate. My mum's. That's where he's going. South of Millwall Park." Lynley thrust open his door. Jean said, "I *tol'* you where he's going. We can—"

He said, "Drive," to Havers and set off after the boy as his sergeant climbed over to his seat. He heard the engine rev behind him as he struck the first knoll and began to sprint up its side. The ground was moist from the last of April's rain, and his shoes were leather. So he slipped and slid in the crumbly earth, once stumbling to his knees, twice grasping on to the white dead-nettle and the ratstail that flourished in the uncut grass. At the top of the knoll, the wind gusted unimpeded across the open expanse of land. It flung back his jacket and watered his eyes, and he was forced to stop and blink to clear his vision before going on. He lost four seconds, but he saw the boy.

Jimmy had the advantage of the trainers he was wearing. He'd made it through the knolls and was descending into the playing fields beyond them. But it appeared that either he thought he'd lost his pursuers or he'd given in to exhaustion, for he had slowed to a lopsided lope and he was grasping his waist as if he had a stitch in his side.

Lynley ran south along the top of the first knoll. He kept the boy in sight as long as possible before he had to descend and scale the second knoll. At the top of this, he saw that Jimmy had slowed to a walk, and with good reason. A man and a boy in matching red windcheaters were giving two Great Danes and an Irish wolfhound some exercise in the playing fields, and the dogs were tearing round in ambitious circles, from which they barked, snapped, and attempted to snare balls, rubbish, and anything else that moved. Having already experienced the Alsatian on Manchester Road, Jimmy wouldn't want another run-in with an overlarge canine.

Lynley seized the advantage. He scaled the third knoll, half slid down its side, and began to sprint across the playing field. He gave the dogs as wide a berth as possible, but as he came within twenty yards of them, the wolfhound caught sight of him and began to bark. The Great Danes joined in. All three dogs headed in his direction. Their owners shouted. It was enough.

Jimmy looked over his shoulder. The wind took his long hair and threw it in his eyes. He shoved it away. He began to run.

He pounded out of the playing fields and into Millwall Park. Seeing the boy's direction, Lynley allowed himself to slow. For beyond the park, Schooner Estate spread out its two-tiered blocks of grey and tan flats like a hand stretching fingers towards the Thames, and Jimmy headed unerringly towards this. He wouldn't know that Sergeant Havers and his mother had anticipated his movements. By now they would have reached the estate. Intercepting him would be easy enough if he headed into the car park.

His course through the park was unveering. He raced across the grass and thudded through the flower beds that lay in his way. It was only at the final moment at the car park's edge, that he feinted a run towards the flats to the east only to bring himself round at the last moment and charge south instead.

Over the wind, Lynley could hear Sergeant Havers' shout, followed by Jean Cooper's cry. He flew into the car park in time to see the Bentley storming after the boy, but Jimmy had the advantage over the car. He charged into the loop of the horseshoe that formed the southernmost section of Manchester Road. A lorry there crashed on its brakes to miss him. He skipped round it, gained the pavement on the other side, and hurdled over the metre-high fence that bounded the grey, prison-like expanse of the George Green Comprehensive School.

Havers propelled the Bentley onto the pavement. She was flinging herself out of it when Lynley caught her up. The boy had raced along the front of the school and was rounding its western corner.

Jimmy had an unimpeded course on the empty schoolgrounds, and he made the most of it. As Lynley and Havers gained the corner of the building, the boy had already crossed the yard. He'd used a rubbish bin as a mount for the back wall, and he was up and over it before they'd run twenty yards.

"Take the car," Lynley said to Havers. "Go round. He's heading for the river."

"The river? Bloody hell! What's he—"

"Go!"

Behind him, he heard Jean Cooper crying out something inarticulately as Sergeant Havers dashed back in the direction of the car. Her cry faded as he made for the wall. He grasped the top of it, used the rubbish bin to launch himself, and went over.

Another road lay behind the school. On its north side, it was faced by a wall. Its south side was built up with trendy river housing: modern brick communities with electronic security gates. These buildings ran along the crescent of the road in a nearly unbroken line. They ended at a stretch of lawn and trees, bordering the river. This was the only possibility. Lynley ran towards it.

He passed through the entrance where a sign identified the park as Island Gardens. At its far west end, a circular brick building stood, domed in glass and mounted by a white-and-green lantern cupola. A movement of white shimmered against the red bricks, and Lynley saw Jimmy Cooper trying the building's door. It was a dead end, Lynley thought. Why would the boy . . . ? He looked to his left, across the water, and understood. Their run had brought them to the Greenwich foot tunnel. Jimmy was going to cross the river.

Lynley picked up speed. As he did so, the Bentley careened round the far corner. Jean Cooper and Sergeant Havers spilled out. Jean shouted her son's name. Jimmy dragged on the handles of the tunnel door. The door didn't move.

Lynley was closing in quickly from the northeast. Sergeant Havers and Jean Cooper were doing the same from the northwest. The boy looked in one direction, then the other. He took off east, along the river wall.

Lynley began to cut across the lawn to intercept him. Havers and Jean Cooper followed the path. Jimmy produced a final burst of speed and strength, leapt over a bench, and sprang onto the wall. He hoisted himself atop the railing of lime-coloured wrought-iron that fenced the gardens off from the river below them.

Lynley called the boy's name.

Jean Cooper screamed.

Arms flailing, Jimmy plunged into the Thames.

CHAPTER
23

Lynley reached the river wall first. Jimmy thrashed below him in the water. The tide was high, but it was still coming in, so the current flowed swiftly from east to west.

Jean Cooper screamed her son's name as she reached the river wall. She threw herself at the railing and began to climb it.

Lynley pulled her back. He thrust her at Havers. "Phone the river police." He tore off his jacket and kicked off his shoes.

"That's Waterloo Bridge!" Havers protested as she struggled with Jean Cooper, holding her back. "They'll never make it in time."

"Just do it." Lynley climbed onto the wall and hoisted himself atop the railing. In the river the boy was stroking ineffectually, hampered by the current and his own exhaustion. Lynley dropped to the other side of the railing. Jimmy's head sank under the turbid water.

Lynley dived. He heard Havers shouting, "Bloody hell! Tommy!" as he hit the water.

It was North Sea cold. It was moving faster than he would have suspected from looking at it behind the safety wall in Island Gardens. The wind chopped against it. The tide's flux created an undertow. The moment that Lynley surfaced from his dive, he could feel himself being swept southwest, into the river but not towards the opposite shore.

He lashed his arms against the water, trying to keep himself afloat. He searched for the boy. Across the river, he could see the facade of the naval college, to its west the masts of the *Cutty Sark*. He could even make out the domed exit to the Greenwich foot tunnel. But he couldn't see Jimmy.

He let the current take him as it would take the boy. His heart and his breathing thundered in his ears. His limbs felt heavy. Dimly he heard screams from Island Gardens, but with the wind, his heart, and his gasping lungs, he couldn't make out what they were trying to tell him.

He twisted in the water as it carried him on. Treading, trying to locate Jimmy. There were no boats to come to his aid. Pleasure boats wouldn't take chances in the gusty weather, and the last of the tourist crafts were gone for the day. The only vessels afloat in the area were two barges chugging slowly up river. And they were at least three hundred yards away, too far to hail even if they could have built up the speed to reach Lynley in time to find the boy.

A bottle bobbed past him. His right foot kicked against what felt like a net. He began to swim with the river's flow, striking towards Greenwich as Jimmy would be doing.

He kept his head down. He kept his arms and legs moving. He tried to time his breaths.

The water dragged at his clothes and pulled him downward. He fought, but the effort was draining him quickly. He'd done too much running, too much climbing and jumping. And the tide was insistent and just as strong. He gulped in water. He coughed. He felt himself go down. He fought back, rose. He gasped for air. He felt himself go down.

Beneath the surface he found there was nearly nothing. Murk. Air bubbles escaping from his lungs. A liquid tornado in which debris swirled madly. Endless green upon white upon grey upon brown.

He thought of his father. He could almost see him, on the deck of the *Daze* sailing out of Lamorna Cove. He was saying, "Don't ever trust the sea, Tom. She's a mistress who'll betray you given half the chance." Lynley wanted to argue that this wasn't the sea, but a river, a river, for God's sake who could be so stupid as to drown in a river? But his father was saying, "A tidal river. Tides come from the sea. Only fools trust the sea." And the water dragged him down.

His vision went black. His ears roared. He heard his mother's voice and his brother's laughter. Then Helen said distinctly, "Tommy, I don't know. I can't give you the answer you want just because you want it."

Christ, he thought. Still ambivalent. Even now. Even now. When it didn't matter in the least. She would never decide. She would never be willing. Goddamn her. God*damn*.

He scissored his legs in a fury. He threshed his arms through the river. He broke the surface. He shook the water from his eyes, coughing and gasping. He heard the boy.

Jimmy was shrieking some twenty yards to the west. His arms pounded against the water. He twisted round and round like a piece of flotsam. As Lynley struck out towards him, the boy went down again.

Lynley went after him, diving, praying his lungs would hold. The current was on his side this time. He collided with the boy and grabbed his hair.

He swam for the surface. Jimmy fought against him, flailing in the water like a netted fish. When they hit the surface, the boy kicked and punched. He shrieked, "No, no, no!" and tried to struggle away.

Lynley changed his grip from Jimmy's hair to his shirt. He looped one arm underneath the boy's arms and round his chest. He had little breath left for speaking, but he managed to gasp, "Drown or survive. Which one?"

The boy kicked frantically.

Lynley tightened his grip. He used his legs and one free arm to keep them afloat. "Fight me, we drown. Help me swim, we might make it. What's it going to be?" He shook the boy's body. "Decide."

"No!" But Jimmy's protest was weak and when Lynley began to tow him towards the north bank of the river, he no longer had the strength to fight him.

"Kick," Lynley said. "I can't do this alone."

"Can't," Jimmy gasped.

"You can. Help me."

But the final forty seconds of struggle had taken Jimmy to the end of his resources. Lynley could feel the boy's exhaustion. His limbs were dead weight. His head lolled back.

Lynley shifted his grip. He locked his left arm beneath Jimmy's chin. He used what stamina remained in his own muscles to turn himself and the boy towards the north bank of the river. He began striking against the water in that direction.

He heard shouting, but he didn't have the strength to locate it. He heard the low horn of a boat somewhere nearby, but he couldn't risk pausing at this point to try to find it. He knew the only chance they had was centred upon the mindless act of his swimming. So he swam, breathing, counting the strokes, one arm and two legs against sheer exhaustion and the desire to sink and have done with it all.

Dimly, he saw a pebbled stretch of bank up ahead where boats could be launched. He made for this. He kicked with ever growing weakness. His grip on the boy became harder to maintain. As he reached the limit of his endurance, he kicked a final time and his feet struck the bottom. First sand, then pebbles, then larger rocks. He found a foothold, drew breath in a sob, and hauled the boy out of the deeper water behind him. They collapsed in the shallows five feet from a bollard, on their hands and knees.

Furious splashing and shouting followed. Someone was weeping close at his side. Then he heard his sergeant cursing violently. Arms went round him, and he was pulled from the water and laid on the launch of the rowing club, to which he had swum.

He coughed. He felt his stomach pitch. He rolled to his side, rose to his knees, and vomited onto his sergeant's shoes.

One of her hands went into his hair. The other curved firmly round his forehead.

He dragged his hand against his mouth. The taste was foul. "Sorry," he said.

"It's okay," Havers said. "The colour's an improvement."

"The boy?"

"His mum's got him."

Jeannie was kneeling in the water, cradling her son. She was weeping, her head lifted towards the sky.

Lynley began to lurch to his feet. "God. He's not—"

Havers grabbed his arm. "He's okay. You got him. He's all right. He's all right."

Lynley sank back to the ground. His senses began to awaken one by one. He became aware of the rubbish heap in which he was sitting. He heard a babble of conversation behind them and looked over his shoulder to see that the local police had finally managed to arrive and were now holding back a group of spectators among whom were the same journalists who'd been trailing him since he'd left New Scotland Yard. The photographer with them was doing his job, documenting the drama over the shoulders of the Manchester Road police. There would be no need for the papers to hide the boy's identity this time round. A river rescue was news that could be reported in a way unconnected to Fleming's murder. From the shouted questions and the noise of the cameras, Lynley knew that the journalists meant to report it.

"What happened to the river police?" he asked Havers. "I told you to phone them."

"I know, but—"

"You heard me, didn't you?"

"There wasn't time."

"What are you saying? You didn't bother to phone? That was an order, Havers. We could have drowned out there. Christ, if I *ever* have to deal with you in an emergency situation again, I may as well depend upon—"

"Inspector. Sir." Havers' voice was firm although her face was pale. "You were in the water for five minutes."

"Five minutes," he said blankly.

"There wasn't time." She quirked her mouth and looked away from him. "Besides, I . . . I panicked, all right? You went down twice. Fast. I saw that and I knew the river blokes couldn't get here anyway and if that was the case . . ." Roughly, she rubbed her fingers beneath her nose.

Lynley watched her blink quickly and pretend it was the wind in her eyes. He got to his feet. "I was out of line then, Barbara. Put it down to my own panic and forgive me please."

"Right," she said.

They picked their way back into the water where Jean Cooper still cradled her son. Lynley knelt next to them.

Jean's hand held her son's head next to her chest. She was bent to him. His eyes were dull, but not glazed, and as Lynley reached out to touch Jean's arm preparatory to helping them both to their feet, Jimmy stirred and looked up at his mother's face.

She was mindlessly repeating, "Why?"

He worked his mouth as if trying to summon the will to speak. "Saw," he whispered.

"What?" she asked. *"What?* Why won't you say?"

"You," he said. "I saw you, Mum."

"Saw me?"

"There." He seemed to go even limper in her arms. "Saw you there. That night."

Lynley heard Havers breathe the word, "Finally," and he saw her make an initial move towards Jean Cooper. He signalled her to stay where she was.

Jean Cooper said, "Me? Saw me where?"

"That night. Dad."

Lynley could see the horror and the realisation break over Jean Cooper simultaneously. She cried, "You talking about Kent? At the cottage?"

"You. Parked in the drive," he murmured. "Went for the key in the shed. Went inside. Came out. It was dark but I saw."

His mother clutched him. "You've been thinking that I . . . that I . . ." Her grip on him tightened. "Jim, I loved your dad. I loved him, *loved* him. I never would of . . . Jim, I thought *you*—"

"Saw you," Jimmy said.

"I didn't know he was there. I didn't know anyone was in Kent at all. I thought you and him were going on holiday. Then you said he phoned. You said he had cricket business to take care of. You said the holiday'd been postponed."

He shook his head numbly. "You came out. You had some squirmies in your hands."

"Squirmies? Jim—"

"The kittens," Havers said.

"Kittens?" Jean echoed. "What kittens? Where? What're you talking about?"

"You tossed them to the ground. You shooed them 'way. At the cottage."

"I wasn't at the cottage. I was never at the cottage. Never."

"I saw," Jimmy said.

Footsteps began to crunch across the boat launch. Behind them someone shouted, "At least let us have a bloody word with one of them!" Jean turned to see who was coming towards them. Jimmy looked in that direction as well. He squinted to bring the interloper into focus. And Lynley at last understood what had happened and how.

He said, "Your glasses. Jimmy, on Wednesday night. Were you wearing your glasses?"

.　　　.　　　.

Barbara Havers trudged along the path to her cottage at the bottom of the garden. Her feet squished inside her shoes. She'd scrubbed them vigorously under the tap in the Ladies' at New Scotland Yard, so they no longer smelled of vomit. But they were pretty much done for. She sighed.

She was completely knackered. All she wanted was a shower and twelve hours of sleep. She hadn't eaten in ages, but food could wait.

They'd shepherded Jimmy and his mother through the spectators and past the firing camera of the single photographer. They'd driven them home. Jean Cooper had insisted no doctor was necessary to see to her son, and she'd taken him upstairs and run him a bath while her younger two children hovered round them both, crying, "Mummy!" and "Jim!" until Jean had said, "Heat some soup," to the girl and "Turn down your brother's bed," to the boy. They scampered off to do so.

Jean had protested when Lynley said he wanted to talk to her son. "There's been talk enough," she said. But he quietly insisted. When the boy was bathed and put into bed, Lynley climbed the stairs in his sodden clothes and placed himself at the foot of Jimmy's bed. He said, "Tell me what you saw that night," and next to him Barbara could feel his limbs shaking. His jacket and shoes were the only dry clothing he wore, and the adrenaline that had so far kept him going was beginning to give way to chill. She asked Jean for a blanket, but he wouldn't use it, instead saying to the boy, "Tell me everything this time. You won't be incriminating your mother, Jimmy. I know she wasn't there."

Barbara had wanted to ask why Lynley believed a simple denial. She recognised Jean's confusion over the kittens, but she wasn't willing to absolve her of responsibility because she'd acted as if she didn't know about the animals. Killers often were master dissemblers. She couldn't see how or why Lynley had decided that Jean Cooper was neither.

Jimmy told them what he had seen: the blue car pulling up in the drive; the shadowy form of a light-haired woman coming into the garden and slipping into the potting shed; that same woman entering the cottage; less than five minutes later, that same woman returning the key to the potting shed, then leaving. He'd watched the cottage for another half hour. Then he'd gone to the potting shed and nicked the key.

"Why?" Lynley asked him.

"Don't know," the boy said. "Just to do it. Cos I wanted." His fingers plucked weakly at the covers.

Lynley was shaking so badly that Barbara was certain she could feel it through the floor. She wanted to insist that he change his clothes, use the blanket, eat some soup, drink some brandy, do something to take care of himself. But when she was about to suggest they'd heard enough for one night—The boy wasn't going anywhere, was he, sir? They could come back tomorrow if they needed more—Lynley placed both hands on the foot of the bed and leaned towards the boy, saying, "You loved your father, didn't you? He's the last person on earth you ever would have hurt."

Jimmy's mouth quivered—at the tone, its gentleness, and its unspoken message of understanding—and his eyelids closed. They looked purple with fatigue.

Lynley said, "Will you help me find his killer? You've already seen her, Jimmy. Will you help me flush her out? You're the only one who can."

His eyelids opened. He said, "But I didn't have my binns. I thought . . . I saw the car and her. I thought Mum . . ."

"You won't have to identify her. You'll just need to do as I say. It won't be pleasant for you. It will mean I release your name to the media. It will mean we take things a step further, you and I. But I think it will work. Will you help me?"

Jimmy swallowed. He nodded in silence. He turned his head in a weak movement on the pillow and looked at his mother, who sat on the edge of the bed. He licked his lips wearily. "I saw," he murmured. "One day I saw . . . when I bunked off school."

Tears seeped slowly from Jean Cooper's eyes. "What?"

He'd bunked off school, he told her wearily again. He'd bought himself fish and chips at the Chinese take-away. He'd eaten them on a bench in St. John's Park. And then he'd thought about the Watney's in the fridge at home and how no one would be there at this time of day and how he could drink half and fill the bottle with water or maybe drink it all and deny it bold-faced when his mother accused. So he went home. He entered through the back, through the kitchen door. He opened the fridge, uncapped the bottle of Watney's, and heard the noise from above.

He'd climbed the stairs. Her door was closed but not latched shut, and he listened to the creaking and suddenly knew what it was. This is why, he thought and the anger felt like a spike in his neck. This is why he left. This is why. This . . . is . . . why.

He'd nudged the door with his toe. He saw her first. She was clutching the tarnished brass headboard and she was crying. But she was gasping as well and she was arched up high so the bloke could have at her. And the bloke was kneeling between her upraised thighs. Naked, head bent, his body shining like it was oiled.

"No one," he was grunting. "No one . . . ever."

"No one," she was gasping.

"Mine." Then he said it again—mine, mine—and increased his pumping until it was frantic, until she was sobbing, until he reared back and flung his head up, shouting, "Jeannie! Jean!" and Jimmy saw it was his father.

He'd crept downstairs. He'd put his Watney's on the kitchen work top undrunk, and he turned to the table where an unsealed envelope lay. He slipped his fingers inside, brought forth the papers, saw Q. *Melvin Abercrombie, Esq.* scrolled across the top. He scanned the unfamiliar terms and the awkward phrases. When he saw the only word that mattered—*divorce*—he returned the papers to the envelope and left the house.

"Oh God," Jean whispered when her son was finished. "I loved him, Jim. I never stopped. I wanted to, but I couldn't. I kept hoping he'd come home if I was good enough to him. If I was patient and kind. If I did what he wanted. If I gave him time."

"Didn't matter," Jimmy said. "Didn't do no good, did it?"

"But it would of," Jean said. "I know it would of in time, cos I knew your dad. He would of come home if—"

Jimmy shook his head feebly.

"—if he hadn't met her. That's the truth of it, Jim."

The boy closed his eyes.

Gabriella Patten. She was the key. Even when Barbara still wanted to press forward with whatever case they could build against Jean Cooper—"She doesn't have an alibi, sir. She was home with the kids? Asleep? Who can prove it? No one and you know it"—Lynley directed her thoughts to Gabriella Patten. He didn't lay any facts out for her perusal, however. He merely said in an exhausted voice as they drove towards the Yard, "It all turns on Gabriella. God. How ironic. To end where we began."

"If that's the case, then let's get her," Barbara said. "We don't need the kid. We can pull her in. We can give her a grilling. Not now, of course,'' she added hastily as Lynley adjusted the Bentley's heating system to do something about the chill that was shaking him like a victim of ague. "But tomorrow morning. First thing. No doubt she's still in Mayfair, having a romp with Mollison when Claude-Pierre, or whoever he was, isn't giving her muscles a proper pounding.''

"That's not on,'' Lynley said.

"Why? You just said that Gabriella's—''

"Interrogating Gabriella Patten again won't get us anywhere. It's the perfect crime, Barbara.''

That's all he would say. To her demand of "How can it be perfect? We've got Jimmy. We've got a witness. He saw—'' Lynley interrupted with: "What? Whom? A blue car he thought was the Cavalier. A light-haired woman he thought was his mother. No prosecutor's going to try a case against anyone else based on that testimony. And no jury in the world would ever convict.''

Barbara had wanted to press forward with her points. They had evidence, after all. As flimsy as it was, they still had evidence. The Benson and Hedges. The matches used to make the incendiary device. Surely these counted for something. But she could see that Lynley was drained. Whatever resources he had left were being devoted to controlling his shivering as she guided the Bentley through the evening traffic back to New Scotland Yard. When they had pulled up next to her Mini in the underground car park, he repeated what he'd already told Chief Superintendent Hillier. Despite their having the best intentions in the world, she needed to prepare herself for the fact that they might not be able to break this case.

"Even with the boy's help, it's going to come down to conscience,'' he said. "And I can't say conscience is going to be enough.''

"For what?'' she'd demanded, feeling the need to argue as well as to understand.

But that's all he would say, other than, "Not now. I need a bath and a change of clothes,'' before he left her.

Now, in Chalk Farm as she wrestled her feet from her sodden shoes at her doorway, she attempted to understand his point about conscience. But no matter how she interpreted the facts and the events of the last few days, they all led her in the same direction and it didn't point to anyone needing to have a conscience about anything.

After all, they knew it was arson, so they knew it was murder. They had a cigarette that could be tested for saliva. No matter the length of time it might take for Ardery's people to complete the tests, if sufficient saliva had been deposited by the arsonist—all right, by Gabriella Patten because apparently Lynley had set his sights on her from the very first and not on Jean Cooper—at the end of the testing they would know about ABH antigens, ABO genotype, and Lewis-reaction relationships. Providing, of course, that Gabriella Patten was a secretor. If she wasn't, they were back to square one. And then they'd be relying upon . . . what? Conscience? Gabriella Patten's conscience? What sort of sense did that make? Did Lynley actually expect that the woman would feel compelled to confess that she murdered Kenneth Fleming because he'd thrown her over? And when would she do it? Between boffing Guy Mollison to take her mind off Fleming's untimely demise and his even more untimely rejection of her? Bloody hell, Barbara thought. No wonder Lynley was saying they might not be able to close the case.

This sort of failure happened to everyone. But it had never happened to Lynley. And, by association since he was the DI with whom she'd worked longest, it also had never happened to her.

This wasn't, however, the best of cases to fail with. Not only were the media focussed on the crime, provoking more public interest than would attend the murder of someone with a less familiar face and name, but also their superiors at New Scotland Yard were worrying the investigation like schoolboys loosening scabs on their knees. This combined interest from media and superiors did not promise to serve either Lynley or Barbara well. It guaranteed to damage Lynley because from nearly the first he had followed a course that violated one precept of efficacious police work: He had decided to play with the media and was continuing to play with them towards an end of his own devising, one which he had obviously failed thus far to reach. It guaranteed to damage Barbara because she was guilty by association. And Chief Superintendent Hillier had signalled that fact to her when he saw to it that she was present at the only meeting he'd had with Lynley about the case.

She could almost hear the castigation that would accompany her next performance evaluation. *Did you once voice an objection, Sergeant Havers? You occupy a subordinate position in the partnership, true, but since when does one's subordinate position obviate the ability to speak one's mind in a matter of ethics?* It wouldn't matter to Chief Superintendent Hillier that she *had* spoken her mind to Lynley during the investigation. She hadn't done so overtly, which meant that she hadn't done so in the meeting that Hillier had called.

Hillier had wanted her to point out to Lynley that the media made disastrous lovers. They were at best faithless, tirelessly dogging the object of their lust until they managed to sate themselves. At their worst, they were ungenerous, taking what they could from the object of their passion, leaving nothing behind when they were satisfied.

But she hadn't said any of that. The ship was sinking and she was about to go down with the crew.

It wouldn't cost either one of them their jobs. Everyone expected a failure now and then. But to fail with the light of publicity shining so unmercifully on them, publicity that Lynley himself was doing nothing to quash, indeed, was on the point of openly encouraging. . . . No one was likely to forget that soon, least of all the higher-ups who had Barbara's future in the palm of their hands.

"Bloody berks, the lot of them," Barbara muttered as she rummaged through her shoulder bag for the key to her door. She was almost too tired to be depressed.

But not tired enough. Inside the cottage, she flipped the light on and looked about. She sighed. God, the place was such a dump. The refrigerator was running and there was mercy in that because at least she'd been able to get rid of the bucket, but otherwise the room was little more than a declaration of personal failure and she knew it. *Alone* was inscribed on it everywhere. Single bed. Dining table with only two chairs—and two was stretching her hopes to the limit, wasn't it, Barb? An old school photograph of a long-dead brother. A snapshot of two parents, one dead and one more than slightly demented. A collection of slim novels—suitable to be read in two hours—in which eternally resisting men broke upon the great wheel of love and were eternally redeemed by the adoration of good women whom those same men swept into their arms or off their feet or into a bed or a stack of hay. And did they live happily ever after, after their sobbing and throbbing reached its grand finale? Did anyone, really?

Get off it, Barbara told herself roughly. You're tired, you're wet from the thighs to the feet, you're hungry, you're worried, you're in a muddle. You need a shower, which you will take right now. You need a bowl of soup, which you will slurp up directly the shower has been taken. You need to phone your mum and let her know that Sunday you'll be in Greenford for a walk on the common and anything else that strikes her fancy. And when you've done that, you need to get into bed and turn on your reading light and wallow in the highly dubious and always vicarious pleasures of love at second hand.

"Right," she declared.

She shed her clothes, left them in a heap, and took herself into the bathroom where she turned on the water in the shower until it was steaming and stepped inside with a bottle of shampoo clutched in her hand. She let the water run over her and as she scrubbed her scalp with great vigour, she sang. She made it an oldies night, a tribute to Buddy Holly. And when she'd got through "Peggy Sue," "That'll Be the Day," "Raining in My Heart," and "Rave On," she dropped into an offkey eulogy to the great one with a very bad rendition of "American Pie." She was standing in her old terry robe with a towel round her head, barking, "The daaaay the muuuusic died," a last time when she became aware of the sound of knocking. She halted her singing abruptly. The knocking halted with her, then started again. Four sharp raps. It was coming from the cottage door.

She said, "Who . . . ?" and padded out from the bathroom on bare feet, retying the belt of her robe. "Yes?" she called out from behind the door.

"Hello, hello. It's me," a small voice said.

"It's you?"

"I visited the other night. Do you remember? That boy gave us your refrigerator by mistake and you were looking at it and I came outside and you invited me to see your cottage if I left a note for my dad and—"

Invited wasn't the word Barbara would have chosen. She said, "Hadiyyah."

"You remember! I knew you would. I saw you come home because I was looking out of the window and I asked my dad if I could come for a visit. Dad said okay because I said you were my friend. So—"

"Gosh, I'm done in, actually," Barbara said, still speaking to the door's panels. "I've only just got home. Can we get together later? Tomorrow, maybe?"

"Oh. I suppose I shouldn't have . . . It's only that I wanted you to . . ." The small voice dropped off dispiritedly. "Yes. Perhaps later." Then with a happier lilt, "I've brought something for you, though. Shall I leave it on the step? Will it be all right? It's rather special."

Barbara thought, What the hell. She said, "Wait a second, okay?" She scooped her discarded clothes from the floor, flung them into the bathroom, and returned to the door. She opened it, saying, "So what've you been up to? Does your dad know—'' and halted when she saw that Hadiyyah wasn't alone.

A man was with her. He was dusky skinned, darker than the child, thin and well dressed in a pin-striped suit. Hadiyyah herself was wearing her school uniform, pink ribbons tying up her plaits this time, and she was holding the man's hand. He wore, Barbara noted, a very fine gold watch.

"I brought my dad," Hadiyyah announced proudly.

Barbara nodded. "He isn't what you were going to leave on the step, is he?"

Hadiyyah giggled and pulled on her father's hand. "She's cheeky, Dad. I said she was, didn't I?"

"You did say that." The man observed Barbara with sombre dark eyes. She observed him back. He wasn't very tall, and his delicate features made him closer to pretty than to handsome. His thick black hair grew straight back from his brow, and a mole high on one cheekbone was so perfectly placed that Barbara could have sworn it was artificial. He could have been anywhere from twenty-five to forty. It was difficult to tell because his skin was virtually unlined. *"Taymullah azhar,"* he said formally to her.

Barbara wondered how she was supposed to respond. Was this some sort of Muslim greeting? She said with a nod that dislodged her towel, "Right," and adjusted the towel round her head once more.

A flicker of a smile moved the man's lips. "I am Taymullah Azhar. Hadiyyah's father."

"Oh! Barbara Havers." She offered her hand. "You moved my refrigerator. I got your note. I just couldn't read the signature. Thanks. It's nice to meet you, Mister—" She knotted her eyebrows, trying to remember what it was these people did with their names.

"Azhar alone is sufficient, as we are to be neighbours," he said. Beneath his jacket, Barbara saw that he was wearing a shirt so white that it looked incandescent in the dying light. "Hadiyyah insisted that I meet her friend Barbara immediately upon my arrival home, but I see that we have not come at a good time."

"Well, right. Rather. Sort of." Why was she babbling? She reined herself in. "I just took a partial dip in the Thames, which is why I'm done up like this. Otherwise, I wouldn't be. I mean, what time is it, anyway? Not time for bed, is it? Would you like to come in?"

Hadiyyah pulled on his hand and made a little dancing movement with her feet. Her father moved his hand to her shoulder, and she was still at once. "No. We would be an intrusion this evening," he said. "But we do thank you, Hadiyyah and I."

"Have you had your dinner?" Hadiyyah asked brightly. "Because we haven't. And we're going to have curry. Dad's going to make it. He's brought us some lamb. We have enough. We have lots. Dad makes a fine curry. If you haven't had dinner."

"Hadiyyah," Azhar said quietly. "School yourself, please." The child became still again, although her face and her eyes didn't alter in brightness. "Do you not have something you wish to leave with your friend?"

"Oh! Yes, yes!" She gave a small jump. Her father removed a bright green envelope from his jacket. He handed it to Hadiyyah. She extended it ceremoniously in Barbara's direction. "This is what I was going to leave on the step," she said. "You don't have to open it now. But you can if you want. If you *really* want."

Barbara slipped her finger under the flap. She pulled out a scalloped piece of yellow construction paper which, unfolded, became a beaming sunflower whose centre had been carefully printed with the message: "You are most cordially invited to Khalidah Hadiyyah's birthday party on Friday evening at seven o'clock. Wonderful Games Will Be Played! Delicious Refreshments Will Be Served!"

"Hadiyyah would not settle herself until the invitation had been delivered this evening," Taymullah Azhar explained politely. "I hope you will be able to join us, Barbara. It will be a—" with a careful glance at the child, "a small gathering only."

"I'll be eight years old," Hadiyyah said. "We're to have strawberry ice cream and chocolate cakes. You don't need to bring a present. I expect I'll have others. Mummy'll send something from Ontario. That's in Canada. She's on holiday, but she knows it's my birthday and she knows what I want. I told her before she left, didn't I, Dad?"

"Indeed you did." Azhar reached for her hand and enclosed it in his own. "And now that you have delivered your invitation to your friend, perhaps it would be best for you to say good night."

"Will you come?" Hadiyyah asked. "We'll have such fun. We will."

Barbara looked from anxious child to sober father. She wondered what waters were running here.

"Chocolate cakes," the girl said. "Strawberry ice cream."

"Hadiyyah." Azhar spoke the name quietly.

Barbara said, "Yeah. I'll come."

The reward was her smile. Hadiyyah skipped back. She pulled on her father's hand to draw him in the direction of their flat. "Seven o'clock," she said. "You won't forget, will you?"

"I won't forget."

"Thank you, Barbara Havers," Taymullah Azhar said simply.

"It's Barbara. Just Barbara," she replied.

He nodded. He gently guided his daughter back to the path. She shot ahead of him, plaits flying round her like twitching ropes. "Birthday, birthday, birthday," she sang.

Barbara watched them until they disappeared round the side of the main house. She shut the door. She looked at the sunflower invitation. She shook her head.

Three weeks and four days, she realised, without a word and without a smile. Who would have thought her first friend in the neighbourhood would turn out to be an eight-year-old girl?

OLIVIA

I've rested for nearly an hour. I should go to bed but I've started to think that if I go to my room without finishing this when I'm so close to the end, I'll lose heart.

Chris wandered out of his room a while ago. His eyes were red-rimmed like they always are when he first wakes up, so I knew he'd been dozing. He had on his striped pyjama bottoms and nothing else. He stood in the doorway of the galley, blinked to clear his eyes. He yawned.

"Reading. Dropped off like a stone. I'm getting old." He went to the sink and poured himself a glass of water. He didn't drink. Instead, he leaned over and sloshed the water against his neck and into his hair, which he ruffled vigourously.

"What're you reading?" I asked him.

"*Atlas Shrugged*. The speech."

"Again?" I shuddered. "No wonder you dropped off."

"What I've always wanted to know is . . ." He yawned again and stretched his arms above his head. He absently scratched at the sparce hair growing in the shape of a feather from his navel to his chest. He looked bonier than ever.

"What you've wondered?" I prompted.

"How long would it take a bloke to talk for sixty-three pages?"

"Any bloke who needs sixty-three pages to make his point isn't worth listening to," I said. I laid my pencil on the table and concentrated hard on making both hands fists. " 'Who is John Galt?' isn't the question unless the answer is 'Who cares?' "

Chris chuckled. He came to my chair and said, "Scooting forward here," and he moved me towards the edge and slipped in behind me.

"I'll fall," I said.

"I've got you. Lean back." He pulled me against him and locked his arms round my waist. He rested his chin on my shoulder. I could feel him breathing against my neck. I touched my head to his. "Go to bed," I said. "I can cope."

He kept one arm round me, holding me on the chair. He stroked the side of my neck with his other hand. "I was dreaming," he murmured. "I was back in school with Lloyd-George Marley."

"Distant relation of Bob?"

"So he claimed. We were facing off a pack of yobs used to hang about the taxi rank near our comprehensive. National Front blokes, these were. Metal-toed boots, the whole bit." His voice was soft. His fingers worked the stiff muscles at the base of my neck. "We came round a corner— Lloyd-George and I—and we saw these blokes, see? And I knew they wanted a dust-up. Not with me, with Lloyd-George. They wanted to bloody him, send a message to his kind. Go back to where you came from, you fucking jungle bunnies. You're polluting the river of our pure English blood. They had knuckle-dusters on. They were swinging chains. I knew we were in for it."

"What'd you do?"

"I tried to yell for Lloyd-George to run, like you do in dreams. But nothing came out. He just kept walking towards them. And they kept coming on. I caught him up and grabbed him. I said let's go, let's go. I wanted to run. He wanted to fight."

"And?"

"I woke up."

"Lucky you."

"That's not it."

"Why?"

I felt his arm tighten round me. "I was glad not to have to decide, Livie."

I twisted to look at him. His nighttime stubble was the colour of cinnamon against his skin. "It doesn't matter," I said. "It was a dream. You woke up."

"It matters."

I could feel his heart beating against me. "It's okay," I said.

"I'm sorry," he said. "All this. What it costs."

"Everything costs something."

"But not this much."

"I don't know about that." I patted his hand and let my eyes close. The galley light was bright as a flare against my eyelids. Still, I fell asleep.

Chris held me the while. When the cramps woke me up, he slid off the chair and saw to my legs. Sometimes I say to him when this is all over he can find a job as a professional masseur. He says either that or a bread maker. "Good at kneading, I am," Chris says. "So am I," I say. And there's the truth of it. Disease makes one conscious of need. It wipes out any thought of independence, of I'll-show-them, of here's-my-life-in-your-face.

Which brings me to Mother.

It was one thing to make the decision to tell Mother about ALS. It was another to do the actual telling. After I decided to do it that night with Chris and Max on the barge, I put it off for a month. I drifted from one scenario to another. I thought I'd ask her to meet me in a public place, perhaps that Italian restaurant on Argyll Road. I'd order risotto—which would give me the least trouble from plate to mouth—and drink two glasses of wine to loosen up. Perhaps I'd order a whole bottle and share it with her. When she was mildly lit, I'd break the news. I'd get there early, before her, and ask the waiter to put my walker out of sight. She'd be miffed that I didn't get to my feet when I saw her, but once she knew why, she'd forgive the affront.

Or I'd ask her to the barge and have Chris and Max there so she could see how my life had changed in recent years. Max would engage her in conversation about cricket, about the pressing responsibilities of factory management, about Victoriana and his passionate attachment to things antique, which he would cooperatively manufacture for the occasion. Chris would be Chris, sitting on the bottom step of the stairs feeding a bit of banana to Panda, which Pan would cooperatively munch while all the time wondering why she was being given such an unexpected treat. I'd have Toast on one side of me and Beans on the other. They'd rather be with Chris but I'd put dog biscuits into my pockets and slip them onto the floor between their paws every now and again when Mother glanced away. We'd present ourselves as a picture of harmony: friends, fellows, compatriots. We'd win her support.

Or I'd have my doctor phone. "Mrs. Whitelaw," he'd say, "this is Stewart Alderson. I'm phoning about your daughter Olivia. May we arrange an appointment?" She'd want to know what it was about. He'd tell her he didn't wish to go into it over the phone. I'd already be in his office when she arrived. She'd see the walker next to my chair. She'd say, "My God. Olivia. What is this, Olivia?" The doctor would speak as I kept my eyes lowered.

I played out each one of these fantasy reconciliations to its logical conclusion. But every time, the conclusion was the same. Mother won, I lost. The circumstances of the meeting itself put me at a disadvantage. The only way I could come out the winner was to meet with Mother under conditions in which she would be forced to shine with compassion, love, and forgiveness. She had to *want* to look good. Since I couldn't reasonably hope that she'd have any desire of looking good for my benefit, I knew that when she and I finally met, Kenneth Fleming would have to be there. So I would have to go to Kensington.

Chris wanted to accompany me, but since I'd lied to him about already having phoned Mother, I couldn't have him with me when she and I met for the first time. So I waited until I knew he had an assault planned, and that same night was the night I chose to announce over dinner that Mother was expecting me at half past ten. He could drop me off in Kensington, I told him, on his way to the research lab in Northampton. I went on hastily to say that it didn't matter if he didn't come for me until the early hours of the morning, as would be necessary if he was out on ARM business. Mother and I had plenty to discuss and she, I said, was as eager to mend our fences as was I. It wasn't an encounter that could be got through in a single hour or two. We had ten years of estrangement to make up for, didn't we?

He said with some reluctance, "I don't know, Livie. I don't like the idea of you being stranded there. What if things don't work out?"

I'd already broken the ice, I told him. What wasn't to work out? I was hardly in a position to start a row with Mother. I was going to see her hat in hand. I was the beggar. She was the chooser. Etcetera, etcetera.

"And if she wants to get nasty?"

"She's not likely to brawl with a cripple, is she? Not in front of her toyboy."

But Fleming might encourage her, Chris pointed out. Fleming might not want to see their situation disturbed as it was likely to be disturbed if Mother and I were to make peace with each other.

"If Kenneth wants to brawl with a cripple," I said, "I'll just phone Max. He can fetch me. All right?"

Chris agreed without liking it.

At twenty-five past ten, we rattled into Staffordshire Terrace. As usual, there wasn't a vacant parking space anywhere, so Chris left the motor running and came round to help me out. He stood the walker in the street, lifted me down to it, said, "Steady?" To which I lied brightly, "As Gibraltar in a gale."

There were seven steps to be managed to get to the door. Together we managed them. We stood on the porch. There were lights on in the dining room. The bay window glowed. Above it, in the drawing room, more lights shone. Chris reached past me to push the bell.

I said, "Wait," and flashed him a smile. "Want to catch my breath." And build my courage. We waited.

I could hear music coming from an open window somewhere above us, nearby. Mother had planted star jasmine in the window box outside the dining room, and it draped a curtain of long, blooming tendrils to overhang the ground-floor windows beneath it. I took a deep breath of the flowers' fragrance and said, "Listen, Chris. I can manage the rest alone. You go on."

"I'll just get you settled."

"No need to trouble. Mother'll do that herself."

"Don't be difficult, Livie." He patted my shoulder, reached past me, and rang the bell.

I thought, That cuts it. I wondered what on earth I was going to say to smooth over Mother's shock when she saw me, uninvited, unexpected, and unforeseen. Chris wasn't going to like having been lied to.

Thirty seconds passed. Chris rang the bell again. Another thirty seconds and he said, "I thought you told me—"

"She's probably in the loo," I said. I took the key from my pocket and prayed that she hadn't changed the lock on the door. She hadn't.

Once inside the entry, with Chris standing behind me in the doorway, I called, "Mother? It's Olivia. I'm here."

The music we'd heard from the porch was coming from upstairs. Frank Sinatra singing "My Way." Old Blue Eyes crooning was enough to cause someone up above to miss the front doorbell as well as my voice.

Chris said, "She's above. Shall I fetch her, then?"

"She's never seen you, Chris. You'll scare her to death."

"If she knows you're coming—"

"She thinks I'm coming alone. No! Chris, don't!" as he made for the stairway at the end of the corridor.

He called out, "Mrs. Whitelaw?" as he began to climb. "It's Chris Faraday. I've brought Livie. Mrs. Whitelaw? I've brought Livie."

He disappeared where the stairs turn at the first mezzanine. I groaned and hobbled into the dining room. There was nothing for it now but to face the music, which wasn't going to be supplied by Frank Sinatra and wasn't going to play sweetly for anyone.

I had to place myself in a position of relative power. I shuffled through the adjoining door into the morning room where against one wall my great-grandmother's ghastly double spoon-backed settee has sat in velvet-and-walnut elegance since the 1850s. This would do.

By the time I had myself arranged upon it with the walker lying on its side and conveniently out of view, Chris had returned.

"She's not here," he said. "Not upstairs at least. God, this place gives me the willies, Livie. It feels like a museum. All this stuff everywhere."

"Her bedroom? Was the door closed?" When he shook his head, I said, "Try the kitchen. Down the corridor, through the door, down the stairs. She wouldn't have heard us if she's in there."

But she would, of course, have heard the doorbell. I didn't mention this as Chris went off again on a search. A minute passed. Frank Sinatra moved on to "Luck Be a Lady," which I thought was a prescient sort of piece.

Below me, I heard the opening of the back door that led onto the garden and I thought, Here she is. I took a calming breath, squirmed for a better position on the settee, and hoped Chris didn't scare her to death when they ran into each other outside the kitchen. But a moment later, I heard Chris calling, "Mrs. Whitelaw?" outside, and I knew he had been the one to open the door. I strained to listen but heard nothing more from him. He seemed to be crossing the garden. I waited impatiently for his return.

She wasn't anywhere, he told me as he re-entered the morning room some three minutes later. But there was a car in the garage, a white BMW, would that be hers?

I had no idea what sort of car she drove, so I said, "It must be. She's probably just stepped out to a neighbour's."

"What about Fleming?"

"I don't know. Perhaps he's gone with her. It doesn't matter. She'll be back in a moment. She knows I'm coming." I concentrated on picking at the fringe of an oriental shawl that lay across the back of the settee. "You've left the van running," I reminded him as gently as I could, considering how anxious I was becoming that he leave the house before my mother returned. "You go on. I'll be fine."

"I don't like to leave you alone like this."

"I'm not alone, Chris. Come on. Don't be difficult. I'm not an infant. I'll cope."

He crossed his arms and studied my face from his position by the door. I knew he was taking a seismic reading to measure the veracity of what I was saying, but in the truth-and-lie department, Chris Faraday had never been a match for me.

"Go," I said. "The assault unit's waiting for you."

"You'll phone Max if there's trouble?"

"There won't be trouble."

"But if there is?"

"I'll phone Max. Now go. You've got business to attend to."

He came to the settee, bent, kissed my cheek. "Right," he said. "I'm off, then." Still he hesitated. I thought he was about to guess the truth, to say, "Your mum doesn't know a thing about all this, does she, Livie?" when instead he chewed for a moment at his upper lip before saying, "I've let you down."

"Cock," I said. I touched his fingers with my fist. "Go. Please. What's going to be said between Mother and me needs to be said without you here."

Those were the magic words. I held my breath until I heard the front door shut behind him. I leaned back against the heavy walnut scrolling that fanned along the top of the old settee and tried to listen for the gunning of the mini-van's motor. Over Frank Sinatra, who was going on about luck with ever growing intensity, I couldn't hear street sounds. But as the minutes ticked by, I felt my body relax against the velvet upholstery, and I knew I'd managed to carry off at least one part of my plan without discovery.

The car was in the garage, Chris had said. The lights were on. The CD was playing. They were somewhere nearby—Kenneth Fleming and my mother. I had the advantage of being inside the house without their knowledge, so I had attained for myself the benefit of surprise. Now, to think of how best to use it.

I began to plan. How to hold myself, what to say, where to ask them to sit, whether to say ALS or merely talk vaguely about my "condition." Frank Sinatra went on: from "New York, New York," to "Cabaret," to "Anything Goes." Then came silence. I thought, This is it, oh God they were in the house all along, Chris didn't check the top floor did he, they were in my old room, here they come, on the stairs, in a moment we'll be face to face, I must—

A tenor began to sing. It was opera, Italian, and the singer's voice climbed notes dramatically. Each number put the tenor through such rigourous paces that I knew I had to be listening to an operatic version of some composer's greatest hits. Verdi, perhaps. Who else wrote Italian operas? I wondered about this and tried to come up with names. Eventually another silence fell. Then it was Michael Crawford and Sarah Brightman, doing *Phantom*. I looked at my watch. Sinatra and the tenor had sung for more than an hour. It was quarter to twelve.

The lights in the dining room suddenly went out. I started. Had I dozed without realising and missed Mother's return? I called out, "Mother? Is that you? Hello?" to no response. My heart began to thump. I was saying, "Mother? It's Olivia. I'm here in the morning—" when the morning room lamp switched off as well. It was on a table in the bay window that overlooks the back garden. It had been lit when I entered the room, and I hadn't switched on another, so now I sat in absolute darkness and tried to decide what the hell was going on.

For the next five or ten minutes—which seemed to crawl by at the speed of months—nothing more happened. Crawford and Brightman completed their duet of "All I Ask of You" and Crawford made his way into "The Music of the Night." Some ten bars along, the singing stopped, midnote, as if someone said, "Enough of this wailing!" and pulled the flex out of the socket. Once the music stopped, the silence swept in like autumn leaves blown from a tree to the ground. I waited for another sound—footsteps, hushed laughter, a sigh, the squeak of furniture springs—that would betray a human presence. Nothing followed. It was as if the ghosts of Kenneth Fleming and my mother had taken themselves off to bed.

I called out, "Mother? Are you here? It's Olivia," and my voice seemed to fade among the scarves that hung from the fireplace mantel, against the iron and bronze firescreen with its one-legged pelicans gazing at each other upon it, among the hundred and one prints on the walls, within the monstrous arrangements of dried flowers on the table-tops, against the Victorian clutter of that claustrophobic room that seemed, for some reason, to grow more claustrophobic as I sat there in the darkness and told myself to breathe breathe breathe, Livie, breathe.

It was the house, of course. Being thrust into unexpected darkness inside that creepy mausoleum was enough for anyone to forget common sense.

I tried to remember where the closest lamp was to the settee. The light that filtered into the dining room from the street lamps on Staffordshire Terrace formed a wedge of illumination against the carpet of the morning room. Objects began to take shape: a guitar on the wall, a clock on the mantelpiece, the pseudo-Greek sculptures on their marble pedestals in two corners of the room, that hideous floor lamp with the tasselled shade. . . .

Yes. There it was, standing at the other end of the settee. I dragged myself towards it, leaned out, and informed my arms that they would grab it. Which they did. I switched it on.

I pulled myself back to my original position and craned my neck to see past an oversized chesterfield to the table in the bay window on which the lamp sat. I followed the flex with my eyes. It looped to the carpet and climbed to an electrical socket at the edge of the curtains. There I could see the flex was not plugged into the socket but into a timer that was itself plugged into the socket.

I congratulated myself with a "Nice work, Sherlock," after which I lay against the back of the settee and thought about what to do next. The BMW in the garage aside, they'd obviously gone off with no intention of returning tonight, leaving lights and CD player on electrical timers to give the appearance of being home so as to thwart potential housebreakers. Although it seemed to me that if housebreaking was in order, the lolly would have to be carted directly to the Victoria and Albert. In fact, I thought, had I gone off for a romantic tryst with my young lover, I'd have left the front door standing open in the hope that someone would clear the place out and save me the bother.

For the first time I wondered how I would be able to manipulate a wheelchair round these rooms if that's what it came down to. Unlike those in the barge, the doorways were wide enough, but the rest of the place was an obstacle course. I felt uneasiness begin to settle over me. It seemed that my future lay not in Staffordshire Terrace with Mother and her lad but in a nursing home or a hospital where the corridors were wide, the rooms were bare, and the terminal patients sat staring at the telly, waiting for the end.

Well, so what, I thought. Who cares? The point is to bring Mother into the picture so that when things get to the stage that Chris and I need help, she'll be ready to offer it in whatever form she decides. Hospital, nursing home, a flat of my own made over to accommodate the medical paraphernalia I was fast acquiring, a bank account from which I could draw the funds I needed to care for myself, a nice blank cheque arriving in the post once a month. She didn't need to refurbish this tomb to make room for me. She just needed to help us out. And she would do that, wouldn't she, once she had all the facts?

Which meant I was going to have to tell her about ALS, not make veiled references to my condition. Which meant I was going to have to stir her heart and her compassion. Which meant I was going to have to talk to her with Kenneth Fleming sitting in the room. So where was he? she? they? I looked at my watch. Nearly half past twelve.

I let my head loll back against the arm of the settee and I stared at the ceiling, which, like the walls, had been hung with William Morris paper. The pattern, like that in the dining room, was of pomegranates, that magical fruit. Eat a ruby-red seed and . . . what? Make a wish? Have your dreams come true? I couldn't remember. But I could have done with a pomegranate or two.

Well, I thought, so much for the plan. Got to phone Max to fetch me. Got to think of something to tell Chris. Got to develop Plan B. Got to—

The telephone rang, jarring me fully awake from the doze I'd been falling into. It sat across from me on the table in the window. I listened to its trilled double ring and wondered if I should . . . Well, why not. It might well be either Chris or Max, wondering how I was faring in the lion's den. Ought to set their minds at rest. Perfect opportunity to lie. I reached for my walker, shoved myself to my feet, dodged past the chesterfield, and reached the phone as it completed its twelfth *brinngg-brinngg*. I picked it up, said, "Yes?"

I heard music in the background, as if at a distance: rapid classical guitar, someone singing in Spanish. Then something clinked against the phone. A harsh gasp came over the wire.

I said, "Yes?"

A woman's voice said, "Bitch. You filthy *bitch*. You got what you wanted." She sounded half-drunk. "But it's not over. It . . . is . . . not . . . over. Do you understand? You're a hag-face cunt. Who do you think—"

"Who is this?"

A laugh. A sharp, indrawn breath. "You know damn well who it is. Just you wait, granny. Lock your windows and doors. Just . . . you . . . wait."

The caller rang off. I replaced the receiver. I rubbed my hand against the leg of my jeans and stared at the phone. She must have been drunk. She must have needed to vent her spleen. She must have . . . I didn't know. I shuddered and wondered why I was shuddering. I had nothing to worry about. Or so I thought.

Still, perhaps I ought to phone Max. Return to the barge. Come back another time. Because it was obvious that Mother and Kenneth were gone for the night, perhaps two or three. I would have to return.

But when, *when*? How many weeks did I really have before the wheelchair was imperative and my life on the barge at an end? How many more opportunities would fall my way before that time, when Chris was out on an assault and I could once again claim to have made an appointment to see Mother alone? Nothing was working out as I planned. It was maddening to think about going through this charade with Chris another time.

I sighed. If Plan A wasn't working, Plan B was worth a try. Near the door that led to the dining room sat Mother's davenport. There would be paper and pens within it. I would write her a letter. It wouldn't have the same power of surprise, but that couldn't be helped.

I found what I was looking for and sat down to write. I was tired, my fingers didn't wish to cooperate. After every paragraph, I had to stop and rest. I was four pages into the project when resting my fingers became resting my eyes became resting my head on the davenport's sloped writing surface. Five minutes, I thought. Let me take five minutes, then I'll go on.

The dream took me upstairs to the top floor of the house, into my old bedroom. I had my rucksacks with me, only when I opened them to unpack, they contained no clothes but instead the bodies of those long-ago kittens we'd rescued from the spinal cord experiment. I thought they were dead, but they weren't. They began to crawl, dragging themselves across the counterpane on the bed with their twisted little back legs stretched out uselessly behind them. I tried to gather them up, these kittens. I knew I had to get them out of sight before Mother came in. But every time I caught one of the kittens, another appeared. They were under the pillows and on the floor. When I opened a drawer in the chest to hide them, they had already multiplied in there as well. And then, in that bizarre scene-switching way of dreams, Richie Brewster was there. We were in my mother's room now. We were in her bed. Richie was playing his saxophone with a snake on his shoulder. It crawled across his chest and went beneath the covers. Richie smiled and gestured with his saxophone and said, "Blow, baby. Blow, Liv," and I knew what he wanted but I was afraid of the snake and afraid of what would happen if my mother came in and saw us in her bed but I went beneath the covers anyway and I did what he wanted but when he said, "Huh huh huh," in a groan, I raised my head and it was my father. He smiled and opened his mouth to speak. The snake slithered out. I gave a gasp and woke up.

My face was damp. My mouth had hung open as I slept and I'd smeared the page I'd been writing on. I thought, Thank God one can wake oneself up from dreams. Thank God dreams don't really mean anything. Thank God . . . and then I heard it.

I hadn't awakened myself at all. A noise had. A door was closing somewhere beneath me, the garden door.

The phone call, I thought. So I said nothing as my heart began to pound. Footsteps climbed the stairs from the kitchen. I heard the door open at the rear of the corridor. It closed. More footsteps. A pause. Then they came rapidly on.

The phone call, I thought. Oh God, oh God. I looked towards the telephone and willed myself to fly across the room and punch those triple nines so that I could yell my head off to the police. But I couldn't move. Never had I been so aware of what the present meant and what the future promised.

CHAPTER
24

Lynley concluded his meeting with Superintendent Webberly by gathering up the manila folders as well as the last three days of newspaper coverage. This latter material began with Jimmy Cooper's plunge into the Thames on Tuesday evening. It continued with accounts of his being taken into custody on Wednesday morning—led from the George Green Comprehensive School with his head hanging and his shoulders sloping as he walked between two uniformed constables. Thursday, with headlines announcing that murder charges were about to be brought against the son of Kenneth Fleming, it pursued everything from graphics depicting the workings of the juvenile justice system to interviews with Crown prosecutors expressing their opinions about the age at which children should be tried as adults, and it ended with this morning's recapitulation of the crime itself along with pertinent information about the Fleming family as well as a review of the career of the eminent batsman. All of the stories bore the same subtextual message: The case was closed and the trial was pending. Lynley couldn't have hoped for more.

"You're certain the Whitelaw woman's story checks out?" Webberly asked him.

"In every respect. Has done from the first."

Webberly heaved himself from the chair he'd taken at the circular table at the beginning of their afternoon meeting. He strolled to his filing cabinets and scooped up a picture of his only child, Miranda. She was happily posing on the river terrace of St. Stephen's College in Cambridge, her trumpet tucked under her arm. Webberly regarded her reflectively. He said to Lynley without raising his eyes, "You're going to be asking a lot, Tommy."

"It's our only hope, sir. In the last three days, I've had the entire team go over every shred of evidence and every interview. Havers and I have been out to Kent twice. We've met with the Maidstone crime scene team. We've spoken to each neighbour within sighting distance of Celandine Cottage. We've combed the garden and the cottage itself. We've been to all of the Springburns and nosed round there. We've come up with nothing more than what we have already. As far as I can tell, there's only one avenue left and that's the one we're following."

Webberly nodded but didn't look particularly happy with Lynley's answer. He replaced Miranda's photograph and wiped a speck of dust from its frame. He said in the same reflective tone, "Hillier's worked himself into a froth over this."

"I'm not surprised. I've let the press come in close. I've abandoned established procedure. He wouldn't like that, no matter the circumstances."

"He's called for another meeting. I've managed to put it off till Monday afternoon." He shot Lynley a look that successfully communicated the unspoken peroration to his remarks: Lynley had until Monday to bring the case to a close. At that point, Hillier would pull rank on them all and assign another DI.

"Right," Lynley said. "Thank you for keeping him out of my way, sir. That can't have been easy."

"I won't be able to hold him off much longer. And not at all after Monday."

"I don't think you'll need to."

Webberly cocked an eyebrow at him. "That confident, are you?"

Lynley tucked the folders and the newspapers under his arm. "Not when all I've got to work with is a single untraceable telephone call. I can't build a case on that."

"Have at her, then." The superintendent strolled back to his desk where he unearthed another case report from the general litter. He nodded Lynley on his way.

Lynley went to his own office where he deposited the case files but not the newspapers. He met Sergeant Havers on his way to the lift. She was flipping through a sheaf of typescript, frowning and muttering, "Hell, hell, hell," and when she saw him, she halted, reversed direction, and matched her stride to his. She said, "Are we off somewhere, then?"

Lynley unhooked his pocket watch and flipped it open. Quarter to five. "Didn't you mention a party this evening? 'Wonderful Games Will Be Played/Delicious Refreshments Will Be Served'? Shouldn't you be heading out to get ready?"

"Tell me, sir. What the hell am I supposed to buy for an eight-year-old girl? A doll? A game? A chemistry set? Nintendo? Roller blades? A flick knife? Water colours? What?" She rolled her eyes, but it was largely for effect. Lynley could tell she was pleased to be troubled with the task. "I could get her a Diablo," she went on, chewing on the pencil she'd been using to tick against the typescript. "At Camden Lock, there's a shop that sells them. Magician's gear as well. I wonder . . . What d'you think about magician's gear for an eight-year-old, sir? Or a costume? Kids like to play dressing up, don't they? I could get her a costume."

"What time is this party?" Lynley asked as he rang for the lift.

"Seven. What about war toys? Model cars? Airplanes? Rock and roll? D'you think she's too young for Sting? David Bowie?"

"I think you'd be wise to start your shopping immediately," Lynley said. The lift doors slid open. He stepped inside.

She was saying, "A skipping rope? A chess set? Backgammon? A plant? Great. What an idiot. A plant for an eight-year-old. What about books?" as the lift doors closed.

Lynley wondered what it would feel like to have so little to worry about on a Friday night.

Chris Faraday walked slowly along Warwick Avenue, from the underground station towards Blomfield Road. Beans and Toast loped ahead of him. They obediently dropped to their haunches at the street corner, anticipating the shouted command, "Walk, dogs!" that would permit them to cross Warwick Place and continue on their way to the barge. When the command didn't come, they dashed back to rejoin him, and ran yelping circles round his legs. They were used to a consistent run, start to finish. He was the one who'd always insisted upon that. Given their preference, they would have chosen to dawdle, snuffling round rubbish bins and chasing stray cats whenever the opportunity arose. But he'd trained them well, so this break in routine left them confused. They expressed their bemusement with their vocal cords. They yapped. They collided with each other. They bumped into his legs.

Chris knew they were there, and he knew what they wanted: speed, action, and the late-afternoon's breeze flapping back their ears. They wouldn't have objected to dinner as well, or a rubber ball thrown in the air for them to catch. But Chris was preoccupied with the *Evening Standard*.

The newspaper, which he'd purchased along the route of their run, featured yet another variation on the story it had been printing since midweek. It had managed the coup of having a photographer on the Isle of Dogs when the boy had made his break from the police, and its editors appeared to be underscoring that fact. Today—Friday—with the accompanying headline "East End Drama," the newspaper was committing a full page to the murder of Kenneth Fleming, the subsequent investigation, the Isle of Dogs chase after Fleming's son, the near-drowning which had concluded that chase, and the sensational one-man rescue that followed. The river photographs were grainy because a telephoto lens had been used to shoot them, but the point they made was clear enough: The long arm of the law reached out to ensnare the guilty no matter what efforts were made to avoid it.

Chris folded the newspaper. He tucked it under his arm with the rest. He scuffed through the cherry blossoms that covered the pavement on Warwick Avenue, and he thought about his conversation with Amanda, late last night after he'd settled Livie in bed. All he'd been able to tell her truthfully was, "I don't think it's likely to work out the way we hoped."

He had heard the fear in her voice despite her effort to sound collected. She'd said, "Why? Has something happened? Has Livie changed her mind?" And he could tell from her tone that she wasn't so much afraid of the truth as she was afraid of being hurt by the truth. He knew she was saying without really saying, "Are you choosing Livie over me?"

He'd wanted to tell her that it wasn't a matter of choosing anyone. The situation was far simpler than that. The path that had previously seemed logical and essentially uncomplicated was now not only tortuous but nearly impossible. But he couldn't tell her that. To tell her that would be extending an inadvertent invitation to ask more questions, which he would want to answer even as he knew that he couldn't.

So he'd told her that Livie hadn't changed her mind, but that the circumstances revolving round her decision had altered. And when she asked how and said, "She's rallied, hasn't she? Oh God, what a horrible question to ask. I've been reduced to sounding as if I want her to die, and I don't, Chris, I *don't*," he said, "I know that. It isn't that, anyway. It's just that Livie's—"

"No," she'd said. "You're not to tell me. Not like this, with me wheedling on the phone like an adolescent. When you're ready, Chris, when Livie is, you can tell me then."

Which made him want to tell her all the more and to ask for her advice. But he'd said only, "I love you. That hasn't changed."

"I wish you were with me."

"I wish the same."

There was nothing more to say. Still, they had remained on the phone, prolonging the contact for another hour. It was after one in the morning when she'd said gently, "I must ring off, Chris."

"Of course," he'd said, "you've work at nine, haven't you? I'm being selfish, holding on like this."

"You're not selfish. Besides, I want you holding on."

He didn't deserve her. He knew that, even as he kept himself going day after day solely, it seemed, with the thought of her.

The dogs had raced back to the corner of Warwick Avenue and Warwick Place. Tails wagging, they awaited his command. He caught them up and checked for traffic. He said, "Walk, dogs," and sent them hurtling on their way.

Livie was on the deck where he'd left her, huddled into one of the canvas chairs with a blanket round her shoulders. She was staring at Browning's Island where the willow trees looped leafy branches towards water and ground. She looked more wizened than he'd ever seen her, a presage of what the coming months held.

She roused herself when Beans and Toast clambered up onto the deck and snuffled at her left hand, which hung limply from the chair. She raised her head and blinked.

Chris laid the newspaper on the deck next to her, saying, "Nothing's changed, Livie." He went to fetch the dogs' bowls from below as she began to read.

He gave the dogs fresh water. He poured out the food. Beans and Toast tucked in. While they gobbled and slurped, Chris leaned against the top of the barge's cabin and turned his attention to Livie.

Since Saturday morning, she'd had him gather every newspaper for her. She read through each one, but she hadn't allowed him to throw any of them away. Instead, after Saturday's visit from the police, she'd had him carry the papers to her room and stack them next to her narrow bed. During the past few nights while he restlessly waited for sleep to come, he watched the striation that her reading light made against the open door of his room and he listened to her quietly turning the newspaper pages as she perused them a second and third time. He knew what she was reading. But he hadn't known why.

She'd held her tongue longer than he would have thought possible. She'd always been the sort of person to shoot from the hip and regret it later when it came to speaking her mind, so at first he'd thought her withdrawal merely indicated an uncharacteristic contemplation of the events that had overtaken them all with Kenneth Fleming's death. She'd finally told him everything because she'd had no choice. He'd been in Kensington on Sunday afternoon. He'd seen and he'd heard. All that was left was his quiet insistence that she share with him the burden of the truth. When she did so, he saw how his plans for his life would be altered. Which, he assumed, was why she hadn't wanted to tell him in the first place. Because she knew, if she told him, that he would exhort her to come forward and speak. And if he did that, both of them knew that they would then be tied to each other until she died. Neither of them spoke of this consequence of her act of confession. They didn't need to discuss the obvious.

Beans and Toast finished their meal and went to Livie's canvas chair. Beans lay at her side, his head within petting distance should the whimsy take her. Toast lowered himself gingerly in front of her and rested his chin on her heavy-soled shoe. Livie bent over the newspaper. Chris had already read the front page story, so he knew she was noting the relevant words *chief suspect in the crime, charges due to be brought, troubled youth with a history of delinquency.* She lifted her hand to the pictures, dropped it to the largest one that was centred among the others. In it, the boy lay like a sodden scarecrow in his mother's arms, with the river lapping round their waists and the soaked DI from Scotland Yard bending over them. As Chris watched, Livie's hand began to crumple the picture. Whether the action was deliberate or the result of a fibrillation of her muscles, he couldn't tell.

He went to her side. He cupped his hand round her cheek and pressed her head to his thigh.

"It doesn't mean they'll actually bring charges," she said. "It doesn't mean that, Chris. Does it?"

"Livie." His tone was gently admonishing. It said, Lie if you must, but not to yourself.

"They won't bring charges." She drew the photograph into a wrinkled mass beneath the palm of her hand. "And even if they do, what can happen to him? He's just turned sixteen. What do they do with kids who break the law when they're only sixteen?"

"That's not actually the point, is it?"

"They send them to Borstal or a place like that. They make them go to school. At school they get trained. They take the GCSE. Or they learn a trade. The paper says he hasn't been in school, so if someone *made* him go, if he had no choice because there was nothing else for him to do once he got there . . ."

Chris didn't bother to argue the point. Livie wasn't a fool. In a moment she would see the sand upon which she was constructing her suppositions, even if she didn't want to admit to the fact.

She let the newspaper go. She brought her right arm to her stomach and hugged herself as if she ached inside. Slowly, she lifted her left arm from where it dangled and curved it round Chris's leg, leaning into him. He stroked her cheek with his thumb.

"He confessed," she said, although her words lacked the conviction that had underscored her comments about Borstal. "Chris, he confessed. He was there. The newspapers said he was there. They said the police have evidence to prove it. If he was there and if he confessed, then he must have done it. Don't you see? Maybe I'm the one who's misunderstanding what happened."

"I don't think so," Chris said.

"Then *why?*" She grasped his leg harder as she said the second word. "Why have the police kept after him like they have? Why's he confessed? Why's he telling the police he killed his dad? It doesn't make sense. He must know he's guilty of something. That's it. It has to be. He's guilty of something. He just isn't saying what. Don't you think that's what's happening?''

"I think what's happening is he's lost his dad, Livie. He's lost him all at once when he wasn't expecting to lose him at all. Don't you think he might be reacting to that? Because how does it feel to have your dad alive one day and then have him dead the next without even having a chance to say good-bye?''

Her arm dropped from his leg. "That's not fair," she whispered.

He persisted. "What did you do, Livie? Shag some bloke you picked up in a pub, didn't you? He offered you a fiver if you'd let him give you a length and you were drunk that night, weren't you, and you were feeling so low that you didn't give a shit what happened to you next. Because your dad was dead and you hadn't even been allowed to go to his funeral. Isn't that what happened? Isn't that how you got started at the game? Weren't you acting crazy? Because of your dad? Even though you didn't want to admit it?''

"It's not the same."

"The hurt's the same. How you deal with the hurt is what's different."

"He's not saying what he's saying to deal with hurt."

"You don't know that. And even if you did, what he's doing and why he's doing it isn't the point in the first place."

She moved to dislodge his hand from her head. She smoothed out the newspaper and began to refold it. She placed it on the others he'd brought her that morning, but she didn't make any effort to turn her attention to them. Instead, she raised her head to Browning's Island. She resumed the position she'd been in when he'd returned from his run with the dogs.

He said, "Livie, you've got to tell them."

"I don't owe them anything. I don't owe anyone anything."

Her face was settled into the stony look she adopted whenever she wanted to dismiss a subject. To argue further was useless at this juncture. He sighed. He touched his fingers to the top of her head, where her chopped-up hair grew wild, like weeds.

He said, "But it *is* about owing, whether you like it or not."

"I don't bloody owe them—"

"Not them. Yourself."

. . .

Lynley went home first. Denton was in the midst of his afternoon tea, cup in hand, feet up on the drawing room coffee table, head back against the sofa, eyes closed. Andrew Lloyd Webber was blasting from the stereo as Denton bellowed along with Michael Crawford. Lynley wondered idly when *Phantom of the Opera* would go out of style. Soon wouldn't be soon enough, he thought.

He crossed to the stereo and lowered the volume, which left Denton howling, ". . . the music of the niiiiiiiiiight," into a moderately silent room.

"You're flat," Lynley said drily.

Denton jumped to his feet. He said, "Sorry. I was just—"

"Believe me, I have the general idea," Lynley interrupted.

Denton hastily put his teacup on the table. He brushed imaginary crumbs from its surface onto the palm of his hand. He deposited the same onto the tray on which he'd thoughtfully arranged sandwiches, biscuits, and grapes for himself. He said sheepishly, "Tea, m'lord?"

"I'm on my way out."

Denton looked from Lynley to the door. "Haven't you just come in?"

"Yes. I'm glad to say I was regaled by only the last twenty seconds of your warbling." He headed out of the room, saying, "Carry on without me. But, if you will, at a lower volume. Dinner at half past eight. For two."

"Two?"

"Lady Helen's joining me."

Denton brightened visibly. "Is it good news, then? Rather, have you and she . . . What I mean to ask is—"

"Half past eight," Lynley said.

"Yes. Right." Denton made much of gathering up teapot, plates, and cup.

As he climbed the stairs, Lynley reflected upon the fact that there was no real news to impart about Helen, to Denton or to anyone for that matter. Just a late-night phone call on Wednesday after she'd seen the newspaper stories covering his Tuesday evening run through the Isle of Dogs. She'd said, "My God, Tommy. Are you quite all right?" He'd said, "Yes. Fine. I've missed you, darling." But when she'd begun to go on with a careful, "Tommy. I've been thinking since Sunday morning. As you asked me to do," he discovered that he couldn't cope with holding a conversation that might touch upon their lives. So he said, "Let's talk at the weekend, Helen." And they'd agreed on dinner.

In his bedroom he went to the wardrobe and began pulling out clothes. Blue jeans, polo shirt, a worn pair of gym shoes, a tatty pair of white socks. He changed from his suit, tossing jacket, trousers, and waistcoat onto the bed. He looked into the cheval mirror on the chest of drawers and studied his reflection. The hair was all wrong. He ran a hand through it, dishevelling as he went. He fetched his car keys from his trousers and left.

The heavy traffic of late Friday afternoon slowed his progress from Belgravia to Little Venice. It was particularly thick in the vicinity of Hyde Park where a tourist coach had stalled on Park Lane, leaving a trail of vehicles stranded behind it.

Past the park, conditions weren't much better on the Edgware Road. Everyone, it seemed, was intent upon leaving the city for the weekend. He couldn't blame them. The weather was May perfect, an invitation to either the country or the coast. He wished coast or country were his destination. He didn't savour the thought of the hours to come, what might follow those hours, or how much depended upon them.

He parked on the south side of Little Venice and, newspapers once again tucked under his arm, he took the long way round Warwick Crescent to the bridge that spanned Regent's Canal. There he paused. He gazed at the murky water where five Canada geese were paddling in the direction of the pool and Browning's Island.

He could see Faraday's barge quite well from here. Although it was still light out and would be for another two hours, no one was on the deck of the barge and lamps had been lit inside it. They cast bands of yellow-gold against the glass. As he watched, he saw the yellow-gold waver as someone within passed between the window and the light. Faraday, he thought. Lynley would have preferred to meet with Olivia alone, but he knew how unlikely it was that she would ever agree to a meeting without her companion present.

Faraday met him at the door to the cabin, before Lynley had the chance to knock. He was halfway up the stairs, dressed in running gear, and the dogs were milling round his legs. One scratched at the step upon which Faraday stood. The other yelped.

Faraday didn't speak. He merely stepped back down into the cabin of the barge and when the dogs began to hurtle themselves up the stairway towards Lynley and the out-of-doors, he said, "Dogs, no!"

Lynley descended. Faraday watched, his face chary. His eyes flicked to the newspapers under Lynley's arm, then to his face.

"She's here?" Lynley said.

A crashing of metal against lino in the galley answered him. Olivia's voice said, "Damn. Chris, I dropped the rice. It's gone everywhere. I'm sorry."

Faraday called over his shoulder, "Leave it."

"*Leave* it? Goddamn it, Chris, stop treating me like—"

"The inspector's here, Livie."

Abrupt silence fell. Lynley could sense that Olivia had drawn in her breath and was holding it as she tried to decide how and if she could avoid this final confrontation. After a moment in which Faraday looked towards the galley and the dogs trotted to see what was what, the sound of movement began. The aluminium walker creaked as it took her weight. Shoe soles dragged sloppily against the floor. Olivia grunted, then said, "Chris, I'm stuck. It's the rice. I can't get round it."

Faraday went to her. He said, "Beans! Toast! Go lie down!" and the sound of their nails against lino faded as they went obediently to the front of the barge.

Lynley switched on the remaining unlit lamps in the main room. Olivia could still play with the disease if she wished to avoid him, but he wouldn't allow her any further variations of shadows and light. He looked for a table on which he could lay out the newspapers he'd brought, but aside from Faraday's worktable against the far wall, there was nothing he could use except one of the armchairs and they wouldn't do. He laid the papers on the floor.

"Well?"

He swung about. Olivia had worked her way to the opening between the galley and the main room. She was slung between the handrails of her walker, her shoulders caving against her weight. Her face appeared at once paste-coloured and shiny, and as she inched forward, she avoided his eyes.

Faraday trailed her, one hand held up, palm outward, a foot or so from her back. She paused when her lowered eyes caught sight of the newspapers, but she gave another grunt—sounding somewhere between derision and disgust—and struggled carefully round them to place herself in one of the corduroy armchairs. When she lowered herself into it, she kept the walker in front of her, as a line of defence. Faraday started to move it. She said, "No." And then, "Will you fetch my fags, Chris?"

She used her lighter against a cigarette that he shook from the packet. She blew out smoke in a thin grey stream. She said to Lynley, "Are you done up for a masquerade, or something?"

He said, "I'm off duty."

She inhaled and blew out another grey stream. Her lips were pursed and made her expression look angry, as perhaps she intended or perhaps she was. "Don't give me that. Cops're never off duty."

"Perhaps. But I'm not here as a cop."

"Then what're you here as? A private citizen? Visiting the sick in your free time? Don't make me laugh. A cop's always a cop, on duty or off." She cranked her head away from him to Faraday. The other man had gone to sit at the kitchen table, his chair turned round so it faced theirs in the sitting room. "You got the tin over there, Chris? I need the tin."

He brought it to her, then retreated once again. She tucked the tin between her legs and tapped a bare millimetre of ash from her cigarette. She was wearing a silver hoop through her nostril and a line of silver studs on one ear, but the rings that had decorated all of her fingers had given way to bracelets stacked along her left arm. These jangled together as she smoked.

"So what d'you want this time?"

"Just to talk to you, actually."

"Haven't got the darbies with you? Haven't made arrangements for my bed-sit in Holloway?"

"That won't be necessary, as you can see."

She followed his lead by clumsily using her foot to indicate the news-papers, which he'd laid on the floor. She said, "So it's Borstal, then. Tell me, Inspector. What's a yob like that get in our current justice system for doing the business on his own dad? A year?"

"The length of the sentence is up to the court. And the skill of his barrister."

"So it's true."

"What?"

"That the kid did it."

"You've no doubt read the papers."

She lifted the cigarette to her mouth and inhaled, watching him over the glowing tip. "Why're you here, then? Shouldn't you be out celebrating?"

"There's not much to celebrate in a murder investigation."

"Not even when the bad guys are caught?"

"Not even then. I've found the bad guys are rarely as bad as I would like them to be. People kill for all sorts of reasons, but the rarest is malice."

She inhaled another time. He could see the wariness in her eyes and her posture. Why's he here? she was wondering, and her expression told him she was making an attempt to suss him out.

"People kill for revenge," he said easily, as if he were a lecturer in a criminology classroom with nothing at stake. "They kill in a sudden fit of temper. They kill because of avarice. Or in self-defence."

"That's not murder, then."

"Sometimes they become embroiled in territorial disputes. Or they attempt to secure justice. Or they need to cover up another crime. Other times they commit an act of desperation, in trying to secure freedom from bondage, for example."

She nodded. Behind her, Faraday shifted on his chair. Lynley could see that the black-and-white cat had stolen silently into the galley as he was speaking and leapt to the table where she was weaving between two empty glasses. Faraday didn't appear to notice the animal.

"Sometimes they kill because of jealousy," Lynley said. "Because of thwarted passion, obsession, or love. Sometimes they even kill by mistake. They aim in one direction, but they shoot in another."

"Yeah. I expect that happens." Olivia tapped her cigarette against the tin. She returned it to her mouth and used her hands to pull her legs closer to the chair.

"That's what happened in this case," Lynley said.

"What?"

"Someone made a mistake."

Olivia gave her attention to the newspapers briefly, seemed to think this was avoidance, and returned her gaze to Lynley. She kept it there as he went on.

"No one knew that Fleming was going to Kent last Wednesday night. Are you aware of that, Miss Whitelaw?"

"As I didn't know Fleming, I haven't given it much thought."

"He told your mother he was going to Greece. He told his teammates much the same. He told his son he had cricket business to take care of. But he didn't tell anyone he was going to Kent. Not even Gabriella Patten, who was staying at the cottage and whom he no doubt wished to surprise. Curious, isn't it?"

"His kid knew he was there. The papers said."

"No. The papers said Jimmy confessed."

"That's logic chopping. If he confessed to killing him, he had to know he was there to do the job."

"It doesn't work that way," Lynley said. "Fleming's killer—"

"The kid."

"I'm sorry. Yes. The boy—Jimmy, the killer—knew that someone was in the cottage. And that someone was indeed the intended victim. But in the killer's mind—"

"In Jimmy's mind."

"—that someone in the cottage wasn't Fleming at all. It was Gabriella Patten."

Olivia ground her cigarette against the tin. She sent Faraday a look. He brought her another. She lit up again and held the smoke in. Lynley could imagine it swirling through her blood to buzz round her skull.

"How'd you come up with this?" she finally asked.

"Because no one knew Fleming was going to Kent. And his killer—"

"The boy," Olivia said tersely. "Why d'you keep saying 'Fleming's killer' when you know it's the boy?"

"Sorry. Force of habit. I'm falling back on police terminology."

"You said you were off duty."

"And I am. Bear with my lapses if you will. Fleming's killer—Jimmy —loved him but had good reason to hate Gabriella Patten. She was a disruptive influence. Fleming was in love with her, but their affair kept him in turmoil, which he was unable to conceal. Beyond that, their affair promised great changes in Fleming's life. If he actually married Gabriella, his circumstances would alter dramatically."

"Specifically, he'd never go back home." Olivia sounded comfortable with this conclusion. "Which is what the boy wanted, isn't it? Didn't he want his dad to come home?"

"Yes," Lynley said, "I dare say that was the motive behind the crime. To keep Fleming from marrying Gabriella Patten. It's ironic, however, when you think about the situation."

She didn't say, What situation? She merely lifted her cigarette and observed him from behind its smoke.

Lynley continued. "No one would have died at all had Fleming himself had less masculine pride."

In spite of herself, Olivia drew her eyebrows together.

"His pride is the basis for the crime in the first place," Lynley explained. "Had Fleming only been less proud, had he only been willing to reveal that he was going to Kent to end the affair with Mrs. Patten because he'd discovered he was just one in a long line of her lovers, his killer—forgive me, I'm doing it again; Jimmy, the boy—would have had no need to eliminate the woman. There would have been no mistake about who was staying in the cottage that night. Fleming himself would still be alive. And the kil— And Jimmy wouldn't go through the rest of life tormented by the thought of having murdered—by mistake—someone he loved so much."

Olivia took a moment to examine the tin's contents before she ground her cigarette out against its side. She placed the tin on the floor and folded her hands in her lap. "Yeah," she said. "Well, what do they say about always hurting the one we love? Life's rotten, Inspector. The kid's just learning early."

"Yes. He is learning, isn't he? All about what it's like to be branded a parricide, to have charges brought against him, to be fingerprinted and photographed, to face a criminal trial. And after that—"

"He should've thought first."

"But he didn't, did he? Because he—the killer, Jimmy, the boy—thought the crime was perfect. And it almost was."

She watched, wary. Lynley thought he could hear her breathing change.

He said, "There was only one detail that marred it."

Olivia reached for her walker. She intended to rise, but Lynley could see that the depth of the armchair made it difficult for her to do so without assistance. She said, "Chris," but Faraday didn't move. She jerked her head in his direction. "Chris. Give a hand."

Faraday looked at Lynley and asked the question, which Olivia was avoiding. "What detail marred it?"

"Chris! Goddamn—"

"What detail?" he asked again.

"A telephone call made by Gabriella Patten."

"What about it?" Faraday asked.

"Chris! Help me. Come on."

"It was answered as it should have been," Lynley said. "But the person who allegedly answered doesn't even know the phone call was made. I find that curious when—"

"Oh too right," Olivia snapped. "Do you remember every phone call you get?"

"—when I consider the time the call was made and the nature of the message. After midnight. Abusive."

"Maybe there was no call," Olivia said. "Did you ever think of that? Maybe she lied about making it."

"No," Lynley said. "Gabriella Patten had no reason to lie. Not when lying extended an alibi to Fleming's killer." He leaned towards Olivia, resting his elbows on his knees. "I'm not here as a policeman, Miss Whitelaw. I'm here simply as a man who'd like to see justice done."

"It's being done. The kid confessed. What more do you want?"

"The real killer. The killer that you can identify."

"Bollocks." But she wouldn't look at him.

"You've seen the papers. Jimmy's confessed. He's been arrested. He's been charged. He'll go to court. But he didn't kill his father, and I think you know it."

She reached for the tin. Her intentions were obvious. But Faraday wouldn't accommodate her.

"Don't you think the boy's been through enough, Miss Whitelaw?"

"If he didn't do it, then let him go."

"That's not the way it works. His future was mapped out the moment he said he murdered his father. What happens next is a trial. After that, prison. The only way he can clear himself is if the real killer is apprehended."

"That's your job, not mine."

"It's everyone's job. That's part of the price we pay for choosing to live among others in an organised society."

"Oh, is it?" Olivia shoved the tin to one side. She grasped the walker and pulled herself forward. She grunted with the strain of lifting and moving the uncooperative mass of her muscles. Beads of perspiration began to dot her forehead.

"Livie." Faraday got up from his chair and came to her side.

She shrank away from him. "No. Forget it." By the time she was upright, her legs were quaking so badly that Lynley wondered if she would be able to remain on her feet much more than a minute. She said, "Look at me. Look . . . at . . . me. Do you know what you're asking?"

"I know," Lynley said.

"Well, I won't. I *won't*. He's nothing to me. They're nothing to me. I don't care about them. I don't care about anyone."

"I don't believe that."

"Try. You'll manage."

She wrenched the walker to one side and followed it with her body. With painful slowness, she faltered from the room. As she passed the table in the galley, the cat sprang to the floor, twined between her legs, and followed her out of sight. More than a minute went by before they heard the sound of a door closing behind her.

Faraday looked as if he wanted to follow her, but he stayed where he was, standing next to her chair. Although he kept his gaze pointed in the direction Olivia had taken, he said to Lynley in a low rapid voice, "Miriam wasn't there that night. Not when we got there. But her car was there and the lights were on and she'd left music playing so we both assumed . . . I mean it was logical for us to assume she'd just popped over to a neighbour's for a minute."

"Which is what anyone who happened to knock on her door was meant to think."

"Except we didn't knock. Because Livie had the key. We let ourselves in. I . . . I looked round the house to tell her Livie had arrived. But she wasn't there. Livie told me to shove off, so I did." He turned to Lynley. He asked, sounding desperate, "Is that enough? For the boy?"

"No," Lynley said and when Faraday's expression became even more bleak, "I'm sorry."

"What's going to happen? If she doesn't tell the truth?"

"A sixteen-year-old boy's future hangs in the balance."

"But if he didn't do it—"

"We have his confession. It's perfectly solid. The only way we can negate it is by identifying who did."

Lynley waited for Faraday to respond in some fashion. He hoped for a single clue as to what might happen next. He'd reached the absolute bottom of his bag of tricks. If Olivia didn't break, he'd smeared the name and the life of an innocent boy for nothing.

But Faraday didn't make a reply. He merely went to the table in the galley, where he sat and dropped his head into his hands. His fingers pressed into his skull until their nails were white.

"God," he said.

"Talk to her," Lynley said.

"She's dying. She's afraid. I don't have the words."

Then they were lost, Lynley concluded. He picked up his newspapers, folded them, and went out into the evening.

OLIVIA

The footsteps came on. They were certain, determined. My mouth got dry as they closed in on the morning room door. They stopped abruptly. I heard someone take a sharp breath. I turned in my chair. It was Mother.

We stared at each other. She said, "God in heaven," with her hand on her breast, and she stayed where she was. I waited for the sound of Kenneth following her. I waited for his voice saying, "What is it, Miriam?" or "Darling, is something wrong?" But the only sound was the grandfather clock in the corridor bonging out three o'clock. The only voice was Mother's. "Olivia? *Olivia?* My God, what on earth . . ."

I thought she would come into the room, but she didn't. She remained in the dark corridor just beyond the doorway, where she reached with one hand for the jamb and climbed the other to the collar of her dress. This she pinched closed. She was fairly hidden in the shadows, but I could see enough to know she wasn't wearing one of her Jackie Kennedy sheaths. Instead she had on a bright spring number of green with a pattern of daffodils climbing from the hem to a gathered waist. It looked like something one might notice in a C & A window display heralding the change in seasons. It wasn't like anything Mother had ever worn before, and it emphasised her hips in an unflattering manner. I felt odd, seeing her dressed like that, and I wondered if she'd hung a gay straw boater with streamers on the hook just inside the garden door. I half expected to look at her feet and see sweet little white T-strap shoes upon them. I was embarrassed for her. It didn't take an advanced degree in human psychology to delve past the costume to the intention beneath it.

"I was writing you a letter," I said.

"A letter."

"I must've fallen asleep."

"How long have you been here?"

"Since half past ten. Something like that. Chris—bloke I live with— he dropped me off. I was waiting for you. Then I decided to write. He'll be by in a while, Chris. I fell asleep."

I felt thick-headed. This wasn't working out the way I had planned. I was supposed to be at ease and in control, but when I looked at her, I found that I didn't know how to go on. Come on, come on, I told myself roughly, who gives a shit what she's doing with herself to keep her honey lamb interested? Be first to establish the whip hand here. Surprise is on your side, just like you wanted.

But surprise was on her side as well, and she wasn't doing anything to make things less awkward between us. Not that she owed me an easy transition back into her world. I'd given up all rights to chummy mother-daughter chats some years ago.

Mother's eyes held mine. She appeared determined not to look at my legs, not to notice the aluminium walker sitting next to the davenport, and not to question what my legs, the walker, and most of all my presence in her house at three in the morning meant.

"I've been reading about you in the papers from time to time," I said. "You. Kenneth. You know."

"Yes," she said, as if my admission was only to be expected.

I could feel that my armpits were wet. I longed to blot them with a handkerchief or something. "Seems like a nice enough bloke. I remember him from when you were a teacher."

"Yes," she said.

I thought, Shit damn hell. Where was this going? She should be saying, What's happened to you, Olivia? I should be saying, I've come to talk, I need your help, I'm going to die.

Instead I sat in a chair in front of the davenport, half turned in her direction. She stood in the corridor with the floor lamp shooting light along the hem of her silly shirtwaister. I couldn't move to her without making an awkward scene of it. And clearly, she had no intention of moving towards me. She was clever enough to know that I'd come to ask for something. She was vindictive enough to make me crawl across coals of discomfort in order to ask it.

All right, I thought. I'll give you your petty victory. You want me to crawl? I'll crawl. I'll be the artist of crawl.

I said, "I've come to talk to you, Mother."

"At three in the morning?"

"I didn't know it would be three."

"You said you've written a letter."

I looked down at the sheets of paper I'd filled. I couldn't use a biro any longer. She'd had no pencils in the davenport. The scrawl came from the hand of an unschooled child. I raised my hand to the papers. My fingers crumpled them.

"I need to talk to you," I repeated. "This doesn't say it the way . . . I need to talk. I've made a hash of this, obviously. I'm sorry about the time. If you want me to come back tomorrow, I'll ask Chris—"

"No," she said. Apparently, I'd crawled long enough to satisfy. "Let me change. I'll make tea."

She left me quickly. I heard her go up the first then the second flight of stairs to her room. It was more than five minutes before she came down again. She passed the morning room door without looking inside at me. She went down to the kitchen. Ten more minutes creeped by. She was going to make me stew for a while. She was going to enjoy it. I wanted to even the score, but I didn't exactly know how to do it.

I got up from the balloon-back chair by the davenport, positioned myself behind the walker, and began to shuffle in the direction of the settee. I made the perilous turn-around prior to lowering myself onto the old velvet and looked up to see that Mother stood in the doorway, a tray of tea in her hands. We gazed across the room at each other.

"Long time no see," I said.

"Ten years, two weeks, four days," she said.

I blinked, turned my head to the wall. It was still hung with a mishmash of Japanese prints, small portraits of dead Whitelaws, and a minor old master of the Flemish school. I stared at this as Mother came into the room and set the tea tray on a games table next to the chesterfield.

"The same?" she asked me. "Milk and two sugars?"

Damn her, I thought, damn her, goddamn her. I nodded. I looked at the Flemish painting: a centaur with forelegs pawing the air, clasping a woman on to his back, his left and her right arm raised for some reason into an arch. They looked as if they both wanted it this way, the monstrous creature and the bare-legged woman who would be his prize. She wasn't even fighting to escape him.

"I've got something called ALS," I said.

Behind me I heard the comforting and so familiar sound of hot liquid splashing against a porcelain cup. I heard a clink as the cup in its saucer tapped against the table. Then I felt her near me, next to me. I felt her hand on the walker.

"Sit down," she said. "Here's your tea. Shall I help you?" Her breath, I thought. She smelled of alcohol, and I realised she'd fortified herself for this encounter while she was changing her clothes and making the tea. It comforted me to know that. She said again, "Do you need help, Olivia?"

I shook my head. She moved the walker to one side when I'd lowered myself to the settee. She handed me the teacup, placing its saucer on my knee and holding it there until I reached for it and steadied it myself.

She'd changed into a navy dressing gown. She looked more like a mother I could recognise.

"ALS," she said.

"I've had it for about a year."

"It gives you difficulty walking?"

"At the moment."

"The moment?"

"For now, it's walking."

"And later?"

"Stephen Hawking."

She'd lifted her teacup to drink. Over the top of it, her eyes met mine. She put the cup back into its saucer slowly, the tea undrunk. She put the saucer and cup onto the table. So careful were her movements that she made no noise. She sat at the corner of the chesterfield. Our bodies were at right angles to each other, our knees separated by less than six inches.

I wanted her to say something. But her only response was to raise her right hand to her temple and press her fingers against it.

I considered saying that I could come back at another time. Instead I said, "Two to five years, basically. Seven if I'm lucky."

She dropped her hand. "But Stephen Hawking—"

"He's the exception. Which doesn't exactly matter because I don't want to live like that anyway."

"You can't know that yet."

"Believe me, I can."

"An illness allows one to define life differently."

"No."

I told her how it started, with the stumble on the street. I told her about the physical examinations and the tests. I told her about the futile programme of exercise, about the healers. Finally, I told her about the disease's progress. "It's on its way into my arms," I finished. "My fingers are weakening. If you look at the letter I was trying to write you—"

"Damn you," she said, although the words contained no element of passion. "Damn you, Olivia."

Now was the time for the lecture. I had wanted the whip hand. I had wanted to win. But how could I have expected either? I'd not returned to Staffordshire Terrace triumphant. I'd returned like a prodigal, ruined physically instead of financially, holding on to aphorisms like "Blood's thicker, isn't it?" as if they could rebuild a bridge that I had so much enjoyed destroying. I waited to live through what she believed I should hear at the moment: This is what you get. . . . How does it feel to have your body go to pieces. . . . You broke your father's heart. . . . You destroyed every one of our lives. . . .

I'd live through it, I thought. They were only words. She needed to say them. Once she had done, we could move from recriminations over the past to arrangements for the future. To get the lecture over with as soon as possible, I gave her an opening.

"I did some stupid things, Mother. . . . I wasn't as clever as I thought. I was wrong and I'm sorry."

The ball was in her court. I waited, resigned. Let her have at me, I thought.

She said, "As am I, Olivia. Sorry, that is."

Nothing more came. I hadn't been looking at her, had been picking instead at a loose thread in the seam of my jeans. I raised my eyes. Her own looked watery, but I couldn't tell if the water meant tears, exhaustion, or an effort to fight off a migraine. Age seemed to be coming on her quickly. However she had appeared in the doorway a half hour earlier, she was looking close to her years at the moment.

I asked the question without knowing I would ask it: "Why did you send me that telegram?"

"To hurt you."

"We could have helped each other."

"Not then, Olivia."

"I hated you."

"I blamed you."

"Do you still?"

She shook her head. "Do you?"

I considered the question. "I don't know."

She smiled briefly. "You've become honest, it seems."

"Dying does that to you."

"You mustn't say—"

"It's part of the honesty." I began to place my teacup on the table. The cup rattled like dried bones against the saucer. She took it from me. She put her hand over my right fist. "You're different," I said. "Not what I expected."

"Loving does that to you."

She said it without the least trace of embarrassment. She didn't sound either proud or defensive. She spoke as if merely stating a fact.

I said, "Where is he?"

She frowned, looking perplexed.

"Kenneth," I said. "Where is he?"

"Ken? Greece. I've just seen him off to Greece." She seemed to realise how odd the remark sounded, coming at nearly half past three in the morning because she shifted in her chair before she added, "The flight was delayed."

"You've come from the airport."

"Yes."

"You've done good by him, Mum."

"I? No. He's done most of it himself. He's a worker and a dreamer. I've simply been there to listen to the dreams and encourage the work."

"Still . . ."

She smiled fondly, as if I hadn't spoken. "Ken has always made his own world, Olivia. He takes dust and water and turns it into marble. I think you'll like him. You're of an age, you know, you and Ken."

"I hated him." I adjusted the statement. "I was jealous of him."

"He's a fine man, Olivia. Truly fine. The things he's done for me out of sheer generosity . . ." She raised her hand slightly from the arm of the chesterfield. "What can I do to make your life lovely, he's always wanted to know. How can I repay what you've done for me? Cook the meals? Talk over the issues of the day? Share my world? Ease the pains in your head? Make you part of my life? Make you proud to know me?"

"I've done none of that for you."

"It doesn't matter. Because things are different now. Life is different now. I never thought life could alter as much as it has. But it does if you're open to it, darling."

Darling. Where were we heading? I took a course blindly. "The barge I live on. It's like . . . I'm going to need a wheelchair, but the barge is too . . . I've been trying to . . . Dr. Alderson tells me there're private nursing homes."

"And there are homes," Mother said. "Like this, which is yours."

"You can't really want—"

"I want," she said.

And that was the end of it. She stood and said that we needed to eat. She helped me into the dining room, sat me at the table, and left me there while she went below to the kitchen. She returned in quarter of an hour with eggs and toast. She brought strawberry jam. She brought fresh tea. She sat not opposite me but next to me. And while she had been the one to suggest food, she ate practically nothing herself.

I said, "It's going to be awful, Mum. This. Me. The ALS."

She put her hand on my arm. "We'll talk about all that tomorrow," she said. "And the tomorrow after that. And the next one as well."

I felt my throat get tight. I set my fork down.

"You're home," Mother said. I knew she meant it.

CHAPTER
25

Lynley found Helen in the back garden of his town house, moving among the rose bushes with a pair of secateurs. She was not gathering either buds or flowers, however. Rather, she was in the process of cutting off the dead remains of roses that had already bloomed and faded. She was letting these fall away to the ground.

He watched her from the dining room window. It was drawing towards dusk, and the failing light glinted softly against her. It shot her hair with streaks coloured like brandy. It made her skin luminous, ivory touched by gold. She was dressed in the expectation of continued good weather, in an apricot tunic and matching leggings, with thin-soled sandals on her feet.

As she moved from one bush to the next, he reconsidered her question about love. How to explain it, he wondered. Not only to her and to her satisfaction but to himself.

She wanted something analysed which did not make itself available to analysis, at least not by him. Love was to him one of life's larger mysteries. He couldn't adequately explain why his heart had decided to settle itself upon her any more than he could explain how the moon maintained a force upon the movement of the ocean, how the earth spun on an ever-tilting axis that effected seasons, how despite the furious spinning of this planet, what stood upon it stood upon it and did not hurtle into oblivion. Some things were provided for by nature. Love was one of them.

If he could have made a rational choice, it probably wouldn't have been Helen Clyde. It would have been someone more likely to appreciate a hike out to Chysauster Village and a ramble through the stones of those ancient prehistoric dwellings without saying, "Good Lord, Tommy. Can you imagine what this ghastly wind must have done to those poor women's skin in those days?" It would have been someone more likely to say, "Ashby de la Zouch? *Ivanhoe*, of course. The great joust. And Lord Hastings as well, but we know what happened to him, don't we, darling?" It would have been someone who walked through the musty remains of Alnwick Castle and thought of Hotspur and what he had lost through giving in to the thrall of his own ambition. But the someone who might have meditated upon Chysauster, waxed poetic about Ashby, and evidenced the appropriate degree of mourning for the spilled blood of Northumberland would not have been Helen. With her exasperating indifference to the millennium of history that surrounded them, with her insouciant ability to enjoy what life offered in the here and now, with her utterly spurious frivolity. She was out of place, she was out of time, she was of different people and another century altogether. They stood not a candle-flicker's chance in a gale of surviving more than a year if they married. And he wanted her anyway.

Perdition catch my soul, he thought, and he smiled grimly and then laughed aloud to think of what *that* particular love had come to. It didn't bode well that the Moor's declaration of passion sprang to his mind when he considered Helen. But on the other hand, if they kept their bed free of pillows and Helen free of handkerchiefs, they might have nothing to worry about.

Isn't it all about risking anyway? he asked himself. Isn't it all about believing in another soul's power to redeem us? That's the why of it, Helen. Love doesn't arise from similarity of education, similarity of background, similarity of experience. Love arises from nothing and creates as it goes. And without it, chaos is indeed come again.

Outside, she ceased her work with the secateurs, stooped, and began to pick up the fallen, dead flowers. She'd forgotten to take a rubbish bag into the garden with her, so she used the front of her tunic as an apron and tossed the remains of the roses there. He went out to join her.

"The garden needs work," she said. "If you leave roses on the bush once the roses have died, the bush keeps putting energy into them and ends up blooming less. Did you know that, Tommy?"

"I didn't."

"It's true. But if you cut off the flowers once they've begun to fade, the energy's constantly diverted into fresh buds." She scooted forward, half-standing and half-bent to her task. She wasn't wearing gloves and her hands were getting dirty. But she was, he saw, still wearing his ring. There was hope in that. There was promise as well. And an end to chaos.

She looked up suddenly and caught his eyes on her hands. She said, "Tell me."

He searched for the words. "Would you agree," he said, "that Elizabeth Barrett loved Robert Browning?"

"I suppose so, but I don't know much about them."

"She eloped with him. Cut herself off from her family for the rest of her life—from her father in particular—in order to spend her life with him. She wrote a series of love poems to him."

"The Portuguese sonnets?"

"Yes. Those."

"And?"

"And yet in the most famous of those sonnets, she can't tell him why, Helen. She tells him that, she tells him how—freely, purely, with childhood's faith—but she never tells him why. So Browning had to take her at her word. He had to accept the that and the how without the why."

"Which is what you'd have me do. Is that it?"

"Yes. That's it."

"I see." She nodded thoughtfully and picked up a few more of the cut, dead flowers. The petals broke away from the sepals within her grasp. The sleeve of her tunic caught on a thorn from one of the bushes and he freed it for her. She covered his hand with hers. "Tommy," she said and waited for him to lift his eyes. "Tell me."

"There's nothing more, Helen. I'm sorry. I've done my best."

Her face softened. She gestured from him to herself and said, "I didn't mean this, us, this business of love, darling. I meant tell me what's happened. The newspaper said it was over, but it isn't over. I can tell that by looking at you."

"How?"

"Tell me," she repeated, more gently this time.

He lowered himself to the lawn that edged the bed of roses. And as she crawled among the plants, scooping up the cuttings, smudging her tunic and her leggings, dirtying her hands, he told her. About Jean Cooper and her son. About Olivia Whitelaw. About her mother. About Kenneth Fleming and three women's love for him and what had happened because of that love.

"I'll be off the case on Monday," he finished. "Frankly, Helen, it's just as well. I'm out of ideas."

She came to sit next to him, cross-legged on the lawn, her lap full of the remains of the roses. "Perhaps there's another way," she said.

He shook his head. "I've got nothing but Olivia. All she has to do is hold fast to her story, and she has every reason in the world to do so."

"Except the reason she needs," Helen said.

"Which is?"

"That it's the right thing to do."

"I don't get the impression that right and wrong have a great deal of meaning in Olivia's life."

"Perhaps. But people can surprise you, Tommy."

He nodded and found he didn't want to talk about the case any longer. It was too much with him, and it made the promise of staying too much with him over the next few days. At least for the moment, for the evening as well, he could choose to forget it. He reached for her hand. He rubbed the specks of dirt from her fingers.

"That was why, by the way," he said.

"What was?"

"When you asked me to tell you and I misunderstood. That was the why of it."

"Because you misunderstood?"

"No. Because you asked me to tell you. You looked at me, you knew what was wrong, and you asked. That's the why of it, Helen. That will always be the why."

She was silent for a moment. She seemed to be examining the manner in which his hand held hers. "Yes," she finally said in a quiet, firm voice.

"So you understand?"

"I understand. Yes. But I was answering you, actually."

"Answering me?"

"The question you asked me last Friday night. Although it wasn't really a question, was it? It sounded more like a demand. Well, perhaps demand isn't right, either. More like a request."

"Friday night?" He thought back. The days had passed so quickly that he couldn't even remember where he had been and what he had been doing last Friday night. Except that they'd been scheduled to hear Strauss and the evening had been ruined and he'd gone to her flat round two in the morning and . . . He looked at her quickly and found her smiling.

"I wasn't asleep," she said. "I love you, Tommy. I suppose I always have in one way or another, even when I thought you would always and only be my friend. So yes. I will. Whenever you choose. Wherever you want."

OLIVIA

I've been watching Panda, who's still lying on the dresser in an artfully arranged pile of letters and bills. She looks quite peaceful. She's made herself into a perfect ball, head touching rear end, paws tucked under tail. She's given up trying to understand why her bedtime rituals have been disrupted. She doesn't question why I've sat in the galley hour after hour instead of removing myself to my room in her company and plumping up the blankets to make her a nest at the foot of the bed. I'd like to take her from the dresser and set her on my lap for a while. There's a certain comfort that only comes from a cat's condescension to be held and petted. I make kitty-kitty sounds to get her attention. Her ears move in my direction, but her position doesn't alter. I know what she's telling me. It's no different from what I've been telling myself. What I'm going to go through, I've got to go through alone. This is like a dress rehearsal for death.

Chris is in his room again. It sounds like he's keeping himself awake by earnest spring housecleaning. I keep hearing drawers slide open and cupboards snap shut. When I call out that he should go to bed, he calls back, "In a while. I'm looking for something." I ask what. He says, "Picture of Lloyd-George Marley. He wore dreadlocks, did I tell you? And Persian slippers with pointed toes." I comment that Lloyd-George Marley sounds quite the snappy bloke. Chris says, "He was." I say, "Did you lose touch with him or something? Why's he never been round the barge to see us?" I hear a drawer slide open and its contents get dumped onto Chris's bed. I say, "Chris, why's he never—" And Chris interrupts. "He's dead, Livie." I repeat the word *dead* and ask how did he die. Chris says, "Knifed." I don't ask Chris was he with him when it happened. I already know.

I don't think the world has much to offer in the way of happiness and contentment, do you? There's too much grief and too much pain. They're born of knowledge, attachment, and involvement.

It's a useless activity, but still I wonder how things might have been had I never gone to Julip's all those years ago and met Richie Brewster. If I'd finished university, taken up a career, made my parents proud. . . . How many needs of other people are we required to fulfill in our lifetimes? How much blame are we to take upon ourselves for our failure to supply the appropriate degree of another's fulfillment? The pat answer to each question is none and none, as any of the agony aunts will tell you. But life's messier than the agony aunts would have it.

My eyelids burn. I don't know what time it is, but it seems to me that the screen of black that lies across the galley window is beginning to lighten to grey. I tell myself that I've written enough for now, that I can go to bed. I need my rest. Hasn't every doctor and healer told me that? Conserve your strength, conserve your energy, they say.

I call for Chris. He pokes his head into the corridor. He's dug up a red-and-gold fez from his cupboard, and he's wearing it perched on the back of his head. He says, "Yes, memsahib?" with his hands folded on his chest. I say, "Wrong country, twit. You need a turban. Will you sit with me, Chris?" He says, "You're there, then?" I say, "Yes." He says, "Right," and flips his head back to toss the fez into his room. He comes into the galley. He slides Panda off the dresser and onto his shoulder. He sits opposite me. The cat doesn't react. She knows it's Chris who's got her. She lies like a beanbag curved over his shoulder. She begins to purr.

With his other hand, Chris reaches across the table. He opens my left palm and carefully places his fingers between mine. I watch my fingers twitch before I can make them close over his. Even when they do, I can tell my grip isn't firm any longer. His fingers close after mine do. "Go on," he says.

So I do.

Mother and I talked in the early hours of that morning in Kensington. We talked until Chris arrived to fetch me. I said, "He's my friend. I think you'll like him," to which she replied, "It's good to have friends. A single good friend, in fact, is more important than anything." She ducked her head and added somewhat diffidently, "That's what I've found, at least."

Chris came in, looking like he'd been worn down from boulder to gravel. He had a cup of tea with us. I said, "It was all right?" He didn't look at me as he said, "All right." Mother glanced between us curiously, but she asked no questions. She said, "Thank you for caring for Olivia, Chris." He said, "Livie tends to care for herself." I said, "Pooh. You keep me going and you know it." Mother said, "That's the way it should be." I could tell she thought there was more than friendship between me and Chris. Like most women in love, she wanted everyone else to have a share in the feeling. I wanted to say, "It's not like that between us, Mum," but I felt a twinge of jealousy that she should have managed to grasp what was out of my reach.

We left after dawn, Chris and I. He'd already met with Max, he said. The rescued animals had already been seen to. He said, "I've got some new members in the unit. Have I mentioned them? I think they're going to work out well," and I imagine he was trying to tell me about Amanda even then. He must have felt a measure of relief. I was on the road to being taken care of, which meant that I would be taken off his hands as the ALS progressed. If he wanted to pursue Amanda despite the rules of ARM, he could do it without the worry of hurting me. All of these thoughts were probably on his mind, but I didn't notice his quiet as we drove back to Little Venice. I was too full of what had passed between my mother and me.

"She's changed," I said. "She seems like she's at peace with herself. Did you see that, Chris?"

He hadn't known her before, he reminded me, so he couldn't tell what was different about her. But she was the first woman he'd ever met who at five o'clock in the morning, after a night without sleep, seemed as sharp as a scalpel. Where did she get the excess energy? he wanted to know. He himself was knackered and I looked done in.

I said it was the tea, the caffeine, the strangeness and the excitement of the evening. "And love," I said. "It was that as well." I spoke more truth than I realised.

We went home to the barge. Chris took the dogs for a run. I filled their food and their water bowls. I fed the cat. I took real pleasure in puttering through the simple chores I could still perform. Everything is going to be all right, I thought.

My body reacted with a vengeance to the long night in Kensington. The day that followed, I fought off an onslaught of fibrillations and weakness by telling myself that it was exhaustion. I had support for that conclusion from Chris, who himself slept until mid-afternoon and left the barge only to take the dogs for two runs.

I more than half expected to hear from my mother during that day. I'd made the first move in her direction. Surely she would make the second move in mine. But each time the telephone rang, it rang for Chris.

Of course, Mother and I hadn't left things so that she needed to phone. And she'd been up all night like us, so she'd probably be sleeping like us as well. Or if she wasn't, no doubt she'd gone to the printworks to see to business. I'd let a few days go by, I decided. Then I'd phone her and ask her to come to the barge for a meal. Better yet, I'd wait till Kenneth was back from Greece. I'd use that holiday as an excuse to phone. It's welcome home and come over for a meal, I would say. What better way for Mother to see that not only was I eager to end the years of enmity between us, but also I wasn't judgemental about her association with a much younger man. In fact, perhaps it wouldn't be such a bad idea if I became familiar with the current news in the cricket world. I'd want to be able to talk to Kenneth when I finally met him, wouldn't I?

When Chris took the dogs for their run the next morning, I asked him to bring me a newspaper. He returned with *The Times* and the *Daily Mail*. I turned to the back to find the news about sport. Articles on boxing, rowing, and cricket filled the page. I began to read.

Nottinghamshire was at the top of the championship table. Three men batting for Derbyshire had each scored a century in the final day of four against Worcestershire. Cambridge University had kept Surrey in the field until after the tea interval before they won. The Test and County Cricket Board were going to have a momentous special meeting at Lord's to discuss the future of domestic cricket. Aside from scoreboards, fixtures, and leading first-class averages, the only mention of the England team and the coming test matches between England and Australia was in an article about the differing styles of their captains: England's Guy Mollison—affable and accessible to the media in contrast to Australia's Henry Church—short-tempered and aloof. I made a mental note about Church. He was something to discuss. I could say, "Tell me, Kenneth, do you find Australia's captain as prickly as the newspapers do?" to break the ice.

I laughed inwardly even as I thought about ice-breaking. What was happening to me? I was actually thinking of putting someone at ease. When in my life had I ever worried about that? Despite the fact that, until his fall from grace with Jean Cooper, he'd haunted my adolescence, I found I wanted to like Kenneth Fleming, I wanted him to like me, I wanted all of us to get on. What on earth was bloody *happening* here? Where were grudge-bearing, ill-will, and distrust?

I hobbled to the loo to have a good look at myself in the mirror, thinking that if I no longer felt myself seething inside at the mere idea of my mother, I must probably look different outside as well. I didn't. And even my looks confused me. The hair was the same, as were the nose ring, the studs, the thick circles of black I still managed to paint round my eyes each morning. Externally, I was the same person who had thought of Miriam Whitelaw as a bitch and a cow. But my heart had changed if my appearance hadn't. It was like a part of me had disappeared.

I decided what had effected the change in me was the change in Mother. She hadn't said, "I washed my hands of you ten years ago, Olivia," or "After everything you've done, Olivia," in a need to rehash and relive the past. She offered, instead, unconditional acceptance. That gesture asked for unconditional acceptance in return. This change in her I assumed to be the result of her involvement with Kenneth Fleming. And if Kenneth Fleming could influence her behaviour that much, I was more than ready to like and accept him.

I remember now that I wondered fleetingly about Jean Cooper, about where she fitted in, about how, when, and if Mother had dealt with her. But I decided that the triangular aspect of the Mother-Kenneth-Jean affair was their business, not mine. If Mother had no worries about Jean Cooper, why should I?

I pulled Chris's collection of vegetarian cookbooks off their shelf above the cooker and carried them one at a time to the table. I opened the first book and thought about the meal Chris and I would serve my mother and Kenneth. Starter, main course, pudding, and cheese, it would be the real thing. We'd even have wine. I began reading. I reached for a pencil from the tin to make notes.

As I thought and planned, Chris studied a piece of moulding in the workroom. Our pencils scratched away on paper for a large part of the afternoon. Aside from that noise and the stereo playing, nothing disturbed or distracted us until Max came to see us later that evening.

He announced himself by calling out quietly, "Chris? Girlie? You below, are you?" as he clambered with a grunt onto the barge. The dogs began to bark. Chris called out, "It's open," and Max stepped carefully down the stairs. He tossed dog biscuits the length of the workroom and smiled as Toast and Beans tore after them. I'd been half-dozing in the old orange armchair. Chris had been sprawled on the floor at my feet. Both of us yawned.

Chris said, " 'Lo, Max. What's up?"

A white grocery bag dangled from Max's right hand. He lifted it slightly. For a moment, he looked oddly awkward and even more oddly unsure of himself. "I've brought you some grub."

"What's the occasion?"

Max unpacked red grapes, a block of cheese, biscuits, and a bottle of Italian wine. "I'm falling back on an age-old response to crisis. When disaster descends upon a family in the village, the neighbours bring food. It's an activity second cousin to brewing tea."

Max went into the galley. Chris and I looked at each other, perplexed. Chris said, "Disaster? What's going on, Max? Are you all right?"

He said, "I?" He returned to us with glasses, plates, and the corkscrew. He placed these on the workbench and turned to face us. "Have you not listened to the radio tonight?"

We shook our heads. "What's happened?" Chris said. And then his face altered quickly. "Shit. Have the cops caught one of the units, Max?"

"It's nothing to do with ARM," Max said. He looked at me. "It's to do with your mother."

I thought, Oh God. Heart attack, stroke, hit-and-run accident, mugged on the street. It felt like a cold hand passed over my face.

"And that lad of hers," Max went on. "You've not yet heard about Kenneth Fleming?"

I said, "Kenneth?" rather stupidly and, "What, Max? What's happened?" In that rapid way ideas zip through one's mind, I thought, Plane crash. But there had been no mention of a crash in this morning's paper, and if a plane had gone down on the way to Greece, wouldn't every paper be announcing that fact? And I had a paper, hadn't I? I had two, in fact. I had yesterday's as well. But neither had said. . . .

I heard only fragments of Max's response. "Dead . . . fire . . . in Kent . . . near the Springburns."

"But he can't be in Kent," I said. "Mother said . . ." I stopped myself. My thinking stopped with my words.

I knew Chris was watching me. I did what I could to show nothing in my face. My memory began to race from detail to detail of those hours I'd spent alone and then with my mother in Kensington. Because she'd said . . . she'd *said* . . . It was Greece. The airport. She'd taken him there. Hadn't she said that?

". . . on the news," Max was saying, ". . . don't know much else yet . . . perfectly rotten for everyone."

I thought of her standing in the darkened corridor. That odd shirtwaister, the declaration that she needed to change, the smell of gin on her breath after she took too long to slip out of a shirtwaister and into a dressing gown. And what had Chris noticed about her when he joined us? The energy flowing from her at five in the morning, so odd in a woman of her age. What was going on?

A spanner seemed to be tightening round my neck. I prayed that Max would leave as soon as possible because I knew if he didn't, I'd break down and babble like a fool.

But babble about *what?* I must have misunderstood her, I thought. I was nervous, after all. She woke me up out of a disturbing sleep. I wasn't paying close attention to her words. I was intent on getting through our initial meeting without it disintegrating into accusation and incrimination. So she must have said something that I misinterpreted.

In bed that night, I examined the facts. She said she'd taken him to the airport . . . No. She said she'd come from the airport, hadn't she? His flight, she said, had been delayed. Okay. All right. Then how did it play out? She wouldn't have wanted to leave him there at loose ends. So she would have stayed, they would have had drinks. Finally, he would have told her to go home. And then . . . what then? He would have left the airport and dashed over to Kent? Why? Even if the flight had been delayed, wouldn't he have already checked in, waited in the international lounge, or in one of those special executive lounges where people without tickets weren't even admitted . . . just as they were not admitted into the international lounge in the first place so why was I thinking that Kenneth and Mother would have been having drinks together as he waited for the flight? That wasn't on. I needed something different.

Perhaps the flight had been cancelled altogether. Perhaps he'd gone from the airport to Kent to use the cottage for his holiday. He hadn't told Mother because he hadn't known he'd be going in the first place because when she'd left him at the airport he hadn't known the flight would be cancelled. Yes. Yes, that was it. So he went to Kent. Yes, he went to Kent. And in Kent he died. Alone. A fire. Wiring gone bad, sparks shooting out, carpet smouldering, then the flames and the flames and his body incinerated. A horrible accident. Yes, yes. That was what had happened.

The relief I felt at this conclusion was incredible. *What* had I been thinking? I wondered. And why on earth had I been thinking it?

When Chris came in with my morning tea, he set the mug on the shelf next to the bed. He sat on the edge, and said, "When shall we go?"

I said, "Go?"

"To see her. You want to see her, don't you?"

I mumbled a *yes*. I asked him would he get me a paper. I said, "I want to know what happened. Before I talk to her. I need to know so I can decide what to say to her."

He brought me *The Times* again. And the *Daily Mail*. As he made our breakfast, I sat at the table and read the stories. There were few details that first morning after Kenneth's body had been discovered: the name of the victim, the name of the cottage in which he'd been found, the owner of the cottage, the name of the milkman who discovered the fire scene, the time of discovery, the names of the principal investigators. Following these facts was the background story on Kenneth Fleming himself. And at the end were posited the current theories waiting to be affirmed by the postmortem and the subsequent investigation. I read this final section over and over, dwelling on the words *arson specialist* and on the speculated time of death. I stared at the sentence: "Prior to the postmortem examination, the medical examiner on the scene has determined the time of death to be approximately thirty to thirty-six hours before discovery of the body," and I did the mathematical calculation in my head. That put the time of death sometime round midnight on Wednesday. My chest felt sore. No matter what Mother had said to me in the early hours of Thursday morning about Kenneth Fleming's whereabouts, one fact remained clear. He couldn't have been in two places at once: in her company on the way to or at the airport and in Celandine Cottage in Kent. Either the medical examiner was wildly incorrect, or Mother was lying.

I told myself that I had to know. I phoned her, but there was no answer. I phoned all day and into the evening. And the following afternoon I broke down.

I asked Chris could we go to Kensington now. I said I wanted to see Mother alone if he didn't mind. Because things had been awkward between Mother and me for so long, I said. She'd be grieving, I said. She wouldn't want someone who's not family there, I said.

Chris said he understood. He'd drop me off, he said. He'd wait for me to phone him and then he'd fetch me back.

I didn't ring the bell when I'd made the muscle-aching climb up those seven front steps. Instead, I let myself in with my key. I closed the door behind me and saw that the dining room door was shut as was the farther door to the morning room. Curtains were drawn over the distant window that overlooked the back garden. I stood in the resulting near-darkness of the entry. I listened to the profound silence of the house.

"Mother?" I called with as much self-assurance as I could muster. "Are you here?" Like Wednesday night, there was no response. I made my way to the dining room and opened the door. Light filtered into the entry, falling against the newel-post at the foot of the stairs. A shoulder bag hung from this. I went to it. I ran my fingers along the soft leather. A floor board creaked somewhere above me. I raised my head, called, "Mother?" and then added, "Chris isn't with me. I've come alone."

I squinted up the stairs. They ascended into darkness. It was early afternoon, but she'd managed with curtains and doors to turn the house into a nighttime tomb. I couldn't see anything but shapes and shadows.

"I've read the papers." I directed my voice to where she had to be, on the second floor of the house, standing just outside her bedroom door, leaning against the panels, her hands behind her clutching the knob. "I know about Kenneth. I'm so sorry, Mother." Pretend, I thought. Pretend nothing has changed. "When I read about the fire, I had to come," I said. "How awful for you. Mother, are you all right?"

A sigh seemed to float down from above although it might have been a gust of wind lightly hitting the curtained window at the end of the corridor. A rustle followed. And then the stairs themselves began to creak slowly as if a hundredweight were being lowered an inch at a time.

I moved myself back from the newel-post. I waited and wondered what we would say. How can I carry off this pretence, I wondered. She's your mother, I told myself in reply, so you'll have to. I riffled through my mind for something to say as she made her way down the first flight of stairs. As she moved across the passage above me, I opened the door to the morning room. I pulled the curtains away from the far corridor window. I went back to meet her at the foot of the stairs.

She paused on the mezzanine. Her left hand clutched the banister. Her right hand made a fist between her breasts. She was wearing the same dressing gown she'd put on at three in the morning on Thursday. But unlike three in the morning on Thursday, she seemed unpossessed of what Chris had seen as unusual energy and what I now realised had been tautly strung nerves.

I said, "When I read about him, I had to come. Are you all right, Mother?"

She descended the last half-flight of stairs. The telephone began ringing in the morning room as she did so. She didn't give any indication that she heard the noise. It went on insistently. I looked towards the morning room and wondered about answering it.

Mother said, "Newspapers. Vultures. Plucking at the corpse."

She was standing on the bottom stair, and in the light I'd let in from the open doors and uncurtained window, I could see how deeply the last day had altered her. Although she was dressed for it, she couldn't have slept. Lines had become gouges on her face. Pouches of flesh hung beneath her eyes.

I saw she was holding something in her fist, mahogany coloured against the ash of her skin. She raised the fist to her cheek and pressed her cheek against whatever she held.

She whispered, "I didn't know. I *didn't*, my darling. I'm swearing it. Now."

"Mother," I said.

"I didn't know you were there."

"Where?"

"In the cottage. I didn't. I didn't know."

All at once my mouth felt like I'd been walking a month in the desert as she destroyed every possibility of pretence between us.

I felt the only answer against going faint was to concentrate on something outside the realm of my own spinning thoughts, so I concentrated on counting the double rings of the phone that still shrilled in the morning room. When the ringing finally stopped, I moved my concentration to what my mother still held to her cheek. I saw it was an old cricket ball.

"After your first century." She whispered, with her eyes fixed on something only she could see. "We went to dinner. A group of us. What you were like that night. Buoyant. Life and laughter, I thought. So splendid and young." She raised the ball to her lips. "You gave me this. In front of all those people. Your wife. Your children. Your parents. Other players. 'Let's give credit where credit is rightly due,' you said. 'I lift my glass to Miriam. She's given me the courage to pursue my dreams.' "

Mother's face crumpled. Tremors shook her hand. "I didn't know," she said against the worn leather ball. "I didn't know."

She walked past me as if I wasn't there. She went down the corridor and into the morning room. I followed slowly and found her at the window, tapping her forehead against the glass. With each tap, she increased the force. She said only, "Ken," with every tap.

I felt immobilised by fear, dread, and my own disability. What to do, I wondered. Who to talk to. How to help. I couldn't even go below to the kitchen and engage in the simple task of fixing her a meal which she no doubt needed because I couldn't bring it up to her once I'd cooked it and even if I could have done, I was terrified to leave her alone.

The telephone began to ring again. As it did so, she increased the strength with which she was hitting her head against the glass. I felt my legs start to cramp. I felt my arms weaken. I needed to sit. I wanted to run.

I went to the phone, lifted the receiver, then replaced it. Before it had a chance to begin ringing again, I punched in the number of the barge and prayed that Chris had gone directly back once he'd dropped me off. Mother continued to bang her head against the window. The panes of glass rattled. As the phone rang on the other end of the line, the first pane cracked. I said, "Mother!" as she increased both the force and the rhythm of her pounding.

When I heard Chris answer, I said, "Come back. Hurry," and I hung up the phone before he could respond. The pane of glass broke. Its pieces shattered on the windowsill and then on the floor. I went to Mother. She'd cut her forehead, but she didn't seem to notice the blood that ran in a trickle into the corner of her eye and then down her cheek like a martyr's tears. I took her arm. I tugged on it gently. I said, "Mother. It's Olivia. I'm here. Sit down."

She said only, "Ken."

"You can't do this to yourself. For God's sake. Please."

A second pane broke. Glass tinkled to the floor. I could see the new cuts begin to ooze blood.

I jerked her back towards me. "Stop it!"

She pulled away. She went back to the window. She continued to pound.

"Goddamn you!" I shrieked. "Stop it! Now!"

I struggled to get closer to her. I reached around her. I grabbed her hands. I found the cricket ball, snatched it from her, and threw it to the floor. It rolled into a corner beneath an urn stand. Her head turned then. She followed the ball with her eyes. She lifted a wrist to her forehead and brought it away smeared with blood. Then she began to weep.

"I didn't know you were there. Help me. Dearest. I didn't know you were there."

I guided her to the chesterfield as best I could. She shrank into a corner with her head against the arm and her blood dripping onto the ancient lace antimacassar. I watched her helplessly. The blood. The tears. I shuffled into the dining room where I found the decanter of sherry. I poured myself one and threw it down my throat. I did the same to another. The third I clutched in my fist and, eyes on it to keep from spilling, I returned to her.

I said, "Drink this. Mother, listen to me. Drink this. You've got to take it because my hands don't work well enough to hold it for you. D'you hear me, Mother? It's sherry. You need to drink it."

She'd stopped speaking. She seemed to be staring at the silver buckle on my belt. One of her hands plucked at the antimacassar beneath her head. The other gripped the tie of her dressing gown. I inched my hand forward and held the sherry out to her.

"Please," I said. "Mother," I said. "Take it."

She blinked. I set the sherry onto the games table next to her. I blotted her forehead with the antimacassar. The cuts weren't deep. Only one of them continued to bleed. I pressed the lace to it as the doorbell rang.

Chris took over with his usual competence. He took one look at her, rubbed her hands between his own, and held the sherry to her mouth until she'd drunk it down.

"She needs a doctor," he said.

"No!" I couldn't imagine what she'd say, what a doctor would conclude, what would happen next. I modulated my voice. "We can deal with it. She's had a shock. We need to get her to eat. We need to get her to bed."

Mother stirred. She lifted her hand and examined the wrist that was smeared with blood, dried now to the colour of wet rust. "Oh," she said. "Cut," she said. She put the wrist to her mouth. She cleaned herself with her tongue.

"Can you get her something to eat?" I asked Chris.

"I didn't know you were there," Mother whispered.

Chris looked her way. He started to respond.

I said, "Breakfast," in a hurry. "Cereal. Tea. Anything. Chris, please. She needs food."

"I didn't know," Mother said.

"What's she—"

"Chris! For God's sake. I can't get down to the kitchen."

He nodded and left us.

I sat next to her. I kept one hand gripped on to the walker just to feel something solid and unchangeable beneath my fingers. I said in a low voice, "You were in Kent on Wednesday night?"

"I didn't know you were there. Ken, I didn't *know*." Tears slid from the corners of her eyes.

"Did you set a fire?"

She brought her fist to her mouth.

"Why?" I whispered. "Why did you do it?"

"Everything to me. My heart. My mind. Nothing will hurt you. Nothing. No one." She bit her index finger as she began to sob. Between her teeth, she took the meaty part of the finger from knuckle to first joint. All the while she wept.

I covered her fist with my hand. I said, "Mother," and tried to pull it away from her mouth. She was far stronger than I would have imagined.

The phone began to ring again. It was cut off abruptly, so I supposed Chris had picked it up in the kitchen. He would fend off journalists. We had nothing to fear there. But as I watched my mother, I realised that it wasn't the phone calls of journalists I feared. I feared the police.

I tried to calm her by putting my hand on the side of her head, by smoothing down her hair. I said, "We'll think this through. You'll be all right."

Chris returned with a tray that he took into the dining room. I heard the sound of plates and cutlery clicking onto the table. He came into the morning room. He put his arm round Mother's shoulders, saying, "Mrs. Whitelaw, I've made you some scrambled eggs," and he helped her to her feet.

She clung to his arm. One of her hands climbed his chest to rest on his shoulder. She examined his face so closely it looked as if she was committing it to memory. She said, "What she did to you. The pain she caused you. It was mine when it wasn't. I couldn't bear that, darling. You weren't meant to suffer any longer at her hands. Do you see?"

I could tell Chris was glancing my way, but I kept my face averted by concentrating on rising from the chesterfield and positioning myself within the three-sided protection of the walker. We went into the dining room. We sat ourselves on either side of Mother. Chris picked up a fork and put it in her hand. I drew the plate closer to her.

She whimpered. "I can't."

Chris said, "Have some, won't you? You'll need your strength."

She let the fork clatter to the plate. "You told me you were going to Greece. Let me do this for you, darling Ken. I thought. Let me solve this problem."

"Mother," I said quickly. "You need to have something to eat. You'll be talking to people, won't you? Journalists. The police. The insurance . . ." I dropped my eyes. The cottage. Insurance. What had she done? Why? God, what a horror. "Don't talk any more while the food's getting cold. Eat first, Mother."

Chris scooped up some eggs and returned the fork to her hand. She began to eat. Her movements were sluggish. Each one of them seemed thought out at great length before it was made.

When she had eaten, we took her back into the morning room. I told Chris where to find blankets and pillows, and we made a bed for her on the chesterfield. The phone began ringing as we worked. Chris picked it up, listened, said, "Unavailable, I'm afraid," and left it off the hook. I found the cricket ball where I had thrown it, and when Mother lay on the chesterfield and let Chris cover her, I handed her the ball. She clutched it just beneath her chin. She started to speak, but I said, "You rest. I'll sit right here." Her eyes closed. I wondered when it was that she'd last slept.

Chris left. I stayed. I sat on the velvet settee. I watched my mother. I counted the quarter hours as the grandfather clock chimed them. The sun slowly moved the shadows across the room. I tried to think what to do.

She must have needed the insurance money, I thought. My surmises scattered like birdshot from there: She hadn't run the printworks as well as she might have done. Things were getting tight. She didn't want to tell Kenneth because she didn't want to worry him or to distract him from his career. Things were getting tight for him. He was supporting his family. The children were getting older. There were more demands placed upon him financially. He was in debt. He had creditors hounding him. They decided to throw convention to the wind and to marry but Jean was demanding a single time payment of so much cash before she'd allow a divorce. The oldest son wanted to go to Winchester. Kenneth couldn't afford it at the same time as he paid Jean off. Mother wanted to help so that they could be married. She had cancer. One of the children had cancer. He had cancer. The money was needed for a special cure. Blackmail. Someone knew something and was making her pay. . . .

I leaned my head against the back of the settee. I couldn't think what to do because I couldn't understand what had been done. The sleeplessness of the previous nights began to take its toll on me. I couldn't make a decision about anything. I couldn't plan. I couldn't think. I slept.

When I awoke, the light had faded. I lifted my head and winced with the pain of the position I'd been in. I looked at the chesterfield. Mother was gone. My mind leapt into action. Where was she? Why? What had she done? Could she possibly be . . .

"You've had a good sleep, darling." I swung my head to the doorway. She'd bathed. She'd dressed in a long black tunic and matching trousers. She'd put on lipstick. She'd seen to her hair. She wore a plaster on her forehead where she'd cut herself.

"Are you hungry?" she asked. I shook my head. She came into the room. She went to the chesterfield and folded the blankets we'd used to cover her. She smoothed them down neatly and stacked them. She folded the stained antimacassar into a square. This she placed in the centre of the stacked blankets. Then she sat exactly where she had sat in the early hours of Thursday morning, in the corner of the chesterfield that was nearest my place on the settee.

Her gaze didn't falter as she looked at me. She said, "I am in your hands, Olivia," and I saw that the power had come to me fully at last.

How odd it felt. There was no triumph in the knowledge, only dread, fear, and responsibility. I wanted none of those sensations, least of all the last.

"Why?" I asked her. "Tell me that much. I need to understand."

Her eyes flickered off mine for an instant, moving to the Flemish painting on the wall above me. Then they returned to my face. "How ironic I find it," she said.

"What?"

"To think that, after all the anguish you and I have caused each other through the years, at the end of both our lives it's come down to need."

She gazed at me steadily. Her expression didn't change. She looked perfectly calm, not resigned but ready.

"It's come down to someone being dead," I said. "And if there's need involved, it's going to come from the police. They need answers. What're you going to tell them?"

"We've come to need each other," she said. "You and I, Olivia. That's where it stands. Here. At the end of things."

I was held by her gaze like a mouse gets held by the gaze of a snake just before he becomes the snake's dinner. I forced my eyes to the fireplace, to the massive ebony chimneypiece whose centre clock had been stopped forever the night Queen Victoria died. It had been my great-grandfather's symbolic act of mourning the end of an era. For me, it had long served as a demonstration of the hold the past maintains upon us.

Mother spoke again. Her voice was quiet. "Had you not been here when I got home, had I not been made aware of your . . ." She faltered, apparently looking for a euphemism. "Had I not seen your condition—what this disease is doing to you and going to do to you—I would have taken my life. I would have done it on Friday evening without the slightest hesitation when I was told that Ken was dead in the cottage. I had the razors here. I filled the bathtub to make the bleeding easier. I sat in the water and held the razor to my wrist. But I couldn't cut. Because to leave you now, to force you to face this horrible death without me here to help even in the smallest way . . ." She shook her head. "How the gods must be laughing at both of us, Olivia. For years I wanted my daughter to come home."

"And I came," I said.

"You did."

I ran my hand back and forth on the old velvet upholstery, feeling the rise and fall of its worn nap. "I'm sorry," I said. "Timing," I said. "God, what a mess I've made of things." She didn't respond. She appeared to be waiting for something more. She sat perfectly still in the dying light of the afternoon, and she watched me as I formulated the question and gathered the resources to ask it again. "Why? Mother, why did you do it? Have you. . . . Do you need money or something? Were you thinking of the insurance on the cottage?"

Her right hand sought the wedding ring on her left. Her fingers closed on it. "No," she said.

"Then what?"

She rose. She walked to the bay window where she replaced the telephone receiver into its cradle. She stood there for a moment with her head bent, with the tips of her fingers resting on the table-top. She said, ''I must sweep up this broken glass.''

I said, ''Mother. Tell me the truth.''

''The truth?'' She raised her head. She didn't turn back to me. ''Love, Olivia. That's always the beginning of things, isn't it? What I didn't understand is that it's also the end.''

OLIVIA

I've learned two lessons. First, there is the truth. Second, neither admitting nor acknowledging truth makes you free.

I've also learned that no matter what I do, someone is going to suffer at my hands.

At first, I thought I could bury knowledge. All the loose ends surrounding that Wednesday night–Thursday morning affair didn't exactly tie up, and Mother wouldn't clarify what she meant about love other than to say she'd done it for him, and I didn't know—and I didn't want to know —who the *she* was that Mother had been referring to in conjunction with Kenneth. All I knew for certain was that it was an accident that Kenneth Fleming had died in the cottage that night. It *was* an accident. And Mother's punishment, if punishment was required, would be having to live with the knowledge that she had started the fire that killed the man she loved. Wouldn't that be punishment enough? Yes, it would, I concluded. It would.

I decided to keep what I knew to myself. I wouldn't tell Chris. What would be the point?

But then, the investigation heightened. I followed what I could of it in the newspapers and on the radio news. A deliberate fire had been started by an incendiary device the nature of which the police wouldn't reveal. But it was the nature of the device, apparently, and not solely its presence that encouraged the authorities to begin using the words *arson* and *murder*. Once those words were employed, their companions began making appearances in the media: *suspect, killer, victim, motive*. Interest grew. Speculation flourished. Then Jimmy Cooper confessed.

I waited for Mother to phone me. She's a woman of conscience, I told myself. She'll come forward now. Any minute. Any hour. Because this is Kenneth Fleming's son we're talking about. This is Kenneth's son.

I tried to label the turn of events convenient for all of us. He's only a boy, I thought. If he stands trial and is found guilty, what can the criminal justice system do with a sixteen-year-old convicted killer? Wouldn't they just send him to a place like Borstal for a few years' useful rehabilitation? And couldn't that be seen as a social advantage? He'd be cared for there, he'd be educated, he'd be given employment skills that he no doubt needed desperately. He'd probably end up all the better for having had the experience.

Then I saw his photograph, when he was taken from his comprehensive by the police. He was walking between two constables, trying his best to look like he didn't give a fig for what was happening to him. He was trying to seem like he couldn't be touched. He was playing it tough and taking himself to a place where his answer to every question would be a sneer. Oh, I know that look Jimmy had on his face. It said, "I've got armour," and "I don't care about nothing." It communicated the fact that the past didn't matter because he had no future.

I phoned Mother then. I asked her did she know about Jimmy. She said the police were merely talking to him. I asked what was she going to do. She said that she was in my hands.

"Olivia," she said, "I'll understand your decision, whatever it is."

"What'll they do to him? Mother, what'll they do?"

"I don't know. I've already arranged for a solicitor. He's been talking to the boy."

"Does the solicitor know? What really . . . I mean . . ."

"I can't think they'll put him on trial, Olivia. He may have been in the vicinity that night, but he wasn't in the cottage. They've no proof of that."

"What happened?" I asked her. "That night. Mother, at least tell me what happened."

"Olivia. Darling. You don't want to know. You don't want to be burdened this way."

Her voice was soft, so reasonable. Not the voice of the Miriam Whitelaw who once vigourously pursued good works around London, but the voice of a woman altered forever.

"I need to know," I told her. "You need to tell me." So that I would know how to act, what to do, what to think, how to be from this moment forward.

So she told me. So simple it all was, really. The house left to look occupied—lights on, music playing, and both on timers to wear the guise of the inhabitant's logical movements that night. Slipping out through the back garden and down the mews under cover of darkness, careful to make no sound and not taking the car because the car wouldn't be needed at all.

"But how?" I asked. "How did you get out there? How did you manage?"

It was more than simple. An underground ride to Victoria Station, where the trains run twenty-four hours a day to Gatwick, where the car hire agencies are open twenty-four hours as well, where without any difficulty a blue Cavalier can be hired for a drive—not a terribly long drive, really—out to Kent, where the key to the cottage can be easily nicked shortly after midnight, when the lights are out and the cottage's sole inhabitant is asleep so that she doesn't hear an intruder who takes less than two minutes to fade into the cottage, to plant in an armchair a cigarette bound with matches, a cigarette taken from a packet bought from any tobacconist, anywhere, a common cigarette really, the most common cigarette imaginable. And then back through the kitchen—pausing only to scoop up two kittens because the kittens are innocent, they haven't chosen to be there, they aren't meant to die in a fire with her, a great conflagration in which the cottage is sacrificed but that doesn't matter, she doesn't matter, nothing matters except Kenneth and putting an end to the pain that she causes him.

"You meant to . . . Then it wasn't an accident." What was there left to hold on to, I wondered.

Accident? No. It wasn't an accident. It wasn't an accident at all. An accident couldn't be this carefully planned, drifting back into the night, driving back to the airport, where the trains still make the return trip into London, where outside Victoria Station a cab from the rank will take a lone woman to a darkened house midway up Argyll Road from which the trip to Phillips Walk isn't far and a silent return in the early hours of the morning—no car's engine to attract any notice—will go unregarded. So simple really. Because who would think that Victoria Station and Gatwick Airport and a car hired for the evening would ever be connected to a fire in Kent?

But I am in your hands, Olivia.

What's it to me, I thought, but more shakily now, and with less conviction. I don't know this kid. I don't know his mother. I don't know his siblings. I never met his father. If he was dim enough to take himself to Kent on the very night that his father died, wasn't that his problem? Wasn't it? *Wasn't* it?

And then you came to the barge, Inspector.

ARM, I tried to tell myself at first. You were asking about Kenneth Fleming, but the real reason you'd come was to do a recce. No one had ever before associated us with the movement, but there was always a chance. Chris had taken up with Amanda in violation of the rules, hadn't he? Perhaps she was a copper's nark. She'd gathered information, passed it along to her superiors, and here you were to suss things out. It seemed logical enough. Never mind your talk about a murder investigation, you were here to look for evidence to connect us to ARM.

Which I've given you. Here. In this document. Are you wondering why, Inspector? You, so determined that I should commit an act of betrayal. . . . Would you like to know?

Well, that street runs in both directions. Walk along it. See how it feels beneath your feet. Then decide. Like me. Decide. Decide.

We were sitting on the deck of the barge when I finally told Chris what I knew. I'd hoped to convince him that you were really only there sussing things out, relative to ARM, but Chris isn't a fool. He'd known something was wrong the moment he saw my mother in Kensington. He'd been at the house, he'd seen her condition, he'd heard her words, he'd seen me pore over the newspapers, he'd seen me try and fail to stop reading them. He asked did I want him to know what was going on.

I was in my canvas chair. Chris was on the deck with his knees drawn up and his jeans hiked and his white socks rucked so that a band of pale flesh showed on each leg. It made him look vulnerable, that position. It made him look young. He clasped his hands round his legs and his wrists slipped out of his jacket sleeves. So knobbly, they were. Just like his elbows, his ankles, and his knees.

He said, "We'd better talk."

"I don't think I can."

"It's to do with your mother." He didn't phrase it as a question and I didn't bother to deny it as a form of reply. Instead, I said, "I'll be a rag doll soon, Chris. I'll probably have to be tied to a wheelchair. There'll be tubes and respirators. Think how bad it's going to be. And when I die—"

"You won't be alone." He reached out and gripped my ankle with his fingers. He gave my leg a little tug. "That's not what this has been about, Livie. I give you my word. I'll take care of you."

"Like the dogs," I whispered.

"I'll take care of you."

I couldn't look at him. Instead I looked at the island. The willows, their branches skimming the ground, provided a shelter that in a few more weeks would become a screen behind which lovers could lie in that depression in the ground where scores of lovers had lain before them. But I would not be one of them.

I extended my hand to Chris. He took it, shifting his position so that he sat next to me, gazing as I was, at the island. As I told him what had happened that night in Kensington, he listened. When I was done, he said, "You don't have many options here, Livie."

"What can they do to him? If there's a trial, chances are he won't be found guilty."

"If he stands trial—guilty or not—what d'you imagine the rest of his life will be like?"

"Don't ask me to do this. Please don't ask me."

I felt his lips press against the back of my hand. He said, "It's getting cold. I'm getting hungry. Let's go below, all right?"

He made dinner. I sat in the galley and watched. He brought our plates to the table, sat opposite me in his usual place, but unlike the usual, he didn't fall to with enthusiasm. He reached across the table and lightly touched my cheek.

"What?" I said.

"That," he said. He forked up a mound of squash. "Nothing seems right, Livie. What to do. How to be. Sometimes it's all confused."

"I don't care about what's right," I said. "I just want what's easy."

"You and everyone else in the world."

"You too?"

"Yeah. It's no different for me."

But it's seemed to be different for Chris. He's always seemed so sure of where he was going and what he was doing. Even now, sitting across the table from me, holding my hand, he still seems sure. I raise my head.

"So?" he says.

"So I've done it," I say. I feel his fingers tighten on mine. I say, "If I send this to him, Chris, I can't go home. I'm here. We're stuck. You and I. Me. The mess that I am. You can't . . . You and . . . You won't be able to . . ." I can't quite say the rest. The words are so easy—You and Amanda can't be together the way you'd like to be while I'm still here and I'm still alive, Chris. Have you thought of that?—but I can't say them. I can't say her name. I can't put her name with his.

He doesn't move. He watches me. Outside the light is growing steadily. I hear a duck flap on the surface of the canal, taking off or landing, impossible to tell.

"It's not easy," Chris says evenly. "But it's right, Livie. I do believe that."

We look at each other and I wonder what he sees. I know what I see and my chest feels full with the need to split open and say all the words that are in my heart. What a relief it would be. Let Chris carry the burden for a while. But he gets to his feet and comes round the table to lift me up and help me to my room and I know that he has burdens enough.

CHAPTER
26

With a "Trust me, darling. It's the best thing for us. I absolutely promise you won't regret it," Helen led Lynley to Hyde Park on Sunday morning. They wore the running clothes she'd purchased for them the previous
week, and she insisted that, if they were sincere about getting themselves
fit, they had to begin by engaging in a brisk march from Eaton Terrace to
Hyde Park Corner, which she had chosen as their starting point. Having
decided that they were "warmed up quite enough," she set off north, in
the distant direction of Marble Arch.

She established an admirable pace for them. They passed at least a
dozen other joggers without the slightest trouble. Behind her, Lynley
paced himself and concentrated on not getting winded too soon. She was
remarkable, really, he thought. She ran beautifully, with her head flung
back, her arms bent at the elbow, and her dark hair flying. In fact, he was
beginning to think that she had been secretly keeping to a fitness programme in order to impress him when she started to fade just as the

Dorchester came into view across Park Lane. He came up next to her, saying, "Too fast a pace, darling?"

She huffed. "No. No." She flung out her arms. "Wonderful, isn't it? . . . Air . . . this exercise."

"Yes, but you're going rather red in the face."

"Am I?" She continued to chug along determinedly. "But that's . . . good . . . isn't it? Blood . . . Circulation. That sort of thing."

They pounded forward another fifty yards.

"I should think . . ." She was gulping down air like a survivor of asphyxia. "Very good for one . . . don't you?"

"Indeed," he said. "A cardiovascular workout is probably the best exercise there is in the world. I'm glad you suggested it, Helen. It's time we made an effort to get in better shape. Shall we slow the pace?"

"Not . . . no . . . at all." Beads of perspiration were emerging on her forehead and her upper lip. "Good . . . this . . . lovely, isn't?"

"Quite." They made a circle round the Joy of Life fountain, and Lynley called out, "Towards Speakers' Corner or into the park?"

She waved an arm in a northerly direction. "Corner," she wheezed.

"Right. Speakers' Corner it is. Slower? Faster? What?"

"This . . . fine. Wonderful."

Lynley stifled a smile. "I don't know," he said. "I think we need to put more into this, if we're going to be serious about exercising regularly. We might start carrying weights as well."

"What?"

"Weights. Have you seen them, darling? You can wear them on your wrists and work your arms while you run. You see, the trouble with running—if we can even call it trouble because God knows it makes me feel absolutely wonderful, doesn't it you?"

"Yes . . . Yes."

"The trouble, though—here, let's increase our speed a bit, I think we're slowing up—is that the heart gets a workout and the lower body is shaped up, but the upper body can go straight to hell. Now if we were to wear weights on our arms and exercise them as we ran, we would—"

She stumbled to a sudden halt. She stood, hands on knees, her chest heaving and her breath coming in what could have been taken for shrieks.

"Something wrong, Helen?" Lynley ran in place. "A complete circuit of the park should take us only . . . I don't know. What's the circumference? Six miles?"

"My God," she gasped. "This . . . My lungs . . ."

"Perhaps we ought to rest. Two minutes, all right? One doesn't want to cool down. You can strain a muscle if you get too cool and then start off again. We don't want that."

"No. No." It took her the two minutes to catch her breath, body flung on the grass and head raised to the sky. When she could finally breathe normally, she didn't rise to her feet. Instead, she lay back, closed her eyes, and said, "Find me a taxi."

He joined her, leaning back on his elbows. "Nonsense, Helen. We've only begun. You need to work up to it. You need to get used to it. If I set the alarm for five each morning and we're faithful about getting up when it goes off, I dare say you'll be able to run round this park two times over in no more than six months. What do you say?"

She opened one eye and fixed it on him. "Taxi. And you're a beast, Lord Asherton. How long have you been running without telling me, please?"

He smiled and fingered a lock of her hair. "November."

She turned her head away in disgust. "You unconscionable rat. Have you been laughing at my expense since last week?"

"Never, darling." And he coughed abruptly to cover a laugh now.

"Have you been getting up at five?"

"Six mostly."

"And running?"

"Hmm."

"And do you propose to continue to do so?"

"Of course. As you yourself said, it's the best exercise there is and we need to keep in shape."

"Right." She gestured towards Park Lane and flopped her arm to the ground. "Taxi," she said. "I'll exercise later."

Denton intercepted them on their way up the stairs to shower off their morning's exertion. He was on his way out, a bouquet of flowers in one hand, a bottle of wine in the other, and the words *lady killer* practically incised upon his forehead. He paused, changed directions, and went into the drawing room, saying to Lynley, "A bloke popped by not ten minutes after you'd gone." He came back out with a large manila envelope tucked under his arm. Lynley relieved him of it as he said, "He brought this by. Didn't want to stay. He said just to give it to the inspector as soon as he gets back."

Lynley unfastened the envelope's clasp, saying, "Are you off, then?"

"Picnic in Dorking. Box Hill," Denton said.

"Ah. Seeing a Janeite these days?"

"Pardon, m'lord?"

"Nothing. Just stay out of trouble, will you?"

Denton grinned. "Always." They could hear him whistling as he shut the front door behind him.

"What is it, Tommy?" Helen returned to him from the stairway as he pulled out the contents of the envelope: a stack of yellow lined pads, each covered with an uneven scrawl rendered in pencil. He read the first words on the top pad—*Chris has taken the dogs for a run*—and then he drew a deep breath and let it out.

"Tommy?" Helen said.

"Olivia," he answered.

"She took your bait, then."

"It appears that she did."

But Lynley found that she had laid her own bait as well. While Helen showered, washed her hair, dressed, and did whatever else it was that women found necessary to eat up at least ninety minutes, he read by the window in the drawing room. And he saw what Olivia had meant him to see. And he felt what she had meant him to feel. When she first revealed the information about ARM—so unnecessary to what he needed from her to bring the investigation into Kenneth Fleming's death to a successful conclusion—he thought, Wait, what is this, why? But then he saw what she was doing, and he knew it arose from the anger and despair with which she had faced the act of betrayal that he had asked her to commit.

He was reading the final pad of writing when Helen rejoined him. She picked up the other pads. She began to read as well. She said nothing when he completed his reading, tossed the pad down, and left the room. She merely continued, flipping the pages quietly, her bare feet and slim legs stretched out on the sofa, a pillow at her back.

Lynley went to shower and change. He thought about some of the ironies of life: meeting the right person at the worst possible time, deciding upon a course of action only to have it bring about one's own downfall, having a cherished belief proven fallacious, attaining what one desperately wants only to discover one doesn't actually want it at all. And this one, of course, this final irony. Having thrown down a gauntlet comprising half-truths, outright lies, and deliberate misinformation only to have a gauntlet of fact thrown down in return.

Decide, he could hear her taunting him. So decide, Inspector. You can do it. Decide.

When he rejoined Helen, she was midway through the stack of pads. As she read, he went to the breakfront cabinet against the wall and began restlessly flipping through a line of CDs. He didn't know what he was looking for any more than he would know when he found it.

Helen continued to read. He aimlessly chose Chopin. Opus 53 in A-flat Major. It was his favourite piece by a composer non-Russian. When the music began to pour from his stereo, he went to the sofa. Helen drew up her feet and changed her position. He sat next to her, kissed the side of her head.

They didn't speak until she had finished reading, and by then another piece of music had begun.

She said, "So you were right." And when he nodded, "You knew it all."

"Not all. I didn't know how she'd managed it. And I didn't know who she had hoped would be arrested if it came down to it."

"Who?" Helen asked.

"Jean Cooper."

"The wife? I don't see—"

"She hired a blue Cavalier. She dressed in a fashion she never would have worn otherwise. Had either she or the car been seen at the cottage that night, the description any witness gave would match Jean Cooper."

"But the boy . . . Tommy, didn't the boy say the woman he saw had light hair?"

"Light hair, grey hair. He wasn't wearing his glasses. He recognised the car, he only half saw the woman, he assumed the rest. He thought his mother had come to see his father. And she had reason to see him, reason to kill Gabriella Patten as well."

Helen nodded thoughtfully. "If Fleming had told Miriam Whitelaw that he was going to Kent to end his affair with Gabriella . . ."

"He'd still be alive."

"So why didn't he tell her?"

"Pride. He'd made a mess of his life once before. He wouldn't have wanted her to know how close he'd come to making a mess of it again."

"But she would have known eventually."

"True. But he could have presented his breaking off the affair as having outgrown Gabriella, having had enough of her, having realised what sort of woman she was. Which is what he probably would have told Miriam eventually. He just wasn't ready to tell her that yet."

"So it was all about timing."

"In a sense, it was." Lynley reached for her hand and watched as her fingers naturally found their way to twine with his. He was unexpectedly moved by that twining, by what it promised and what it revealed.

Helen said hesitantly, "As to the rest. The animal rescue business."

"What about it?"

"What're you going to do?"

He was silent, pondering the question, evaluating the implications behind each answer he might give her. When he didn't reply, she went on.

"Miriam will go to Holloway, Tommy."

"Yes."

"And do you know who's working on the other ones? The animal rescue cases? Who's investigating them?"

"It's easy enough to find out."

He felt her fingers tighten on his. "But if you turn Chris Faraday over to whoever's working on the break-ins and the rescues . . . Tommy, she won't have anyone left. She'll have to go into a home or a hospital. All this—what you've asked her to do—it will be for nothing."

"It will be to bring a murderer to justice, Helen. That's hardly nothing."

He wasn't looking at her but he could sense that she was searching his face, trying to read behind and beneath his expression in order that she might know what he intended to do. Which he didn't know himself. Not now. Not yet.

I want things simple, he thought. I want them cut and dried. I want to draw lines that no one thinks of crossing. I want an end to the play when sometimes it's only an interlude in the action. That's the miserable fact of my life. That fact has always been my curse.

Decide, Inspector. He could almost hear Olivia's voice. Decide. Decide. And then live afterwards with the decision. As I will. As I do.

Yes, Lynley thought. In an odd sort of way he owed her that much. He owed her his own distinct act of bearing the burden of choice, the weight of conscience, and the lifelong knowledge of responsibility.

"This is a homicide investigation," he finally said in answer to Helen's unasked question. "That's where it began. That's where it ends."

ACKNOWLEDGMENTS

I would like to extend grateful acknowledgment to the people in England who assisted with background material for this novel. I thank Alex Prowse for time, conversation, and photographs on his barge in the Pool of Little Venice; John Gilmore for a tour of the Clermont Club; Susan Monson for an introduction to the East End; the docents of Linley-Sanbourne house for fielding my questions on Victoriana; Sandy Shafernich for assistance with background material on the anti-vivisection movement; Ruth Schuster for risking life, limb, and liberty all in the name of verisimilitude; David Crane, John Blake, and John Lyon for the herculean task of schooling an American in the mysteries of that most elegant of games: cricket; Joan and Colin Randall for hours and days of hospitality and kindness in Kent. I thank also my favorite old Carthusian, Tony Mott, as well as Vivienne Schuster for everything they do to smooth the way.

In the United States, many thanks to Orange County fire investigator John McMasters and to Investigator Gary Bale of the Sheriff's Department for background in arson and arrest; to Ira Toibin for patiently living through yet another fourteen months of the creative process; to Suzanne Forster and Roger Angle for being there to prop up the pieces when the going gets rough; to Julie Mayer for reading yet another rough draft; to Kate Miciak for constant editorial support; to Deborah Schneider for belief and abiding friendship.

It should be noted that although the places mentioned in this novel do exist in London, they are being used fictitiously. It should also be noted that any errors or missteps found herein are mine alone.